Fred Campbell

JANEY

JOHN DICKSON CARR

Four Complete Dr. Fell Mysteries

ABOUT THE AUTHOR

JOHN DICKSON CARR was born in 1906 in Uniontown, Pennsylvania, and died in 1977. His numerous books are known for their ingenuity of plot, and he was perhaps most widely recognized as the true genius of the locked-room murder genre. His broad sense of humor and strong sense of the bizarre create an often palpable atmosphere of mystery. Carr was a former president of the Mystery Writers of America, and received their Grand Master award. An extraordinarily prolific writer, he also wrote many books under the pseudonym of Carter Dickson.

Dr. Fell, Carr's famous detective/historian, has for his ancestry the model of G. K. Chesterton, whom Carr greatly admired. His true relative, in name only, was the seventeenth-century Dr. Fell, dean of Christ Church, Oxford, and bishop of Oxford, who inspired Thomas Brown to change an epigram by Martial into the following famous satirical verse:

> I do not love thee, Dr. Fell;
> The reason why I cannot tell;
> But this I know and know right well:
> I do not love thee, Dr. Fell.

As for Dr. Fell's character and reputation, that may be well vouched for in this collection.

JOHN DICKSON CARR

Four Complete Dr. Fell Mysteries

Complete and Unabridged

THE BLIND BARBER

TO WAKE THE DEAD

THE CROOKED HINGE

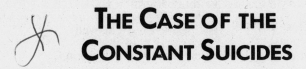

THE CASE OF THE CONSTANT SUICIDES

AVENEL BOOKS

New York

This edition contains the complete and unabridged texts of the original editions. They have been completely reset for this volume.

This omnibus was originally published in separate volumes under the titles: *The Blind Barber,* copyright © MCMXXXIV, renewed MCMLXI by John Dickson Carr. *To Wake the Dead,* copyright © MCMXXXVIII, renewed MCMLXVI by John Dickson Carr. *The Crooked Hinge,* copyright © MCMXXXVIII, renewed MCMLXVI by John Dickson Carr. *The Case of the Constant Suicides,* copyright © MCMXLI, renewed MCMLXIX by John Dickson Carr.

This 1988 edition is published by Avenel Books, distributed by Crown Publishers, Inc., 225 Park Avenue South, New York, New York 10003, by arrangement with Harper & Row, Publishers, Inc.

Printed and Bound in the United States of America.

LIBRARY OF CONGRESS CATALOGING-IN-PUBLICATION DATA

Carr, John Dickson, 1906–1977.
  [Novels. Selections]
  Four complete novels : Dr. Fell mysteries / John Dickson Carr.
    p. cm.
  Contents: The crooked hinge—To wake the dead—The case of the constant suicides—The blind barber.
  1. Fell, Gideon (Fictitious character)—Fiction. 2. Detective and mystery stories, American. I. Title. II. Title: 4 complete novels.
PS3505.A763A6   1988   88-16804
813'.52—dc19   CIP

  ISBN 0-517-65956-5
  h g f e d c b a

CONTENTS

THE BLIND BARBER

CONTENTS

PART I
Chapter I

STRANGE CARGO

hen the liner *Queen Victoria* left New York bound for Southampton and Cherbourg, it was said that two fairly well-known
people were aboard, and it was whispered that a highly
notorious third person was aboard also. Moreover, there was a fourth—
but inconspicuous—person who will take rather a large part in this rowdy
and topsy-turvy chronicle. Although he did not know it, this young man
had in his luggage something more valuable than the marionettes of M.
Fortinbras or the emerald elephant of Lord Sturton, which partly explains
why there were puzzles and high carnival in the sedate bosom of the
Queen Victoria, and monkey business not altogether according to the
customary pattern.

No more dignified ship than the *Queen Victoria* flies the house-flag of
any British line. She is what is sometimes described as a "family" boat:
which means that no hilarity is permitted in her state-room after 11 p.m.,
and all the cross-ocean changes in time are punctiliously observed—so
that the bar always closes three-quarters of an hour before you expect it,
and makes you swear. Melancholy passengers sit in her glazed writing-
room and seem to be composing letters to the relatives of the deceased. In
the heavily-ornamented lounge there is soft conversation, not so loud as
the creaking of woodwork when the green swell lifts and glitters past the
portholes; and knitting is in progress before some electric lights arranged
to represent a fire. There is a semblance of gaiety when a serious-minded
orchestra plays in the gallery of the dining-saloon at lunch and dinner.
But there was one east-bound crossing, in the spring of last year, which
Commander Sir Hector Whistler will never forget. Under his professional
bluff *camaraderie* Captain Whistler possesses the most pyrotechnic temper of any skipper who has forsaken sail for steam, and the richness of his
language is the admiration of junior officers. When, therefore—

The *Queen Victoria* was to dock at Southampton on the afternoon of
May 18th, after the weirdest voyage she had ever made. On the morning
of the next day Mr. Henry Morgan was ringing the bell of Dr. Fell's new
house at No. 1 Adelphi Terrace. Henry Morgan, it may be remembered,
was that eminent writer of detective-stories who took his own profession
with unbecoming levity, and who had made Dr. Fell's acquaintance
during the case of the Eight of Swords. On this particular morning—when

there was a smoky sun on the river and the quiet gardens below Adelphi Terrace—Morgan's long, bespectacled, deceptively-melancholy face wore an expression which might have been anger or amusement. But he certainly looked like a man who had been through much; as he had.

Dr. Fell boomed a welcome, greeted him warmly, and pressed upon him a tankard of beer. The doctor, his guest saw, was stouter and more red-faced than ever. He bulged out over a deep chair in the embrasure of one of the tall windows overlooking the river. The high room, with its Adam fireplace, had been set to rights since Morgan had seen it some months before, when Dr. and Mrs. Fell moved in. It was still untidy, for that was the doctor's way; but the five-thousand-odd books had been crammed somehow into their oak shelves, and the litter of junk had found place in corners and nooks. Dr. Fell has an old-fashioned weakness for junk, especially for bright pictures of the hunting-print of Dickens variety, and scenes showing people getting out of stage-coaches and holding up mugs of beer before country inns. He also likes carved procelain tankards with pewter lids, curious book-ends, ash-trays filched from pubs, statuettes of monk or devil, and other childish things which, nevertheless—in the sombre room with the oak bookshelves, with the frayed carpet on the floor—formed a fitting background for his Gargantuan presence. He sat in his chair in the window embrasure, before a broad study table littered with books and papers; there was a grin under his bandit's moustache, and a twinkle in his eye as he blinked at his visitor over eyeglasses on a broad black ribbon. And when the cigars had been lighted Dr. Fell said:

"I may be mistaken, my boy, but I seem to detect a professional gleam in your eye." He wheezed and folded his big hands on the table. "Is there anything on your mind, hey?"

"There is," said Morgan grimly. "I have to unfold just about the rummiest story you've ever listened to, if you've got time to hear it. It's rather a long one, but I don't think it'll bore you. And—if you want any corroboration—I've taken the liberty of asking Curt Warren to come round here. . . ."

"Heh " said Dr. Fell, rubbing his hands delightedly. "Heh-heh-hehe! This is like old times. Of course I've got time. And bring round anybody you like. Replenish that glass again and let's have the details."

Morgan took a deep drink and a deep breath.

"First," he said, in the manner of one commencing lecture, "I would direct your attention to a group of people sitting at the captain's table on the good ship *Queen Victoria*. Among whom, fortunately or unfortunately, I was one.

"From the beginning I thought it would be a dull crossing; everybody seemed to be injected with virtue like embalming fluid, and half an hour after the bar had opened there were only two people in it, not counting myself. That was how I made the acquaintance of Valvick and Warren.

"Captain Thomassen Valvick was a Norwegian ex-skipper who used to command cargo and passenger boats on the North Atlantic route; now retired, and living in a cottage in Baltimore with a wife, a Ford, and nine children. He was as big as a prize-fighter, with a sandy moustache, a lot of massive gestures, and a habit of snorting through his nose before he laughed. And he was the most genial soul who ever sat up all night telling incredible yarns, which were all the funnier in his strong squarehead accent, and he never minded if you called him a liar. He had twinkling, pale-blue eyes half-shut up in a lot of wrinkles and a sandy, wrinkled face, and absolutely no sense of dignity. I could see it was going to be an uncomfortable voyage for Captain Sir Hector Whistler.

"Because, you see, Captain Valvick had known the skipper of the *Queen Victoria* in the old days before Whistler became the stuffed and stern professional gentleman at the head of the table. There was Whistler—growing stout, with his jaw drawn in like his shoulders, strung with gold braid like a Christmas tree—there was Whistler, his eye always on Valvick. He watched Valvick exactly as you'd watch a plate of soup at a ship's table in heavy weather; but it never kept the old squarehead quiet or muzzled his stories.

"At first it didn't matter greatly. We ran into heavy weather immediately and unexpectedly; rain-squalls, and a dizzying combination of pitch-and-roll that drove almost all the passengers to their state-rooms. Those polished lounges and saloons were deserted to the point of ghostliness; the passages creaked like wickerwork being ripped apart, the sea went past with a dip and roar that slung against the bulkhead or pitched you forward on the rise, and navigating a staircase was an adventure. Personally, I like bad weather. I like the wind tearing in when you open a door; I like the smell of white paint and polished brass, which they say is what brings the sea-sickness, when a corridor is writhing and dropping like a lift. But some people don't care for it. As a result, there were only six of us at the captain's table: Whistler, Valvick, Margaret Glenn, Warren, Dr. Kyle, and myself. The two near-celebrities we wanted to see were both represented by vacant chairs. . . . They were old Fortinbras, who runs what has become a very swank marionette-theatre, and the Viscount Sturton. Know either one of them?"

Dr. Fell rumpled his big mop of grey-streaked hair.

"Fortinbras!" he rumbled. "Haven't I seen something about it recently in the highbrow magazines? It's a theatre somewhere in London where the marionettes are nearly life-size and as heavy as real people; he stages classic French drama or something—?"

"Right," said Morgan, nodding. "He's been doing that to amuse himself, or out of a mystic sense of preserving the Higher Arts, for the past ten or twelve years; he's got a little box of a theatre with bare benches, seating about fifty people, somewhere in Soho. Nobody ever used to go there but all the kids in the foreign colony, who were wild about it. Old Fortinbras's *pièce de résistance* was his dramatisation of 'The Song of Roland,' in French blank verse. I got all this from Peggy Glenn. She says he took most of the parts himself, thundering out the noble lines from back-stage, while he and an assistant worked the figures. The marionettes' weight—nearly eight stone, each of 'em stuffed with sawdust and with all the armour, swords and trappings—was supported by a trolley on which the figures were run along, and a complicated set of wires worked their arms and legs. That was very necessary, because what they did mostly was fight; and the kids in the audience would hop up and down and cheer themselves hoarse.

"The kids, you see, never paid any attention to the lofty sentiments. They probably didn't even hear them or understand what it was all about. All they knew was that out would stagger the Emperor Charlemagne on the stage, in gold armour and a scarlet cloak, with a sword in one hand and a battle-axe in the other. After him would come bumping and reeling all the nobles of his court, with equally bright clothes and equally lethal weapons. From the other side would come in the Emperor of the Moors and *his* gang, armed to the eyebrows. Then all the puppets would lean against the air in various overbalanced positions while Charlemagne, with a voice of thunder said, 'Pry, thee, friend, gadzooks, gramercy, what ho, sirrah!', and made a blank-verse speech lasting nearly twenty minutes. It was to the effect that the Moors had no business in France, and had better get to hell out of there—or else. The Emperor of the Moors lifted his sword and replied with a fifteen-minute address whose purport was 'Says you!' And Charlemagne, whooping out his war-cry, up and dots him one with the battle-axe.

"That was the real beginning, you see. The puppets rose from the stage and sailed at each other like fowls across a cockpit, thrashing their swords and kicking up a battle that nearly brought down the roof. Every so often one of them would be released from the trolley as dead, and would crash down on the stage and raise a fog of dust. In the fog the battle kept on whirling and clashing, and old Fortinbras rushed behind the scenes screaming himself hoarse with noble speeches, until the kids were delirious with excitement. Then down would tumble the curtain; and out would come old Fortinbras, bowing and puffing and wiping the sweat off his face, supremely happy at the cheers of the audience; and he would make a speech about the glory of France which they applauded just as loudly without knowing what he was talking about. . . . He was a happy artist; an appreciated artist.

"Well, the thing was inevitable. Sooner or later the highbrows would 'discover' him, and his art; and somebody did. He became famous overnight, a misunderstood genius whom the British public had shamefully neglected. No kids could get into the place now; it was all top-hats and people who wanted to discuss Corneille and Racine. I gather that the old boy was rather puzzled. Anyhow, he got a thumping offer to exhibit his various classic dramas in America, and it was one long triumphal tour. . . ."

Morgan drew a deep breath.

"All this, as I say, I got from Miss Glenn, who is—and has been long before the thing grew popular—a sort of secretary and general manager for the foggy old boy. She's some sort of relation of his on her mother's side. Her father was a country parson or schoolmaster or something; and when he died, she came to London and nearly starved until old Jules took her in. She's devilish good-looking, and seems prim and stiffish until you realise how much devilment there is in her, or until she's had a few drinks; then she's a glittering holy terror.

"Peggy Glenn, then, made the next member of our group, and was closely followed by my friend, Curtis Warren.

"You'll like Curt. He's a harum-scarum sort, the favourite nephew of a certain Great Personage in the present American Government. . . ."

"What personage?" inquired Dr. Fell. "I don't know of any Warren who is—"

Morgan coughed.

"It's on his mother's side," he replied. "That has a good deal to do with my story; so we'll say for the moment only a Great Personage, not far from F.D. himself. This Great Personage, by the way, is the most dignified and pompous figure in politics; the glossiest Top-Hat, the neatest Trouser-Press, the prince of unsplit infinitives and undamaged etiquette. . . . Anyhow, he pulled some wires (you're not supposed to be able to do this) and landed Curt a berth in the Consular Service. It isn't a very good berth: some God-forsaken hole out in Palestine or somewhere, but Curt was coming over for a holiday round Europe before he took over the heavy labour of stamping invoices or what-not. His hobby, by the way, is the making of amateur moving-pictures. He's wealthy, and I gather he's got not only a full-sized camera, but also a sound apparatus of the sort the news-reel men carry.

"But, speaking of Great Personages, we now come to the other celebrity aboard the *Queen Victoria,* also paralysed with sea-sickness. This was none other than Lord Sturton—you know—the one they call the Hermit of Jermyn Street. He'll see nobody; he has no friends; all he does is collect bits of rare jewellery. . . ."

Dr. Fell took the pipe out of his mouth and blinked.

"Look here," he said suspiciously, "there's something I want to know before you go on. Is this by any chance the familiar chestnut about the fabulous diamond known as the Lake of Light, or some such term, which was pinched out of the left eye of an idol at Burma, and is being stalked by a sinister stranger in a turban? Because, if it is, I'll be damned if I listen to you. . . ."

Morgan wrinkled his forehead sardonically.

"No," he said. "I told you it was a rummy thing; it's much queerer than that. But I'm bound to confess that a jewel *does* figure in the story—it was what tangled us up and raised all the hell when the wires got crossed—but nobody ever intended it to figure at all."

"H'm " said Dr. Fell, peering at him.

"And also I am bound to admit that the jewel got stolen—"

"By whom?"

"By *me,*" said Morgan unexpectedly. He shifted. "Or by several of us, to be exact. I tell you it was a nightmare. The thing was an emerald elephant, a big pendant thing of no historical interest but of enormous intrinsic value. It was a curiosity, a rarity; that's why Sturton went after it. It was an open secret that he had been negotiating to buy it from one of the busted millionaires in New York. Well, he'd got it right enough; I had that from Curt Warren. The Great Personage, Curt's uncle, is a friend of Sturton's, and Curt's uncle told him all about it just before Curt sailed. Probably half the people on the boat heard the rumour. I know we were all waiting to catch a glimpse of him when he came aboard—queer, sandy old chap with ancient side-whiskers and a hanging jaw; only attendant a secretary. He popped up the gangway all swathed round in checked comforters, and cursed everybody in reach.

"Now it's a very odd thing, for a variety of reasons, that you should have mentioned the old familiar story about the fabulous jewel. Because, on the afternoon when all the trouble started—it was the late afternoon of the fourth day out, and we were to dock three days later—Peggy Glenn and Skipper Valvick and I had been discussing this emerald elephant, in the way you do when you're lying back in a deck-chair with a robe across your knees, and nothing much to think about except when the bugle will blow for tea. We discussed whether it was in Lord Sturton's possession or locked in the captain's safe, and, in either case, how you could steal it. Peggy, I know, had evolved a very complicated and ingenious plan; but I wasn't listening closely. We had all got to know one another pretty well in those four days, and we stood on very little ceremony.

"As a matter of fact," said Morgan, "I was more than half-asleep. Then—"

Chapter II

INDISCRETIONS OF UNCLE WARPUS

Low along the sky there was a liquid yellow brightness, but twilight had begun to come down, and the grey sea wore changing lights on its white-caps when the *Queen Victoria* shouldered down against a heavy swell. The skyline tilted and rose above a boiling hiss; there was a stiff breeze along the almost deserted promenade-deck. Lying back drowsily in a deck-chair, well wrapped against the cold, Morgan was in that lethargic frame of mind when the booming sea-noises are as comfortable as a fire. He reflected that shortly lights would go on along the ship; tea would be set out in the lounge while the orchestra played. Both his companions were momentarily silent, and he glanced at them.

Margaret Glenn had dropped her book in her lap; she was lying back in the deck-chair with eyes half-closed. Her rather thin, pretty, impish face—which ordinarily wore such a deceptive look of schoolmistress primness—now seemed puzzled and disturbed. She swung shell-rimmed reading-glasses by one ear-piece, and there was a wrinkle above her hazel eyes. She was muffled in a fur coat, with a wildly-blowing batik scarf; and from under her little brown hat a tendril of black hair danced above the windy deck.

She observed: "I say, what can be keeping Curt? It's nearly tea-time, and he promised to be here long ago; then we were going to round you two up for cocktails. . . ." She shifted, and her earnest eyes peered round at the porthole behind as though she expected to see Warren there.

"*I* know," said Morgan lazily. "It's that bouncing little blonde from Nashville; you know, the one who's going to Paris for the first time and says she wants to gain experiences for her soul."

Turning a wind-flushed face, the girl was about to rise to the remark when she saw his expression, and stuck out her tongue at him instead.

"Bah!" she said, without heat. "That little faker; I know her type. Dresses like a trollop and won't let a man get within a yard of her. You take my advice," said Miss Glenn, nodding and winking wisely. "You stay clear of women who want to gain deep experience for the soul. All that means is that they don't want to employ the body in doing it." She

7

frowned. "But I say, what *can* have happened to Curt? I mean, even with the notorious unpunctuality of American men—"

"Ha-ha-ha!" said Captain Thomassen Valvick, with an air of inspiration. "I tell you, maybe. Maybe it is like de horse."

"What horse?" asked Morgan.

Captain Valvick uttered one of his amiable snorts and bent his big shoulders. Even though the deck was rolling and pitching in a way that made the deck-chairs slide into each other, he stood upright without difficulty. His long sandy-reddish face was etched out in wrinkles of enjoyment, and behind very small gilt-rimmed spectacles his pale-blue eyes had an almost unholy twinkle. He wrinkled them up; he snorted again, hoarsely, through his sandy moustache, pulled down his large tweed cap over one ear, and made a massive gesture that would have been as heavy as a smaller man's blow.

"Ha-ha-Ha!" thundered Captain Valvick. "Ay tell you. In my country, in Norway, we haff a custom. When *you* wont to make a horse stop, you say, 'Whoa!' But we don't. We say, '*Brubublubluoooo-bl-oooo!* ' "

Shaking his jowls and lifting his head like Tarzan over a fresh kill, Captain Valvick here uttered the most extraordinary noise Morgan had ever heard. It cannot be reproduced into phonetic sounds, and so loses its beauty and poignancy. It was something like the noise of water running out of a bath-tub, but rising on a triumphant note like a battle-cry, and trembling on in shadings of defective drains and broken water-pipes; as though Mr. Paul Whiteman (say) had built a symphony round it, and come out strongly with his horns and strings.

"*Bru-bloo-bulooooluloo-buloooooo!*" crowed Captain Valvick, starting low with his shakings of head and jowl, and then rearing up his head at the climax.

"Isn't that a lot of trouble?" inquired Morgan.

"Oh, no!" Ay do it easy," scoffed the other, nodding complacently. "But ay was going to tell you, de first time I try it on a English-speaking 'orse, de 'orse didn't understand me. Ay tell you how it was. At dat time, when I was young, I was courting a girl who lived in Vermont, where it always snow like Norway. So ay t'ink ay take her out for a sleigh-ride, all nice and fine. I hire de best horse and sleigh dey got, I tell de girl to be ready at two o'clock in de afternoon, and I come for her. So of course I want to make a good impression on my girl, and I come dashing up de road to her house, and I see her standing on de porch, waiting for me. So ay t'ink it be fine t'ing to make de grand entrance, and ay say, '*Brubu-bluooo-bloo!*' fine and strong to de 'orse so ay can turn in de gates. But he don't stop. And ay t'ink, 'Coroosh! What is wrong wit' de goddam 'orse?' " Here Captain Valvick made a dramatic gesture, "So I shout, '*Brubu-bloooo-bloooo!*' and lean over de footboard and say it again. And dis time de 'orse turn its head round to look at me. But it don't stop, you bet. It keep right on going, straight past de house where de girl is standing, and it only gallop faster when I keep saying, '*Brubu-blubluoooo-bl-oooo!*' And my girl open her eyes at me and look fonny, but de 'orse fly straight on up de road; and all I can do is stand up in de sleigh and keep taking off my hat and bowing to her w'ile all de time ay go farder and farder away from her; and still ay am doing dat we'en we go round a bend and ay can't see her no more. . . .."

All this was recited with much pantomime and urging the reins of an imaginary horse. With an expiring sigh Captain Valvick shook his head in a melancholy fashion, and then twinkled benevolently.

"Ay could never get dat girl to go out again. Ha-ha-ha!"

"But I don't see the point," protested Peggy Glenn, who was regarding him in some perplexity. "How is that like Curt Warren?"

"Ay don't know," admitted the other, scratching his head. "Ay yust wanted to tell de story, ay guess. . . . Maybe he is sea-sick, eh? Ha-ha-ha! Ah! Dat remind me. Haff ay ever told you de story about de mutiny ay 'ave when de cook always eat all de peas out of de soup and—"

"Sea-sick?" the girl exclaimed indignantly. "Bosh! At least—poor old fellow, I hope not. My uncle is having a terrible time of it, and he's suffering worse because he's promised to give a performance of his marionettes at the ship's concert. . . . Do you think we'd better go and see what's wrong with Curt?"

She paused as a white-coated steward struggled out of a door near by and peered round in the darkening light. Morgan recognised him as his own cabin steward—a cheerful-faced young man with flat black hair and a long jaw. He had, now, a rather conspiratorial manner. Sliding down the gusty deck, he beckoned towards Morgan and raised his voice above the crash and hiss of water.

"Sir," he said, "it's Mr. Warren, sir. 'Is compliments, and 'e'd like to see you. And 'is friends too. . . .."

Peggy Glenn sat up. "There's nothing wrong, is there? Where is he? What's the matter?"

The steward looked dubious, and then reassuring, "Oh no, miss! Nothing wrong. Only I think somebody's 'it him."

"What?"

"Hin the eye, miss. And on the back of th 'ead. But 'e's not a bit upset, miss, not 'im. I left 'im sitting on the floor in the cabin," said the steward, rather admiringly, "with a towel to 'is 'ead and a piece of movie film in 'is 'and, swearing something 'andsome. And 'e'd taken a nasty knock, miss; that's a fact."

They stared at each other, and then they all hurried after the steward. Captain Valvick, puffing and snorting through his moustache, threatened dire things. Tearing open one of the doors, they were kicked by its recoil in the wind into the warm, paint-and-rubbery odour of the corridor. Warren's cabin, a large double which he occupied alone, was an outside one on C deck, starboard side. They descended heaving stairs, struck off past the gloomy staircase to the dining-room, and knocked at the door of C 91.

Mr. Curtis G. Warren's ordinarily lazy and good-humoured face was now malevolent. The odour of recent profanity hung about him like garlic. Round his head a wet towel had been wound like a turban; there was a slight cut of somebody's knuckles. Mr. Warren's greenish eyes regarded them bitterly out of a lean, newly-scrubbed face; his hair, over the bandage, stuck up like a goblin's; and in his hand he had a strip of what resembled motion-picture film with perforations for sound, torn at one end. He sat on the edge of his berth, faintly visible in the yellowish twilight through the porthole, and the whole cabin was wildly disarranged.

"Come in," said Mr. Warren. Then he exploded. "When I catch," he announced, drawing a deep breath like one who begins an oration, and spacing his words carefully—"when I catch the white-livered, greenly empurpled so-and-so who tried to get away with this—when I get one look at the ugly mug of the lascivious-habited son of a bachelor who runs around beaning people with a blackjack—"

Peggy Glenn wailed, "Curt!" and rushed over to examine his head, which she turned to one side and the other as though she were looking behind his ears. Warren broke off and said, "Ow!"

"But, my dear, what happened?" the girl demanded. "Oh, why do you *let* things like this happen? Are you hurt?"

"Baby," said Warren in a tone of dignity, "I can tell you that it is not alone my dignity which has suffered. By the time they have finished stitching up my head, I shall probably resemble a baseball. As to my deliberately encouraging all this to happen. . . . Boys," he said, appealing moodily to Morgan and the captain, "I need help. I'm in a jam, and that's no lie."

"Ha!" growled Valvick, rubbing a large hand down across his moustache. "You yust tell me who smack you, eh? Ha! Den ay take him and—"

"I don't know who did it. That's the point."

"But why . . . ?" asked Morgan who was surveying the litter in the cabin; and the other grinned sourly.

"This, old son," Warren told him, "is right in your line. Do you know if there are any international crooks on board? The Prince or Princess Somebody kind, who always hang out at Monte Carlo? Because an important State document has been pinched. . . . No, I'm not kidding. I didn't know I had the damned thing; never occurred to me; I thought it had been destroyed. . . . I tell you I'm in bad trouble, and it's not funny. Sit down somewhere and I'll tell you about it."

"You go straight to the doctor!" Peggy Glenn said, warmly. "If you think I'm going to have you laid up with amnesia or something—"

"Baby, listen," the other begged, with a sort of wild patience; "you don't seem to get it yet. This is dynamite. It's—well, it's like one of Hank's spy stories, only it's something new along that line, now that I come to think of it. . . . Look here. You see this film?"

He handed it to Morgan, who held it up for examination against the fading light through the porthole. The pictures were all of a portly, white-haired gentleman in evening clothes, who had one fist lifted as though making a speech and whose mouth was split wide as though it were a very explosive speech. There was, moreover, a very curious, bleary look about the dignified person; his tie was skewered under one ear, and over his head and shoulders had been sprinkled what Morgan at first presumed to be snow. It was, in fact, confetti.

And the face was vaguely familiar. Morgan stared at it for some time before he realised that it was none other than a certain Great Personage, the most pompous starched-shirt of the Administration, the potent rain-maker and high priest of quackdoodle. His cheerful, soothing voice over the radio had inspired millions of Americans with dreams of a fresh, effulgent era of national prosperity in which there should be instalment plans without ever any payments demanded, and similar American conceptions of the millennium. His dignity, his scholarship, his courtly manners—

"Yes, you're right," Warren said wryly. "It's my uncle. Now I'll tell you about it . . . and don't laugh, because it's absolutely serious.

"He's a very good fellow, Uncle Warpus is; you've got to understand that. He got into this position through the ordinary, human behaviour that might happen to anybody, but others mightn't think so. All politicians ought to have a chance every once in a while to blow off steam. Otherwise they're apt to go mad and chew off an ambassador's ear, or something. With the whole country in a mix-up, and everything going wrong, and wooden-heads trying to block every reasonable measure, there are times when they explode. Especially if they're in congenial company and have a social highball or two.

"Well—my hobby is the taking of amateur moving-pictures, with, Lord help me, sound. So about a week before I was to sail I was due to visit Uncle Warpus in Washington for a good-by call." Warren put his chin in his hands and looked sardonically on the others, who had moved backwards to find seats. "I couldn't take my movie apparatus abroad with me; it was much too elaborate. Uncle Warpus suggested that I should leave it with him. He was interested in such things; he thought he might get some pleasure in tinkering with it, and I should show him how to work everything. . . .

"On the first night I got there," pursued Warren, taking a deep breath, "there was a very large, very dignified party at Uncle Warpus's. But he and a few of his Cabinet and senatorial cronies had sneaked away from the dancing; they were upstairs in the library, playing poker and drinking whisky. When I arrived they thought it would be an excellent idea if I arranged my apparatus, and we took a few friendly talking-pictures there in the library. It took me some time, with the assistance of the butler, to get it all arranged. Meanwhile, they were having a few friendly drinks. Some of 'em were a good deal the strong, silent, rough-diamond administrators from the prairies; and even Uncle Warpus was relaxing considerably."

Warren blinked with reminiscent pleasure at the ceiling.

"It all began with much seriousness and formality. The butler was camera man, and I recorded the sound. First the Honourable William T. Pinkis recited Lincoln's Gettysburg Address. *That* was all right. Then the Honourable Secretary of Interstate Agriculture did the dagger scene from *Macbeth,* a very powerful piece of acting, with a bottle of gin as the dagger. One thing led to another. Senator Borax sang 'Annie Laurie,' and then they got up a quartet to render 'Where is my Wandering Boy Tonight?' and 'Put on Your Old Grey Bonnet.' . . . "

Sitting back in the berth with her back against the wall, Peggy Glenn was regarding him with a shocked expression. Her pink lips were open, her eyebrows raised.

"Oh, I say!" she protested. "Curt, you're pulling our legs. I mean to say, just fancy our House of Commons. . . ."

Warren raised his hand fervently. "Baby, as Heaven is my witness, that is precisely—" He broke off to scowl as Morgan began laughing. "I tell you, Hank, this is serious!"

"I know it," agreed Morgan, growing thoughtful. "I think I begin to see what's coming. Go on."

"Ay t'ank dey did right," said Captain Valvick, nodding vigorously and approvingly. "Ay haff always wanted to try one of dem t'ings too. Den ay giff my imitation of de two cargo-boats in de fog. It is very good, dat one. I show you. Ha-ha-ha!"

Warren brooded.

"Well, as I say, one little thing led to another. The signal for the fireworks was when one Cabinet member, who had been chuckling to himself for some time, recounted a spirited story about the travelling saleman and the farmer's daughter. And then came the highlight of the whole evening. My uncle Warpus had been sitting by himself—you could almost see his mind going round *click-click—click-click*—and he was weighed down by a sense of injustice. He said he was going to make a speech. He did. He got in front of the microphone, cleared his throat, squared his shoulders, and then the cataract came down at Lodore.

"In some ways," said Warren, rather admiringly, "it was the funniest thing I ever heard. Uncle Warpus had had to repress his sense of humour for some time. But I happened to know of his talent for making burlesque political speeches. . . . Wow! What he did was to give his free, ornamental, and uncensored opinion of the ways of government, the people in the government, and everything connected with it. Then he went on to discuss foreign policy and armaments. He addressed the heads of Germany, Italy, and France, explaining exactly what he thought of their parentage and alleged social pastimes, and indicating where they could thrust their battleships with the greatest possible effect. . . ." Warren wiped his forehead rather dazedly. "You see, it was all done in the form of a burlesque flagwaving speech, with plenty of weird references to Washington and Jefferson and the faith of the fathers. . . . Well, the other eminent soaks caught on and were cheering and applauding. Senator Borax got hold of a little American flag, and every time Uncle Warpus made a particularly telling point, Senator Borax would stick his head out in front of the camera, and wave the flag for a second, and say, 'Hooray!' . . . Boys, it was hair-raising. As an oratorical effort I have never heard it surpassed. But I know two or three newspapers in New York that would give a cool million dollars for sixty feet of that film.

Peggy Glenn, struggling between laughter and incredulity, sat forward, with her bright hazel eyes fixed on him; she seemed annoyed. "But I tell you," she protested again, "it's absurd! It—it isn't *nice,* you know. . . ."

"You're telling me," said Warren, grimly.

" . . . and all those awfully nice high-minded people; it's disgusting! you can't really tell me! . . . Oh, it's absurd! I don't believe it."

"Baby," said Warren gently, "that's because you're British. You don't understand American character. It's not in the least unreasonable; it's simply one of those scandals that sometimes happen and have to be hushed up somehow. Only this one is a scandal of such enormous, dizzying proportions that—Look here. We'll say nothing of the explosion it would cause at home. It would ruin Uncle Warpus, and a lot of others with him. But can you imagine the effect of those pronouncements on, say, certain dignitaries in Italy and Germany? They wouldn't see anything funny about it in the least. If they didn't jump up and down, tearing out handfuls of hair, and rush out and declare war immediately, it would be because somebody had the forethought to sit on their heads. . . . Whoosh! T.N.T.? T.N.T.'s as mild as a firecracker compared with it."

It was growing dark in the cabin. Heavy clouds had massed up; there

was a tremble through the ship above the dull beat of her screws, and a
deeper thunder and swish of water as she pitched. Glasses and waterbottle were rattling in the rack above the washstand. Morgan reached up
to switch on the light. He said:

"And someone stole it from you?"

"Half of it, yes. . . . Let me tell you what happened.

"The morning after that little carnival, Uncle Warpus woke up with a
realisation of what he'd done. He came rushing into my room, and it
appears he'd been bombarded with phone-calls from other offenders since
seven o'clock. Fortunately, I was able to reassure him—as I thought,
anyhow. What with other difficulties, I'd taken in all only two reels. Each
reel was packed into a container like this. . . ."

Reaching down under his berth, Warren pulled out a large oblong box,
bound in steel, with a handle like a suitcase. It was unlocked, and he
opened the snap-catch. Packed inside were a number of flat circular tins
measuring about ten inches in diameter painted black, and scrawled with
cryptic markings in white chalk. One of these had its lid off. Inside had
been jammed a tangled and disarranged spool of film from which a good
length seemed to have been torn off.

Warren tapped the tin. "I was taking some of my better efforts with
me," he explained. "I've got a little projector, and I thought they might
amuse people on the other side. . . .

"On the night of Uncle Warpus's eloquence, I was a little tight myself.
The packing up I left to the butler, and I showed him how to do the
marking. What must have happened—I can see it now—was that he got
the notations mixed. I carefully destroyed two reels that I thought were
the right ones. But, like an imbecile"—Warren got out a pack of
cigarettes and stuck one askew into his mouth—"like an imbecile, I only
examined one of the reels with any care. So I destroyed the Gettysburg
Address, the Dagger Scene, and singing of 'Annie Laurie.' But the rest of
it . . . well, I can figure it now. What I got rid of were some swell shots of
the Bronx Park Zoo."

"And the rest of it?"

Warren pointed to the floor.

"In my luggage, without my knowing it. Never a suspicion, you see,
until this afternoon. Gaa! what a situation. Well, you see, I had an urgent
radiogram I had to send off to somebody at home—"

"Oh?" said Miss Glenn, sitting up and eyeing him suspiciously.

"Yes. To my old man. So I went up to the wirelessroom. The operator
said he'd just received a message for me. He also said, 'This looks like
code. Will you check it over and make sure it's all right?' Code. Ho-ho! I
glanced over it, and it seemed so queer that I read it aloud. You must
remember, what with the excitement of going away and things on board

here and all, I'd forgotten that little performance entirely. Besides, the radiogram was unsigned; I suppose Uncle Warpus didn't dare. . . ." Warren shook his head sadly, a weird turbaned figure with the cigarette hanging from one corner of his mouth and his face scrubbed like a schoolboy's. Then he took the cable from his pocket. "It said, '*found traces in sweeping out. Hiller—*' that's his butler; old family retainer; wouldn't squeal if Uncle Warpus pinched the silver out of the White House—'*Hiller nervous. They look like bears. Is this real reel. Urgent no hitch in sarcasm effaced. Advise about bears.*' "

"Eh?" demanded Captain Valvick, who was puffing slowly.

"That's the closest he could take a chance on coming to it," Warren explained. "Bears in the zoo. But it's not the sort of thing that makes much sense when it's sprung on you unexpectedly. I argued it out with the wireless operator, and it wasn't until ten minutes later that it struck me—how the devil was I to know Uncle Warpus had sent it? So I couldn't connect up the words; then suddenly it hit me.

"Well, I rushed down here to my cabin. It was getting dark, and besides, the curtain was drawn over the porthole . . . but there was somebody in here."

"And of course," said Morgan, "you didn't see who it was?"

"When I get that low-down"—snarled Warren, going off at a tangent and glaring murderously at the waterbottle—"when I find—no, damn it! All I knew was that it was a man. He had my film-box over in the corner, half the tins with their lids off (I found this later) and had the right roll in his hands. I dived for him, and he let go a hard one at my face. When I grabbed him I grabbed a piece of the film. He cracked out again—there isn't much space in here, and the boat was pitching pretty heavily—then we staggered over against the washstand while I tried to slam him against the wall. I didn't dare let go of the film. The next thing I knew the whole cabin went up like a flashlight powder; that was his blackjack on the back of my head. I didn't quite lose consciousness, but the place was going round in sparks; I slugged him again, and I was bent over the part of the film I had. Then he yanked the door open and got out somehow. I must have been knocked out for a few minutes then. When I came to, I rang for the steward, sloshed some water on my head, and discovered—" With his foot Warren raised the tangle of film on the floor.

"But didn't you *see* him?" asked the girl, in her fluttering concern, again taking hold of his head and causing an agonised "Ow!" She jumped. "I mean, old boy, that, after all, you were fighting with him. . . ."

"No, I didn't see him, I tell you! It might have been anybody. . . . But the question is, what's to be done? I'm appealing to you for help. We've got to get that piece of film back. He got—maybe fifty feet of it. And that's as dangerous as though he'd got all of it."

Chapter III

TRAP FOR A FILM THIEF

"Well," Morgan observed thoughtfully, "I admit this is the rummiest kind of secret-service mission that a self-respecting hero was ever called on to undertake. It rouses my professional instincts."

He felt a glow of pleasurable excitement. Here was he, an eminent writer of detective stories, involved in one of those complicated spy plots to recover a stolen document and preserve the honour of a great Personage. It was the sort of thing that would have been nuts to Mr. Oppenheim; and, Morgan reflected, he himself had often used the background of a luxurious ocean liner, sweeping its lighted decks through waters floored with stars—full of monocled crooks sipping champagne; of pale, long-necked Ladies with a Purpose who are not interested in love-making; and of dirty work in general. (The women in a secret-service story seldom *are* interested in love-making; that is the trouble with it.) Although the *Queen Victoria* was scarcely the boat for such goings-on, Morgan considered the idea and found it good. Outside, it had begun to rain. The liner was bumping like a tub against the crash of the swell, and Morgan lurched a little as he stalked up and down the narrow cabin, revolving plans, pushing his glasses up and down his nose, becoming each second more excited with the prospect.

"Well?" demanded Peggy Glenn. "Say something, Hank! Of course we help him, don't we?"

She still seemed hurt by the behaviour of the eminent soaks; but her protective instincts had been roused and her small jaw was very square. She had even put on her shell-rimmed reading-glasses, which lent a look of unwonted sombreness (or flippant make-believe, if you like) to the thin face. And she had removed her hat, to show a mop of black bobbed hair. Sitting with one leg curled under her, she regarded Morgan almost fiercely. He said:

"My girl, I wouldn't miss it for—well, for a good deal. Ha! It is obvious," he continued, with relish, and hoped it was true, "that there is aboard a wily and clever international crook who is determined to secure that film for purposes of his own. Very good. We therefore form a Defensive Alliance. . . ."

"Thanks," said Warren, in some relief. "God knows I need help and—you see, you were the only people I could trust. Well, then?"

"Right. You and I, Curt, will be the Brains. Peggy will be the Siren, if we need one. Captain Valvick will be the Brawn—"

"Hah!" snorted the captain, nodding vigorously and lifting his shoulders with approval. He twinkled down on them, and raised his arm with terrific gusto. " 'For God! For de cause! For de Church! For de laws,' " he thundered unexpectedly. " 'For Charles, King of England, and Rupert off de Rhine!' Ha-ha-ha."

"What the devil's that?" demanded Morgan.

"Ay dunno yust what it mean," admitted the captain, blinking on them rather sheepishly. "Ay read it in a book once, and ay t'ink it iss fine. If ay ever get stirred up in de heart—hoooo-o!—Ay say it." He shook his head. "But ay got to be careful wit' de books. When ay finish reading one, ay got to be careful to write its name down so I don't forget and go back and read it all over again."

He looked on them with great amiability, rubbing his nose, and inquired, "But what iss dere you want me to do?"

"First," said Morgan, "it's agreed that you don't want official steps taken, Curt? I mean, you could tell Captain Whistler—?"

"Lord, no!" the other said violently. "I can't do that, don't you see? If we get this back at all, it's got to be under the strictest cover. And that's where it's going to be difficult. Out of the whole passenger-list of this boat, how are we going to pick out the person who might want to steal the thing? Besides, how did the fellow know I had that film, if I didn't know it myself?"

Morgan reflected. "That wireless message—" he said, and stopped. "Look here, you said you read it aloud, And it was only a very short time afterwards that the chap tried to burgle this cabin. It seems too much to be a coincidence. . . . Was there anybody who might have overheard you?"

The other made scoffing noises. In the pure absorption of the debate he had absent-mindedly fished out a bottle of whisky from one of his suit-cases. "Bunk!" said Warren. "Suppose there were a crook of some description aboard. What would that cock-eyed message mean to him? It took some time for *me* to figure it out."

"All right. All right, then! It's got to mean this. The thief was somebody who already knew about the film; that is, that there had been one made. . . . That's possible, isn't it?"

Warren hesitated, knocking his knuckles against his turbaned forehead.

"Ye-es, I suppose it is," he admitted. "There were all sorts of rumours afloat next day; you know how it is. But we were in the library with the door locked, and naturally it can't be any of the people who were in the game. . . . I told you there was a reception downstairs, but how anybody down there could have known—"

"Well, evidently somebody *did* know," Morgan argued. "And it's at a crush of a reception like that, at the home of some big pot, where you'd expect to find a specimen of the gentry we're looking for. . . . Put it this way, just for a starter." He meditated, pulling at his ear-lobe. "The thief—we'll call him, say, Film-Flam—gets wind of your important document. But he thinks it's been destroyed and abandons any idea of pinching it. Still, he is travelling abroad on the *Queen Victoria*—"

"Why?" inquired Miss Glenn practically.

"How should I know?" Morgan demanded, with some asperity. His imagination had been working on opulent ballrooms full of tiaras and red shirt-ribbons; and sinister whiskery strangers smoking cigarettes round the corners of pillars. "Maybe it was accident, maybe Film-Flam is a professional diplomatic crook who dashes about from capital to capital and hopes for the best. Anyway, you've got to admit it was somebody who'd been in Washington and heard all about the indiscretion. . . . Righto, then. He's abandoned the idea, but all the same he happens to be travelling aboard the same boat as Curt. If you looked at the passenger-list, Curt, would you recognise the name of anybody who'd been at your uncle's house that night?"

Warren shook his head.

"There were millions of 'em and I didn't know anybody. No, that won't work. . . . But you mean this. You mean that this bird (after abandoning the idea) overhears that cable in the wireless-room, tumbles to it before I do, and takes a long chance on stealing it before I've got time to realise what I'm carrying?"

"He'd have to work fast, man. Otherwise, as soon as you knew you'd chuck it overboard. And here's another thing," crowed Morgan, stabbing his finger into his palm as the idea grew on him. "The field of search isn't as wide as you'd think at first. Again this is only a theory, but look here!—isn't this chap pretty sure to be somebody who has scraped an acquaintance with you already? I mean, if I were an international crook, even though I didn't think you were carrying that roll of film, I'm jolly certain *I'd* try to get into your good graces. As Uncle Warpus's favourite nephew, you'd be a valuable person to make friends with. . . . Doesn't that sound reasonable?"

By this time they were all eagerly engrossed in the business, floundering as they tried to stand or sit in the creaking cabin, and each playing with theories. Warren, who had produced paper cups and was pouring out drinks, stopped. He handed a cup carefully to Peggy Glenn before he spoke. Then he said:

"It's a funny thing you should say that. . . ."

"Well?"

"Aside from yourselves, I know very few people aboard this tub. The weather's been too bad, for one thing. But it's funny." He blew into a folding paper cup savagely to open it; then he looked up. "There were—let's see—there were five people in the wireless-room at the time my cable came through, aside from the operator and myself. There was Captain Whistler, who was having some kind of whispered row with the operator; he walked out in a turkey-cock rage. There was a girl I hadn't seen before. Wash out the captain and that girl, and there were three men. One of 'em I didn't know; didn't notice him at all. . . . But the last two are the only other people I *do* know. One was that fellow Woodcock, the travelling salesman for the bug-powder firm; and the other was Dr. Kyle, who sits at our table."

There was a hoot of derision from Peggy Glenn at the mention of the latter name. Even Morgan, whose profession of necessity made him doubly suspicious of any respectable person, inclined to agree with her. They had both heard of Dr. Kyle. He was one of the more resounding names in Harley Street—a noted brain specialist who had figured as alienist in several murder trials. Morgan remembered him at the table—a tall, lean, rather sardonic Scot, slovenly except for his well-brushed hair, with shrewd eyes under ragged brows whisking upwards at the outer corner, and two deep furrows running down his cheeks. To imagine this distinguished loony-doctor in the role of Film-Flam strained even Morgan's credulity. If he were given a choice in crooks, he would have preferred to fasten on the bouncing Mr. Charles Woodcock, commercial traveller for "Swat," the instant eradicator of insects. But, distinctly, Dr. Kyle must be counted out.

However, when he pointed out this difficulty to Warren, it seemed to make the American all the more certain Dr. Kyle was the culprit.

"Absolutely!" said Warren excitedly. "It's always people like that. Besides—suppose somebody's impersonating him? There's an idea for you! What better disguise would there be for an international crook than as the respectable head of a bughouse? Say, if we were to tax him with it—jump on him suddenly, you see—"

"You want to be shoved in the psychopathic ward?" demanded Morgan. "No, we can't do that; not with Kyle. Besides, it's nonsense! We've got to rule out Kyle, and get a good working plan. . : ."

Captain Valvick shifted from one foot to the other.

"Excuse me," he suggested, with a sort of thunderous timidity, and beamed on them. "Ay got a idea, ay haff."

"H'm!" said Morgan dubiously.

"Ay tell you," pursued the captain, peering round to be sure they were not overheard, "dis feller dat bat you one, he hass got only half de film, eh? Well, den, ay tell you what. He got only half de film; den maybe he iss going to come back, eh? So we stand watch and when he come back we say, 'Hey—!' ''

"Yes, I know," interrupted Warren, with a gloomy air. "I'd thought of that, too, but it won't work. That's what always happens in the stories; but you can bet your last shirt this bird is too cagy for that. He knows I'm wise to him, he knows I'll take good care of that film; *if* I don't pitch the rest of it overboard right away. No, no. He won't take any risk like that."

For some time Peggy Glenn had been sitting silent, her chin cupped in her hands, studying the matter. Her glossy hair was tousled across her forehead, and now she suddenly looked up with such an expression of diabolical brightness and practicality that she almost crowed.

"You men," she said, rather scornfully—"you men—just messing about, that's all! Now you let *me* tell you what to do, and you'll have your film back to-night. Yes, I mean it. I fancy I've got an idea"—she struggled to conceal the pleasure that was making her tilt up her chin and grow as excited as Warren—"and it's a *ripping* idea! Whee! Listen. In a way, Captain Valvick is right. We've got to trap this chap into coming back for the rest of the film. . . ."

Warren made a weary gesture, but she frowned him down.

"Will you listen to me? I tell you we can do it. Because why? Because *we* are the only people on the whole boat—we four—who know Curt was attacked and why he was attacked. Very well. We give it out publicly that we came in here and found Curt lying on the floor unconscious, dead to the world with a bad scalp wound. We have no suspicions that there was an attack or theft. We don't know how it happened; we suppose that he must have come in here drunk or something, and staggered about and finally fell and bashed himself over the head—"

Warren raised his eyebrows.

"Baby," he said with dignity, "it is not that I myself have any objection to the charming picture you have just described. But I only want to remind you that I am a member of the American Diplomatic Service. The DIPLOMATIC Service, Baby. The rules laid down for the strictness of my behaviour would cause annoyance among the seraphim and start a riot in a waxworks. I dislike offering suggestions, but why don't you say that in the course of my customary morning opium debauch I went cuckoo and batted my head against the wall? My chief would like that fine."

"Oh, all right," she conceded primly, "if you must keep to your nasty old rules. Then—say you were ill or sea-sick; anyway, that it was an accident. Well, that you haven't recovered consciousness. . . ."

Morgan whistled. "I begin to see this. Curt, I believe the wench has got something!"

"Yes," said Warren, "and in another minute I'm going to tell you what it is. Go on, Baby. Here, have another drink. After I am picked up insensible, what then?"

"Then," the girl continued, beaming excitedly, "we tell everybody you were taken to the infirmary, where you are still in a stupor. You see, if we tell it at the table it will go all about the boat. It's supposed to be an accident, so there'll be no investigation. In the meantime here will be the cabin, open and unguarded. Don't you think this crook will see his opportunity? Of course he will. He'll come back straightaway—and there you are."

She tossed up her head, her hazel eyes shining and her lower lip folded over the upper in defiant triumph. There was a silence.

"By God! it's good!" exploded Morgan, driving his fist into his palm. Even Warren was impressed; he sat like a thoughtful Indian prophet, staring at the paper cup, while Captain Valvick chuckled and Peggy said: "Hoo!" in a pleased tone. "But wait a bit," Morgan added, "what about the steward, the one you sent to tell us? *He* knows."

"Stewards never talk," the girl said wisely; "they know too much as it is. Make it certain with a good tip. Then you can go ahead. . . . By the way, Curt, is the cabin next to this one vacant? That's where you want to hide and wait for him, if it is."

"Why not in here?"

"He'd see you straightaway, you silly! And you've got to catch him with the goods. It's no good saying, 'Cough up, you villain!' unless you can catch him dead to rights. He'd only say he'd got into the wrong cabin by mistake, and then where are you? He must have the film on his person—then," she added judicially, "I dare say you may land him one, dear, if you like."

"Ah-hh!" Warren breathed, and dreamily fingered a large fist. "Yes, Baby, the next cabin is unoccupied, as it happens. Tell you what. I'll install myself in there, and get the steward to bring me some dinner. Captain Valvick can keep watch with me. You two go down to dinner and spread the glad news. Then you can join us afterwards. We'll probably have a long wait. The ingredients for cocktails might not be out of place. . . ."

"But we mustn't get drunk," said Miss Glenn, as though she were uttering a careful definition of terms.

"Oh, no!" said Warren vigorously. "Not at all. Of course not. Ha-ha! The idea is absurd. But look here, I wish we had more dope on our mysterious crook. If we could only find out something about him. . . ." He frowned. "Wait a minute. I've got an idea. Captain, you know Captain Whistler pretty well, don't you?"

"Dat old barnacle?" inquired the other. "Coroo! Ay know him when he wass not so stuck up, you bet. He got a hawful temper, I tell you. De first time ay know him wass in Naples, when he come in wid de cargo-boat where de chief mate hass de religious mania and go crazy and t'ink he is Yesus." The breath whistled through Valvick's large moustache; his sandy eyebrows rose and he illustrated the drama. "De chief mate walk up on de bridge and fold his arms and say, 'Ay am Yesus.' De captain say, 'You are not Yesus.' De chief mate say, 'Ay am Yesus and you are Pontius Pilate,' and *smack*—he haul off and bust Captain Whistler in de yaw, and dey got to put 'im in irons. Iss a fact. Ay t'ank of it w'en you say Dr. Kyle iss a mad doctor, because Captain Whistler don' like de people which go nutty. Anudder time—"

"Listen, old man," begged Warren. "Spare the Odyssey for a minute. If there were any big international crook aboard, or there were a rumour of it, Captain Whistler would be the one to know about it, wouldn't he? They'd wireless him, wouldn't they, even if he kept it under cover?"

Valvick massively lifted his head sideways and scratched his cheek.

"Ay dunno. It depend on wedder dey know it at de port. Maybe. You want me to hask him?"

"Well—not exactly. Sort of sound him out, you see? Don't let on you know anything. You might do it before dinner; and then we'd be all ready to keep watch."

The other nodded vigorously, and Warren looked at his watch. "Nearly time for the bugle to dress for dinner. We're all set, then?"

There was an enthusiastic chorus in the affirmative. For all these people had within them the true, glorious hare-brained spirit of adventure; and Warren poured them a quick one as a toast to the new gamble as lights came on through the vibrating sleekness of white decks, and rain-squalls spattered the portholes, and the voice of a bugle began to brattle past state-room doors, and the stately *Queen Victoria* shouldered on towards the wild business that was to be.

Chapter IV

A MATTER OF SKULLS

"But didn't you know it?" inquired Peggy Glenn, in her sweetest and most surprised tone.

Her voice was clear in the almost deserted dining-saloon, its lights winking against polished rosewood and its vast height wrenched with ghostly cracklings. The roof writhed in the fashion of tottering blocks; Morgan was not at all sure about that glass dome. To eat (or do nearly anything else) was a sporting performance in which you must look sharp for sudden rushes of the crockery from any corner of the table, from the snake-like dart of the water-glass to the majestic ground-swell of the gravy. Morgan felt like a nervous juggler. The dining-saloon would slowly surge up with an incredible balloon swell, climb higher, tilt, and plunge down from its height with a long-drawn roar of water that dislodged stewards from their pillars and made diners—clutching their chairs—feel a sudden dizziness in the pit of the stomach.

There were possibly a dozen people to stem a clattering avalanche of dishes and silver. In general, they were eating away grimly but cautiously, while a gallant orchestra attempted to play "The Student Prince." But none of this bothered Peggy Glenn. Suave in black velvet, with her black bobbed hair done into some sort of trick wave that lent a hoydenish air to her thin face, she sat at Captain Whistler's elbow and regarded him with naïve surprise.

"But didn't you know it?" she repeated. "Of course Curtis can't help it, poor boy. It runs in the family, sort of. I mean, I shouldn't exactly call it insanity, of course. . . ."

Morgan choked on a bit of fish and peered sideways at her. She appealed to him.

"I say, Hank, what was the name of that uncle of his Curt was telling us about? I mean the one who had the fits-and-gibbers or something in his sleep, or maybe it was claustrophobia, and used to give a terrific spring out of bed because he thought he was being strangled?"

Captain Whistler laid down his knife and fork. He had obviously been in an ill temper when he came to the table; but he had concealed it under gruff amiability and absentminded smiles. Wheeling round his chair he had announced that he must return to the bridge and could stay only for one course or two. Captain Whistler was stout and short of breath. He had protruding eyes of a pale brown colour, something like the hue of pickled onions, a ruddy face, and a large loose mouth which was always booming a professional and paternal "Ha-ha" to nervous old ladies. His gold braid blazed, and his short white hair stood up like the foam on a beer-glass.

Now he addressed Peggy with coy heartiness. "Come, come," he said in his best nursery manner, "and what is the little lady telling us now? Eh, my dear? Something about an accident to a friend of yours?"

"A *dreadful* accident," she assured him, looking round to make sure the dining-room would overhear. The only people at their own table were the captain, Dr. Kyle, Morgan, and herself; so she wanted to make sure. She described Warren's being picked up unconscious, with a wealth of graphic detail. "But, of course, poor boy, he isn't responsible for his actions when he gets into those fits. . . ."

Captain Whistler looked concerned, and then rather alarmed. His fleshy face grew redder.

"Ah, hurrumph!" he said, clearing his throat. "Dear me! Dear me!"—it speaks much for the captain's social polish that he could sometimes force himself to say "Dear me!"—"Bad, bad, Miss Glenn! But there's nothing—ah—seriously wrong with him, is there?" He peered at her in gruff anxiety. "Is it maybe something in Dr. Kyle's line now?"

"Well, of course, I shouldn't like to say—"

"Have you known cases of the kind, Doctor?"

Kyle was not a man of many words. He was methodically disposing of grilled sole—a lean, long-faced figure with a bulging shirt-front, and traces of a thin smile had pulled down the furrows in his cheeks. He glanced at Peggy from under grizzled eyebrows, and then at Morgan. Morgan received the impression that he believed in Warren's lurid ailment about as much as he believed in the Loch Ness monster.

"Oh, yes," he replied in his heavy, meditative voice. "Not unknown. I've met it before." He looked hard at Peggy. "A mild case of *legensis-pullibus*, I should think. Patient'll recover."

In a harassed way Captain Whistler wiped his mouth with his napkin.

"But—ah—why wasn't I told of this?" he demanded. "I'm master here, and it's my right to be told of things like this. . . ."

"I did tell you, Captain!" Peggy protested indignantly. "I've been sitting here the whole time telling you; I told you three times over before you understood. I say, what *is* worrying you?"

"Eh?" said the captain, jumping a little. "Worrying me? Rubbish, my dear! Rubbish! Ha-ha!"

"I mean, I hope we're not going to hit an iceberg or anything. That would be dreadful!" She regarded him with wide hazel eyes. "And, you know, they *do* say the captain of the *Gigantic* was drunk the night they hit the whale, and—"

"I am not drunk, madam," said Captain Whistler, his voice taking on a slight roar. "And I am not worried either. Rubbish!"

She seemed to have an inspiration. "Then I know what it is, poor dear! Of course. You're worried about poor Lord Sturton and all those valuable emeralds he's got with him. . . ." Commiseratingly she looked at the chair which a very sea-sick peer had not yet occupied on the voyage. "And I don't blame you. I say, Hank, just fancy. Suppose there were a notorious criminal aboard—just suppose it, I mean—and this criminal had decided to pinch Lord Sturton's jewels. Wouldn't it be thrilling? Only not for poor Captain Whistler, of course; because he'd be responsible, wouldn't he?"

Under the table Morgan administered an unmannerly kick towards the shins of his beaming partner. His lips framed "Easy on!" But undoubtedly a number of diners had pricked up their ears.

"My dear young lady," said the captain, in an agitated voice, "for Go—ah—please kindly get that nonsense out of your pretty little head. Ha-ha! You'll alarm my passengers, you know; and I can't have that, can I? (*Lower your voice, will you?*) The idea's fantastic. Come, now!"

She was appealing. "Oh dear, have I said anything I shouldn't? I mean, I was only supposing, to sort of relieve the monotony; because it *has* been rather dull, you know, and there hasn't been anything really funny, dear Captain Whistler, since I saw you playing handball on the boat-deck. But if there were a notorious criminal on board, it would be exciting. And it might be anybody. It might be Hank. Or it might be Dr. Kyle—mightn't it?"

"Verra likely," agreed Dr. Kyle composedly, and went on dissecting fish.

"But if I did have anything on my mind," declared the captain, in heavy joviality, "it would be about your uncle, Miss Glenn. He's promised to give us a full-dress performance of his marionettes at the ship's concert. And that's to-morrow night, my dear. He mustn't be ill for that, you know. He and his assistant—ah—well, they're—they're improving, aren't they?" said the captain, his voice rising to a desperate bellow as he tried to divert her. "I have looked forward, I have hoped, I have waited for the—ah—pleasure, the supreme honour," yelled Captain Whistler, "of being present at a performance. And now you really must excuse me. I mustn't forget my duties, even at the expense of your charming company. I must—er—go. Good night, my dear. Good night, gentlemen."

He rolled away. There was a silence. Of the diners left at roundabout tables, Morgan noticed swiftly, only three people glanced after him. There was the sharp-edged, bony, shock-haired face of Mr. Charles Woodcock, the commercial traveller, who peered out motionless with his soup-spoon poised above his mouth as though he were going to pose for a figure of a fountain. At another table some distance away Morgan saw a man and a woman—both thin and well-dressed, their pale faces looking curiously alike except that the woman wore a monocle and the man a floating blond moustache like a feather waving from his lip. They stared after the captain. Morgan did not know who they were, but he saw them every morning. They made endless circuits of the promenade-deck, in absolute silence walking rapidly, with their eyes fixed straight ahead. One morning, in dull fascination, Morgan had watched them make one hundred and sixty-four circuits without a word. At the hundred and sixty-fifth they had stopped; the man said, "Eh?" and the woman said, "Ah!" and then they both nodded and went inside. It had occurred to Morgan to speculate how their marital relations were conducted. . . . Anyhow, they seemed to be interested in the movements of Captain Whistler.

"The captain," said Morgan, frowning, "seems to have something on his mind. . . ."

"Verra likely," agreed Dr. Kyle composedly. "I'll have the tripe and onions, steward."

Peggy Glenn smiled at him. "But I say, Doctor, do you think there might be a mysterious master criminal aboard?"

"Why, I'll tell you," said the doctor, bending his head. His shrewd eyes were amused; under the ragged brows whisking upwards at the corners, and with the furrows deepening round his mouth, Morgan thought uncomfortably that he looked a little too much like Sherlock Holmes. "And I'll put in a word of warning gratis. You're a clever young lady, Miss Glenn. But don't pull Captain Whistler's leg too hard. He'd be a bad man to have on the wrong side of anybody. Please pass the salt."

The dining-saloon soared up on another swell, and tilted amid sour notes from the orchestra. "But, really," said Peggy, "I mean, it's perfectly true about poor old Curt. . . ."

"Oh, ah!" said Dr. Kyle. "Was he sober?"

"Doctor," she told him, lowering her voice confidentially, "I hate to tell it, but he was terribly, *terribly* drunk, poor boy. I mean, it's all right to speak of these things to a medical man, isn't it? But I pitied him from the bottom of my heart, poor boy, when I saw. . . ."

Morgan got her away from the table after a brief and telegraphic exchange of kicks. They navigated the big staircase and stood in a breezy, lurching hall upstairs while Morgan said things. But Peggy, her prim little face beaming, only chortled with pleasure. She said she must go to her cabin and get a wrap, if they were going to watch with the others; also that she ought to look in on her Uncle Jules.

"By the way," she said, doubtfully, "I don't suppose you'd care to be a Moorish warrior, would you?"

"Not particularly," said Morgan, with conviction. "Is this relevant to the issue?"

"All you'd have to do, you know, would be blacken your face and put on some gilt armour and shawls and things; and stand at one side of the stage with a spear while Uncle Jules speaks the prologue. . . . I wonder if you're tall enough, though? I say, Captain Valvick would make a *ripping* Moorish warrior, wouldn't he?"

"Oh, unquestionably."

"You see, there have to be two extras, a French warrior and a Moor, who stand on either side of the stage for effect. The stage isn't high enough for them to be on it; they're outside, on a little platform. . . . When the play begins they go backstage, and sometimes they help move the figures—the unimportant ones that have nothing to do. Only my uncle and Abdul (that's his assistant) move the chief figures; they're the only ones with speaking parts. . . . I say, it would be simply awful if Uncle Jules can't play. There's a professor or somebody aboard who's written all kinds of articles about his art. Abdul's all right and he could take the main part in place of uncle. But I'm the only other one and I couldn't very well say the men's lines, could I?"

They had gone down into a tangle of passages on D deck, and Peggy knocked at a door. In response to a spectral groan, she pushed the door open. The cabin was dark except for a faint light over the washstand. That scene—with the cabin twisting sideways, and rain slashing the porthole—gave Morgan a slight shiver. Two or three witless-looking dummies were sprawled against the bulkhead in a seated position, and swayed with the motion as though they were moving their heads in a horrible chorus. The straps and hooks for their wires rattled eerily; they were solid lumps about four and a half feet tall; they glittered with gilt armour, red cloaks, and gaudy jewelled accoutrements. Their faces, bearded formidably in dark wool, smirked from under spiked helmets. While they swayed, a powerful-looking man with a flattish dark face sat on the couch with another dummy across his knee. In the dim light he was mending the figure's cloak with a long needle and blue thread. Occasionally he glanced towards the dark berth where something heavy was burrowing and groaning.

"*Je meurs!*" whispered a voice from the berth, dramatically. "*Ah, mon Dieu, je meurs! Ooooo! Abdul, je t'implore. . . .*"

Abdul shrugged, squinted at his needle, shrugged again, and spat on the floor. Peggy closed the door.

"He's no better," she said, unnecessarily, and they started back to the cabin where Warren was waiting. Morgan, in fact, was not eager for more than a glimpse into that cabin. Whether it was merely night and the rain in the middle of a shouting Atlantic, or merely that dull after-dinner feeling which is not dispelled on shipboard without bibulous hilarity, still he did not like the look of those smirking dummies. Moreover, such an irrelevant impression as that had given him another impression—of trouble ahead. There was no Q.E.D. about it, or even a rational subtlety. But he glanced round rather sharply when they reached the side passage that led to Warren's cabin.

It opened off a main corridor, and its short length contained two cabins on either side. Warren's was an end one on the left, beside a door opening out on C deck. It was dark, and the white-painted door was hooked open. Morgan knocked in the manner agreed on at the door beside it, and they slipped inside.

Only the light inside the lower berth was on. Warren sat gingerly on the edge of the berth. And he looked worried.

Morgan said sharply, but in a low voice, "Anything wrong?"

"Plenty," said the other. "Sit down and keep as quiet as you can. I think we've got a long time to wait, but you never can tell what *this* joker will be up to. Valvick's gone for some soda-water. And we're set now." He nodded towards the ventilator high in the wall, communicating with the next cabin. "If anybody goes in there, we can hear him in a second. Then we nab him. Moreover, I've got the hook on the door wedged so that, no matter how quiet he tries to be, he'll make a racket as loud as an alarm clock."

Warren paused, rubbing his jaw rather nervously and peering about the dim-lit state-room. He had discarded the towel round his head, but absorbent gauze and sticking-plaster along the back of the skull still made his dark hair stand up in a goblin-like way. The glow in the berth illumined one side of his face, and they could see a vein beating in his temple.

"Curt," said the girl, "what *is* wrong?"

"All hell, I'm afraid. Old Valvick went to see Captain Whistler before dinner. . . ."

"Yes?"

"Well, I don't know how much in earnest you people were when we were sitting in there piling up theories about fancy crooks. But the impossible happened. We were right. There's a very badly wanted little joker aboard, and no joke about it. He's after old Sturton's emerald. And—he's a killer."

Morgan felt in the pit of his stomach an uneasy sensation which was partly the motion of the ship. He said:

"Are you serious, or is this—?"

"You bet I'm serious. So is Whistler. Valvick got the information from him, because Whistler badly needs advice. Old Valvick's story is pretty muddled; but that much is clear. Whistler wonders whether to keep it dark or broadcast the news to the ship. Valvick advised the latter: it's customary. But Whistler says this is a respectable boat, a family boat, and the rest of that stuff. . . ."

Morgan whistled. Peggy went over and sat down beside Warren. She protested stoutly that it was nonsense and she didn't believe it.

"Who is he, Curt? What do they know about him?" she demanded.

"That's just it. Nobody seems to know, except that he's travelling under an alias. You remember, I told you this afternoon that when I was in the radio-room old Whistler seemed to be having a row with the wireless operator? . . . Well, that was it. He'd got a radiogram. Fortunately, Valvik had the sense to persuade Whistler to let him take a copy of it. Have a look."

From his inside pocket he took an envelope, on the back of which was sprawled in crooked handwriting:

COMMANDER S.S. *QUEEN VICTORIA*, AT SEA. SUSPECT MAN
RESPONSIBLE FOR STELLY JOB IN WASHINGTON AND MACGEE
KILLING HERE SAILED UNDER ALIAS YOUR SHIP. FEDERAL OFFI-
CER ARRIVING TO-NIGHT FROM WASHINGTON AND WILL SEND
FULLER INFORMATION. LOOK OUT FOR SMOOTH CUSTOMERS AND
ADVISE IF ANY SUSPECTS.

                              ARNOLD, COMMISSIONER N.Y.P.D.

"I don't know anything about this MacGee killing, whatever it is, in
New York," Warren went on, "but I know a little about the Stelly
business because it raised such a row and looked like magic. It was tied
up with the British Embassy. Stelly seems to have been a pretty well-
known English jewel-cutter and appraiser. . . ."

"Hold on!" said Morgan. "D'you mean that Bond Street fellow, the
one who's always designing the necklaces for royalty and having pictures
of his work in the newspapers?"

Warren grunted. "Probably. Because it seems he was staying in Washington, and the wife of the British ambassador asked him to reset or
redesign a necklace for her. I don't know the details of it—nobody knows
much about it. But he left the British Embassy with the necklace one
night, as safe as you please, and about four hours later they found him
somewhere out Connecticut Avenue way. He was sitting on the kerbstone
with his back propped up against a street lamp, and the back of his head
smashed in. He didn't die, but he'll be a paralysed moron for the rest of
his life, and never speak a word. That seems to be a quaint habit of this
joker. He doesn't exactly kill; but he has a knack of softening their heads
so that they're worse than dead. . . ."

"By the Lord!" said Warren, clenching and unclenching his hands,
"I'm wondering whether that's what *I* nearly got in the other cabin, only
the fellow missed his aim when the ship rolled."

There was a silence, made portentous by creaking bulkheads and the
blustering roar outside.

"I say, Peggy," Morgan observed, thoughtfully, "you'd better get out
of this, old girl. It isn't funny. Go up to the bar and entice some gullibles
into a bridge game. If this basher comes along and tries to pinch the rest
of the film, we'll let you know. Meantime—"

The girl said, with vehemence, "Bah! You can't scare me. You *are* a
cheerful lot, though. Why don't you start telling ghost stories? If you start
off by being afraid of this chap—"

"Who's afraid of him?" shouted Warren. "Listen, Baby. I've got
something to settle, I have. When I get *at* him—" Satirically he watched
her jump a little when there was a knock at the door. Captain Valvick
bearing two large siphons of soda-water, bent his head under the door and
closed it behind him with a mysterious air.

Morgan always remembered the ensuing two hours (or possibly three) on account of the interminable game of Geography that was played to pass away the time. Captain Valvick—cheerfully twinkling, in no whit disturbed—insisted that they should turn out the light, hook the door partly open, and get enough light from the dim bulb in the passage. First he administered to each a hair-raising peg of whisky, which made them feel anew the excellence of the adventure; then he placed them in a weird circle on the floor, with the bottle in the middle like a camp fire; finally, he filled up the glasses again.

"Skoal!" said the captain, raising his glass in the dim light. "Ay tell you, diss iss de life. Coroosh! But ay got to feel bad about Captain Whistler. Ho-ho! Dat poor old barnacle iss near crazy. you bet, on account of de crook which like to steal de jewellery. He iss afraid diss crook going to rob de English duke, and he try to persuade de duke to let him lock up de hemereld helephant in de captain's safe. But dat duke only give him de bird. He say, 'It be safer wit' me dan in your safe, or wit' de purser or anybody.' De captain say no. De duke say yes. De captain say no. De duke say yes. . . ."

"Look here, you can omit the element of suspense," said Morgan, taking another drink. "What did they decide?"

"Ay dunno yust what dey decide. But ay got to feel bad about dat poor old barnacle. Come on, now; we play Geography."

This game was trying, but in many senses lively. As the whisky diminished, it led to long and bitter arguments between Warren and the captain. The latter, when stumped for a place-name, would always introduce some such place as Ymorgenickenburg or the River Skoff, in Norway. Warren would heatedly cast slurs on his veracity. Then the captain would say he had an aunt living there. As this was not considered *prima facie* evidence, he would embark on a long and complicated anecdote about the relative in question, with accounts of such other members of his family as happened to occur to him. Morgan's watch ticked on, and the stir about the boat gradually died away into a roaring night, as they heard about the captain's brother, August, his Cousin Ole, his niece Gretta, and his grandfather who was a beadle. Footsteps went by in the main corridor, but none of them turned into the side passage. It was growing stuffy in the cabin. . . .

"I—I think he probably won't come," Peggy whispered, reverting to the subject for the first time. There was an uneasy hopefulness in the way she said it.

"It's hotter than hell in here," muttered Warren. Glassware rattled faintly. "I'm tired of the game, anyhow. I think—"

"Listen!" said Morgan.

He had scrambled up and was holding to the side of the berth. They all felt it—a terrific draught blowing through the passage outside, rattling the hooks of the doors, and they heard the deeper tumult of the sea boiling more loudly. The door to D deck had been pushed open.

But it did not close. They were all standing up now, waiting to hear the swish and slam of that door as it closed against the compressed-air valve. Those doors were heavy; and in a wind you dodged inside quickly. But for an interminable time something seemed to be holding it partly open, while the draught whistled. The *Queen Victoria* rose, pitched, and went over in a long roll to starboard, but still the door stayed open. It was impossible to distinguish smaller noises above the crazy wickerwork creaking, but yet Morgan had an eerie sense that the door did not close because it could not; that there was something caught there, trapped in a snare and in pain, between the black sea and warm security inside.

They heard a moan. A faint voice seemed to be muttering something, muttering and repeating thinly in the passage. "Warren!" they thought it said. And again, *"Warren. . . ."* until it died off in pain.

Chapter V

ENTER THE EMERALD ELEPHANT

Morgan almost pitched head foremost into the wardrobe as his clumsy fingers fumbled at the hook on the door. He righted himself, squeezed outside, and called to Valvick to follow.

There was something caught there. It was small and broken-looking, snapped between the jamb and the heavy door—a woman fallen forward across a sill six inches high. She wore no hat, and her dishevelled brown hair, which had tumbled down along one side, blew wildly in the draught. They could not see her face. Her hands, flung forward out of the sleeves of a green, fur-edged coat, were groping in weak movements—horribly, as though she were tapping at the keys of a piano. The head and body rolled with the ship. As they did, a splashing of blood ran thinly along the rubber matting of the floor.

With his shoulder, Morgan forced the door wide while Captain Valvick picked the woman up. Then the door boomed shut once more with a cessation of draught that made them shiver.

"Dat blood," said Valvick, suddenly, in a low voice. "Look! It iss from her nose. She been hit on de back off de head. . . ."

Her head lay limply in the crook of the captain's arm; and he moved his arm as though with a notion he must not touch her there. She was a sturdy, wiry girl with thick eyebrows and long lashes—not unattractive under a pallor that made her rouge stand out, but with one of those straight Greek-coin faces which have a look of heaviness rather than beauty. Her throat quivered as the head lolled over. Breathing raspingly, with eyes squeezed shut, she seemed to be trying to move her lips.

"In here," Warren's voice said in a whisper from the door of the dark cabin. They carried her in, a trembling Peggy making way for them, laid her down on the berth, and switched on the dim lamp inside. Morgan closed the door.

Peggy was very pale, but with some sudden mechanical impulse she seized a towel off the rack and wiped the blood from the nose and mouth of the inert girl.

"Who—who is she? What—?"

"Get some whisky," said the captain, curtly. Blinking his pale blue eyes, he puffed slowly through his moustache; there was a scowl on his face as he ran one finger along the base of the women's skull. "Ay dunno, but she may be hurt bad. Ha! Turn her on de side, and you wet de cloths. Ay haff to know somet'ing of what de doctor know because dere is no doctor on de cargo-boat. . . . Ha! Maybe—"

"I've seen her before," said Warren. He steadily poured out whisky and put it to the girl's lips as the captain eased up her head. "Hold it. . . . I'll see if I can force her teeth apart. Damn it! she's jerking like a mule. . . . She was the girl in the wireless-room this afternoon, the one who was there when I got my cable. You think her skull's fractured?"

"She might—" Peggy observed, in a small voice—"she might have fallen—"

"Haaaah!" growled the captain, jerking his neck. "She fall like Mr. Warren fall in de next cabin, you bet." His fingers were still exploring; his face looked heavy and puzzled. "Ho! Ay dunn, but ay don't t'ink she got de skull fractured; don't feel like it. See, it pain her when ay feel, eh? And dat iss not de way dey act if dey are bad 'urt. . . ." He drew a wheezing breath. "Try de whisky again. So."

"I'll swear I heard her saying my name," Warren whispered," "Got those wet towels, Hank? Put 'em on. Come on—er—ma'am" he said, with a kind of wild, coaxing note, "take some of this liquor. . . . Up you go! . . . Come on!"

His face wore a rather weird encouraging smile as he clicked the glass against her locked teeth. A shudder went over the white face. The *Queen Victoria* pitched down in a long foam of water, diving with such a deeper cyclone plunge that it flung them all against the forward bulkhead, and they could feel the thick shaking as the propellers beat out of water. But they could hear something else also. It had been done softly. with little draught and no slam whatever, but the door to D deck had again been opened and closed.

They were silent amid the rattling of the cabin. Warren, who had been cursing in a whisper when the contents of the glass splashed wide, turned round sharply. His face, under the wild goblin hair, wore a look of triumphant malevolence. Clinging to furniture, they waited. . . .

Somebody was trying the latch-hook of the cabin next door.

There was an elaborate pantomime of communication. Morgan's lips elaborately writhed to frame, "Let him get inside," as he jerked his thumb at the next cabin. Valvick and Warren nodded; they were all making fierce gestures, and nodding to one another, and trying to reach the passage-door without sprawling full-length. Warren glared at Peggy, and his lips formed, "You stay *here*," as he pointed at the girl in the berth and then savagely stabbed his finger at the floor. Giving him an answering glare, she folded over her under-lip mutinously and shook her head until the hair obscured her eyes. He repeated his order, first pleadingly and then with a graphic pantomime of somebody being strangled. Rearing out of the trough, the ship was climbing again on a steep upward slant. . . .

The light in the next room was switched on. . . .

Here on the floor, the whisky-bottle was rolling and bumping wildly. Captain Valvick made a dart for it, as a man chases his hat in a gale. The pantomime still went on, grotesque against the dim light in the berth, where that pale-faced figure was twisting. . . .

The door of the next cabin slammed.

Whether or not it was the wind, they could not tell. Warren tore open the door of his state-room, the sticking-plaster on his head going before like a banner, and lurched into the passage. Plunging out after Valvick's big figure, Morgan seized the handrail in the passage just in time to steady himself as the ship plunged once more. *The door opening out on C deck was closing again.*

Either he had been too quick for them or he had been frightened away. With a rather satiric wink, the rubber edging of the door caught and contracted; the gilt piston closed softly. Over the tortured wrenching and bone-cracking of the woodwork, when the whole ship seemed to be heeling over down a colossal chute, Warren let out a howl and charged for the door. The inrush of wind smashed over them as he got it open; they were whirled sideways in the trough of the wave, and the wind carried away something Captain Valvick was crying, about "be careful," and "hold de rail," and "close to water line."

The spray took Morgan in the face as he clambered out into darkness. Between spray and bellowing wind, he was momentarily blind. The wind cut through him with paralysing chill, and his foot slipped on the wet iron plates. A whistle and drumming went by in the halloo of the blast. A few lights from high up in the ship gleamed out across a darkness shot with ghostly white. The lights shone on creaming white flickers; on a curl of grey-black swell that shone like grained wood, and then a mist of spray as the wet deck tilted sickeningly and the crash of water rose high in a spectral mane. Morgan seized at the bulkhead rail, steadied himself, and shaded his eyes.

They were on the windward side. D deck was long, rather narrow, and very dimly lighted. He saw it go up before them on the rise—and he saw their man. A little way ahead, not holding to the rail, but, head down, a figure was hurrying towards the bows. Even in the dull yellow flicker in the roof they could see that this figure carried something under its arm. And this was a circular black box, flattish, and about ten inches in diameter. . . .

"Steady, boys!" said Warren, exultantly, and flapped against the rail. "Steady, boys! Here we go down again. Hang on!" He stabbed his finger ahead. "And *there's* the son-of-a—"

The rest of the sentence was lost, although he seemed to keep on speaking. They were after him. Far ahead, Morgan could see the lamp on the tall foremast swing up, rear, and swerve like a diver. He thought (and thinks to this day) that they did not so much run down that deck as hook their elbows to the rail and sail down it like a stupendous water-chute. They were going so fast, in fact, that he wondered whether they could stop in time, or whether they would go straight at the big enclosure of glass that protected the fore part of the deck from the wind's full violence. Their quarry heard them now. He had reached the turn of the deck by the glass enclosure when he heard the clatter of pursuit; he was almost in darkness, and he whirled round towards them. Juggled on flying water, the liner crested another rise. . . .

"HAAA!" screamed Warren, and charged.

To say that Warren hit the man would be a powerful understatement. Morgan afterwards wondered why that crack did not jar the other's head loose from his spine. Warren landed on his quarry's jaw, with the weight of his own thirteen stone and the catapult-start of the Atlantic Ocean behind. It was the most terrific, reverberating smack since Mr. William Henry Harrison Dempsey pasted Mr. Luis Angel Firpo clean over the ropes into the newspapermen's laps; and it is to be recorded that, when the other hit the glass enclosure, he bounced. Warren did not afterwards even give him time to fall. "You'll go around smacking people with a blackjack, will you?" he demanded—a purely rhetorical question. "You'll come into a guy's cabin, hey! and crack him one with a lead pipe? Oh, you will, will you?" inquired Mr. Warren, and waded in.

Both Captain Vavick and Morgan, who had been ready to lend assistance, clutched the rail and stared. The circular tin box slid from the victim's arms, clattered on the deck, and rolled. Valvick caught it as the deck was carrying it overboard.

"Yumping Yudas!" said the captain, his eyeballs bulging. "Ho! Hey! Go easy! Ay t'ank you going to kill him if you keep on. . . ."

"Whee!" said a voice behind them. "Darling! Sock him again!"

Reeling, Morgan turned round to see Peggy Glenn, without hat or coat, capering in the middle of the spray-drenched deck. Her hair was blowing wildly, and she beamed as she spun to keep her footing. She had the whisky-bottle in one hand ("in case somebody needed it," as she afterwards explained), and she was waving it encouragingly.

"You blasted little fool," yelled Morgan, "go back!" He seized her arm and dragged her to the inside rail, but she broke loose and stuck out her tongue at him. "Go back, I tell you! Here, take this—" he got the tin box from Valvick, and thrust it into her hands—"take this and go back. We'll be there. It's all over. . . ."

It was, and had been for some seconds. By the time she was persuaded to work her way back some distance. Warren had arranged his tie, smoothed the hair over his sticking-plaster, and come up to them with the deprecating air of a person who regrets having caused a fuss.

"Well, boys," he said, "I feel a little better. Now we can examine this blackjacker-user and see if he's carrying the first part of the film on him. If not, we can easily find out his cabin." He drew a deep breath. A high wave careered, swung and broke close to the deck, drenching him; but he only adjusted his tie and wiped the water from his eyes in a negligent fashion. He was beaming. "This isn't a bad night's work. As a member of the Diplomatic Service, I feel that I have earned considerable thanks from Uncle Warpus, and—What the devil's the matter with—!"

The girl had screamed. Even with the sea noises, it went up shrill and thin above them, paralysing on the darkened liner.

Morgan whirled round. She had taken the lid off the tin box, and Morgan noted in fascinated horror that the lid had a hasp and a hinge, which he did not remember having seen. . . . Holding tight to the rail, he wove his way to where the girl, under sickly electric bulb, was holding the box out and staring into it.

"Coroosh!" said Captain Valvick.

The box was not tin; it was thin steel. Inside, it was padded and lined with gleaming white satin. Bedded into a depression in the middle was a glow of green brilliancy which shifted and burned under the moving light. There were two rubies for eyes in the exquisitely carven thing; a piece of subtle Persian workmanship somewhat larger than a Vesta matchbox, and wound with gold links into a pendant.

"*Hold it!*" shouted Morgan, as a jerk of the deck nearly carried the box

overboard. He clutched it in. Wet splashes flashed out on the satin. . . .
"Thought," he yelled, "gone overboard. . . ."

He swallowed hard, and a nauseating suspicion struck him as he peered over his shoulder.

"By the Lord! had he pinched the emerald elephant?" demanded Warren. "Look here; we did better than we knew. Getting this back—ha! Why old Sturton'll—What's the matter with you all? What are you thinking about?" His eyes suddenly widened. They all stared at one another under the wild screaming of the night. "Look!" muttered Warren, swallowing hard. "That is, you don't think—*hurrum?*"

Captain Valvick groped his way down to where a stout mass in a waterproof, dead to the world, was wedged into an angle of the glass enclosure. Bending down, and sheltered by the enclosure, they saw the spurt of a match.

"Oh, Yesus!" said the captain, in an awed voice. He got up. He pushed back his cap and scratched his head. When he came back to them his leathery face had a queer, wrinkled, wryly amused expression, and his voice was matter-of-fact.

"Ay t'ank," he observed, scratching his head again—"ay t'ank we haf made a mistake. Ay t'ank we are in one most hawful yam. Ay t'ank de man you haff busted in de yaw is Captain Whistler."

Chapter VI

THE MISSING BODY

Morgan reeled, in a more than merely literal sense. Then he recovered himself, after a long silence in which everybody stared at everybody else. He hooked his arms in the rail and took a meditative survey of the deck. He cleared his throat.

"Well, well!" he said.

Captain Valvick suddenly chuckled, and then let out thunderous guffaws. He doubled up his shoulders, shook, writhed in unholy fashion, and there were tears in those honest old eyes as he leaned against the rail. Warren joined him; Warren could not help it. They chortled, they yowled, they slapped one another on the back and roared. Morgan eyed them in some disapproval.

"Not for the world," he observed, in a thoughtful yell, "would I care to be a spirit of Stygian gloom upon the innocent mirth and jollity of this occasion. Go on and gather rosebuds, you fatheads. But certain facts remain for our consideration. I am not thoroughly familiar with maritime law. Beyond the obvious fact that we have compounded and executed a felony, I am therefore not fully aware of the exact extent of our offence. But I have my suspicions, gentlemen. It would strike me that any sea-going passenger who wilfully up and busts the captain in the eye, or is found guilty of conniving at the same, will probably spend the rest of his life in clink. . . . Peggy, my dear, hand me that bottle. I need a drink."

The girl's lips were twitching with unholy mirth, but she put the steel box under her arm and obediently handed over the whisky. Morgan sampled it. He sampled it again. He had sampled it a third time before Warren got his face straight.

"It's aaal-ri-whooooosh!" roared Warren, doubling up again. "It's all riii-whi-choosh! I mean, wha-keeeee! It's all right, old man. You people go on back to the cabin and sit down and make yourselves comfortable. I'll throw some water over the old walrus and confess to him. Huh-huh-huh!" His shoulders heaved; he swallowed and straightened up. "I pasted him. So I'll have to tell him. . . ."

"Don't be a howling ass," said Morgan. "You'll tell him what?"

"Why, that—" said the other, and stopped.

"Exactly," said Morgan. "I defy anybody's ingenuity to invent a reasonable lie as to why you came roaring out of your cabin, slid down sixty yards of deck, and bounced the captain of the *Queen Victoria* all over his own deck. And, when that walrus comes to, my boy, he's going to be WILD. If you tell him the truth, then the fat's in the fire and you've got to explain about Uncle Warpus—not that he'd probably believe you, anyway. . . ."

"Um," said Warren, uneasily. "But, say what do you suppose *did* happen, anyway? Hell! I thought I was hitting the fellow who tried to break into my cabin. . . ."

Morgan handed him the bottle. "It was his captainly solicitude, my lad. Peggy told him all about your accident at dinner. Now that I come to think of it, what she neglected to tell him was that you were supposedly taken to the infirmary. So he came to call on the wreck. . . ."

"After—" shouted Captain Valvick excitedly—"after he hass persuaded de English duke to give him dat hemerald helephant, and he take it wit' him to put in de safe. . . .' "

"Exactly. He glanced in your cabin, saw you weren't there, went out, and—*bang*," Morgan reflected. "Besides, my lad, there's another good reason why you can't confess. The one thing we'll be forced to report to him is that girl—the one in the cabin now—with a crack over the back of the head. You'll certainly be for it if you admit slugging the captain. To our friend Whistler's forthright intelligence, the explanation would be simple. If one of your simple pleasures is to go about assaulting the skippers of ocean liners, then you would consider beaning his lady-passengers with a blackjack as only a kind of warming-up exercise. Especially as—Holy Mike!" Morgan stopped, stared, and then seized the rail again as the ship roared down. "Now that I remember it, our good Peggy informed the captain at dinner that she was afraid you suffered from bats in the belfry. . . ."

"Oooo, I never did!" cried the girl, and undoubtedly believed it. "All I said was—"

"Never mind, Baby," said Warren, soothingly. "The point is, what's to be done? We can't stand here arguing, and we're soaked to the skin. I'm pretty sure the old what-not didn't recognise me, or any of us. . . ."

"You're positive of that?"

"Absolutely."

"Well, then," said Morgan, with a breath of relief, "the only thing to do is to shove the box inside his coat and leave him where he is. Every second we stay here we're in danger of being spotted, and then—whaa! I—er—don't suppose there's any danger of his rolling overboard, is there?" he added, doubtfully.

"Noooo, not a chance!" Captain Valvick assured him, with cheerful scorn. "He be all right where he iss. Ay fold him up against de bulkhead, Ha-ha-ha! Giff me de box, Miss Glenn. Ah, you shiver! You should not haf come out wi'out de coat. Now you giff me de box and go back where it iss warm. Dere iss not'ing to be afraid of now, because we haf—"

"*Captain Whistler,* sir!" cried a voice, almost directly above their heads.

Morgan's heart executed a somersault over a couple of rowdy lungs. He stared at the others, who were stricken silent, and stayed motionless without daring to look up. The voice seemed to have come from the top of the companionway to B deck, near which Warren and Valvick were standing. They were in shadow, but Morgan feared the worst. He glanced at Peggy, who was petrified, and who held the steel box like a bomb. He saw what was passing in her mind. She looked at the rail, as though she had a wild impulse to toss the box overboard, and he gestured a savage negative. Morgan felt something knocking at his ribs. . . .

"Captain Whistler, sir!" repeated the voice, more loudly. The sea battered back in answer. "I could've sworn," the voice continued, in tones which Morgan recognised as belonging to the second officer, "I heard something down there. What's happened to the old man, anyway? He said he'd be up. . . ." The rest of it was lost in the gale, until a second voice—it sounded like the ship's doctor—said:

"It sounded like a woman. I say, you don't suppose the old man's up to any funny business with the ladies, do you? Shall we go down?"

Feet scuffled on the iron companion-ladder, but the second officer said: "Never mind. It might've been imagination. We'll—"

And then, to the horror of the little group by the glass enclosure, the captain's corpse sat up.

"!!!!¾½&£!?!??°???" roared Captain Whistler—weakly it is true, and huskily, but with gathering volume as his sticky wits ceased to whirl. "!&£&/£/!" He gasped, he blinked, and then, as the full realisation smote him, he lifted shaking arms to heaven and set soaring his soul in one hoarse blast: "!!!!&/£—!!?????&—&£/!!/?⅔¾4⅓!? THIEVES! MURDERERS! HELP!"

"That's torn it," breathed Morgan, in a fierce whisper. "Quick! There's only one. . . . What are you doing?" he demanded, and stared at Peggy Glenn.

After saying, "Eiee!" the girl did not hesitate. Just behind her there was the porthole to somebody's cabin, open and fastened back. As the obliging boat rolled over to assist her aim, she flung the steel box inside. It was a dark cabin, and they heard the box bump down. Without looking at the others, who were staring aghast, she had turned to run, when Morgan caught her arm. . . .

"Gawd lummy!" said the ghostly voice from the top of the companion-way, as though it were coming out of a trance, "that's the old man! Come on!"

Morgan was shooing his charges before him like chickens. He spoke so fast, under cover of the crashing swell, that he wondered if they heard him: "Don't try to run, you fatheads, or Whistler'll see you! He's still groggy. . . . Stick in the shadow, make a lot of noise with your feet as though you'd heard him and were running to help! Say something! Talk! Run about in circles. . . ."

It was an old detective-story trick, and he hoped it would work. Certainly their response was magnificent. To Captain Whistler, opening gummy eyes as he sat on the deck, it must have seemed that he was being rescued by a regiment of cavalry. The din was staggering especially Captain Valvick's realistic impersonation of a horse starting from far away and growing louder and more thunderous as it galloped near. Morgan's stout-hearted trio also cut the gale with such cries as, "What is it?" "What's wrong?" "Who's hurt?" They had timed themselves to spin round the forward bulkhead just as the second officer and the doctor came pelting up, their waterproofs swishing and the gilt ensigns on their caps gleaming out of the murk. There was silence while everybody clung to what was convenient, and several moments of hard breathing. The second officer, bending down, snapped on his flashlight. One good eye— undamaged, although the pickled-onion blaze of its pupil was distended horribly—one good eye smouldered and glared back at them out of a face which resembled a powerful piece of futurist painting. Captain Whistler was breathing hard. Morgan thought of the Cyclops, and also of incipient apoplexy. Captain Whistler sat on the wet deck, supporting himself with his hands behind him, and his cap was pushed back over his short white hair. He did not say anything. He was incapable, at that moment, of saying anything. He only breathed.

"Gor!" whispered the second officer.

There was another silence. Without removing his gaze from that terrifying face, the second officer beckoned behind him to the doctor. "I—er—" he faltered; "that is, what happened, sir?"

A certain terrible spasm and shiver twitched over the captain's face and chest, as though a volcano were trembling at its crust. But he still said nothing, and continued to wheeze noisily. His Cyclopean eye remained fixed.

"Come on, sir!" urged the second officer. "Let me help you up. You'll—er—catch cold. What happened?" he demanded, bewilderedly, turning to Morgan. "We heard—"

"So did we," agreed Morgan, "and came running when you did. I don't know what happened to him. He must have fallen off the bridge or something."

Among the dusky figures Peggy pressed forward. "It *is* Captain Whistler!" she wailed. "Oh, the poor dear! This is awful! Whatever can have happened to him? I say—" She seemed to have a shocking presentiment. Although she lowered her voice, there was only a hissing recoil of waters on the rise, and her shocked whisper to Warren carried clearly. "I say, I hope the poor man hasn't been drinking, has he?"

"What's that rattling on the deck?" demanded Warren, who was peering about him in the gloom. Following his glance, the uneasy second officer directed the beam of the flashlight down on the deck. . . .

"I—I do believe it's a whisky-bottle," said Peggy, earnestly contemplating the object that rolled there. "And—er—it seems to be empty. Oh, poor man!"

Morgan looked at her over his misted spectacles. A fair-minded person, he was bound to consider that this was laying it on a bit thick. Besides, he was momentarily afraid that Captain Whistler might have an apoplectic stroke. There were even richer hues blooming in the Cyclopean-eyed face; there were gurglings and rattlings and mysterious internal combustions which apparently defied nature. The second officer coughed.

"Come along, sir," he urged, soothingly. "Let me help you up, now. Then the doctor can—"

Captain Whistler found his voice.

"I WILL NOT GET UP!" he roared, gasping. "I AM PERFECTLY SOBER!" But so violent was the steam pressure that it even blocked the escape-valve; he could only gurgle insanely, and the pain of his swollen jaw made him grimace and stop, clapping a hand to it. Yet one thought remained burning. "That bottle—that bottle. That's what they hit me with. I AM PERFECTLY SOBER, I TELL YOU. That's what they hit me with. There were three of 'em. Giants. They all jumped on me at once. And—my elephant. O, my God! what's happened to my elephant?" he demanded, galvanised suddenly. "They stole my elephant! Don't stand there like a dummy, damn you! Do something. Look for it. Find that elephant or, strike me blind? I'll have the ticket of every crimson immoral landlubber on this. . . ."

There is no discipline like that of the British merchant service. The second officer stiffened and saluted. His not to reason why.

"Very good, sir. A search shall be instituted immediately, sir. It cannot have got far. In the meantime," he continued crisply, and turned to the others with a jealous safeguarding of the captain's reputation, "while the hunt for the commander's elephant is in progress, it is his instructions that all of you go below. Captain Whistler feels that it will be unnecessary for any of his guests to mention what has occurred to-night. . . . Let me help you up, sir."

"Sure thing," said Warren affably. "You can trust us. We'll keep quiet. If there's anything we can do—"

"But do you really think it's safe?" Peggy asked the second officer in some anxiety. "I mean, poor man, suppose he sees the elephant sitting up on top of the smokestack or something, making faces at him, and orders one of you to go and coax it down. . . ."

"Smell my breath!" cried the captain passionately. "Smell my breath, blast you; that's all I ask. I tell you I have not taken one single scarlet drink since five o'clock this evening."

"Look here," said the ship's doctor, who had been kneeling beside the anguished commander, "you people be sensible. He's not—upset. He's quite all right, Baldwin. There's something very queer going on here. Steady on, sir; we'll have you feeling top-notch in a moment. . . . We can get you up to your room without anybody seeing you, you know. . . . No?" Evidently Captain Whistler's soul shrank from encountering passengers or crew at that instant. "Well, then, there's a recess forward here on the leeward side, with some tables and chairs. It Mr. Baldwin will hold the flashlight I've got my bag. . . ."

This, Morgan felt, was the psychological moment for a retreat. The real object in remaining so long had been to ascertain definitely whether Captain Whistler had recognised his assailant. And it seemed they were safe. But he felt that suspicion was growing in the air. The doctor's sharp words had roused the first officer, who now seemed uneasy, and glanced several times at them. Doctor and officer were hoisting up their commander. . . .

"Wait a minute!" shouted Whistler, as there began to be a general melting-away of spectators. The good eye glared. "Hold on, there, you, whoever you are! You thought I was drunk, did you? Well, I'll show you! I want to ask you a lot of questions in a very few minutes. Stop where you are. I'll show you how drunk—"

. "But look here, Captain," protested Warren, "we're wet through! *We'll* stay, if you like, but let this young lady go back to her cabin—to get a coat, anyway. She hasn't got a coat! There's no reason why she should stay, is there? None of us can run away and—"

"YOU'LL TELL ME WHAT TO DO, WILL YOU?" said the captain, his chest swelling. "YOU'LL GIVE ORDERS ABOARD MY SHIP, WILL YOU? Haa! Strike me blind! There! Now just for that, my lad, you'll all stop exactly where you are; you won't move as much as a fraction of an inch from where you are, or sink me! I'll put the whole crew of you under arrest! Sink me! I'll put *everybody* under arrest, that's what I'll do. And when I find the so-and-so who hit me with a bottle and stole that emerald—"

"Don't!" Morgan said to Warren in a fierce whisper, as he saw the other lowering his head curiously and shutting up one eye as he regarded Captain Whistler, "for the love of God don't say anything, Curt! In another minute he'll be making us walk the plank. Steady."

"You won't move," pursued Captain Whistler wildly, lifting up his hands, squinting at them, and holding them a fraction of an inch apart before his face, "you won't move so much as *that* distance from where you are. You won't even move that far. You won't stir. You won't— Who was that who spoke?" he broke off to demand. "Who's there anyway? Who are you? What was that about a coat? Who had the nerve to ask me something about a blasted coat, eh?"

"My name's Warren, Captain. Curtis Warren. You know me. I hope you don't think *I'm* the crook you're after?"

Whistler stopped, stared, and seemed tumultuously to reflect.

"Ah!" he said in a curious tone. "Warren, hey? Warren. Well, well! And who is with you?" When three voices spoke up simultaneously he took on a grim but rather nervous tone. "Stay where you are now! Don't move. . . . Mr. Baldwin, you watch them. I mean, watch *him*. You've been wandering round the boat, have you, Mr. Warren? And what's that on your head? Come into the light. Sticking plaster. Oh, yes. You hurt your head. . . ."

Warren made a gesture. "Yes, I did. And that's what I want to tell you. If you won't let us go, at least send somebody back to my cabin. Send the doctor, you old fool! You're all right. Send the doctor, I tell you. There's a young girl back there—unconscious—maybe dead—I don't know. Have some sense, can't you? She's been hit over the head and knocked unconscious. . . ."

"*What?*"

"Yes. Somebody cracked her over the head and then—"

Between them, the doctor and the second officer got the captain away to a sheltered recess, where he did not stop talking. He would hear of nothing, not a step or a movement. He insisted that the four conspirators should remain within reach of the eye of Mr. Baldwin, who was holding up the flashlight for the repair-work. So they huddled against a glass front that was stung with whips of rain; Warren took off his coat and wrapped it round the girl, and they took whispered communion.

"Listen," said Morgan, peering over his shoulder to make sure they were out of earshot. "We're going to be jolly lucky if we don't get shoved in the brig. Scuttle my hatches, the old man's raving. He's insane, and you don't want to cross him. What fathead dropped that whisky-bottle beside him, anyway?"

"Ay did," replied Captain Valvick, thumping his chest. He beamed proudly. "Ay t'ank dat was a touch of yenius, eh? What iss wrong? Dere wass no more whisky in it, honest. Eh, eh; you t'ink dere be fingerprints on it, maybe?"

Warren frowned and ran a hand through his goblin hair. "Say, Hank," he muttered uneasily, "that's an idea. If it occurs to the old boy. . . . And there's another thing. Baby, what possessed you to fire that box through the porthole of somebody's cabin?"

She was indignant. "Well, I like that! With those officers coming down on us—you didn't want me to chuck it overboard, did you? Besides, I think it was a splendid idea. It can't be blamed on us, and it won't be blamed on anybody else. I don't know whose cabin that was. But there'll be a hunt for the box. And then whoever has the cabin will wake up to-morrow morning and find it on the floor; then he'll take it to the captain and explain it was thrown through the porthole, and there you are."

"Well," said Warren, drawing a deep breath, "all I can say is that we had a piece of luck. I tell you, I damn near died when you did that. I had visions of somebody sticking his head out the porthole just as those officers were coming up, and saying, 'Hey, what's the idea of throwing things through my window?' "

He brooded, staring out through the glass at the murky night ahead, dimly luminous from the glow above on the bridge; at the sharp bows shouldering up in mist; at the white torrent that poured, swirled, and fell away round stubborn winches. From far above smote the clang of the liner's bell—*one-two, one-two, one-two*—that is the drowsiest of sea noises by night. The wind had a flat whine now; it was dying, and rain had ceased to tick on the glass. Stately as a galleon, the tall foremast rose, swung, and tilted as the bows smashed down again into a fan of spray. . . .

Warren glared straight ahead.

"I've let you people in for all this," he said in a low voice. "I'm—I'm damned sorry."

"Dat iss de bunk, son," said Captain Valvick. "Ay ain't had so much fun in a long time. De only t'ing, we got to agree on a story dat we are all going to tell. . . ."

"I got you into this," continued Warren doggedly, "and I'm going to get you out. Don't worry about that. You let me do the talking, and I'll convince him. There's nothing wrong with my diplomatic talents. I very, very seldom go off half-cocked"—Morgan coughed but the others obviously believed what he was saying, so nobody spoke—"and I'll fix it. All that burns me up—" declared Warren, lifting a heavy fist high and bringing it down on the rail—"all that makes me burn and sizzle with bright murderous flames is that there really is a lousy, low-down, black-jack-using crook aboard this tub, and he's giving us the merry horse laugh right now. Goroo! This was made to order for him. And I'm mad now. I'm good and mad. I'll catch him. I'll get him, if it's the last thing I ever do, and if I have to sit up every night and wait for him to come after the fi—"

He stopped, stiffening, as an idea struck him. Slowly he turned round a lean, hollow-eyed, startled face.

"Film!" he said, clutching at the ends of his spiked hair. "Film! In my cabin. The rest of it. Unguarded! The rest of poor old Uncle Warpus's speech, and he's probably pinching it right now. . . ."

Before anybody could stop him, he had whirled round and was stumbling back towards his cabin along the slippery deck.

"Curt!" said Morgan, with a groan which ended deep in his stomach. "Listen! Hey! Come back! The captain—"

Over his shoulder Warren called out a suggested course of action for the captain. Whistler was out of his alcove at a bound and trumpeting. He shouted to the second officer to follow; then he stood and gibbered while Baldwin pursued the flying shirt-sleeved figure down the deck. Warren got inside the door, and Baldwin after him. In vain stout Valvick attempted to pacify his fellow skipper. Captain Whistler, *imprimis,* objected to being addressed as "barnacle," and described horrible surgical tortures he would like to perform. He was in no better mood when presently Warren, with Second-Officer Baldwin keeping a firm grip on his arm, emerged from the door. Warren seemed to be expostulating as they skidded back down the deck.

"But haven't you got any heart?" he demanded. "All I ask you to do, one little thing, is go into that next cabin and see whether that poor girl is alive—whether she needs help—whether—Or let *me* go. But no. I've got a good mind," said Warren, closing one fist with a meditative air, "to—"

"What was he up to?" Whistler demanded eagerly, as the culprit was led up. "Why did he bolt?"

A very harassed-looking Baldwin regarded Warren in some uneasiness.

"I don't know, sir. He rushed in 'is own cabin, and when I got there he was kneeling on the floor throwing motion-picture films over his shoulder and sayin, 'Gone! Gone!"

"Yes," agreed Warren. Wryly he shook his head as he glanced from Peggy to Morgan. "The little joker's been there in the meantime. He's swiped it all right."

"What is gone, young man?" inquired Captain Whistler.

A little of the first shock of rage had gone from him. He was still in a thrice-dangerous mood, but the insult of the attack had been partly put aside in favour of appalling reflections as to its consequences. Evidently what bulked large in the captain's rather small brain, larger than whisky-bottles or upper-cuts, was the fact that an emerald trinket worth fifty thousand pounds had been stolen while in his possession. And Lord Sturton had a crusty reputation. Captain Whistler savagely waved aside the doctor, who had not yet completed his ministrations. A few strips of sticking-plaster lent an even subtler Cézanne touch to his purple countenance; he narrowed his good right eye, squared his shoulders, and repeated with hoarse control of his temper: "What is gone, young man?"

"I can't tell you," returned Warren. "And anyway it's not important. To you, anyway. It doesn't concern whatever he stole from you. All I would beg and plead of you, if you have any heart, is don't let that poor girl lie there, maybe dying. . . .!"

"Mr. Warren," said the skipper, with a tense and sinister calmness, "I *will* have some sense out of this. . . . I will start at the beginning, and I will tell you that there is known to be aboard this ship a dangerous criminal who has stolen from me an object of enormous value. . . ."

"Ay told you, Barnacle," interposed Valvick, shaking his head gloomily—"ay told you it be better to post a notice and warn all de people. Now look at what iss done."

"Never you mind what you told me, sir. You keep out of this, Sharkmeat. You stow your t'g'lant-royals and come off the high mighty when you talk to me, Sharkmeat. I remember the time—" He caught himself up. "Hurrum! No matter, I will continue, Mr. Warren. You are the nephew of a very distinguished gentleman and were confided especially to my care. I have read Mr. Morgan's stories; he has travelled with me before, and I know him. Captain Valvick, God knows, I am familiar with. I am not drunk or mad, sir. I do not believe that any of you is this notorious criminal. Kindly understand that. But I do believe, Mr. Warren, that from the time Miss Glenn told me about you at dinner to-night, you have been guilty of very odd behaviour. Now, when you tell me about a young lady who has received an injury to the back of her head, I insist on hearing your full story."

"Right!" said Warren, with the air of one coming to an agreement. "That's fair enough, Skipper, and here you are. We don't know anything about the attack on you. It happened this way. We were all together, you see, when this unknown girl staggered in, badly hurt. We knew somebody had hit her, so we rushed out to see whether we could find the assailant. While we were on deck we heard your yell—"

("Not bad for a start," thought Morgan uneasily. "Steady now.")

"I see," said the captain. "And where were you then?"

"Eh?"

"I said," repeated the captain, looking so curiously like the headmaster at old St. Just's that Morgan shivered a little, "where were you when this alleged unknown woman came in? You weren't in your cabin. I looked in there and I know."

"Oh! Oh! I see! No, of course not," Warren answered, with some heat. "Naturally not. We were in the empty cabin next door."

"Why?"

"Why? Well—er—well, it was just an idea, you see. A kind of idea I had. I mean," said Warren, his wits clicking out words desperately in the hope of finding the right ones, "I mean, I thought it would be a good idea. Anyway, we *were* there, damn it! You can ask any of them. They were sort of taking care of me. . . ."

"Taking care of you," repeated Captain Whistler heavily. "And what were you doing there?"

"Well, we were sitting on the floor playing Geography. And then we heard the door to C deck open, and this girl who was attacked started calling my name. I don't know who she is; I only saw her once before," pursued Warren, acquiring greater assurance and fluency as he hurried on, "and that was in the wireless-room, when I got the cablegram about—euh!—I mean, when I got the cablegram—about the bears, you see."

"What bears?"

Warren's jaws moved. He glanced wildly at Morgan for assistance.

"It's quite all right, Captain," the latter explained as smoothly as he could. He had a lump in his throat and a feeling that if Warren kept on explaining he would go insane himself. "Naturally Curt's a bit upset, and I suppose he tells things in rather an odd way. But it's quite simple, after all. It's about some stocks—you understand. The bears were raiding the market, you see, and his stocks had depreciated."

"Oh! He's been worried about financial matters has he? Yes, yes," said the captain heavily. "But let's come down to terms, Mr. Morgan? Do *you* vouch for the truth of this crazy story?"

"Go and see, why don't you?" shouted the exasperated Warren. "That's what I've been asking you to do from the first, if you'd had any sense. Here you're keeping Miss Glenn shivering in my coat, and all of us standing out here on a zero deck when that poor girl may be dying. Aren't you coming, Doctor?"

"We are all coming," said the captain, with sudden decision. He beckoned his two subordinates, and the weird little procession went down to the door. Warren tugged it open, while they all piled through; a pale-faced Peggy, trembling and breathing deeply in the warm air. For a moment they blinked against the light.

"All right, there you are," said Warren, himself shivering as he stood against the wall of the white passage. "There's where she got caught in the door. You see the blood on the rubber matting. . . ."

The captain looked at him.

"Blood? What blood? I don't see any blood."

There was none, although Morgan knew it had been there. He took off his spectacles, wiped them, and looked again without result. And again he felt in the pit of his stomach that uneasy sensation that behind this foolery there was moving something monstrous and deadly.

"But—!" said Warren desperately. He stared at the captain, and then threw open the door of the state-room beside his.

The light in the roof was burning. The berth on which they had laid the injured girl was empty; the pillow was not disarranged, or the tucked-back sheets wrinkled. There was not even the smeared towel with which Peggy had wiped blood from the girl's face. A fresh towel, white and undisturbed, swung from the rack of the washstand.

"Yes?" said Captain Whistler stormily. "I'm waiting."

Chapter VII

INTO WHICH CABIN?

In its own way that was the beginning. It was the mere prospect of an empty bed and a clean towel, not in themselves especially alarming things, which sent through Morgan a sense of fear such as he had not known even in the past during the case of the Eight of Swords, or was to know in the future during the case of the Two Hangmen. He tried to tell himself that this was absurd and was a part of the crack-brain comedy on C deck.

It wasn't. Afterwards he realised that what had struck him first was something about the position of those sheets. . . .

During the brief moment of silence while they all looked into the white state-room, he thought of many things. That girl—he saw again her straight, heavy, classic face, with its strong eyebrows, twitching and blood-smeared against the pillow—that girl *had* been here. There was no question about that. Ergo, there were three explanations of why she was not here now.

She might have recovered consciousness, found herself alone in a strange cabin, and left it for her own. This sounded thin, especially as her injury had been severe and as a normal person on recovering consciousness would have called for help, kicked up a row, rung for the steward, at least shown sign of weakness or curiosity. But there was an even stronger reason. Before leaving the cabin, she would not have remade the bed. She would not carefully have put on *fresh sheets and a pillow-case,* in addition to disposing of a soiled towel and hanging another exactly in its place. Yet this had been done. Morgan remembered that, as they put her down, there had been spots of blood flicked on the sheet. He remembered that a lurch of the ship had caused the contents of a whisky-glass to soak the pillow and a part of the top sheet. The bed had been remade! but why and by whom?

The second explanation was a piece of fantasy which even Morgan doubted. Suppose the girl had been acting? Suppose she was in league with their friend the joker; that she had only pretended being hurt to distract their attention while somebody rifled Warren's cabin? Ridiculous or not, that film had very dangerous potentialities in countries where it is not considered humorous to direct raspberries at the Chancellor. The world wags, and Progress brings back the solemn nonsense of autocracy. In England or the United States the thing would be regarded with levity, as the sort of diplomatic howler often perpetrated by a Tophat; but elsewhere—? Still, Morgan did not believe in any such abstruse plot. Aside from the fact that the joker could gain very little freedom of movement merely because he had got a woman to sham injuries in the next cabin, there was the question of the girl's condition. The dangerous contusion along the skull, the blood of a real cerebral hæmorrhage, the white eyeballs uprolled in unconsciousness, were not feigned. She had been hurt, and badly hurt.

The third explanation he did not like to think of. But he was afraid of it. It was five miles, they said, to the bottom of the sea. As he saw weird images in the stuffy little cabin, he felt a jerk of relief—yes, in a way—that Peggy Glenn had disregarded orders and had not stayed at the bedside. *Somebody* would have come in and found her there.

These thoughts were so rapid that Captain Whistler had spoken no more than one sinister sentence before Morgan turned round. The captain, his fat figure hunched into a waterproof, had lowered his head nearly into the collar. Under the full electric light the colours of his swollen face were even more of the paint-palette variety, especially the left eye that had closed up behind a purpling hatch. He knew that they were looking at this, and it made him madder still.

"Well?" he said. "What kind of a joke is this? Where's the woman you said was dying? Where's the woman you begged me to help? Blast my compass with lightning! What's your idea in wasting my time when there's fifty thousand pounds' worth of emeralds stolen somewhere on this ship? There's nobody in the bunk. There's *been* nobody in that bunk." A ghoulish thought seemed to strike him. "You don't tell me there's anybody there now, do you? Come on, young man; you don't seriously think you see anybody there now, do you?"

He backed away a little, his eyes on Warren.

"Barnacle," said Captain Valvick violently, "dere iss no yoke. Ay tell you he iss right! Ay saw her—ay have my fingers on her head. Ay carry her in here. She wass—" Words failed him. He strode over, seized the pillow out of the berth and shook it. He peered under the berth, and then into the one above. "Coroosh! You don't t'ink we are in de wrong place, do you?"

Peggy, who had been stretching her arms out of Warren's loose blue coat to push the hair from her eyes, seized the captain's arm.

"It's true, Captain. Oh, can't you see it's true? Do you think we could have been mistaken about a thing like that? There's my compact, see? I left it on the couch. She was here. I saw her. I touched her. Maybe she just woke up and left. She had on a yellow crêpe de chine frock, a dark green coat with—"

Captain Whistler inspected each one of them with his good eye and then shut it up. Then he passed the back of his hand across his forehead.

"I don't know what to make of you," he said. "So help me Harry! I don't. Forty years I've been at sea, thirteen in sail and seventeen in steam, and I never saw the beat of it. Mr. Baldwin!"

"Sir!" answered the second officer, who had been standing outside the door with a blank expression on his face. "Yes, sir?"

"Mr. Baldwin, what do *you* make of all this?"

"Well, sir," replied Mr. Baldwin doubtfully, "it's all these elephants and bears that bothers me, sir. Not knowing, can't say; but I'd got a bit of a notion we were trying to round up a bleeding Zoo."

"I don't want to hear anything about elephants and bears, Mr. Baldwin. WILL YOU SHUT UP ABOUT ELEPHANTS AND BEARS? I asked you a plain question and I want a plain answer. What do you think of this story about the woman?"

Mr. Baldwin hesitated. "Well, sir, they can't *all* be loonies, now, can they?"

"I don't know," said the captain, inspecting them. "My God! I think I must be going mad, if they're not. I know all of them—I don't think they're crooks—I know they wouldn't steal fifty thousand pounds' worth of emeralds. And yet look here." He reached over and touched the berth. "Nobody's lain on that, I'll swear, if there was the blood they say. Where's the towel they say they used, hey? Where's the blood they say was outside the door? The woman didn't change the linen on that bed and walk off with the towel, did she?"

"No," said Morgan, looking straight at him. "But somebody else might have. I'm not joking, Captain. Somebody else might have."

"You, too, eh?" said Whistler, with the air of one whom nothing surprises now. "You, too?"

"The whole bed was changed, Captain, that's all. And I'm just wondering why. Look here—it won't take a second. Lift off the bedding and look underneath at the mattress."

This, allied with Morgan's absent expression as he blinked at the bed, was too much for the captain's grim-faced attempt to listen to everybody's side of the case. He picked up the pillow and slammed it down on the berth.

"I'll do no such damn fool thing, sir!" he said in what started to be a bellow but trailed off as he remembered where he was. "I've had about enough of this. You may be right or you may not. I won't argue, but I've got more important things to attend to. To-night I'm going to call a conference and start one of the finest-toothed-comb searches that you ever heard of on sea or land. That elephant's aboard, and, strike me blind, I'll find it if I have to take this tub apart one plate from another. That's what *I'm* going to do. And to-morrow morning every passenger will come under my personal observation. I'm master here, and I can search the cabin of anybody I like. That's what *I'm* going to do. Now, if you'll kindly get out of my way—"

"Look here, Skipper," said Morgan, "I admit we wouldn't be much help, but why don't we join forces?"

"Join forces?"

"Like this. I admit appearances are against us. We've told you a story you don't believe, and nearly given you apoplexy. But in all seriousness, there's a very sound reason behind everything. It's a big thing—bigger than you know. And why don't you believe us?"

"I believe," said the captain grimly, "what I see and hear, that's all."

"Yes, I know. That's what I'm kicking about," the other nodded. He got out his pipe and absently knocked the bowl against his palm. "But we don't. If we did, what do you suppose we should have thought when we walked up and found you sitting bunged-up and gibbering on a wet deck, with an empty whisky-bottle beside you and babbling wildly about your lost elephant?"

"I WAS PERFECTLY SOBER," said the captain. "If any illegitimate lubber," said the captain, lifting a shaking arm. . . . "if any illigitimate lubber refers again to what was pure misfortune—"

"I know it was, sir. Of course it was. But it's six of one and half a dozen of the other, don't you see? The misfortunes are precisely alike. Symbolically speaking, as Mr. Baldwin says, they are elephants and bears. And if you insist on having your elephants, why shouldn't you allow Curt his bears?"

"I don't understand this," said the captain dazedly. "I'm a plain man, sir, and I like plain speaking. What are you getting at? What do you want?"

"Only this. If I were to sit down at the breakfast table to-morrow morning and tell only what I had *seen* to-night—Oh, I don't say I *would,* of course," said Morgan, assuming a shocked expression and also closing one eye significantly. "I only use the illustration as an example, you understand—"

This was the sort of plain speaking the captain clearly comprehended. For a moment his head rose in appalling wrath out of the collar of the waterproof.

"Are you," he said thickly, "trying to blackmail—"

It took all Morgan could do, with a swift tactical change, to smooth him down. But it was like a shrewd lawyer's inadmissable question to the witness at a trial which the judge orders the jury to disregard: the suggestion had been put forth, and the effect made. An effect had been made, unquestionably, on the captain.

"I didn't mean anything," Morgan insisted. "Lord knows, we won't be much help. But all I wish you'd do is this. We're as interested as you are in catching this crook. If you'd keep us posted as to any developments—"

"I don't see any reason why I shouldn't," growled the other after a pause, during which he cleared his throat several times. Whistler's eye and jaw were paining him considerably, as Morgan observed; it was much to his credit that he could keep his temper down to a simmering point. Still, ramifications were beginning to suggest themselves to him, and it was apparent that he did not like them. "I don't see any reason why I shouldn't. I tell you straight, right here and now, to-morrow morning I'm going to haul all of you up to Lord Sturton and make you tell him the story you told me. If it weren't so late, I'd take you all up now. Oh, you'll be in it, right enough. . . .

"I'll tell you frankly, Mr. Warren," he added, in a rather different tone, and swung round on him, "that if it weren't for your uncle, you certainly wouldn't get the consideration you are getting. And I'll be fair. I'll give this cock-and-bull story of yours a chance."

"Thanks," said Warren dryly. "And I can take my oath Uncle Warpus will appreciate it if you do. And how?"

"Mr. Baldwin!"

"Sir?"

"Make a note of this. To-morrow morning you will institute an inquiry, with whatever reason or pretext you like, to find out whether any passenger on this boat got an injury along the lines you've heard described. Be discreet, burn you! or I'll have your stripes. Then report to Mr. Morgan. Now I've done all I can for you," he snapped, turning round, "and I'll bid you good night. But, mind I expect co-operation. CO-OPERATION. I've done a good deal already, and if so much as one word of all this is breathed, God help you!. . . . And you want to know the truth, Mr. Warren," said Captain Whistler, his Cyclops eye suddenly bulging past all control, "I think you're mad, sir. I THINK YOU'RE STARK, RAVING MAD, and these people are shielding you. On more questionable action, sir, just one more questionable action, and into a strait-waistcoat you go. That's all !!!'&—£&&'''£&£⅔¼⅘¾⁴⅛!!!???! . . . Good night."

The door closed with a dignified slam, and they were alone.

Brooding, Morgan stared at the floor and chewed at the stem of his empty pipe. Besides, his eyes would keep wandering to the berth; and he did not like to think of that. The *Queen Victoria* was pitching less heavily now, so that you could feel the monotonous vibration of the screw. Morgan felt cold and unutterably tired. He jumped as voices began to sing and glanced up dully. Peggy Glenn and Curtis Warren, with seraphic expressions on their faces (at two o'clock in the morning) had their heads together and their arms round each other's shoulders; they were swaying slowly as they uplifted throats in harmony:

"Oh, a life on the ocean wave [sang these worthies]
A ho-ome on the ro-olling deep . . . !
A life on the ocean wave . . ."

"Shut it, will you?" said Morgan, as Captain Valvick uttered a hoot of approval and joined his unmusical bass to the chorus. "Aside from the fact that there are people hereabouts trying to sleep, you'll have the captain back in here."

This threat quieted them in the middle of a bar. But they shook hands all around, gleefully, and Warren insisted on shaking Morgan's hand in a shoulder-cracking grip. The Englishman studied them: Valvick draping himself affably over the washstand, and Peggy and Warren chortling on the berth. He wondered if they had any idea what had really happened. He also wondered if it would be wise to tell them.

"Boy," said Warren in admiration, "I don't mind telling you it was a swell piece of work. It was great. It was *the nuts.*" He waggled his hand high in the air and brought it down on his knee. "That crack about elephants and bears, and the horrible threat to spill the beans on that incorrigible souse, Captain Whistler . . . yee! Great! You are hereby elected Brains of this concern. Henceforth anything you say goes. As for me, I'm going to be good, and how. You heard what the old sea-terrier said."

"Au, sure," agreed Valvick, with a ponderous gesture. "But it iss going to be all right in de morning. He find de emerald. Whoever hass de cabin where Miss Peggy t'row it in iss going to wake up in de morning and see it. And dere you be."

Warren sat up, impressed by this new thought. "By the way, Baby, whose cabin *did* you throw it in, anyway?"

"How should I know?" she asked, rather defensively. "I don't know who has every cabin on the deck. It was just a convenient porthole, and I sort of obeyed the impulse. What difference does it make?"

"Well, I was only wondering. . . ." He peered at the light, at a corner of the roof, at the wardrobe door. "I—that is, I don't suppose by any chance you heaved it on somebody to whom it would—er—prove a temptation?"

"Caroosh!" said Captain Valvick.

By one accord they looked at Morgan. The latter would have immensely enjoyed the throne to which this trio of genial idiots had elected him, that of Brains in the combine to catch the joker, if it were not for that disturbing, nagging doubt which was apparently shared by none of his lieutenants. He did not want to examine that berth, and yet he knew he must. Meanwhile his lieutenants—ready to go off at any new tangent, and obsessed now with a thought which had nothing to do with the main problem—were regarding him in expectancy.

"Well," he said rather wearily, "if you really want to know whose cabin it is, that ought to be easy. Pick out the cabin that's attached to the porthole in which you threw that box (am I making myself clear?) and spot its number. Then look up the number in the passenger-list, and there you are. . . . What porthole did you throw it through, Peggy?"

The girl opened her mouth eagerly and shut it again. Her brows contracted. She wriggled, as though to assist thought.

"Dash it!" she said in a small voice. "I think—well, honestly, I don't remember."

Chapter VIII

Blood Under a Blanket

Warren hopped up.

"But, Baby," he protested, "you've *got* to remember. Why shouldn't you remember? It's a cinch: there's a row of portholes, and they're all near the companionway on the starboard side. All right. You were standing near one, and all you've got to do is remember which one. Besides—" A new aspect of the matter struck him. "Say, I never thought of it before, but this is terrible! Suppose by some chance you slung that box into the *criminal's* cabin? By Jiminy!" said Warren, now almost convinced that this was the case, "he's got away with a lot, but I won't stand for this! I've got a score to settle with that guy. . . ."

"Son," said Morgan, "permit me to suggest that we have enough difficulties on our hands without your imagining fresh ones. That's foolish! You're only getting the wind up about nothing."

"Yes, I know, but it bothers me," returned Warren, moving his neck uncomfortably. "The thought of that fellow getting away with a thing like that would make me wild. After he's walked in as easy as pie, and stolen my film, to have us deliberately hand him the emerald elephant as well! . . . Baby, you've got to remember which porthole it was! Then, if we went down to that cabin and sort of busted down the door, you see, and said, 'Hey, you! . . .'"

Morgan lowered his head to cool it, and swallowed hard in a dry throat. Never before had he seen the true extent of American energy.

"So now," he said, "so now you want to go around breaking down doors, do you? Kindly reflect a moment, Curt. Consider what you have already done to Captain Whistler's blood pressure. You fathead, why don't you go up and smash down the captain's door and get put into a strait-waistcoat and have done with it? You said I was to give the orders, and I'm giving some now. You're to stop absolutely quiet. Do you understand?"

"Ay haf an idea," volunteered Captain Valvick, who was scratching his short sandy hair. "Coroosh! Ay yust t'ink of it. Suppose de port where you t'row dat elephant wass in de cabin of dat English duke which own de

54

elephant in de first place? Corrrsh! But he iss going to be surprised if he wake up in de morning and find it dere. Maybe he t'ink Captain Whistler hass got mad at him for somet'ing and come down in de night and t'row dat elephant back at him t'rough de port."

"No, that won't work," said Warren. "Old Sturton's got a suite on B deck. But we've got to find out who does sleep in that cabin. Think. Baby! Get your brain working."

Peggy's face was screwed up with intense concentration. She made slow gestures to bring the scene back.

"I've got it now," she said. "Yes, I'm sure. It was either the second or third porthole from the end of the wall where we were standing. They look so much alike and *you* ought to remember it yourself. But it was either the second or third porthole."

"You're absolutely sure of that, are you?"

"Yes, I am. I won't say which one, but I'll swear it was one of those two."

"Den dass all right," rumbled Valvick, nodding. "Ay go out right now and find de numbers on dem cabins, and we look it up in de passenger-list. Also ay got anudder bottle of Old Rob Roy in my locker, and ay get it and we out of it a nightcap haff, hey? Yumping Yudas, but ay am t'irsty! Hold on. Ay won't be a minute."

Morgan protested in vain. The captain insisted that he would only be a minute, and went out foraging, with the approval of the other two lieutenants.

" . . . Also," Morgan continued, turning to them when Valvick had gone, "what the devil's the use of bothering about that emerald now? Has it occurred to you what happened in this place to-night? What about that woman? What happened to *her?*"

Warren made a savage gesture. "I've got it all figured out," he snapped. "I knew it the minute we came back in here, but I didn't very well see how I could tell old Popeye. We've been outsmarted, that's what. They got us to fall for that as neat as you please, and it's another thing that makes me mad. . . . Why, that girl was our crook's accomplice, don't you see? They arranged it between them for her to pull a fake faint, calling my name, mind you—which wasn't natural to begin with. . . ."

"And you don't think the injury was real?"

"Of course it wasn't real. I read a story once about a bird who could suddenly make funny noises and go into a cataleptic fit, and while the doctor was poking him his gang came in and robbed the doctor's house. I thought it was a low-down dirty trick at the time; but that's what they've done. Yes, and don't you remember in your own books, in *Aconite in the Admiralty?* where that detective what's-his-name gets into the master criminal's luxurious den in Downing Street, and they think they've stabbed him with the poisoned needle?"

"The literary formula," agreed Morgan, "is excellent. Still, I doubt it in this case. Granted that the crook was watching us, knew where we were, and all that, I don't see how it would help him much. He knew we'd certainly take the girl into one of these two cabins, so it wouldn't be much easier. It was only chance in old Whistler's coming in when he did, so that we were dragged away and the crook had a clear field."

Peggy also refused to listen to this line of argument. Warren had got out a damp package of cigarettes, and he and Peggy lit one while Morgan filled his pipe. The girl said, between short puffs, as though she were rather angrily trying to get rid of the smoke:

"But, I say, it's going to be *easy* now, isn't it? It was rather a dreadful bloomer on their part, wasn't it? Because we shall know that girl when we see her again, and then we've got 'em. She wasn't disguised, you know. She hardly had any make-up on, even. That reminds me—my compact. Give it me, Curt. I say I must look a sight! Anyway, we can't miss her. She's still aboard the boat."

"Is she?" said Morgan. "I wonder."

Warren, who was about to make some impatient comment, glanced up and saw the other's expression. He took the cigarette out of his mouth; his eyes grew curiously fixed.

"What—what's on your mind, General?"

"Only that Peggy's right in one sense. If that girl was an accomplice, then the thing would be too easy, much too easy for us. On the other hand, if that girl had been coming here to try to warn you about something. . . . I know you didn't know her, but let's suppose that's what she was doing. . . . Then the thief gets after her and thinks he's done the business. But he hasn't. Then—"

The droning engines seemed to vibrate loud above creaking woodwork, because the wind had died outside, deep tumult was subsiding, and the *Queen Victoria* was rolling almost gently as though she were exhausted by the gale. All of them were relaxed; but it did not help their nerves. Peggy jumped then as the door opened and Captain Valvick returned with the passenger-list in one hand and a quart of Old Rob Roy in the other.

"Ay told you ay only be a minute," he announced. "It wass easy to find de ports, and den de cabin numbers from inside. One is C 51 and the other C 46. Ay t'ank. . . . Hey?" he said, peering at the strained faces in the room. "What iss de matter, hey?"

"Nothing," said Morgan. "Not for a minute, anyhow. Come on, now. Set your minds at rest. You wanted to know. Find out who occupies those cabins first, and then we can go on."

With a jerk of her head, still looking at him, Peggy took the passenger-list. On the point of speaking, she said nothing, and opened the list instead. But she rose and sat on the couch this time. Under cover of Captain Valvick's talk, Warren helped him take the extra glasses off the rack and pour drinks. They all glanced furtively at Morgan, who had begun to wonder whether he were merely flourishing a turnip ghost. He lit his pipe during a queer silence while Peggy ran her finger down the list, and the ship's engines beat monotonously. . . .

"Well?" said Warren.

"Wait a bit, old boy. This takes time. . . . Mmmm. Gar—Gran—Gulden—Harris—mmm—Hooper, Isaacs mm, no—Jarvis, Jerome. . . . I say, I hope I haven't missed it; Jeston, Ka-Kedler—Kennedy. . . . Hullo!" She breathed a line of smoke past her cigarette, and glanced up with wide eyes. "What was it, skipper? C 46? Righto! Here it is. "C 46 *Kyle, Dr. Oliver Harrison."* Fancy that! Dr. Kyle has one of those cabins. . . ."

Warren whistled.

"Kyle, eh? Not bad. Whoa! Wait a bit," said the diplomat. He struck the bulkhead. "My God! wasn't he one of the suspects? Yes, I remember now. This crook is probably masquerading. . . ."

With difficulty Morgan shut him up, for more and more was Warren impressed by the general rightness and poetic reasonableness of a crook with a taste for using the blackjack adopting the guise of a distinguished Harley Street physician. His views were based on the forthright principle that, the more respectable they looked, the more likely they were to turn out dastardly murderers. He also cited examples from the collected works of Henry Morgan in which the authors of the dirty work had proved to be (respectively) an admiral, a rose-grower, an invalid, and an archdeacon. It was only when Peggy protested that this was merely the case in detective stories that Morgan took his side.

"That's just where you're wrong, old girl," he said. "It's in real life that the crooks and killers always go in the most solidly respectable dress. Only, you see them at the wrong end—in the dock. You think of them as a murderer, not as the erstwhile churchgoing occupant of Number 13 Laburnum Grove. Whisper softly to yourself the names of the most distinguished croakers of a century, and observe that nearly all of them were highly esteemed by the vicar. Constance Kent? Dr. Pritchard? Christina Edmunds? Dr. Lamson? Dr. Crippen—"

"And nearly all of 'em doctors, eh?" inquired Warren, with an air of sinister enlightenment. He seemed to brood over this incorrigible tendency among members of the medical profession to go about murdering people. "You see, Peggy? Hank's right."

"Don't be a lop-eared ass," said Morgan. "Wash out this idea of Dr.

Kyle's being a crook, will you? He's a very well-known figure . . . oh, and get rid of the notion, too, that somebody may be impersonating him while the real Dr. Kyle is dead. That may be all right for some person who never comes in contact with anybody; but a public figure like an eminent physician won't do. . . . Go on, Peggy. Tell us who's in C 51, and then we can forget it and get down to real business."

She wrinkled her forehead.

"Here we are, and this is odd, too. 'C 51. *Perrigord, Mr. and Mrs. Leslie.*' So-ho!"

"What's odd about that? Who are they?"

"You remember my telling you about a very, very great highbrow and æsthete who was aboard, and had written reams of ecstatic articles about Uncle Jules's genius? And I said I hoped for his sake as well as the kids who wanted to see the fighting that there'd be a performance tomorrow night?"

"Ah! Perrigord?"

"Yes. Both he and she are awfully æsthetic, you know. He writes poetry—you know, the kind you can't understand, all about his soul being like a busted fencer-rail or something. And I believe he's a dramatic critic, too, although you can't make much sense out of what he writes there, either. *I* can't anyway. But he says the only dramatists are the French dramatists. He says Uncle Jules has the greatest classic genius since Molière. Maybe you've seen him about? Tall, thin chap with flat, blond hair, and his wife wears a monocle?" She giggled. "They do about two hundred circuits of the promenade-deck every morning, and never speak to anybody, those people!"

"H'm!" said Morgan, remembering the dinner-table that night. "Oh, yes. But I didn't know you knew them. If this fellow has written all that stuff about your uncle—"

"Oh, I don't know them," she disclaimed, opening her eyes wide. "They're English, you see. They'll write volumes about you, and discuss every one of your good and bad points minutely; but they won't *say* how-de-do unless you've been properly introduced."

All this analysis was over the head of the good Captain Valvick, who had grown restive and was puffing through his moustache with strange noises, as though he wanted to be admitted through a closed door.

"Ay got de whisky poured out," he vouchsafed. "And you put in de soda. Iss it decided what we are going to do? What *iss* decided, anyway? Sometime we got to go to bed."

"I'll tell you what we're going to do," said Warren, with energy, "and we can sketch out the plan of battle now. Tomorrow morning we're going to comb the boat for that girl who pulled the fainting-act in here. That's the only lead we've got, and we're going after it as hard as Whistler goes after the emerald. That is—" He turned round abruptly. "Let's have it out, Hank. Were you only trying to scare us or were you serious when you made that suggestion?"

Obviously this had been at the back of his mind from the beginning, and he did not like to face it. His hands were clenched. There was a silence while Peggy put the passenger-list aside and also looked up.

"What iss de suggestion?" asked Captain Valvick.

"It's a queer thing," said Morgan. "We don't want our pleasant farce to turn into something else, do we? But why do you think new sheets and maybe blankets were put on that berth?"

"All right," said Warren, quietly. "Why?"

"Because there may have been more blood afterwards than *we* saw there. Steady, now."

There was a silence. Morgan heard the breath whistling through Captain Valvick's nostrils. With a jerk Warren turned round; he regarded the berth for a moment and then began tearing off the bedclothes.

The cabin creaked faintly. . . .

"You may be wrong," said Warren, "and I hope you are. I don't believe anything like that. I *won't* believe it. Pillow—top-sheet—blanket—under-sheet of the bed. . . . It's all right. Look." He was holding them up, a weird figure in shirt-sleeves, with a brown blanket and a whirl of linen about him. "Look at it, damn you! Everything in order. What are you trying to scare us for? See, this sheet of the bed. . . . Wait a minute. . . !"

"Take it off," said Morgan, "and look at the mattress. I hope I'm wrong as much as you do."

Peggy took one look, and then turned away, white-faced. Morgan felt a constriction in his throat as he stepped up beside Warren and Valvick. A blanket had been neatly spread under the sheet and over the mattress; but stains were already soaking through it. When they swept off the blanket, the colours of the blue-and-white striped mattress were not very distinguishable in a great sodden patch spread for some length down.

"Is it . . . ?" asked Morgan, and took a deep draw on his cigarette. "Is it . . . ?"

"Oh, yes. It iss blood," said Captain Valvick.

It was so quiet that even across that distance Morgan imagined he could hear the liner's bell. They were moving almost steadily now, with a deep throb below decks in the ship and a faint vibration of glassware. Also Morgan imagined the pale classic-faced girl lying unconscious, with the dim light burning above her in the berth, and the door opening as somebody came in. . . .

"But what's happened to her? Where is she now?" Warren asked, in a low voice. "Besides," he added, with a sort of dull argumentative air—"besides, he couldn't have done *that* with a blackjack."

"And why should he do it, anyway?" asked Peggy, trying to control her voice. "Oh, it's absurd! I won't believe it! You're scaring me! And—and, anyway, where did he get the linen for the bed? Where is she, and why? . . . *Oh, you're trying to frighten me, aren't you?"*

"Steady, Baby," said Warren, taking her hand without removing his eyes from the bed. "I don't know why he did it, or what he expected to gain by making the bed over. But we'd better cover that up again."

Carefully putting down his pipe on the edge of the thrumming wash-stand, Morgan choked back his revulsion and bent over to examine the berth. The stains were still wet, and he avoided them as much as he could. So strung up was he into that queer, clear-brained, almost fey state of mind that sometimes comes in the drugged hours of the morning, that he was not altogether surprised when he heard something rattle deep down between mattress and bulkhead. He yanked over a corner of the sheet, wound it round his fingers, and groped.

"Better not look, old girl," he said after a pause. "This won't be pretty."

Shielding the find with his body so that only Captain Valvick could see, he pulled it up in the sheet and turned it over in his palm. It was a razor, of the straight, old-fashioned variety, and closed; but it had recently been used. Rather larger than the ordinary size, it was an elaborate and delicate piece of craftsmanship with a handle so curiously fashioned that Morgan wiped the blood away to examine it.

The handle was of a wood that resembled ebony. Down one side ran a design picked out in thin silver and white porcelain. At first Morgan took it for an intricate nameplate, until, under cleaning, it became a man's standing figure. The figure was possibly three inches high, and under it was a tiny plate inscribed with the word *Sunday*.

"Ay know," said Captain Valvick, staring at it. "It iss one of a set of seven, one for every day of de week. Ay haff seen dose before. But what iss dat thing on it, like a man?"

The thin figure, in its silver and white and black, was picked out in a curious striped medieval costume, which recalled to Morgan's mind vague associations with steel-cut engravings out of Doré. Surgeon, surgeon—barber, that was it! There was the razor in the thing's fist. But most ugly and grotesque of all, the head of the figure was subtly like a death's head, and a bandage was across the eyes so that the barber was—

"Blind," said Warren, who was looking over his shoulder. "Put it away, Hank! Put it away. Blind . . . death and barber . . . end of the week. Somebody used that, and lost it or left it here. Put it away. Have a drink."

Morgan looked at the evil and smeared design. He looked at the door, then at the white-painted bulkhead in the bunk, the tumbled bedclothes and the spotty brown blanket. Again he tried to picture the girl in the yellow frock lying here under a dim light, while the outside door was opening. So who was the girl, and where was she now, wrapped round in the soaked sheets that were here before? It was five miles to the bottom of the sea. They would never find her body now. Morgan turned round.

"Yes," he said, "the Blind Barber has been here to-night."

Chapter IX

MORE DOUBTS AT MORNING

As the hands of the travelling-clock at the head of Morgan's bed pointed to eight-thirty, he was roused out of a heavy slumber by the sound of an unmusical baritone voice singing with all the range of its off-keys. The voice singing, "A Life on the Ocean Wave." It brought nightmares into his doze before he struggled awake. As he opened his eyes, the heartening bray of the breakfast bugle went past in the gangway outside, and he remembered where he was.

Furthermore, it was a heartening morning. His cabin—on the boat-deck—was filled with sunshine, and a warm salt-spiced breeze fluttered the curtain at the open porthole. It was winelike May again, with a reflected glitter of water at the porthole; and the ship's engines churning steadily in a docile sea. He drew a deep breath, feeling a mighty uplift of the heart and a sensual longing for bacon and eggs. Then somebody threw a shoe at him, and he knew Warren was there.

Warren sat across from him on the couch under the porthole, smoking a cigarette. He wore white flannels, a careless blue coat, and a sportive tie; he showed not at all the rigours of last night, nor any depression of spirit. His hair was brushed smoothly again, unpropped by sticking-plaster. He said:

"Howdy, General," and tipped his hand to his head. "Wake up, can't you? Wow! it's a beautiful morning! Even our old sea-beetle of a skipper is going to be in better temper to-day. All the sea-sick lads are beginning to creep out of their holes and say it was only something they ate, no doubt. Haaaaa!" Breathing deeply, he arched his chest, knocked his fists against it, and beamed with seraphic good-humour. "Get ready and come down to breakfast. This is an important morning in the lives of several people, including Captain Whistler."

"Right," said Morgan. "Find something to amuse yourself with while I catch a bath and dress. . . . I suppose there's some kind of story all over the boat about last night's activities, isn't there? We were doing a good deal of shouting out on that deck, now I remember it."

The other grinned.

"There is. I don't know how it happens, but there's a kind of wireless telegraphy aboard these tubs that always get a story even if it's a little cockeyed. But I've only heard two versions so far. When I came out this morning, I heard an old dame in 310 raising hell with the stewardess. She was furious. She says six drunken men were standing outside her porthole all night, having a terrible argument about a giraffe, and she's going to complain to the captain. I also passed two clergymen taking a morning stroll. One of them was telling the other some kind of a complicated story—I didn't get much of it. It was something to the effect that the boat's got in her hold a cargo of cages full of dangerous wild beasts, only they're keeping it quiet so as not to alarm the passengers. In the storm last night the cages worked loose and the Bengal tiger was in danger of getting out, but a seaman named Barnacle got it back in its cage. The preacher said A. B. Barnacle was armed only with a whisky-bottle. He said the sailor must be a very brave man, although he used horrible language."

"Come off it," said Morgan, staring.

"So help me, it's absolutely true!" the other declared fervently. "You'll see for yourself." His face clouded a little. "Look here, Hank. Have—have you thought any more about that *other* business?"

"The film?"

"Ah, hang the film! I'll trust you. We'll get it back somehow. No, I meant the—the *other* business, you know. It gives me the jitters. If it weren't for that . . . that, and the fact that when I get my hands on the lousy, low-down skunk who—"

"Save it," said Morgan.

His steward tapped on the door to tell him the bath was ready as usual; Morgan slid into a dressing-gown and went out into the breezy passage. Passing the outer door, he pushed it open a little way to put his head out and breathe the full exaltation of the morning. The warm air blew on him in a splendour of sunlight broadening along the horizon behind long pinkish-white streamers of cloud. There was a deep grey-green sea, stung with flecks of whitecaps and wrinkling under a glitter of sun that trembled up like heat haze. He looked up ahead to the long lift and fall of the bows; at the sweep of white cabins; at the red-mouthed air-funnels and brass-work of portholes awink with morning; he heard the monotonous break and swish of water past the bows, and felt that it was good. Everything was good. He even had a fleeting tenderness for Captain Whistler, who was probably now sitting with a beefsteak at his eye and sighing because he could not go down to breakfast. Good old Captain Whistler. There even occurred to him a wild idea that they might go to Whistler straight-forwardly, man to man, and say, "Look here, skipper, it was a blinking shame we had to paste you in the eye last night and strew whisky-bottles all over your deck, and we're sorry; so let's forget it and be friends. Shall we?" But more sober reflection suggested to him that not all the good omens of the morning presaged enough magic to wangle this. Mean-while, he dreamily sniffed the morning. He thought in joyous content-ment of England and his wife Madeleine who would meet him at South-ampton; of the holiday in Paris they would take on the money he had contrived to hypnotise out of gimlet-eyed publishers in America; of the little white hotel by the Ecole Militaire, where there were eels in the fountain of a little gravelled garden; and of other things not relevant to this chronicle.

But, while he bathed and shaved he reviewed the unpleasant side of the problem. He could still feel the horrible shock of finding that grotesque razor in the berth, and the blood under his fingers to mark the way of the Blind Barber. In a conference lasting until nearly four in the morning they had tried to determined what was best to do.

Warren and Valvick, as usual, were for direct action. The former thought it would be best to go straight to Whistler, taking the razor, and saying, "Now, you old so-and-so, if you think I'm crazy, what do you think of *this*?" Morgan and Peggy had dissented. They said it was a question of psychology and that you had to consider the captain's frame of mind. In the skipper's momentarily excited state, they said, Warren might just as well tell him he had gone back to his cabin and discovered a couple of buffaloes grazing on the furniture. Better wait. In the morning Whistler would institute a search and find a woman missing; then they could go to him and vindicate themselves. Ultimately, it was so agreed.

With the razor safely locked away in Morgan's bag, and the berth on C deck made up in case a steward should become curious, Morgan again discussed the plan with Warren while he dressed that morning. For the moment, Morgan deliberately kept himself from speculating on the hows and whys of the (alleged) murder last night. There were things to come first. Shortly the ship would be buzzing with the news of the recovery of the emerald elephant. Afterwards, with this weight removed from the skipper's microscopic intelligence, they could soothe him back to belief in a throat-cutting. Then would come the real duel with the Blind Barber.

"What I want to know," said Warren, as they descended to the dining-saloon, "is whether it'll be Dr. Kyle or the Perrigords who find the emerald. I still have my suspicions. . . ."

"Of the medical profession?" asked Morgan. "Nonsense! But I would rather like to see Dr. Kyle shaken out of his calm. Jove! you were right!

The boat's waking up. We'll have the sick-list down to a minimum by this afternoon. Look at all the kids. If old Jules Fortinbras has got his sea legs—"

The dining-saloon was full of sunlight and murmurous with an eager clatter of knives and forks. Stewards beamed and did tricks with trays. There were more people out for breakfast at the unholy hour of eight-thirty than there had been for dinner last night. But at the captain's table sat only one solitary figure—Dr. Kyle, sturdily plying knife and fork. Dr. Kyle was a trencherman after the fashion of the lairds in Sir Walter Scott. He could mess up a plate of fried eggs with a dispatch that would have roused the envious approval of Nicol Jarvie or that foreigner, Athelstane.

"Good morning!" said Dr. Kyle, with unexpected affability, and rolling round his shoulder, he looked up. "A fine day, a fine day. Good morning, Mr. Warren. Good morrrrning, Mr. Morgan. Sit down."

The other two looked at each other and strove to dissemble. Every morning, hitherto, Dr. Kyle had been perfectly polite, but hardly interested or communicative. He had conveyed an impression that his own society was all he cared to cultivate. A solid large-boned figure in black, with his well-brushed greyish hair and the furrows carven down his cheeks, he had devoted himself to food with the concentration of a surgical operation. Now he had an almost raffish appearance. He wore a tweed suit, with a striped tie, and his grizzled eyebrows were much less Mephistophelian as he welcomed them with a broad gesture. It was, Morgan supposed, the weather. . . .

"Er—" said Warren, sliding into his chair, "good morning, sir. Yes, indeed, it's a fine morning! Did you—er—did you sleep well?"

"Ah, like a top!" said the doctor, nodding. "Though, mind," he added, remembering his habits of thought and correcting himself cautiously, "I don't say, fra my own experience, that I should judge it a well-chosen worrrd as applied to tops. Accurately speaking (fra my own expeerience as a boy) I should say it was mair to the purpose for tops in general to refrain fra sedentary habits. However, that's as may be. I'll have more of the bacon and eggs, steward."

This was the first morning, incidentally, in which Dr. Kyle had given the letter "r" its full-wristed spin. He looked benevolently on them, and at the green glitter of the sea dancing outside the portholes.

"I mean," pursued Warren, looking at him curiously, "you didn't—that is, everything was all right when you woke up, was it?"

"Everything," said Dr. Kyle, "was fine." He paused, drawing down his brows thoughtfully. "Ah! Ye may be referring to that disturbance in the night, then?"

"Disturbance?" said Morgan. "Was there a disturbance?"

The other regarded him shrewdly, and in a way that disturbed him.

"I see, I see. You hadn't hearrd of it, then? Well, well, it didn't disturb *me*, Mr. Morgan, and all I heard was some speerited currsing on the deck. But I heard an account of it this morning, from a person of my acquaintance—which account I can't vouch for, you understand—"

"What happened?"

"*Rape*," said the doctor, succinctly, and closed one eye in a startlingly raffish fashion.

"Rape?" yelped Morgan. There are certain words which have a mysterious telepathic power. Although there was a buzz in the dining-room which drowned his voice, several heads were twitched in their direction. "Rape? My God! Who was raped? What happened?"

"I can't say," replied Dr. Kyle, chuckling. "However, my inforrmant distinctly heard the girl's scream when set upon. My inforrmant declares that some scoundrelly dastard approached the poor girrul by telling her of his adventures while hunting big game in Africa. Weel, weel, then, that he offered her an emerald brrooch worth a fabulous sum. But, failing in his foul design, the rrascally skellum struck her over the head with a bottle o' whisky. . . ."

"Great—Cæsar's—ghost!" said Warren, his eyeballs slightly distended. "You—you didn't hear any names mentioned in the business, did you?"

"My inforrmant made no secret of it," Dr. Kyle answered philosophically. "She said the abandoned wretch and seducer was either Captain Whistler or Lord Sturton."

"And this woman's story is all over the boat?" asked Morgan.

"Oh, it will be," said Kyle, still philosophically. "It will be."

Dr. Kyle continued to talk on affably while the others attacked breakfast; and Morgan wondered what would be the ultimate version of the tale that would be humming through the *Queen Victoria* by midday. Evidently Dr. Kyle had not found any emeralds. There remained only the stony-faced Mr. Perrigord and his monocled wife. Well? The ship's miniature newspaper lay beside his plate, and he glanced over it between deep draughts of coffee, his eye slid over what appeared to be an article or essay on the back page, stopped, and returned to it. It was headed "RENAISSANCE DU THEATRE," and under it appeared, *"By Mr. Leslie Perrigord, reprinted by permission of the author from the Sunday 'Times' of Oct. 25, 1932."*

Skirling notes of harps celestial [began this effusion, with running start] sweeping one old reviewer, *malgré lui,* counterclockwise from his *fauteuil,* while *nuances* so subtle danced and slithered, reminding one of Bernhardt. Will you say, "Has old Perrigord gone off his chump this Sunday?" But what is one to say of this performance of M. Jules Fortinbras, which I journeyed to Soho to see? As Balzac once said to

Victor Hugo, *"Je suis étonné, sale chameau, je suis bouleversé."*
(Molière would have said it better.) A thrilling performance, if that is
consolation to the poor British public, but why speak of *that?* For sheer
splendour and beauty of imagic imagery, in these subtle lines spoken by
Charlemagne and Roland, I can think of nothing but that superb soliloquy
in the fifth act of Corneille's tragedy, *"La Barbe,"* which is spoken by
Amourette Pernod, and begins, *"Monâme est un fromage qui souffle dans
les forêts mystérieuses de la nuit. . . ."* Or shall I speak of wit? Almost it
approaches some of Molière's gems, say, *"Pour moi, j'aime bien les
saucissons, parce qu'ils ne parlent pas français. . . ."*

"What's all this?" demanded Warren, who was reading the article also
and making strange whistling noises rather like Amourette Pernod's soul.
"Do you see this attack of dysentery on the back page? Is this our
Perrigord?"

Morgan said, "You have no cultural feelings, I fear. As Chimène said
to Tartuffe, *"Nuts."* Well, you've got to *get* cultural feelings, old son.
Read that article very carefully. If there's anything in it you don't
understand, ask me. Because—" he checked himself, but Dr. Kyle had
finished his last order of bacon and eggs and was rising genially from the
table. Dr. Kyle bade them good morning, and said he had half a mind to
play deck-tennis. Altogether he was so self-satisfied, as he strode away
from the table, that in Warren's face Morgan could see newly awakened
suspicions gathering and darkening. "Listen!" hissed Warren in a low
voice, and stabbed out dangerously with his fork. "He *says* he didn't find
any emerald when he woke up this morning. . . ."

"Will you forget about Dr. Kyle?" said the exasperated Morgan. "It's
all right; it simply wasn't his cabin, that's all. Listen to me. . . ."

But an uneasy possibility had struck him. Dr. Kyle didn't find the
emerald. Very well. Suppose the Perrigords hadn't found it, either? It
was an absurd supposition, yet it grew on him. Assuming both parties to
be entirely honest, what the devil could have happened to the emerald?
They could not have missed it, either of them; he himself had heard the
steel box bump on the floor. Again assuming them to be honest, it might
mean that Peggy had mistaken the cabin. But this he doubted. There was
shrewdness, there was certainty, in that girl's prim little face. Well—
alternatively, it might mean that the Blind Barber was up to tricks. They
had ample proof that he was somewhere close at hand during the wild
business on C deck. He might very well have seen what happened. Later
that night it would have been a simple matter to go after that emerald. . . .

Irritably Morgan told himself that he was flying at theories like Warren. Warren, taking advantage of the other's blank silence, was going on
talking with vehemence; and the more he talked the more strongly he
convinced himself; so that Dr. Kyle's character had begun to assume hues

of the richest and most sinister black. Morgan said, "Nonsense!" and again he told himself there was no sense to this doubt. The Perrigords had found the emerald, and that was that. But his real irritation with himself was for not thinking before of a simple possibility like that of the Blind Barber's having been in attendance. If those æsthetes really hadn't found the thing, after all. . . .

"There's this that's got to be done," he said, breaking in on the other's heated discourse. "Somehow, we've got to ask Kyle a few questions, tactfully—whether he's a light sleeper, whether he keeps his door bolted at night. . . ."

"Now you're showing some sense," said Warren. "Trip him up, eh? Mind, I don't say that necessarily he's the—the barber. What I do say is that fifty thousand pounds' worth of emerald, chucked in on him like that when he thought nobody'd be the wiser. . . . Did you notice his expression? Did you hear the crazy story he told us, knowing the thing'd get so tangled up that nobody would be able to accuse . . .?"

"Read that article in the paper," the other ordered, tapping it inexorably. "We've got to make the acquaintance of the Perrigords, even if it's only a red herring; and you've got to be able to talk intelligently about *nuances*. What's the matter with your education? You're in the diplomatic or consular service, or whatever it is. Don't you have to know French to get in that?"

He had hoped that this crack would divert Warren. It did. The young diplomat was stung.

"Certainly I know French," he returned, with cold dignity. "Listen. I had to pass the toughest examination they can dish out, I'll have you know; yes, and I'll bet *you* couldn't pass it yourself. Only it's commercial French. Ask me anything in commercial French. Go on, ask me how to say, "Dear sir. Yrs of the 18th inst. to hand, and enclose under separate cover bill of exchange, together with consular invoice, to the amt. of sixteen dollars (or perhaps pounds, francs, marks, lire, roubles, kopecks, or kronen) and forty-five cents (or perhaps shillings, centimes, pfennigs. . . .' "

"Well, what's the matter with you, then?"

"I'm telling you, it isn't the same thing. The only other French I know is some guff I remember from preparatory school. I know how to ask for a hat which fits me, and I know how to inquire my way in case I should feel a passionate desire to rush out and visit the Botanical Gardens. But I never had the least desire to go to the Botanical Gardens; and, believe me, if I ever go into a hat-shop in Paris, no pop-eyed Frog in the world is going to sell me a lid that slides down over my ears. . . . Besides, not having a sister who's a shepherdess kind of cramps my conversational style."

"Hullo!" said Morgan, who was paying no attention. "It's begun. Good work. She thought of it. . . ."

Down the broad polished staircase into the dining-saloon came the tall and majestic figures of Mr. and Mrs. Leslie Perrigord; well-groomed, moving together in step. And between them, talking earnestly, walked Peggy Glenn.

Peggy came just a trifle above Mrs. Perrigord's shoulder. Evidently as a sort of intellectual touch, she had put on her shell-rimmed spectacles and an exuberant amount of make-up. Her frock was what looked to Morgan like a batik pattern. She was speaking with animation to the monocled Mrs. Perrigord, who seemed to convey *nuances* of reply by ghostly silent movements of eyebrow and lip. At the foot of the stairs Morgan expected her to break off and come to their table; but she did nothing of the kind. To Morgan she made an almost imperceptible signal; of what, he was not sure. Then she went on with the Perrigords to their table.

Warren muttered something in muffled surprise, after which they noted something else. Coming down the staircase a short distance behind them shuffled the big and amiable figure of Captain Valvick, whose sandy hair was brushed up straight and his leathery face once more netted with wrinkles as he listened to some tale. The tale was being told him, in fact, by Mr. Charles Woodcock. Mr. Woodcock, who freely described himself as the Bug-powder Boy, seemed excited. Invariably, when excited his thin frame seemed to hop and twist; an optical illusion, because he kept his eyes fixed on your face while he poured out a rapid string of words in a confidential undertone.

"What's Valvick up to?" demanded Warren. "All the allies seem to be working except us. Have you noticed our square-head's been keeping away from Woodcock, because they're both powerful yarn-spinners and they put each other out like a couple of forest fires? Well, then look how quiet he's keeping and tell me what's on his mind."

Morgan didn't know; he supposed it was Mr. Woodcock's version of what had occurred last night. If so conservative a Presbyterian as Dr. Oliver Harrison Kyle had suggested rape, then he shuddered to think of the goings-on that would present themselves to the versatile imagination of the Bug-powder Boy. The dining-saloon was rapidly filling up, pulsing now with a joyous babble and clamour as of prisoners released, but they heard Mr. Woodcock's hearty voice. He said, "All right, old socks. Don't forget to tell your pals," and slapped Captain Valvick on the back as he went towards his own table.

With a puzzled expression Valvick lumbered towards their table. He beamed a good morning, swung round his chair, and uttered the word:

"Mermaid!"

Morgan blinked. "Don't," he said. "For God's sake stop! That's enough. If anybody tells me that Captain Whistler was chasing a mermaid around C deck last night, the last shred of my sanity will be gone. Don't say it! I can't bear to hear any more!"

"Eh?" said Valvick, staring. "What iss dis? Ay nefer hear anyt'ing like dat, dough ay haff a mess-boy once who say he hass seen one. Dis iss Mr. Woodcock's invention—ay tell you about it, but ay haff to listen to him a lot because he know a lot about diss crook. . . ."

Valvick sat down.

"Listen! Ay got bot' de hatches full off news. Ay tell you all about it, but first ay tell you de most important. Captain Whistler want all of us up in his cabin after breakfast, and—coroosh!—he t'ink he know who de criminal is."

Chapter X

DRAMATIS PERSONAE

After the captain had ordered porridge and the table steward had gone, a rather nervous Warren put down his coffee-cup.

"Knows who the criminal is? He's not getting any funny ideas, is he? About us, I mean?"

Chuckling, Valvick made a broad gesture. "Coroosh, no! Not at all. Dat ain't it. Ay dunno yust what it is, but he send Sparks to my cabin to say we all got to come up after mess. Sparks say de captain get a wireless message, but he will not tell me what iss in it until we see old Barnacle."

"I wonder," said Morgan.

"So dat remind, and ay say to Sparks—iss de wireless-operator; all de wireless-operators iss Sparkses, you see—ay say, 'Sparks, you wass on duty yesterday afternoon, eh?' And he say, 'Yes.' And den ay say, 'Sparks, do you remember when de old man receive dat first message about de crook, and hass a row wit' you? Wass dere some odder people in de cabin wit' you at de time?' When he says yes, den ay describe dat girl we find cracked on de head last night, and ay say, 'Sparks, was *she* dere?' (All Sparkses is hawful wit' de ladies, so ay know he remember her if she wass.) Halso, if she send or receive a message, he iss going to know her name, eh?"

"Neat!" said Warren. "Swell! Who was she?"

"Ahhhh, dass de trouble. He remember her, but he dunno. Dere was several people, and halso a cousin of Sparks which is travelling as a passenger. She came in, and see dere is people in a waiting-line, so he guess she don't want to wait and she turn round and go out; he say she hass got 'ands full of papers. No matter! We find out when we know who iss missing. *Now* is de part I want to tell you. . . ."

The porridge had arrived. Captain Valvick emptied the creamjug over it, bent his vast shoulders, adjusted his elbows in a wing-like spread, and spoke between excavations.

"Well, we get to talking, you see, and ay give him a drink of Old Rob Roy, and he say, 'Coroosh! Captain, but my cousin Alick could haff use dis whisky last night.' Den he tell me his cousin Alick hass suffered somet'ing hawful with de yumping toothache, and de doctor hass give him somet'ing to put on it, but it don't do no good. And ay say, 'So-ho?' ay say, 'den he should haff come to me, for ay know somet'ing dat cure him bing-bing.' It iss composed—"

"Not to interrupt you, Skipper," said Morgan, who was keeping a wary eye out for a signal from Peggy at the Perrigords' table, "but are you sure this is strictly—"

"Ay am sure, you bet!" returned the other, with snorting excitement. "Listen. He say, 'Den ay wish you would go see him,' Sparks say; 'he iss only round in C 47. . . .' "

"Sorry," said Morgan, and jerked his head back. "C 47, eh? Well?"

"So we go to C 47, which iss in de gangway just hopposite Dr. Kyle's. Eh? And hiss cousin is walking round in circles with de 'ot-water-bag, and sometimes he go and bump his head on de bulkhead, and say, 'Coroosh! ay wish ay wass dead,' and ay pity de poor fallar hawful. So ay write out what he hass to get at doctor's, and send Sparks for it. In fife minutes dat pain go, and de poor fallar can't believe it, and he got tears in his eyes when he t'ank me. Oh, ay forgot to tell you he iss a prizefighter which is called de Bermondsey Terror. He hask me if dere is somet'ing he can do for me. Ay say no, and ay give *him* a drink of Old Rob Roy, but ay got a hidea yust de same."

With a massive finger the captain tapped the table.

"Like diss. In de night ay am t'inking to myself, and all of a sudden ay yump up in my bunk, and t'ink, 'Coroosh! Maybe de doctor and de odders iss honest people, but suppose diss crook sneak into de cabin where Miss Glenn t'row dat hemerald? . . .' "

Morgan nodded. The old skipper was no fool. It took some time for his clicking mind to mesh its wheels, but he arrived. This idea, bringing new implications to worry Warren, caused a silence to fall on the table.

"You don't mean"—Warren gulped—"you don't mean—?"

"Oh! no! But ay t'ank ay better ask de Bermondsey Terror. Ay say,

'You wass up all night wit' de toothache?' He say yes. Ay say, 'Did you hear any yumps and yitters out on de deck?' He say, 'Yes, ay t'ank ay hear a woman say, "Sock him again," but ay feel too bad to go see what it iss; besides,' he say, 'ay haf de port closed so ay don't catch cold in de yaw, and can't hear much, but,' he say, 'it iss close in de cabin, and ay haff de door fastened open.' Dat is de way wit de lime-yuicers. Dey iss hell on cold air. Ay wass in yail once in Boston wit' a lime-yuicer, and all he do all de time iss to squawk about dat yail because it hass got steam heat. . . ."

"And the Bermondsey Terror," said Morgan, "was up all night, and could see Kyle's door?"

"Dat iss right," agreed the captain. "And he swear nobody go down dere all night. So ay got *somet'ing* off my mind." He heaved a wheezy sigh.

Observing that Warren was about to construe this into further proof of Kyle's guilt, Morgan said, hastily: "You've accomplished lots of work before breakfast, Captain. Was there anything else? What's this you say about Woodcock knowing something?"

"Ah! Yes, yes. Ay almost forget!" The captain gave a mighty flip of his spoon. "But ay dunno yust what to make of it. Dat Woodcock iss a funny fallar, you bet. Efery time he talk business, he try to use de subtlety and den ay dunno what he iss talking about. But he say it iss a business proposition. He say he want to speak to Mr. Warren, and he got a deal to make if Mr. Warren will talk turkey. First, he knows what happen last night. . . ."

"I'll bet he does," said Warren, grimly. "What's *his* version?"

"No, no, no! Dat iss de funny part. Ay t'ank he know most of it for sure, all except about de girl."

Warren seized the edge of the table. "You don't mean he knows about Uncle Warpus or that film?"

"Well, he knows somet'ing about a film, ay tell you dat. He iss a smart man. What all he know ay dunno, but he sort of hint he know plenty about diss crook." Valvick stroked his moustache, scowling. "You better talk to him. De point iss diss. He has invented something. It iss a bug-powder gun wit' a helectric light."

"A bug-powder gun with an electric light?" repeated Morgan, rather wildly. He dismissed the idea that this might be some singular kind of nautical metaphor. "What the hell is a bug-powder gun with an electric light? This strain is gradually sapping my mental powers. I'm going mad, I tell you. Skipper, haven't we got enough on our minds without you babbling about bug-powder guns and electric lights?"

"Ay am not babbling!" said the captain, with some heat. "Dat is yust what he tell me. Ay dunno how it vurk, but it iss somet'ing you use to kill de mosquitoes in de dark. He say it will refolutionise de bug-killing profession, and he iss going to call it de Mermaid. He say it can also be used on bedbugs, cockroaches, earwigs, caterpillars, red ants, horse-flies. . . ."

"I have no doubt," said Morgan, "that it will enable a good shot to bring down a cockroach at sixty yards. But get back to the subject. Whether or not it has something to do with us, we have more immediate concerns. Dr. Kyle, skipper, did *not* find the emerald in his cabin this morning. Thanks to you and the Bermondsey Terror, we've proved that the Blind Barber didn't get in to pinch it, either. . . . That leaves the Perrigords. It's got to be the Perrigords. They're our last hope. Of course the Perrigords have got it! That's why Peggy is staying so long over there. . . ."

Warren tapped his arm.

"She's giving us the high sign now," he said, in a low voice. "Don't turn round too obviously now, but have a look. No, wait a minute. It's no secret stuff. She wants us to come over to the table."

"De odder people haff got de emerald?" inquired Valvick, peering over his shoulder. "Haa! Den dat iss all right. Ay tell you ay wass worried."

"Lord! I hope so," said Morgan, fervently. "But Peggy doesn't look too pleased. Finish your breakfast, Skipper, and then join us. Get ready, Curt. Did you finish that article?"

"Sure I did," retorted Warren. He spoke out of the corner of his mouth as they moved out across the dance floor towards the other table. "And don't go making any cracks about my education either. I can tell you all about it. It seems Peggy's uncle is the goods. As a classic dramatist he is an eight-cyclindered wow, and there's been nobody like him since Molière. If any impertinent criticism of his jewelled lines can be made by one, one would say a certain *je ne sais quoi*. I should possibly suggest the introduction of certain deft touches of *realism* into the speech of, say, so human and breathing a figure as the Knight Roland or the crafty Banhambra, Sultan of the Moors which would lend an element of graphic power. . . ."

"An element," said the loud, concise voice of Mr. Leslie Perrigord in the flesh, "of graphic power. And that is all."

Morgan looked him over as he sat stiffly upright at the breakfast-table, holding a fork with its prongs against the cloth and e-nun-ci-a-ting his words through stiff jaws. There was nothing effeminate or lackadaisical about Mr. Leslie Perrigord, that element which most irritated Morgan in the species intellectual. Mr. Perrigord looked as though he could pull his weight in a crew or handle a skittish horse. A tall lath with thin blond hair, a hooked nose, and a mummified eye, he simply talked. He looked at nothing in particular. He seemed far away. If you had not seen the feathery blond moustache floating as in an icy breeze, you would have sworn it was an effect of ventriloquism. But (once started) he showed no disposition to leave off talking.

A measured stream of hooey flowing from Mr. Perrigord's lips in concise cadences was checked by Peggy only when it became necessary for Perrigord to wind himself up with ice-water. She said:

"Oh, I say, excuse me! I'm so sorry to interrupt you, but I must present two very good friends of mine. Mr. Warren, Mr. Morgan. . . ."

"De-do?" said Mrs. Perrigord, sepulchrally.

"Oh?" said Mr. Perrigord. He seemed vaguely annoyed. He had just kicked Shakespeare in the eye and mashed the hat of Ben Jonson; and Morgan felt he was ruffled at being interrupted. "Oh? Delighted, I'm sure. I was—ah—mentioning some of the more elementary points, *en passant,* in the talk I have been asked to deliver at the ship's concert to-night." He smiled thinly. "But—ah—I fear I shall bore you. It is merely a talk serving as an introductory speech to the performance of M. Fortinbras's marionettes. I fear—"

"But of course they'll be interested, Mr. Perrigord!" crowed Peggy, with enthusiasm. "Curt, I was just telling Mr. and Mrs. Perrigord about the time in Dubuque when the Knight Oliver got his pants split in the battle with the Moors, and they had to lower the curtain because all the sawdust came out of him, and he had to be sewed up again before uncle would go on with the play. Mr. Perrigord said it was charming, a charming detail. Didn't you, Mr. Perrigord?"

"Quite, Miss Glenn," said the oracle, benevolently (for him), but he looked as if he wished the others would go and let him get back to literature. He showed that heavy sort of politeness which grows acutely uncomfortable in the air. "Quite charming. These little details. But surely I am boring these gentlemen, who can have no conceivable interest. . . . ?"

"But just fancy," continued Peggy, appealing to Morgan. "Hank, you villain, I've lost my bet to you, after all. And now I'll have to stand the cocktails, and it's a terrible shame. Don't you think so, dear Mr. Perrigord?"

Warren did not like this at all.

"Bet?" he said. "What bet? Who made a bet?"

Somebody kicked him in the shins. "Because," the girl went on, "after all my tam-o'-shanter *didn't* blow in the porthole of Mr. Perrigord's cabin last night. It's beastly luck, because now I've probably lost it; but it didn't, and there's that. Just before Mr. Perrigord began talking so wonderfully"—here she raised earnest, awed, soft eyes for a moment and kept them fixed on Perrigord's countenance. He cleared his throat. A sort of paralytic leer passed over his face. Warren saw it. So did Mrs.

Perrigord—"just before Mr. Perrigord began talking so *wonderfully*, he told me he'd found nothing in the cabin at all, and I'm afraid now I *must* have lost that nice tam of mine."

"No deu-oubt," said Mrs. Perrigord, giving Peggy a nasty look through her monocle. "It was *quayte* dark on deck, wasn't it, my de-ah?"

"Quayte. And, I say, these men do take such advantage of us, don't they, Mrs. Perrigord? I mean, I think it's simply awful; but after all what can one *do?* I mean, it's much better to submit than cause a terrible lot of fuss and bother, isn't it?"

"Well, re-aolly!" said Mrs. Perrigord, stiffening. "I confess I scarcely kneow. To—to one at a time, perhaps. But—ah—reaolly, my deah, since I am olmost certain I heard at least six intoxicated men carousing out the-ah, I confess I should not have been at oll surprised to find on our floor considerably moah than a tam-o'-shanter. As I observed to the steward at the time—"

"To the steward?" asked Peggy wonderingly. "But, Mrs. Perrigord, wherever was your husband?"

Mrs. Perrigord's husband, who now seemed to despair of getting back to the serious business of sitting on literary hats, interposed:

"Most refreshing, Miss Glenn. Most refreshing. Ha-ha! I like the outspoken views, the free and untrammelled straightforwardness of our youth to-day, which is not by ancient prejudice cabined, cribbed, and confined. . . . " At this point, Mrs. Perrigord looked as though, if she were not by ancient prejudice cabined, cribbed, and confined, she would up and dot him one with a plate of kippers. "I—in short, I like it. But you must not mind my wife. Ha-ha!"

"Oh?" said Mrs. Perrigord.

"Come, come, Cynthia. *Jeunesse, jeunesse.* A trifle of exuberant 'seizing the moment,' so to speak. Remember what D. H. Lawrence said to James Joyce. Ha-ha-ha!"

"My deah Leslie," said Mrs. Perrigord coldly, "Babylonian orgies and revels of Ishtar *à la Pierre Louys* are oll very well in books. But if it is to youah æsthetic taste to have these rites peahfoahmed oll ovah the deck of a respectable linah undah youah window at 2 a.m., I must say I caon't agree. And I must insist on explaining to this young lady that muh relations with the cabin steward were—ah—puahly those of business—"

"Coo!" said Peggy.

"—and were confined," went on Mrs. Perrigord, in a louder voice, "to ringing the bell, unbolting the doah, and asking him whethah (as my husband will inform you) something could be done to stop the noise. I can assuah you that I slept no moah oll night."

Mr. Perrigord said mildly that you had got to remember what James

Joyce said to D. H. Lawrence. Morgan felt that he had better do something to culminate this exchange of dirty digs before it reached the hair-pulling stage. All the same, he was aghast. The emerald had to be *somewhere*. He held no brief for either Lord Sturton or Captain Whistler, but the fact remained that they had pinched a fifty-thousand-pound jewel and thrown it through the porthole of one of those two cabins. If the emerald had somehow incredibly vanished, it meant the vanishing of Sturton's money and probably Whistler's official head. Something was wrong. Kyle said it wasn't in *his* cabin, and there was testimony to prove the Barber could not have lifted it from there. On the other hand, the Perrigords were awake; noticed the row; would certainly have noticed anything thrown in, and certainly could not have missed it this morning. His bewilderment grew, and he desperately sought for a new lead. . . .

So Morgan assumed his most winning smile (although he felt it stretch like a hideous mask) and spoke flattering, soothing, cajoling words to Mrs. Perrigord. She was not at all bad-looking, by the way; and he went to work with gusto. While Warren stared at him, he sympathised with her and apologised angrily for the behaviour of whatever disgusting revellers had disturbed her sleep. He intimated that, no matter what might have been the conversation between those two notorious old rips James Joyce and D. H. Lawrence, it had been in very bad taste.

" . . . But to tell you the truth, Mrs. Perrigord," said Morgan, leaning confidingly over her chair, "I heard that disturbance, too; and, though I can't say, since of course I wasn't there, you understand . . ."

"Oh, quayte!" said Mrs. Perrigord, relaxing a good deal and much less stiffly indicating that he had her royal ear. "Yes?"

" . . . still, I should have said it sounded less like—well, shall we say Dionysian revelry?—than simply a free-for-all scrap. Er, fisticuffs, you know," explained Morgan, seeking the highbrow *mot juste*. "Especially as (if you'll forgive my saying so, Mrs. Perrigord) that a lady of your charm and knowledge of refinements in sensual indulgence would probably take a light view of men's and women's frailties if only they were staged with any degree of delicacy. Furthermore—"

"Well, no, reaolly!" said Mrs. Perrigord, looking arch. "Come now, Mr. Morgan, you can scarcely expect muh to agree *all*together with that, can you? Heh-heh-heh!"

"Sure! Absolutely, Mrs. Perrigord!" said Warren. He perceived that Hank was trying to win the old girl over, and stoutly tried to help the good work along. "We know you're a good sport. Absolutely. Remember what the travelling salesman said to the farmer's daughter."

"Shut up," said Morgan out of the corner of his mouth. "And naturally I suppose this idea of a fight occurred to you, too. Gad! I wonder you didn't get up and bolt the door, Mrs. Perrigord, in case those drunken ba—ah—in case those revellers should decide—"

"But I did!" cried Mrs. Perrigord. "Oh, the doah was bolted, I assuah you! From the very first moment I heard a woman's voice imploring someone to—to strike someone ageyne, it was bolted. I did not close an eye oll night. I can most certainly tell you that no one came into the cabin."

(Well, that tore it. Morgan glanced at his companions. Peggy looked upset. Warren angry and mystified. The puzzle was growing worse jumbled and also it was Mr. Perrigord who now seemed to be giving the nasty looks. Morgan felt that they had better go off and cool their heads before going up for the interview with Captain Whistler. He prepared some discreet words. . . .)

"But tell me," said Mrs. Perrigord, apparently struck with an idea. "Someone said—are you the Mr. Morgan who writes the detective stories?"

"Why—er—yes. Yes, I believe so. Thank you very much, Mrs. Perrigord, and you too, sir. It's been delightful to have made your acquaintance, and I only hope we shall have the opportunity—"

"I adore detective stories," said Mrs. Perrigord.

Her husband remained motionless. But on his glassy-eyed countenance was a curious expression. He looked as a familiar of the Spanish Inquisition might have looked if, on the morning of an *auto-da-fé,* Fra Torquemada had announced an intention of dismissing the poor blighters with a warning.

"Do you indeed, my dear?" inquired Leslie Perrigord, frostily. "Most extraordinary. Well, we must not detain them, Cynthia. Miss Glenn, I hope I shall have the pleasure of conferring with you to-day—and also your excellent uncle, to whom I look forward to meeting—and arrange matters for the performance to-night. *A bientôt!"*

"But we shall see you at the concert, of course," observed Mrs. Perrigord. On her face was a narrow-eyed smile which somehow reminded Morgan of Mr. Stanley Laurel. "Les-leh and I have bean conferring with the pursah to arrange it. I shall *so* hope to see you, deah Miss Glenn. An excellent programme has bean arranged. Madame Giulia Leda Camopsozzi will sing *morceaux* from the more modern masters, accompanied by her husband, Signor Benito Furioso Camopsozzi. I—ah—believe," she added, frowning as though this did not appeal to her, "that the pursah, a certain Mr. Macgregor, has persuaded Dr. Oliver Kyle to recite selections from the works of Robert Burns. This will of course precede M. Fortinbras's performance. *A bientôt."*

"Cheero-ho," said Peggy, rising from the table, "and thanks most awfully for all the information. You *must* come and see me, Mr. Perrigord, and tell me all about those fascinating things—but, I say—er—if you're going to see my uncle—"

"Yes?" inquired Mr. Perrigord. He lifted his eyebrows at her worried expression.

"Don't think me foolish, but I really know him awfully well. And please promise me, if he's up and about—I mean, I know how *awful* some of you terribly intelligent people are," she really seemed to be in earnest this time, and even Mrs. Perrigord condescended to look at her as she hesitated; "but promise me you won't give him anything to drink. I know it sounds silly, but he really hasn't got a strong head; and—and you'd never believe it, but he has a most awful weakness for gin. I have to watch him, you see, because one night when we were to give a performance in Philadelphia—"

"I never touch spirits, Miss Glenn," said Perrigord, swiftly and rather curtly. " 'Why should I put a thief in my mouth to steal away my brains?' as T. S. Eliot somewhere puts it. It is abominable. I am also a vegetarian. M. Fortinbras will be quite safe in my care. Good day."

In silence the three conspirators hurried away from the table. Morgan, locked up with his own bewildering thoughts, did not speak. Peggy looked scared. It was Warren who broke the silence.

"You see?" he demanded, savagely. "Those two dumb chucks wouldn't steal anything. Now take my advice before it's too late. It's that fake doctor, I'm telling you. My Lord! the thing didn't just disappear! It's in his cabin. . . ."

"Peggy," said Morgan, "there's no other explanation. You must have mistaken the cabin."

They had reached the foot of the staircase, and she waited until a passing steward was out of earshot. "I didn't, Hank," she told him, quietly and earnestly. "I'm absolutely positive I didn't. I was out on deck again this morning, putting myself just where I stood last night. . . ."

"Well?"

"I wasn't mistaken. It was one of those two, because there are only two portholes anywhere near. It was one of those two; and I *think,* I say I think, it was Dr. Kyle's."

"As far as I'm concerned, I don't see what more evidence you want," remarked Warren, rather querulously. "I'll do what the Brains says, and no questions asked, but I've got my own theories. Come on. We've got to go up and see Captain Whistler."

A voice just above them said: "Excuse me, Mr. Warren. I don't want to bust up anything; but if you've ten minutes to spare, I think I can make it worth your while."

Leaning over the gilt banister, tapping it with his finger, Mr. Charles Woodcock was regarding them in a very curious fashion.

Chapter XI

ONE WHO SAW THE BLIND BARBER

M r. Woodcock's countenance wore such an expression of tense and alert seriousness that Morgan felt a new uneasiness. He remembered Valvick's remarks to the effect that Woodcock had hinted of things, nebulous but dangerous things, the man claimed to know. Never thoroughly at ease before live-wire business men, because his mind could not move as fast as theirs along their own lines, Morgan thought of several disturbing possibilities, including blackmail. And so it was that they encountered a feature of the case which (a week before) Morgan would have considered an absurdity or a frank impossibility, yet which to others was serious: one of the deadly serious things which underlay a tissue of misdirection and nonsense.

Woodcock was a wiry, restless, shock-headed man with a bony face and good-humoured eyes which were nevertheless rather fixed. Round his sharp jaw were wrinkles as though from much talking; the talking, in fact—as he strolled about the ship hitherto—had been rapid, lurid, jovial and winking. He seemed desirous of conveying the impression that he was a bouncing, engagingly mendacious good fellow with little on his mind. Now he leaned over the banister, his sharp eyes moving swiftly right and left.

"Now I spoke to the old skipper," he went on in a rapid and con-fidential undertone, "because I didn't have any idea of shoving myself in, you understand, where I mightn't be wanted. All right!" said Mr. Wood-cock lifting his palm in a gesture as though he expected an objection. He did this each time he said, "All right!" It was a means of noting that he had made a point; and could go on from there with a certainty that, so far, everything was understood. "All right! But I know how it is with these things, and I want to make it man to man, and fair and square, so that I can convince you you'll be doing a thing you'll never regret if you come in on my proposition. All right! Now, all I want, Mr. Warren, is ten minutes of your valuable time—alone. Just ten minutes. You can take out your watch and put it on the table, and if I haven't interested you in just ten minutes—" Here he made a significant gesture of his wrist and raised his eyebrows—"then there's absolutely no more to be said."

"Not at all, not at all," said Warren rather vaguely. He was flustered at this new intrusion, and clearly had the idea Woodcock was trying to sell him something. "Glad to give you all the time you want. Well—we'll have a drink and talk it over. But not just now. My friends and I have an important date—"

Woodcock leaned closer.

"Exactly, old man. Exactly. I know. With the captain. It's all right now; it's all right," he whispered, raising his hand. "I understand, old man."

The conspirators stared at each other, and Woodcock's eyes swept from one to the other of them. "What," said Warren, "what's on your mind?"

"Ten minutes," said the other, "alone?"

"Well—yes. But my friends have got to be there. You can tell all of us, can't you?"

Woodcock seemed to scent a bluff somewhere. His eyebrows went up, but he spoke in a tone of pleasant and fatherly chiding, anxiously.

"Look, old man. Are you sure you've got it straight? Are you sure you'd like to have the young lady there?"

"Why not? Good God! what have you got into your head, anyhow?"

"All right, old man, if that's what you want!" He was affable. "I admit I'd rather talk to you alone, but I won't argue. Suppose we go up to the writing-room, where it'll be quiet."

On the way he talked steadily and with sprightly bounce of other matters, laughing heartily, amid many jocose references. The white-panelled writing-room was deserted. He led them to an embrasure of full-glass windows, where the morning sun was muffled by thick curtains, and quiet was broken only by the pounding of the engines. Here, when they were seated, he ran a hand through his bristly hair, fidgeted, and suddenly shot into action.

"Now, I want to help you, old man," he explained, still confidentially, "but you see, it's a case of mutual benefits, you see? You're young, and you don't understand these things. But when you get older and have a wife and family, ah!" said Mr. Woodcock. He made an impressive gesture. "Then you'll understand that business isn't only a matter of favours. All right! Now, frankly, you're sort of in a jam, aren't you?"

"Shoot," said Warren briefly.

"Well then. I don't know what went on on the boat last night, that everybody's talking about; I don't *want* to know. It's none of my business, see? But I do know what happened yesterday afternoon. A roll of film was stolen from your cabin, wasn't it? No, no, don't answer, and don't interrupt.

"I'm going to show you," continued Mr. Woodcock, after a pause in which he demonstrated himself an admirable showman—" 'm going to show you," he went on, rather sharply, "a little moving-picture of my own as to what might have happened. I don't say it *did* happen, y'unna-stand. You wouldn't expect me to pin myself down to that, would you? I say it *might* have happened. All right! Now here's my little moving-picture. I'm coming along the gangway down on C deck, see? about ha'-past four yesterday afternoon, and I've just been up sending off a radio to my firm, and there's nothing on my mind. All of a sudden I hear a noise behind me when I'm passing one of those little offshoots of the gangway, and I turn around in time to see a guy ducking out of it, and across the gangway into the wash-room. All right! And I see this bozo's got a whole mess of movie film that he's trying to stuff under his coat—

"*U-uh,* now!" said Mr. Woodcock warningly, "don't interrupt! Well, suppose I see this guy's face so that if I haven't seen it before I'd know it again wherever I saw it; just suppose that. I wonder what it is, but I figure it's none of my business. Still, I think there may be a angle to it, see, so I sort of go down and take a peek. But all I can see is a door sort of open and a lot of film and film-boxes scattered around on the floor; and I see a guy—maybe yourself—sort of getting up from the floor with his hands to his head.

"And I think 'Whu-o, Charley! You'd better get out of this, and not be mixed up in any trouble,' see? Besides, the guy was coming round and didn't need any help, or I'd have stopped. But then I get to thinking—"

"You mean," said Warren, rather hoarsely, "you saw who—?"

"Now go easy, old man, go easy. Let me show my picture now!"

His picture, they discovered, exhibited a sort of strange interlude in which Mr. Woodcock's memory spoke to him. Apparently he was a great hand at reading the tabloids and scandal sheets, explaining also that he was a subscriber to the magazine *True Sex-Life Stories.* One of the papers, it appeared, had recently published a red-hot, zippy item straight from the capital city. It was couched in the form of innuendo, inquiring what Big Shot had a nephew who could always get a job turning a camera crank in Hollywood; furthermore, was it possible that the afore-mentioned Big Shot, in a sportive mood, had been indiscreet before a camera; and, if this were within the limits of possibility, who was the woman in the case?

"Woman?" said Warren uncontrollably. "*Woman?* There's no woman! Why, my un—"

"Steady," interrupted Morgan, his face stolid. "Mr. Woodcock's doing the talking."

Woodcock did not even smile or contradict. He probably expected this. He was still helpful, concerned; but there were tighter wrinkles round his jaw and his eyes were expressionless. "So maybe I'm thinking to myself," he pursued, jerking his wrist and shoulder with a curiously Hebraic gesture while the sharp eyes fixed Warren, "about a very funny cable-gram I overhear in the wireless-room. And maybe I don't make much sense out of it, see? because I don't hear much of it; except that it's about a movie film and also about somebody being *bare*. Now, now, old man, you needn't look so funny at me—I understand how these things are. But I think, 'Charley, maybe you're wrong. Maybe it was just an ordinary stick-up job. And if it was, then of course there'll be a noise about it this evening, and Mr. Warren'll report he's been robbed.' All right! Only," concluded Mr. Woodcock, leaning over and tapping Warren on the knee, "there wasn't, and he didn't."

During the silence they could hear some children crying out and pelting past the door of the writing-room. The engines throbbed faintly. Slowly Warren passed his hand over his forehead.

"There've been some funny interpretations put on all this," he said in a strained voice, "but this is *the limit*. A woman! . . . All right to you, old horse," he added, with sudden crispness. "You're wrong, of course; but this isn't the time to discuss that. WHO WAS THAT MAN WHO STOLE THE FILM? That's what we want to know. What is it you want? Money?"

Clearly this had never occurred to the other. He jumped on the seat of the window. "I may not be as big as you," he said quietly, "but you try offering me money again, and, by God! you'll regret it. What do you think I am, a blackmailer? Come on, old man"—his voice changed and his eyes had a hopeful and propitiatory gleam—"come on now. I'm a business man and this is the biggest chance of my life. I'm only trying to do my job, after all. If I can put this across, I'll be in line for an assistant-vice-presidency. I'm giving it to you straight: if I'd thought that anything really important'd been stolen, or anything like that, I wouldn't hold out on you for a second. But I figure it this way. What's happened? An old guy, who ought to know better, has played sugar-daddy and got himself into a jam with a woman, and there's a picture of it. All right! I don't wish him any bad luck—I sympathise, and *I offer to help*. I offer to tell you who's got it, so's you can get it back . . . well, whatever way you like. But I figure *I* rate a favour in return. And if that's not fair, I don't know what is."

The man was desperately serious. Morgan studied him, trying to understand both the man's ethics and the man's nature. He was a problem aside from both the grim and the comic. That a governmental stuffed-shirt had been caught in a compromising position with a woman before somebody's moving-picture camera he thought of as neither serious nor ridiculous; in all probability he simply supposed that, if a government official got into difficulties they would *be* difficulties of that nature, to be judged solely from how he could use the fact in a legitimate business fashion. Morgan looked at Warren, and he could see that the latter considered it all fair enough.

"Good enough," said Warren, nodding grimly. "You've got a right to proposition me. Fire away. But what the devil can *I* do for you?"

Woodcock drew a deep breath.

"I want a signed testimonial, with a picture," he said, "for the newspapers and magazines."

"Testimonial? Hell, yes, I'll give you a testimonial for anything," Warren returned, staring. "But what good can I do you? What—Wait a minute. Holy smoke! You don't mean a *bug-powder* testimonial, do you?"

"I mean," said Woodcock, "I want a recommendation for a certain article which my firm is about to place on the market and which I invented. Mind, old man, if I didn't know this thing was a world-beater I wouldn't try to sell you the idea. I'm not going to ask you to accept anything sight unseen. I'm going to *show* you," said Mr. Woodcock, suddenly taking out a long package from under his coat like an anarchist who gets has victim in a corner with a bomb. "I'm going to show you that this little gadget will really do everything we claim for it in the advertising campaign. Yes, I want a testimonial, old man. . . . But not from you."

"He means, Curt," said Peggy, regarding Mr. Woodcock with a fascinated horror—"he means, you see—"

Woodcock nodded. "You get it lady. I want a testimonial of endorsement from the Hon. Thaddeus G. Warpus for the Mermaid Electrically-fitted Mosquito Gun, fitted with Swat No. 2 Liquid Insect Exterminator; saying that he personally uses it at his country home in New Jersey, and warmly recommends it. This is my chance, and I'm not going to miss it. For years we've been trying to get testimonials for our stuff from the big shots or the society women. And we can't. Because why? Because they say it isn't dignified. But what's the difference? Cigarettes, toothpaste, face cream, shaving soap—you'll get *them* recommended all right, and what's the difference? I'm not asking you to recommend a bug-powder, but a neat, svelte-looking, silver-plate and enamel job. Let me show it to you, let me explain how it works—that combines all the advantages of a double-sized electric torch with—"

Eagerly, as though to press an advantage, he began to take off the wrappings of the parcel. Morgan, as he looked at Curtis Warren, was more and more startled. This business, which had the elements of howling farce, was not farce at all. Warren was as serious as the Bug-powder Boy.

"But, man, have some sense!" he protested, waving his arms. "If it had been anything else, toothpaste, cigarettes. . . . It can't be done. It'ud make him out to look foolish. . . ."

"Yeah?" said Woodcock coolly. "Well, answer me this. Which is going to make him look more foolish, which is going to show he's more of a mug, this neat little apparatus or that film? Sorry, old man, but there you are. That's my offer. Take it or leave it."

"And otherwise you won't tell who stole that film?"

"That's what I said," agreed the other, almost cordially. "I'll tell you what, old man. You get the cablegrams working; you tell him his bare skin'll be saved if he plays ball with Charley Woodcock. . . ."

"But he'd never do it!"

"Then it'll be just too bad for him, won't it?" asked the other candidly. He folded his arms. "Now you're a nice fellow and I like you. There's nothing personal in it. But I've got to look out for myself. . . . Oh, and don't try to start anything either," he suggested, as Warren suddenly got to his feet. "You start any funny business, and I may not get my testimonial, but the story of T. G. Warpus's brief movie stardom is going to be all over the world as fast as I can broadcast it. Get me? In fact, old man," said Mr. Woodcock, trying to keep his confidential suavity, but breathing a little hard now, "if I don't get some assurance before we leave this boat that T. G. Warpus is a right guy who can take his medicine, *I* might get indiscreet when I'd had a drink too many in the bar."

"You wouldn't do that!" said Peggy.

There was a long silence. Woodcock had turned away to stare past the curtain at the sea, his hand fluttering at his bony chin. The hand dropped and he turned round.

"All right, lady," he said in a rather different voice. "I suppose you win there. No, I guess I wouldn't." He addressed Warren fiercely. "I'm not a crook. I just got mad for a minute, that was all. At least you don't have to worry about that part of it. I may try to pull some fast ones, but I'm not a lousy blackmailer. I've made you a straight proposition, and it stands. Come on, now; I apologise. What about it?"

Warren, slowly hammering his fist on one knee, said nothing. He looked at Peggy. He looked round at Henry Morgan. Morgan said:

"I'm glad you said that, Mr. Woodcock."

"Said what? Oh, about not being a crook? Thanks," the other answered bitterly, "for nothing, I'm not one of those smooth boys who can scare you into doing anything, only they call it successful salesmanship. . . . Why?"

"For instance," said Morgan, trying to keep his voice steady. He had an idea, and he only prayed that he would not bungle it. "For instance, would you like to be tried as accessory after the fact in a murder?"

"Oh, cut it," said Woodcock. "I've been wondering when the bluff would start."

All the same, his pale blue eyes briefly flashed sideways. He had got out a handkerchief and begun to mop his forehead as though he were tired of the whole business; but his bony hand stopped. The word "murder" comes rather startingly in a business discussion. As the idea grew on Morgan—he thought that in a few minutes, if he kept his jugglery going with a steady hand, they might hear the Blind Barber's name—he had still more difficulty to keep from showing his nervous excitement. *Easy, now.* Easy does it. . . .

"Let's see. You know the name of the man who stole a piece of film from Curt Warren's cabin?"

"I could point him out to you. There's not much chance of his leaving the boat."

"He committed a murder last night. He cut a woman's throat in the cabin next to Curt's. I thought you'd better be warned, that's all. Do you want me to show you the razor he did it with?"

"For God's sake," said Woodcock, jerking round, "be yourself!"

It was dusky and stuffily warm in the white writing-room, with its parade of gold-leafed mirrors and mortuary chairs. The white glass-topped desks, the ink-wells and pen-racks rattled slightly with the slight roll of the *Queen Victoria;* and, with the motion, a drowsy curling swish of water would rise in the silence. Morgan reached into the breast pocket of his coat and took out a folded dark-smeared handkerchief. He opened it just beneath a long beam of sunlight that came through the curtains, and a dull glitter shone inside.

Again there was silence. . . .

But Mr. Woodcock was not having any. Morgan saw him sitting there very straight, his hands relaxed, and a very thin smile fluttered across his face. It was a curious psychological fact, but the very production of evidence, the very display of a blood-stained razor with such sudden convenience, was what seemed to convince Woodcock that he was being elaborately bluffed.

He shook his head chidingly.

"Oh, I remember now, Hank, old man. You're the fellow who writes the stories. Say, I've got to hand it to you at that. You had me wondering for a second." The man looked as though he honestly relished this. "It's all right. I appreciate a good try. I've done the same thing myself. But put it back, old man; put it back and let's talk turkey."

"We don't know who the girl was," Morgan went on, but with a desperate feeling that he had lost his game; "that is, not yet. We were just going up to the captain to find out. It'll be very easy to prove. . . ."

"Now listen," said Woodcock, with an air of friendly if slightly bored tolerance. "The gag's all right, unnastand. It's swell. But why keep on with it? I've told you I'm not falling for it; I'm too old a bird. So why not talk business?"

"It's true, Mr. Woodcock!" Peggy insisted, clenching her hands. *"Won't* you see it's true? We admit we don't know who was killed yet—"

"Well, well!"

"But we will know. Can't you tell us. Can't you give us a *hint?"*

"You'd never suspect," said Woodcock. He smiled dreamily, and looked at the roof with the expression of one who knows the answer in a guessing game that is driving all the players wild. It was having just that effect on these three. To know that the answer was locked up in the bony skull of the man before them, yet to be told coolly they were not to hear it. . . . "I'll give you the answer," observed the Bug-powder Boy, "the moment *I* get the right answer back from T.G. Not before."

"I'll try," began Warren, but the other pointed out *that* was no guarantee.

"You don't believe," Morgan went on grimly, "that there's been a murder by the man who stole that film. Well, suppose you were convinced of it. Wait a bit now! You had your hypothesis, so at least pass an opinion on mine. Suppose there had been a murder and we could prove it, so that you'd be withholding evidence if you kept quiet. Would you tell us then?"

Woodcock lifted his shoulder, still with the pale, tolerant smile on his face. "We-el, old man! No reason why I shouldn't concede that point—in theory. Yes, indeed. If there'd been a murder done, if somebody's been killed, that would be a different thing. I sure would tell you."

"You promise that?"

"Word of honour. Now, if we can just get back to business—"

"All right," said Warren, coming to an abrupt decision. He got up. "We're going to see the captain now. And I'll make a little deal with you. If we can convince you by to-day that a murder's been committed, then you tell what you know. If we can't, then somehow or other, I give you my solemn word I'll get that testimonial from Uncle Warpus."

For the first time Woodcock seemed a little shaken. "I don't know what the gag is," he remarked critically, "and I'm damn sure there's a gag somewhere; but my answer is, You're on. . . . Put 'er there, old man; shake on it. All right! In the meantime, just as a favour to me, you take the little Mermaid along and test it, will you? There are full directions for use inside, but maybe I'd better explain some of the salient points; some features, I'm telling you, that will make the Mermaid Automatic Electric Mosquito Gun the most talked-about item in the advertising world. For example, gentlemen! The old-fashioned, out-moded type of squirt-gun for insects you had to work by hand—working a plunger in and out by hand—didn't you? Exactly. Now, the Mermaid here is automatic. Simply twist this small enamelled button, and electricity does the rest. From the nozzle issues a fine stream of liquid insect exterminator, which can be regulated to greater or less power and range; also to spray in fan-like

fashion over a wide area, all by means of buttons. Then again, gentlemen, there is our own unique feature of the electric light. How will you
find those troublesome mosquitoes that, under cover of darkness, are
making you lose sleep and undermining your health? I'll show you.
Simply press this button. . . ."

Warren took the gift from the Greek and Morgan and Peggy hurried
him out in case he grew violent in an effort to make Mr. Woodcock
disgorge information. Woodcock stood teetering on his heels, smiling
tightly, as they left him. In the passage outside they leaned against the
wall, rather breathless.

"The low-down crook!" breathed Warren, shaking in the air the Mermaid Automatic Electric Mosquito Gun. "The dirty double-crosser! He
knows! He knows, and he won't—"

"But was he serious about that testimonial?" asked Peggy, who could still
not get this part of the matter untangled. "I mean, fancy! He can't really
mean that he wants your uncle to appear in the newspapers saying, 'I'm wild
about Woodcock's bug-powder,' can he? I mean, that would be awful!"

"Baby, that's just it. He's as serious—well, he's as serious as Uncle
Warpus trying to swing an international treaty and protect somebody's
neutrality. You don't know," said Warren, with some violence, "how
self-complacent modern advertising is. They call it public service. Come
on. Let's go up and see the old horse-thief upstairs. What Uncle Warpus
would say to me if I forced him into endorsing bug-powder is more than a
drinkless stomach allows me to contemplate. I have a feeling that the
sooner we see Captain Whistler, the old herring, and get this business
about the girl straightened out, the sooner I'm going to feel well again.
Come on."

"And *I* have a feeling—" said Morgan, and stopped.

He did not continue. But he was right.

Chapter XII

INDISCRETIONS OF CURTIS WARREN

When they knocked at the door of Captain Whistler's cabin just
abaft the bridge, it was opened by a melancholy steward who
was making up the berth and clearing away breakfast dishes in
a large, comfortable, rosewood-panelled cabin with curtains of rather
startling pattern at the portholes.

"Commander ayn't 'ere, sir," the steward informed them, squinting at Warren in a rather sinister fashion. " 'E's gorn to see Lord Sturton, 'e said you wos to wait, *if* you please."

Warren tried to be nonchalant, but he showed his apprehension.

"Ah," he said, "Ah! Thanks, steward. How is the old mackerel feeling this morning? That is—er—"

"Ho!" said the steward significantly, and punched at a pillow as he arranged it.

"I see," said Warren. "Well, we'll—er—sit down."

The steward pottered about the cabin, which gave evidence that the captain had fired things about in some haste, and finally doddered out with the breakfast tray. The nasty look he gave them over his shoulder confirmed their hypothesis that the beauties of nature did not induce in Captain Whistler any mood to stand on the bridge and sing sea-shanties.

"I guess he's still peeved," was Warren's opinion. "And this is kind of a delicate matter, Hank. You do all the talking now. I don't think I care to risk it."

"You bet your sweet life I'll do all the talking," agreed Morgan. "I wouldn't answer for any of us if the skipper walked in here and saw you with this razor in your hands. Especially as he's just gone to see Sturton, he is not likely to be in a playful frame of mind. Understand—you are to keep *absolutely silent* throughout the whole interview. Not a word, not a movement unless you're asked to confirm something. I refuse to take any more chances. But I don't know—" He sat down in a leather chair, ruffled his hair, and stared out of one porthole at the pale sky. The sunlit cabin, swaying with drowsy gentleness in a murmurous swish of water conveyed no sense of peace. "I don't know," he went on, "that I feel altogether right about it myself. For the moment let Woodcock keep his information and blast him. *What has happened to that emerald?* That's the question."

"But after all, Hank, it isn't any business of ours," Peggy pointed out, with a woman's practical instinct. She took off her shell-rimmed glasses with a pleased air of having solved the thing, and shut them into her handbag with a decisive snap. "*I* shouldn't bother, old boy. What's the odds?"

"*What's the odds?*"

"Yes, of course I'm jolly sorry for Lord Sturton, and all that; but, after all, he's got pots of money hasn't he? And all he'd do would be to lock the emerald up in some nasty old safe, and what's the good of that? . . . Whereas this film of Curt's is really important, poor boy. I know what *I'd* do if I were a man," she declared scornfully. "I'd take that nasty little Woodcock chap and torture him until he told. Or I'd lock him up somewhere, the way they did to that baron what's-his-name, in *The Count of Monte Cristo,* and not let him have anything to eat and hold soup

under his nose and laugh ha-ha until he was willing to tell me. You men
Bah! You make me tired."

She made a gesture of impatience.

"Young lady," said Morgan, "both your ruthlessness and your logic are
scandalous. I have sometimes observed a similar phenomenon in my own
wife. Aside from the practical impossibility of holding soup under the
bug-powder king's nose and laughing ha-ha, there's the sporting element
to consider. Don't say bah. The fact remains that we have pinched old
Sturton's emerald and the responsibility—What the devil's that noise?"

He jumped a little. For some moments he had been conscious of a low,
steady, hissing noise somewhere about him. In his present frame of mind,
it sounded exactly like the sinister hissing which Dr. Watson had heard at
midnight in the dark bedroom during the Adventure of the Speckled
Band. It was, in fact, the Mermaid Automatic Bug-Powder Gun.

"Curt," said Peggy, whirling suspiciously, "what are you up to *now?*"

"Handy little gadget at that," declared Warren, in some admiration.
His eyes were shining, and he bent absorbedly over the elaborate silver
and enamel tube. It was a stream-lined cylinder full of scrolls and
flutings, with a complicated array of black buttons. From the nozzle a
thin wide spray, as advertised, was flying out across the captain's papers
on the centre table. Warren moved it about. "All the buttons are marked,
you see. Here's "Spray"—that's what I've got on now. Then there's
"Half Power" and "Full Power." . . .

Peggy put a hand over her mouth and began to gurgle. This unseemly
mirth annoyed Morgan still more. Besides, the spray was peculiarly
pungent.

"Turn the damn thing off!" he howled, as a thin spray began to glitter
all about them. "No, don't turn it at the wardrobe, you fathead. Now
you've got the captain's spare uniform. Turn it—"

"All right, all right," said Warren, rather testily. "You needn't get
griped about it. I was only trying the thing out. . . . All I've got to do, you
see, is press this dingus and—What's the matter with the fool thing?
Hey!"

The pressing of the dingus, it is true, did away with the spray. It
substituted what to the skilful engineers who designed it was presumably
"Half Power." A thin but violent stream of liquid bug-powder ascended
past Warren's shoulder as he tried to look at the nozzle and somewhat
frantically twisted buttons. All he succeeded in doing was turning on the
electric light.

"Give *me* the swine," said Morgan. "I'll fix it. Do something, can't
you? It's raining bug-powder; the place is becoming impregnated with
bug-powder! Don't turn it on yourself, you blithering idiot. Turn it. . . .O
my God, *no!* Not in the captain's berth. Take it out of the captain's berth.

. . . No, you can't shut it off with a pillow. Not under the bedclothes, dummy! You're—"

"Well, it's better than having it soak up the room, isn't it?" inquired Warren's hoarse voice, out of a luminous mist of bug-powder. "All right. Don't get apoplexy. I'll shut it off. I'll—" He avoided Morgan's arm, a fiendish expression on his face, and rushed to the middle of the cabin. "No, you don't. I turned this thing on and, so help me, I'll turn it off!" He gestured with the Mermaid, which was hissing like an enthusiastic cobra. "And this is the lousy thing my uncle is asked to endorse, is it? It's a cheat! It's no damn good! I'll find Woodcock and tell him so! I've turned every lousy knob. . . ."

"Don't stand there orating!" shouted Morgan, whom the clammy mist had begun to envelop. "Do something. Fire it out the port-hole. . . ."

"I know what I'll do!" said Warren, with fiendish inspiration. "I know what it is. I'll try *Full Power.*" That's probably the only thing that'll shut the swine off. That's it! If Woodcock had told the truth about it—"

Woodcock had told the truth about it, and could have exhibited a pardonable pride in its response. From the nozzle a fine stream of liquid insect exterminator shot with the force and violence of a fire-hose. Nor could Mr. Woodcock have in the least complained of its accuracy. In fact, it sizzled across the cabin full and true into the face of Commander Sir Hector Whistler just as he opened the door.

Morgan shut his eyes. In that moment of blasting and appalled silence he did not wish to look upon Captain Whistler's countenance. He would sooner have tried to outstare Medusa. Moreover, he wished he could summon his muscles to dive out of the room and run. But he could hear the Mermaid still hissing on the door-post beside the captain's head; and he risked one eye to look, not at Whistler, but at Warren.

Warren found his voice.

"I couldn't help it, Skipper!" he yelled. "I swear by all that's holy I couldn't help it. I tried everything. I pressed every button, but it wouldn't stop. Look! See, I'll show you! Look . . .!"

There was a sharp click. Instantly the stream gurgled, fell, and died away from the Mermaid's nozzle. It stopped. The Mermaid was as innocuous as she had been before.

Morgan afterwards realised that only one thing saved them then. Peering over the captain's shoulder in the doorway he had seen the startled countenance of Captain Valvick. Only the strangled words, "So—it's—*you!*" issued from the quivering lungs of the *Queen Victoria*'s commander before Valvick had shot a big hand over his mouth. With one hand over his mouth and the other impelling him by the sack of the trousers, he hustled the insane skipper into the cabin and kicked the door shut.

"Qvick!" rumbled Valvick. "You get somet'ing to gag him wit' till he cool down, or he call de chief mate and den maybe we iss all in de brig. Ay am hawful sorry, Barnacle, but ay got to do diss. . . ." Frowning, he turned a glance of angry reproachfulness on Warren. "What you want to playing for, anyway, eh? Diss iss no time for playing, ay tell you. After ay take al de time to smoot' old Barnacle down and tell him what we are doing, den it iss no time for playing. Coroosh! What iss dat stuff ay smell in de air?"

"It's only bug-powder, Skipper," insisted Warren. "After all, it's only bug-powder!"

A spasm racked the stout frame of Captain Whistler; his good eye bulged, but his internal noises beat in vain against the Gibraltar of Valvick's hand across his mouth. Nevertheless, Valvick had to use two hands to keep him quiet.

"Honest, Barnacle, diss iss for your own good!" Valvick begged, dragging him over to the chair before his desk and pushing him in. He was answered by a variety of muffled sounds like a steam-calliope heard underground. "Odderwise you are going to do somet'ing you regret. Dese yentlemen can explain; ay know it! If you promise to do not'ing, ay let you loose. Ay mean, you kin svear all you like if it reliefs your mind, but you are not to *do* not'ing. Odderwise we got to gag you, eh? . . . Ay tell you it iss for your own good! . . . Now! You iss a man of your word. What about it, eh?"

A noise of assent and an inclination of the head like the Dying Gladiator answered him. Valvick stepped back, removing his hand.

The ensuing half-hour is one of the things in Morgan's life that he likes to forget. To say that it was nerve-racking would be to employ a spiritless word, and one without those *nuances* which Mr. Leslie Perrigord declares are essential to the power of classic drama. There was much classic fire at one point in the captain's remarks—that at which he frequently clutched his throat, stabbed a shaking finger at Warren like Macbeth seeing the ghost, and kept repeating "He's mad, I tell you! He tried to poison me! He's a homicidal maniac! Do you want him to murder my passengers? Why don't you let me lock him up?"

If, eventually, more sober counsels prevailed, it was due to a circumstance which Morgan did not at the moment understand. Captain Whistler, he was compelled to admit, had certain reasonable grounds for protest. Aside from all questions of personal dignity (the Mermaid's aim had gone straight as Locksley's good clothyard shaft into the skipper's damaged left eye), there was reason for complaint in the general omnipresence of bug-powder. The cabin was haunted by bug-powder. It rose in ghostly waves from his dress uniform; it soaked his berth, pervaded his linen, clung round his shoes, made fragrant his log-book, and whispered sweet nothings from his correspondence. In short, you could safely have wagered that not for months would even the most reckless cockroach be daredevil enough to venture within smelling-distance of anything that was Captain Whistler's.

Therefore it considerably astonished Morgan that in the short space of half an hour he was prevailed on to accept their explanations. True, he placed the Mermaid Automatic Electric Mosquito Gun in the middle of the floor and jumped on it. True, he no whit retreated from his declaration that Curtis Warren was a dangerous lunatic who would shortly be cutting somebody's throat if not placed under observation. But (whether due to Peggy's blandishments or to another cause shortly to be indicated, you shall decide) he consented to give Warren just one more chance.

"Just one more chance," he proclaimed, leaning forward in the chair and bringing his hand down on his desk, "and that's ALL. If there's one more suspicious move out of not only him, but any of you—*Any of you, do you understand?*—then he goes to the brig under guard. That's my last word." Glaring he sat back and sipped the healing whisky-and-soda that had been brought him. "Now, if you don't mind, we'll get down to business. And first I'll tell you this. I promised to share any information I might get, Mr. Morgan, because I considered you at least a sane man. Well, I have some information, although I admit it puzzles me. But before I tell you, there's something I want to point out. The young maniac, and you three as well, have caused me more trouble than anybody I ever had aboard a craft of mine. *I could murder all four of you!* You've caused me more trouble than anybody except the man who stole that emerald; and, in a way, you're involved in that. . . ."

("Steady," thought Morgan.)

"But that's more important. And, if you liked, you could, I say, you *could,* help me a little in return. . . . Are you sure there's nobody listening at that door?"

His tone was so gruffly and uneasily conspiratorial that Valvick peered out the door and closed all the portholes. Peggy said, earnestly:

"I don't think, Captain, you have the least idea how glad we'd be to make it up to you. If there's anything we can do—"

Whistler hesitated. He took another sip of whisky.

"I've just seen his lordship," he went on, as though he hated to make a confession, but that Hector Whistler was a desperate man. "He's— haaa—up in the air, because the emerald wasn't insured. He *had the cheek to say I was drunk or careless, the* ??!!!£!!!/???¾½¼¾⅜¼!!! *old?!!!£?£¾!*—that's what he said! He said it would never have happened if I had left it with him. . . ."

"You haven't found it, by any chance, have you?" asked Morgan.

"*No!* I have searched this ship with fifteen picked men from fo'c's'le-head to rudder, and I have *not* found it, young man. Now, then, be quiet and listen. I don't think he'll sue the line. But there's a question of law to be considered. That question is: Was I, or was I not, guilty of careless conduct? The emerald was technically in my possession, although I had not locked it in my safe. Show me the lubber," snarled Captain Whistler, glaring from one to the other of them, "who says I was guilty of careless conduct—contributory negligence—just show him to me, that's all. Let me so much as glimpse his sky-s'ls, and I'll make him regret the day his father first went courting. Am I guilty of careless conduct if four armed Dagoes take me from behind and give me the marlinspike with a bottle? Am I? *No,*" was Captain Whistler's reply, delivered with a gesture like that of the late Marcus Tullius Cicero, "no, I am not. Well, then. If somebody would tell old Sturton that I was murderously set on without a chance to defend myself. . . . Mind, I don't want to tell him you *saw* me attacked. If there's any lying to be done, sink me! I can do it myself. But if you could tell him you are able to swear, from your own observation at the time, that you believed me to be the victim of a ruthless attack . . . well, the money don't count much with him, and I'm pretty certain he won't sue. . . . How about it?" inquired the captain, suddenly lowering his voice to a startlingly more normal tone.

There was a chorus of assent.

"You'll do it?" Whistler demanded.

"I'll do more than that, Skipper," said Warren, eagerly. "I'll tell you the name of the son of a bachelor who's got that emerald right now."

"Eh?"

"Yes. I'll give it to you straight from the table. And the man who's got that emerald at this very minute," announced Warren, leaning over and pointing his finger in the captain's face, "is none other than the dastardly crook who's masquerading on this boat as Doctor Oliver Harrison Kyle."

Morgan's spirit, uttering a deep groan, rose from his body and flapped out the porthole on riddled wings. He thought: It's all up now. This is the end. The old mackerel will utter one whoop, go mad, and call for assistance. Morgan expected many strange, possibly intricate observations from the captain. He expected him to order a strait-waistcoat. He expected, in fact, every conceivable thing except what actually happened. For fully a minute Whistler stared, his handkerchief at his forehead.

"You, too?" he said. "You think so, too?" His voice awed. "Out of the mouths of babes and—and lunatics. But wait. I forgot to show you. That was why I wanted you here. I don't believe it. I can't believe it. But when even the maniacs can see it, I've got to hard my helm. Besides, it may not mean that. I don't believe it. I'm going insane myself. Here! Here! Read this!" He whirled to his desk and rummaged. "This was what I wanted you to see. It came this morning."

He held out a radiogram, delicately scented with Swat Number 2 Instantaneous Insect Exterminator, and handed it to Morgan.

COMMANDER, S.S. *QUEEN VICTORIA,* AT SEA [it ran]. FEDERAL AGENT REPORTS UNKNOWN MAN PICKED UP SUPPOSEDLY DYING CHEVY CHASE OUTSIDE WASHINGTON MARCH 25. THOUGHT VICTIM AUTO ACCIDENT CONCUSSION OF BRAIN. NO IDENTIFICATION NO PAPERS OR MARKS IN CLOTHING. PATIENT RUSHED TO MERCY HOSPITAL IN COMA. TWO WEEKS DELIRIOUS UNTIL YESTERDAY. STILL INCOHERENT BUT CLAIMS TO BE PERSON ABOARD YOUR SHIP. FEDERAL AGENT THINKS CROOK RESPONSIBLE STELLY AND MACGEE JOBS. FEDERAL AGENT THINKS ALSO PHYSICIAN IS IMPOSTOR ON YOUR SHIP. WELL-KNOWN FIGURE AND MUST BE NO MISTAKE MADE OR TROUBLE, AND MEDICAL PROFESSION INFLUENTIAL CARE ALL SIDES. . . .

Morgan whistled. Warren uttered an exclamation of triumph as he read the message across the other's shoulder.

"You've come to that, have you?" demanded Captain Whistler. "If that message is right, I don't know what to think. There's no other physician than Dr. Kyle aboard the ship—except the ship's doctor, and he's been with me seven years."

WILL NOT BE DEFINITE CASE TROUBLE. ARREST NOBODY YET. AM SENDING MAN INSPECTOR PATRICK KNOWS ACCUSED PERSONALLY. PATRICK SAILED S.S. *ETRUSCA* ARRIVE SOUTHAMPTON ONE DAY BEFORE YOU. AFFORD HIM FACILITIES. ADVISE.

ARNOLD, COMMISSIONER N.Y.P.D.

"Ha-ha!" said Warren. He threw out his chest. He took the radiogram from Morgan and flourished it over his head. "Now say I'm crazy, Skipper! Go on, say it—if you can. By God! I knew I was right. I had him figured out. . . ."

"How?" demanded Captain Whistler.

Warren stopped, his mouth slightly open. They all saw the open trap into which, with cheers and wide eyes, Warren had deliberately walked. To tell why he thought Dr. Kyle guilty was exactly the one thing he could *not* do. Morgan froze. He saw his companion's eyes assume a rather glassy look in the long silence. . . .

"I'm waiting, young man," said Whistler, snappishly. "Sink me! I'd be eternally blasted if I'd let the police get all the credit for a capture on *my* ship, sink me! provided I could think of a way to trap that—Go on! Speak up! Why do you think he's guilty?"

"I tell you I've said it from the first. Ask Peggy and Hank and the captain if I haven't! I've sworn he was posing as Dr. Kyle, ever since he batted me over the head in my cabin. . . ."

He stopped suddenly. Captain Whistler, who had started to take a healing pull at his whisky-and-soda, choked. He put down the glass.

"Dr. Kyle batted you over the head in your cabin?" he said, beginning to look curiously at the other. "When was this?"

"I mean, I was mistaken. That was an accident! Honest it was, Captain. I fell and hit my head—"

"Then I'll give you the benefit of the doubt, young man. *I will not be trifled with any longer*. You made an accusation, and it seems— I say it *seems*—to be right. Why did you accuse Dr. Kyle?" Warren ruffled his hair. He gritted his teeth feverishly.

"Well, Captain," he said, after a pause, "I knew it! He *looked* guilty. He—had a kind of guilty look about him when he was so pleasant at breakfast and said somebody'd been raped; that's why. . . . You don't believe me, do you? Well, I'm going to show you, and I'm going to prove that he's got to be put under lock and key! So I'll tell you why I came up here to see you. There was a murder committed aboard this boat last night, you old sturgeon! Hank," said Warren, whirling around, "*give me that razor.*"

It is a literal fact that Captain Whistler shot at least six inches into the air. Without doubt this was due partly to the extraordinary power in his sea-legs that uncoiled him from his chair like a spring; but behind this materialistic explanation there surged a stronger spiritual ecstasy. And he did not forget what to do. Even as he was descending, his hand flashed into the drawer of the desk and emerged levelling an automatic pistol.

"All right," he said. "Steady, me lads. . . ."

"Captain, it's absolutely true," said Morgan, seizing his arm. "He's not mad and he's not joking. This criminal did commit a murder; I mean, the impostor on the boat. If you'll give me one minute, I'll prove it. Come on, Valvick. To hell with his gun. Let's hold him back in his chair and sit on him until we can jam the truth down his throat. By this time your second officer will have made the rounds of the boat, and he'll find a woman missing. That woman was murdered last night, and she's overboard now—"

There was a knock at the door.

Everybody froze; why, none of them knew, except that it may have been some latent idea they were all making outstanding asses of themselves. A silence fell while Whistler gibbered a command to come in.

"Beg leave to report, sir," said the crisp voice of the second officer.

"And"—his eyes flashed over—"*and* to Mr. Morgan, as you ordered. Two of us have made a complete round of the ship. We have investigated every passenger and member of the crew. There was nobody hurt last night."

A vein was beginning to beat in Morgan's temple. He controlled his voice. "Right-ho, Mr. Baldwin. But we're not looking for a person who was merely hurt. We're looking for a woman who is murdered and missing. . . ."

Baldwin stiffened. "Well, sir, you may be," he said in a tone of regret. "But you won't find her. *I have checked over personally everybody on this ship, and there is nobody missing, either.*"

"Is that so, Mr. Baldwin?" inquired Whistler, almost genially. "Well, well."

Warren was escorted to the brig, under heavy guard, at exactly 11:45 Eastern daylight-saving time.

INTERLUDE

OBSERVATIONS OF DR. FELL

In the great book-lined room above Adelphi Terrace the warm May sun threw flat shadows on the floor and the river glittered under its blaze. Through the open windows they could hear the distant bang of the clock in Westminster Tower beating out twelve. Cigar stumps had accumulated, and Morgan was growing hoarse from his recital.

Sitting back in the chair, his eyes half-closed behind the eyeglasses on the ribbon, his chins upheaving in chuckles under the bandit's moustache, Dr. Fell shifted his gaze from the distant traffic along the Embankment.

"Noon," said Dr. Fell. "Now, break off for a minute and I'll order up some lunch. A long cool draught of beer will do you an uncommon amount of good." Wheezing, he pulled a bell-cord. "First, my boy, allow me to say that I would have given a year of my already wasted life to have been with you on that voyage. Heh! Heh-heh-heh! And at the moment I will ask only one question. Is there more to come? Is it really possible for any given group of people to get in *more* trouble than your excellent band has already done?"

Morgan croaked slightly.

"Sir," he said, with a deep gesture of earnestness, "what I've already told you is a—a microscopic atom, an invisibility, a microbe concealed in a drop of water in the vast comprehensive ocean of trouble which is to come. You have heard nothing yet, nothing. That my brain is still whole I am prepared to admit, but why it is still whole I can't tell you. After the sinister episode of the gold watches . . . but that's yet to come."

He hesitated.

"Look here, sir. I know your interest in detective plots, and if I came to ask your aid, I'd want to get everything straight first. That is, I like my own plots to be clean-cut. If it's going to be really a murder story, in spite of all entangled nonsense, I want to know that so that I can be prepared, and not have the whole thing sprung on me as a hoax. I like to see the body on the floor. When somebody disappears in a story, you've nothing solid to go on. It might be—and generally is—a dastardly trick to prove that there's been no murder, or that the wrong person's been murdered, or something that only annoys you. . . . That's from the analytic side, you understand, and not the human side. But, as to the murder, if you ask me at this moment whether there's really been a murder, I've got to admit I can't tell you."

Dr. Fell grunted. He had a pencil in one hand, with which he had been tapping some notes.

"Well, then," he said, blinking over his eye-glasses, "in that case, why don't you ask *me?*"

"You—er—think—?"

"Yes, there's been a murder," replied Dr. Fell. He scowled. "I dislike having to tell you that. I dislike having to think of it, and I hope I may be wrong. There is one thing that, inevitably, you have got to tell me, which will settle any doubts. But one thing I insist on. Don't be afraid of the nonsense. Don't apologise for the vast Christian joy of laughing when an admiral slips on a cake of soap and sits on his own cocked hat. Don't say that it has no place in a murder case, or that a murderer himself can't laugh. Once you set him up as a waxworks horror, leering over his red hands, you will never be able to understand him and you will probably never see who he is. Damn him if you will, but don't say that he isn't human or that real life ever attains the straight level of ghastliness to be found in a detective-story. That's the way to produce dummy murderers, and dummy detectives as well. And yet—"

He stabbed at the notes with his pencil.

". . . and yet, my lad, it's both logical and ironical that this particular case should produce what is in a sense a dummy murderer. . . ."

"A dummy murderer?"

"I mean a professional criminal; an expert mimic; a mask. In short, a murderer who kills for the sake of expediency. How can a person who's playing a part as somebody else be anything more or less than a good or bad copy of the original? So he eludes us in his own personality, and all we've got to judge by is how well he speaks stolen lines. H'm! It makes for better analysis, I dare say, and the mask is undoubtedly lifelike. But, as for seeing his real self in the mask, you might as well question one of M. Fortinbras's marionettes. . . ." He stopped. The small, lazy eyes narrowed. "You jumped a little there. Why?"

"Well—er," said Morgan, "as a matter of fact, they've—er—they've got old Uncle Jules in the brig."

For a moment Dr. Fell stared, and then his vast chuckle blew a cloud of sparks from his pipe. He blinked thoughtfully.

"Uncle Jules in the brig?" he repeated. "Most refreshing. Why?"

"Oh, not for murder or anything like that. I'll tell you all about it. Of course they're going to let him out to-day. They—"

"Humf. Harrumph! Now let me see if I understand this. Let him out to-day? Hasn't the boat docked yet?"

"That's what I was getting at, sir. It hasn't. Thank the Lord for what you've said, anyhow, because that's why I'm here. . . . You know Captain Whistler, don't you? And he knows of you?"

"I have had some experience," replied Dr. Fell, shutting up one eye meditatively, "with the old—um—cuttlefish. Heh! Heh-heh-heh! Yes, I know him. Well?"

"We were to dock early this morning. The trouble was that at the last minute there was a mix-up about our dock or berth or whatever they call it; the *Queen Anne* didn't get under way so that we could move in, and we were left lying in the harbour, with no chance of docking until about two o'clock this afternoon. . . ."

Dr. Fell sat up. "And the *Queen Victoria* is still—?"

"Yes. Due to something you shall hear of in due course, I was able to persuade Whistler to let me go ashore with the pilot; I had to sneak it, of course, or the others would have been wild. But," he drew a deep breath, "Whistler knowing you, I contrived to convince him that, if I could get to you before the passengers left that ship, there might be *kudos* in it for him. Actually, sir, you'll say I had the hell of a nerve, but what I did was practically promise him you'd land him an outstanding crook with credit for it if I could get to you before the passengers left the *Queen Victoria*."

He sat back and shrugged his shoulders; but he watched Dr. Fell closely.

"Nerve? Ha! Heh-heh-heh!" Nonsense!" rumbled the doctor, affably. "What's Gideon Fell, for, I ask you, if not for that? Besides, I owe Hadley one for doing me in the eye over that Blumgarten business last week. Thank'ee, my boy, thank'ee."

"You think—?"

"Why, between ourselves, I rather think we'll land the Blind Barber. I have rather a strong suspicion," said Dr. Fell, scowling, with a long rumbling sniff through his nose, "who this Blind Barber is. If I'm wrong, there'll be no harm done aside from a little outraged dignity. . . . But, look here, why is it necessary? What about this New York man who was supposed to arrive on the *Etrusca* this morning?"

Morgan shook his head.

"I suppose it's bad to run ahead of my story," he said, "but we've had so many mix-ups, setbacks, and dizzy confusions that one more out of place is comparatively small. The *Etrusca* arrived right enough, but Inspector Patrick isn't on her. He didn't sail at all. I don't know why; I don't make any sense of it at all; but the fact remains that if something isn't done the Barber will walk off that ship a free man in exactly three hours."

Dr. Fell sat back in his chair and for a moment he sat looking vacantly, and in a cross-eyed fashion, at the notes on the table.

"Um! H'm, yes! Hand me that A.B.C. on the tabouret there, will you? Thanks. . . . What train d'jou take this morning? Seven fifty-three to Waterloo? So. Now, then. . . . H'm yes! This would do it. I don't suppose by any chance you have a passenger-list of that ship with you?"

"Yes. I thought—"

"Hand it over." He flicked the pages rapidly until he found a name. Then he went very slowly through it, his fingers following the list of cabins. When he found what he seemed to want, he made a comparison; but it was on the other side of the table and Morgan could not see precisely what had been done. "Now, then, excuse the old charlatan a moment. I am going to make some telephone-calls. Not under torture would I reveal what I intend to do, or where's the fun of mystifying you, hey? Heh! There's no pleasure like mystification, my boy, *if* you can pull it off. . . . As a matter of fact, I'm just going to wire the name of the murdered woman to Captain Whistler, with a few suggestions. Also it would be a good idea to ring up a branch of Victoria 7000 and make other suggestions. Have another bottle of beer."

He lumbered across the room, chuckling fiendishly and stamping his cane. When he returned, he was rubbing his hands in exultation behind a woman laden with the largest, most elaborately stocked lunch-tray Morgan had seen in a long time.

"Mash and sausage," he explained, inhaling sensuously. "Down here, Vida. . . . Now, then. Let's get on with our story. There are several points on which I want to be enlightened, if you feel up to talking over the food. Your case, my boy, is the best surprise-package I've opened yet. With each separate event, I discover, there is no telling whether the thing is a water-pistol or a loaded automatic until you pull the trigger. In a way it's unique, because some of the best clues are only half-serious. . . ."

"Question," said Morgan.

"Exactly. Have you ever reflected," boomed Dr. Fell, tucking a napkin under his chin and pointing at his guest with a fork in the serene assumption that he had never reflected, "on old proverbs? On the sad state of affairs which makes old proverbs so popular, and so easy to quote, precisely because those old platitudes are the only maxims which to-day nobody believes? How many people really believe, for instance, 'honesty is the best policy'?—particularly if they happen to be honest themselves. How many people believe that 'early to bed and early to rise' have the effect designated? Similarly, we have the saw to the effect that many a true word is spoken in jest. A true application of that principle would be too exciting; it would call for much more ingenuity and intelligence than most people are able to display; and it would make social life unendurable if anybody for a moment believed that a true word *could* be spoken in jest—worse, for instance, than going out to dinner with a crowd of psycho-analysts."

"What's all this?" said Morgan. "You can't hang a man on a joke."

"Oh, they're not jokes. You have no idea as to the trend of this?"

"No."

Dr. Fell scribbled rapidly on a sheet of paper, and passed it over.

"Here, for your further enlightenment," he said, frowning, "I have tabulated eight clues. Eight suggestions, if you will. Not one of 'em is direct evidence—it's the direct evidence I'm looking for you to supply in your next instalment of the story. I feel fairly certain you will mention the evidence I want; and my hunch is so strong that I—like several others—will risk Whistler's official head on it. Eh?"

Morgan took the paper, which read

1. The Clue of Suggestion.
2. The Clue of Opportunity.
3. The Clue of Fraternal Trust.
4. The Clue of Invisibility.
5. The Clue of Seven Razors.
6. The Clue of Seven Radiograms.
7. The Clue of Elimination.
8. The Clue of Terse Style.

"It doesn't mean a devil of a lot to me," said Morgan. "The first two you could apply in any way you like. . . . Wait! Don't puff and blow, sir!—I say 'you,' meaning myself. And I don't like to consider the suggestion of the third. . . . But what about seven razors? We didn't find seven razors."

"Exactly," boomed the doctor, pointing his fork as though that explained it. "The point is that there probably *were* seven razors, you see. That's the point."

"You mean we ought to have looked for them?"

"Oh, no! The Barber would have got rid of the others. All you should have done was remember that they were seven. Eh?"

"And then," said Morgan, "this point about seven radiograms. . . . What seven radiograms? There are only two radiograms I mentioned in my story."

"Ah, I should have explained about that," said Dr. Fell, skewering a sausage. "Seven—mystic number; rounded, complete, suggestive number with a curious history. I use it advisedly in place of the word 'several,' because we assume there were several. The interesting thing is that I am not referring to any radiograms you saw. You didn't see 'em. That's very significant, hey?"

"No, I'll be damned if it is," said Morgan, somewhat violently. "If we didn't see 'em—"

"Proceed, then," requested the doctor, waving a large flipper. "I feel positive that before you have finished I shall have noted down eight more clues—sixteen, say—by which we finish and round out our case."

Morgan cleared his throat and began.

PART II
Chapter XIII

TWO MANDARINS

Among unthinking chroniclers it is much the fashion, at certain movements of mysticism, to embark on a reflection as to how, if it were not for such-and-such a small thing happening, then such-and-such a larger thing would not have happened, and so on until they have ultimately proved King Priam's bootblack responsible for the fall of Troy. Which is, demonstrably, nonsense.

Doubtless such a historian would say that all would yet have been well, when Curtis Warren was installed in a padded cell on D deck, if it were not for two tiny circumstances harmless in themselves. In proof of this he would point out that—if they had only known it—the conspirators were within an ace of catching the Blind Barber himself at least once that day; and there would have been no more lurid happenings aboard the *Queen Victoria*. The present chronicler does not believe it. Men go straight as a stream of liquid exterminator from the nozzle of the Mermaid Automatic Electric Bug-Powder Gun along the line that is determined by their characters, nor can any horseshoe nail affect their destinies. Curtis Warren, as may have been observed from time to time, was a fairly impetuous young man much influenced by the power of suggestion. If he had not got into more trouble one way, it would have been in another; and only a thoughtless quibbler could lay the blame on such excellent articles as a detective novel and a bottle of Scotch whisky.

Sic volvere parcæ! To solace him in captivity they could not share, Peggy Glenn presented him with a bottle of whisky (full size) and Henry Morgan with one of his old detective-novels.

Thereby, incidentally, they showed their own characters. If anybody says Morgan should have known better, it will shortly be indicated how much he had on his mind. Morgan was fighting mad at the perverse orneriness of the Parcæ, and his own none-too-good sense reduced to a minimum. Besides—as he agreed with Peggy—if that stormy petrel, Curtis Warren, were not safe from causing trouble when locked and bolted in a padded cell, where the devil *would* he be safe?

Now let's quit this philosophising and get down to business.

There had been an almost touching scene of farewell after Warren had been shot into the padded cell by three sturdy seamen, of whom two had to undergo considerable repairs in the doctor's office immediately afterwards. It would also take too much time to dwell on their progress down from the captain's cabin to D deck, which resembled an erratic Catharine wheel of arms and legs whirling down companionways and causing pale-faced passengers to bolt like rabbits. With a last heave he was fired into the cell and the door slammed; yet, damaged but undaunted, he still continued to shake the bars and hurl raspberries at the exhausted sailors.

Peggy, in a tearful frenzy, refused to leave him. If they would not let her stay with him, she made a loyal attempt to kick Captain Whistler in a vital spot and get locked up herself. Morgan and Valvick also loyally insisted that, if the old sea-cow thought Warren off his onion, they were loony, too, and demanded their rights of being imprisoned. But this Warren—either with a glimmer of sense or a desire to make a gallant gesture—would not hear of.

"Carry on, old man!" he said, grimly and heroically, shaking hands with Morgan through the bars of the cell. "The Barber's still loose, and you've got to find him. Besides, Peggy's got to help her uncle with those marionettes. Carry on, and we'll nail Kyle yet."

That Whistler did not accede to their demands for a uniform imprisonment, both demand and consent being made in the heat of rage, Morgan afterwards attributed solely to his desire to produce them as witness to Lord Sturton that he had been treacherously attacked. This did not occur to him at the time, or he would have made use of it as a threat; and Captain Whistler would have been saved trouble, as shall be seen, with the choleric peer. All the three conspirators knew was that their ally had been locked away in the bowels of the ship: down a dark companionway, through a steel-plated corridor pungent with oil and lit by one sickly electric bulb which quivered to the pounding of the ship's engines, and behind a door with a steel grill through which he stared out like King Richard in exile. A sailor with a whistle, reading *Hollywood Romances,* had been stolidly posted on a chair outside, so that the possibility of a jail-break was *nil*.

There was, however, one consolation. The rather sardonic ship's doctor—who believed not at all in Warren's insanity, but found it prudent from long experience not to cross Captain Whistler before his temper subsided—made no objection to supplying the maniac with cigarettes and reading-matter. If he saw the bottle of whisky which Peggy smuggled through in a roll of magazines, he made no sign.

Morgan's contributions to the captive were a box of Gold Flake and a copy of one of his earlier novels called *Played, Partner!* Now, if you are a very prolific writer of detective-stories, you will be aware that the details of earlier ones tend to fade from your mind even more quickly than they do from the reader's. Morgan remembered in a general way what the book was about. *Played, Partner!* was the tale of Lord Gerald Derreval, known to West End clubland as a wealthy idler, *dillettante,* and sportsman; but known to Scotland Yard under the enigmatic and terrible pseudonymn of The Will-o'-the-Wisp. As a gentleman burglar, Lord Gerald was hot stuff. His thrilling escapes from captivity under heavy guard made Mr. Harry Houdini look like a bungler who had got out of clink only with a writ of *habeas corpus.* Of course, there was never anything really crooked about Lord Gerald. All he did was pinch the shirt off any old reprobate who had been low-minded enough to get rich, thereby qualifying Lord Gerald for a high place in the Socialist literature which is so popular nowadays. Besides, he was redeemed by his love for the beautiful Sardinia Trelawney. In the end he trapped the real villain who had tried to saddle a murder on him; and made it up with Inspector Daniels, the man who had sworn to get him and was in general so weak-minded and got the bird so often that even in the midst of pitying him you wondered how he contrived to hold his job.

These were the details that had faded from Morgan's mind, but such was the dynamite placed in the hands of Mr. Curtis Warren along with an imperial-quart of Old Rob Roy. It would, perhaps, have been wiser to give him a Bradshaw or a volume of sermons; but the moving finger writes, and, having writ, moves on; and, besides, philosophical remarks on this question have already been made. After Peggy had bidden him a tearful good-bye, and Morgan and Valvick had shaken hands with him, they went up in a thunder-fraught mood to see the captain.

"Honest, now," said Valvick rather broodingly, as they crossed the boat-deck in the sunlight that Warren was forbidden to see, "do you t'ank we are right, or iss dere a mistake? Dat wass no yoke, what dey tell us. If dey say dere is nobody missing, den ay don't see how dere is somebody missing. Maybe we talk about a murder and dere is no murder."

"I tell you we're right!" snapped Morgan. "We're right, and it's got to be proved somehow. First thing, I'll tackle Whistler in as cool a frame of mind as I can. I'll challenge him to get that blood on the razor and in the berth tested. The ship's doctor can do it, or maybe Dr. Kyle. . . ."

"Kyle?" said Peggy, staring at him. "But Dr. Kyle—"

"Will you get your mind off that tedious joke?" said Morgan, wearily. "Let's dispose of it once and for all. Don't you realise that Kyle is the one person on the whole ship who can't possibly be guilty?"

"Why?"

"Because he's the one man who's got an alibi, old girl. Look here, Skipper. You're pretty sure your friend with the toothache, the Bermondsey Terror, is honest; aren't you?—all right. And what did he say? He said that he didn't lose sight of Kyle's door all night; that he heard the row on deck from the beginning. . . . Wait a bit. You didn't know about that, did you, Peggy?" He rapidly sketched out the Bermondsey Terror's information, and also gave Valvick the evidence of the Perrigords. "So what? The Blind Barber stole the rest of that film and killed the girl while the row was going on out on deck. Nobody went in or out of Kyle's door all night. So how did Kyle get out and back? It won't wash, I tell you."

"It's you that's the blind one, Hank," she informed him, scornfully. "He needn't have been in his cabin at all, need he? Alibis! Bah! What's the good of an alibi. They always turn out to be fakes, anyway."

Morgan gestured.

"All right. It's easily settled. We're going into action at once, and by the Lord we're going to prove our case. Here's a commission for you, Skipper. Go down and see your friend the Bermondsey Terror and question him. Also see the cabin steward and make any inquiries you think of. . . ."

"Now?" asked Valvick, scratching his head.

"Now. We'll prove it one way or another. To continue," he said to Peggy, as the other muttered a few reflections and lumbered off, "I'll tackle Whistler about that blood. I'll swear it's human blood; and, if it is, we can safely point out to him that nobody could have lost so much and still show no sign of being hurt this morning. Nobody, old girl! Then we'll make the whole round of the ship ourselves, if necessary. And we'll show 'em."

He looked rather malevolently about the boat-deck, which was crowded and noisy. Warren's triumphal progress to the brig had taken place belowdecks and by a devious way, but the news was already flying, so that there was a note of shrillness in the clatter of talk. Somnolent figures in deck chairs, set out to dry themselves under the sun, were sitting up from their rugs; a game of shuffleboard had been suspended and two deck-tennis players came up to the net for a conference. The ship's reigning belle—there is always one—had stopped her professional smiling, her beret pushed over one ear and a cigarette half-way to her mouth, and was bending to listen in a whispering group of admirers. She stood on a raised platform by a lifeboat, her gaudy green scarf blowing against the sky. Far above their heads, on one of the three vast black funnels that showed a faint stain of smoke, the liner's whistle emitted a sudden hoarse *Whooo!* as though it were giving an alarm. A suggestion of lunch was now in the air. There was a good deal of laughter. Morgan scowled.

They found Whistler getting his cabin set to rights and being particularly rough on the steward.

"I won't discuss it," he said, "any more. Maybe I was hasty. I won't say I wasn't. But I acted within my rights, and I'll let that young drunkard or lunatic stop there until I damned well get ready to let him out. We'll say nothing of his story. But take a look around my cabin, just *look* at it, and then tell me whether I didn't do the right thing." He thrust out his jaw, the good eye narrowed in his battered face, and the gold stripes on his sleeves gleamed as he jammed his fists on his hips. But there was something curiously conciliating about him. "Come now!" he said suddenly. "We're alone. There's no need for you to defend your friend. What's the truth of the matter?"

They could hear the breath whistling from his nose.

"Does this mean, Captain," said Peggy, after a pause in which she seemed taken aback, "that you really don't think Curt is mad, after all? Oooh, you villain! After you ordered those nasty men to *manhandle* and," she gasped, "and mistreat—"

"I want the truth, madam. The truth, that's all. In my position—"

"I say, Captain," said Morgan, after another pause in which Whistler shut his teeth hard, "does this mean something new has happened?"

"Why should it?"

"Oh, I only wondered. . . ." He was looking quickly round the cabin, searching a clue, and then he saw it. Rolled into a wad at one side of the wardrobe lay what looked very much like a sheet tied round stained blankets. "So," said Morgan, "do you mean to tell us a steward saw something queer about the cabin next to Curt's? And went in and found the berth full of bloodstained sheets? And then reported to you? Excellent. Here's the razor that was used in the killing." He took it out of his pocket and laid it on the table, while Whistler stared at him fixedly. "Now everything is fine. All you've done is accuse the wrong man of being a liar and a lunatic, and locked him up under guard. If old Sturton can only get you convicted of criminal negligence to the extent of fifty thousand pounds, the officials of this steamship line will be in an even better humour."

As a matter of fact, he was (despite himself) feeling sorry for the old mackerel. A persistent voice told him that the whole mess was their own fault. All that made him wild was that circumstances seemed conspiring to prevent belief in something he still fiercely felt to be true.

"*Murder!*" said the captain, in a sort of gulp. "Murder! You have the nerve to stand there and talk to me of murder when there's nobody not accounted for on the whole ship? Where's the murdered person? . . . And don't try to talk to me about what my superiors will think. I put that young lunatic in confinement for an offence against discipline. That's all. An offence against discipline, and that's my right. My word is *law,* and any maritime court—"

"It would make a good story, though," the other pointed out, "printed in the newspapers. Impassioned Defence of Captain Whistler. 'The Dastardly Villain Set on Me with a Bug-powder Gun.' That also would gratify the Green Star Line. Yes, it would. In your eye.''

The captain seemed slightly awed.

"Isn't there any justice?" he inquired suddenly, and looked rather blankly about the cabin. "In all God's green earth, isn't there any justice? What have I done to deserve this?"

It was only the beginning of a genuinely powerful, if rather pathetic, oration, for which there was undeniably some justification. It was pitched in a rather Biblical strain. Captain Whistler pointed out and enumerated his afflictions. Masked foreigners, he said, attacked him with stilettos and bottles. Uninsured jewels belonging to ?!£&/!! viscounts were stolen while murdering thieves posed as Harley Street doctors at his table. Blood-stained blankets and razors mysteriously appeared in the cabins; women vanished but did not vanish; the nephews of eminent American administrators first went mad and gibbered of bears and geography then ran amok with bug-powder guns, tried to poison him and finally threatened him with razors. Indeed, an unprejudiced listener would have decided that the situation aboard the *Queen Victoria* was past hope. An unprejudiced listener would have said this boat had been chosen for the annual convention of the Ancient Order of Sorcerers, and that the boys must have been showing off a bit. Captain Whistler said it was too much. He said he was a strong man, but he would rather be thrown to the sharks.

"I know it, Captain," Morgan agreed, uncomfortably, when the typhoon began to die and the skipper went to pour himself a drink with shaking hands. "And, believe it or not, we feel as badly about it as you do. So the first thing we must do—"

"There is nothing to do," said the other, with finality, "except maybe get drunk."

". . . is to join forces and start to unwind this tangle. So here's a guarantee of good faith. We'll go with you to Sturton and clear you absolutely. We'll say we saw you suddenly struck down without a chance to defend yourself; for all you know, it may be true. . . ."

"You'd do that?" demanded the skipper, sitting up. "I was damned if I'd ask a favour of you, but if you would—could . . . man, I'll do anything. I'll even let that madman out of the brig."

Morgan reflected. "As a matter of fact," he said, hesitantly, "for the next few hours I'd rather you didn't."

"Hank!" said Peggy. But she stopped.

"Yes, you see how it is," nodded Morgan, after some thought. "When we thought the captain wouldn't listen to reason, we'd have blown the wall down to get him out. But if we do have co-operation—have we Captain?"

"To the water-line, man."

"Then it may be much the best thing to leave him where he is for the moment. He's thoroughly comfortable, and we have a breathing-space while he's in a place where he can't possibly get into trouble. At least," Morgan amended, rather doubtfully, "I don't *see* how he can get into trouble. The whole thing was in your attitude, Captain. If you'd like us to talk to Sturton now, we're ready."

They met storm signals at the door of the peer's large and rather elaborate suite of cabins on B deck. The door to the drawing-room was on the latch, and they penetrated into a stuffy finery of curtains drawn at the portholes, gilt furniture disarranged, and an array of medicine-bottles sprawled round a chaise-lounge on which Sturton had evidently taken his hitherto sea-sick rest. Whether his recovery had been due to smooth weather or the loss of the emerald they did not know; but he had definitely recovered. From behind the door of the bedroom rose a dry, quick, high-pitched voice in a sort of pounce.

". . . and take a radiogram. Ha. Now. 'Messrs. Kickwood, Bane, and Kickwood, Solicitors.'. . . Spell it? Damn it, Miss Keller, you spell it the way it's pronounced: K-i-c-k-w-o-o-d, Kickwood. Ha. '31B King's Bench Walk.' Or is it 31A? Why can't these confounded lawyers make up their minds? How should *I* remember their infernal addresses? Wait a minute, wait a minute. . . ."

The door popped open in the gloom. A lean figure in a shabby grey dressing-gown, with a worsted plaid shawl wrapped round its shoulders, stared at them. Even indoors it wore a broad-brimmed black hat, and the greyish face underneath had so queer a look, in the midst of Lord Sturton's costly trinkets strewn about the drawing-room, that it reminded Morgan of one of those pictures of wizards in an Arthur Rackham illustration. Also, Morgan wished somebody would open a porthole.

The figure said, "Hah!" and stalked over. It was observable that before this man Captain Whistler looked exactly as Warren had looked before Captain Whistler.

"Well?" said Lord Sturton. "I'm waiting, I'm waiting." He took a thin finger and thumb and flicked at one of his side burns. "Have you got that emerald?"

"If you'll only be patient, sir," replied Whistler, as though he were trying to swell himself out with affability and be his public beaming self, "I—ha-ha! Of course we shall get it."

"Then you haven't got the emerald. Very well. Why don't you say so?"

"I only wished to say—"

"Rubbish, rubbish, rubbish! Answer me, yes, or no. If you haven't got the emerald, why are you here?" Sturton shot out his neck.

"It was about that little matter we were discussing—ha-ha!" returned

Whistler, with a broad gesture of paternal friendliness. "You know I said, your Lordship, that I could bring witnesses to show I had behaved within my duties. You said I was responsible—"

"So you are, so you are. I have your signed receipt. Here."

"The great line of which I have the honour to be one of the senior commanders has always wished, your Lordship, to avoid unpleasantness," began the captain, in a rolling voice. "However, having its best interests at heart. . . ."

"Pfaa!" snapped the other, suddenly sitting down against the back of the chaise-longue and hunching his shawl round his shoulders. "Why don't you say what you mean? You mean that you've been caught fair and square; but what you want is a sporting run. Eh? Eh?"

"That, your Lordship, is putting it harshly. . . ."

Sturton thrust his finger out of the shawl and pointed. "I'll give it you. Damn no man without proof. Bible says so. Prove it to me; no damage suit. There."

Morgan got the impression that he immensely enjoyed being arbiter of somebody's official head; that it tickled a nerve of perverted humour under his dry ribs. He could humour a whim—but the whim had to have its compensations. Morgan realised that, with this sharp-eyed old lad questioning, a lie had to be good. Well, he should be beaten. In a way, Morgan thought, that was incentive enough to save Whistler's bacon! Sturton was leaning back, hugging the shawl round his head. On the table at his elbow was a curious trinket of his own: a Mandarin-head that would wag on its pedestal, and had two rubies for eyes. At intervals he would reach out and set it wagging.

"Well?" he said, abruptly. "Anything to say?"

"A while ago, your Lordship, you intimated to me—as I told this lady and gentleman—that, if I could offer you the proof I said I could," Whistler cleared his throat, "you would not—ah—"

"Well? Well? Where's the proof? I don't see it?"

"These witnesses, you see—"

Morgan got ready, steadying himself. It was unnecessary.

"Who are *you*, young man? Are you the nephew of a friend of mine? Are you Warpus's nephew? Eh?"

"No, your Lordship," interposed the captain. "This is Mr. Henry Morgan, the very distinguished writer, who I thought would offer evidence acceptable. . . ."

Sturton laughed. It was not a pleasant sound. Morgan glanced at Peggy, who had begun to grow frightened. Sturton laughed again.

"Fail first count. *You'd* make no lawyer. I want witnesses I know of. Er—Commander, you stated to me, I think, that you believed you could produce this nephew. Where is he?"

He leaned out and flung the question with a snap of impatience.

The Parcæ were at it again. Morgan could have whistled in admiring astonishment, or sworn from the same situation.

"This morning," continued Sturton, "you stated to me that you could bring him. Why isn't he here? Won't he come?"

Whistler jerked himself out of his hypnotised stare. "Yes, yes, of course. Your Lordship. I—ah—that is, I'm sure he'll be glad to come."

"I repeat to you," squeaked the other, snapping his finger on the Mandarin's head until the rubies winked demoniacally, "that, as this little trial by the court may cost me fifty thousand pounds, I must insist on a direct answer. Don't quibble with me. Don't spoil my entertainment. He was the witness I especially asked for, and the only witness I especially asked for. Why didn't you bring him?"

"It was not exactly *convenient*. . . ." said Whistler, his voice beginning to rise to a roar despite himself. His eye rolled round at Morgan, who could only shrug.

"Ah!" said Sturton. "Signals, eh? Signals. Now then. . . ."

"If you will allow me to go and find him, your Lordship—"

"Once and for all, I demand, I insist on an answer! Where is he?"

All caution boarded the Flying Dutchman and sailed away. "He's in the *brig;* you dried-up lubber!" roared Captain Whistler, exploding at last. "*He's in the brig.* And now I'm going to tell you what I think of you and your ruddy elephant and your—"

Sturton was laughing again.

It was an unholy noise in that gloomy, ill-smelling place, with the rubies winking on the table and Sturton's head bobbing under the broad hat. "Ah." he said, "that's better! That's more like yourself. I'd heard the news, you see. He's in the brig. Yes, yes. Exactly. Why did you put him there?"

"Because he's stark, raving mad, that's why! He attacked me with a razor. He tried to poison me. He gabbled about bears. He—"

"Indeed?" said Sturton. "Mad, is he? Well, well. And this is the man, I think, you wished to call as a witness to your spotless behaviour? This is your star witness, who was to testify how you lost the emerald? . . . Captain Whistler, are you sure that you yourself are entirely in your right mind?"

Peggy went over and patted the skipper on the back, speaking soothing words to him. Her feminine instincts were deeply aroused, for he was almost at the point where there were tears in those honest old eyes. And again he was speechless before the evil weaving of Lachesis. He must now be beginning, Morgan fancied, to have a faint conception of how Warren had felt.

"I am waiting," said Sturton.

Again the mirth tickled his rusty ribs. But he was watching Whistler wind himself up for a few sulphurous remarks, and forestalled him by holding up a scraggy hand.

"Rubbish rubbish rubbish. Wait. Don't say it, Commander. You'd regret it. *I* have something to say. It is only fair to you. The joke has been excellent, excellent. excellent. It has amused me, although, as a lawyer, Commander—tut, tut! But it is time to end it now. I have enjoyed myself long enough. . . . Captain, there will be no suit."

"No suit?"

"None. My secretary informed me of the rumour in the ship. That the nephew of my old friend had been imprisoned for trying to kill some-body. I could not resist amusing myself. Well! Time's ended. Joke's up. I have business. . . . No suit. Finished, ended, done. Don't want to hear of it again."

"But that emerald . . . !"

"Oh, yes! Yes, yes. The stone, of course. Very funny things go on aboard this ship. But why should there be a suit? Maybe the thief reformed; got qualms of conscience. How should *I* know? Anyhow—"

He fumbled in the pocket of his dressing-gown.

He laughed again, shaking his lean shoulders.

Before their astounded eyes he held up, twisting on its gold chain and glittering as it slowly revolved, the emerald elephant.

Chapter XIV

CAN THESE THINGS BE?

"**D**on't know how it happened," continued Sturton, rather carelessly, "and don't care, now I've got it back. I know *you* didn't recover it. Ha! . . . Found it lying on the middle of the table there," he stabbed his finger, "half an hour ago. Saw nobody, heard nobody. There it was. Somebody walked in and put it down—Here's your receipt back, Commander. You won't get this elephant again."

Again his squeaky mirth rose as he blinked at their faces. The receipt fluttered out and fell at Whistler's feet.

Morgan only half heard him. He was getting to the point where too many surprises were as deadening as too much pain. Staring at the little Mandarin-head smirking and wagging on the table, he heard Whistler gabbling something, the peer assuring him there would be no trouble, and the end of the latter's squeaky tirade:

". . . find out who stole it? Go on, if you like. *I* won't stop you. But I've got it back, and that's all I care. *I'm* not going to prosecute anybody. Ha! Got enough lawsuits as it is. Let the beggar go. Why bother? Shouldn't be surprised if it got stolen by mistake, and somebody returned it. Never mind. Now get out. Get out! . . ."

He was flailing his arms at them like a banshee, with the emerald gleaming on its chain from one hand. They were shooed into the gangway and the door closed behind them. Then they stood in the corridor on B deck and looked at one another.

"You're quite right, Captain," agreed Morgan, after listening thoughtfully to the skipper's rather weak-voiced comments. "If anything, I should think the adjectives were conservative. But the question remains, who, how, and why?"

After Whistler had recovered himself, swabbing his face with a handkerchief, he was weakly jubilant. He had the air of one who had endured blessed martyrdom in the arena, and suddenly sees ahead of him not the cruel countenance of Nero Ahenobarbus, but a cheering St. Peter at the head of a celestial brass band. The captain drew himself up. His face subtly altered. Taking his receipt for the emerald, he tore it into small pieces and blew them away. Over the battered face, with its plum-coloured eye, there spread a benevolent smile.

"My friends," he said, placing an arm around the shoulders of Peggy and Morgan, "I don't know who returned that ruddy elephant, and I don't care. Whoever it was, he did me a good turn that Hector Whistler will never forget. I could forgive him anything, I could almost forgive him"— momentarily the face darkened, but only for a moment—"*this*. Yes, even the foul blow, foully struck when I wasn't looking. If old Sturton doesn't care—My friends, to-morrow night, our last night at sea, is the captain's dinner. My friends, I will give such a dinner as has never been seen on blue water since the days of Francis Drake. Champagne shall bubble at every table, and every lady shall wear a corsage. And this, my friends, reminds me. I think, I say I *think* that I have in my locker at this moment a bottle of Pol Roger 1915. If it will now please you to come with me and accept the hospitality of an old, rough sea-dog—"

"But, hang it, Captain," said Morgan, "the difficulties aren't one-tenth over. Not a tenth. There's the little matter of a murder. . . ."

"Murder?" inquired the old, rough sea-dog genially. "What murder, lad?"

Mysterious are the ways of psychology.

"But, Captain Whistler!" cried Peggy, "that poor girl . . . down in the cabin beside Curt's . . . that awful razor. . . ."

"Ah, yes, my dear!" agreed the captain tolerantly benevolent. "Yes, of course. You mean that little joke of yours. Of course. Yes. Ha-ha-ha!"

"But—"

"Now, my dear," the other pursued, with radiant kindliness, "you listen to me. Come! You take a bit of advice from a rough old seafaring man old enough to be your father. From the first I've liked the cut of your jib, Miss Glenn, and the swing of your spanker-boom. Aye, lassie, I might have had a daughter like you if the Mrs. W. that was hadn't been dead and gone these twenty years, rest her sweet soul. It was in a sou'wester off Cape Hatteras, I mind. . . . But you don't want to hear of that. This is my advice, lassie. When a murder's been committed, in my experience, there's somebody dead," Captain Whistler pointed out, with irrefutable logic. "And if somebody's dead, that person can't be breathing heaven's free air on my deck. There's nobody missing, and nobody's complained, which they generally do in case of a murder. So—come, now; until somebody complains, I'm a free man. Just between ourselves, wasn't somebody having you on?"

"But you promised, Captain, that you'd co-operate and help us and—"

"And so I will, Miss Glenn," he told her, heartily, patting her shoulder. "You two—and old Sharkmeat also, if he likes—shall have the freedom of the ship, to question whom you like, and say I sent you. If you have news, ha-ha-ha! come to me. . . . By the way, would you like me to release that poor lad from his cell? No? Well, remember that I offered. I'll tell you what I'll do. I'll send him a fine basket of fruit, with my compliments, and a specially cooked capon for his dinner. How's that? Then, when we touch England day after to-morrow, we'll see what can be done about obtaining the services of the finest mental-specialist in London. . . ."

He stopped.

"Yes," said Morgan, seizing the opportunity, "and that reminds us all of Dr. Kyle, doesn't it? Not that I believe he's the Blind Barber, but it takes us back to that radiogram from the Police Commissioner, and the fact that—whatever else you believe or don't believe—there's a damned dangerous criminal aboard."

"H'm!" said Whistler. "H'm! Possibly. In any case, I've been in-structed not to do anything, haven't I, in case there's a mistake, eh? And the more I think it over, sink me!" he said with a happy flash of inspiration, "the more I'm convinced there *has* been a mistake. Why? I'll tell you. Because dangerous criminals don't steal fifty-thousand-pound jewels and then *return* 'em, do they? Sink me! you know, if I hadn't been assured by old Sturton that the emerald was returned to him while young Warren was in the brig—well I'd be fairly sure it was more of his mad vapourings. But I know it couldn't have been young Warren. . . ."

"Thank God for *that*," said Morgan.

"Anyhow," continued Whistler, assuming his hearty manner again, "I'll think it over. I believe it's a mistake and there's no crook aboard at all. Though—h'm—it would be a feather in the cap of the Green Star Line if I could have the honour of nabbing a notorious criminal before that New York detective arrived. I'll think it over. So, if you won't drink a health in Pol Roger—eh—no? Well, good day, good day, good day!"

He was off, saluting jauntily, before the stupefied allies could stop him. He swung his shoulders, his thumbs hooked in his pockets, and he was hoarsely humming a tune to the effect that Captain Ball was a Yankee slaver, blow, blow, blow the man down! His smile was radiant.

When he had gone, Peggy looked about hopelessly.

"Hank," she said, "it's no good. We can't beat Providence. Let's give it up. Let's go to the bar and get screamingly drunk."

Morgan replied grimly: "We will not. Give it up, I mean. But a couple of quick ones in the bar might fortify us before we comb this boat from stem to stern. . . . Why's the place so quiet, anyway?" He peered round. "They're all at lunch, that's it! We've missed lunch, and I didn't even hear the bugle. Never mind; we can get a sandwich in the bar. Come on. This thing has got to be thrashed out. Girl, that emerald's turning up puts the absolute lid on it! . . . What do you suppose could have happened?"

"Oh, drat the emerald!" she sniffed, with some pettishness. "Who cares about their nasty old emerald, anyway? We'll find out about this girl, if you like. But, honestly, Hank, I'm beginning to think we must be wrong, after all. H'm! I'll bet she was a hussy, anyway. . . ."

"She was calling Curt's name," her companion reminded her. He was determined not to lose his last ally. "She knew something that concerned him, don't you see? So if you want to help him, she'll be your first concern. It probably concerns the film; remember *that* my wench! Besides, have you forgotten another thing? Curt promised that chap Woodcock—definitely gave him his word—that he'd demonstrate by to-day there'd been a murder committed, or else force a bug-powder endorsement out of old Warpus."

She put her hand to her forehead. "Oh, I say, but I'd forgotten all about that awful little man! Oh, Hank, this is dreadful! And when I think of my poor Curt languishing behind prison bars, sitting there forlornly with his poor head in his hands. . . ." A sob caught her throat; she choked, and the tears overflowed her eyes. "Oh, it's awful, awful, awful!"

"Well, my God! don't cry about it!" said Morgan, waving his arms desperately. He peered round to make sure there was nobody in sight. "Look here. I didn't know you felt like that about it. Listen! *Stop* yowling, will you? It's all right. You heard what the skipper said. We'll go right down and get him out—"

"Oh, I w-wouldn't g-get him out f-for anything!" she gulped, forlornly, over the handkerchief she was jabbing at the corners of her eyes. Her breast heaved jerkily. "He—h-he'd only d-do some perfectly m-mad thing straight-away and g-get p-put right—right b-back in again. But, oh, d-dear! when I think of the p-poor d-darling l-languishing, p-positively—l-languishing—in—in a—foul d-dun—*bubuloo!*" choked Peggy, and burst into a spasm of weeping.

These, reader, are the times that try men's souls: when tears flow by reason of some inexplicable logic that escapes you, and all you can do is to pat her shoulder whilst desperately wondering what is wrong. He tried remonstrance—an error. He pointed out that it was not as though Warren had been shoved in the Bastille, never again to see the light of day; adding that the maniac was quite comfortable there and had been promised a specially cooked capon for his dinner. She said she wondered how Morgan thought the poor boy would have the heart to eat it. She said he was a cruel, callous beast ever to think of such a thing; and went off the deep end again. After this crushing retort, all he could think of was to rush her to the bar for a couple of stiff drinks as quickly as possible.

That her tears were dried was due to a new cause for worry, which he saw presented itself to her as soon as they entered the bar.

The bar (quaintly called smoking-room) was a spacious oak-panelled cathedral at the rear of B deck, full of stale smoke and a damp alcoholic fragrance. There were tables in alcoves of deep leather lounges, and a number of gaunt electric fans depending from the pastoral-painted ceiling. Except for one customer, who stood at the bar counter with his back towards them, it was deserted. Sunlight streamed through windows of coloured mosaic glass swaying gently on the floor; only peaceful creakings of woodwork and the drowsy murmur of the wake disturbed its cathedral hush.

Peggy saw the one customer, and stiffened. Then she began to advance stealthily. The customer was a short, stocky man with a fringe of black hair round his bald head, and the arms and shoulders of a wrestler. He was just raising his glass to his lips when he seemed warned by some telepathic power. But before he could turn Peggy had pounced.

"*Ah!*" she said, dramatically. She paused. She drew back as though she could not believe her eyes. "*Tiens, mon oncle! Qu'est-ce que je vois? Ah, mon Dieu, qu'est-ce que je vois, alors?*"

She folded her arms.

The other started guiltily. He turned round and peered up at her over the rim of his glass. He had a reddish face, a large mouth, and an enormous curled grey-streaked moustache. Morgan observed that the moment Peggy fell into the Gallic tongue her gestures corresponded. She became a whirlwind of rattling syllables. She rapidly smacked her hands together under the other's nose.

"*Eh bien, eh bien! Encore tu bois! Toujours tu bois! Ah, zut, alors!*"

She became cutting. *"Tu m'a donné votre parole d'honneur, comme un soldat de la France! Et qu'est-ce que je trouve? Un soldat de la France, hein! Non!"* She drew back witheringly. *"Je te vois en buvant le* GIN!*"*

This, unquestionably, was Uncle Jules sneaking out with the laudable purpose of knocking off a quick one before his niece caught him. A spasm contorted his face. Lifting his powerful shoulders, he spread out his arms with a gesture of extraordinary agony.

"Mais, chérie!" he protested in long-drawn, agonised insistence like a steamer's fog-horn. *"Mais, ché-é-riii-e! C'est un très, très, très petit verre, tu sais! Regards-toi, chérie! Regards!! C'est une pauvre, misérable boule, tu sais. Je suis enrhumé, chérie*—he coughed hollowly, his hand at his chest—*"et ce soir—"*

"Tu parles! Toi," she announced, pointing her finger at him and speaking in measured tones, *"toi, je t'appelle dégoutant!"*

This seemed to crush Uncle Jules, who relapsed into a gloomy frame of mind. Morgan was introduced to him, and he followed them to a table while Morgan ordered two double-whiskies and a milk-and-soda. Uncle Jules appealed in vain. He said he had never had so bad a cold in his life, coughing hideously by way of demonstration, and said that if nothing were done about it he would probably be speechless by five o'clock. Peggy made the obvious retort. She also adduced examples from a long list of Uncle Jules' past colds, including the time in Buffalo when he had been brought back to the hotel in an ash-cart.

He brightened a little, however, as he described the preparations for the performance that night. Preparations marched, he said, on a scale superb. Three hand-trucks had been provided to convey his fifty-eight separate marionettes (housed in a cabin of their own adjoining his, although they were *not* sea-sick, happy *gosses*) together with all the vast machinery of his theatre, to the hall of concert. The three costumes, one in which he spoke the prologue, and two for his extras, the French and Moorish warrior, were now being given a stroke of the iron; the piano and violin for off-stage music were installed behind the scenes as the theatre was set up in the hall of concert. A hall of concert magnificent, situated on B deck, but with a backstage staircase leading up from the dressing-room on C deck. Which reminded him that, while investigating the dressing-room, he and his assistant, Abdul, had met M. and Mme. Perrigord.

"A husband and his wife," pursued Uncle Jules, excitedly, "very charming, very intelligent, of whom the cabin finds itself near by. Listen, my dear! It is he who has written of me those pieces so magnificent which I do not understand. One thousand thunders, but I am enchanted! Yes, yes, my dear. Among us we have arranged the order of the performance. Good! Also we have met a Dr. Keel, a medicine Scottish, who will make recitations. Good! All is arranged. Two professors of a university who voyage shall be our warriors; M. Furioso Camposozzi at the piano and M. Ivan Slifovitz at the violin have arranged for accompanying my sitting with music of the chamber which I do not understand, see you? but, ah, my dear, what a triumph of intelligence. For me, I shall be superb? I—"

"Dear uncle," said Peggy, taking a soothing draught of whiskey neat and sighing deeply afterwards, "it is necessary that I speak with this monsieur. Go to your cabin and couch yourself. But attend! It is I who speak! *Nothing to drink.* Nothing! Is it understood?"

M. Fortinbras swore that an old soldier of France would cut his throat sooner than break his promise. He finished his milk-and-soda with a heroic gesture, and doddered out of the bar.

"Listen, Hank," said Peggy, dropping the language of Racine. She turned excitedly. "Seeing the old boy has just brought me back to business, I've got to see that he keeps sober until after the show; but it's given me an idea. . . . You're determined on questioning everybody on this boat, seeing everybody face to face. . . ."

"I'm letting nobody by," returned Morgan grimly, "except the people we *know* to be aboard. I'm going to take a passenger-list, and get a crew-list from the captain, and check everybody if it takes all afternoon. It would be devilish easy for somebody to conceal an absence when that first officer went round. 'Oh, no, she wasn't hurt—sorry she isn't here; she's lying down; but I can give you my word. . . .' Peggy, that girl hasn't vanished. She's somewhere on the boat. She's a real person! Hang it, we saw her! And she's going to be found."

"Righto. Then I'll tell you your pretext."

"Pretext?"

"Of course you've got to have a pretext, silly. You can't go roaring about the ship after somebody who was murdered and starting an alarm, can you? Fancy what Captain Whistler would say, old dear. You've got to do it without arousing suspicion. And I've got the very idea for you." She beamed and winked, wriggling her shoulders delightedly. "Get hold of your dear, dear friend Mrs. Perrigord—"

Morgan looked at her. He started to say something, but confined himself to ordering two more whiskies.

". . . and it's as easy as shelling peas. You're looking for volunteers to do amateur acts at the ship's concert. *She's* in charge of it. Then you can insist on seeing everybody without the least suspicion."

Morgan thought it over. Then he said:

"Ever since last night, to tell the truth, I have been inclined to scrutinise any idea of yours with more than usual circumspection. And this one strikes me as being full of weak points. It's a comparatively simple matter if I encounter a lot of shy violets who are averse to appearing in public. But suppose they accept? Not that I personally would object to an amateur mammy-singer or a couple of Swiss yodellers, but I don't think it would go well with the chamber-music. How do I persuade Mrs. Perrigord to accompany me, in the first place, and to put all my crooners on the programme, in the second?"

Peggy suggested a simple expedient, couched in even simpler language, to which Morgan rather austerely replied that he was a married man. "Well, then," Peggy said excitedly, "it's even easier than *that,* if you're going to be fussy and moral about it. Like this. You tell Mrs. Perrigord that you're after material for character-drawing, and you want to get the reactions of a number of diversified types. On Being Approached to Make Exhibitions of Themselves in a Public Place. . . . Now don't misunderstand me and get such a funny look on your face! She'll eat it up. All you've got to do is suggest getting somebody's reactions to some loony thing that nobody's ever thought of before, and the highbrows think it's elegant. Then you might jolly her along and sort of make goo-goo eyes at her. As for the volunteers, bah! You can turn 'em all down after you've heard 'em rehearse, and say it won't do. . . ."

"Woman," said Morgan, after taking a deep breath, "your language makes my gorge rise. I will *not* make goo-goo eyes at Mrs. Perrigord, or anybody else. Then there is this question of rehearsing. If you think I have any intention of sitting around while amateur conjurers break eggs in my hat and wild sopranos sing 'The Rosary,' you're cockeyed. Kindly stop drivelling, will you? I've been through too much to-day."

"Can you think of any better plan?"

"It has its points, I admit; but—"

"Very well, then," said Peggy, flushed with triumph and two whiskies. She lit a cigarette. "I'd do it myself with *Mr.* Perrigord, only I have to help uncle. I'm the Noises Off-stage, you know: the horses, and Roland's horn, and all that, and I've got to get my effects set up this afternoon. I'll get it over as quickly as I can, because we *must* find that film. What I really can't understand is why our crook returned that emerald and yet didn't—I suppose he really didn't put the film back in Curt's cabin, did he? Do you think, we ought to look?"

Morgan made an irritable gesture.

"Don't you see that it wasn't the barber who did that? Off-hand, you'd say that there was only one explanation of it. When we chucked it away, it landed either in Kyle's cabin or in the Perrigords'. The obvious answer is that one of 'em found it in the cabin, meditated keeping it, then got scared at the row and sneaked it back to Sturton. But, damn it all! I can't believe that! Does it sound like Kyle? It does NOT. Conversely, if Kyle is a masquerading crook you can lay a strong wager that a cool hand like the Blind Barber wouldn't return that emerald—as Whistler said. Wash out Kyle either because he's a crook or because he isn't. If he's genuinely a great brain specialist he wouldn't do one thing, and if he's genuinely a great crook he wouldn't do the other. . . . And what have we left?"

"You think," demanded Peggy, "that nasty Mrs. Perrigord—?"

"No, I don't. Or friend Leslie, either. I can see Leslie handing over the emerald to Sturton with immense relish, and giving a long dissertation on the bad taste of gaudy baubles, but—Ah! News! Enter our squarehead."

He broke off and gestured to Captain Valvick, who had just shambled into the bar. The captain was puffing hard; his leathery face looked redder than ever, and, as he approached, he distilled like a wandering oven a strong aroma of Old Rob Roy.

"Ay been talking wi' Sparks and de Bermondsey Terror," he announced, somewhat unnecessarily and wheezed as he sat down. "And, ay got proof. Dr. Kyle iss not de crook."

"You're sure of that?"

"Yess. De Bermondsey Terror iss willing to swear. He iss willing to swear Dr. Kyle has gone into his cabin last night at half-past nine and he hass not left it until de breakfast bugle diss morning. He know, because he hass heard Dr. Kyle iss a doctor, and he wonder whedder he can knock on de door and ask him if he can cure de bad toot'. He didn't do it because he hass heard Kyle is a great doctor who live in dat street, you know, and he iss afraid of him. But he knows."

There was a silence.

"Hank," Peggy said, uneasily, "more and more—that radiogram from New York, where they were so sure—don't you think there's a dreadful mistake somewhere? What *can* be happening, anyhow? Every time we think we know something, it turns to be just the other way round. I'm getting frightened. I don't believe anything. What can we do now?"

"Come along, Skipper," said Morgan. "We're going to find Mrs. Perrigord."

Chapter XV

HOW MRS. PERRIGORD ORDERED CHAMPAGNE, AND THE EMERALD APPEARED AGAIN

Clear yellow evening drew in over the *Queen Victoria* moving steadily, and with only a silken swishing past her bows, down towards a horizon darkening to purple. So luminous was the sky that you could watch the red tip of the sun disappear at the end of a glowing path, the clouds and water changing like the colours of a vase, and the crater of glowing clouds when the sun was gone. The dress bugle sounded at the hush between the lights. And the *Queen Victoria,* inspired for the first time by that mild fragrance in the air, woke up.

Sooner or later on any voyage this must happen. Hitherto-blank-faced passengers rouse from their deck-chairs and look at one another. They smiled nervously, wishing they had made more acquaintances. The insinuating murmur of the orchestra begins to have its suggestion on them; they see broad Europe looming, and lamps twinkling in the trees of Paris. A sudden clamour of enjoyment whips the decks like the entrance of a popular comedian. Then they begin by twos and threes to drift into the bar.

Activity had begun to pulse this night before it was quite dark. The beautiful, mongoose-eyed shrew who was going to Paris for her divorce searched out her shrewdest evening-gown; so did the little high-school teacher determined to see the Lake Country. Love affairs began to flicker brightly; two or three bridge games were started; and the disused piano in the screened deck off the bar was rolled out for use. The dining-saloon was in a roar of talk. Diffident ladies had come out with unexpected rashes of jewels, optimists ordered from the wine-list, and the orchestra was for the first time encouraged. When Henry Morgan—tired, disgusted, and without energy to dress for dinner—entered with his two companions towards the close of the meal, he saw that it was the beginning of what for the sedate *Queen Victoria* would be a large night.

His own ideas were in a muddle. After four exasperating hours of questioning, he was almost convinced that the girl with the Greek-coin face had never existed. She was not aboard, and (so far as he could ascertain) had never been aboard. The thing was growing eerie.

Nobody knew her, nobody remembered having seen her, when at length in desperation he had dropped the pretext of searching for music-hall talent. On the tempers of some already harassed people, in fact, this latter device had been ill-timed. Its effects on Lord Sturton, on an Anglo-Indian colonel and his lady not yet recovered from *mal-de-mer,* on a D.A.R. from Boston and kindred folk, had been a bouncer's rush from the cabin before the request was fully out of his mouth. Even Captain Valvick's easy temper was ruffled by receptions of this kind.

Mrs. Perrigord, on the other hand, had been invaluable. Although she must have been aware that there was more in the tour than Morgan would admit, she had been impassive, helpful, even mildly enthusiastic. She took on herself a duty of cutting things short in a way that the easy-going novelist admired but could not imitate. When a proud mother eagerly went into long explanations of how her daughter Frances, aged nine, could play "Santa's Sleigh-Bells" on the violin after only six lessons, and how Professor E. L. Kropotkin had confidently predicted a concert future, then Mrs. Perrigord had a trick of saying, "I reolly don't think we need waste your time," in a loud, freezing voice which instantly struck dumb the most clamorous. It was an admirably frank trait, but it did not add to Morgan's comfort through those long, hot, gabbling, foodless hours in which he acquired a distaste for the entire human race.

Mrs. Perrigord did not mind at all. She said she enjoyed it, chatting volubly all the while, and coyly taking Morgan's arm. Moreover, she took quite a fancy to Captain Valvick, who, she confided to Morgan in a loud side-whisper, was so fresh and unspoilt, a definition which the skipper seemed to associate vaguely with fish, and which seemed to fret him a good deal. Another curious, puzzling circumstance was the behaviour of Warren, when they looked in on him in the padded cell just before going down to dinner.

It was growing dark, but he had not switched on the light in his cell. He was lying at full length on the bunk, his face turned to the wall as though he were asleep. In one hand was a closed book with his finger marking the place in the leaves. He breathed deeply.

"Hey!" said Morgan, whistling through the bars. "Curt! Wake up! Listen . . . !"

Warren did not stir. An uneasy suspicion assailed his friend, but he thought he could see the whisky-bottle also, and it appeared to be only slightly depleted: he could not be drunk. Mrs. Perrigord murmured, "Pooah lad!" The sailor on guard duty, who had respectfully risen, said the gentleman 'ad been like that all afternoon; was exhausted-like.

"Ay don't like dis," said Valvick, shaking his head. "Аноу!" he roared, and pounded at the bars. "Mr. Warren! Аноу!"

The figure moved a little. It raised its head cautiously in the gloom and there was a fiendish expression on its face. Placing a finger on its lips, it hissed "Sh-h-h!", made a fierce gesture for them to go away, and instantly fell somnolent again.

They went. Whatever the meaning of the episode, it was driven from Morgan's mind by the prospect of food and drink. The fragrance and glitter of the dining-room soothed his rattled nerves; he breathed deeply once more. But—there was nobody whatever at the captain's table, not even Dr. Kyle. In the middle of the crowd and clatter, every chair remained ominously empty. He stared.

" . . . Now you *must,*" Mrs. Perrigord was saying, "you really *must* come and dine at ouah table to-night, you kneow. Whatevah is worrying you, Mr. Morgan, I must insist on youah forgetting it. Come!" Her smile became mysterious as she took her rather dazed guests across the room. "Les-leh will not be with us to-night. He will dine on milk and dry biscuit, and prepare himself foah his talk." She leaned close to Morgan. "My husband, you know, has rather extrooordinry principles, Mr. Morgan. But I, on the othah hand—"

Again she smiled. That was how she came to order champagne.

After the soup, Morgan felt a warmth steal through him. After the fish, his wolfish silence began to wear thin and his spirits stirred from their depths. In the midst of a tender steak, done rare between crisp marks of the grill and smoking between those smooth-slipping chipped potatoes whose edges have no hardness, he suddenly felt a pleased sense of relaxation. The music of the orchestra did not sound far away, and he rather liked the appearance of the faces about him. Life looked less like a heap of unwashed dishes, and the warm lights were comforting. Champagne nipped warm and soothing. Captain Valvick said, "Ahh-h!" on a long-drawn note. When the steak disappeared, to be replaced by mysteriously tinted ice-cream and smoking black coffee, his spirits commenced to soar. He appreciated the noise that people were making around him. The champagne nestled through his innards, causing him to beam round on Mrs. Perrigord and the captain; to find himself keeping time with his foot when a reckless orchestra ventured into Gilbert and Sullivan.

"Ta-ti-ta-ta-ta-, ti-ta-ta-ta-*ti;* sing, 'Willow, tit-willow, tit-willow,' " murmured Henry Morgan, wagging his head expansively. He smiled, and Mrs. Perrigord spread effulgence in reply. " 'Iss it veakness of intellect, birdie, ay cried—!' " whoomed Captain Valvick, drawing back his chin for a thoughtful rumble; " 'Or a tough worm in youah little in-side—' " gently speculated Mrs. Perrigord, beginning to giggle; and all three together, inspired with a surge of mirth, whirled out together:

> *"With a shake of his poor little head he replied,*
> " *'Willow,*
> " *'Tit-willow,*
> " *'Tit-willow* ' (WHEE!)"

"Oh, I say, you know," protested Mrs. Perrigord, whose face was growing rather flushed and her voice more loud, "we reolly shouldn't be doing this at oll, should we? Oh, I *say!* Heh-heh-heh! Shall we have anothah bottle?" she beamed on them.

"You yust bet we do!" boomed Captain Valvick. "And diss one iss on me. Steward!" A cork popped, pale smoke sizzled, and they raised glasses. "Ay got a toast ay like to giff. . . ."

"Oh, I say, you know, I reolly mustn't!" breathed Mrs. Perrigord, putting her hand against her breast; "just fancy! What would deah Les-leh say? But if you two positively outrageous people positively insist, you know. . . . Heh-heh-heh! Here's loud cheaahs!"

"What I mean to say is this," said Morgan vigorously. "If there's any toast to be drunk, first off there ought to be a toast drunk to Mrs. Perrigord, Skipper. She's been the best sport in the world this after, Skipper, and I'd like to see anybody deny it. She came with us on a fool's errand, and never asked one question. So what I propose—"

He was speaking rather loudly, but he would not have been heard in any case. The entire dining-saloon had begun to converse in an almost precisely similar vein, with the exception of one or two crusty spoil-sports who stared in growing amaze. They could not understand, and would go to their graves without the ability to understand, that mysterious spirit which suddenly strikes and galvanises ocean liners for no reason discernible to the eye. Laughter in varying tones broke like rockets over the tumult; sniggers, giggles, guffaws, excited chuckles growing and rushing. More corks popped and stewards flew. It being against the rules to smoke in the dining-saloon, for the first time a mist of smoke began to rise. The orchestra smashed into a rollicking air out of *The Prince of Pisen;* then the perspiring leader came to the rail of the balcony and bowed to a roar of applause, dashed back and whipped his minions into another. Jewels began to wink as total strangers drifted to one another's tables, made appointments, gesticulated, argued whether they should stay here or go up to the bar; and Henry Morgan ordered a third bottle of champagne.

" . . . Oh, no, but I say, reolly!" cried Mrs. Perrigord, sitting back in a sort of coy alarm and talking still more loudly, "you mustn't! You two outrageous people are positively outrageous, you know! It's simply dreadful how you take advantage of a pooah, weak woman who"— gurgle, gurgle, gurgle—"it's reolly lovely champagne, isn't it?—who can't defend herself, you know. Just fancy, you wicked men, I shall be positively *tight,* you know. And that would be owful, wouldn't it?" She laughed delightedly. "Simply screamingly, deliciously owful if I am tight when I am tight, and—"

"What ay say iss diss," declared Captain Valvick, tapping the table and speaking in a confidential roar. "De champagne iss all right. Ay got not'ing against de champagne. But it iss not a man's drink. It do not put hair on de chest. What we want to drink iss Old Rob Roy. Ay tell you what. After we finish diss bottle we go up to de bar and we order Old Rob Roy and we start a poker game. . . ."

" . . . but I say, you mustn't be so owfully, owfully *formal,*" said Mrs. Perrigord chidingly. "*Henry.* Theah! I've said it, haven't I? Oh, deah me! And now you'll think I'm positively"—gurgle, gurgle, gurgle— "positively *dreadful,* won't you? But I have so *many* things I should like to discuss with you, you know. . . ."

A new voice chirped:

"Hullo!"

Morgan started up, rather guiltily, to see Peggy Glenn, in a green evening gown that looked rather disarranged, negotiating the last step of the staircase and bearing down on them. She was beaming seraphically, and something in her gait as she moved through the layers of smoke struck Morgan's eye even out of a warmth of champagne. Mrs. Perrigord turned. "Why, my deah!" she cried, with unexpected and loud affection. "Oh, how reolly, reolly *wonderful!* Oh, do, do come heah! It's simply wonderful to see you looking so spic hic, so sick and span after oll those owful things that happened to you last night whee! And—"

"Darling!" cried Peggy ecstatically.

"Peggy," said Morgan, fixing her with a stern eye, "Peggy, you—have—been—drinking."

"Hoo!" cried Peggy, lifting her arm with a conquering gesture by way of emphasis. Her eyes were bright and pleased.

"*Why* have you been drinking?"

"Why not?" inquired Peggy, with the air of one clinching a point.

"Well then," said Morgan magnanimously, "have another. Pour her a glass of fizz, Skipper. All I thought was after all that bawling and screaming this afternoon—"

"You did. You bawled and screamed this afternoon about Curt being shut up in a foul dungeon with the rats, and—"

"I hate him!" Peggy said passionately. She became tense and fierce, and moisture came into her eyes. "I hate and loathe him and despise him, that's what I do. I don't ever want to hear his name again, ever, ever, ever! Gimme a drink."

"My God!" said Morgan, starting up. "What's happened *now?*"

"Ooo, how I loathe him! He wouldn't even speak to me, the f-filthy w-wretch," she said, her lip trembling. "Don't ever mention his name again, Hank. I'll get blind, speechless drunk, that's what I'll do, and *that'll* show him, it will, and I hope the rats gnaw him, too. And I had a big basket of fruit for him, and all he did was lie there and pretend he was asleep, that's what he did; and I said, "All right!", so I went upstairs and I met Leslie—Mr. Perrigord—and he said, would I like to listen to his speech? And I said yes, if he didn't mind my drinking, and he said he never touched spirits, but he didn't mind if I did; so we sort of went to his cabin—"

"HAVE ANOTHER DRINK, MRS. PERRIGORD—CYNTHIA!" roared Morgan, to drown out the possibilities of this. "Pour everybody a drink. Ha-ha!"

"But, Henry!" crowed Mrs. Perrigord, opening her eyes wide, "I think it's p-perfectly wonderful, reolly, and so screamingly funny, don't you know, because oll deah Leslie evah does is tolk, you see, and the pooah darling must have been most dreadfully disappointed. Whee!" Gurgle, gurgle, gurgle.

"Ay like to see de young foolks have a good time," observed Captain Valvick affably.

" . . . and for Curt to act like that just when everything was nice and arranged for the performance to-night, when I'd finally succeeded in keeping Uncle Jules sober! And it *was* such a ghastly task, you know," explained Peggy, wrinkling up her face to keep back the tears, "because four separate times I caught him trying to sneak out after that horrible old GIN!" The thought of that horrible old gin almost overcame her with tears, but she turned a grim if wrinkled face steadily towards them. "But at last I made him see reason, and everything was all right, and he came down here in lovely shape to the dining-room to eat his dinner, and everything is nice—"

"Your Uncle Jules," said Morgan thoughtfully, in the midst of a curious silence, "came down *where* to eat his dinner?"

"Why, down here! And—"

"No, he didn't," said Morgan.

Peggy whirled round. Slowly, painstakingly, with misted eyes and lips slowly opening, she scanned the dining-saloon inch by inch. Babble and riot flowed there under a fog of smoke; but Uncle Jules was not there. Peggy hesitated. Then she sat down at the table and burst into sobs.

"Come on!" said Morgan, leaping to his feet. "Come on, Skipper! There's a chance to salvage the wreck if we work fast. He'll be in the bar if he's anywhere. . . . How long's he been on the loose, Peggy?"

"Th-thrree-qu-quarr*bolooo!*" sobbed Peggy, beating her hands against her forehead. "And only an hour unt-t-il the *bolooo*. Oh, w-why w-was the aw-ful st-stuff ever invented, and w-why do beastly m-men drink—?"

"Can he drink much in three quarters of an hour?"

"G-gallons," said Peggy. "*Whoooo!*"

"My de-deah," cried Mrs. Perrigord, the tears starting to her own eyes, "do you reolly mean that that*cher* M'skieux Fortinbras has really m'usk-ic, hic, has reolly got himskehelp *tight?* Oh, my deah, the horrible, owful, drunken—"

"Lady, lady," thundered Captain Valvick, hammering the table, "ay tell you diss is no time for a crying yag! Come on, Mr. Morgan; you take care of one and ay take care of de odder. Stop it, bot' of you! Come on now. . . ."

By dint of holding firmly to Mrs. Perrigord's arm while the captain took Peggy's, they slid through the rollicking, friendly crowd that was now streaming upstairs for a head-long rush on the bar before the hour of the ship's concert. The bar, already crowded and seething with noise, seemed even more crowded and noisy to Morgan. Each of his trio had consumed exactly one bottle of champagne; and, while he would have scorned the imputation that he could become the least sozzled on a quart of fizz, he could not in honesty deny certain insidious manifestations. For example, it seemed to him that he was entirely without legs, and that his torso must be moving through the air in a singularly ghostly fashion; whereas the more lachrymose became the two ladies over Uncle Jules going off on the razzle-dazzle, the more it impressed him as an excellent joke. On the other hand, his brain was clearer than normal; sights, sounds, colours, voices took on a brilliant sharpness and purity. He felt in his pores the heat and smoke and alcoholic dampness of the bar. He saw the red-faced crowd milling about leather chairs under the whirring fans and the pastoral scenes of the roof. He saw the amber lights glittering on mosaic glass in the windows, and heard somebody strumming the piano. Good old bar! Excellent bar!

"Come on!" said Captain Valvick. "Shovf de ladies into chairs at de table here and we make de round. *Coorosh!* Ay vant to see that mario- nette show myself. Come on. We start along de side and work ofer. You see him anywhere? Ay dunno him at all."

Morgan did not see him. He saw white-coated stewards shuttling in and out of the crowd with trays; but everybody in the crowd seemed to get in his way. Twice they made the circuit of the room: and no Uncle Jules.

"It's all right, I think," said Morgan, mopping his forehead with a handkerchief when they drew back towards a door giving on B deck. "He's probably gone down to take a last look at the marionettes. It's all right. He's safe, after all, and—"

" *'When chapman-billies leave the street,'* " intoned a sepulchral voice just behind them, " *'and drouthy neighbours neighbours meet—When market-days are wearin' late, and folk begin to tak the gate.'* . . . Not bad, not bad," the voice broke off genially. "Guid evening to ye, Mr. Morgan!"

Morgan whirled. A hand was raised in greeting from a leather alcove in a corner, where Dr. Oliver Harrison Kyle sat bolt upright in a solitary state. On Dr. Kyle's rugged face there was an expression of Jovian pleasure; a trifle frozen, it is true, but dreamy and appreciative. He had stretched out one hand levelly, and his eyes were half-closed as he rolled out the lines. But now he gestured hospitably.

Dr. Kyle was full of reaming swats that drank divinely. Dr. Kyle was, in fact, cockeyed.

" *'Auld Ayr, wham ne'er a town surpasses,'* " announced Dr. Kyle, with a gesture that indicated him to be a local boy and proud of it, " *'for honest men and bonnie lasses'!* Aye! A statement ye ken, Mr. Morgan, frae the wairks o' the great Scottish poet, Rabbie Burrrns. Sit down, Mr. Morgan. And perhaps ye'll tak a drap o' whusky, eh? *'The souter tauld his queerest stories—'* "

"Excuse me, sir," said Morgan. "We can't stop now, I'm afraid, but maybe you can help us. We're looking for a Frenchman named Fortin- bras; short, stocky chap—perhaps you saw—?"

"Ah," said the doctor reflectively. He shook his head. "A guid horse,

Mr. Morgan, a guid horse, but ower hasty. Weel, weel! I could ha' tauld him frae his ain exuberance at clearing the firrst sax hurdles he wadna gang the courrse. Ye'll find him *there,*" said Dr. Kyle.

They hauled Uncle Jules out from under the lounge, a pleasant far-off smile on his red face, but unquestionably locked in slumber. Peggy and Mrs. Perrigord arrived just as they were trying to revive him.

"Quick!" Peggy gulped. "I knew it! Stand round, now, so nobody sees him. The door's right behind you . . . carry him out and downstairs."

"Any chance of reviving him?" inquired Morgan, rather doubtfully. "He looks—"

"Come *on!* Don't argue! You *won't* say anything of this, will you, Dr. Kyle?" she demanded. "He'll be perfectly all right by curtain-time. Please don't mention it. Nobody'll ever know. . . ."

The doctor assured her gallantly the secret would be safe with him. He deplored the habits of inebriates, and offered to give them assistance in moving Uncle Jules; but Valvick and Morgan managed it. They contrived to lurch out on the deck and below without more than the incurious observation to stewards. Peggy, stanching her tears, was a whirlwind.

"Not to his cabin—to the dressing-room at the back entrance to the concert-hall! Oh, be careful! Be careful! Where can Abdul have been? Why wasn't Abdul watching him? Abdul will be furious; he's got a fearful temper as it is. . . . Oh, if we can't revive him there'll be nobody to speak the prologue; and Abdul will have to take *all* the parts himself, which he probably won't do. . . . Listen! You can hear the hall filling up already. . . ."

They had come out into the corridor in the starboard side of C deck aft, and Peggy led them up a darkish side-passage. At its end was a door opening on a steep stairway, and beside it the door of a large cabin whose lights she switched on. Faintly, from up the staircase, they could hear an echoing murmur which seemed to come chiefly from children. Panting hard, Morgan helped Valvick spill on a couch the puppet-master, who was as heavily limp as one of his own puppets. A small whistle escaped the lips of Uncle Jules as his head rolled over. He murmured, *"Magnifique!"* and began to snore, smiling sadly.

Peggy, weeping and cursing at once, rushed to an open trunk in one corner of the cabin. It was a cabin fully fitted up as a dressing-room, Morgan saw. Three superb uniforms, with spiked helmets, broadswords, scimitars, chain mail, and cloaks crusted in glass jewels, hung in a wardrobe. A scent of powder was in the air; on a lighted dressing-table were false whiskers of varying hues, wigs in long fighting-curls, face creams, greasepaints, spirit gum, make-up boxes, and pencils of rich soft blackness. Morgan breathed deeply the air of the theatre and liked it. Peggy snatched from the trunk a large box of baking-soda.

"You neffer do it," said Captain Valvick, looking gloomily at Uncle Jules. "Ay seen lots of drunks in my time, and ay tell you—"

"I will do it!" cried Peggy. "Mrs. Perrigord, please, *please* stop crying and pour out a glass of water. Water, somebody! I got him round once in Nashville when he was nearly as bad as this. Now! Now, if somebody will—"

"Oh, the poah *deah!*" cried Mrs. Perrigord, going over to stroke his forehead. Immediately, with a deep snore which rose to crescendo in a reverberating whistle, Uncle Jules slid off the couch on the other side.

"Up!" wailed Peggy. "Hold him—lift him up, Captain! Hold his head. That's it. Now tickle him. Yes, tickle him; you know." She dropped a lump of baking-soda into a glass of water and advanced warily through an aroma of gin that was drowning the odour of grease-paint. "Hold him now. Oh, *where* is Abdul? Abdul knows how to do this! Now, hold him and tickle him a little. . . ."

"*Gla-goo!*" snorted Uncle Jules, leaping like a captured dolphin. An expression of mild annoyance had crossed his face.

"*Viens, mon oncle!*" whispered Peggy soothingly. Her steps were a little unsteady, her eyes smearily bright; but she was determined. "*Ah, mon pauvre enfant! Mon pauvre petit gosse! Viens, alors. . . .*"

The *pauvre enfant* seemed vaguely to catch the drift of this. He sat up suddenly with his eyes closed; his fist shot out with unerring aim, caught the glass full and true, and carried it with a crash against the opposite bulkhead. Then Uncle Jules slid down and serenely went on snoring. "Haah, whee!" breathed Uncle Jules.

There was a knock at the door.

Peggy nearly screamed as she backed away. "That can't be Mr. Perrigord!" she wailed. "Oh, it can't be! He'll ruin us if he learns this. He *hates* drinking, and he says he's going to write an account again for the papers. Abdul! Maybe it's Abdul. He'll have to do it now. He'll have to. . . ."

"Dat," said Captain Valvick suddenly, "is a very funny knock. Lissen!"

They stared, and Morgan felt a rather eerie sensation. The knock was a complicated one, very light and rapid, rather like a lodge signal. Valvick moved over to open it, when it began to open of itself in a rather singular and mysterious way, by sharp jerks. . . .

"Ps-s-sst!" hissed a voice warningly.

Into the room, after a precautionary survey, darted none other than Mr. Curtis Warren. His attire was much rumpled, including torn coat and picturesquely grease-stained white flannels; his hair stood up, and there was some damage done to his countenance. But a glow of fiendish triumph shone from it. He closed the door carefully and faced them with a proud gesture.

Before they could recover from the shock of stupefaction and horror, he laughed a low, satisfied, swaggering laugh.

Thrusting his hand into his pocket, he drew it forth and held up, winking and glittering on its gold chain, the emerald elephant.

"I've got it back!" he announced triumphantly.

Chapter XVI

DANGER IN CABIN C46

Morgan said nothing. Like Captain Whistler on several occasions too well known to cite, he was incapable of speech. His first sharp fear—*viz.*, that his eyes were deceiving him, and that this might be a grotesque fantasy of champagne and weariness—was dispelled by sombre reality. Warren was here. He was here, and he had the emerald elephant. What he might have been up to was a vision which Morgan, for the moment, did not care to face. All he distinctly remembered afterwards was Valvick saying, hoarsely, "Lock dat door!"

"As for you—" continued Warren, and made a withering gesture at Peggy. "As for you—that's all the faith and trust you put in me, is it? That's the help I get, Baby! Ha! I put through a deep-laid plan; but do you trust me when I'm shamming sleep? No! You go rushing off in a tantrum. . . ."

"Darling!" said Peggy, and rushed, weeping into his arms.

"Well, now—" said Warren, somewhat mollified. "Have a drink!" he added, with an air of inspiration, and drew from his pocket a bottle of Old Rob Roy depleted by exactly one pint.

Morgan pressed his fists to his throbbing temples. He swallowed hard. Trying to get a grip on himself, he approached Warren as warily as you would approach a captured orang-outang, and tried to speak in a sensible tone.

"To begin with," he said, "it is no use wasting time in futile recriminations. Beyond pointing out that you are intoxicated as well as off your onion, I will say nothing. But I want you to try, if possible, to collect yourself sufficiently to give me a coherent account of your movements."

A horrible suspicion struck him. "You didn't haul off and paste the captain again, did you?" he demanded. "O God! you didn't assault Captain Whistler for the third time, did you? No? Well, that's something. Then what have you been up to?"

"You're asking *me?*" queried Warren. He patted Peggy with one hand and passed the bottle to Morgan with the other. Morgan instantly took a healing pull at it. "You're asking *me?* What did Lord Gerald do in Chapter Nine? It was your own idea. What did Lord Gerald do in Chapter Nine?"

To the other's bemused wits this was on a par with that cryptic query touching the manifesto said to have been thundered forth by W. E. Gladstone in the year 1886.

"Now, hold on," said Morgan, soothingly. "We'll take it bit by bit. First, where did you pinch that emerald again?"

"From KYLE, the dastardly villain! I lifted it out of his cabin not five minutes ago. Oh, he had it, all right! We've *got* him now; and if Captain Whistler doesn't have me a medal. . . ."

"From Kyle? . . . Don't gibber, my dear Curt," commanded Morgan, pressing his hands to his temples again. "I can't stand any more gibbering. You couldn't have got it from Kyle's cabin. It was returned to Lord—"

"Now, Hank, old man," interposed Warren with an air of friendly reasonableness. "*I* ought to know where I got it, oughtn't I? You'll at least admit that? Well, it was in Kyle's cabin. I sneaked in there to get the goods on the villain, the way Lord Gerald did when Sir Geoffrey's gang thought they had him imprisoned in the house at Moorfens. And I've *got* the goods on him. . . . Oh, by the way," said Warren, remembering something exultantly. He thrust his hand into the breast pocket of his coat and drew out a thick bundle. "I also got all his private papers, too."

"You did *what?*"

"Well, I sort of opened all his bags and trunk and briefcases and things. . . ."

"But, I say, howevah did the deah boy get out of gaol?" inquired Mrs. Perrigord. She had dried her tears, adjusted her monocle again, and she watched breathlessly with her hands against her breast. "I think it's most, owfully, screamingly, delightfully clevah of him to. . . ."

There was a quick knock at the door.

"They're after him!" breathed Peggy, whirling round with wide eyes. "Oh, they're a-after the p-poor darling to p-put him back in that horrible brig. Oh, *don't let them take*—"

"Sh-h-h!" rumbled Valvick, and made a mighty gesture. He blinked round. "Ay dunno what he done, but he got to hide. . . ."

The knock was repeated. . . .

"Dere iss no cupboard—dere iss no—Coroosh! Ay got it! He hass got to put on de false whiskers. Come here. Come here, ay tell you, or ay bust you one! You iss cuckoo! Don't argu wit' me," he boomed as a spluttering Warren was hauled across the cabin. "Here iss a wig. Mr. Morgan, get a robe or something out of dat locker. . . ."

"But why, I ask you?" demanded Warren. He spoke with a difficult attempt at dignity from behind a threatening bush of red whiskers with curled ends, and a black wig with long curls which Valvick had jammed over one eye. When he began to shake one arm and declaim, Morgan wrapped round him a scarlet bejewelled robe. "I've got proof! I can prove Kyle is a crook. All I've got to do is to go to Whistler and say, 'Look here, you old porpoise—' "

"Shut up!" hissed Valvick, clapping a hand over the whiskers. "Now. We iss ready. Open dat door. . . ."

They stared tensely, but the sight, as Morgan opened the door, was not very alarming. Under ordinary circumstances they would have deduced that their visitor was, if anything, a shade more nervous than they. A stocky A.B. in dungarees and a striped jersey was pulling at his forelock, shifting his feet, and flashing the whites of his eyes. Before anybody could speak, the A.B. burst out rapidly, in a hoarse confidential voice.

"Miss! Wot we want to 'ave clearly understood, my mates and me, which I was delegyted 'ere to sy, is that my mates and me is in naow wy responsible. Miss! Stryke me blind, so 'elp me, miss, if we're responsible! Like this. Not that we didn't feel like it, wot with 'im ordering us abaht like we wos dirt, and 'im only a ruddy Turk, yer see—but it's abaht that bloke Abdul, miss—"

"Abdul?" said Peggy. "Abdul! Where is he?"

"Right 'ere, miss, yer see. I've got 'im outside, miss. In a wheelbarrow, miss."

"In a wheelbarrow?"

"Like this, miss. So 'elp me! All dy me and my mates wos a-working wheeling them ruddy dummies, miss, and a-working *'ard,* so 'elp me. And Bill Pottle, my mate, says to me, 'e says, 'Gawd lummy, Tom, d'you know 'oo we've got on this 'ere tub?' 'e says. 'It's the Bermondsey Terror, Tom, the bloke we see knock out Texas Willie larst year.' So all of us thought we'd go and tyke a look at 'im, and a real top-notch good sport 'e wos, miss, 'oo said 'ed been a-drinking, wiv a Swede, and, 'Come in,' 'e says, 'all of yer!' So 'e begins a-telling us 'ow 'e beat the Dublin Smasher in eighteen seconds. And just when we wos all interested, miss, in walks this 'ere Abdul, yer see, miss, and starts rysing a row. And somebody says, 'Gorn' yer ruddy frog-eater,' 'e says, 'gorn back to yer ruddy 'arem,' 'e says. Then Abdul gets narsty and says, 'Ow, well, 'e'd rather be a frog-eater than a—Britisher a-stuffing fuller roast beef,' 'e says. And the Bermondsey Terror gets up and says, 'Ow, yerce?' And Abdul says, 'Yerce.' So Bermondsey sorter reaches out and taps him a couple, yersee, miss. . . ."

"But he's all *right,* isn't he?" cried Peggy.

"Sure, 'e's all right, miss!" the other hastened to assure her, with a gesture of heavy heartiness. "Except 'e can't *talk,* yer see. Bermondsey 'it 'im in the vocal cords, once, yer see, miss. . . ."

With her eyes brimming over, Peggy glared. "Oooh, you—oh, you nasty, brawling fighting. . . . Can't *talk?* You take him back, do you hear? You work over him, do you hear? If he isn't in shape in half an hour I'll walk straight up and tell the captain, and I'll—"

She herself was incapable of speech. She dashed at the door, the thoroughly scared A.B. ducking out before her wrath. He was mumbling something rather defiantly to the effect that that was what Abdul had croaked out, and the Bermondsey Terror said *he* didn't care, and if any games was tried on *him*—Peggy slammed the door.

"Coroosh!" said Captain Valvick, wiping his forehead. He shook his head despondently. "Ay tell you ay seen roughneck ships before, but diss one of Old Barnacle's iss de worst. It iss hawful. Ay haff a cook once on de old *Betsy Yee* which get mad and chase de whole fo'c's'l round and round de deck wit' a carving-knife; and ay t'ank now ay could get him a job on diss ship and he be right at home. Coroosh! what iss going to happen next?"

A faint, pleasant, gurgling noise behind them caused them to turn. The neck of a bottle had been tilted up among a brush of savage red whiskers. It descended. Red-whiskered and black-wigged, Curtis Warren regarded them affably.

"Good for the old Bermondsey Terror!" he said. "I'd like to meet that fellow. He'd make a good addition to our crowd. It reminds me a little of the way I served old Charley Woodcock about an hour ago. . . . What does Abdul weigh, Peggy? Woodcock's fairly light."

Cool despair settled on Morgan, so that he felt pleasant and collected now. Nothing more, he was certain, could happen. They might as well bow before the Parcæ and enjoy the gyrations of those relentless sisters.

"Ha-ha-ha!" he said. "Well, old boy, what did you do to Woodcock? What's Woodcock got to do with this?"

"How do you think I got out of the jug, anyhow?" demanded Warren. "It was a stratagem, I'm telling you, and a damned good stratagem, if you ask me. I asked you before, What did Lord Gerald do in Chapter Nine? And I'll tell you. The trick was this. If they thought he was safely locked up, then he could prowl as he liked and get the evidence that would hang the guilty man. That was *my* position. . . . So I had to have a substitute to take my place so they wouldn't suspect anything. And if I do say it myself, I worked it pretty well—though I'll have to hand the real credit to you, Hank." He removed his whiskers to talk the better.

"Woodcock was definitely the one person I could summon to me so that he'd come any time I liked, wasn't he? Right. Well I carefully prepared my ground by seeming to sleep all afternoon, so they'd get used to it; I refused dinner and everything. Then I wrote a note to Woodcock. I said I had news from my Uncle Warpus, and to come down to the brig at exactly seven o'clock. Just before this, I told him to have a message sent in the captain's name to the sailor on guard—I'd learned his name—to get him away for ten minutes, so there'd be nobody to hear when we talked business. I asked the sailor whether I could send a mesage, and he said he supposed it was all right, but he couldn't leave to take it; so they sent a pageboy. The only thing was, I was afraid somebody might read it, so—" Warren glanced round with triumphant glee, rubbing his hands.

"Masterly," said Morgan in a hollow voice.

"So what did I do? I ripped the book apart. There's always the heavy mucilage sticking the cover to the inside flaps of the book; and I tore out one of the flaps and sealed it. *And it worked!* Good old Charley came through. The sailor didn't like to leave when the fake message came through; but he saw there were bolts on the outside of the door I couldn't move, and I was asleep, anyway." Warren made a gesture. "Down comes Woodcock and says, 'You've got it, have you?' And I said, 'Yes; just pull back those bolts and open the door for a second; I don't want to get out, but I'll have to give you this.' So he opened the door. And I said, 'Look here, old man, I'm damned sorry, but you know how it is,' and I let him have it in the jaw. . . ."

"Darling!" said Peggy. "Oh, you poor dear idiot. Why didn't you make him *tell* before you hit him? . . . Oh, confound it all, if you'd only done what I wanted you to, if you'd only tortured him before you hit him! Oh, dear . . . and now look what's happened, with all this nasty fighting and torturing!" She wrung her hands. "Abdul and Uncle Jules, look at them! And unless we can get them on their feet there'll be no performance. Listen! I can hear the crowd upstairs already. . . ."

She snatched the bottle from Warren's hand and strengthened herself with a draught. A wheel seemed to go round behind her eyes. "The n-nasty d-drunken b-beasts!" said Peggy; "the—"

"My deah!" said Mrs. Perrigord, "Oh, I say, I don't know what has kick-happened, but I think it was most owfully clevah of Mr. Joyce to torture oll those people, and get out of gaol, I do, reolly, especially as it was Henry's idea, and I think we reolly might have the courtesy to offer Mr. Lawrence a glass of champagne. . . ."

"Silence!" roared Morgan. "Listen, Peggy, the performance doesn't matter now; hasn't that occurred to you? Have you realised that we're

saddled again with that blasted emerald . . . which Curt swears he got out
of *Kyle's* cabin? Curt, come to your senses. You couldn't have got it out
of Kyle's cabin, I tell you! Lord Sturton—"

Warren shook his head tolerantly, agitating the curls of the savage
black wig that was jammed over one ear.

"No, no, old man," he said. "You don't understand. Not Lord Sturton—Lord Derreval. Lord Gerald Derreval. If you don't believe me, go
down to Kyle's cabin—it isn't far from here—and look behind the
wardrobe trunk just under the porthole. The steel box is there; I left the
box there so the crook would maybe think the emerald was still in it. . . ."

Valvick whirled on Morgan.

"Maybe," he said, "maybe it been dere all de time! Coroosh! You t'ink
dere is *two* emeralds, and one of dem a fake, and somebody hass returned
de fake to dat English duke, eh?"

"Impossible, Skipper," returned Morgan, who was feeling queerly
light-headed. "Don't you think Sturton would know a real emerald from a
fake? Unless, somehow, the real emerald was returned to him. . . . I don't
know! The thing's driving me insane. Go on, Curt. Go on from the
consummation of your crafty scheme to entice Woodcock to the brig.
What then?"

"Well, I got in a neat upper-cut, you see. . . ."

"Yes, yes, we know that. But afterwards?"

"I tore the sheet up, bound and gagged him securely, and tied him to
the berth so he couldn't move; then I put a blanket over him, so when the
sailor came back he'd only look into the cell and think I was there. . . .
Neat, eh?"

"I have no doubt," agreed Morgan, "that at the present moment Mr.
Woodcock thinks very highly of your forethought. If the idea had ever
previously occurred to him to tip over the beams concerning your Uncle
Warpus. I should think it would recommend itself strongly to him now.
You're a wonder, you are. Carry on."

"So I sneaked away and made straight for Kyle's cabin to get the goods
on him. I wasn't afraid of running into Kyle because I looked through a
porthole and saw him in the bar; besides, I knew he was due at the
concert. And—there you are. The proof! Also, I've got his papers. All I
was afraid of was what Captain Whistler had said about maybe catching
Kyle, but everything was fine. Now all we've got to do is examine his
papers, and we'll find evidence that he's really the crook who's impersonating Dr. Kyle. . . ."

"Yess, dere is de papers, too," rumbled Captain Valvick. "It is a
hawful offence, ay tell you. Worst offence on de high seas to steal a
man's papers. What we going to do *now?*"

Morgan stalked up and down the cabin, slapping his hand against the
back of his head.

"There's only one thing. We've got to get Curt back to the brig before the captain learns he's on the loose. I don't see how it's to be done without—*Mrs. Perrigord,*" he said whirling round, "*what are you doing?*"

"But, my own Henry," protested Mrs. Perrigord, jumping involuntarily. Her face wrinkled up in anguish. "Oh, I do so hope I didn't offend you! Reolly, I was only ringing the bell for the steward. Pierre Louys wants a bottle of champagne, you know, and you know it would be dreadfully rude if we didn't kick-offer. . . . But I reolly didn't know which was the b-bell, so what could I do but ring *oll* the bells, you see. . . ."

Morgan reeled. He dived and caught her arm just as she was about to press a last push-button, hitherto overlooked, and labelled "*Fire Alarm.*"

"Peggy," he said, "if you ever showed any sense and speed, show 'em now. If those bells don't bring down a mob, at least there'll be a crowd of highbrows swarming in to see if things are all ready for the performance. At the moment, this is the safest place on the ship for Curt if you'll do as I tell you. Black his face—fit him out in wig and whiskers. . . ."

"I will, Captain!" said Peggy grimly. "The poor darling sha'n't go back to that horrible old brig if *I* can help it. But what—?"

Morgan took her hands and looked her steadily in the eye.

"CAN I TRUST YOU AND CURT HERE FOR JUST FIVE MINUTES—just five minutes, that's all I ask—without your getting in more trouble. You *can* stay out of more trouble for five minutes, can't you?"

"I swear it, Hank! But what are you going to do?"

"The skipper and I are going to take those papers back to that cabin before anybody discovers they're gone. There's no chance of being caught; the only chance and danger is here. Give me that emerald, Curt. I don't know what's happened or what it is, but we'll take it back and be quit of the responsibility. Hand it over!"

"Are you stark, raving crazy?" shouted Warren. "I risk life and limb and my position in the Diplomatic Service to get the goods on a murdering crook, and now you ask me to hand back—"

Morgan lowered his voice, perceiving this was the only way of handling the matter, and fixed him with a hypnotic eye.

"This is subtle, Curt. A subtle, deep scheme, you see. We only pretend to do it. But the moth is in our net now. A pin, a cork, and a card, and we add him to our Baker Street collection! You see? You trusted the wit and resource of Lord Gerald in a tight spot; now trust it again. . . . Eh? Ah, that's it. That's it, old chap. Papers all here? Good! And—er—go light on the whisky, will you, or what there is left of it, until we get back? Stout fellow. . . . Now, remember, Peggy, you've promised there'll be no trouble. I rely on you. Come on, Skipper. . . ."

He backed away gingerly, as a lion-tamer might swerve to get out of a cage. Mrs. Perrigord said she wanted to go with Henry. She insisted on going with Henry. Exactly how she was dissuaded from this intention Morgan never knew, since he and Valvick slid out a fraction of a second before the closing door.

The gangway was empty, although a more confused buzzing and laughing, mingled with the deep note of people shuffling chairs, swept down from the staircase up to the stage.

"Well, remarked the skipper musingly, "we is de only two people left wit' any sense, and ay don't t'ink much of diss Lord Gerald, whoever he iss. Coroosh! Ay don't believe de government off de United States need to care much about dat movie-film. Ay dunno if dey know it, but dey have bigger worries. All dey got to do iss send dat young Warren out in de Diplomatic Service and dey are going to have a war every week. It iss up to us. We got to save de situation."

"We'll save it, Skipper. Easy, now! . . . Damn it! Don't walk like a crook! We're only out for a stroll. Take these papers. Round the corner here. At least, thank the Lord *we've* kept out of trouble so far. If anybody saw Curt sneaking back to Kyle's cabin, he'd be pounced on in a second. We haven't got a chance to put Kyle's papers back where they were—he'll know there's been a burglary—but at least there'll be nothing missing. In the ensuing search *this* emerald. . . . Look here, do you think somebody's pinched it *back* from Sturton?"

"Ay not be surprised. Ay not be surprised at anyt'ing. Sh-h-h, now! Here is where we turn off. Listen!"

At a dim side-passage off the main corridor they stopped and peered down. All the noises of the ship were away from them, in the dim tumult of the throng milling up on B deck towards the concert-hall. Here it was so quiet the sea's rush and murmur became again discernible, and the low creaking of woodwork. But there were voices somewhere. They listened a moment before they could place them as coming from behind the closed door of C 47 in the passage.

"It iss all right," whispered the captain, nodding. "Dat iss ony Sparks and hiss cousin, de Bermondsey Terror. Ay haff start de Bermondsey Terror off on Old Rob Roy, and ay bet he don't want to stop. But don't disturb 'em, or we haff to explain. Walk soft. . . . !"

C 46, Dr. Kyle's cabin, had its door closed. They tiptoed down, and Morgan felt his heart rise in his throat, growing to an enormous pounding, as he softly turned the knob. He pushed it open. . . .

Nobody inside.

One danger passed. If there had been somebody. . . .

Again he felt hot fear as he switched on the light, but there was nobody. It was a large cabin, with what he supposed to be a bathroom attached, and now in a wild state of confusion. Not even a private detective could have called Warren's methods in the least subtle.

Under the porthole stood a large wardrobe trunk with its leaves apart, its lid propped up and top shelf streaming ties. He pointed.

"Look there, Skipper. If that steel box were thrown in *this* porthole last night, it would land behind that trunk and nobody would ever see it unless the trunk were moved. . . ."

Valvick closed the door softly. He was peering at two valises open on the floor, and an unlocked brief-case lying across the berth.

"Come on," he said; "we haff to work fast. Take a handful of these papers and shove 'em somew'ere. Coroosh! Ay feel like a crook! Ay don't like diss. What you doing?"

Morgan was groping behind the trunk. His fingers touched metal, and he withdrew the circular box with the hinged lid. He stared at it a moment, and handed it to Valvick.

"There it is, Skipper. And here's the elephant"—he stared at Warren's trophy in his hand and shivered. "Come on; let's put it back. The less we have to do. . . ."

"*Listen!*" said Valvick, cocking his head.

Nothing. The porthole was open; they heard the curtain thrumming in the breeze, and the multitudinous rustlings of the sea. Also, very faintly, they could hear the murmur of voices from the gangway opposite, where sat Sparks and the Bermondsey Terror. Nothing else.

"Come on," whispered Morgan. "You're getting nerves, Skipper. Stuff those things away somewhere, and let's get out of here. We'll put this little job through without any hitch, and they'll never suspect us. . . ."

A voice said:

"*You think so?*"

Morgan felt his skin crawl, and his head bump forward against the trunk as he knelt. The voice was not loud, but it brought the universe to a standstill like a dead clock. After it the silence was so heavy that he seemed unable to hear the sea or the thrumming curtain.

He looked up.

The door to the bathroom, previously closed, was standing open. Captain Whistler stood with one hand on the knob and the other on a trigger. He was wearing full-dress uniform, an arabesque of gold braid against the blue, from which the breeze (Morgan noticed even in that glassy, frozen moment) brought a wave of Swat Number 2 Liquid Insect Exterminator. Captain Whistler's good eye had a malignant gleam as at the realisation of some obvious fact that had hitherto escaped him. . . . Behind him, Second-Officer Baldwin was looking over his shoulder . . .

His glance travelled to the emerald in Morgan's hand.

"So you two," said Captain Whistler, "*were* the real thieves, after all. I might have known it. I was a fool not to see it first off last night. . . . Don't move! All right, Mr. Baldwin. Move out and see if they're armed. Steady now. . . ."

Chapter XVII

BERMONDSEY CARRIES ON

There were, as they afterwards reflected, several courses that thoughtful men might have pursued. Even thoughtful men, however, would have conceded that these two conspirators were fairly in the soup. If at one time explanations might have been made to Captain Whistler, both Morgan and Valvick realised that by this time the Parcæ had so tangled matters up that it was practically impossible to explain *anything*. Morgan himself doubted whether even half an hour's lucid thought would enable him to explain the situation to himself. Yet there are certain courses which thoughtful men deplore—those courses are elementary, like a reflex action, and spring to the muscles from a prompting older than reason. Captain Valvick, for instance, might have held out the steel box. He might have thrown the box on the floor at Whistler's feet, and surrendered in explanation.

Captain Valvick did nothing of the kind.

He threw that steel box, in fact, straight at the light in the roof of Cabin C 46, where it spattered glass and extinguished the same in one reverberating pop. Then he nearly yanked Morgan's arm from his socket swinging him out before himself into the passage and slamming the door behind.

Morgan dimly heard Whistler's avenging yell. Flung against the opposite bulkhead, he bounced back in time to hear a weight of bodies thud against the door inside.

"Dat old Barnacle!" roared Valvick, whose powerful hands were firmly clamped on the knob at the door as he held it. "Dat!&—£/&???(!! *ay show him!* He t'ank we iss t'ieves, eh? By yumping Yudas, ay show him; Nobody effer tell me dat before; NOBODY! Ay show him. Qvick, lad; rope! Ve got to get rope and tie de door shut. . . ."

"*Wassermarrer?*" inquired a voice behind Morgan.

The voice had to speak loudly and hoarsely, because insane riot banged at the door inside, mingled with baffled bellowings from the *Queen Victoria*'s skipper. Morgan spun round, to see that the door of Cabin C 47 was open. Framed in the doorway, his shoulders filling it and wriggling out at either side, stood a young man who was likewise so tall that he had to bend his head to peer out. He had a flattened countenance and a ruminating jaw like a philosophical cow.

"Coroosh!" roared Valvick, with a blast of thankfulness. He panted. "Bermondsey! Iss dat you?"

"Ho!" said the Bermondsey Terror, his face lighting up. "Sir!"

"Bermondsey—qvick—dere is no time to argue. Ay haff done you a good turn wit' de toot-ache, eh?"

"Ho!" said the Bermondsey Terror.

"And you say you like to do me a good turn? Good! Den you do diss, eh? You hold diss door for me until we can go for help and get aw—can get rope to tie dem up. Here, you hold. . . ."

Uttering his significant monosyllable, the other leaped from the door with a crack of his head on the doorpost which he seemed to mind not at all, and lent his weight to the knob.

"Wot's up?" he inquired.

"Dey iss robbers," said Captain Valvick.

"Ho?"

"Dey steal my pearl cuff-links," rumbled Captain Valvick, with rapid pantomime, "and de platinum studs which my old mudder gave me. Dey steal dis yentleman's watch and his pocket-book wit' all de money. . . ."

"Robbed *you?*"

"Yess. All ay want you to do iss hold de door v'ile—"

"Ho!" said the Bermondsey Terror, letting to the door to hitch up his belt. "Lemme at 'em!"

"No!" roared the captain, with a hideous insight of what he had done with his burst of poetic fancy. "No! Not dat! Only hold de door! Ay tell you it is de capt—"

The Bermondsey Terror's somewhat diminutive mind was concentrated on business. He hurled his fifteen stone at the door without pausing for explanation or protest. There was a thud and crackle; then a sound suggesting that two rather heavy bodies had been catapulted back across the cabin like bowling-pins. Then Bermondsey plunged into the dark cabin.

"We've got to stop him!" panted Morgan, trying to get through the door. He was stopped by Valvick's arm. "Listen! he'll—"

"Ay don't t'ink we can do not'ing but run," said Valvick. "*No!* Stay back. Ay am sorry for old Barnacle, but—"

From the cabin issued hideous muffled noises, language reminiscent of King Kong, and the clean inspiriting crack of knuckles against bone and flesh. A large suit-case sailed out of the darkness, as though from a lively spiritualist séance; banged against the opposite wall and showered underwear, socks, shirts, and papers. The passage began to be inundated with Dr. Kyle's possessions. Morgan, breaking loose, made another effort to dive in at the door. It was a gallant attempt, which might have succeeded if at that moment somebody had not thrown a chair.

Then he had a vague impression that somebody was dragging him away. Dimly he heard the Bermondsey Terror's hoarse voice announcing in muffled accents, between cracks, that he would teach people to steal pearl cuff-links and gold watches that their mothers gave them. When Morgan's wits cleared a second or more later, he was some distance from the scene of tumult. A new sound struck him—a deepening, gathering buzz and laughter. They were in the passage leading to the back stairs of the concert-hall.

"You ain't hurt!" Valvick was saying in his ear. "It yust bump you. Brace up! Qvick, now! De hunt be up in a second, and we got to find a place to hide if we don't want to be put in irons. . . . Sh-h-h! Walk careless! Here iss somebody. . . ."

Morgan straightened up, feeling his eyes crossed in a buzzing head, as somebody stalked round the corner into the narrow gangway. It was a steward bearing a large tray on which there were six tall gilt-foil bottles. Paying no attention to them, the steward swung past and knocked at the door of the dressing-room. In response to his knock there was poked out a face of such appalling hideousness that Morgan blinked. It was a brown face with tangled black hair, murderous squint-eyes, and whiskers.

"Champagne, sir," said the steward, crisply, "for a Mr. D. H. Lawrence. That'll be six pounds six, sir."

The cut-throat leered. On his head he placed rather rakishly a spiked helmet of brass set with emeralds and rubies; so that he could the better reach under an elaborate green robe, where he fumbled a moment, and then laid on the tray two American twenty-dollar bills. The bottles were mysteriously whisked inside by what appeared to be feminine hands behind the warrior. Then, as the steward hastened away, the warrior drew from its scabbard a broad curved scimitar and squinted evilly up and down the passage. Seeing Valvick and Morgan, he beckoned.

"Well?" inquired the voice of Curtis Warren, as the two conspirators tumbled into the dressing-room and Valvick locked the door. "Did you get it back all right? Did you . . . ?" The warrior stared. Thoughtfully he pushed his helmet forward and scratched his wig. "What's the idea, Hank? You've still got the emerald! Look. . . ."

Morgan nodded wearily. He glanced round. Uncle Jules was on the couch again, sprawled wide, while Peggy was trying to raise his head and insinuate a second dose of baking-soda under his twitching nose. There was a sharp plob as Mrs. Perrigord dexterously opened a bottle of champagne.

"You explain, Skipper." said Morgan, sadly juggling the emerald in his palm. "Suffice it to say that the game is up. U-up. Go on, Captain."

Valvick sketched out a rough outline. "You mean," said Warren, quakes and bubbles beginning to show under his ferocious moustache— "you mean the Bermondsey Terror is down there murdering the old sardine for stealing Hank's watch? Why, oh *why* wasn't I there to see it? Yee-ow! I'd have given anything to see it! Curse the rotten luck, why do I have to miss every good thing . . .?"

Tears had come into Peggy's eyes again.

"But," she protested, "why, oh *why* can't you lay off the poor old captain? What have you got against him, anyway? Why must you go about assaulting the poor dear captain every time you get out of my sight? It isn't fair. It isn't just, after he said he almost had a daughter like me off Cape Hatteras. It—"

"Owful!" said Mrs. Perrigord, clucking her tongue reprovingly. "You owful, naughty boys, you. Have some champagne."

"Well, why hass he got to *be* dere, anyway?" demanded Valvick, hotly. "Ay tell you de old Barnacle call me a t'ief, and now ay am mad. Ay going to find out who iss at de bottom of diss business if ay haff to sving from de yard-arm for it. And ay mean it."

"He was only trying to do his duty, Skipper," said Morgan. "We ought to have been warned. You heard what he said this afternoon: he wanted to have the honour of nabbing Kyle for himself. He and the second officer were probably there searching the cabin when they heard us coming. They ducked into the bathroom and when they opened the door and saw us they thought . . . well, what would *you* have thought? Skipper, it's no go. They'll be having a search party out for us in five minutes. The only thing to do is to go to Whistler, try to explain, and take our medicine. God knows what they'll do to us; plenty, I should think. But . . . there you are."

Valvick brought his arm down in a mighty gesture. "Ay will not! Ay am mad now, and ay will NOT! Barnacle iss not going to put me in de brig like a drunken A.B. while diss crook laughs ha-ha. We are going to hide somewhere, dat iss what, so he don't catch us, and den—"

"What's the good of that?" Morgan wanted to know. "Calm yourself, Skipper. Even if we could hide, which I doubt, what good would it do? We land day after to-morrow, and they'd be bound to catch us. We couldn't stay on the ship. . . ."

"Haff you forgotten dat de New York detective iss coming aboard at Southampton to identify diss crook, eh?"

"Yes, but—"

"And de charge we got to avoid iss stealing de emerald. . . ."

"With others, including Curt's jail-break, assault and battery of Woodcock; to say nothing of—"

"Bah! What iss Woodock? All you got to do iss promise him de bug-powder testimonial and he be all right. As for de odders, what iss dey? When dat detective point out de right man, do you t'ink Whistler going to get away wit' accusing us of stealing? Ay bet you not. Dey only t'ink he iss cuckoo, and den we threaten to tell de newspapers about dat bug-powder gun and dey will giff him de bird something hawful if he open his mouth about de rest! Coroosh! It iss easy. Ay will not be put in dat brig! Dat iss my last word. *'For God. For de cause! For de Church! For de laws!'* Liberty for ever, hooray! Are you wit' me, Mr. Warren?"

"Man, you never said a truer word!" said the Moorish warrior, and gripped his hand. "We'll show 'em, we will! Let 'em try to put me back in that brig!" He flourished his scimitar. Peggy rushed into his arms, beaming through her tears. He burst into song.

> *"May the serr-vice united ne-'er se-ver,*
> *But hold to its co-oolours so true!"*

sang the Moorish warrior, enthusiastically, and Valvick took it up,

> *"Theee ar-my and naaa-avee forever—*
> *Three cheers for the red—white—and blue!"*

"Sh-h!" howled Morgan as the three of them clasped hands in a dramatic gesture. "All right! Have it your way. If you must do it, I suppose I can be as mad as anybody else. Lead on; I'll follow. . . . The point is, where do you propose to hide? . . . Yes, thanks, Mrs. Perrigord, I *will* have some champagne."

Peggy slapped her hands together. "I've got it! I've got it! I know where you'll hide so they won't put you in that nasty brig. You'll hide with the marionettes."

"With the marionettes?"

"Of course, silly! Listen! The marionettes have a cabin of their own, haven't they? Adjoining Uncle Jules's, isn't it? And the stewards are all afraid to go in there, aren't they? And you have three uniforms like the marionettes, haven't you, and false whiskers? And food can be passed in to you from Uncle Jules's cabin, can't it? And if they did look in they'd only see marionettes lying in the berth. Darling, it's wonderful and it'll work, too. . . ."

"I'm glad to hear that," said Morgan. "Without wishing to be a spoil-sport, it would damp my ardour considerably if I had to hang on a hook all day and then found it *didn't* work. Besides, I think enough strain has already been put on Captain Whistler's reason without having a marionette sneeze in his face when he looked into the cabin.

YOU'RE MAD, PEGGY. Besides, how can we get away with it? We're wasting time. The highbrows will be roaring down on this cabin in a minute, asking if Uncle Jules is ready to begin performing, and then we're discovered. This cabin is probably surrounded at the moment, and we can't even get to our hideaway. I also think it probable that a searching-party would feel considerable curiosity concerning three full-panoplied Moorish warriors seen strolling arm in arm down C deck."

Peggy pointed her finger at him.

"No, we're not caught, either! Because you three will climb into those clothes this minute, *and we'll put on the whole performance ourselves.* They won't know you in disguise, and you can help wheel the marionettes back to the cabin and stay there."

There was a silence. Then Morgan got up, with his head in his hands, and danced helplessly.

"Baby, the idea is a knockout!" breathed Warren. "But how are we going to work it? I can stand in front of the stage with a battle-axe right enough; but what about the rest of it? I can't even work those marionettes, to say nothing of what they say. . . ."

"Listen to me. Quick, champagne, somebody!" She snatched a bottle from the beaming Mrs. Perrigord, and after a moment, brilliant with inspiration, she continued: "We'll save Uncle Jules's bacon yet. To begin with, there isn't a real Frenchman aboard this ship, with the exception of Uncle Jules and Abdul. The audience will be mostly kids, or else people with only a smattering of French, out to see the fighting. . . ."

"What about Perrigord?" inquired Warren.

"I'm not forgetting him, darling. That's where Hank comes in. Hank will be the Emperor Charlemagne and also the crafty Banhambra, Sultan of the Moors. . . ."

"Good for you, old man!" applauded Warren, radiating kindliness and slapping the Emperor Charlemagne on the back.

" . . . because I've heard his accent, and it's at least good enough to deceive Perrigord. People will think he *is* Uncle Jules, because we'll stuff him with pillows and disguise him; and when he speaks the prologue it's behind a lighted gauze screen at the back of the stage, and nobody can tell who it is. Yee, this is wonderful, now I think of it! The rest of the time he's out of sight. I have a typewritten copy of his part, and all he has to do is read it. . . . As for working the marionettes, you can master that in ten minutes while Madame Camposozzi is singing and Kyle's reciting and Perrigord is talking. All you need is to be strong in the arms, which is where Curt and the skipper excel, and you can make 'em *fight,* can't you? Well—"

"Yess, but where do ay come in?" asked Valvick. "Ay dunno no French except one or two words. Ay can juggle plates, dough," he suggested hopefully, "and play de piano. . . ."

"You can play the piano? Then," declared Peggy excitedly, "we're absolutely all right. Because, you see, the only other speaking parts are very small—the Knight Roland, the Knight Oliver, and Bishop Turpin. Those parts will be taken by Curt. I'll prompt him roughly, just a few words; but it won't matter what he says, because the skipper will be playing the piano, loud and hard, with appropriate music. . . ."

Morgan roared. He couldn't help it. The strengthening sizzle of champagne cried, "Whee!" along his windpipe; weariness dropped from him. He looked round at the radiant Mrs. Perrigord, who was now seated on the stomach of the prostrate Uncle Jules and looking coyly at him. Again plans began to twist and shift in his brain.

"Right you are!" said he, slapping his hands together. "By Gad! we'll go down in a burst of glory if we do nothing else! It's mad, it's risking a thunderbolt from above, but we'll do it. Up and at 'em! Come on, Skipper; into those uniforms we go—there's no time to be lost. . . ."

There was not. From above began to sound now a measured and steady clapping; a deeper buzz and hum which rattled the lights of the dressing-table. Stopping only to execute a brief gleeful round-the-mulberry-bush with Warren, Peggy rushed to set out the cosmetics.

"And this," continued Morgan, excitedly stripping off his coat, "is where Mrs. Perrigord comes in. Sing your prayers, lads, to the blessed stars that sent her to us to-night. . . ."

"*Gloo!*" crowed Mrs. Perrigord. "Oh, you positively owful man, you mustn't say things like that! Whee!"

" . . . because," he said, tapping Warren on the chest, "she's going to get rid of the people who were to be extras in our places to-night. Don't you see? We can't have anybody behind the scenes but ourselves. Wasn't this Madame Camposozzi to play the piano, and some Russian the violin; yes, and a couple of professors to be warriors . . . ?"

"O Lord! I'd forgotten that!" cried Peggy, freezing. "Oh, Hank, how can we—?"

"Easy! Mrs. Perrigord simply puts on one of those chilly stares of hers when they come down here, and says the places have been filled. We have the organiser of the concert talking for us, and she'll be obeyed; otherwise there'd be a row and we could never wangle it. . . . Listen!" he whirled round to her. "That's all right, isn't it? Mrs. Perrigord—CYNTHIA—you'll do it for me, won't you?"

There was a world of pleading in his voice. The organiser of the concert did not give him a chilly stare. She said, "Oh, you owful man!" and got up and put her arms round his neck.

"No, listen! Wait a bit—listen, Cynthia!" said Morgan desperately. "Listen to what I have to say. Let go, damn it! I tell you we can't lose time! Let me get my waistcoat off. . . ."

"I don't think you're making yourself quite clear," observed Warren critically. "Suppose your wife could see you now, you old rip? Let the poor woman go, can't you?"

"You've *got* to get her in shape to face 'em, Hank!" cried Peggy, flying across the room. "Oh, it's p-perfectly a-aful the w-way we're p-persecuted and t-tortured with these n-nasty drunken p-people . . . !"

"Who's a nasty drunken people, may I ask?" inquired Mrs. Perrigord, suddenly raising a flushed face from Morgan's shoulder.

"All I was saying, darling—"

A fusillade of knocks on the door froze the conspirators where they stood.

"Signor Fortinbras!" exclaimed a voice with a broad rolling accent. The knocks were redoubled.

"Signor Fortinbras! It ees-a me, Signor Benito—Furioso—Camposozzi! Signor Perrigord he weesha to know eef you are alla-right. He—"

Peggy raised a quavering voice. "He is quite all right, Signor Camposozzi. He ees-a—I mean, he is dressing now. Please come back in five minutes. Mrs. Perrigord wishes to speak to you."

"Ah! Good! Tenn-mee-*noots* and we start. Good! Good! I am averra-glad to hear it. Signor Ivan Slifovitz hasa tolda me," bawled Signor Camposozzi, with deplorable Latin lack of reticence, "that he thought you might hava drink too moocha *Gin*. . . ."

"*Gin?*" repeated a sudden, thoughtful, sepulchral voice just behind Morgan. It seemed to come from deep down in the earth. "Gin?"

Uncle Jules abruptly sat up. He slid off the couch. With eyes half-closed and face intent, as though some illuminating idea had come to him, he walked straight to the door.

"*Je vais chercher le gin,*" he explained hurriedly.

Valvick was after him at a bound, but, since his hand was on the knob of the door, nothing less than a full-sized miracle could have prevented discovery if Signor Camposozzi's attention had not been momentarily distracted.

"Eee!" squeaked Signor Camposozzi, for a reason they could not discern. "*Sangua della madonne,* who are you? Go away! You been-a fighting; you area onea begga crook. . . ."

"Now look 'ere, Guv'nor," protested a hoarse voice, "don't run awy, will yer? '*Ere!* Come back! I've got 'ere," continued the Bermondsey Terror, "two gold watches, two sets of cuff-links, two pocket-books, but only one set o' studs. I'm looking for a chap nymed Cap'n Valvick, 'oo owns part of it, and I wants ter 'ave 'im tyke his choice. 'Ere! Come back—I only wanted to ask where I could find—"

There were two sets of frantic footsteps rushing away as the Bermondsey Terror pursued him.

Chapter XVIII

GOLD WATCHES AND DISAPPEARANCE

"A little more larceny, of course," said Morgan, "added to the list of our other offences won't matter a great deal. All the same, Skipper, you'd better stop the Bermondsey Terror and give him time to think up some excuses. Also, it mightn't be a bad idea to retrieve Captain Whistler's best studs and cuff-links."

Valvick took Uncle Jules, who was smiling vacantly, and propped him against the wall with one hand while he unlocked the door. He called "Bermondsey!" and one set of footfalls stopped. Then Valvick set up Uncle Jules like a sign on a couch just beside the door.

"He's coming round," said Warren, inspecting the red face of the puppet-master. "Look here, Baby, what happens to our new scheme if the old geezer wakes up? He may not be too tight to play, after all. Better give him another drink."

"We'll do nothing of the kind!" snapped Peggy. "We don't need to abandon our scheme. If he does come round, we can still hide in the back of the stage. Take off your helmet, Curt, and fill it with water. We'll slosh him down, and then maybe—"

She stopped as the Bermondsey Terror, laden with his plunder, stooped his head under the door. Except for a torn necktie and a scratch down one cheekbone, the Terror was undamaged. A drowsy smile went over his face.

"Ho!" said the Terror. " 'Ere's the stuff, sir. You and t'other gentleman just pick out whatcher want."

Valvick peered out hastily, drew him into the cabin, took the booty from his hands and slid it out of sight along the couch.

"Listen, Bermondsey," he growled, wiping his forehead: "Ay am afraid dere has been a mistake. Ay 'tank you haff smack de wrong men. Ay—"

"Ho?" inquired the Terror. His smile deepened. He wagged his head and closed one eye portentously. 'I sorter thought so, d'yer see, when I see 'oo they wos." Shaken by hoarse mirth, he winked again. "Never yer mind, Guv'nor. Did me good, that workout. Wot's the game? I sorter thought there wos something up when first I see somebody go into the sawbones' room and come out with the green jule thing as *that* gentleman's got now," he nodded at Morgan, who had disentangled himself from Mrs. Perrigord, "and then I see you two take it back. None o' my ruddy bursness, yer see, till you asks for 'elp."

Again he laughed hoarsely. Morgan, to whom had come a glimmer of hope that might avert Peggy's insane idea, took it up.

"Look here, Bermondsey. About those two robbers—just how much damage did you do to them?"

The Terror smiled complacently. He counted a few imaginary stars, closed his eyes, and uttered a snore.

"Out," inquired Morgan.

"Cold," said the Terror.

"Did they see you? Would they know you again, I mean?"

"Ho!" said the Terror. "Not them! Wosn't no light, yer see. 'Ad ter strike a match ter tear the watches orf 'em. Ho-ho-ho!"

"Bermondsey," said Warren, enthusiastically, as the other stared dully at his costume, "I want to shake your hand. I also want to offer you a drink of champagne. . . . What's on your mind, Hank?"

Morgan had begun to stalk about excitedly. He picked up the watches and examined them. Then he put them down on the couch with the emerald elephant.

"If this idea works out," he said, swinging round, "then there'll be no need to lie under a heap of marionettes and play dead for two days. Nor will there be any need to go to the brig, either, for any of us except Curt. . . ."

"That's fine," said Warren. "That's great. Well, all I've got to say is, and I take my oath on it, I am not going back to that damned padded cell, whatever happens! Get me? Furthermore—"

"Shut up, will you?—and listen! You'll need to go back for not more than an hour. The whole point is, Captain Whistler doesn't know you're *out* of the brig, does he? Right. Now don't interrupt. So what have we got? We've got in Bermondsey a witness who can definitely prove we were not stealing that emerald out of Kyle's cabin, but were *returning* it, together with Kyle's papers. Our witness needn't say anything about Curt's having taken it from there. Then—"

"Ahoy dere!" protested Valvick. "Coroosh! you are not going to try to see Barnacle *now*, are you?"

"Listen! Then this is the way it's to be done:

"Peggy takes the note-cases, watches, and the rest of it, including the emerald. She goes to Whistler and says, 'Captain, do you know what the two people you thought were thieves have done? They've saved your

bacon and saved the emerald when it was nearly stolen a second time.'
She then tells a story of how, as we were passing by, the skipper and I
saw a mysterious masked stranger—"

"Horse feathers!" said Warren, with some definiteness. "You're
drunk."

Morgan steadied himself. "All right, we'll omit the mask then. We saw
this stranger sneaking out of Kyle's cabin laden with Kyle's papers and
the emerald. We set on him; and, although he got away without our
learning who he was, we retrieved the whole thing. . . ." A howl of
protest arose, and Morgan regarded them sardonically. "Actually, the
reason why you oppose it is that you want to hide in with the marionettes
and put on that damned show, don't you? Isn't that true?"

"Yes, ay know," Valvick growled stubbornly, "but what about dem
getting beaten up?"

"That's part of it. You don't honestly imagine even old Whistler would
believe *we'd* pinch his watch and cuff-links, do you? Very well: Admittedly we were in a bad position and acted hastily when we ran out on him.
But our mythical crook, who was ever in attendance, is on the watch;
and, thinking Whistler's got the emerald from us, bursts in. By the use
of a bottle as a weapon—that's Whistler's own story, remember, and
he's got to stick to it whether he believes it or not—the crook lays
low the captain and the second officer, and he makes a clean haul of everything. . . ."

He stopped, feeling that the story sounded thin even to his own ears;
yet also convinced that their own plan was even more impracticable. It
was a case of Mephistopheles or deep water, a toss-up of two insanities,
but at least his scheme might do something towards soothing the gigantic
wrath of Captain Whistler. Warren grunted.

"And then you and Valvick attack this crook again, I suppose?" he
asked. "Hank, it's the bunk. I'm surprised at you."

"*No!* You don't understand. The crook, groggy from Captain Whistler's powerful smashes, staggers away to fall. We, roused by the noise,
return. We find the plunder again. At first we daren't take it to Whistler,
knowing what he'll think. But Peggy, seeing we have nothing to fear
from our noble conduct, persuades us—"

He saw that Valvick was wavering and scratching his chin, and said
desperately:

"Let's put it to a vote. We do this, while Curt returns to the brig and
pacifies Woodcock by a definite promise to get him the testimonial.
Listen!" An inspiration struck him. "Do you realise that, while Captain
Whistler's authority only extends over the high seas, Woodcock is a
private citizen and can prosecute in the civil courts? He can get a
thousand pounds damages for that, and *he's* not got any false dignity to

restrain him. Do you want to go to jail, Curt? Well, if you leave Woodcock tied up there much longer—and they may not discover him until to-morrow—he'll be so wild that a bug-powder testimonial from the President himself wouldn't keep him quiet. For God's sake, get the champagne out of your brains for three seconds and think! You needn't stay in the brig any longer than you like, Curt. Whistler's promised to let you out."

"I still vote No," said Warren. A babble of voices arose, while they got together in the middle of the cabin waving their arms and shouting. Mrs. Perrigord said it was oll owfully clever, and she voted as Henry did.

"Eee! Stop it!" cried Peggy, clapping her hands to her ears. "Listen. Let *me* talk. I'll admit I think it would be rather nice to go to the captain and make goo-goo eyes at him, sort of. Wait! But we'll let it rest on Uncle Jules and—I don't care what you say, he's my uncle, and I won't have him g-guyed because they s-say he's too drunk to—"

"Steady now!" said Warren, as she shook her fists desperately.

". . . to play. And we'll let it rest at that. If he's sober enough to play inside of, say fifteen minutes or half an hour, we can hold the curtain until then; we'll adopt Hank's idea. If not, then we'll carry on as we'd intended. . . . What's that noise?" She broke off suddenly. Her smeary eyes travelled past Morgan's shoulder and widened. Then she screamed.

"Where," said Peggy, *"is Uncle Jules?"*

The door of the cabin was lightly banging with the slight roll of the ship.

Uncle Jules was gone. Also missing were the watches, the cuff-links, the note-case, the studs, and the emerald elephant.

Chapter XIX

INDISCRETIONS OF UNCLE JULES

The Moorish warrior removed his spiked helmet and flung it on the floor.

"Sunk!" he said wildly. "Sunk! Done brown. Come on, take our vote if we want to, but we can't do either one thing or the other now. I'm getting sick of this. What's the matter with the old soak? Is he a kleptomaniac?"

"You let him alone!" cried Peggy. "He can't help it. He's drunk, poor darling. Oh, *why* didn't I think? He's done it before. Only mostly it's only motor-car keys, and there's not an awful lot of harm done, in spite of what awful people say. . . ."

"What do you mean, motor-car keys?"

Her eyes wrinkled up. "Why, the keys of the cars, you know; things you turn on the ignition with. He waits till somebody goes away, leaving the key in the car, and then he sneaks up ever so softly and pinches the key out. Then he goes away somewhere until he can find a fence, and throws the key over it. After that he goes on to find another car. There was a most horrible row in St. Louis because he got loose in a ground where they park cars, and pinched thirty-eight keys at one haul. . . . But why don't you *do* something? Go after him! Get him back before they find—"

"HAH!" cried a furious voice.

The door was flung open. Fat-faced, with vast trembling cheeks, sinister beetle brows and vast moustachios, a tubby little man stood in the doorway. He pointed at Peggy.

"So! So! You have trieda to de-ceive me, eh? You have a trieda toa deceive Signor Benito Furiosa Camposozzi, eh? *Sangua della madonne,* I feex you! You tella me he eesa all-right, eh? Haah! What you call all-aright, eh? I tell you, signorina, tó youra face, he ees-a DRUNK!" Signor Camposozzi was breathing so hard that he choked. Peggy hurried up to him.

"You saw him? Oh, please tell me! Where is he?"

Signor Camposozzi raised one arm to heaven, slapped his forehead, and the whites of his eyes rolled up horribly.

"Sooah? You aska me if I see heem? Haah! I weela tella you! Never have I beena so *insulted!* I go up to him. I say, 'Signor Fortinbras!' He say, 'Shhh-h!' In heesa hands he hasa got fourteen gold watches and pocket-books. He open theesa pocket-books and handa me—ME—he handa me wan pound *note.* He say, 'Sh-hh! You buya me onea bottle of gin, eh? Sh-h!' Den he go off asaying, 'Shh-h!' and a pooshing wan pound note under every door he see. I say—"

"There goes the old swordfish's dough," said Warren, staring from under his villainous eyebrows. "Look, Mr. Sozzi, listen. Did you see—I mean, did he have a kind of a jewel thing with him? A sort of green thing on a gold chain?"

"Haah! Dida I *see* it?" inquired Signor Camposozzi, with a withering leer. "He hasa fasten it around his neck."

Morgan turned to Valvick. "The fat's in the fire now anyway, Skipper," he said. "Whatever else we do, we can't be marionettes. But if it occurs to Uncle Jules to give that emerald away to somebody . . . well, we can't be in more trouble than we are. We'd better go after him. No, Curt! No! You're not coming, do you hear?"

"Certainly I'm coming," said Warren, drawing his scimitar again and placing a bottle of champagne in the pocket of his robe. "Think I'm going to miss this? It's absolutely safe. My own mother wouldn't recognise me in this outfit. If we run into the old haddock or anybody, I can simply gesture and say, 'No speeka da Eenglish.' See?"

As a matter of fact, he was the first one out the door. Nobody protested. The fat was now sizzling and flaring in the fire anyway; and, Morgan reflected, at least three people were better than two at nobbling Uncle Jules—provided they could find him—before he gave away Captain Whistler's watch to somebody and left a trail of Captain Whistler's money all along C deck. Also, they were joined by the Bermondsey Terror.

"Head for the bar!" said Morgan as the three of them charged up the passage. "He'll go in that direction by instinct. No, not that way. Turn round and go by the port side, or we may run into Whistler and his crowd. . . ."

They stopped. A confused noise was beginning to bellow down in the direction of cabin C 46; the patter of running feet, excited voices, and a stentorian ocean-going call to arms. The four allies instantly shifted their course and made for the forward part of the boat—a fortunate circumstance, since they picked up Uncle Jules's trail within a few seconds. Indeed, nobody but Messrs. Lestrade, Gregson, and Athelney Jones could have missed it. Two or three doors were open, and infuriated passengers, clad only in dress trousers, and dress shirts hanging out over them, were dancing stockingless in the doors while they bawled at a dazed steward.

"I couldn't *'elp* it!" protested the steward. "I tell you, sir—"

"You!" said Warren, presenting the point of his scimitar at the steward's breast, an apparition which nearly brought a scream bubbling from between the other's lips. "You!" he repeated, as the steward strove to run. "Have you seen him? A bald-headed drunk with a prizefighter's shoulders and his hands full of stuff?"

"Yes! Y-yes, sir! Take that thing away! Just gone! Did he get yours too?"

"My what?"

"Shoes!" said the steward.

"I'll have the law on this line!" screamed one maddened passenger, laying hold of the steward's collar. "I'll sue 'em for the biggest damages ever awarded in a court. I'll complain to the captain. I put my shoes outside my door to be polished, and when I go to get 'em what do I see but—"

"He's stolen every damn shoe that was outside a door!" snorted another, who was sniffing after shoes up and down the passage like a terrier. "Where's the captain? Who was it? Who—"

"Come *on*," said Captain Valvick. "Out on de deck and go round."

They found a door forward, and plunged out on C deck—on the same deck and the same side that had seen the hurricane of the night before. As before, it was dimly lighted, but this time peaceful. They paused and stared round, breathing cool air after the thick atmosphere inside. And Morgan, as he peered down a companion-way leading to D deck, came face to face with Mr. Charles Woodcock.

Somebody swore, and then there was silence.

Mr. Woodcock was coming slowly and rather painfully up the steps. Aside from rumpled clothes, he was undamaged, but every joint was cramped from his long trussing in torn sheets. His bush of hair waved in the breeze. He writhed his shoulders, cracking the knuckles of his hands; and on his bony face, as he looked up and saw who stood there, was an expression—

Morgan stared as he saw that look. He had expected many things from the unfortunate bug-powder representative, triumph, threats, rumpled dignity swearing vengeance, sinister joviality, at all events hostility. But here was an expression which puzzled him. Woodcock had stiffened. His tie was blown into his face and seemed to tickle his nose and terrify him like the brushing of a bat in the dark. His bony hand jerked. There was a silence but for seething water. . . .

"So it's *you* again," said Warren, and slapped the scimitar against his leg.

Woodcock recognised the voice. He glanced from Warren to Morgan.

"Listen!" he said, clearing his throat. "Listen! Don't fly off the handle now. I want you to unnastand something. . . ."

This looked inexplicably like retreat. As startled by Woodcock's appearance as he had evidently been by theirs, Morgan nevertheless cut in before Warren could speak again.

"Well?" he demanded, and assumed by instinct an ominous tone. "Well?"

The pale smile fluttered on Woodcock's face. "What I wantcha to unnastand, old man," he said, writhing his shoulders again and speaking very rapidly, "is that *I* wasn't responsible for you being stuck in that brig, even if you think I was; honest to God I wasn't. Look, I'm not mad at you, even if you've hurt me so bad I'll maybe have to go to the hospital. That's what you've done—but you can see I'm not mad, can't you, old man? Maybe it was right for you to take a sock at me—from what you thought, I mean. I know how it is when you get mad. A guy can't help himself. But when I told you—you know, what I did tell you—it was absolutely in good faith. . . ."

There was something so utterly suspicious and guilty-seeming about the man that even the Bermondsey Terror, who had evidently no idea what this was all about, took a step forward.

" 'Ere!" he said. "Oo's *this?*"

"Come up here, Mr. Woodcock," said Morgan quietly. He jabbed his elbow into Warren's ribs to keep him quiet. "You mean that you really didn't see that film stolen out of Curt Warren's cabin, after all?"

"I did! I swear I did, old man!"

"Attempted blackmail, eh?" asked the Moorish warrior, who had opened his eyes wide and was fiddling with the scimitar.

"No! No! I tell you it was a mistake, and I can prove it. I mean, it may *look* like the man I saw isn't on board at all, but he is! He's got to be. He must have been disguised or something. . . ."

A dim suspicion that at last the Parcæ had got tired of tangling things up for their particular crowd, and had begun on somebody else, began to grow hopefully in Morgan's mind.

"Let's hear your side of the story," he said, playing a chance. "Then we'll decide. What do you have to say about it?"

Woodcock came up to the deck. A scowl, of which neither of them probably knew the reason, had overspread the rather grim faces of large Valvick and even larger Bermondsey. Woodcock saw it, and veered like a sloop in a windward breeze.

Clearing his throat, he set himself amiably for a hypnotic speech.

"So listen, old man. I *did* see that guy; word of honour. But after I talked to you to-day I said to myself, I said, 'Charley, that fellow Warren's a real white man, and he's promised to get the testimonial for you. And you're a man of your word, Charley,' I said," lowering his voice, 'so you'll get the name of the man for him'. . . ."

"You mean you didn't know his *name?*" demanded Woodcock urgently. "Think what I said! Remember what I said! And what I said was, I'd know him if I saw him again. And, damn it! he had to be on the boat, didn't he? So I thought I'd look around and find out who it was. Well, all the possible people were at meals to-day, and I looked, and he wasn't there! So I thought, 'What the hell?' and I began to get scared," he swallowed hard; "so I went to the purser, and described the man as somebody I wanted to meet. I couldn't miss him; I remembered everything, including a funny-looking ear and a strawberry mark on the fellow's cheek. And the purser said, 'Charley,' he said, 'there's nobody like that aboard.' And then I thought, 'Disguise!' But yet it couldn't have been anybody I'd already seen, because I'd have known 'em disguise or no disguise—shape of the face, no whiskers, all that." He was growing unintelligible, but he rushed on. "And then I heard you'd been put in the brig because the captain had accused you of making a false accusation about somebody; and I thought, 'O God, Charley, this is all your fault and he won't believe you really did see that.' When I got your note to come down, I thought you mightn't blame me after all; but as soon as you hit me—Listen, I'll make it up to you. I'm no crook, I swear. . . ."

Good old Parcæ! Morgan felt a rush of gratitude even for this small favour of averting charges of assault and battery, or whatever else might have occurred to Mr. Woodcock in a more rational moment.

"You hear what Mr. Woodcock says, Curt?" asked Morgan.

"I hear it," Warren said, in a curious tone. He smoothed at his whiskers and looked meditatively at the scimitar.

"And you're willing to admit the mistake," pursued Morgan, "and let bygones be bygones if Mr. Woodcock is? Righto! Of course Mr. Woodcock will realise from a business point of view he no longer has any right to ask for that testimonial. . . ."

"Hank, old man," said Mr. Woodcock, with great earnestness, "what I say is, To hell with the testimonial. And the bug-powder business too. This isn't my game, and I might as well admit it. I can sell things— there's not a better little spieler on the European route than Charley R. Woodcock, if I do say it myself—but for the big business side of it, *ixnay*. No soap. Through. But I'm entirely willing, old man, to give you all the help I can. You see I kept bumping myself against the wall down there in that cell until the sailor looked in; and finally I got the gag out of my mouth. Well, he released me and went off to find the captain. And I'd better tell you—"

From somewhere on the other side of the deck rose a shout. A door wheezed and slammed, and the clatter of feet rushed nearer.

"*There he goes!*" said a voice and, rising above it, they heard the view-halloo bellow of Captain Whistler.

"Don't run!" wheezed Valvick. "Don't run, ay tell you, or you may run into him. Down de companion-ladder—'ere!—all of you. Watch! Maybe dey don't see. . . ."

As the distant din of pursuit grew, Valvick shoved the Moorish warrior down the steps and the Bermondsey Terror after him. The Bug-powder Boy, full of new terrors, tumbled down first. Crouching on the iron steps beside Valvick, Morgan thrust his head up to look along C deck. And he saw a rather impressive sight. He saw Uncle Jules.

Far up ahead, faint and yet discernible in the dim lights, Uncle Jules turned the corner round the forward bulkhead and moved majestically towards them. The breeze blew up his fringe of hair like a halo. His gait was intent, determined, even with a hint of stateliness; yet in it there were the cautious indications of one who suspects he is being followed. A lighted porthole attracted his attention. He moved towards it, so that his red, determined, screwed-up face showed leering against the light. He stuck his head partly inside.

"Sh-h-h!" said Uncle Jules, lifting his finger to his lip.

"Eeee!" shrieked a feminine voice inside. "EEEEEE!"

A look of mild annoyance crossed Uncle Jules's face. "Sh!" he urged. After peering cautiously around, he searched among the bundle of articles he was carrying, selected what appeared to be a gold watch, and carefully tossed it through the porthole. *"Onze!"* he whispered. They heard it crash on the floor inside. Uncle Jules moved towards the rail of the boat with an air of impartiality. With fierce care he selected a pair of patent-leather dancing-pumps and tossed them overboard.

"Douze!" counted Uncle Jules. *"Treize, quatorze—"*

"Eee!" still shrieked the feminine voice as a stream of articles began to go overboard. Uncle Jules seemed annoyed at this interruption. But he was willing to indulge the vagaries of the weaker sex.

"Vous n' amiez-pas cette montre, hein?" he asked solicitously. *"Es-ce-que vous aimez l' argent?"*

The din of pursuit burst with a crash of sound round the corner of the deck ahead, led by Captain Whistler and Second-Officer Baldwin. They stopped, stricken. They were just in time to see Uncle Jules empty the contents of Captain Whistler's wallet through the porthole. Then, with swift impartiality, he flew to the rail. Overboard, clear-sailing against the moonlight, went Captain Whistler's watch, Captain Whistler's cuff-links, Captain Whistler's studs—and the emerald elephant.

"Dix-sept, dix-huit, dix-neuf, VINGT!" whispered Uncle Jules triumphantly. Then he turned round, saw his pursuers and said *"Sh-hhh!"*

There are times when action is impossible. Morgan laid his face against the cold iron step, his muscles turning to water, and groaned so deeply that under ordinary circumstances the pursuers must have heard him.

But they did not hear him. Not unreasonably, they had failed to observe the strict letter of Uncle Jules's parting injunction. The noises that arose as the pack closed in on Uncle Jules awoke the sleeping gulls to scream and wheel on the water. They were terrifying noises. But, just as Morgan and Warren were rising again, the implications of one remark struck them motionless.

"So that," bellowed the appalled voice of Captain Whistler, strangled with incoherent fury, "so *that's* the man, is it, who burst in there and—and launched the m-most murderous attack on us that—"

"Sure it is, sir," said the hardly less sane voice of Second-Officer Baldwin. "Look at him! Look at those arms and shoulders! Nobody but somebody used to swinging those—marionettes day after day could've had the strength to hit like that. There's nobody on the ship who could've done it else. . . ."

"Ho?" muttered the Bermondsey Terror, starting violently.

"Shh!" hissed Captain Valvick.

". . . No, sir," pursued Baldwin, "he's not a crook. But he's a notorious drunkard. I know all about him. A drunkard, and that's the sort of thing he does. . . ."

"Pardonnez-moi, messieurs," rumbled a polite if muffled voice from

under what appeared to be many bodies. *"Es-ce-que vous pouvez me donner du gin?"*

"He—he threw that—that emer—" Whistler gulped amid strange noises. "But what about—those—young Morgan—Sharkmeat—those—"

Somebody's heels clicked. A new voice put in: "Will you let me offer an explanation, sir? I'm Sparks, sir. I saw part of it from my cousin's cabin. If you'll let me tell you, sir, that young fellow and the Swede weren't trying to steal—you know. They were trying to return it. I saw them. They're close friends of Miss Glenn, this man's niece; and I should think they were trying to cover him up after the old drunk had stolen it. . . ."

"FROM DR. KYLE'S CABIN? What the hell do you mean? They—"

"Sir, if you'll listen to me!" roared Baldwin. "Sparks is right. Don't you see what happened? This kleptomaniac souse is the man who stole the emerald from you last night! Who else could have hit you as hard as that? And didn't he act last night exactly as he's acting to-night, sir? Look here: you were standing near where you are now. And what did he do? He did exactly what we saw him do to-night—he chucked that jewel through the nearest port, which happened to be Dr. Kyle's, and it landed behind the trunk. . . . He's drunk, sir, and not responsible; but that's what happened. . . ."

There was an awed silence.

"By God!" said Captain Whistler. "By God! . . . But wait! It was returned to Lord Sturton—"

"Sir," said Baldwin wearily, "don't you realise that this souse's niece and their crowd have been trying to protect him all the time? One of 'em returned it, that's all, and I sort of admire the sport who did. The drunk stole it again, so they decided they'd put it back in the doc's cabin where the drunk had a fixed idea it ought to go, and then tip off somebody to find it. Only we wouldn't let them explain, sir. We—er—we owe 'em an apology."

"One of you," said the captain crisply, "go to Lord Sturton; present my compliments, and say that I will wait on him immediately. GET ME SOME ROPES AND TIE THIS LUBBER UP. YOU!" said Captain Whistler, evidently addressing Uncle Jules, "is—this—true?"

Morgan risked a look. Captain Whistler's back was turned among the group of figures on the deck, so that Morgan could not see the new damage to his face. But he saw Uncle Jules struggling to sit upright among the hands that held him. With a fierce expression of concentration on his face, Uncle Jules wrenched his vast shoulders and flung off the hands. A solitary pair of shoes remained gripped close to him. With a last effort he sent the shoes sailing overboard; then he breathed deeply, smiled, rolled over gently on the deck, and began to snore. "Ha, whee!" breathed Uncle Jules, with a long sigh of contentment.

"Take him away," said Whistler, "and lock him up."

A trampling of feet ensued. Morgan, about to get up, was restrained by Valvick.

"It iss all right!" he whispered fiercely. "Ay know how seafaring men iss. Dey get hawful mad, but dey will not prosecute if dey t'ink a mann iss drunk. De code iss dat whatever you do when you iss drunk, a yentleman goes light on. Shh! Ay know. Listen—!"

They listened carefully while Captain Whistler relieved his mind for some moments. Then he took on a more tragic note in mourning his watch and valuables, thus gradually working himself up to a dizzy pitch when he came to the last trouble.

"So that's the thief I was supposed to have aboard, eh?" he wanted to know. "A *common drunk,* who throws fifty-thousand-pound emeralds overboard, who—who—"

Baldwin said gloomily: "You see now why that young Warren pretended to act like a madman, sir? He's more or less engaged to the girl, they tell me. Well, they made a good job of it shielding him. But I've got to admit we've been a bit rough on—"

"Sir," said a new voice, "Lord Sturton's compliments, sir, and—"

"Go on," sneered the captain, with a sort of heavy-stage-despair. "Don't stop there. Speak up, will you? Let's hear it!"

"Well, sir—he—he says for you to go to hell, sir. . . ."

"What?"

"He says—I'm only repeating it—he says you're drunk, sir. He says nobody's stolen his emerald, and he got it out and showed it to me to prove it. He's in a bit of a temper, sir. He says if he hears one more word about that bleeding emerald—if anybody makes a row or so much as mentions that bleeding emerald to him again—he'll have your papers and sue the line for a hundred thousand pounds. That's a fact."

"Here, Mitchell!" snapped Baldwin. "Don't stand there like a dummy! Come and give me a hand with the commander. . . . Get some brandy or something. Hurry, damn you, hurry!"

There was a sound of running footsteps. Then up from behind Morgan, an expression of dreamy triumph on his face, rose Curtis Warren full panoplied in Moorish arms. He pushed past the others and ascended the ladder. Drawing his bejewelled cloak about him, shooting back the cuffs of his chain mail, he adjusted the spiked helmet rakishly over the curls of his wig. He drew himself up with a haughty gesture. Before the bleary eyes of the *Queen Victoria*'s skipper, who was reeling dumbly against the rail and almost toppling overboard, Warren strode forward with ringing footfalls.

He paused before Whistler. Lifting the scimitar like an accusing finger, he pointed it at the captain.

"Captain Whistler," he said in a voice of shocked and horrified rebuke, "after all your suspicions of innocent men . . . Captain Whistler, AREN'T—YOU—ASHAMED OF YOURSELF?"

Chapter XX

DISCLOSURE

In a certain big room above Adelphi Terrace, a misted sun was beginning to lengthen the shadows. It was beginning to make a dazzle against a huddle of purpling towers westward at the curve of the river; and from one of these towers Big Ben had just finished clanging out the hour of four. A very hoarse story-teller listened to the strokes reverberating away. Then Morgan sat back.

Dr. Fell removed his glasses. With a large red bandana he mopped a moisture of joy from his eyes, said, "Whoosh!" with a wheezing and expiring chuckle, and rumbled:

"No, I'll never forgive myself for not being there. My boy, it's an epic. Oh, Bacchus, what I'd give for one glimpse of Uncle Jules in his last *moment suprême!* Or of the old mollusc, Captain Whistler, either. But surely that's not all?"

"It's all," said Morgan wearily, "I have the voice to tell you now. Also, I imagine, it's all that's relevant to the issue. If you think the fireworks ended there, of course, you still haven't plumbed the spiritual possibilities of our crowd. I could fill a fair number of pages with the saga of pyrotechnics between nine-fifteen night before last, when Uncle Jules threw his last gallant shoe, until 7 A.M. this morning, when I slipped away from a ship accursed. But I can give you only a general outline. . . . Besides, I hesitated to include all the things I have. It was hair-raising action, if you like, but it seemed to me not to have any bearing on the vital issues. . . ."

Dr. Fell finished mopping his eyes and subsided in dying chuckles. Then he blinked across the table.

"Curiously enough, that's where you're wrong," he said. "Now I can say positively that it's a pleasure to me to find a case in which the most important clues are jokes. If you had omitted any point of that recital I should have been cheated of valuable evidence. The cuckoo's call is the lion's roar, and a jack-in-the-box has a disconcerting habit of showing a thief's face. But the clues are sealed now; you've provided me with my second eight. H'm! Four o'clock. It's too late to do anything more, or hear anything that can help me further. If I'm right, I should know it shortly. If not, the Blind Barber has got away. Still—"

There was a ring downstairs at the bell.

For a moment Dr. Fell sat motionless, only his great stomach heaving, and he seemed flushed and rather uneasy.

"If I'm wrong—" he said. Then he struggled to his feet. "I'll answer that ring myself. Just glance over this notation, will you? Here's a list of my second eight clues. See if they convey anything?"

While he was gone Morgan drew out a full bottle of beer from the troop of dead guardsmen that stood at attention on the table. He grinned. Whatever had happened, it was something to write in the note-book. "?" he said, and read on the slip of paper:

9. The Clue of Wrong Rooms.
10. The Clue of Lights.
11. The Clue of Personal Taste.
12. The Clue of Avoided Explanations.
13. The Clue Direct.
14. The Clue of Known Doubles.
15. The Clue of Misunderstanding.
16. The Clue Conclusive.

He was still frowning over it when Dr. Fell stumped back, leaning on his two canes. Under one arm Dr. Fell held a package wrapped in brown paper, and in the other an envelope ripped open. Many things he could conceal: the insight and strategy of his nimble, rocket-brilliant, childlike brain, and these he could conceal because, out of a desire to spring his surprise, he liked to fog them round with genial talk. But a certain relief he could not conceal. Morgan saw it and half rose from his chair.

"Rubbish, rubbish!" boomed the doctor, nodding jovially. "Sit down, sit down! Heh! As I was about to say—"

"Have you—?"

"Now, now! Let me get comfortab . . . aah! So. Well, my boy, whatever's done is already done. Either the Blind Barber has got away or he hasn't. If he has got away, I think it's highly likely we shall catch him sooner or later. I don't think he intended to keep his present disguise after he had landed in either France or England; then, safely out of it, he could perform another of his quick changes and disappear. He's by way of being a genius. I wonder who he really is?"

"But you said—"

"Oh, I know the name he's using at the moment. But I warned you long ago that the garb was only a mask and a dummy; and I should like to see how his real mind works. . . . In any event, the boat has docked. Didn't you tell me that young Warren was coming to see me? What arrangements have you made about that?"

"I gave him your address and said to look up the phone number if he needed to communicate. He and Peggy and the old man are coming on to London as soon as they can get the boat train. But listen! *Who is it?* Is he going to get away, after all? What, in God's name, is the real explanation of the whole thing?"

"Heh!" said Dr. Fell. "Heh-heh! You read my last eight clues and still don't know? You had the evidence of that steel box staring you in the face and still couldn't make your wits work? Tut, now, I don't blame you. You were doing too much action to think. If a man's required to turn round every second and pick up a new person who has been knocked out by somebody, he isn't apt to have much time for cool reflection. . . . You see this parcel?" He put it on the table. "No, don't look at it just yet. We've still some time before a final consultation, and there are a few points on which I should like enlightenment. . . . What was the upshot of the matter after Uncle Jules was haled away to clink? Does Whistler still think Uncle Jules was the thief? And what about the marionette show? The thing seems to me to be incomplete. From the very first, as a matter of fact, I had a strong feeling that your band would somehow be enticed into that marionette show and would be forced by the Parcæ into putting on a performance. . . ."

Morgan scratched his ear.

"As a matter of fact," he said, "we did. It was Peggy's fault for insisting on our saving Uncle Jules's bacon. She said if we didn't she'd go straight to the captain and tell him everything. We pointed out that, whatever the explanations might have been, Uncle Jules really had left a brilliant trail of shoes in our wake; that Captain Whistler was not in the mood to smile indulgently when his fifty-guinea watch sailed overboard; and after all Uncle Jules was better off in the brig. We also pointed out that, just prior to his capture, he had been seen marching through the bar and placing a shoe in the hand of any person who took his fancy. Consequently, we said, it would not appear probable to the passengers that he could work his marionette show that night."

"And then?"

Morgan shook his head gloomily.

"Well, she wouldn't hear of it. She said it was our fault that he'd done all of it. She pointed out that most of the passengers were in the concert-hall, applauding for the show to go on, and the person she was really afraid of was Perrigord. Perrigord had prepared an elaborate and powerful speech commemorating Uncle Jules's genius, and had just begun it at the moment Uncle Jules was firing shoes overboard. Peggy said if a good performance didn't go on, Perrigord would be made out such an ass that he'd never let up on Uncle Jules in the papers, and their success depended on him. The girl was loony and wouldn't see reason. At last we promised her we'd do it if she'd consent to allow Uncle Jules to stay in the brig. It was the best way out for everybody, for they'll forgive a drunk's insanities when they'll prosecute an honest mistake. Curt insisted on paying for the damage, which amounted, all in all, to close on two hundred pounds. And we felt it was time for peace to descend on the *Queen Victoria.* . . ."

"Well?"

"It didn't," said Morgan gloomily. " I begged and pleaded with Peggy. I told her some damned thing was bound to happen if we tried to work that show, and Perrigord would be more infuriated than though there'd been no performance. She wouldn't see it. She wouldn't even see it when we had one brief rehearsal of the first scene. My portrayal of Charlemagne, I flatter myself, would have been eloquent and kingly, but Curt, in the role of Roland got stage-struck at the rehearsal and insisted on dictating a long consular report in French about the facts and figures in the export of sardines from Lisbon. Captain Valvick at the piano would have been an error. It was not merely that he wanted to greet the entrance of the Frankish army with the strains of 'La Madelon,' but since somebody had informed him in general terms that Moors were 'black men,' then the crafty Sultan of the Moors would have made his entrance with 'Old Man River.' Next—"

"Hold on!" said Dr. Fell, whose eyes were growing bright with tears again, and who had clapped a hand over his mouth as he trembled. "I don't quite understand this. It should have been one of your high lights, *Why are you so reluctant to talk about it?* Out with it now! Was there, or wasn't there a performance?"

"Well—yes and again no," replied Morgan, shifting uneasily. "It started, anyway. Oh, I'll admit it saved our lives in a way, because the old dabble Parcæ were working for us now; but I'd rather not have had it saved in that way. . . . Have you noticed that I've not seemed too cheerful to-day! Have you also noticed that I'm not accompanied by my wife? She was supposed to meet me at Southampton, but at the last minute I sent her a radiogram not to come, because I was afraid some of the passengers might—"

Dr. Fell sat up.

"If I've got to tell it," said Morgan wryly, "I suppose I must. Fortunately, we got no farther than the first scene, wherein Charlemagne speaks the prologue. I was Charlemagne. Charlemagne wore long white whiskers; his venerable head was adorned with a gold crown studded with diamonds and rubies; a mantle of scarlet and ermine swathed his mighty shoulders; a jewelled broadsword was buckled about his waist, and under his chain mail his stomach was stuffed with four sofa-pillows to give him *embonpoint*. I was Charlemagne.

"Charlemagne spoke the prologue behind an illuminated gauze screen, like a tall picture-frame, at the rear of the stage. Yes. And how. Mr. Leslie Perrigord had just concluded an impassioned speech lasting fifty-five minutes to the tick. Mr. Perrigord said that this performance was the goods. He said he hoped his hearers, with minds made torpid by the miasmatic sluggishness of Hollywood, would receive a refreshing shock as they watched enthralled this drama in which every gesture recorded an aspiration of the human soul. He said to watch closely, even though they would not fully appreciate its lights and shadings, its subtle groupings and baffling harmonies of line, its bold chords on the metaphysical yearning of man, not surpassed in the mightiest pages of Ibsen. He also said a number of complimentary things about the prowess of Charlemagne. I was Charlemagne.

"When at length he ran out of breath, he stopped. There were three hollow knocks. Captain Valvick, despite all that could be done to stop him, played an overture consisting of 'La Marseillaise.' The curtain flew up a bit prematurely, I fear. Among eighty-odd others, Mr. Perrigord saw the gauze screen glowing luminous against darkness, and full of rich colour. He saw the venerable Charlemagne. He also saw his wife. The position was—er—full of subtle groupings and baffling harmonies of line. Yes. That was the moment at which the chain mail split and the sofa-pillows flew out as though they had been fired from a gun. I was Charlemagne. . . . Now, maybe you understand why I do not care to incorporate it into the body of the story. I have no doubt that the audience received a refreshing shock as they watched enthralled this drama in which every gesture recorded an aspiration of the human soul."

Morgan took a deep drink of beer.

Dr. Fell turned his face towards the window. Morgan observed that his shoulders were quivering as though with shock and outrage.

"In any event, it saved us, and it saved Uncle Jules for ever. The roar of applause which went up pleased everybody except possibly Mr. Perrigord. Such an instantaneous success was never achieved in any theatre by a performance which lasted only long enough for somebody to drop the curtain. Uncle Jules's marionette theatre in Soho will be crowded to the end of his days whether he's drunk or sober. And rest solemnly assured that, whatever he happens to feel about it, Mr. Leslie Perrigord will never write in the newspapers a word to condemn him."

The declining sun drew lower across the carpet, resting on the brown-wrapped parcel in the middle of the table. After a time, Dr. Fell turned back.

"So—" he observed, his face gradually becoming less red as quiet settled down—"so it all ends happily, eh? Except perhaps for Mr. Perrigord and—the Blind Barber."

He opened a penknife and weighed it in his hand.

"Yes," said Morgan. "Yes, except in one sense. After all, the fact remains that—whatever little game *you're* playing—we still don't know a blasted thing that's important. We don't know what happened on that ship, although, in spite of all the foolery, we know there was a murder. And a murder isn't especially funny. Nor is, actually, the fact that Curt hasn't recovered his film, and, however ridiculous that looks, to him and to others it's as desperately serious a matter as any."

"Oh?" grunted Dr. Fell. "Well, well!" he said, deprecatingly, and winked one eye, "if that's all you want. . . ."

Suddenly he reached across the table and cut the strings of the parcel with his knife.

"I thought—" he added, beaming, as his hand dived among the wrappings and lifted up a tangled coil of film like a genial Laocoön, "I thought it might be better to have it sent up here before the police rake over the Blind Barber's effects and cause scandal by finding this. I'll hand it over to young Warren when he arrives, so that he can destroy it immediately; although, in return for the favour, do you think he would consent to running it privately, just once, for my benefit? Heh-heh-heh! Hang it all, I think I can insist on *that* much reward, hey? Of course, it's holding back evidence, in a way. But there'll be enough to hang the Barber without it. It was my price for pointing out the culprit to Captain Whistler and handing him the credit of capturing a dangerous criminal. I felt the old sea-horse would comply. . . ."

Tossing the rustling coil across on Morgan's arm, Dr. Fell sat back and blinked. Morgan was on his feet, staring.

"You mean, then, the man is under arrest already?"

"Oh, yes. Caught neatly by the brilliant Captain Whistler—who will get a medal for this, and completing everybody's happiness—an hour before the ship docked. Inspector Jennings, at my suggestion, went down from the Yard in a fast car and was ready to take the Barber in charge when he landed. . . ."

"Ready to take *who* in charge?" he demanded.

"Why, the impostor who calls himself Lord Sturton, of course!" said Dr. Fell.

Chapter XXI

THE MURDERER

"I perceive on your face," continued the doctor affably, as he lit his pipe, "a certain frog-like expression which would seem to indicate astonishment. H'm! puff, puff, haaaa! You should not be in the least astonished. Under the data given, as I have tabulated in my sixteen clues, there was only one person who could conceivably have been guilty. If I were wrong on my first eight—which, as I pointed out to you, were mere suggestions—then no harm could be done by testing my theory. The second eight confirmed it, and so I had no fear of the result. But, not to leap in too sylph-like a fashion at conclusions, I did this. Here is a copy of the telegram I dispatched to Captain Whistler."

He drew a scribbled envelope from his pocket, on which Morgan read:

MAN CALLING HIMSELF VISCOUNT STURTON IS IMPOSTOR. HOLD HIM UNDER PORT AUTHORITY AND ASK TO SPEAK TO HILDA KELLER, SECRETARY TRAVELLING WITH HIM. HE WILL NOT BE ABLE TO PRODUCE HER; SHE IS DEAD. MAKE THOROUGH SEARCH OF MAN'S CABIN AND PERSON. YOU WILL FIND EVIDENCE TO SUPPORT YOU. AMONG POSSESSIONS YOU WILL PROBABLY FIND FILM. . . .

(Here followed a description.)

IF YOU WILL SEND THIS TO ME SPECIAL MESSENGER TRAVELLING TRAIN ARRIVING WATERLOO 3:50, KINDLY SAY CAPTURE WAS YOUR OWN IDEA. RELEASE FORTINBRAS FROM BRIG. ALL REGARDS.

GIDEON FELL.

"What's the use of special authority," inquired Dr. Fell, "if you don't use it. Besides, if I had been wrong, and the girl was not really missing, there wouldn't have been an enormous row. But she was. You see, this bogus Sturton was able to conceal her presence or absence admirably so long as you never had any suspicions of *him*. Lad, at several places he was in devilish tight positions; but his very position, and the fact that he was the one who seemed to suffer most from the theft, kept him entirely immune from being suspected. . . . Don't choke, now; have some more beer. Shall I explain?"

"By all means," said Morgan feelingly.

"Hand me back my list of clues, then. H'mf! I'll see if I can have a modest shot at proving to you that—always supposing your data to be correct and complete—Lord Sturton was the only person aboard the *Queen Victoria* who could fill all the requirements for the Blind Barber.

"We commence, then, on one assumption: one assumption on which the whole case must rest. This assumption is that there is an impostor aboard, masquerading as somebody else. Fix that fact firmly in mind before beginning; go even to the length of believing a police commissioner's radiogram, and you will have at least a direction in which to start."

"Wait a bit!" protested Morgan. "We know that now, of course; and, since you were the only one who saw who it was, you ought to have the concession. But that radiogram accused Dr. Kyle, and therefore—"

"No, it didn't," said Dr. Fell, gently. "That is precisely where your whole vision strained away into the mist. It went wrong on so small but understandable a matter as the fact that people don't waste money by sending punctuation in radiograms, and you were misled by the absence of a couple of commas. With that error I shall deal in its proper place, under the head of The Clue of Terse Style. . . . For the moment, we have only the conception of an impostor aboard. There is another point in connection with this, stated to you so flatly and frankly that I have not even bothered to include it as a clue. As in other cases of mine, I seem to remember, it was so big that nobody ever gave it a thought. At one sweep it narrowed the search for the Blind Barber from a hundred passengers to a very, very few people. The Police Commissioner of the City of New York—not unusually timorous or faint-hearted about making arrests, even if they happen to be wrong arrests—wires thus: 'Well-known figure and must be no mistake made or trouble,' and adds, 'Will not be definite in case of trouble.' Now, that is suggestive. It is even startling. The man, in other words, is so important that the Commissioner finds it advisable not to mention his name, even in a confidential communication to the commander of the ship. Not only does it exclude John Smith or James Jones or Charles Woodcock, but it leads us towards men of such wealth or influence that the public is (presumably) interested in newspaper photographs of them (or anybody else) playing golf. This coy reticence on the part of the New York authorities may also be due partly to the possibility that the eminent man is an Englishman, and that severe complications may ensue in case of an error. But I do not press the point, because it is reasoning before my clues."

He had clearly been listening absently for the doorbell; and now, as the doorbell rang, he nodded and lifted his head to bellow:

"*Let 'em in, Vida!*"

There was a tramping of footfalls up the steps. The door of Dr. Fell's study opened to admit two large men with a prisoner between them. Morgan heard Dr. Fell say, "Ah, good afternoon, Jennings; and you, too, Hamper. Inspector Jennings, this is Mr. Morgan, one of our witnesses. Mr. Morgan, Sergeant Hamper. The prisoner, I think you know. . . ."

But Morgan was looking at the latter, who said, almost affably:

"How do you do, Doctor? I—er—I see you're looking at my appearance. No, there's no deception and damned little disguise. Too tricky and difficult. . . . Good afternoon, Mr. Morgan. I see you're surprised at the change in my voice. It's a relief to let down from the jerky manner; but I'd got so used to it it almost came natural. Rubbish rubbish rubbish!" squeaked the bogus Lord Sturton, with a sudden shift back to the manner he had previously used, and crowed with mirth.

Morgan jumped a little when he heard that echo of the old manner. The bogus Lord Sturton was in sunlight now, where Morgan remembered him only in the gloom of a darkened cabin like a picture-book wizard: his head hunched into a shawl, his face shaded by a flopping hat. Now he was revealed as a pale, long-faced, sharp-featured man with a rather unpleasant grin. A checked comforter was wound round his scrawny throat, and his clothes were weird. But he wore a bowler hat pushed back on his head, and he was smoking a cigar. Yet, although the grotesquerie had been removed, Morgan liked his look even less. He had an eye literally like a rattlesnake's. It measured Dr. Fell, swivelled round to the window, calculated, and became affable again.

"Come in!" said Dr. Fell. "Sit down. Make yourself comfortable. I've been wanting very much to make your acquaintance, if you're willing to talk. . . ."

"Prisoner's pretty talkative, sir," said Inspector Jennings, with a slow grin. "He's been entertaining Sergeant Hamper and me all the way up on the train. I've got a note-book full and he admits—"

"Why not?" inquired their captive, lifting his left hand to take the cigar out of his mouth. "Rubbish rubbish rubbish! Ha-ha!"

" . . . But all the same, sir," said Jennings, "I don't think I'll unlock the handcuff just yet. He says his name's Nemo. Sit down, Nemo, if the doctor says so. I'll be beside you."

Dr. Fell lumbered to the sideboard and got Nemo a drink of brandy. Nemo sat down.

"Point's this," Nemo explained, in a natural voice which was not quite so shrill or jerky as the Lord Sturton impersonation, but nevertheless had enough echo of it to make Morgan remember the whole scene in the darkened ill-smelling cabin. "Point's this. You think you're going to hang me? You're not. Rubbish!" His snaky neck swivelled round, and his eye smiled on Morgan. "Haha, no, no! I've got to be extradited first. They'll want me in the States. And between that time and this—I've got out of worse fixes."

Dr. Fell put the glass at his elbow, sat down opposite, and contemplated him. Mr. Nemo worked his head round and winked.

"Point is, I'm giving this up because I'm a fatalist. Fatalist! Wouldn't *you* be? Best set-up I ever had—meat—pie—easy; ho-ho, how easy? Wasn't as though I had to be a disguise expert. I told you there was no deception. I'm a dead ringer for Sturton. Look so much like him I could stand him in front of me and shave by him. Joke. But I can't beat marked cards. Sweat? I never had such a bad time in my life as when those God-damned kids—" again he twisted round and looked at Morgan, who was glad he had not a razor in his hands at the moment—"when those God-damned kids tangled it all up. . . ."

"I was about to tell my young friend," said Dr. Fell, "at his own request, some of the points that indicated you were—yourself, Mr. Nemo. . . ."

The doctor was getting great if sleepy enjoyment as he sat back against the dying light from the window and studied the man. Mr. Nemo's lidless eyes were returning the stare.

"Be interested to hear it myself," he said. "Anything to—delay things. Good cigar, good brandy. You listen, m'boy," he said, leering at Jennings. "Give you some pointers. If there's anything you don't know—well, when you've finished I'll tell you. Not before."

Jennings gestured to Sergeant Hamper, who got out his notebook.

Dr. Fell settled himself to begin with relish:

"Sixteen clues, then. Casting my eye over the evidence presented—you needn't take all this down, Hamper; you won't understand all of it—I came, after the obvious give-away of the impostor being an important man. . . ."

Mr. Nemo bowed very gravely, and the doctor's eye twinkled.

" . . . to what I called the Clue of Suggestion. It conveyed the idea. It opened the door on what first seemed a mad notion. During a heated argument between you, Morgan, and your friend Warren, while Warren was enthusiastically pleading the guilt of Dr. Kyle on the basis of detective fiction, you yourself said: 'Oh, and get rid of the idea that somebody may be impersonating him. . . . That may be all right for somebody who seldom comes in contact with anyone, but a public figure like an eminent physician won't do.' "[1]

---

[1](Numbers indicating major clues.) Page 58.

"It wasn't evidence. It only struck me as a curious coincidence that there really was aboard the ship somebody who seldom came in contact with anyone; who was known, I think, you said, as 'The Hermit of Jermyn Street.' 'He'll see nobody,' you remarked; 'he has no friends; all he does is collect rare bits of jewellery.'[2] These were only supporting facts to my real clue of suggestion; but undeniably Lord Sturton filled the qualifications of the radiogram. Merely a coincidence. . . .

"Then I remembered another coincidence: Lord Sturton was in Washington. A Sturton, real or bogus, had called on Uncle Warpus and told him of the purchase of the emerald elephant, which is the Clue of Opportunity.[3] Whether he was at the reception on the night of Uncle Warpus's indiscretion some time later, and learned about the moving-picture film . . ."

"He was," said Mr. Nemo, and chortled suddenly.

" . . . this I didn't know. But what we do know is that the Stelly affair occurred next in Washington, as Warren explained. This account of the Stelly business is what I call the Clue of Fraternal Trust.[4] It was described as a crime that looked like magic and was connected with the British Embassy. Stelly was a shrewd, careful, well-known jewel-collector who didn't omit any precautions against thieves, ordinary or extraordinary, as he thought. He left the Embassy one night, and was robbed without fuss. What looked like magic was his being decoyed or robbed by any ordinary criminal, and also how the criminal should have known of the necklace to begin with. . . . But it is not all magical if two well-known jewel-collectors exhibit their treasures to each other and have a tendency to talk shop. It is not at all magical for an eminent peer, even if he is so hermit-like that nobody knows him, to be welcomed at the Embassy in a foreign country, provided he has the documents to prove his identity. These coincidences, you see, are piling up.

"But this peer doesn't travel entirely alone. He is known to have a secretary. The first glimpse we have of him in the narrative is his rushing up the gangplank of a ship (so notoriously eccentric that he can wrap himself round in concealing comforters) and accompanied by this secretary.[5] In the passenger-list I find a Miss Hilda Keller occupying the same suite as Lord Sturton, as I think you yourselves found later.[6] But for the moment I put that aside. . . ."

There was a gurgling noise as Dr. Fell chuckled into his pipe.

"Definitely, things began to happen after some days out (during all of which time Lord Sturton has kept entirely to his cabin, and the secretary

[2](Markings indicate minor clues.) Page 5.
[3]Page 6.
[4]Page 29.
[5]Page 6.
[6]Page 57.

with him).[7] The first part of the film was stolen. The mysterious girl appeared, obviously trying to warn young Warren of something. There was the dastardly attack on Captain Whistler—the absence of the attackers on deck for some half an hour—and the subsequent disappearance of the girl. You believed (and so did I) that she had been murdered and thrown overboard. But, putting aside the questions of who the girl was and why she was killed, we have that curious feature of the bed being remade thoroughly, a soiled towel even being replaced. That is what I call, from deductions you will see in a moment, the Clue of Invisibility. . . ."[8]

Mr. Nemo wriggled back in the chair. He put down his glass; his face had gone more pale and his mouth twitched—but not from fear at all. He had nothing to conceal. He was white and poisonous from some emotion Morgan did not understand. You felt the atmosphere about him, as palpably as though you could smell a drug.

"I was crazy about that little whore," he said, suddenly, with such a change in voice and expression that they involuntarily started. "I hope she's in hell."

"That's enough," said Dr. Fell, quietly. He went on: "If somebody wished (for whatever reason) to kill her, why was she not merely killed and left there? The inference first off was that she would be more dangerous to the murderer if her body were discovered than if she were thrown overboard. By why should this be. Disappearance or outright murder, there would still be an investigation. . . . Yet observe! What does the murderer do? He carefully makes up the berth and replaces the towel. This could not be to make you think the stunned girl had recovered and gone to her own cabin. It would have exactly the opposite effect. It means that the murderer was trying to make those in authority think—meaning Captain Whistler—that the girl was nothing but a mythical person; a lie invented for some reason by yourselves.

"Behind the apparent madness of this course, since four people had seen her, consider what the murderer's reasons must have been. To begin with, he knew what had happened on C deck; he hoped Whistler would spot young Warren as the man who had attacked him, and yourselves as the people who had stolen the emerald; he knew that Whistler would not be likely to credit *any* story you told, and give short shrift to your excuses. But to adopt such a dangerous course as pretending she was a myth meant (*a*) that the girl would be traced straight to him if she were found dead, and that he could not stand the light of *any investigation whatever by police authorities afterwards*. It also meant (*b*) it was far less dangerous to conceal her absence, and that he had good reason to think he could conceal it.

"Now, this, gentlemen, is a very remarkable choice indeed, when you try to conceal an absence from a community of only a hundred passengers. Why couldn't he stand *any* investigation? How could he hope to convince investigators that nobody was missing?

"First ask yourself who this girl could have been. She could not have been travelling alone: a solitary passenger is not connected closely enough with anybody else to lead absolutely damning evidence straight to him among a hundred people, and to make it necessary to pretend the girl had never existed; besides, a solitary passenger would be the first to be missed. She was not travelling in a family party, or, as Captain Whistler shrewdly pointed out, there might possibly have been complaint at her disappearance. She was travelling then, with just one other person—the murderer. She was travelling as wife, companion, or what you like. The murderer could hope to conceal her disappearance, first, because she must have made no acquaintances and have been with him every moment of the time. That means the murderer seldom or never had left his cabin. He might conceal it, second, because he was so highly placed as to be above suspicion—*not otherwise*—and because he himself was the victim of a theft that directed attention away from him. But, if he were all this, why couldn't he stand any investigation whatever? The not-very-complicated answer is that he was an impostor who had enough to do in concealing his imposture. If you then musingly consider what man was travelling with a single female companion, what man had kept to his cabin every moment of the time, what man was so highly-placed as to be above suspicion; what man had been the victim of a theft; and, finally, what man there is whom we have some slight reason to think as an impostor; then it is remarkable how we swing round again to Lord Sturton. All this is built up on the clue of a clean towel, the clue of invisibility. But it is still coincidence without definite reason, though we find rapid support for it.

"I mean that razor incautiously left behind in the berth. . . ."

Mr. Nemo, who had been mouthing his cigar for some time, twitched round and looked at each in turn. His pale, bony face had worn an absent look, but now it had such a wide smile of urbanity and charm that Morgan shivered. "I cut the little bitch's throat," offered Mr. Nemo, making a gesture with the cigar. "Much better for her. *And* more satisfactory for me. That's right, old man," he said to the staring Hamper; "write it down. It's much better to damage their skulls. A surgeon showed me all about that once. If you practise, you can find the right spot. But it wouldn't do for *her*. I had to take one of Sturton's set of razors to do it, and throw the others away. It hurt me. That case of razors must have cost a hundred-odd pound."

He jerked with laughter, lifted his bowler off his head as though in tribute, smirked, kicked his heels, and asked for another drink.

"Yes," said Dr. Fell, staring at him curiously, "that's what I mean. I asked my young friend here not to think of one razor, but of seven in a set. I asked him to think of a set of razors as enormously expensive as those carven, silver-studded, ebony-handled rarities, which were obviously made to order.[9] No ordinary man would have had them. The person likeliest to have them, said my Clue of Seven Razors, was the man who went after costly trinkets, who bought the emerald elephant, 'because it was a curiosity and a rarity, of enormous intrinsic value.' . . . [10] And the razors bring us back again to the question of who the girl was.

"Her solitary appearance in public was in the wireless-room, where she was described by the wireless-operator as 'having her hands full of papers'; and this I call, symbolically, my Clue of Seven Radiograms.[11] What does that appearance sound like? Not a joyous tourist dashing off an inconsequential message home. There is a businesslike look to it. A number of messages—a businesslike look—and we begin to think of a secretary. The edifice rears. Our Blind Barber becomes not only an impostor masquerading as a highly placed recluse who kept to his cabin, and travelled with a female companion; but the girl becomes a secretary and the recluse an enormously wealthy man with a taste for grotesque trinkets. . . ."

Dr. Fell lifted his stick and pointed suddenly.

"Why did you kill her?" he demanded. "Was she an accomplice?"

"You're telling the story," shrugged Mr. Nemo. "And while I'm bored, I'm bored as hell with it, because just at the moment *I* feel like talking, still—your brandy's not at all bad. Ha-ha-ha. Ought to get hospitality. Go on. *You* talk. Then I'll talk, and I'll surprise you. Give you a little hint, though. Yes. Sporting run for your money, like old Sturton would. . . . Didn't I come down on old Whistler, though! Ho-ho! Yes. . . . Hint is, she was what you'd call virtuous in the way of being honest. She wouldn't step into my game with me when she found out who I was. And when she tried to warn that young fellow—Tcha! Bloody little fool! Ha-ha! Eh?" inquired Mr. Nemo, putting back his cigar with a portentous wink.

"Did you know," said Dr. Fell, "that a man named Woodcock saw you when you stole the first part of that film?"

[9]Page 60.
[10]Page 6.
[11]Page 70.

"Did he?" asked Mr. Nemo, lifting one shoulder. "What did I care? Remove sideburns—they're detachable—little wax in mouth; strawberry mark on cheek; who'll identify me afterwards, eh?"

Dr. Fell slowly drew a line through one line on a sheet of paper.

"And there we had the first direct evidence: of Elimination.[12] Woodcock said definitely that you were a person he'd never seen before. Now, Woodcock hadn't been sea-sick. He'd been in the dining-room at all times, and after the sea-sick passengers came out of their lairs he would have spotted the thief—if the thief hadn't been still among the very, very few who kept to their cabins. Humf! Ha! I was wondering whether anybody had fantastic suspicions of—well, say Perrigord or somebody of the sort. But it ruled out Perrigord, it ruled out Kyle, it ruled out nearly everybody. The thing is plain enough, but where everybody went off on the wrong scent was over that radiogram from New York." Dr. Fell wrote rapidly on a sheet of paper and pushed it across to Morgan.

FEDERAL AGENT THINKS CROOK RESPONSIBLE FOR STELLY AND MACGEE JOBS. FEDERAL AGENT THINKS ALSO PHYSICIAN IS IMPOSTOR ON YOUR SHIP. . . .

"Well?" said Morgan. The doctor made a few marks, and held it out again.

"The Clue of Terse Style," said Dr. Fell, "indicates that the word "also" is a supernumerary, is out of place, is a word merely wasted in an expensive radiogram if what it means is, "Federal agent *also* thinks. . . ." But read it thus."[13]

FEDERAL AGENT THINKS—ALSO PHYSICIAN—IS IMPOSTOR ON YOUR SHIP. . . .

"Meaning," said Dr. Fell, crumpling up the paper, "an entirely different thing. The remark about 'medical profession influential' simply means that the doctor in attendance is making a row; he is insisting that, despite the patient at the hospital being apparently out of his head in insisting he is Sturton, the doctor believes it and they mustn't disregard it. But, good God! Do you seriously think that, if he had meant Dr. Kyle was a murderer, the whole medical profession would have wanted to shield him? The idea was so absurd that I wonder anybody considered it. It refers to Sturton! Sweep away the whole flimsy tangle, now. Let's have one point piled on top of the other until you'll realise it couldn't have

[12]Page 80.
[13]Page 93.

been anybody; let's come at last to the gigantic and damning proof."

He flung the paper on the table with an angry gesture.

"You visit Sturton to pacify him over the loss of the emerald. Do you see his secretary? No! You hear him *apparently* talking to somebody behind a door in the bedroom.[14] But, though you don't make any noise or speak, out he darts to see you and closes the door.[15] He knew you were there already, and he put on that show for your benefit. The mistake, the Clue of Wrong Rooms, was—why in the bedroom? It wasn't in the drawing-room where he'd been apparently lying, with his medicine-bottles around; that was his haunt. But he had to be out of sight. . . ."[16]

Morgan heard Mr. Nemo's shrill laughter and the steady scratching of a pencil; but Dr. Fell went on:

"Then there was the business of Lights: curtains always drawn, shawl round his shoulders, hat on, always back to the light.[17] There was the straight suggestion of his Personal Taste: the toy trinket with real rubies for eyes, winking and leering at you as he deliberately tapped it while he bamboozled you; and still you didn't see the connection between the wagging Mandarin-head and the costly trinket of the razor.[18] And what happened," said Dr. Fell, rapping his stick sharply on the table, "when you and Captain Valvick and Mrs. Perrigord went round with the grim intention of finding the missing girl? You combed the boat through—but yet in sublime innocence of heart you did not demand to see Sturton's secretary; you went there, you asked a question, and you let him rush you out of the cabin without ever going any further!" . . .[19] After a pause Dr. Fell wheeled round and looked at Inspector Jennings. "I'm going off my base, Jennings. I suppose you don't understand any of this?"

The inspector smiled grimly. "I understand every word of it, sir. That's why I haven't interrupted you. Nemo here regaled us with a whole account of it on the train. It's fine. Eh, Nemo?"

"Rubbish rubbish rubbish!" squeaked Nemo, in repulsive glee at his successful imitation. "Mad Captain Whistler. Prosecute the line! And all the while I was wondering. . . . Eh, Inspector?"

The inspector studied him curiously. He seemed to wish he were farther away than handcuffed to Nemo's wrist.

"Oh, it's a great joke," he said coolly. "But you'll hang for all of it, you filthy swine. Go on, Dr. Fell."

Nemo straightened up.

[14]Page 108.
[15]Page 108.
[16]Page 108.
[17]Page 108.
[18]Page 109.
[19]Page 120.

"I'll kill you for that, one day," he remarked, just as coolly. "Maybe to-morrow, maybe next day, maybe a year from now." His eye wandered round the room; his face was slightly paler, and he breathed hard. Morgan felt he was keeping his spirits up with desperate jocularity. "Shall *I* talk now?" he asked suddenly.

Chapter XXII

EXIT NEMO

It was growing shadowy in the room. Nemo took off his hat and brushed its brim across his forehead. He gestured with it.

"I'll tell you," he said, "why you can't beat what's cut out for you at birth. I'll fill up your story. I'll show you how a trick nobody could help cheated me out of the cushiest soft spot on earth. And those kids—they thought it was funny. . . .

"I won't tell you who I am," he said, looking round at them with a curious expression which reminded Morgan of Woodcock squinting at the ceiling in the writing-room. "I might be anybody. You'll never know. I could say I was Harry Jones of Surbiton, or Bill Smith of Yonkers—or maybe somebody not very much different from the man I was impersonating. I'll tell you what I am, though—I'm a ghost. Reason that out how you like; *I'm* not telling. I'll never have any occasion to tell."

He grinned. Nobody spoke. The yellow twilight outside showed in queer colour his face peering at Dr. Fell, at Jennings, at Morgan.

"Or maybe I'm only Mad Tommy, of . . . who's going to tell? But what I will tell you is that I put through that trick neatly. I passed as Sturton without anybody being suspicious, but I won't tell you how I managed it, because it might get others in trouble. I deceived his secretary. I admit she'd only been with him for a month or two—but I deceived her. If I was an eccentric who couldn't remember my business affairs, *she* took care of it. She was nice." He stroked the air and chortled. "I did it so well that I thought, 'Nemo, you only intended to impersonate Sturton long enough to make a haul; but why not keep on?'

"I kept her with me. I shouldn't have killed MacGee in New York; but he was a diamond man, and I couldn't resist diamonds. When I sailed aboard that ship I had unlimited cash of Sturton's—ever see me imitate a signature?—and nearly five hundred thousand pounds in jewels. The only thing people knew I had was the emerald elephant. And what did I intend to do? Pay duty on it, like an honest man; no fuss at all. For the rest, I was the well-known Sturton; *I* wouldn't smuggle in other things, and they'd be very careless about my luggage. I knew that, being close to me aboardship, Hilda—Miss Keller, my Hilda—might find out who I was. But I wanted her to. I was going to say: 'You're in deep; too deep; I'm the one you'll have to stick with; so' "—he made a gesture and spoke in a rather, thick ghastly voice—" 'so move your belongings into my berth, Hilda,' I'd say to her. Ha! . . ."

"If you had all that money," said Dr. Fell, sharply, "why did you want to steal the film?"

"Trouble," said Nemo, tapping his free hand on the side of his nose. "To make trouble for—oh, everybody I could, do you see? No, you don't. I meant to give away that film, free, to whoever could do the most damage with it. You don't see? But I do. I'm like Sturton. I might be Sturton's ghost; I hate—people." He laughed, and massaged his head. "I'd heard of it in Washington. Hilda, still not knowing who I was, came to my cabin that afternoon. She told me all about a very, very curious radiogram she'd overheard. Then my wits—*my* wits—remembered. And I thought, 'Here's my chance to break it to her gently.' I'd get the film, I'd show it her, and we'd appreciate—both of us—how much trouble we could make.

"I did," said Nemo, in a sudden loud, harsh voice like a crow. "But she didn't understand. That was why I had to kill her.

"And what happened just before that? Eh? Eh? I had *another* inspiration, to make her love me still more. When I first planned to rob old Sturton, I hadn't intended to impersonate him; never mind all that; I was after the elephant, and I had a nearly perfect duplicate made to switch on him. That was the way I meant to work it. . . .

"But I thought, why not make a clean sweep? Why pay duty on the real emerald at all? And it would be easy. I would take the imitation emerald across with me, and the real one hidden, and it would be the imitation I'd offer to the customs men. They'd say, 'This isn't real,' when I was offering to pay the enormous duty. I would say, 'What?' . . ." Here Mr. Nemo chuckled with delight. A curious wondering expression, however, had come into his eyes. . . . "They would say, 'Your Lordship, you've been had. This isn't real.' And there would be a terrific joke at my expense, and I would curse and jump, and give them big tips to keep quiet about it. And walk off with it in my luggage. . . . So, to make it look more real, I let the captain lock it in his safe. . . .

"But what happened. IT WENT WRONG. God damn the whole world! IT WENT WRONG! Those kids—"

Dr. Fell cut him off. "Yes," he said, quietly, "and that was where you made a mistake; and what I call the Clue Direct. The last thing you wanted was the emerald to be stolen, especially as it was false, because *that meant there would be an inquiry on the ship and afterwards a police inquiry,* which was the one thing you couldn't risk. The only thing you could do was shut off investigation by producing the real emerald and saying it had been returned to you. That would stop things. The Clue Direct, and your whole mistake, was that you acted entirely out of character for the first time; you did something Lord Sturton would never have done; you said, *"I don't know how it happened, and I don't care, now I've got it back."* [1] Not one word of all that rang true, friend Nemo. What puzzled me for a moment, though I see the explanation now, is why you left the bogus emerald lying in the steel box behind the cabin trunk; and risked having it found. You must have known where it was, if you were on hand and saw the whole scene. Anybody could have seen it was your work from the time young Warren found the bogus emerald there. . . ."

"Wait a bit!" protested Morgan. "I don't see that. How so?"

"Well, there were obviously two emeralds. If one had been lying all the time in a box behind Kyle's trunk, it couldn't be the one in Sturton's hands. Yet—the box containing the emerald was the one which Captain Whistler had received straight from Sturton's hands! Sturton gave it to him; it was presumably the real emerald; yet here is Sturton flourishing *another* elephant which he says is genuine! The Clue of Known Doubles lies simply in *your* own statement that, if there were two emeralds, Sturton would surely know a true from a false. . . .[2] Certainly he would; but, if the emerald he gave in the steel box to Whistler were real, then the one returned to him couldn't have been; and yet he said it *was* real. It is not a very abstruse deduction, is it? And it leads straight back to our gallant impostor." Dr. Fell stared at him. "But what I didn't see for a second, friend Nemo, was why you risked the bogus emerald lying in Kyle's cabin and the deadly chance of having it brought forward."

Nemo was so inexplicably excited that he overturned and smashed his glass. The excitement seemed to have been growing on him for some time, as though he were waiting for something that did not happen.

"I thought it had gone overboard," he snarled. "I knew it had gone overboard! I heard that—that swine"—he stabbed his finger at Morgan— "distinctly say—there was a lot of noise on the deck from the waves—but I was listening, and I heard him say, 'Gone overboard. . . .' "[3]

"You missed part of it, I fear," said Dr. Fell, composedly, and ran his pencil through the Clue of Misunderstanding. "And the final proof con-

[1] Page 111
[2] Page 134.
[3] Page 36.

clusive—it must have shaken you—was when the other emerald did turn up. Even to the last you screamed that there had been no robbery, and went so ridiculously far as to forbid anybody mentioning it.[4] As it was, your goose was burned to a cinder and your identity out with a yell if anybody hadn't been fairly sure before. What you should have done was try even the thin tale that you had been robbed again. And yet (bow, friend Nemo, and prostrate yourself before the Parcæ) for a second you were saved by good old Uncle Jules chucking it overboard."

Mr. Nemo straightened up. He twisted his neck.

"I may be a ghost," he said with a glassy-eyed and absolute seriousness which was not absurd, but rather terrible; "and yet, my friend, I'm not omniscient. Ha-ha! Well, I shortly shall be; and then I'll come back with a razor, some night, when you aren't looking."

He exploded into mirth.

"What the devil ails him?" demanded Dr. Fell, and got slowly to his feet.

"That little bottle," said Nemo. "I drank it an hour ago, just when we left the train. I was afraid it wasn't working; I've been afraid, and that's why I had to talk. I drank it. I tell you I'm a ghost. A ghost has been sitting with you for an hour; I hope you remember it and think about it at night."

In the eerie yellow light, against which Dr. Fell's great bulk was silhouetted black, the mirth of the prisoner bubbled, and his body made a rustling sound which froze Morgan. . . . And then, in the silence, Inspector Jennings got slowly to his feet. He face was impassive. They heard the creak and clink of the handcuffs.

"Yes, Nemo," said Inspector Jennings, with satisfaction, "I thought you'd try that. That's why I changed the contents of it. Most of 'em try the trick. It's old. You're not going to die of poison. . . ."

The mirth struck off in a choking sound, and the man began to flap at the handcuffs. . . .

"You're not going to die of poison, Nemo," said Inspector Jennings, moving slowly towards the door. "You're going to hang. . . . Good night, gentlemen, and thanks."

[4]Page 157.

TO WAKE THE DEAD

CONTENTS

Chapter 1

THE CRIME OF HAVING BREAKFAST

A t just after daybreak on that raw January morning, Christopher Kent stood in Piccadilly and shivered. The air seemed painted grey as though with a brush. He was only a dozen yards from Piccadilly Circus, and the Guinness clock told him that it was twenty minutes past seven. The only thing moving in the Circus was a taxi whose motor clanked with great distinctness; it circled Ares's island and throbbed away down a quiet Regent Street. A wind had begun to blow from the east, shaking the bitter air as you might shake a carpet. Christopher Kent noticed a flake of snow, and then another, blown suddenly past him. He eyed them without animosity, but he was not amused.

At the bank round the corner, he could draw a cheque for whatever he liked. But he had not a penny in his pocket, nor was it likely that he would have one for twenty-four hours more. That was the trouble. He had not eaten since yesterday's breakfast, and he was so hungry that it was beginning to cramp him.

As though by instinct he was almost at the doors of the Royal Scarlet Hotel. It fascinated him. One day later—to be exact at ten o'clock on the morning of February 1st—he would walk into that hotel and meet Dan Reaper, as had been arranged. Then the whole matter under debate would be over. There would be satisfaction in winning from Dan; but, at the moment, hunger and light-headedness were turning his earlier amusement to a mood of sullen anger.

As usual, the events leading to that meeting of the ways were unreasonable. He was the son of the late Kent's South African Ales. South African by bringing-up, he had lived in nearly every country except his own; and he had not seen England since they had taken him away at the age of two. Something had always happened to prevent it. Kent's Ales required attention, though he was nowadays too lazy to pay much attention to them beyond the drinking. He had other views. Having been brought up on sound principles by his father, with whose judgments he agreed on everything except the fascination of business, he had early acquired a liking for sensational fiction. In the middle twenties he began to write it, and at that trade he worked like a Kaffir to make the stuff good. But Dan Reaper was not pleased.

Standing on the more-than-hard London pavement, he remembered a more pleasant day three months ago, with iced drinks at hand, and the noise of the surf coming up from Durban beach. He was arguing, as usual, with Dan. He remembered Dan's heavy red-brown complexion, his crisp-moving gestures, his flat positiveness. At fifty Dan had prospered in a young man's country, and was one of those who have made Johannesburg a new Chicago. Though Dan was nearly twenty years older than Kent, they had been friends for a long time, and enjoyed arguing the worth or trash of all created things. Dan was a Member of the Assembly, and was working his way towards becoming an important man politically. And (again as usual) he was laying down the law.

"I haven't got time to read novels," Dan said as usual. "Biographies, histories: yes. That's my line. It's real. I want something that Repays Study. About the other stuff, I feel like old Mrs. Patterson: 'What's the use? It's all a pack of lies.' But if people must turn out novels, at least they ought to write out of experience—out of a full knowledge of life—like mine, for instance. I sometimes think I could—"

"Yes," said Kent. "I know. I seem to have heard all this somewhere else. Nonsense. The job's a trade, like any other good trade; and it's got to be learned. As for your cursed experience—"

"You don't deny it's necessary?"

"I don't know," Kent had admitted honestly. He remembered studying the colours of blue water and sky through his glass. "One thing has always struck me, when I've read the brief biographical notices of writers tucked away on the back flap of the book. It's astonishing how alike they all are. In nine cases out of ten you'll read, 'Mr. Blank has been lumberman, rancher, newspaperman, miner, and barman in the course of an adventurous life; has travelled through Canada; was for a time—' and so on. The number of writers who have been ranchers in Canada must be overwhelming. One day when I'm asked for a biographical note, I am going to break this tyranny. I am going to write, 'I have *not* been lumberman, rancher, newspaperman, miner, or barman; and, in fact, I never did an honest day's work in my life until I took up writing.' "

This stung Dan on the raw.

"I know you didn't," he retorted grimly. "You've always had all the money you wanted. But you couldn't do an honest day's work. It would kill you."

From there the argument, stimulated by a John Collins or two, had taken a sharper and more business-like turn, while Dan grew still more heated.

"I'll bet you a thousand pounds," cried Dan, who had a romantic imagination, "that you couldn't stand up to a test that I've been through myself. Look here, it's an idea. You couldn't start at Johannesburg without a penny in your pocket, say; you couldn't work or beat your way to the coast—Durban, Capetown, Port Elizabeth, anywhere you like— you couldn't work your way to England aboard ship, and turn up to meet me there at a given rendezvous on a date, say, ten weeks from now. I mean, you couldn't do it without cashing a cheque or using your own name to be helped along. Bah!"

Kent did not tell him that the idea, in fiction, was not original. But it interested him.

"I might take you up on that," he said.

Dan regarded him suspiciously; Dan looked for a catch in everything.

"Are you serious? Mind, if you did a thing like that—or tried to do it—it would do you all the good in the world. Teach you what Life is like. And you'd get material for some real books instead of these footling stories about master-spies and murders. But you don't mean it. You'll think better of it to-morrow morning."

"Damn your hide, I believe I do mean it."

"Ho ho!" said Dan, and gurgled into his glass. "All right!" He pointed a heavy finger. "At the beginning of January I've got to go to England on business. Melitta's going with me, and your cousin Rod, and Jenny; and probably Francine and Harvey as well." Dan always travelled like an emperor, with a suite of friends. "I've got to go down to Gay's place in Sussex when we first get there. But on the morning of February 1st, sharp, we're to be in London. Do you think you could make that trip and meet me in my suite at the Royal Scarlet Hotel at ten o'clock on the morning of the first? Think it over, my lad. A thousand pounds you can't—no cheating, mind."

Two more snowflakes curled over in the air and were blown wide by that bitter wind. Kent looked up Piccadilly, figuratively tightening his belt. Well, he had done it. Here he was; or, at least, he would have done it in twenty-four hours more if he could hold out until then. And his chief impression now was that nearly everything Dan had so confidently predicted was wrong.

Experience? Material for books? At the moment he did not know whether to laugh or swear. None of these things had come on adventurous wings. To Dan himself, going out to South Africa in a cattle-boat after the War, there might have come some vision of high adventure or mystic twilights: though Kent doubted this. Exhilaration be hanged. It had been nothing but monotony and work; bone-cracking work, which—if he had not been solidly put together—would have broken him in the first two weeks. His own stubbornness had carried him through. He could have learned as much about human nature from a boarding-house in Johannesburg, and nearly as much about adventure.

But here he was. Nearly a week ago he had landed from the *Volpar* at Tilbury, with a trimmer's pay in his pocket; and had spent most of it in one glorious bust with a couple of messmates. Possibly, with time to lend joke and point, a sense of adventure on the high seas would come in retrospect. At the moment he knew only that he was devilish hungry.

He moved a little closer to the great revolving doors of the Royal Scarlet Hotel, which towered up in white stone over Piccadilly. Inside he could see charwomen finishing their work on the marble floors; carpets were being put down again, silently; and the hush of early morning was disturbed only by the echo of footsteps.

The Royal Scarlet was an imposing but not expensive place. Dan Reaper always preferred to go there, though as a rule he hired half a floor and in the end paid nearly as much as he might have paid at the Savoy. It was the principle of the thing, Dan said, never to let high-priced hotels make you pay for a name. Besides, the manager was a fellow South-African and a friend of his. For Coronation year they were building a top-floor annex which was predicted to be something new in the way of luxury rooms, and which had also attracted Dan.

Christopher Kent moved closer. It was warm inside those glass doors; warm and drowsy; and you might rest even hungry innards in a comfortable chair. Looking through into the lobby, he was conscious of an irrational resentment against Dan—Dan, expansive *père de famille* without any family, Dan, who exulted in going to all kinds of trouble if he could get a ten-shilling article for nine and elevenpence three farthings. At this moment Dan would still be at Gay's house in Sussex, snugly tucked into bed. But he would be here presently, with his suite of friends and employees. Kent ran them over in his mind. Melitta, Dan's wife. Francine Forbes, his niece. Rodney Kent, Christopher's cousin, and Rodney's wife Jenny: Rodney was Dan's political secretary. Harvey Wrayburn, a great friend of the family, would probably have made the trip too. And in another day they would be descending on London. . . .

That was a real cramp in the stomach this time. He would not have thought it possible to be so hungry.

Something white, something that was too large to be a snowflake, caught the corner of his eye. It was drifting down from the sky; it slipped past his shoulder; and automatically he put out his hand for it. It was a little folded card, of the sort they gave you when you were assigned to a room. It said in red letters:

THE
ROYAL SCARLET
HOTEL

DATE: 30/1/37.

ROOM: 707.

CHARGE: 21/6 (Double).

The charge includes room, bath, and breakfast. No responsibility can be accepted for valuables unless they are placed in the manager's safe.

"Room, bath, *and* breakfast—" Kent stared at the card; first the idea occurred to him as a good thing for a story, and then with a rush of hesitant surprise he realised that it might be practical.

He remembered how these things were done. You walked into the dining-room and gave your room-number either to the waiter or to someone sitting at the entrance with a book. Then you were served with breakfast. If he walked in boldly and gave the number of a room certain to be occupied, he could breakfast well—and then walk out again into the void. Why not? How were they to know he wasn't the occupier of the room? It was now barely seven-thirty. The chances were slight that the real occupant of the room would be down so early; and, in any case, it was something that would have to be risked.

The idea appealed to him enormously. Though he had pawned most of his possessions, and needed a haircut, still his suit was presentable; and he had shaved the night before. He pushed through the revolving doors into the foyer, removing his hat and overcoat.

It was a mild enough form of swindle; but Kent suddenly realised that he had never felt so guilty in his life. An empty stomach gives very little assurance; still, he wondered whether they were all looking at him hard or peering at the thoughts in his head. He had to get a grip on himself to prevent himself from hurrying across the foyer as though he were pursued. Only a hall-porter—in the neat dark-blue uniform naturally adopted by any hotel calling itself the Royal Scarlet—seemed to be looking at him. He strolled casually through the foyer, then through a palm-lounge, and into a big dining-room which seemed to be just waking up from sleep.

There were, he was relieved to see, already several people at the tables. If he had been the first there, and a swindler at that, he might have bolted. He almost did bolt at the sight of so many waiters. But he tried to walk with cool assurance, like a man carrying a morning paper. Then a head waiter bowed to him; and the thing was done.

He has afterwards admitted that his heart was in his mouth when the waiter drew out a chair for him at an isolated table.

"Yes, sir?"

"Bacon and eggs, toast, and coffee. Lots of bacon and eggs."

"Yes, sir," said the waiter briskly, and whipped out a pad. "And the number of your room?"

"Seven-o-seven."

It seemed to excite no surprise. The waiter noted it down, tore out a duplicate slip made on carbon-paper underneath, and hurried away. Kent sat back. It was pleasantly warm; the scent of coffee in the air made him a little more light-headed; but he felt like a man unsteadily getting his grip at last. Before he had time to wonder whether it might be snatched away from him, there was put before him a plate of what seemed the finest eggs and the most succulent bacon he had ever seen. A rack of toast and a coffee-service of polished pewter added silver to the already bright colours of the table: the yellow and red-brown of bacon and eggs, against shining white china and cloth, might make a painting of rare quality.

"Banners," he thought, looking at the eggs, " 'banners yellow, glorious, golden, From its roof did float and flow—' "

"Sir?" said the waiter.

" 'We fight to the finish, we drink to the dregs,' " quoted Kent recklessly, " 'And dare to be Daniels on bacon and eggs.' That's all, thanks."

Then he dug in. It was difficult at first, for his insides appeared to be opening and shutting like a concertina; but presently a soothing sense of well-being began to creep into him. He sat back drowsily, feeling at peace with the world, and wished for something to smoke. But that would not do. He had had his meal; now he must get out of here before—

Then he noticed the two waiters. One had just come into the dining-room; they were looking towards his table and conferring.

"That's done it," he thought. But he felt almost cheerful.

Getting to his feet with as much dignity as he could, he started to walk out of the room. Behind the waiters, he noticed, was a hotel-attendant of some sort, wearing the dark-blue uniform. He could guess what that meant even before the attendant stepped out and spoke to him.

"Will you come this way, sir, please?" asked the man, with what seemed a very sinister inflection.

Kent drew a deep breath. That was that, then. He wondered if they put you in jail for this sort of thing. He could imagine Dan Reaper's roars of laughter (and the laughter of everyone else) if they arrived next day and found him in clink for cadging a breakfast; or washing dishes to pay it off.

It made him furious, but there was no way out unless he ran for it; and he was not going to do that. He walked as sedately as he could beside the attendant, who led him through the palm-lounge, and then to the lodge of the hall-porter. That dignitary, a burly man with a sergeant-major's moustache and bearing, did not look sinister; he looked polite and disturbed. After glancing round as though he suspected the presence of enemy spies, he addressed Kent with confidential heartiness.

"I'm very sorry to trouble you, sir," he said; "but I wonder if you'd be good enough to help us out of a difficulty? You're the gentleman in 707?"

"Yes, that's right."

"Ah! Well, sir, it's like this. The room you're in—707—was occupied up to yesterday afternoon," again the sergeant-major looked around, "by an American lady who's sailing home in the *Directoire* late to-day. She rang us up late last night; but of course we didn't like to disturb you until you were up and about. The fact is, sir, that when she left here she forgot a very valuable bracelet; pushed it down in the drawer of the bureau, it seems, inside the paper lining, and clean forgot about it. The lady prizes it very highly, she tells us, and doesn't want to go home without it. It's too bad the chambermaid didn't spot it when the room was made up yesterday before you came in; but you know how these things happen. Now, sir, I know it's an imposition on you; but if we found that bracelet right now, we could get it to Southampton in time to catch her boat. I wonder if you'd mind just stepping upstairs with me, and looking in that drawer?"

Kent had begun to feel a trifle ill.

"I'm afraid I have to go out," he said slowly. "But there's no reason why *you* shouldn't go upstairs and look—or the maid, or whoever wants to. You have my full permission, and you could get in with a pass-key."

The hall-porter assumed an even more heavily reluctant air.

"Ah, but that's just the trouble, sir," he pointed out, shaking his head. "Under the circumstances—"

"What circumstances?"

"Your good lady being asleep up there, and having hung a 'quiet' sign on the door," said the porter, with an air of handsome frankness, "you can see we hardly liked—"

"My good lady?"

"Your wife. It would hardly do for us to wake anyone up with a request like that. But I thought if you wouldn't mind going in and explaining to your wife—"

Even as his mind registered the word "sunk," Kent found himself being urged by some hypnotic power in the direction of the nearer of the two lifts.

Chapter 11

THE CRIME OF MURDER

There were, he afterwards realised, very few courses open to him. No course, in fact, except that of walking sternly and quickly out of the hotel: an action into which his inflamed conscience put an interpretation of guilt bringing about immediate pursuit. Also, with a stomach now lined with good food, he began to take a pleasant interest in the situation. It was like a situation in one of his own books; and it stirred in him the quality of devilment. Apparently he would have to break into the room of a blameless husband and wife, now asleep upstairs—and get away with it somehow. Adventures (he could have told Dan Reaper) are to be found within walls, not on the plain.

Going up in the lift, the hall-porter was affable.

"Have a good night, sir? Sleep well?"

"Pretty well."

"I hope you weren't disturbed by the men in the hall getting ready that second lift. That top floor where you are, you know, is very new; we're quite proud of it; and it isn't quite finished. They haven't finished installing the second lift. They're working double-time to get all that floor ready in time for Coronation. Ah, here we are."

The seventh floor of the Royal Scarlet was constructed on the principle of fewer and larger rooms. It had four wings, of which wing A (immediately to your right as you stepped out of the working lift) was the only one with which Kent ever had any concern. A broad descending staircase faced the two lifts, set side by side, and on the second lift workmen were now tinkering with the mechanism under a powerful light.

Wing A was spacious and luxurious enough, although Kent could have wished for a little of the less frantically modern note in chromium, glass, and murals. To the right of the lifts, a broad corridor ran some distance down before turning again at right angles. Underfoot was a very thick grey carpet; and the walls were decorated in a way which suggested the smoking-room or lounge of a liner. On one side ran a full-length representation of a scene round a prize-ring, and the other side appeared to be composed of a coloured alphabet gone mad. Dim lights illuminated it with a chrysalis effect. It was very new, and not quite out of its smooth rawness; you could almost smell the stream-lining as you could smell the paint.

Kent was growing even more uneasy as he came to face it. Number 707 was in the corner at the turning of the corridor, its door being round the corner and out of sight from the direction of the lifts. Kent, a little ahead of the hall-porter, was the first to see that door. Outside it stood a pair of woman's brown shoes: of what material he could not tell or did not notice. And hanging from the knob was one of those cardboard notices reading, "Quiet is requested for the benefit of those who have retired." But that was not what made him stop dead, instinctively shielding the card with his body. Across the notice had been scrawled, half-writing, half-printing, in red ink:

DEAD WOMAN

In Kent's mind it took on a weird clearness. At the end of this bend in the corridor there was a window, and outside the window a fire-escape; he seemed to notice a dozen things at once. He noted also the linen-closet at the end of the corridor: there was a bright light inside it, and a chambermaid in a blue-and-white uniform. Yet it all concentrated on those words, "Dead Woman," hanging helpfully outside the door.

Surely if the chambermaid had already passed the door, those words would have been noticed? His own voice sounded very queer when he said:

"I'm afraid I haven't got my key."

(Well, should he own up now, or bolt for it?)

"Oh, that's all right, sir," the hall-porter assured him, in a surprisingly natural tone. "We'll have the maid here in half a tick. S-sss-t!"

He was already hurrying down the hall to get the maid. Christopher Kent remained where he stood: he did nothing because he could think of absolutely nothing to do. But one thing he did not like. He put out his hand quickly and reversed the card, so that its inner side (printed in the same way except for that curious note in red ink) was now outwards.

"Here we are, sir," said the hall-porter. The key clicked in the lock and the door opened an inch. Even if the porter had not tactfully stood aside, Kent was instantly in front of him.

"If you'll just wait here a moment—?" he said.

"Of course, sir. No hurry."

Gritting his teeth, Kent slipped in and let the door swing shut after him; it was one of those which automatically lock on closing.

The room inside was almost dark. Heavy cream-coloured blinds had been drawn full down on its two windows, and made opaque blurs against the gloom. Neither window could have been up, for the place smelt heavily stuffy. In the wall to his left he could dimly make out the line of twin beds; and he momentarily expected someone to sit up in one of them and ask him what the devil he was doing there. But nothing stirred, not even the quilted counterpane on either, and he saw that both beds were empty. Nothing stirred, that is, except his own scalp; for he began to realise that the notice on the door was probably true.

A little way out in the big room he could discern a wardrobe trunk, of the sort that stands on end and opens out like a book. It now stood part way open towards him, and something was projecting along the floor from between its leaves. First it was a dark mass; then it had a leg in a grey silk stocking; then a hand. It was a woman's body lying on its side with the head between the leaves of the trunk. Something white was partly draped over the shoulder.

Those interested in such matters have argued what an ordinary man in the street would do if he were thrown into a bad position with a dead person before him; Kent had argued it himself. He did nothing. The time he actually spent in that room he afterwards computed as about three minutes.

First he must bring himself to go and look. His hand was moving uncertainly in the air, and to the right of the door his fingers brushed something which made him draw back. A little table stood there: on the table was a huge pile of neatly-folded bath-towels.

He did not think of turning on a light or raising a blind. In his pocket he had a box of matches, with two or three left. He went over to the woman as quietly as he could, bent down, and hurriedly struck a match. That this was murder he had not doubted from the first. And, after a quick look, he blew out the match with equal haste: swallowing to keep down that feeling of revulsion which creeps on you before you are aware of it.

To the best of his knowledge, he had never seen the woman before. She seemed to be young, and had brown bobbed hair: which was one of the few details of which he could be sure. She was fully dressed, in a dark grey tailored suit and white silk blouse, except that instead of shoes she wore soft black slippers trimmed with fur. Evidently she had been strangled: the murderer having wrapped on his hands, to avoid leaving any marks, the ordinary crumpled face-towel which now lay across her shoulder. But this was not all that had been done. Her face had been heavily beaten or stamped on—undoubtedly after death, for there was not a great deal of blood despite the damage of that vicious afterthought. She was quite cold.

Kent crept across the room. There was a chair near the window and he sat down on the edge of it, though he automatically refrained from touching anything. He said to himself, coolly and half aloud, "My lad, you're in one terrible mess."

He had claimed he had spent that night in the room, with a woman he did not know from Eve. Logically, one thing ought to sustain him: he was in no danger of eventual arrest or hanging. The woman had been dead many hours. He had spent the night at a coffee-stall on the Embankment, and he could prove it by much congenial company; fortunately, his alibi was secure.

But that was only eventually. If he did not wish to spend the next day or so in a cell—to say nothing of being obliged to reveal his real name, losing a thousand-pound wager to Dan, and making himself a laughing-stock—he would have to get out of there somehow. All his stubbornness butted against this mess. Flight? Certainly; why not, if it could be managed? But in decency he could not leave that woman lying there—

There was a discreet knock at the door.

Kent got up quickly, searching for the bureau. One name and address now stood out in his mind as clearly as the lettering on the card. It was the name and address of a man whom he had never met, but with whom he frequently corresponded: Dr. Gideon Fell, number 1 Adelphi Terrace. He must call Dr. Fell. In the meantime, if he could find that infernal bracelet which someone had left behind in the bureau, he might get rid of the hall-porter.

He found the bureau, which was between the two windows; he had to touch things now. Through the sides of the blinds, pale light illuminated it. But he did not find the bracelet, because it was not there. A sense of something even more crooked and dangerous stirred in Kent's brain: he did not exactly suspect the waxed moustaches of the hall-porter, now waiting patiently outside the door, but he thought there must be something wrong besides murder. There was nothing at all in the bureau, whose drawers had each a clean paper lining.

Gingerly lifting a corner of the window-blind, Kent peered out. The windows of the room opened out on a high enclosed air-well faced with white tiles. Something else was wrong as well. A little while ago, the folded card bearing the number 707—the card that had brought him here—had floated down from some high window into his hand. But he had been standing in front of the hotel. Ergo, it had come from someone else's room. . . .

The discreet knock at the door was repeated. This time he thought he could hear the hall-porter cough.

Kent turned round and studied the room. In the wall now on his right there was another door; but this side of the room formed the angle with the two corridors outside. He made a quick and correct calculation. Unless it were a cupboard, that door must open directly into the corridor on the side out of sight of the hall-porter. It did: he drew back the bolt and opened it, now in sight of the men working on the lift. Accept what the gods give; in other words, here goes! Slipping out, he closed the door behind him and made off towards the stairs. Fifteen minutes later, in the midst of a thickening snowstorm, he was ringing the door-bell at number 1 Adelphi Terrace.

"*Aha!*" said Dr. Fell.

The door was opened by the doctor himself. He stood as vast as the door itself, projecting thence like a figurehead on a ship, and beaming out into the snow. His red face shone, as though by the reflection of firelight through the library windows; his small eyes twinkled behind eye-glasses on a broad black ribbon; and he seemed to peer down, with massive and wheezy geniality, over the ridges of his stomach. Kent restrained an impulse to cheer. It was like meeting Old King Cole on his own doorstep. Even before the visitor had mentioned his name or his errand, Dr. Fell cocked his head affably and waited.

His visitor arrived at a decision.

"I'm Christopher Kent," he said, breaking the rule and losing his bet. "And I'm afraid I've come six thousand miles to tell you I've walked into trouble."

Dr. Fell blinked at him. Though his geniality did not lessen, his face had become grave. He seemed to hover in the doorway (if such a manoeuvre were possible), like a great balloon with an ivory-headed stick. Then he glanced round at his own uncurtained library windows. Through them Kent could see a table laid for breakfast in the embrasure of the bay, and a tall, middle-aged man pacing round as though with impatience.

"Look here," said Dr. Fell seriously, "I think I can guess why and who. But I've got to warn you—you see that chap in there? That's Superintendent Hadley of the Criminal Investigation Department; I've written to you about him. Knowing that, will you come in and smoke a cigar?"

"I'd like to."

"Aha!" said Dr. Fell, with a pleased chuckle.

He lumbered into a big room lined to the ceiling with books; and the watchful, cautious, explosive Hadley, whose mental picture Kent had been able to build up already, stared when he heard the visitor's name. Then Hadley sat down quietly, smoothing out his noncommittal face. Kent found himself in a comfortable easy-chair by the breakfast-table, a cup of coffee in his hand, and he told his story with directness. Now that he had decided to lose his bet and let Dan's triumph go hang, there was satisfaction in feeling like a human being again.

"—and that's the whole story," he concluded. "Probably I was a fool to run out of there; but, if I'm going to jail, I'd rather be sent to jail by the head-man than explain to the hotel-staff how I cadged a breakfast. I didn't kill the woman. I never saw her before in my life. And, fortunately, I'm pretty sure I can prove where I was last night. That's the full list of my crimes."

Throughout this Hadley had been regarding him steadily. He seemed friendly enough, if very worried.

"No, it wasn't the thing to do," Hadley said. "But I don't suppose there's any great harm done, if you can prove what you say. And in a way I'm glad you did. (Eh, Fell?) The point is—" He drummed his fingers on his brief-case, and moved forward in the chair. "Never mind about last night. Where were you last Thursday fortnight: the 14th of January, to be exact?"

"On the *Volpar,* from Capetown to Tilbury."

"That ought to be easy enough to prove?"

"Yes. But why?"

Hadley glanced at Dr. Fell. Dr. Fell was sitting back in an enormous chair, several of his chins showing over his collar, and looking in an uneasy fashion down his nose. Over Kent's account of the wager he had made rumbling noises of approval; but now his noises were of a different sort.

"It would not be either striking or original," he observed, clearing his throat, "if I observed that I did not like this. H'mf. Ha. No. The business itself is neither striking nor original. It is not very bizarre. It is not very unusual. It is merely completely brutal and completely unreasonable. Dammit, Hadley—!"

"Look here, what's up?" demanded Kent. He had felt a tension brush that snug and firelit room.

"I know you found a woman in that room," Hadley said. "The news was phoned to me here not five minutes before you arrived. She had been strangled. Then, presumably after death, her face had been so battered as to be almost unrecognisable. You saw her by the light of a match with her head against the floor. Now, Mr. Kent, I assume you're telling the truth." His eyelids moved briefly. "And therefore I'm afraid I've got some bad news for you. If you had got a better look at her, you might have recognised her. The lady was Mrs. Josephine Kent—the wife of your cousin, Mr. Rodney Kent."

He looked from Hadley to Dr. Fell, and saw that neither of them was in the mood for joking.

"Jenny!" he said. "But that's—"

He stopped, because he did not know what he meant himself. It was simply that the two ideas, Jenny Kent and death, would not coincide; one was a stencil that would not go over the other. He tried to build up a picture of her. Small, plump, neat woman; yes. Brown hair; yes. But the description would fit a thousand women. It seemed impossible that it should have been his cousin's wife over whom he had struck a match not half an hour ago; yet why not? That piece of clay beside the trunk would not carry Jenny's extraordinary attractiveness.

Hadley looked hard at him. "There's no doubt it is Mrs. Kent if that's what you're thinking," the superintendent said. "You see, Mr. Reaper's party arrived at the Royal Scarlet last night, and they're occupying that wing on the seventh floor."

"The whole party? Then they were already there when I walked in?"

"Yes. Did you know Mrs. Kent well?"

"I suppose I should have expected that," muttered Kent, reflecting that much trouble could have been saved had he known it. He tried to arrange his thoughts. "Jenny? I don't know," he answered, honestly doubtful. "She wasn't the sort you did know well, and yet everybody in the world liked her. It's difficult to explain. I suppose you could call her 'nice.' Not unpleasantly nice; but you couldn't imagine her on a party or doing anything that wasn't strictly according to Hansard. And she was amazingly attractive without being beautiful: bright complexion, very quiet. Rod worshipped her; they've been married only a year or two, and—" He stopped. "Good God, that's the worst of it! This will just about kill Rod."

The figure of his cousin Rodney was very distinct in his mind then. He sympathised more with Rod than with the woman who was dead, for he had grown up with Rod and liked him very well. To Christopher Kent things had always come easily. To Rodney they came by plodding. Rodney was in simple earnest about everything. He was admirably suited to be Dan Reaper's political secretary; to answer letters with interest and thoroughness; to assemble the facts for Dan's speeches (Rodney Kent's facts could never be questioned); and even to write the sincere prose into which Dan stuck a tail-feather of rhetoric.

"The double room at the hotel, of course." Kent remembered it suddenly. "Rod would have been with her. But where was he? Where was he while she was being murdered? He wasn't there this morning. I tell you, it'll just about kill him—"

"No," said Dr. Fell. "He has been spared that, anyhow."

Again he became aware that both Dr. Fell and Hadley were looking at him.

"We may as well get this over with," the superintendent went on. "You may have wondered how I come to know so much about you and your affairs. I knew about this wager of yours; Mr. Reaper told me. We have been trying to get in touch with you, but nobody knew what ship you would be on or even what name you would use. . . . This isn't the first time I've been in touch with that party. Your cousin, Mr. Rodney Kent, was murdered on the 14th of January in exactly the same way that his wife was murdered last night."

Chapter III

The Statement of Ritchie Bellowes

"Consequently," pursued the superintendent, "I think you can help us." For the first time a human look appeared on his face, the shadow of an exasperated smile. "I've come to *this* duffer for help," he nodded towards Dr. Fell, who scowled, "because it seems to be another of those meaningless cases which delight his heart so much. Here are two young people, a happily married couple. It is universally agreed (at least, it's agreed by everyone I've spoken to) that neither of them had an enemy in the world. They certainly hadn't an enemy in England, for neither of them has ever been out of South Africa up until now. There seems no doubt that they were as harmless a pair as you'd find anywhere. Yet somebody patiently stalks and kills them—one at Sir Gyles Gay's place in Sussex, the other here at the Royal Scarlet Hotel. After killing them, the murderer stands over them and batters their faces with a vindictiveness I've not often seen equalled. Well?"

There was a pause.

"Naturally I'll help all I can," said Kent with bitterness. "But I still can't believe it. It's—hang it, it's indecent! As you say, neither of them had an enemy in—By the way, how is Jenny fixed? I mean, does she need money or anything, for—no, I forgot; she's dead. But haven't you got any idea who did it?"

Hadley hesitated. Then, pushing his finished breakfast-plate to one side, he opened his brief-case on the table.

"There's a fellow we've got in jail: not on a charge of murder, of course, though that's actually why he's there. Fellow named Bellowes. A good deal of the evidence points to him as the murderer of Rodney Kent—"

"Bellowes," said Dr. Fell blankly, "has now become the most important figure in the case, if I understand you properly."

"I don't think you do understand. Whether or not Bellowes killed Rodney Kent, I'm ruddy sure he didn't kill Mrs. Kent, because he's in jail."

A long sniff rumbled in Dr. Fell's nose. The light of battle, never very far away between these two, made them momentarily forget their visitor. Dr. Fell's face was fiery with controversy.

"What I am patiently attempting to point out," he returned, "is that Bellowes's statement, which seemed so ridiculous to you at the time—"

"Bellowes's statement can't be true. In the first place, his finger-prints were in the room. In the second place, when any man, drunk or sober, seriously maintains that he saw a man in the resplendent uniform of a hotel attendant walking about a Sussex country house at two o'clock in the morning—"

"Here!' protested Kent.

"I think," said Dr. Fell mildly, "that we had better enlighten our friend about a few things. H'mf. Suppose you go over the evidence again, Hadley, and ask for any information you want. Speaking for myself, I cannot hear too much of it. It's like one of Lear's nonsense rhymes: it flows so smoothly that for a second you are almost tricked into thinking you know what it means. The hotel attendant in a country house is a difficulty, I admit; but I can't see it's a difficulty that tells against Bellowes."

Hadley turned to Kent. "To begin with," he asked, "do you know Sir Gyles Gay?"

"No. I've heard Dan talk a lot about him, but I've never met him. He's something in the government, isn't he?"

"He used to be. He was under-secretary for the Union of South Africa: that means, I gather, a sort of buffer or liaison-officer between Whitehall and Pretoria. But he retired about a year ago, and it's been less than a year since he took a house at Northfield, in Sussex, just over the border of Kent." Hadley reflected. "Reaper's chief reason for coming to England was to see him, it seems. It was a business-deal: some property in Middelburg that Reaper was either buying or selling for Sir Gyles, and a friendly visit as well. Gay is a bachelor, and seems to have welcomed a lot of company in his new country house."

Again Hadley reflected. Then, as though frankly getting something off his chest, he got up and began to pace about the room, measuring the spots in the carpet while he talked. His voice was as indeterminate as his clipped moustache. But Kent had an impression that his watchfulness never relaxed.

"On Tuesday, January 12th, Reaper and his party went down from London to Northfield; they had arrived in England the day before. They intended to stay there for a little over a fortnight, and return to London on the evening of January 31st—that's actually to-day—in time for Reaper to meet you at the Royal Scarlet *if* you won the wager and appeared to-morrow. Everybody in the party seems to have been speculating about it.

"In the party at Northfield there were six persons. Sir Gyles Gay himself, the host. Mr. and Mrs. Reaper. Miss Francine Forbes, their

niece. Mr. Harvey Wrayburn. And your cousin, Mr. Rodney Kent,"
continued Hadley. He was as formal as though he were giving evidence.
"Mrs. Kent was not there. She has two aunts in Dorset—we checked up
on them—and she decided to pay them a visit; she had never seen them
before, although she had heard about them for years. So she went down
there before coming on to Northfield. I suppose you know all the persons
in Reaper's party?"

"Oh, yes," said Kent, thinking of Francine.

"And you'll be willing to supply any information I need about them?"
Kent faced him frankly.

"Look here, it's no good saying I don't see your implication. But you'll
never find a murderer in that group. It's a funny thing, too: I know most
of them better than I knew my own cousin."

"Oh, a murderer—!" said Hadley, with a slow and dry smile, as though
he brushed the matter aside as being unimportant. "At the moment we're
not finding a murderer; we're merely finding facts.

"Now the facts about the business are simple enough. Nobody was
running about the place at the wrong times. No group of people cross
each other's trails or contradict each other's stories. But the background
is the unusual part of the business, which seems to appeal to Fell.

"The village, Northfield, is an attractive sort of place such as you find
frequently in Kent and Sussex. It consists of a village green with a
church, a pub, and a dozen or so houses round it. It's rather secluded, set
in the middle of all those thousand little lanes designed exactly like a
maze for motor-cars; it runs to half-timbering and an 'old-world' atmosphere."

Dr. Fell grunted.

"This back-handed lyricism," he said, "is inspired by the fact that
Hadley, in spite of being a Scot, is a good Cockney who hates the
country, and profoundly resents the circumstance that roads antedated
motor-cars."

"That may be," admitted Hadley quite seriously. "But all the same I
was looking for a hint in it. Say what you like, it can't be—it wasn't—a
very exciting place in the dead of winter. I was just wondering why *all*
Reaper's party wanted to go down there for a fortnight and dig in. You'd
think they'd prefer to stay in town and see some shows.

"Well, for the past forty years one of the great local characters thereabouts was old Ritchie Bellowes: the father of our chief suspect. He's
dead now, but they thought a lot of him. Old Bellowes was both an
architect and a practical builder, with a taste for doing a lot of the work
with his own hands. He built half the modern houses in the district. He
seems to have had a fondness for wood-carving and all sorts of gadgets;
but his particular hobby was building replicas of Tudor or Stuart houses

so cleverly faked, with beams and floor-boards out of other houses, that the most expert architect would be deceived about the age of the house. It was a sort of village joke, and the old man seems to have had rather a queer sense of humour himself. He loved putting in trick doors and se-cret passages—stop! I hasten to assure you, from absolute knowledge, that there's no secret passage or the like in the house I'm telling you about.

"This house, the one he built for his own use, was bought by Sir Gyles Gay some months ago. It's a fairly large place—eight bedrooms—and stands at the foot of a lane going down past the church. It's an imitation Queen Anne place, and a really beautiful job if you don't mind something on the heavy and grim style. Some of the windows look straight out across the churchyard, which is hardly my idea of rural grandeur.

"What we have to consider is the position of young Ritchie Bellowes, the old man's son. I tell you quite frankly I'm damned if I see how he fits into this, and I should feel happier if I could. He's a character also. He was born and brought up in that house. From what I've been able to learn, he's had the best of educations, and he's certainly a clever chap. What seems to impress everyone is his phenomenal power of quick observa-tion, drunk or sober: the sort of person before whom you can riffle a pack of cards and he can afterwards name you consecutively every card he saw. As a matter of fact, he gave a little entertainment of this kind, mental tests, before Sir Gyles's guests during the first few days they were at the house.

"He was left very well off when the old man died. Then the dry rot set in. He doesn't seem to have had any actual vices: he was simply plain lazy, added to a slight paralysis in the left arm, and he liked the drink. The slide down the incline was first gradual, and then abrupt. First his business dropped to pieces; the slump hit him and he didn't improve it by the way he squandered money. Then his wife died of typhoid at the seaside, and he caught it too. He kept on quietly drinking. By this time he's become something like the village drunk. He gives no trouble and makes no fuss. Every night of his life he leaves the bar-parlour of the Stag and Glove under his own steam, with great politeness. Finally, he had to sell his favourite fake Queen Anne house—Four Doors, it's called—for whatever it would bring. He's been living in lodgings with a pious widow; and almost haunting the old place since Sir Gyles Gay bought it. That may have been the root of the trouble.

"Now we come to the bare facts about the night of the murder. Exclusive of servants there were six persons in the house. Sir Gyles and his five guests all slept on the same floor. They all occupied separate rooms (Mr. and Mrs. Reaper were in connecting ones); and all the rooms opened on a central passage running the breadth of the house. Like a hotel, you'll say. The household retired together about midnight. So far as I can find out, there had been absolutely nothing unusual, abnormal, or even suspicious about anyone or any event that night; on the contrary, it seems to have been a fairly dull evening. After midnight only one person—according to the testimony—left his room at any time. At about five minutes past two o'clock Mr. Reaper woke up, put on his dressing-gown, turned on the light, and went out in the hall to go to the bathroom. Up to this time it is agreed that no noise or disturbance of any kind had been heard.

"Next, compare this with our knowledge of Bellowes's movements for that night. Bellowes left the Stag and Glove, which is off the village green about two hundred yards from the lane leading to Four Doors, at just ten o'clock: closing time. He had drunk no more than usual that night; six pints of ale, the landlord says. But on the last round he called for whisky, and, when he left, he bought a half-bottle of whisky to take with him. He then seemed to be his usual self. He was seen to walk off along the road towards Porting, the next village, and to branch from there into a lane leading to a wood called Grinning Copse: another favourite haunt of his, where he often sat and drank alone. The 14th was a cold night, with a very bright moon. There we lose sight of him.

"At five minutes past two, then, Reaper at the house opened his bedroom door and walked out into the main passage. Along one wall of this passage—not far outside the door of the room occupied by Rodney Kent—there is a leather-covered sofa. By the moonlight through the window at the end of the passage, Reaper could see a man stretched out on this sofa, asleep and snoring. In that light he didn't recognise the man; but it was Bellowes, unquestionably dead drunk.

"Reaper turned on the lights and knocked at Sir Gyles's door. Sir Gyles knew Bellowes, of course, and seems to have sympathised with him. They both assumed that Bellowes, drunk, had simply come here by instinct, as he had been doing all his life: a key to the house was found in his pocket. Then they noticed that the door to Rodney Kent's room was wide open."

Outside the windows the snow was falling with silent insistence, shadowing this book-lined room. In a sort of hypnosis induced by reaction or firelight, Christopher Kent was trying to fit the person he had always known under warmer skies—ginger-haired, serious-minded Rodney—into this bleak atmosphere of a sham Queen Anne house by a churchyard. During the recital Dr. Fell had not moved, except to ruffle his big mop of grey-streaked hair.

"Well," Hadley went on abruptly, "they found your cousin dead there, Mr. Kent. He was lying at the foot of the bed. He wore his pyjamas and dressing-gown, but he had not yet gone to bed when the murderer caught him. He had been strangled by hands wrapped in a face-towel; the towel itself, which came from the wash-hand-stand, was lying across his shoulder. (That particular room is furnished in heavy eighteen-sixties style, with marble-topped bureaux and the old massive stuff.) After being strangled, his face had been bashed in by about a dozen blows—our old friend the blunt instrument, of course—but the blunt instrument wasn't found.

"It was a nasty bit of work, because the blows must have been delivered some minutes after his actual death, out of deliberate hatred or mania. But it was not enough to prevent positive identification, so there's no doubt as to the victim. Finally the murderer must have caught him almost as soon as he'd retired to his room, because the medical evidence showed he had been dead nearly two hours. Is all that clear?"

"No," said Dr. Fell. "But go on."

"Stop a bit," interposed Kent. "There's something even more queer here. Rod was thin, but he was as tough as wire. The murderer must have been very quick and very powerful to catch him like that without any noise; or was there a struggle?"

"Not necessarily. No, there was no sign of a struggle. But on the back of his head there was a bad bruise which did not quite break the skin. It might have come from the scrollwork and curves on the footboard of the bed—you know the sort of thing—when he fell. Or the murderer might have stunned him with the instrument that was later used to batter him."

"So you arrested this fellow Bellowes?"

Hadley was irritable. His measurement of the spots in the carpet had now become a matter of painful preciseness.

"Not on a charge of murder. Technically, of housebreaking," he retorted. "Naturally he was the suspect. First of all, his finger-prints were found in the room, round the light-switch: though he says he has no recollection of being in the room and is willing to swear he didn't go in. Second, he is the only person likely to have committed the crime. He was drunk; he may have suffered from a sense of grievance about the house; he may have come back there and gone berserk—

"Wait!" Hadley interrupted himself, forestalling objection. "I can see all the holes in it, and I'll give you them. If he killed his victim at midnight and then went out and fell asleep on the sofa in the hall, what happened to our blunt instrument? Also, there was no trace whatever of blood on him or on his clothes. Finally, it so happens that his left arm is partially paralysed (one of the reasons why he never took to work), and the doctor is of the opinion that he couldn't have strangled anybody. The drunken motive is also weak. If he had a grievance against anybody, it would have been against Sir Gyles Gay. He would hardly have walked in and—(with malice aforethought, since there was a weapon)—assaulted a complete stranger at random, especially as he didn't make the least noise in doing it. I also admit that nobody in a village where he's been drinking for a good many years has ever found him savage or vindictive, no matter how much he had aboard. But there you are.

"Then there's his statement, which seems a mass of nonsense. He wasn't coherent until the next day, and even in jail he didn't seem to realise what was happening. When he told his story for the first time, Inspector Tanner thought he was still drunk and didn't even bother to write it down; but he repeated it when he was cold sober, and he's stuck to it since.

"According to him—well, here you are."

Opening his brief-case, Hadley took a typewritten sheet from among a sheaf of others and ran his finger down it.

I remember being in Grinning Copse, going there after the pub closed, and I remember drinking most of the bottle I had. I have no idea how long I was there. At one time I thought there was someone talking to me; but I may have imagined this. The last thing I remember distinctly is sitting in the copse on one of the iron seats. The next thing I knew I was back at Four Doors, sitting on the sofa in the upstairs hall.

I cannot tell you how I got there; but it did not seem strange to find myself there. I thought, "Hullo, I'm home," that's all. Since I was already on the sofa and did not feel like moving, I thought I would just stretch out and take a nap.

At this time I do not think I went to sleep immediately. While I was lying there I saw something; I think I looked round and saw it. It was bright moonlight in the hall; there is a window at the end of the hall, on the south side, and the moon was high then. I do not know how it caught the corner of my eye, but I saw him in the corner there, by the Blue Room door.

I should describe him as a medium-sized man wearing a uniform such as you see in the big hotels like the Royal Scarlet or the Royal Purple. It was a dark blue uniform, with a long coat, and silver or brass buttons; I could not be sure about colours in the moonlight. I think there was a stripe round the cuffs, a dark red stripe. He was carrying a kind of tray, and at first he stood in the corner and did not move.

Question: What about his face?

A.: I could not make out his face, because there seemed to be a lot of shadow, or a hole or something, where his eyes ought to be.

Then he moved out of the corner, and moved or walked down where I could not see him, past my head. His walk also made me think of a hotel attendant.

Q.: Where did he go?

A.: I do not know.

Q.: Did it not surprise you to see a hotel-attendant walking along the hall with a tray in the middle of the night?

A.: No, I did not even think much about it that I remember. I rolled over and went to sleep; or at least I do not remember anything more. Besides, it was not a tray he had; it was more like a salver to carry visiting-cards.

"Which," commented Hadley, slapping the typewritten sheet down on the table, "makes it all the more nonsensical. A salver, mind you! Blast it, Fell, this is either delirium tremens or prophecy or truth. A salver for what? For carrying the weapon? I don't say this fellow Bellowes is guilty; just among the three of us, I don't think he is. But if he's quite sincere in telling this, and if the hotel-attendant isn't the same kind of vision as a brass-buttoned snake, where are we?"

"Well, I'll tell you," said Dr. Fell modestly. He pointed his ivory-headed stick at Hadley, and sighted along it as though it were a rifle. "That toper of yours, you recall, is the same man who can describe a shop-window full of articles after one glance at 'em. A little *causerie* with Ritchie Bellowes, now languishing in clink, is indicated. Dig into that statement; find out what he really saw, or thinks he saw; and we shall probably have a glimmer of the truth."

Hadley considered.

"Of course," he said, "there's the theory that Bellowes committed the first murder while drunk; and that some other person merely used it, used the way of the crime and Bellowes's story about a phantom hotel-attendant, to kill Mrs. Kent later at the Royal Scarlet Hotel—"

"Do you believe that?"

"Frankly, no."

"Thank'e," said Dr. Fell. He wheezed for a moment, regarding Hadley with what can only be called ruddy dignity. "These two murders are the work of one person: anything else, my boy, would be artistically wrong: and I have an unpleasant feeling that someone behind the scenes is managing matters with great artistry." For a time he remained blinking, in a vacant and somewhat cross-eyed fashion, at the hands folded over his stick. " 'Mf. Take this business at the Royal Scarlet last night. All of Reaper's party were present again, I take it?"

"All I know," said Hadley, "is what Betts told me over the phone a few minutes ago. Yes. And Gay himself was with them again—making six persons, just as there were at Four Doors."

"Gay went with 'em to the hotel? Why?"

"Instinct to stick together, I suppose. Gay and Reaper are as thick as thieves."

Dr. Fell looked at him curiously, as though interested by the choice of phrase. But he turned to Kent. "This," rumbled the doctor apologetically, "is hardly what you would be inclined to call fine old English hospitality. I've been looking forward to meeting you, because there are one or two points concerning sensational fiction which I should like to debate with some vehemence. But, frankly, I should like to ask some questions now. These friends of yours—I haven't met any of them, and I want you to describe them for me. Not (heaven forbid) any complicated backgrounds. Just give me one word or phrase about them, the first word or phrase that jumps into your head. Eh?"

"Right," said Kent, "though I still think—"

"Well: Daniel Reaper?"

"Talk and action," replied the other promptly.

"Melitta Reaper?"

"Talk."

"Francine Forbes?"

"Femininity," said Kent, after a pause.

Hadley spoke in a colourless voice. "I understand from talking to Mr. Reaper that you were a good deal interested in the young lady."

"I am," the other admitted frankly. "But we don't get on very well. She is vitally concerned with the importance of new political movements, new theories of all kinds; she *is* The Intelligent Woman's Guide to Socialism, Capitalism, Sovietism, and so on. I'm not. In politics, like Andrew Lang, I never got any farther than being a Jacobite; and I think that, if a man's got the gumption to go out and make himself a fortune, more power to him. Consequently, she regards me as a pig-headed Tory and reactionary. But one of the main reasons why I took up this fool bet was to show her—"

"Heh," said Dr. Fell. "Heh-heh-heh. I see. Next name on our list: Harvey Wrayburn."

"Acrobat."

"Is he?" inquired Dr. Fell, opening his eyes. "I say, Hadley, this is interesting. Do you remember O'Rourke in the Hollow Man case?"

"He's not an acrobat literally," interposed Hadley. "But I think I see what you mean." His eyes narrowed as he regarded Kent. "Very versatile fellow, Fell. He seems to know a good deal about, or to have had some personal experience with, every subject you could mention. He buttonholed me on the subject of crime, and was spouting encyclopaedia after your own heart. He seems a decent sort and," added Hadley, with innate caution about saying this of anyone, "straightforward enough."

"He is," agreed Kent.

"And that's the lot. Now," argued the superintendent, "I don't want to say too much before we've got all our facts. But, by George! a more sterile, harmless lot, as far as suspicion is concerned, I never came across. We've looked up the pasts of all these people. I've talked to them until I'm blue in the face. No one hated or disliked anyone else. No one is financially crooked or even financially crippled. There is not even a hint of a last stand-by in someone's having a love-affair with someone else's wife. There seems to be absolutely no reason why two ordinary young people, whose death would not benefit or even please anyone, should be carefully stalked and murdered. But again—there you are. They were not only murdered: they were battered with patient fury after death. Unless some member of that group is homicidally mad (which I refuse to believe, because I never met a case of it in which signs didn't crop out plainly even when the person was not in a seizure), it makes no sense. What do you make of it?"

"There's just one thing, Hadley. After the man was murdered, you at least had his wife to question. Couldn't she tell you anything to throw any light on it?"

"No. Or she said she couldn't, and I'll swear she was telling the truth; so why should anyone kill her? As I told you, she was with the aunts in Dorset when it happened. She went half out of her mind, and took to her bed under the soothing hysterics of the aunts. She only got out of the doctor's care long enough to rejoin the rest of the party in London: and on her first night here *she's* murdered. I still ask, what do you make of it?"

"Well, I'll tell you," said Dr. Fell. He puffed out his cheeks, seeming to loom even vaster as he leaned back in the chair. "I can give no assistance at the moment, I regret to say. I can only indicate the things which seem intriguing. I'm interested in towels. I'm interested in buttons. And I'm interested in names."

"Names?"

"Or their permutations," said Dr. Fell. "Shall we get on to the hotel?"

Chapter IV

HOTEL-SERVICE FOR MURDER

When they were introduced to the manager of the Royal Scarlet Hotel, Kent had expected to meet a suave autocrat in a morning coat, a sort of super head-waiter, of foreign and possibly Semitic extraction. Quite to the contrary, Mr. Kenneth Hardwick was a homely, comfortable, and friendly island product, who wore an ordinary grey suit. Kenneth Hardwick was a grizzled man of middle age, with a strong face, a hooked nose, and a twinkling eye; the keynote of himself, as of his hotel, seemed to be an untroubled efficiency which was shaken by a murder but prepared to deal with it without fuss.

Superintendent Hadley, Dr. Fell, and Kent sat in the manager's private rooms on the seventh floor. The ordinary business office was downstairs; but two rooms on the new floor, in Wing D, had been set apart for him. His living-room, a severe but comfortable place in dark oak, had two windows looking out on the white-tiled air-well. Hardwick sat behind a big desk, where a desk-lamp was burning in the gloom of the day, and tapped a plan of Wing A spread out before him. He constantly put on and took off a pair of eyeglasses, his only sign of perturbation in a business-like recital.

"—so," he concluded, "before the other Mr. Kent came here this morning, that was the position. Mr. Reaper booked the rooms for his party six weeks ago, and asked particularly to have the accommodations on this floor. Of course I knew about Mr. Rodney Kent's death two weeks ago, and a bad business it was." He seemed to draw himself together, setting his glasses on more firmly. "Although there was practically nothing about it in the Press, and certainly no hint of anything except—um—a drunken attack. . . ."

"No," said Hadley. "The Home Office have instructed us to keep it out of the public eye. The inquest has been adjourned."

"I see." Hardwick leaned a little farther forward. "Now the position is this, superintendent. Ordinarily I should be a fool if I asked whether this affair could be kept quiet. I had and have no intention of asking that. But what's the situation? If there has been a certain amount of secrecy about Mr. Kent's death, does the same thing apply to Mrs. Kent? Right up to this minute nobody, except those immediately concerned, knows anything about it. Business as usual, you see. This has been easy, because Mr. Reaper's party are the only persons in Wing A; they're more or less cut off—"

"Cut off," repeated Hadley. "Until I get my instructions, it will certainly be kept quiet. Now for details. Just which rooms are these various persons occupying?"

Hardwick pushed the plan across the desk. "I've marked them here," he explained. "You'll see that number 707 says, 'Mr. and Mrs. Rodney Kent.' It was down like that in our books; and it was not changed. That was why, this morning, the staff saw nothing odd in there being a second occupant of the room when someone asked for breakfast."

There was a knock at the door. Sergeant Betts, Hadley's aide-de-camp, came in with a note-book significantly displayed.

"Doctor's just finished, sir," he announced. "He'd like to see you. I've checked up on the other points you asked about."

"Right. Where are the—guests?"

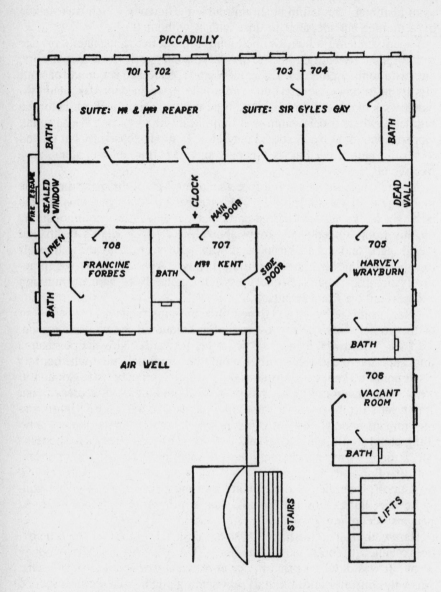

PICCADILLY

701 - 702

SUITE: MR & MRS REAPER

703 - 704

SUITE: SIR GYLES GAY

BATH

FIRE ESCAPE

SEALED WINDOW

← CLOCK

MAIN DOOR

DEAD WALL

BATH

LINEN

708

FRANCINE FORBES

BATH

707

MRS KENT

SIDE DOOR

705

HARVEY WRAYBURN

BATH

BATH

706

VACANT ROOM

AIR WELL

BATH

STAIRS

LIFTS

PLAN OF WING A
SEVENTH FLOOR, ROYAL SCARLET HOTEL

"All in their own rooms. I had a bit of difficulty with Mr. Reaper, but Preston is standing guard in the hall."

Hadley grunted, hitching his chair closer to study the plan. There was a long silence. The light of the desk-lamp shone on Hardwick's face, moulded with attention, a half-smile fixed there. Dr. Fell, a great bandit figure in the black cape, with his shovel-hat in his lap, stared down over Hadley's shoulder. Faintly they were aware of the music of the orchestra from the lounge below, coming up the air-well; but it was a background, a vibration, rather than something actually heard.

"I see," the superintendent began abruptly, "that all the rooms have private bathrooms. And only one of them is unoccupied."

"Yes; number 706 is unoccupied. Nearest the lifts. The workmen are still there, and I was afraid it might disturb anybody who was too close."

"Do you take charge of these arrangements personally?"

"Not ordinarily, no. But in this case, yes; I know Mr. Reaper, and I used to live in South Africa myself."

"Were these rooms assigned some time ago?"

"Oh, yes. The only difference was that the party arrived here a day earlier than they had intended."

"How was that? Do you know?"

"Well, Mr. Reaper rang me up from Northfield yesterday afternoon. He said—their nerves were all on edge, you see—" Hardwick made a slight deprecating gesture; "he felt they had better not stay in the country any longer, and the police had no objection to their coming to London. It was easy enough to fit them in; this is a slack season. As a matter of fact, only one of the rooms had been occupied—707—by a lady who was vacating it yesterday afternoon."

Hadley glanced at Kent. "That's the American lady who said she left a valuable bracelet behind in the bureau of the room?"

"Said?" repeated the manager. "I don't know what you mean by that exactly. She *did* leave a bracelet in the bureau. Myers, the day hall-porter, found it there at the same time he found—Mrs. Kent."

Christopher Kent stared at him. He had too vivid a recollection of that maplewood bureau, with its sleek-moving drawers and their paper linings, to let this pass.

"Wait. There's a mistake here somewhere," he interposed. "During my little adventure this morning I looked all through that bureau; and I'll swear by anything you like that there was no bracelet in it then."

Hardwick spoke after a pause. The small lines had returned to his forehead; it was as though they were poised there. He looked quickly from one to the other of his guests.

"I don't know what to say. All I know is that I have the bracelet now; a fairly clinching argument. Myers brought it to me when he came to report the other business. Here, have a look at it."

He pulled out a drawer at the left-hand side of his desk. Tearing open a sealed envelope, he put down the bracelet under the light. It was of white gold, set in broad links, and in the centre was one stone of curious design. Square, black, polished and dully gleaming, it had engraved on it two lines in Roman script just large enough to read. *Claudite jam rivos, pueri,* said the inscription, *sat prata biberunt.* Behind Hadley's shoulder Dr. Fell was making vast and seething noises of excitement.

"Yes, it's unusual," Hardwick commented. "That stone—obsidian, black opal, what is it?—looks as though it had been taken out of a ring and set into the bracelet. But the inscription is still more unusual. The remains of a once-passable stock of Latin don't help me. I should render it irreverently as, 'Shut up the liquor, boys; the meadows have had enough to drink'—which seems to be nonsense."

He regarded Dr. Fell with a dry and inquiring grin, which had a sudden keenness in it.

"Oh, Bacchus!" growled Dr. Fell, not informatively. "I say, no wonder she wants to get this back! The stone is not intrinsically valuable; but there are several museum-curators who would cut your throat to get it. If it's what I think it is, there must be very few of them extant. As for the inscription, you're not far off. It's a string of metaphors in Virgil's coyest style; his injunction to the shepherds; and a schoolbook softener would render it, 'Cease to sing, lads; recreation enough has been taken.' H'mf. Ha. Yes, I should say this had certainly been taken out of a ring and set into the bracelet. White gold; broad links—nothing there. Only the stone is old. Of course the scheme originated in Greece, and was only copied by the Romans. It's unique! Wow! Dammit, Hadley, you are looking at one of the most ingenious devices of the ancient world."

"Ingenious devices?" demanded Hadley. "Ingenious device for what? You mean it's a poison-stone or bracelet or something?"

"The professional touch," said Dr. Fell with austerity. He stared at it. "No, nothing of that sort; and yet it is as severely practical as one. The Romans were a practical race. Who is the owner of this, Mr. Hardwick?"

The manager looked puzzled. "A Mrs. Jopley-Dunne. I have her address here."

"You don't happen to know her, do you?"

"Yes, quite well. She always stays with us when she is in England."

Wheezing, Dr. Fell sat down again and shook his head. An exasperated Hadley waited for him to speak; but, when the doctor's eye wandered off towards vacancy, Hadley gave it up in favour of more practical matters.

"The bracelet can wait; one thing at a time. Just at the moment, we're following Mr. Reaper's party. At what time did they arrive here?"

"About six o'clock last evening."

"What were they like then? I mean, what was the mood of the party?"

"Definitely glum," said Hardwick, with a gravity which Kent felt was hiding a bleak smile. It did not pass unnoticed by Hadley.

"Go on," said the superintendent. "What happened then?"

"I met them, and took them upstairs. As I told you, I know Mr. Reaper personally. Well, under the circumstances, I advised him to take his friends out and see a show, preferably something funny. You know."

"And did he?"

"Yes; he took six tickets for *She Will When She Won't.*"

"Did they all go?"

"Yes. I don't think Mrs. Kent wanted to go, but she was persuaded. I happened to be leaving my office—downstairs that is—about a quarter past eleven, and I met the party returning from the theatre. They certainly seemed in much better spirits. Mr. Reaper stopped to buy a cigar, and told me that they had all enjoyed the show."

"And then?"

"They went upstairs. At least," said Hardwick, cocking his head on one side and choosing terms carefully, "they got into the lift. I did not see any of them again. The next thing I knew of the business was next morning, when Myers came in to report the discovery of the body." He removed his eyeglasses, put them into their case, and shut it with a snap. For a time he remained looking meditatively at the blotter. "I am not," he added, "going to make any more comments on the ugly nature of this business. You know it; I know it; and it's bad enough to speak for itself." He looked up. "Have you seen that woman's face?"

"Not yet," said Hadley. "Now one question in particular. You say that there were men working on one of the lifts. Were they working all night?"

"Yes."

"Do you know what time they came on and went off duty?"

"Yes. That shift—three men—began at ten last night and worked until eight this morning. They were still there when the body was discovered."

"Suppose some other person—some outsider, someone not connected with Mr. Reaper's party—had gone into Wing A or come out of it at any time during the night. Those men would have seen him, wouldn't they?"

"I should certainly think so. The wing is lighted all night. A person could have come up or down only by the lift or by the staircase; and the workmen were standing between both."

Hadley gave an interrogative glance at Sergeant Betts, who nodded.

"Yes, sir," agreed the sergeant. "I've got a statement from all three men. They seem straightforward enough and they all tell the same story. They remember Mr. Reaper's party coming upstairs about a quarter past eleven. As a matter of fact, Mr. Reaper stopped and asked them some questions about how the lift worked, and how they were getting on with it. They saw the party separate at the turning of the corridor. Afterwards, they're willing to swear no other person came in or went out of the wing all night."

"So. But is there any other way an outsider could have got in?"

Hadley's question was directed midway between Betts and the hotel-manager. After a pause the latter shook his head.

"Unlikely," he said.

"Why?"

"Look at your plan. I don't say it's impossible, but you're the judge of that." Hardwick twisted the plan round on the table. "There are two other ways, theoretically. An outsider—I suppose you mean a burglar?—might have climbed up the fire-escape to the window at the end of the wing. But, as it happens, that particular window is not only solidly locked on the inside: it was reported to me yesterday as being so stuck in its frame that it couldn't be opened at all. A man was to have seen to it this morning. The only other way in would have been for your burglar to have climbed up the face of the building—either on the outer side towards Piccadilly, or else inside by way of the air-well—barged through some-one else's room without being seen, and got out the same way. Knowing what I do of this hotel, I should say it's so unlikely as to be nearly impossible."

"You see where these questions are leading?"

"Oh, yes. I see it."

Hadley turned to Betts. "Well, excluding outsiders, did *anybody* go in or out of that wing during the night? What about employees of the hotel?"

"Nobody except the chambermaid, sir. She went off duty at half-past eleven."

"Yes, but—" Hadley scowled at his note-book. "What about the Boots? Wouldn't there be a Boots, or whatever you call him? You put your shoes outside the door at night, and they take them away to be polished—"

Betts nodded. "Yes, sir. But the Boots—he's actually an under-porter—wasn't in the wing until early this morning, a good many hours after the murder. It seems they don't pick up your shoes and take them away during the night, in case someone comes in very late. They wait unitl five o'clock in the morning; then they gather up the lot, polish them, and put them back. The Boots went through at five o'clock, and spoke to the men working on the lifts. But only one person in the wing had put out a pair of shoes—Mrs. Kent. And the Boots knew there was some mistake."

"Mistake?" said Hadley sharply.

"In the first place, they were a pair of brown suède shoes; and you can't polish suède. In the second place, they weren't a pair, though they looked alike at first glance. One was a lighter brown than the other, and had a small flat buckle on it. The Boots knew there had been a mistake somewhere, so he left the shoes there and came away."

Dr. Fell interposed, with an expression of painful interest on his face. "Just one moment. I'm interested in the mechanics of this citadel. Just how is a hotel run? Who would be in and out of the place at that time of night?"

"There are some three hundred people employed here," said Hardwick, "and it would take some time to explain how everything is run. But I can tell you this: after eleven-thirty at night, nobody would have any business upstairs at all—nobody—except one of the four under-porters.

"It's like this. The maids, who are on duty to answer bells and the rest of it during the day, go off for the night at eleven-thirty. That's for moral reasons," he explained blandly; "you don't want a crowd of girls about when you're turning in. At that time, also, any employees who would have had occasion to go upstairs during the day (like waiters or page-boys) are also off duty. The upstairs is left to the four under-porters on the staff of the night hall-porter."

"There are two shifts, I suppose?" asked Hadley.

"Oh, yes. The night men come on at eight o'clock, and go on until eight the next morning. Each man takes care of one or two floors, according to how full we are. If a bell rings from his floor, he answers it. If luggage has to be carried up, or a guest forgets his key or comes home tight—all the odd jobs, you see. They also collect the shoes at five in the morning, as the sergeant says."

"The point is," insisted Hadley, "*did* anyone go upstairs last night except the maid?"

"No, sir," said Betts. "That seems to be pretty certain."

With a very brief preliminary knock, the door opened and Dan Reaper walked in. After him came Francine Forbes, as though for a rear-guard.

Kent got up automatically. She saw him, although Dan did not notice anything. More than ever, in London, Kent realised that Dan was built on a large scale like a relief map of Africa, and he required room in which to breathe. Yet, despite Dan's buoyant energy, he looked ill; there was a part of his brain which for ever worried and worried and worried. His hair, turning dry and greyish at the temples, was cut short in the Teutonic style; his very light eyes, in a face whose brick-dust tan had not faded, were surrounded with little wrinkles which made the heavy face seem to have been gone over with a nutmeg-grater. His mouth, which expressed at once generosity and suspicion, had been pulled in so that the lower lip was drawn over the lower teeth.

In appearance Francine offered a contrast, though in a few mental features she might have been his daughter. She was calmer than Dan, possibly even more determined: it was that determination which brought her and Christopher Kent into conflict whenever they met. She was slender, with that very fair skin which does not tan or burn, but seems to keep a kind of glow in its whiteness: emphasised by fair hair curtly bobbed, and dark brown eyes with long lids. She looked—there is no other word for it—overbred, though the overbreeding seemed to have run to vitality rather than anaemia. You knew that her brown dress was an extreme in fashion less because it was so plain than because it was so completely right for her.

"Look here, Hardwick," said Dan, with restraint. He put the palms of his hands flat on the desk, and then he saw Kent.

Dan whistled.

"How in the world—?" he added, with a subdued roar.

"I think," said Hadley, "that you know Mr. Kent?"

"Lord, yes. One of my best—" said Dan. He stopped again, and looked up quickly. "Did you tell him who you were, Chris? Because, if you did—"

"I know: I lose. Never mind the bet, Dan. Forget the bet. We're in the middle of too serious a mess for that. Hello, Francine."

Dan flushed, rubbing the side of his jaw. He looked at a loss, the other thought, because his innate tact was struggling with his innate desire to explain himself.

"Rotten," he said. "Rottenest nightmare I ever stumbled into. We tried to find you, Chris, but of course—Don't worry, though; don't worry a bit. I took care of everything. He was buried in Hampshire; you know his people came from there; everything of the best; cost me over five hundred, but worth it." After these jerky utterances, even Dan's strong nerve seemed to falter. He spoke querulously. "But I wish I were back having a nice comfortable drink at the SAPC. Now it's Jenny. Have you got any idea what's been happening to us?"

"No."

"But you can tell them, can't you, that nobody would want to kill Rod or Jenny?"

"I can and have."

Hadley let them talk, watching both of them. After barely acknowledging Kent's greeting, Francine Forbes waited with that same air of just having emerged from a cold bath; it was a glow of the skin, he thought, as well as a mental atmosphere. But she was not at ease. Although the long eyes did not move, her hands did: nervously brushing the sides of her dress.

"If we are through discussing Chris's gallant gesture," she said in her brittle voice—it made him hot and angry in a fraction of a second— "perhaps we'd better tell you, Mr. Hadley, why we are here. We form a deputation of two to tell you that we're jolly well not going to stay caged up in separate compartments, like isolated cases, until we know what has happened. We know Jenny is dead. And that's all we do know."

Hadley was at his suavest. He pushed out a chair for her, although she declined it with a turn of the wrist which indicated that she saw nothing except the matter in hand.

"I'm afraid it's all we know ourselves, Miss Forbes," the superintendent told her. "We were coming round to see each of you as soon as we had gone over the room where the murder was committed. Yes, murder: the same as the other one, I'm afraid. By the way, let me introduce Dr. Gideon Fell, of whom you may have heard."

She nodded curtly: a salutation which the doctor, who had got up with vast wheezings, acknowledged by sweeping his shovel-hat across his breast. He also surveyed her through his eyeglasses with an expression of vast and benevolent interest which she seemed to find irritating. But she kept her eyes fixed on Hadley.

"Was she—strangled?"

"Yes."

"When?" asked Dan. He seemed to wish to assert himself.

"We don't know that yet; as I say, we haven't been to the room or seen the doctor. I know," pursued Hadley smoothly, "that it's difficult to remain in your various rooms just now. But, believe me, it would help to keep matters quiet and prevent attracting attention to what's happened— and to yourselves as well—if you would just follow my advice and go back there now. Unless, of course, you have anything important to tell us about last night?"

"N-no," said Dan, clearing his throat. "Not that, God knows!"

"I understand your party came back here from the theatre about a quarter past eleven last night?"

"Yes, that's right."

Hadley paid no attention to his suspicious glance. "When you came back, Mr. Reaper, did you visit one another's rooms or did you all go directly to your own rooms?"

"Straight to our own rooms. We were tired."

By this time Francine had assumed so bored an expression that Kent longed to administer a whacking in the proper place. What he could never determine was whether these moods of hers were quite genuine or an elaborate shell of affectation.

"Well, then: did you see or hear anything suspicious during the night?"

"No," said Dan rigorously.

"You, Miss Forbes?"

"Nothing, thank you," said Francine, as though she were refusing something to eat or drink.

"Did either of you leave your room at any time?"

"No," answered Dan, and hesitated. "No; that still goes. I didn't leave the room. I put my head out and looked into the hall, that's all."

"Looked out into the hall? Why?"

"To see the clock. There's a clock on the wall in the hall there, near Francine's door. My watch had stopped. I called out to my wife to ask her if she knew what time it was; but she was in the bathroom with the bath running, and couldn't hear me. So I opened the door," said Dan, making a heavy gesture of lucidity, "and looked out at the clock. That's all."

"At what time was this?"

"At two minutes past midnight," replied the other promptly. "I set my watch then."

Sergeant Betts moved unobtrusively round behind Hadley's chair. He wrote a few words on the margin of his note-book and held it out. Kent, who was sitting nearest, could read it before Hadley noncommittally passed the note-book to Dr. Fell. It read: *Doctor says she died about midnight.*

"Did you see or hear anyone then, Mr. Reaper? Anyone in the hall, for instance?"

"No," said Dan. "Nobody," he added, "except one of the hotel-attendants, outside Jenny's door, carrying a big pile of towels."

Chapter V

THE NEW IRON-MAIDEN

What Kent could not understand was whether or not Dan realised what he had said—even whether he threw it off deliberately, and had come here to do so. It was difficult to think that a man of Dan's practical intelligence would not think of it. But he spoke with his own casual air of flat positiveness, as though the matter were of no importance. Something brushed the atmosphere of that room, and they all felt it.

"But—" protested Hardwick suddenly; then he adjusted his expression and remained polite.

"Sit down for just one moment, Mr. Reaper," Hadley said. "At two minutes past midnight you saw a hotel-attendant in the hall carrying towels? A man?"

"Yes."

This time the atmosphere in the room brushed Dan like a touch on the shoulder. His look responded to it.

"A man in uniform?"

"Yes, naturally. I think so."

"What kind of uniform?"

"What kind have they all got? Dark blue; red stripe on the cuff; brass or silver buttons; something like that." Abruptly Dan's heavy eyes grew fixed, and then opened slightly like those of a man making out something from a great distance away. "Oho!" he said.

"You realise it, then. At the time Mr. Kent was murdered, a man in the dress of a hotel-attendant was seen at Sir Gyles Gay's house—"

Dan summed it up. "Ah, *vootzach!*" he said. After a pause he went on" "I see what you're getting at, of course. But do you think it surprised me to see a hotel-attendant *in* a hotel? Do you think I'd regard it as suspicious? What the blazes should I expect to see? I didn't even notice the fellow, particularly. I simply looked out—saw it out of the tail of my eye—and shut the door again. Like that."

Dan used many gestures when he argued. He was arguing now, with some heat. And there was reason in his position.

"That's not the point, Mr. Reaper. We have evidence, or seem to have evidence, that no employee of the hotel was in that wing between half-past eleven last night and five o'clock this morning."

"Oh," said the other. He assumed his buttoned-up "business" expression, and he had assumed it suddenly. "I didn't know that, superintendent. All I can tell you is what I saw. What evidence?"

"The men working on the lifts say that nobody went upstairs or came down during that time."

"Staircase?"

"Nor by the staircase."

"I see," said Dan abruptly. "Well, what does that make me?"

"An important witness, possibly," Hadley answered without heat. "This man in the hall: did you see his face?"

"No. He was carrying a big pile of—bath-towels! That's it! Bath-towels. Must have been a dozen of 'em. They hid his face."

"He was facing towards you, then?"

"Yes, he was walking along. . . . Just a minute—I've got it now! I was standing in the door of the bedroom of our suite, looking towards the left—towards the clock on the wall, naturally. He was coming towards me. As I was saying, he was just about outside Jenny's door."

"What was he doing?"

"I've told you," replied the other, in a tone as expressionless as Hadley's own, "that I hardly noticed him. I don't suppose I had the door open more than a couple of seconds, just long enough to see the clock. I'd say he was either walking towards me or standing still."

"Which? All I want is your impression, Mr. Reaper."

"Standing still, then."

It was no very terrifying ghost to be found in the halls of an ordinary hotel; but it was a patient kind of ghost which strangled its victims and then battered their faces in. Kent found himself thinking that it was all the more unpleasant because it had been described as "standing still" near Josephine's door.

"Bath-towels," said Hadley. "A number of bath-towels, we've heard, were found in the room where the murder was committed. It looks as though your mysterious man had at least gone into that room. . . ."

"Was her face—?" Francine cried suddenly.

"Yes. And a face-towel was used to strangle her, as in another case we know about," said Hadley. The girl did not falter, or anything of a dramatic nature; but her eyes suddenly grew so bright they thought she was going to cry. Hadley was not uncomfortable. He turned to Dan. "About this man: didn't it strike you as odd to see an attendant carrying bath-towels? Wouldn't it have been a job for the maid?"

"I don't know whose job it was," retorted Dan. "It certainly didn't strike me as odd, and wouldn't have done even if I had noticed all the subtleties you're putting into it. At home, in the hotels, you hardly ever find a maid at all. All the work is done by boys—Indians, mostly. I can see now that it's queer enough; but why should it strike me then?"

"Can you give us any description of this man? Tall, short? Fat, thin?"

"Just ordinary."

Hardwick interposed. He had been standing unobtrusively on the fringe of the group as on the fringe of thought; but he looked so solid and so dependable that Dan turned to him as though he were going to shake hands.

"You have been speaking about a uniform," he said slowly. "What sort of uniform was it? We've got several, you know."

Hadley swung round. "I was coming to that. What uniforms have you got, to begin with?"

"For that time of night, not many: as I told you a moment ago. If this had happened during the day, there would be a pretty broad range. But when you get to a time as late as midnight, there are only three kinds of employees who wear a uniform at all; everybody else, from car-starter to page-boy, is off duty. First, there's the night hall-porter, Billings, and his four under-porters. Second, there are the two liftmen. Third, there are the two attendants in the lounge—you know, serving late drinks. That's all."

"Well?"

"The hall-porter," replied Hardwick, half shutting his eyes, "wears a long blue tunic, frock-coat effect: double-breasted, silver buttons, opening high at the neck: wing collar and black bow tie: red stripe on cuff and collar. The four under-porters wear a double-breasted coat with wing collar and black four-in-hand tie; red insignia. The liftmen wear a short single-breasted coat high at the neck; silver buttons, shoulder epaulets. The lounge attendants have a uniform like blue evening clothes, with silver buttons and red insignia. But as for the last two being upstairs—"

"I had no idea there were so many of 'em," growled Dan. "It's no good. If I try to keep on thinking, I'll only put ideas into my own head and probably lead you wrong. I remember the coat and the buttons; that's all I can swear to. You could see the buttons under the pile of towels. He was holding up the towels in front of his face."

Hadley frowned at his note-book.

"But can you tell us, for instance, whether it was a long or a short coat? Or an open or a closed collar?"

"I couldn't see his collar. I've got a fairly strong impression that it was a short coat; but I wouldn't swear to that either."

Hardwick interrupted with abrupt explosiveness.

"This is a worse business than you think. There's something you'd better know, superintendent, though it won't help you much. Some years ago we had a night under-porter who turned out to be a thief—and as neat and ingenious a thief as I've come across. His method of robbing the guests was very nearly fool-proof. He would have his two floors to attend, as usual. In the middle of the night he would go upstairs to answer a bell, or to 'look round' as they often do. Up there he had hidden a pair of pyjamas and slippers, and sometimes a dressing-gown as well. The pyjamas would go on over his uniform. He had, naturally, a master-key to the rooms in his circuit. So he would simply slip in and steal what he liked. If the occupant of the room woke up, or was disturbed in any way, he had a magnificent excuse which never failed, 'Sorry; wrong room; I've barged in.' In any case he would be taken for a guest. If he were seen coming out of a room, or walking in the halls, he would excite absolutely no suspicion; he was a guest going to the lavatory, or wherever you like. When the robbery was discovered a guest would naturally be suspected. Well, he did that for some time, until one victim refused to accept the 'wrong room' excuse, and grabbed him."[1]

Hardwick paused.

"Don't, he added, with dour amusement, "run away with the idea, please, that you're in a wayside den of thieves. But I thought I had better mention it. It's what made me put up those signs in every room, 'Please bolt your door.' "

[1] It is unwise, I know, to thrust out an editorial head from behind the scenes; but, in case it should be thought that I am plagiarising from fiction, I should like to say that this really happened. For obvious reasons I cannot give the name of the hotel, but it is a large one in Bloomsbury.—J. D. C.

Francine took up the challenge—if it was a challenge. "It seems to me that there is a moral there," she said without inflection. "If an employee can dress up as a guest, a guest can also dress up as an employee."

There was a heavy silence, while the room seemed very warm.

"I beg your pardon, Miss Forbes," said Hardwick, not too quickly. "I honestly did not mean that at all. I—um—merely mentioned it. In any case, I can check up on the movements of all those people last night."

"You might do that immediately," Hadley suggested, and got up with decision. "In the meantime, we'll have a look at the body. Just one more question. You were speaking about 'master-keys'. Are the locks on the doors the same in every room?"

"Hardly. The locks are something of a fine art in gradation. As a rule, each maid has assigned to her a certain number of rooms to do: usually twelve, though it may be less. She carries only one key, which opens any door in her group. And each group of rooms has a different lock. Lock-patterns may be repeated in different parts of the hotel, of course, but there are nearly twenty different combinations. The under-porters carry a master-key which will open any lock on their two floors; and so on up in gradations, until I have a key which will open any door in the building. *But* that general rule does not apply to our top floor, the new addition. We're trying out an experiment, probably not successful, of having Yale locks on all the doors, and no two locks the same. It will be a hundred times more trouble, and cause a lot of confusion; but it's absolutely impossible for any unauthorised person to open even so much as a linen-closet."

"Thank you. We'll go round to 707, then. You had better come along, Mr. Kent." Hadley turned to Francine and Dan. "Will you wait here for us, or would you rather go back to your own rooms?"

For answer Francine went to the chair he had previously drawn out for her, and sat down in it with the air of one who folds her arms. Dan—rather deprecatingly—said that they would stay.

It was very warm in the corridors outside, crossed in zebra-fashion with cold where someone had left open a window or raised a skylight in this hive. The raising of windows gave brief glimpses deep into the life of the hotel, and brought together the noises that make up the hollow hum which is its background. Ghostly voices talked in the air-well. You heard a plate rattle, and the buzzing of a vacuum-cleaner. Indistinct figures crossed the line of vision at windows; Kent felt certain that there would be roast chicken for lunch. All this was built up layer upon layer below them, leading to the sedate modernness of Wing A. The three of them, with Sergeant Betts following, looked down that wide corridor, with its bright mural decorations and each of its lights enclosed in a chrysalis of frosted glass.

"Well?" prompted Hadley.

"I have found the essential clue," said Dr. Fell earnestly. "Hadley, I'll let you into the secret. It's the wrong sort of bogey-man."

"All right," said the other with some bitterness. "I was wondering when it would commence. Fire away, then."

"No, I'm quite serious. For a murderer deliberately to dress up as a hotel-attendant is wrong; and therefore—I say, therefore—it means something."

"I suppose you wouldn't consider the startling theory that the murderer was dressed like a hotel-attendant because he really *is* a hotel-attendant?"

"Perhaps. But that's what I want to emphasise," urged the doctor, plucking at Hadley's sleeve. "In that case the business becomes much worse. We have here a menace which is undoubtedly peering round corners and dogging this party. Now, a menace may or may not be frightening; but it's usually appropriate. Unless it is appropriate there's no point to it. For the first murder we have as a setting an isolated house by a churchyard in Sussex: a setting appropriate to nearly every kind of lurking menace except a hotel-attendant in full canonicals stalking through the passage with a salver. Considering what has happened here in the hotel, I don't think we can dismiss that business at Northfield as a coincidence or the mere hallucination of a drunken man.

"You see, these two murders were committed either by a real hotel-attendant, or by a member of Reaper's party dressed up to look like one. But if it is the first, why should the murderer deliberately put on his workaday uniform to wander through a Sussex country house in the middle of the night? And, if it is the second, why should a member of Reaper's party put on the infernal costume at all?"

Hadley was troubled.

"Here, stop a bit!" he protested. "Aren't you jumping to conclusions all over the place? It seems to me you're being hag-ridden by the idea of a double-murderer in fancy dress. Suppose what Bellowes saw at Northfield was a hallucination: suppose the attendant carrying the towels, here, was an innocent member of the staff who somehow escaped being noticed as he came upstairs—" He stopped, because he could not convince himself of this. But about the principle of the thing he was dogged. "I mean, there's not a shred of actual evidence to show that either Mr. or Mrs. Kent was killed by someone dressed up like that. It seems probable, but where's the evidence?"

"Well," said Dr. Fell mildly, "our friend Hardwick should be able to check up on the movements of his staff last night at midnight. Eh?"

"I should think so."

"H'mf, yes. And suppose they can all account for their whereabouts? That would mean, I think (let's face it) that it was somebody in masquerade? Ergo, what becomes of your innocent figure who is first a hallucination and then an accident?" The doctor was lighting his pipe, and his vast puffs sent the smoke skew-wiff round his face. "I say, Hadley, why are you so opposed to the idea?"

"I'm not opposed to the idea. Only, it seems ruddy nonsense to me. Why should anyone dress up like that? Unless, of course—"

Dr. Fell grunted. "Oh, yes. We can always say (soothingly) that the murderer is a lunatic with a complex for doing his work in that particular kind of fancy costume. I can't quite believe that, because to my simple mind the dress of a hotel-porter is hardly one I should associate with an avenging angel or any form of secret violence. But look at your cursed evidence! The crimes appear to be completely without motive; they are wantonly brutal; and there seems to be no reason why the murderer should insist on strangling his victims with his hands wrapped up in a towel, which I submit would be a clumsy and uncertain process. Finally, there's that."

They had come round the turn in the corridor, where Sergeant Preston was on guard. Dr. Fell indicated the "quiet-is-requested" sign still hanging from the knob of the closed door, with its announcement in red ink of the presence of a dead woman inside. Then he reached out with his stick and touched the brown suède shoes a little to the left of the door.

"Shoes that don't match," he said gruffly. "Mind, I must caution you against too many deductions. But kindly note—shoes that don't match."

Hadley turned to Sergeant Preston. "Anything new?"

"Two sets of finger-prints, sir. They're developing the pictures now; the manager lent us their regular dark-room here. The doctor's waiting for you."

"Good. Go downstairs and get that hall-porter; also the chambermaid who was on duty here last night. Bring them up here, but keep them outside until I call."

Then Hadley opened the door. The cream-coloured blinds were now drawn up on the windows, so that Kent had a good view of the room he had first seen in dimness. For a second or two he was not sure whether he could force himself to go in. He knew what was lying on the floor; he knew now that it was Jenny; and he felt a certain nausea choking him. For several hours he had been telling himself that it was not as though he had lost someone very close to him, either in Jenny or even in Rod. He bore their name in law; but other friends, and particularly Francine, were much closer to his feelings than this amiable young couple who had dodged about on the fringes of his life. But it was the meaningless nature of the crimes which took his nerves; suddenly it disgusted him with his own crime-fiction.

Then Hadley touched his elbow and he went in. Two broad windows opening on the air-well, their grey velvet curtains drawn fully back, showed the white tiling outside like the wall of a cold-storage vault; and snow patched the window-ledges. It was a room about twenty feet square, with a ceiling somewhat low in proportion. Its tint was uniformly grey and blue, with light outlines in the panelling, and sleek maplewood furniture after the prevailing fashion. It showed little sign of disturbance. Towards his left were the twin beds, their blue silk counterpanes un-disturbed. In the wall on the left was the other door leading to the corridor; and, farther on, a dressing-table. The bureau—as he had good reason to know from his first visit—stood between the windows. In the wall on the right he now noticed a door open on a bathroom, and a large wardrobe. Completing the circuit of the room, the pile of bath-towels still lay on the little table to the right of the door.

Evidently Jenny had been unpacking her trunk when the murderer entered. The wardrobe door stood ajar, and he could see just one frock hanging up inside from the many still hanging in the trunk; there were also several pairs of shoes in the wardrobe. But he saw one great difference from this morning. The trunk stood in its former position, facing the door and some eight feet out from the right-hand window, its leaves well open. Yet the body, which formerly had lain on its right side with the head just inside the trunk, now sprawled face upwards some three or four feet closer to the door. He was relieved to see that the towel had now been draped over her face. Then Kent caught sight of his own face reflected in the mirror over the bureau, and dodged back in-stinctively.

"I see," he said, clearing his throat, "you've moved her."

A middle-aged man in glasses, who had been sitting across the room with a medical bag on the floor beside him, got up quickly.

"Moved her?" repeated Hadley. "She certainly hasn't been and wouldn't have been moved. That's how she was found—that right, Betts?"

"Yes, sir," agreed the sergeant. "Aside from the constable, I was the first person here; and that's how I found her."

"Well, it isn't how I found her," said Kent. He described the position. "I've got good reason to know that. Somebody must have pulled her out this distance after I had gone."

Hadley put his brief-case on the bed. "We want that hall-porter. Where the devil's that hall-por—Ah, I've sent for him. Look round, Mr. Kent; take your time. Does anything else look different?"

"No, not so far as I can see. I didn't get a good look at the room; the blinds were down; but everything seems about the same. I didn't notice that wardrobe, though it's unlikely that *it* wasn't here a couple of hours ago. But there's another point besides the position of the body: that missing bracelet which the woman who vacated the room last was supposed to have left behind in the bureau. If that's the bureau you mean,"—he pointed—"I'll swear again there was no bracelet in it at eight o'clock this morning. Yet according to the manager, it was found by the hall-porter after I had gone. I'd like to know how long it was between the time I left the room and the time he opened the door."

"We'll attend to that," said Hadley. "In the meantime—well, doctor?"

Hadley knelt beside the body, twitched the towel off Jenny's face, and grunted noncommittally; Kent was glad that his back hid the sight. The police-surgeon approached with interest.

"So she's been moved," the latter commented, with a quick look at Kent and a beam of satisfaction. "I'm not surprised. That would account for it. If I'm right, this is a new way of committing murder."

"New way of committing murder? She was strangled, wasn't she?"

"Yes, yes, strangled, asphyxiated, what you like; but with a difference. She was probably stunned first, though there are eight blows on her face and head, and I can't tell which of them might have done the stunning. I should say, roughly, that she died about midnight—allow a margin one way or the other." The doctor peered over his spectacles, and then knelt beside Hadley. "But look here! Look at the front and back of the neck."

"Creases. As though," muttered Hadley, "there'd been a cord or wire tied round. But—"

"But there's no cord or wire, and the creases don't extend round as far as the sides of the neck," the other pointed out. "It explains everything, including the towel, though I should have imagined the fellow would have used a thick bath-towel rather than this. Now take a look at that wardrobe trunk. It's a big trunk—plenty of space at one side where the dresses hung—and she's a small woman. You also notice that the dresses inside look a bit rumpled and tossed about. It's a job for you, of course: but I should say her neck was put between the sharp jaws of the trunk as it stood upright, with the towel round her neck so that the edges wouldn't cut. . . ."

Hadley got to his feet, snapping his fingers.

"Oh, yes. Nasty business, of course," agreed the other. "As I say: the towel muffled her neck, and her body was in the part of the trunk where the dresses are hanging. Then the murderer slowly pressed together the edges of the trunk until she was very effectually strangled. Afterwards she was allowed to drop, and the blows were administered for good measure. Neat idea, though. There's death in everything nowadays, isn't there?"

Chapter VI

FIFTEEN BATH-TOWELS

There was a silence, after which Hadley dropped the towel back on the face and drew a deep breath. The big trunk, very suggestive despite the pink frock that hung uppermost in the space to the left, drew all their eyes.

"This is one murderer," said Hadley, closing his hands deliberately, "that I'm going to see hanged if it's the last thing I ever do. Look here, doctor: you examined the other one—her husband—didn't you? *He* wasn't killed with any such hocus-pocus as that, was he?"

"No, that seemed to be a straight case of strangling with the hands wrapped in a towel. Pretty powerful hands, too; or else—" He put his finger to his temple and made a circling motion with it. "Dementia praecox, superintendent. The whole case smells of it; or has so far. The trouble is that this looks like too reasoned and deliberate a plan of campaign. However, that's your job. Unless you want me for anything more, I'll be pushing off. They'll bring the body along whenever you say."

"Thanks, doctor. Nothing else," said Hadley. For a time he moved slowly in a circle, studying the body and the trunk, and making careful notes. "Betts!"

"Yes, sir?"

"That 'quiet' sign on the door: could you find out where it came from?"

"It came from here," said the sergeant. "There's one of them supplied to every room; it's put in the bureau drawer, in case the guest wants it. New-fangled notion, apparently. And as for the writing in red ink on it—here you are, sir."

He walked across the room to a small writing-desk, placed cater-cornered in the far right-hand corner near one window. The dark-blue carpet was so thick that no footfall sounded here when either Hadley or the sergeant moved. Kent also suspected that these new walls were sound-proof. Drawing away the chair before the desk, Betts indicated the blotter. In addition to the hotel pen and inkwell, with stationery in the rack above, there was a small agate-coloured fountain-pen.

"Probably hers," the sergeant suggested. "It's got her initials on the band, and it's filled with red ink."

"It is hers," said Kent, who recognised it even at a distance. The stuffy warmth of the room was growing heavy on his forehead. "She had two of them, one filled with blue and the other with red ink. They were something like—mascots."

Hadley frowned at the pen. "But why red ink?"

"Capable business-woman. She had a part interest in a dress-making shop in Pritchard Street, although she never let it appear. Apparently she thought it wasn't dignified." Suddenly Kent felt tempted to laugh. Many images rose in his mind. The term "capable business-woman" seemed the last to describe Jenny, for it did not convey the extraordinary attractiveness which (in a purely spiritual way) turned so many people's heads. Harvey Wrayburn had once remarked that she appealed to the adolescent mentality. Through those memories he heard Hadley's voice:

"Finger-prints on this?"

"No, sir."

"But if she had two pens, where's the other one?"

"Must be in her trunk," said Betts. "It's not in her handbag, over on the dressing-table."

Disturbed, Hadley examined the trunk. Though solid, it was an old, worn one; and her maiden name, "Josephine Parkes," had almost faded out in white lettering on one side, the surname now being replaced with a bright white, "Kent." The top compartment on the right-hand side of the trunk formed a kind of tray, filled with handkerchiefs and stockings neatly arranged. In the middle of a pile of handkerchiefs Hadley found the second pen, together with a little gold box, the key in its lock, containing costume jewellery. He juggled the two pens in his hand, muttering.

"This won't do. Look here, Fell, what do you make of it? She was undoubtedly beginning to unpack the trunk when the murderer got her. She'd begin with the dresses—my wife always does, anyway, to see that they don't crumple. But she had taken out only one dress and some shoes; the shoes apparently to change them, for she's wearing bedroom slippers. The only other thing she removed was this red-ink fountain-pen, which was buried under a pile of handkerchiefs. Unless, of course . . ."

During this whole examination Dr. Fell had been leaning back against the wall, his shovel-hat over his eyes. Now he roused himself, putting away his pipe.

"Unless the murderer took it out himself. And in that case he knew where to look for it. H'mf, yes," said Dr. Fell, wheezing in slow laborious breaths. "But I say, Hadley, I should be very much obliged if you would just recapitulate what you think happened here. It's rather important. Again we have one blessed gift from heaven. The guests seemed to have remained quietly in their rooms—except the murderer. We are not obliged to remember a complicated time-table of people treading on each other's heels through the halls, or who met whom in going to post a letter at 9.46. What we have got to do is merely to read the indications of the physical evidence. But, oh, Bacchus, I've got an idea it's going to be difficult! Begin, will you?"

"Where?"

"With the entrance of the murderer."

"Assuming that the murderer is the 'attendant' Reaper saw outside the door at midnight?"

"Assuming anything you like."

Hadley studied his note-book. "I know that tone of yours," he said suspiciously. "Just let me tell you this: I'm not going to stand here and get a whole analysis worked out while you merely wave your hand and say you knew it all the time, but that it's not the important point. By the Lord Harry, I'm going to have one case where you play fair. Agree or disagree, I don't give a damn which; but no misleading. Is it a go?"

"You flatter me," said Dr. Fell with dignity. "All right; fire away."

"Well, as I see it, there's one main difficulty. There are eight blows on the face and on the front of the skull, and no blow or bruise on the back of the head. But she certainly couldn't have been conscious when she was put into that Iron-maiden trunk over there; she had to be fitted into the machine; and she'd have cut up a row that would have been heard. I know the walls look fairly solid, but sound-proof walls are like noiseless typewriters: you can still hear through them. This seems to mean that the murderer must have attacked her face to face with our blunt instrument, and that one of the blows from the front stunned her."

"Undoubtedly. Whereas, you remember," Dr. Fell pointed out, screwing up his face, "Rodney Kent was hit on the back of the head."

"If the murderer, then, used a weapon large enough to do what's been done to that face afterwards, how was it that she didn't sing out, or run, or put up some kind of struggle, when she saw him coming? And—in a brightly lighted hotel—how was he able to carry the weapon about without being observed?"

Dr. Fell pushed himself away from the wall. Lumbering over to the tall pile of bath-towels on the table, he began picking them up quickly one after the other, shaking them out, and letting them fall. At the sixth towel, when the floor was littered with them, something dropped with a soft thud and rolled to Hadley's feet. It was an iron poker some two feet long; its head was covered with lint where stains had made it stick to the towel.

"Look here, my boy," said Dr. Fell, turning to Kent apologetically;

"why not go downstairs and get a drink? It can't be very pleasant for you to see her like that, and—"

"I'm all right," said Kent. "It was the way the thing jumped, that's all. So that's how it was done?"

Drawing on his gloves, Hadley picked up the poker and turned it over.

"It's what we want, right enough," he said. "I see. It was not only a good concealment; but, with your hand on the grip of this thing, and the towels hiding the sight of it from the other person, you could whip it out and hit before the other person knew what you were doing."

"Yes. But that's not the only consideration. It is also reasonable to ask: why are there *so many* towels? There are fifteen of the blighters; I counted. If your purpose is merely to hide the poker, why do you stack them up like that and badly encumber your movements when you have to strike? But fifteen towels would not only serve to hide the poker: they would also hide—"

"The face," said Hadley.

Again Dr. Fell got the pipe out of his pocket and stared at it blankly. "The face. Quite. Which leads us to the question: if the murderer is a real hotel-attendant, why should he bother to hide his face either in the halls or before Mrs. Kent? In the halls he is in his proper sphere; open to no suspicion so long as he is not seen entering this room; and carrying such a great pile of towels will actually serve to call attention to him. Before Mrs. Kent, when he knocks at the door, he is a hotel employee with an obvious errand. But if he is some member of her own party—some person she knows very well—he *must* hide his face. He cannot run the danger of being seen walking about in that elaborate uniform with his well-known face bared. Mrs. Kent will certainly be surprised and probably alarmed if she opens the door and sees a friend in fancy-dress: particularly the same sort of fancy-dress that appeared in the house when her husband was murdered. And he must get inside that room before she is suspicious. Add to all this the fact that the liftmen swear no real attendant came up here last night between eleven-thirty at night and five in the morning: you begin to perceive, my boy, that the Royal Scarlet Hotel houses an unco' dangerous guest with an odd taste in clothes."

There was a pause. Hadley tapped on his note-book.

"I've never suggested," he returned, "that she was killed by a complete stranger. But in that case—unless he pinched a real attendant's uniform, the clothes he wore must still be in one of these rooms?"

"So it would appear."

"But why? Why carry about an outfit, and wear it only for murders?"

Dr. Fell clucked his tongue. "Tut, tut, now! Ne'er pull your hat upon your brows. There are other things to claim our attention. Since you won't recapitulate, I will.

"Several things were done in this room besides murder. First, someone picked up a pair of mis-mated brown shoes and put them outside the door. It seems unlikely, to say the least, that Mrs. Kent would have done it. They were not only shoes that did not match; they were suède shoes that could not be cleaned. So the murderer did it. Why?"

"At first glance," replied Hadley cautiously, "you'd say it was because the murderer didn't wish to be interrupted by anybody, as he might have been. He was in the midst of a clutter of shoes. So he picked up a pair, which looked alike to a man in a hurry, and put them outside the door so that it would be assumed Mrs. Kent had gone to bed. That was why he also—hold on!"

"Exactly," agreed Dr. Fell. "That was why, you were going to say, he also hung a 'quiet' sign on the door. But there we take a dismal header. The murderer takes a (hidden) 'quiet' sign out of the bureau drawer; he takes a (hidden) fountain-pen out of Mrs. Kent's trunk; on this card he writes 'Dead Woman' in large letters, and hangs it on the door-knob. It seems rather a curious way of making sure you avoid interruption. Why does he appear to need so much time, and to take so many precautions?"

"Any suggestions?"

"Only to conclude this account by indicating what happened this morning. We assume,"—he pointed his stick towards Kent, who had been swept aside in the backwash of this argument—"we assume that our friend here is telling the truth. H'mf. At about eight o'clock he comes up here with the hall-porter. At this time the bureau does *not* contain a bracelet left behind by an American lady who departed yesterday, the body is lying with head almost inside the leaves of the trunk. While the hall-porter waits, our friend gets out. Presently the porter has the door opened again. The missing bracelet is then found in the bureau, and the body has been moved some feet out from the trunk. The conjuring entertainment is over: ladies and gentlemen, I thank you."

Kent thought that the glance Hadley turned towards him was speculative enough to be ominous.

"If I were judging the matter from outside," Kent admitted, "I should say I was lying. But I'm not lying. Besides, what about that bracelet? I certainly didn't come here last night, pinch a bracelet I'd never seen from a woman I'd never heard of; and then come back here this morning and return it. Where does the bracelet fit in?"

"The alternative being," said Hadley, ignoring this, "that the hall-porter is lying?"

"Not necessarily," said Dr. Fell. "If you will look—"

There was a knock at the door. Preston brought in the hall-porter and the chambermaid.

The girl was an earnest blonde in a starched blue-and-white uniform which made her look stout; she seemed to jingle like the bunch of keys (all Yale keys) at her waist; but she appeared excited rather than frightened, and a nerve twitched beside one eyelid. Myers, the hall-porter, stood in massive contrast. Though Kent again noted his pointed moustaches and slightly pitted face, the most conspicuous thing in all their eyes was the porter's costume: notably the long double-breasted frock-coat with the silver buttons. Myers, after one glance, affected not to notice Kent's presence. That glance was not belligerent; it was one of dignified but hideous reproachfulness.

Hadley turned to the maid first. "Now there's nothing to worry about," he assured her. "Just look here, please, and answer a few questions. What's your name?"

"Eleanor Peters," said the girl, hardly lifting her eyes from studying the figure on the floor. She seemed to carry an atmosphere of strong soap.

"You were on duty here last night, weren't you, until half-past eleven?"

"Yes."

"Look up at me, please; never mind that!—Now. You see these towels? Do you know where they come from?"

A pause. "From the linen-closet down the hall," she answered, reluctantly following instructions. "Or at least I suppose they do. There was fifteen of them gone from there this morning, and the place was pulled all about, sir."

"Do you have charge of that linen-closet?"

"Yes, I do. And I locked it up last night, too, but somebody got in and pulled it all about."

"Was anything else gone?"

"Nothing but one face-towel. That one, I'll bet." She nodded in a fascinated way towards Jenny Kent's body; and Hadley moved over to obscure her sight of it.

"Who else has a key to the linen-closet?"

"Nobody, far as I know."

"What time did you come on duty this morning?"

"Quarter-past seven."

Hadley went over to the door, opened it, and detached the "quiet" sign from outside. Standing well back in the room, Kent could now see out diagonally across the corridor towards the door which, on the plan, had been marked as that of Sir Gyles Gay's sitting-room. This door stood part-way open, and a face was looking out with an air of alert and refreshed interest. If this were Sir Gyles Gay, Kent was conscious of surprise. He remembered Dr. Fell's mention of interest in names, whatever might have been the significance of it. The name itself had a spacious Cavalier ring, as of one who would down tankards on the table and join a businessmen's chorus in full Cavalier style. Actually, he was a little wizened, philosophical-looking man with an air of interest in everything and a complete lack of embarrassment. After giving Hadley an amiable, somewhat marble-toothed smile reminiscent of the portraits of Woodrow Wilson, he withdrew his head and shut the door. The mural design on that wall was a representation of a cocktail party. Hadley closed the door of 707.

"You came on duty at a quarter-past seven," he said to the maid. "I suppose you passed this door?"

"Oh, yes, sir. Naturally."

"Did you notice this card on the door?"

"I noticed the card, but I didn't notice what's written on it. No, I did *not*," said the excited Eleanor, who evidently wished she had.

"Between the time you came on duty and the time this gentleman came upstairs with the porter," he nodded towards Kent, "did you see anyone else in this wing?"

"No. That is, nobody except a page. He came up about half-past seven and looked at the door of number 707 here, and turned round and went away again."

Myers, the porter, was about to come into action. He had been waiting with several slight clearings of the throat, like a nervous orator who has several speakers before him. Now he began, with massive respectfulness, to explain; but Hadley cut him short.

"Just a moment. . . . About last night. Were you in this part of the wing when Mr. Reaper's party got back from the theatre?"

"That's the handsome one in 701," said the maid; and stopped, covered with a pouring confusion. She added rapidly: "Yes, I was."

"Did you see—?" Hadley stood aside and indicated Jenny.

"Yes, I did. I saw them all except the one with the moustache, in 705."

"What was Mrs. Kent wearing then? Do you remember?"

"Same as she's wearing now, but with a mink coat over it. Except that she'd got on shoes instead of slippers," added Eleanor, after another careful inspection. "The other, the fat one"—Melitta Reaper, undoubtedly—"was in evening dress, gold lawn, with a white fur wrap. But this lady, and the hoity-toity one in 708 were both in ordinary clothes."

Myers, evidently furious, was about to quell this style of talk with cold authority; but Hadley's glance at him was even colder.

"Did you hear them saying anything?"

"Only good night, that I remember."

"Did they go directly to their rooms?"

"Yes, sir. They all stood with their hands on the knobs of the doors, looking round, as though they were waiting for a signal or something; and then all of a sudden they all turned round together and went into their own rooms."

Hadley studied his note-book; then he turned to Myers.

"First, about this bracelet: when did you hear it had been left behind in this room?"

"Eight o'clock this morning, sir, when I came on duty," replied the other instantly. He had a good parade-ground manner of giving evidence, and he was on his mettle. His answers bristled up as though you had given him a shake by the shoulders. "I'm the day-porter, you see, and I come on duty at eight. But Billings, the night man, told me about it when he went off duty. Mrs. Jopley-Dunne, who occupied this room last, had telephoned last night about the bracelet. Mrs. Jopley-Dunne was then staying overnight with friends in Winchester, intending to go on to Southampton next day to catch the *Directoire*. But she telephoned so late that Billings would not disturb Mrs. Kent at that hour."

"What hour? Do you know when the call came through?"

"Yes, sir, there's always a record. At 11.50."

"At 11.50?" the superintendent repeated quickly. "Was anyone sent up here to inquire?"

"No, sir, nor even telephone. As I say, he would not disturb Mrs. Kent at that hour."

"Where were you at that time, by the way?"

"Me, sir? I was at my home, in bed." A new, somewhat hoarser tone, had come into Myers's voice; he showed a kind of Gibraltaresque surprise.

"Go on: about next morning."

Myers retold the familiar story. "—so you see, sir, Billings had already sent up a page-boy at seven-thirty, and the page said there was a 'quiet' sign on the door. When I came on duty, and Billings passed the word along to me, Hubbard (that's one of the under-porters) said he thought the gentleman in 707 was just finishing his breakfast in the dining-room. I took the liberty of asking this gentleman, thinking naturally—you understand.

"We went upstairs. I got the chambermaid to open the door, and he went in. He asked me to wait outside, of course. When he had been gone about two or three minutes, and there was no sound out of the room, I tapped on the door: meaning to tell him, you see, sir, that the matter could wait if he could not find the bracelet. There was no answer to that. A minute or so later I tapped again; I was beginning to think it was queer. Then my coat or something brushed that sign on the door. It had been turned round so that the dead-woman part was facing the wall, and I hadn't seen it until then." Myers drew a quick whistling breath. "Well, sir, I knew I was taking a responsibility, but I asked the maid to open the door. And I went in. This gentleman—wasn't there."

"Where was the body lying then?"

"Just where it is now."

"What did you do first when you went in?"

"I went to look for the bracelet."

"For the bracelet?"

"Sir," replied Myers, in a sudden lofty passion, "I had been told to go and get that there bracelet. I did it; and I don't see why everyone should think it was so out of the way. I walked across, like this"—he illustrated—"I opened the right-hand bureau drawer, like this; and there it was, stuck down by the paper lining. I put it in my pocket. Then I went and told the manager I had got it, and that the lady in here was dead. I know there's been mistakes; and I don't *say* this gentleman here killed her; but I've heard nothing about nothing; that's all *I* say."

Hadley turned to Kent.

"How long should you say you were in here before you slipped out that side door into the other angle of the corridor?"

"It's hard to tell. About three minutes, I should think."

"And you?" the superintendent asked Myers. "How long between the time Mr. Kent came in here and the time you followed him?"

"Well, sir, say five minutes."

"While you were waiting outside what we'll call the main door, the one with the sign on it, I suppose nobody went in or out past you?"

"Not by that door they didn't! No, sir!"

"Then here is the order of events, if we say both of you are telling the truth. Mr. Kent comes into this room. After three minutes he goes out by the side door. At the end of five minutes you come in. During the space of two minutes, then, someone has entered by the side door—must have been, because you were planted in front of the only other entrance—someone has put the bracelet in the drawer, moved the body, and gone out the same way. This, I repeat, happened in the two minutes between the time Mr. Kent left the room and the time you entered it. Is that right?"

Myers was aggrieved. "I can't speak for him, sir, that's all I say. But I can speak for myself, and what I say's the truth."

"Just one last thing. While you were outside the main door, you could see the doors of all the rooms in this angle of the corridor?"

"Yes, sir," replied the other—and stopped, evidently taken backwards by a rush of thought.

"During that time, did any of the guests come out of their rooms? Would you have noticed?"

"I should have noticed. And, sir," said Myers, with massive simplicity, "none of 'em did. That I'll swear to."

"What about you?" inquired Hadley, and turned to the maid.

"Stop a bit!" urged that young lady, examining the past. "Yes, I'll agree to that. *I* should have noticed, I'm sure. But there's one door I couldn't see from there; I mean it was round the corner. That's the side door to 705, facing the side door of this one across the hall."

Hadley shut up his note-book. "That's all, thanks. You can go; but don't talk about this, either of you." When they had been dismissed, he looked for Dr. Fell with some satisfaction. "This looks dangerously like a bit of luck. It's what you would call a logical certainty. Either this one is lying—" he put his hand on Kent's shoulder—"which I don't believe. Or *both* the porter and the maid are lying, which I don't believe either. Or—we come to it—the person in this room must have been Harvey Wrayburn, from 705."

Chapter VII

A SQUARE BLACK STONE

D r. Fell had again played his disconcerting trick of never being in the place you expected him, which was a physical as well as a mental trait. When Hadley looked round, the doctor was bending over the dressing-table at the other side of the room, so that they could see only a vast expanse of back and black cape. A red face now turned round and rose to the surface like Leviathan, while he blinked over his eyeglasses.

"Oh, it's possible," admitted the doctor, with a petulant wheeze. "It's still more possible since—" He flourished a snakeskin handbag.

"Since what?"

"Since I can't find her key. The key to this room. I've been looking all over the place for it. You remember, we heard a very interesting account of the spring-locks with which all the doors on this floor are supplied; no two locks alike. Except, I dare say, when one room has two doors, like this one: then the same key would open both. But where is the key? If someone used that side door to sneak in here and return the bracelet in two minutes—well, he had to get in. On the other hand, there are certain curious suggestions which occur to me, especially after a closer examination of that trunk, and they do not fit in with your friend Wrayburn."

There was the sound of an argument outside the partly-open main door to the hall, cut short by a faint "Pah!" Into the room, with the utmost composure, came the wizened and calm-faced man whom Kent had seen peering out of the doorway across the hall. Though he was of middle height, he seemed much shorter by reason of his bony leanness; he was carefully dressed, to the point of the dapper, in a blue double-breasted suit and (very) hard collar. That collar, like the set if pleasant expression which suggested false teeth, seemed to give him a high glaze like the polish on a tombstone. While preserving the most careful decorum, he nevertheless contrived to suggest the same air of refreshed interest. His thin hair, carefully parted, was whitish at the top and dull grey over the ears; its smoothness contrasted with his wizened face. He stopped by the body, as though performing a conventional rite; he shook his head, cast down his eyes, and then looked at Hadley.

"Good morning, superintendent."

"Morning, Sir Gyles."

"And this, I think," the other went on gravely, "will be the celebrated Dr. Fell. And the other—?" Introductions were performed, while Gay's shrewd eye appraised them. "Gentlemen, I have come for you, and I will not be denied. You must come over to my rooms and—

"—and take a cup of China tea," he added, when by some mysterious power of eye he had got them out of the room. "I could not say it in there. I don't know why."

Despite his poise he was a trifle white. Dr. Fell beamed down on him as though on some interesting phenomenon.

"Heh," said the doctor. "Heh-heh-heh. Yes. I particularly wished to speak to you. I want a fresh viewpoint on character, so to speak; the others are able judges, I don't doubt, but they have lived too close to each other to be free from bias."

"You flatter me," said Gay, showing the edge of a marble-toothed smile. "I am entirely at your service."

While Hadley remained behind to give brief instructions to Betts and Preston, Gay took the others into his sitting-room. It was a pleasant place, furnished (surprisingly) in eighteenth-century fashion, though the noise of traffic from Piccadilly boiled up below the windows. From this height you could see far down the slope of grey barrack-like roofs, past the curt solidness of St. James's, to the bare trees of St. James's Park. The dapper old man fitted into this. On a table by the window there was a steaming tea-service; and, when the others refused tea, their host poured a cup for himself with a steady hand.

"You will find cigars in the box beside you," he told Dr. Fell. "And now, gentlemen, to business: though the business will be mostly theory. One thing, though, I can tell you at the start," he said vigorously. "I know no more of this—this bloody business than when that young man was murdered in my house. I did not leave my room last night, and I don't know who did. All I *know* is that we seem to be pursued by an exacting and business-like murderer."

"H'm," said Dr. Fell, who was endangering a frail-looking chair.

"Well, look here: what do you think of Mr. Reaper's party in general?"

Gay drew a deep breath. There was an expression of pleasure on his bony face, which faded as he seemed to reflect.

"Up to the time young Kent was murdered," he answered gravely, "I had never had so much fun in my life."

He paused to let this sink in.

"I must explain. In business I have been known as a terror, a spoiler of the Egyptians and everyone else; and I confess that my conduct in the City, as the Wodehouse story puts it, would have caused raised eyebrows in the fo'c'sle of a pirate sloop. Also, I have been a successful government official: hence my surprising knighthood. Also, there is no arguing with the mirror—and the mirror displays a stern and shrivelled look. Therefore it is taken for granted. Therefore people, coming in contact with my bleak atmosphere, talk about the weather. I think it has been years since anyone invited me to have a second drink. . . . Well, Reaper's party paid no attention to that, or never thought of it. They came into my house, and after a decorous interval they cut loose. They banged the piano. They got up games in which I found myself blind-folded, inadvertently pinning a paper donkey's tail to the posterior of Mrs. Reaper. Young Wrayburn, and even the Grim Reaper himself, when he forgot he was an M.A. and a business man, introduced the novel note of 'Ride 'em, cowboy!' In short, they made the damn place resound!—and I loved it."

He ended with a surprising and deep-throated crow of mirth, lifting his neck to do so, and showing an extraordinary animation which twinkled up to his eyes.

"And murder came next," said Dr. Fell.

The other grew sober. "Yes. I knew I was enjoying myself too much for it to last."

"You're an intelligent man," Dr. Fell went on, in the same sleepy and abstracted fashion. "What do you think happened?"

"Oh, I don't know. If this hadn't happened to me, I should have said, Read your psychology: but those books don't apply—to personal cases. They never do."

"Was Rodney Kent one of the persons who promoted the hilarity?"

Gay hesitated. "No, he was not, though he tried to be. It was not in his nature, I think. He was too conscientious. I think you have met the type. He is one of the persons who stand, smiling but uncertain, on the edge of a group who are enjoying themselves; and you think over and over, 'What in blazes can I do to amuse so-and-so?' till it amounts to a point of desperation. But you never succeed."

It was, Christopher Kent reflected, a perfect description of Rod, who was really in his element only when he had facts to dig out.

"But he was murdered," said Gay.

"What about Miss Forbes?"

"Ah, Miss Forbes," said Gay dryly, and again showed the edge of the marble-toothed smile. "I think you misunderstand her, Dr. Fell. You should have seen her, when *she* forgot herself, standing by the piano and singing a ballad whose drift I need not repeat." He turned to Kent, and added: "She is in love with you, you know."

As startled as though he had got two successive blows in the wind, Kent sat up.

"She's—What makes you think that?"

"Secrets," said Gay reflectively. "You would be surprised at the number of secrets that have been confided to me in the past fortnight. Nothing damaging, nothing helpful, I am afraid; but I was surprised and pleased and a little touched. It is flattering. In the old days nobody would have thought of confiding a secret to me. That person would have been afraid I should use it to extract his back teeth or collar-stud. And I fear he would have been right. But I mention this particular secret in the hope that it may be helpful." He considered. "Now listen, and I'll sum up. In South Africa to-day there is a minority political group called the Dominion Party. They are excellent fellows, although they haven't a dog's chance; the government is eighty per cent *Afrikaans*. But they try to keep up English traditions—including the wholly mythical one of English reserve. Nearly all the members of Reaper's crowd are touched with that brush. Reaper himself is, though he professes to be a United man." He looked at Kent. "*You* are, I suspect. But I don't think Miss Forbes realises that it is not really necessary nowadays to stand on her dignity. The spectacle of me lapping up sherry out of a saucer as a forfeit for failing to do something else equally dignified—I forget what—should have corrected that. You understand, Dr. Fell?"

The doctor chuckled, though he kept a speculative eye on their host.

"I'm not sure I do understand," he rumbled. "Are you trying to tell us something? Do I detect, as a sinister undertone to these games, a suggestion that there is a repression or neurosis which takes the form of murder?"

Gay's face did not change, though it was a second or two before he answered. "I'll be quite candid," he said with a broad air. "I don't know what I bloody well do mean."

"H'mf. Still, there's one person, you know, whose character you haven't described. I mean Mrs. Josephine Kent."

Gay got up, with his dapper walk, and passed round a humidor of good cigars. Each accepted one; and, in a perplexity of thought, Kent looked out across the grey roofs patched in snow. The scratching of a match, and the ritual of cigar-lighting, roused him. Their host was again sitting quietly on the edge of his chair; but his face had hardened.

"You forget," he continued, "that I met the lady for the first time last night, and that I knew her only a few hours before this happened. She was with her aunts during the other business; she met us in London. Nevertheless, I'll tell you what she was. She was a dangerous girl."

"Nonsense!" exploded Kent. "Rod's wife?"

Sir Gyles Gay's face was alight with a great pleasure, so that it seemed to shine as at the discovery of a toy.

"Hadn't you discovered that?"

"Yes," said Dr. Fell. "But go on."

"I don't mean," said Gay, with a quick and sharp look at the doctor, "I don't mean a crooked girl, or an evil one. (By the way, she must be rather older than she looks, you know.) I don't suppose there was ever a consciously crooked thought in her head; I doubt whether she would have recognised one of her worst and most radiant thoughts as being crooked, even if such a thought had been there. Since you object to the term 'dangerous,' though, I'll describe her in another way. She would have made an ideal wife for me. And she knew it."

Kent grinned in spite of himself. "Was that why she was dangerous?"

"You still don't understand. The sort of character she had is common enough, but it's elusive and difficult to describe. So I'll merely tell you something. I met her last evening for the first time. Within fifteen minutes she was making up to me. Object, matrimony. For my money."

There was a pause. "Sir Gyles," Kent said, "you're a very intelligent man, as Dr. Fell has said; but don't you think that's rather an asinine statement?"

The other did not seem offended, though there was a gleam in his eye. On the contrary, he appeared pleased as at more confirmation of a theory. After taking several deep pulls at his cigar, and savouring the smoke, he leaned forward.

"And," he insisted, "I should have fallen. Oh, yes. Was I attracted? Damme, yes! Even though I know—well, I have not got the phrase that describes her. She was the ideal Old Man's Darling. Hadn't you realised all this?" His calm certainty on the point sent through Kent a sudden discomfort that was like a touch of belief. "Tell me if I've read her character correctly on other points. I judge that she was an excellent business woman: probably with a business of her own: very likely something to do with clothes or millinery. I also judge that nobody ever saw her disturbed or out of countenance: that nobody ever really knew her. She slid through things. That little—er—*half pint* (a word I've picked up) could not actually be touched by anything. That, gentlemen, is the quality which would drive our sex crazy; and she had the particular kind of attractiveness, blessed-Damozel and kiss-me-lightly style, which turns a lot of heads to begin with. Of course she would marry a well-meaning chap like Rodney Kent. Of course she would sweetly expect all the favours; and get 'em. But when she saw the possibility of a better match, or was merely tired, she would say he was too gross, or something; that she had been entrapped or sold into the marriage; that her soul had been snatched; and she would pass on to what she wanted amid general murmurs of sympathy. Dignity she had, I've no doubt—and for some curious reason there persists among our countrymen a belief that if you have dignity you're probably right."

It was a thrust so straight and deep that Kent stirred again. Jenny, instead of lying over there with her face covered by a towel, now seemed to walk in the room. Dr. Fell seemed to be half asleep; but you could see the steady shining of intentness in his eyes.

"Forgive the long oration," Gay concluded abruptly.

Dr. Fell examined the end of his cigar. "Not at all," he said with offhand affability. "Do you think that quality had anything to do with her murder?"

"I didn't say anything about the murder. You asked about her character."

"Oh, here! Do you mean that a person's character has nothing to do with his or her murder?"

"Undoubtedly. But I haven't had a chance to deduce anything about the murder yet. I haven't even heard about the circumstances. So I must stick to what I know."

At this invitation Dr. Fell merely opened one eye. "Yes, but—" he said with an air of stubbornness. "Tell me: is there anything you know, or can deduce, which would lead you to suspect that Mrs. Kent wasn't want she seemed?"

"Wasn't what she seemed? I don't understand."

"Then I won't ask it. It is another of those subtleties which grieve Hadley. 'For *nutu signisque loquuntur* is good consistorial law.' It also has some reference to a blind horse, which I may be. I take it you regarded Mrs. Kent, then, as a kind of painted Roman statue, hollow inside?"

"That's it exactly. If you knocked on it, you'd get the same kind of sound. Knock, knock—" Gay paused with another interested expression, as his agile brain seemed to go after a new line of thought. "Ahem! By the way, doctor, I have been introduced in my old age to a game which offers considerable possibilities. It consists in taking various good English words and twisting them out of the shapes God gave them. For example! I say to you, 'Knock, knock.' You are now to reply, 'Who's there?' "

"All right. Who's there?" inquired Dr. Fell, with interest.

"Beelzebub. You now say, 'Beelzebub who?' "

"Beelzebub who?" said Dr. Fell obediently.

What particular gem of this genus was about to be perpetrated Kent never learned, although he was interested by the spectacle of the two grave philosophers playing it. At this point there was, in actual fact, a knock at the door, and Hadley came in. The theories were dispelled. Kent wondered whether the superintendent had been listening at the door, for his face wore a curiously exasperated look.

"Wrayburn," he said to Dr. Fell, "will see us in a minute. He's just getting up, it seems." Then Hadley looked at Gay. "In the meantime, Sir Gyles, would you mind answering a few questions? Also, would you have any objection to this suite being searched?"

"Searched? Not at all; go right ahead. But may I ask what you're looking for?"

"For a hotel-attendant's uniform." Hadley waited, and Gay put down his cigar on the edge of the saucer; he tried to flash his marble-toothed smile, sardonically, but he displayed the first sign of uneasiness he had yet shown.

"Ah, I thought so. I knew it. The ghost has been walking again. I tried, by applying the spur of silence, to extract some information from Dr. Fell. But it doesn't seem to work as well with schoolmasters as with business men or lesser breeds without the law."

Hadley gestured to Sergeant Betts, who went towards the bedroom. "—and also, if possible, we hope to find a key."

"Key? What sort of key?"

On the polished round centre table a key was lying now: a Yale key through whose thumb-hole was threaded a little chromium tag bearing the number 703. Hadley picked it up.

"A key like this. This is yours, naturally?"

"Yes, it's the key to the suite. Why?"

Hadley was at his most offhand. "Someone, presumably the murderer, stole the key to Mrs. Kent's room. It must be somewhere in this wing now, unless it was—thrown out of the window, for instance." The tone of the last few words was curious, though he looked amused. "*You* haven't see it, have you?"

Their host was thoughtful. "Sit down, superintendent; make yourself comfortable. No, I have not seen it. Not since last night, that is."

"Last night?"

"Yes. I noticed Mrs. Kent opening the door of her room with it."

"How was that?"

"It is customary," explained Gay, with icy testiness, "to open doors with a key." He had adopted a harder guard with Hadley than he had attempted with Dr. Fell. "No, see here—it was like this. I don't know whether you've heard it; I suppose you have; but we all went to the theatre last night, and when we came back we turned in immediately. We made a kind of military drill of saying good night, each standing in the door of his own room. Well, Mrs. Kent's room is directly across the hall. She opened the door with her key. She turned on the light just inside. Then, just after she went inside, I remember that she dropped the key in her handbag."

Dr. Fell woke up. "I say, you're sure of that?" he demanded with some excitement. "You're certain she put the key in her handbag?"

"Yes, I'm quite certain of that." Gay's interest was roused again. "Why do you ask? She was standing with her back to me (naturally); but turned round a little towards the left, so that I could see her left arm. I think she was holding the door open with her right knee. She wore a fur coat, and her handbag was snake-skin. She turned round to say good night over her left shoulder; she went in—I am following this carefully— and at this time the bag was in her left hand. She dropped in the key and closed the bag. I remember that left hand because on the wrist she was wearing a white-gold bracelet, with a square black stone in it, and I noticed it when the sleeve of the coat fell back."

He stopped abruptly, aware of the expression on his companions' faces.

Chapter VIII

THE CARD FROM THE WINDOW

"I seem to have startled you," Gay observed, picking up his cigar. "Is anything wrong?"

Though Hadley remained impassive, he wore a heavier look. "A white-gold bracelet with—Are you telling us that Mrs. Kent was wearing Mrs. Jopley-Dunne's bracelet?"

"No indeed, superintendent. I never heard of Mrs. Jopley-Dunne, and I can't say I like the name. I merely said she had on *a* bracelet of that kind. It had a Latin inscription on the stone, I believe; though I didn't get close enough to examine it. I'm fairly sure she had it on at the theatre. One of her friends ought to be able to identify it."

Dr. Fell, after spilling cigar-ash down the ridges of his waistcoat, spoke in a hollow voice. He said:

"That has torn it, Hadley. That has most definitely torn it. Oh, my sacred hat. We grope through a spiritual abyss; and all because, by the innate mental workings of guests at hotels, Mrs. Jopley-Dunne drops a brick. It's a curious fact, worthy of consideration by psychologists, that whenever someone away from home mislays anything, he or she is always firmly convinced that it was Left At The Hotel. Don't you see the sinister significance of it now? The elusive Mrs. Jopley-Dunne didn't leave her bracelet. It wasn't her bracelet at all. It was Mrs. Kent's. . . . There ought to be a house-telephone here somewhere. I strongly advise you to get hold of Hardwick, bring him up here with the bracelet and Reaper and Miss Forbes, round up Mrs. Reaper as well: and if one of them can't identify that thing as belonging to Mrs. Kent, I'm a son of Boetia."

"But, according to everybody, Mrs. Jopley-D. seemed pretty positive she had left it," Hadley muttered. "And why are you so excited? Even if this is true, how does it help us?"

"Help us?" roared Dr. Fell, who was stirring with spark and cigar-ash like the Spirit of the Volcano. "Help us? It is the most enlightening and stimulating thing I have heard this morning. It solves a good many of our difficulties. Grant me the fact that the bracelet belonged to Mrs. Kent," he argued, "and I'll take you a little farther along an exceedingly murky road."

"How?"

"Just tell me this, Hadley: what happened in that room last night?"

"How the hell should I know? That's what—"

"No, no, no," said Dr. Fell testily. "I've had occasion to tell you about this before. You're concentrating so exclusively on the murder that you don't stop to ask yourself what *else* happened there. Why, we were asking a while ago, did the murderer need so much time in that room? Why did he need to be free from interruption for a fairly long time? What was he doing in there?"

"All right. What was he doing?"

"He was making a very careful and intensive search of the room," replied Dr. Fell, making a hideous pantomime face by way of emphasis. "Without, apparently, finding what he wanted or pinching anything. Consider the following points. He found a fountain-pen which had been hidden under a pile of handkerchiefs in the tray of the trunk: therefore he had been through at least that part of the trunk. He found a 'quiet' sign hidden in the bureau drawer: therefore he had been into the bureau. He got the key of the room out of Mrs. Kent's handbag: therefore he had been through the handbag. So much it requires very little cerebral activity to determine, and we are pretty safe in postulating a search. The trouble was that, so far as I could see, nothing appeared to be missing. If we prove that the bracelet belonged to Mrs. Kent, and that for some reason the murderer pinched it last night—"

Hadley was staring at him. "After which the murderer came back and returned it this morning? You call that making things clearer? And, anyway, what's the point of the bracelet? You were making a great fuss about its being one of the most ingenious devices of the ancient world, or some such nonsense; but you haven't said a definite word about it yet."

"Oh, I know," said Dr. Fell despondently. "And yet—and yet—well, I still think you'd better get on to that telephone."

"There it is, on the table," suggested Gay.

Hadley roused himself to the fact that he was indiscreetly talking before witnesses. After asking to be put through to the manager's office, he showed the newspaperman's trick of speaking to the telephone in such a way as to be inaudible four feet off. The others shifted uncomfortably until he put back the receiver again.

"Hardwick will phone through to Mrs. Jopley-Dunne," he said. "Then he'll come round here with Reaper and Miss Forbes. We may as well have them all here. Mr. Kent, you know Mrs. Reaper. Will you go down to their suite and ask her to come here?" (Kent suddenly realised that the superintendent found Melitta a difficult proposition.) "In the meantime, Sir Gyles, those questions . . ."

"I am at your service," assented Gay, with a sort of ancient vivacity. "Though, as I told Dr. Fell, I am afraid I can't help you. Nothing suspicious happened last night so far as I know. I turned in immediately, and read in bed until half-past twelve; but nothing disturbed me in any way. . . ."

That smooth, hard voice was the last thing Kent heard as he went out into the hall. But he did not go immediately to Dan's suite. He stood for a time in that muffled corridor, the stump of the hot cigar almost burning his hand, and tried to rearrange his thoughts.

Two things were becoming apparent now. In spite of himself he was beginning to credit Gay's deadly sharp analysis of Jenny. He had always been credited with being unobservant about people; and certain vague scenes, gestures, inflections, returned to trouble him now. It was like trying to remember a passage or a quotation in a book, in which you can remember the appearance of the book, the page on which the passage occurred, and even the part of the page on which the passage occurred; but you cannot remember the quotation itself. But, even granting all Gay had said, this did nothing to explain her murder—and certainly gave no ghost of a reason why Rod should be killed.

Next, Harvey Wrayburn was in a bad position. You had only to look at this corridor in order to see that. The maid and the hall-porter had been outside one door; they were in a position to testify that nobody else could have stirred out of a room, and Wrayburn's side door was the *only* one they could not see. But why? Why? Why? He thought of Wrayburn, with his brushed-up moustache, his bouncing energy, and his vast mine of information on all the most useless subjects: in appearance a little like that Laughing Cavalier who does not (you recall) really laugh. Then there was this odd business of Wrayburn being still asleep at eleven o'clock in the morning; so far as Kent could remember, he had never done that before.

From hotel-attendant to bracelet to Iron-maiden trunk, it was all a bogging mass of whys. Kent walked slowly down the hall; and, about to knock at the door of Dan's suite, he stopped to inspect the linen-closet. Its door was now ajar; through a frosted-glass window, partly raised, the dull light showed that it served another purpose besides housing the neat shelves of sheets and towels. Other shelves contained tea-services, evidently for those guests who wished early-morning tea before break-fast. He inspected it gloomily, without much enlightenment. Then he knocked at the sitting-room door of Dan's suite, and Melitta's voice told him to come in.

Well, you would not unduly upset Melitta even by the presence of murder, for Melitta lived in a perpetual state of being mildly and stoically upset. It was as though she had taken a tonic which kept her always in the same state of disturbance, and her voice at the same monotone. Twenty years ago she had been a very beautiful woman. She would still have been a beautiful woman if it were not for her soft stoutness, or a certain expression by which the angles of her face seemed to have drooped plaintively out of line: as though the whole woman had been pushed down squatly from above.

But her eyelids were reddish this morning. She sat in a deep chair by a table on which were the remains of a large breakfast, and a box of chocolates. She seldom touched the chocolates, however; she remained bolt upright as a Sphinx, her hands flat along the arms of the chair. The large body was exceedingly well if a little hastily dressed. Her voice struck him like a familiar tune; she showed no surprise at seeing him, but simply picked up the conversation as though it had been broken off five minutes ago, while the handsome blue eyes never left his face.

"—and it is all very dreadful, I know, and of course I know how dreadful it must be for you, and I quite sympathise; but what I say is that it seems so *inconsiderate,* when we had been looking forward to such a nice holiday; but it just does seem as though there would always be something wherever I go. Did you have a nice trip out?"

"Melitta," said Kent, "do you know what's happened? The superinten-dent wants to see you."

Her monotone never noticed a change of subject; she accepted it, and slid into it as easily as though they had been discussing it all the time. But, even while seeming to regard him vacantly, she showed her frequent disconcerting shrewdness.

"My dear Christopher, I got it all out of the maid a little while ago, and gave her a shilling for it too. Not that I begrudge the shilling, heaven knows; though I do think that things in England are *too much,* and when I see the prices on things in the shops I simply gasp, and I cannot understand how they can pay so much when at home I could get that same hat for twenty-seven and six. Poor Jenny; her shop was much nicer, and Parisian models too. Poor Jenny: my heart does bleed for her, it does really,"—and undoubtedly it did—"but I wish Dan would not let them talk such nonsense as they do. But you know how men are, and Dan especially, wanting to get on well with everybody—"

In conversation with Melitta, Kent had discovered, the best policy was to find some train of thought you could understand, and trace it back to its devious beginning: at which time you usually found something worth hearing.

"Nonsense? Nonsense about what?"

"Christopher, you know perfectly well what I mean. Why should any of us do anything like that to Rod or Jenny? We never did at home, did we? I have said before, and I say again, though you needn't repeat it, I do *not* trust that Sir Gyles Gay, even if he has got a title. I have heard about him at home, though of course Dan wouldn't listen, and in business he has the reputation of being nothing better than an absolute Twister. But of course Dan is easy and soft-headed"—it was hardly a description Kent himself would have applied to Dan—"when he finds someone he thinks is a good fellow. Yes, I know what you're going to say, but all men are like that; and I admit he made me laugh, but, as my grandfather used to say, beware of people who make you laugh, because they're usually up to no good."

"That," said Kent, a trifle stunned, "is just about the most cynical remark I've ever heard. But what has it all got to do with Jenny or Rod?"

"I'm sure I don't know," she told him placidly. "But what Rod knew, Jenny knew; you can be sure of that."

"Meaning? It doesn't seem to make any sense."

"Oh, fiddle-de-dee!" cried Melitta, losing a little of her injured air and showing some of that sparkle which could still make Dan Reaper beam with pride. "Who wants to make sense? *I* don't pretend to, thank heaven, though I've always been more sensible than most, and a good deal more sensible than any of you. If you want to know what happened, you just think of everything that could have happened; and one of them is the right explanation; and there you are."

Kent looked at her with a certain reverence. If she had taken just two glasses of champagne at that moment, the hump would have lifted from her face as well as from her feelings, and she would have been a genuinely beautiful woman.

"I suppose it's a sound principle in detective-work," he admitted. "But, since you have a suspicious mind and secrets are coming out all over the place, how did Jenny strike you?"

"Strike me?" she asked quickly.

"I mean what's your version of her character?"

"Version fiddlesticks. People do not have versions of character in families: they take what they can get, and thank heaven it isn't worse, as Uncle Lionel used to say. I do think you ought not to talk in such a silly way, Christopher, though I dare say it's all very well in novels. Jenny was a sweet girl, or as much as could be expected."

"Well, you'd better make up your mind before you see Superintendent Hadley and Dr. Fell." This was the sort of talk from Melitta which always stung him. "There seem to be more niggers in the woodpile than you'd think. As old friend to old friend, Melitta, you're only fifty; don't try to talk like a grandmother before your time."

He was sorry a moment later, that he had said it. It pierced something that was not a fancied complaint. But there was nothing now that could be done. When he took her down to Gay's room, he asked only one more question.

"Did you ever notice in Jenny's possession a white-gold bracelet with one black stone, like an obsidian?"

"No," said Melitta, her first monosyllable.

Yet she was complacent, amiable, even cheerful in Gay's room, where Hadley was concluding his questioning. Gay preserved towards her an attitude of great gallantry, and, when he presented her to Dr. Fell, she was almost effusive. Hadley, his note-book on his knee, forged ahead as steadily as an army lorry.

"—and you did not wake up, Sir Gyles, until half-past nine this morning?"

"That is correct," agreed the other with great gravity.

"How did you first learn of the murder?"

"From one of your men. Sergeant Somebody. I rang for the maid to get hot water for my tea," he nodded towards the table. "The maid answered the bell, but the sergeant came with her. He told me Mrs. Kent had been killed, and asked if I would stay in my suite. I obeyed orders."

"One last question. I believe it is the usual thing, when you take a room at this hotel, for them to issue a little folded card with the number of the room, the price, and so on?"

Gay frowned. "I don't know. It certainly is so at a number of hotels. This is the first time I have ever been here."

"But didn't you get such a card?"

"No."

Hadley's pencil stopped. "I'll tell you why I ask. Mr. Kent here was standing in front of this hotel between seven-twenty and seven-thirty this morning. One of those cards—let me have it, will you?—dropped down out of a window; from up here somewhere, anyhow." He took the card Kent handed him. "This, you see, is for room 707, Mrs. Kent's room. But her room looks out on the air-well. This card, apparently, could only have come from your suite or Mr. Reaper's. What we want to know is how the card for 707 came to be in here, and why it was dropped out of a window at seven-thirty in the morning."

There was a pause. Gay returned the look unwinkingly.

"I don't know, superintendent. So far as I know, it was not dropped out of here."

"Can you tell us anything, Mrs. Reaper?"

"My husband attends to all that," Melitta said vaguely. The lines of dissatisfaction pressed down her face again, so as to make its expression unreadable; Kent guessed that she and Hadley were not favourites of each other. "I remember quite well that there were a number of those little cards. And naturally they gave them to my husband in a batch, because of course he was the host and paid for all the rooms. I am quite *sure* he put them all down on the bureau in our bedroom. And, though I cannot and do not expect to be consulted about it, I should think it was easy. It blew out."

"Blew out?"

"The card blew out," she told him with an air of patience. "Out of the window. And since my husband will insist on sleeping with both of the windows wide open, and they always put the bureau between the windows, I cannot say I am surprised. There must have been a high wind this morning,"—this was true, Kent remembered, for he had been standing out in it when the card whirled down,—"because I know he got up at some time to close the windows, and things were blown all about on the bureau."

Hadley wore a look of unspoken profanity. If this attractive clue turned into a mere gust of wind, it would be a final bedevilment.

"Are you certain the card for 707 was among them?"

"I am not certain; I don't know anything about it. All I know is that I simply glanced at them, to make sure my husband had told me the truth about what the rooms cost. I never noticed the numbers at all. I am afraid, as usual, you will have to ask my husband."

There was an opportunity to ask him. Dan, shouldering in at that juncture, stopped short and seemed disturbed to find her there. Francine was behind him, with a worried-looking Hardwick, the latter carrying a sheet of notes.

"That bracelet—" exploded Dan. "No. You tell 'em, Hardwick. Fire away."

The manager gave a careful and courteous greeting to everyone before he took up a task he did not seem to relish. He resembled a grizzled clerk studying a ledger, and had a pencil poised.

"About the bracelet, as Mr. Reaper says. It belonged to Mrs. Kent; Miss Forbes has just identified it. But we're not through with the other one yet. I've talked to Mrs. Jopley-Dunne on the telephone. Her bracelet is a silver linked one set with small diamonds; it's worth three thousand dollars, and she says that beyond any doubt she left it in that bureau." He looked up. "I think she means it, Mr. Hadley. She—er—she can't claim any liability; but, all the same, we don't want this unpleasantness and I have got to find the bracelet somehow."

Dr. Fell sat up. "Steady!" rumbled the doctor. "Let me understand this. You say there were *two* bracelets in that bureau?"

"It looks like that," admitted Hardwick.

"Two bracelets. Both were stolen, and then one was returned. But the one that was returned was Mrs. Kent's bracelet, which very probably has some meaning in this case. And the one that was taken and *not* returned was a bracelet belonging to Mrs. Jopley-Dunne, a woman whose belongings have absolutely nothing to do with the case at all. If it had been the other way round, we should have had sense. But it isn't and we haven't. Oh, my eye, Hadley! This won't do."

Hadley gave a sharp glance round.

"Not so fast," he snapped. "Anything else, Mr. Hardwick?"

"Yes. I've checked up on the night-staff. I take it," inquired Hardwick, "that you were most interested in the time round midnight? Mr. Reaper saw this 'hotel-attendant' in the hall at two minutes past twelve?"

"That's right. Well?"

The manager peered up over his eyeglasses. "Then every solitary soul employed on the night-staff has what you'd call a complete alibi. It's a long story, but it's all here for your convenience in checking. I've had them routed individually out of their beds as quickly as I could. Shall I read this out?"

"Fine," said Dan without enthusiasm. "I hope that clears the air. But, since I'm chiefly interested in my own tight little circle—You haven't got any mechanism, have you, to prove an alibi for all of us?"

"As a matter of fact, in one case I can." Hardwick forgot himself and put his pencil behind his ear. "It goes along with the alibi of Billings, the night-porter, who was in his lodge downstairs. A telephone-call from up here came through at just midnight. Billings answered it. The guest wanted information, and they talked until three minutes past. Billings is willing to swear to the voice of the guest who spoke to him; and an under-porter heard Billings's side of it. So—er—well, it's your affair; but that seems to let both of them out of it."

"Who was the guest?" demanded Hadley.

"Mr. Wrayburn, in 705."

Chapter IX

MEN IN THE CASE

H adley did not comment; for a short time it was as though he had not heard. But he avoided Dr. Fell's eye and studied the ring of faces which, blank or interested, now included all of the *dramatis personae* except one. A very clever person (had he known it) was then within sound of his voice.

"We'll go into that later," he observed. "Thanks for the information, though. At the moment, have you got that bracelet? Good! Miss Forbes: you identify this as belonging to Mrs. Kent?"

Kent had been looking at her ever since she had come in, wondering about Gay's maunderings, wondering about the nature of the mess in which they had been landed. Francine's expression baffled him as she regarded the bracelet; it was not an expression he knew.

"Yes. She was wearing it last night."

"Will someone else identify it? Mrs. Reaper? Mr. Reaper?"

"I'm sure *I* never saw it before," said Melitta.

"Neither have I," Dan asserted, wheeling round as though surprised. "Funny, too. You'd notice a thing like that, with the inscription and the rest of it. Do you suppose she bought it since she landed over here?"

Hadley gave a quick look at Dr. Fell, who did not respond. "It doesn't look the sort of thing you could buy in Dorset; or possibly even in London, according to the doctor. However! She was wearing this at the theatre last night?"

"Yes, she was," Francine said in a cool tone which gave the impression that her truthfulness might be doubted. "Perhaps the others didn't notice it because she wore her fur coat all last night. But I saw it beforehand. I—"

"We don't doubt you, Miss Forbes," Hadley said at that curious tone, as though to prod her. "When did you see it?"

"Before we went to the theatre, and just before we went out to dinner. I went to her room to ask her whether she was going to dress for the theatre last night."

"Time?"

"About seven o'clock."

"Go on, please."

"She said she was much too tired and queer inside to dress. She said she wouldn't even go to the theatre if it weren't for sticking to the party; she said she thought it wasn't decent." Francine stopped. Under the long eyelids her dark brown eyes, which gave vitality to the too-fair complexion, flashed towards Hadley as though pondering. "She said—"

"Just a moment. She talked about 'sticking to the party.' Do you mean she was alarmed or frightened?"

"No, I don't think so. It would have taken a great deal to frighten her." Another pause. The emotional temperature was so low that Kent wondered about it. "When I went in her trunk was open but not unpacked; she said she would unpack after the theatre. She was standing in front of the dressing-table, with her wrist out, looking at that bracelet. I admired it, and asked whether it was new. She said yes. She also said, 'If anything ever happens to me, which I don't anticipate, you shall have it.' "

Hadley looked up quickly.

"She was a great friend of yours?"

"No. I'm not sure whether she liked me. But I think she trusted me."

This was a curious remark from Francine; both Dan and Melitta Reaper seemed to find it so, for there was a shifting and muttering in the group.

"Anything else, Miss Forbes?"

"Well, she looked very hard at me, I thought, and asked if I had ever seen anything like the bracelet before. I said I hadn't, and looked at it closer. I asked her whether the inscription had any meaning; any personal meaning, that is. She said, 'Only if you're able to read it; that's the whole secret.' "

Again Hadley glanced at Dr. Fell, who seemed intrigued and sardonically amused. " 'Only if you're able to read it; that's the whole secret.' Wait!" muttered the superintendent. "You mean that Latin inscription is, or contains, a cryptogram or cipher of some sort? Oh, Lord, haven't we had enough—"

"Be careful, Hadley," warned Dr. Fell. "I rather doubt that. Anything else, Miss Forbes?"

"No, that was all. I don't know what she meant. I certainly never suspected her of subtlety. So I went back to my room, and she didn't refer to the matter afterwards. May I have it now?"

"Have what?"

"That bracelet. She promised—"

This was so frankly and blatantly out of character that even her voice sounded wrong. Francine corrected herself, with a little husky cough, and tried to assume her earlier impersonal air. Hadley, with a smile that was not pleasant, closed up his note-book; he sat back with a look of luxurious patience.

"Now let's have it, Miss Forbes. What is it you're hiding?"

"I don't think I understand."

"But I do think you understand," said Hadley patiently. "You ought to know the consequences. I'm not going to sit here and howl at you; I simply warn you that I'll act on the assumption you're keeping something back. Some exceedingly dirty work has been done in this hotel and I mean to find out what. I'm going to ask your friends some questions; and then I'm going to ask you again. See that you have something to tell me."

"Oh, really?" said Francine in a high voice. "You don't know how you frighten me. Well, I still have nothing to tell."

Hadley ignored this. "Some general questions, please. I got you all together because, if anyone can add anything to the pool, we want to know it. You all swore to me two weeks ago that there was no reason why Mr. Kent—Mr. Rodney Kent—should have been murdered. Now his wife is killed. You all must know quite well that there is a reason somewhere. Mr. Reaper!"

Dan had sat down in a chair opposite Melitta, with Sir Gyles Gay between them like a referee. When Dan got out his pipe, unrolled an oilskin tobacco-pouch, and began to press in tobacco with a steady thumb, it was as though he were loading a gun: say a twelve-bore shotgun.

"Fire away," he invited, shaking himself.

"I think you told me that Mr. and Mrs. Rodney Kent lived in your house in Johannesburg?"

"Right. They had the top floor."

"So you and Mrs. Reaper must have known Mrs. Kent as well as anybody?"

"Yes, certainly."

"Do you share this general belief that nobody knew her very well?"

"I don't know," said Dan, and stopped. "I never thought of it. What do you mean by 'knowing' her, anyway? Term makes no sense. I didn't watch her go to bed at night and get up in the morning."

Sir Gyles Gay interposed, with Cheshire-cat effect. "I think the superintendent is wondering, though, whether anybody else did. The seeds are taking root."

"*You* put them there," said Hadley. "What I mean, Mr. Reaper, is this. Do you know of any love affair Mrs. Kent may have had before her marriage—or afterwards?"

"Good God, no!" said Dan, who seemed to be genuinely shocked as he dug back into his memory. "That's the last thing I should have thought of Jenny. Afterwards, I mean. I know you hinted at something like that after Rod's death; but I knew you didn't mean it seriously. She wasn't like that. She was a—a kind of sister. Wasn't she, Mel?"

Melitta nodded with such earnestness that she seemed to be waggling her head like a China figure.

"What was her attitude towards divorce, Mr. Reaper?"

"Divorce?" repeated Dan with a blank look.

"She was absolutely and unalterably opposed to it," interposed Melitta suddenly. "She told me so any number of times; she said it was shocking and disgusting the way they go on in Hollywood because someone drops a shoe on the floor or something."

"But what are you getting at?" asked Dan.

"The devilish respectability of many murderers," Sir Gyles Gay put in with the effect of a pounce. "Now that I have got a policeman in a corner, I should like to get his practical opinion on the matter. It's the only thing that's puzzled me about murderers. I don't care what causes crime in general, whether it's the thickness of a gland or the thinness of a lobe or anything that the doctors wrangle about. To my forthright mind the explanation of most crime is simple: somebody wants something and so he simply goes and grabs it—"

Dan grunted approvingly. Hadley did not stop this oration; he was watching the group while Gay, with the pleased expression of a wizened small boy, continued:

"—but one kind of crime is plain nonsense. It's this: A. falls in love with Mrs. B. So, instead of separating from Mr. B., instead of doing anything rational about it, Mrs. B. gets together with A. and they murder Mr. B. This seems to me to be carrying respectability too far. I know it isn't an original thesis. But I'll make an extra point: it's the only kind of murder case which is certain to cause a big splash of notoriety in the Press, to be eagerly followed and read by everyone, and to be remembered for many years in the public mind. Millionaires are shot, chorus-girls are gassed, matrons are dismembered in trunks; that kind of case may or may not attract great notice. But the case of A. and Mrs. B. always does. Think of the criminal cases which most readily jump to your mind, and you'll see what seven out of ten of them are. Now, that seems to indicate that it strikes home. It's close to the great British household. It affects us—a disturbing thought. Maybe A. and Mrs. B. are prowling closer round our own doors than we think. Mrs. B doesn't get a separation, or a divorce, or go and live with A.; she simply has her husband murdered. Why?"

Francine could not keep out of this. "Because," she said curtly, "most people aren't well off and can't afford emotional luxuries. Get a decent social state, and you'll change all that. Under our present state the only emotional luxury the poor can afford is murder."

"They don't really intend to do any dreadful thing like that," said Melitta with the same air of suddenness, "though I suppose most women have thought about it at one time or another, like that terrible woman who wrote all the letters that are shocking, but you wish more of them had been printed in the book. But all of a sudden they get drunk or lose their heads or something, and before they know it it's all over: like adultery, you know."

"What do *you* know about adultery?" said Dan with restraint. He blinked at her, after which a grin crept over his face. "Here! If the parade of epigrams has finished, I'd like to know just what all this has to do with Jenny. She wouldn't—er—lose her head."

Francine, folding her arms, looked straight at Hadley though she addressed Dan.

"Don't you see what they're hinting at? The background of the idea is that someone has fallen in love with Jenny, but *she* knows Rod will never give her up under any circumstances; and above all things she mustn't be touched by any scandal. That would horrify her. So she encourages this man to kill Rod. But for that reason she won't go down to Sussex and stay in the house while the killing is done; so she remains with her aunts. It may be delicacy or caution. Then she discovers that she can't stick the man—possibly she says her soul is revolted, or possibly she wanted Rod killed for some other reason, and now that it's done she needn't encourage the murderer any longer—so she tries to send him about his business. But he kills her."

"Could you believe that about *Jenny?*" demanded Dan. "Didn't she make Rod a good wife?"

"Oh, uncle, my darling," said Francine, "I didn't say it was my theory. But, as for the last part of it, yes. I've watched her making him a good wife, and, frankly, it made me sick. She cared no more for Rod than I do for that lamp-shade."

"I am glad to have my judgment," observed Gay, tilting up his chin with shining pleasure, "confirmed by outside witnesses. I warned Dr. Fell, and later Mr. Hadley, that she was that very dangerous and insidious thing, a sweet and dignified woman."

"Well, I'll be—" said Dan. "What kind of a woman do you want, then? Sour and undignified?"

"*Hey!*" roared Dr. Fell.

There was an abrupt silence after that thunderous blast. Dr. Fell pounded on the floor with his stick, but his eye twinkled over eyeglasses coming askew on his nose. Then he cleared his throat for pontifical pronouncement.

"Much as I dislike to interrupt," he said, "this discussion appears to have turned into an argument about matrimony. I am always willing to argue about matrimony; or, in fact, anything else; and at any other time I shall be happy to oblige. Both murder and matrimony are stimulating and exciting things: in fact, an analogy could be drawn between them as regards the interest they excite. Harrumph! Ha! But Miss Forbes has made at least one point—point of fact—which is so good that we can't let it drop. Eh, Hadley?"

"Thank you," said Francine. Her chilly manner was in contrast to the fervor with which she had spoken last; but in spite of herself she smiled under the beam of Dr. Fell's presence. "I didn't say it was my theory."

"H'mf, no. That odious burden shall rest elsewhere. But in this theory, how did that bracelet fit into it?" He pointed his stick towards the table where the bracelet lay. "Was it a kind of pledge or token given by this X, this unidentified man, to Mrs. Kent?"

"Well—yes."

"Do you believe that to be actually the case?"

"Yes. I—oh, I don't know! That's just it: I don't know anything! I've already said a dozen times more than I intended. . . ."

"Yes," agreed Hadley placidly, "I thought you would." He seemed to gain his point by ignoring her. "Mr. Reaper: let's get back to the subject we started on, before we continue about this. What do you know *about* Mrs. Kent? I met her only once, and she was ill then, or said she was; so it's little enough I got out of her. For instance, where was she from? Johannesburg?"

"No, she was born up country, in Rhodesia. I knew her parents well, when she was a kid in curls. Good old stock; gentlemen-farmers; not very go-ahead."

"Are her parents living?"

"No. I lost touch with them some years ago. They left her very well provided for, though I shouldn't have suspected that. She came to Johannesburg about three years ago; she and Rod have been married for two."

Dr. Fell interposed a sleepy question. "I say, was she fond of travelling? Did she do much of it?"

"No," said Dan, sighting behind his pipe. "Funny you should ask that. She detested it; never did any. Trains and ships made her sick, or something; even coming from Salisbury to Johannesburg was something to set her teeth about. Didn't want to make this trip, either. As it happens," he added, staring down at the packed tobacco with a heavy and lowering embarrassment, "I wish she hadn't. I wish nobody had. And then—" He spoke quietly. "Right down to brass tacks: did you mean all that about A and Mrs. B.?"

"That was Sir Gyles's suggestion." Hadley was still prodding, and he saw Dan look sideways with abrupt suspicion. "I'm merely trying to get at the truth. But do you think someone in your party is a homicidal lunatic?"

"My God, no!"

"Then we've got to look for a motive, if you'll help. Think. Was there *any* reason why someone should have killed both Mr. and Mrs. Kent? By this time you've all got to face it: it wasn't an outsider or a member of the hotel staff. So was there any reason? Money? Revenge? You shake your head—you all do. Then, Mrs. Kent being the sort of person some of you think she was, the only indication we've got is a possible affair in which Rodney Kent is killed by X in collusion with Mrs. Kent, and X later kills Mrs. Kent herself. If," Hadley's tone grew sharper, "Miss Forbes will now tell us what she knows. . . ."

"Which is still nothing," said Francine. "The sum and substance of it is this. I wasn't actually told a word. I inferred, from the way she talked, that some man she was very much interested in had given her the bracelet; someone she either loved or—"

"Or—?"

"Feared, I was going to say. There you are. I couldn't tell you because I didn't want to sound silly," she drew in her breath with hard effect, "like one of Chris's melodramatic novels. Maybe I was imagining it all, because it seems a little too melodramatic to be true. But I did understand that if I looked hard enough at that bracelet I might learn something."

"About what? About the person who gave it to her?"

"Yes."

"And that is why you wanted me to give it to you a while ago?"

"Well, yes."

Hadley picked up the bracelet and turned it over in his hand. "You can see for yourself that there's not a scrap of writing, or place for writing, or any secret hanky-panky, except that Latin inscription. Do you mean there's a secret hidden in that, like an acrostic or some such thing? *Claudite jam rivos, pueri, sat prata biberunt*. This is more in your line, Fell."

"I still think," Gay urged, "that you're making too much of a small thing. If I may suggest it, the inquiries should be broader. If there has been a man in the case, there ought to be traces of him. Find that man, and you'll be a good deal closer to finding the murderer.

"No, you won't," said a new voice.

The door to the hall had opened and Harvey Wrayburn came in. He did not come with his usual bounce or bustle. In appearance he was stoutish and undistinguished, except when some enthusiasm animated him—as it often did. Then his gingery hair and moustache, his alert eyes under a bump of a forehead, would all take on a vividness of self-assurance in which few could disbelieve. He had a fondness for wearing old grey worsted suits, and a habit of jamming his fists into the coat-pockets so that the coat always looked bulging and long. At this time he was self-assured enough, except for a look of strain round his eyes. He seemed poised on the edge of speech, as though he had just been put in front of a microphone and told that the red light would flash on in half a second.

"For the last five minutes," he said, "I've been listening outside that door. Who wouldn't?" he added, raising his neck up a little. "The question was whether I should get our friend Hadley in a corner and explain, or else get it all off my chest in front of all of you—and have done with it. I've decided to get it off my chest. All right: I'm the man you want."

Hadley jumped to his feet. "Mr. Wrayburn, you may make a statement if you like, but I must caution you—"

"Oh, I didn't kill her," said the other rather irritably, as if he had been robbed of an effect. "I was going to marry her; or she was going to marry me. Your grand reconstruction also misfires on one other point: that bracelet. I didn't give the bracelet to her. She gave it to me."

Chapter X

SHIPBOARD IDYLL

Wrayburn's next statement was in a slightly different key. "I feel better," he said in a surprised tone. "No balloon or aneurism seems to have burst. You don't look any different. Oh, hell."

After a violence of expelled breath, he perched himself on the edge of the table as though he were addressing a class, and went on:

"I know about the penalty for suppressing evidence. And that's not all. I've always hated the silly fathead who shoves an important clue into his pocket and causes everybody trouble because he (or usually it's a she) won't speak; and then, when you find it, it's not worth the hunt. All right, here I am. And here's your clue."

From his waistcoat-pocket he took a Yale key with a chromium tag bearing the number 707, and tossed it across to Hadley.

"You mean," said Dan, "that you and Jenny have been—"

"Have been what? Six kisses," said Wrayburn gloomily. "I counted 'em. She said the last one was for luck."

Hadley was curt.

"I think we'd better hear about this from the beginning," he said, only less satisfied than exasperated. "You didn't say anything about it when Mr. Rodney Kent was murdered."

"No, of course I didn't. Why should I? I didn't kill him."

"And yet, if you intended to marry her, his being dead must have simplified matters, didn't it?"

"This isn't going to be as easy as I had hoped," said Wrayburn, fixing his eyes grimly on the door-knob after a quick look at Hadley. "Try to understand this. I didn't think about it simplifying matters at all. I thought about it as an infernal shame and a piece of senseless brutality done by that fellow Bellowes when he was drunk. That's all I thought. It—woke me up."

"How long has this been going on? I mean the affair with Mrs. Kent."

"Well—it only really started on shipboard. Oh, Lord, these ships. The weather was cutting up rough, and only Jenny and I, and sometimes Dan, had our sea-legs. You know how these things happen."

"Mrs. Kent wasn't sea-sick?"

"Not a bit."

"We heard just a minute ago that she couldn't stand ships in any kind of weather."

Wrayburn glanced over his shoulder. As a rule, Kent knew, he was fond of the limelight; but he seemed to regret that he had perched on the table.

"Then all I can say," he retorted querulously, "is that somebody is mistaken. You ought to have seen her. That old tub was jumping about like a ball in a roulette-wheel, and Jenny would stand as cool as though she had just walked into a drawing-room. It was the—the humanest I ever saw her. How that woman liked to see things smashed up! Once the wicker furniture, and the gramophone, and all the rest of the stuff got loose in the palm-room when the ship was pitching badly. It sailed round from one side to the other, and simply busted the whole show to blazes. It was one of the few times I ever saw Jenny really laugh."

There was a stony kind of silence, while some members of the group shifted in their chairs. Dr. Fell was the first to speak.

"You ought to know, Mr. Wrayburn," he said, "that you're making rather a bad impression. That look on Hadley's face—I know it. In other words, you don't show any signs of being a broken-hearted lover."

"I'm not," said Wrayburn, moving off the table. "Now we're getting down to it."

He looked round the circle.

"You must be Dr. Fell. Will *you* explain what happened, even if I can't? I don't know exactly how it came about on that ship. The trouble with sirens, like Jenny, is that they win half their victories by their very reputations. They're attractive; you know they're attractive; but you have no intention of being attracted by them. Then they let you know—inadvertently—how much interested they are in you; and you're so flattered that, like a chump, you wonder if you're not falling. Then you do fall. Finish. You're anaesthetised; for the time being."

"You needn't look so crushed about it," rumbled Dr. Fell cheerfully. "It happens, you know. When did you begin to wake up?"

His manner was so casual that Wrayburn stopped pacing.

" 'Begin.' 'Begin.' Yes, that's the word," he admitted. He dug his hands into the usual pockets; and once his animation had gone, he looked undistinguished again. "Let's see. It was—maybe just after the ship docked. Maybe it was when she told me she wasn't going down to Sussex because she couldn't trust herself to be with me. All of a sudden that struck a wrong note. Bing! I looked at her and knew she was lying. Finally, maybe it was when Rod died."

Dan had been waving a hand for silence.

"Will somebody explain this business about Jenny's 'reputation'?" he insisted. "What reputation? All I can say is that it's complete news to me."

"Of course," said Melitta.

"You mean to say you knew it?"

Melitta's thin voice kept to its monotone. "Of course, my dear, you will *not* listen to anyone; and you say everything is gossip, as it often is, and you're so terribly concerned with your own ideas—you and Chris, too—that naturally nobody ever tells you anything." Melitta was full of impatience. "All the same, I stick to my opinion, and I don't alter it. Jenny was a Sweet Girl. Of course, I know there has been a certain amount of gossip, and my grandfather always used to say that most gossip is probably true because it is what the people would like to do even if they are not doing it. But in Jenny's case there was *absolutely* nothing against her, and I was quite sure she could be trusted not to do anything foolish. And it was really most interesting to see what happened."

"Murder happened," said Hadley.

A wrathful superintendent had been trying to break through this screen of talk.

"It won't be necessary to explain your state of mind, Mr. Wrayburn. Just tell me what you did. Were you in Mrs. Kent's room last night?"

"Yes."

"Very well; let's get that clear. What time did you go in?"

"About twenty-five minutes to twelve. Just after the maid left, any-how."

"At what time did you leave the room?"

"Midnight—I was also in there at seven, and again at eight o'clock this morning."

"And you tell us you did not commit this murder?"

"I did not."

During a strained pause of about ten seconds he met Hadley's eye. Then Hadley turned briskly and nodded to Dr. Fell and Kent.

"Good. Then just come across the hall with me to 707, and explain how you managed it. No! The rest of you, with the exception of these two, will remain here."

He very quickly shut off the protests. Opening the door for the other three, he ushered them out ahead of him and closed the door with a snap. Wrayburn, breathing hard, went out with a stiff gait which suggested that he might have been walking through a more evil doorway than this. In the corridor Hadley beckoned to Sergeant Preston, who was just coming out of the Reapers' suite. From room 707 the body had now been removed, leaving only a few stains on the floor.

"We've nearly finished searching, sir," Preston reported. "And so far, there's not a sign of that unif—"

"Shorthand," said Hadley. "Mr. Wrayburn, your statement will be taken down, and you will be asked to initial it afterwards. Now let's hear just what happened in here."

After looking round quickly, Wrayburn leaned against the foot of the nearest twin-bed and seemed to brace himself. His moustache was not now brushed up, either literally or metaphorically; he looked heavy and a little shabby.

"Well, it was like this. It's no good saying I was entirely out from under the ether. That's partly camouflage for the benefit of —" he jerked his head towards the other side of the hall. "But I was beginning to wonder whether I might have made a fool of myself aboard ship. Besides, we had had a roaring good time at Gay's."

"Wait. Had there been any talk of marriage between you and Mrs. Kent?"

"No, not then. She wouldn't bring it up, and I didn't. You understand, there was always Rod." He looked at Kent. "I swear, Chris, I never meant any harm to him."

"Go on."

"So, you see, I saw Jenny again for the first time last night. Considering what had happened—naturally, I didn't expect her to fly to my shoulder or anything of the sort. I was beginning to wonder whether I wanted her to; I didn't trust her. But I couldn't get an opportunity to speak to her alone. She seemed odd. At the theatre she arranged matters so that we were sitting at opposite ends of the row of seats, and between the acts she monopolised Gay. I had never seen her look—brighter.

"As you can understand, the only time I could get to see her alone was after the others had gone to bed. I waited for fifteen or twenty minutes after we had all closed our doors. Then I nipped across the hall to there," he indicated the side door, "and knocked."

"Yes?" Hadley prompted, as he hesitated.

"I can tell you this. She was frightened about something. After I knocked there was no answer for a second or two. Then I heard her voice very close to the door, asking who it was. I had to repeat my name twice before she opened the door."

"Had she seemed frightened earlier in the evening?"

"No. At least, not noticeably. There was a stealthy kind of air about this; I don't know how else to describe it. And the door was bolted—I remember the noise of the bolt when she drew it back.

"She had changed her shoes for slippers, and was just beginning to unpack her trunk. The trunk, everything, looked just about as it does now. I don't want you to think I'm any more an ass than necessary. But when I saw her again, I didn't know what to say. I simply stood and looked at her; and my chest hurt. That's a devil of a confession to have to make, but it did. She sat down in a chair and waited for me to speak first. She was sitting in that one, over by the writing-desk."

He nodded towards it. The room was now grey with early-afternoon shadows, and the maplewood gleamed faintly.

"So I started in to talk—chiefly about Rod, and how bad it was. Not a word about ourselves. I knew she was waiting for me to do it. And she was listening with a kind of composed expression, as though she were waiting to have her photograph taken. You know: cool, and the corners of the mouth turning down a bit. She was wearing that bracelet with the black stone and the inscription. It was the first time I had ever seen it. As I told you, *I* didn't give it to *her;* she gave it to me, presently.

"There's something else I must tell you, because it fits into the story. I kept on talking, inanely, and wondered why I talked at all. During this time she got up once or twice; in particular, she went over to the dressing-table there, picked up her handbag, and got a handkerchief out of it. I noticed, when she ran through the things in the handbag, that the key to the room—the key with the chromium tag—was inside.

"By the time I was wondering if I ought to make jokes, she came to a decision. You could see it; all at once. Her face softened up a bit. She asked me straight out, in that trustful way of hers, whether I was in love with her. That broke the barriers. I said I was. I said a whole lot. Whereupon she said she was going to give me a keepsake, a pledge, all that kind of thing. She unhooked that bracelet and handed it to me, and I can remember exactly what she said. She said: 'You keep that for always. Then nobody will try to wake the dead.' Don't ask me what it means. I thought it was a high-flown kind of thing to say. Because, mind, one part of my intelligence was still awake. In these romantic moments—arrh!—I didn't seem any closer to her than to a clock ticking beside you. Also, she brightened up immediately afterwards. She said it was late, and what would anybody think if I were found there at that hour?

"I was still fuddled; I wanted to keep on with a good thing. So I had a romantic idea. I said, why shouldn't we get up early in the morning, and have breakfast together and go out and see the town on our own before any of the rest could join us? It would have to be early, because Dan Reaper is always up and roaring round the place just at the time I like to take the best part of sleep. I recklessly said seven o'clock. You understand. I didn't really *want* to go out at seven o'clock. God love you, I wouldn't want to get up at seven o'clock in the morning to walk through the Earthly Paradise with an unveiled Houri. But I stood there and said fool things. She welcomed the idea, with an out-you-go expression. Finally, she asked me whether I wasn't going to kiss her good night. I said of course. Instead of grabbing the wench, as I would have grabbed any other woman, I gave her a couple of chaste and tender salutes. . . . Stop looking so damned embarrassed, coppers; you wanted the truth— and drew away. Then she put out her swan-like neck and said, 'And one for luck.' Then was when I saw her eyes sort of slide past my shoulder. There wasn't much in them; it was an expression like that of a woman in a foyer waiting for the lift to go up; they were blank and blue as marbles. And in that one second the cable was cut. My cable. In short, I saw—"

There was a click, and the wall-lights over the beds came on; Sergeant Preston was no longer sure with his shorthand notes. Nobody except Wrayburn, Kent thought, would have had the nerve to pour all this out to a note-book. He was now regarding them with sour poise and flippancy, his hands dug deep into his coat-pockets. The wall-lamps, behind their frosted-glass shades, made a sleek, theatrical light in the sleek, theatrical room.

"That's it," Wrayburn said complacently, nodding towards them. "Crafty little devil! I knew then; I felt it; though I couldn't imagine what the game was. I might have pursued the subject then, because all of a sudden it was beginning to hurt. But I couldn't—because that was when we heard the knock at the door."

Hadley jerked up his head.

"Knock at the door? Which door?"

"At what I suppose you'd call the main door: the one that had the sign hung on it later."

"What time was this? Do you know?"

"Yes. It was just a few seconds short of midnight. I know, because I looked at my watch when Jenny said good night."

"You were actually *in* the room when you heard this knock?"

"Certainly I was in the room—" Wrayburn was beginning with some asperity, when he stopped, and for the first time his eyes shifted. He added in a lower tone: "Oi! Here! You don't mean it was—Nobody told me—"

"Go on; what happened when you heard the knock?"

"Jenny whispered to me to get out in case I should be found there. So I ducked out of the side door, with the 'keepsake' in my pocket. I think Jenny bolted the door after me. I walked straight across to my own side door and went in."

"The time being—?"

"Oh, midnight. It couldn't have taken more than ten seconds. I admit I was feeling a bit mixed-up, and not too good-humoured; but I was going to see the thing through. In case I should forget it, I rang up the porter on the telephone (or at least I put through a call downstairs) and told him I was to be waked up at a quarter to seven next morning. I also wondered, with a few less romantic fumes in my head, where we should get breakfast at that time; and what in the name of sense we were going to *see* at that hour. Most people get over calf-love by the early twenties. I waited for a brief, bad bout of it until the early thirties. I suppose I saw us riding on a bus in the snow. Anyhow, I asked the porter a lot of questions, and I must have talked for three or four minutes on the phone."

Kent found himself fitting together the pieces of evidence. Wrayburn's story coincided exactly with the ascertained and ascertainable facts as regarded the man himself. He had been speaking on the telephone (according to Hardwick's schedule) from midnight until three minutes past. If any wonder might have been felt as to what could have been the reason for such a fairly long call at so late an hour, there was now a strong and plausible motive behind it. Wrayburn also spoke with an air of weary earnestness which was difficult to disbelieve. The question was now how far this evidence coincided with Dan's. Dan had seen in the hall this goblin, the figure carrying bath-towels, at exactly two minutes past midnight—standing outside Jenny's door. If Dan's statement were accepted (and nobody had questioned it), Wrayburn could not possibly be the elusive figure in uniform.

But there was one extra question. Someone, undoubtedly the figure in uniform, had knocked on the main door at a few seconds before midnight. Would it have remained there for two full minutes after the first knock, without going into or being admitted into the room? Why not? At least, so it appeared to Kent, who was watching Hadley and Dr. Fell.

Hadley drew a design in his note-book.

"Did you see anything of the person who knocked at the door?"

"No," said Wrayburn shortly. "No gratuitous information. I'll answer what you like; but I'm not bubbling over any longer. Thanks."

"Are you sure your watch was right about the times?"

"Yes. She's a good timekeeper, and I set her early in the evening, by the big clock on the wall outside this room."

(The same clock Dan had seen. Well?)

"Just continue your story," Hadley said. "You left this room at midnight, with Mrs. Kent's bracelet—?"

"*And* I didn't sleep. I couldn't. There was no need to ring me; I was awake long before seven. I got dressed, feeling seedy. At seven o'clock I went over and knocked at Jenny's door. There was no answer, even when I knocked harder. That made me mad, rather. It occurred to me that, since she would be sleeping in one of the twin beds, she would be closer to the main door, and would hear me better if I knocked there. I went round to the main door. The shoes were outside it, and the 'quiet' sign was hung from the knob. Now begins the story of my derelictions. I looked at the sign, and saw 'Dead Woman' scrawled on it. I picked up the sign to look at it closer; then I could see, behind it, the key still stuck in the lock outside the main door."

Dr. Fell puffed out his cheeks. So far he had been shutting out the view of one window, but now he lumbered forward.

"The key," he said, "was in the lock outside the door. Kindly take note of that, Hadley. The night before it had been in her handbag. Well?"

"I opened the door with it," said Wrayburn obediently, "and took the key out of the lock. Automatically, I suppose. I stuck my head inside the room, and saw her."

"That door wasn't bolted on the inside, then?"

"Naturally not, or I couldn't have got in. There was a heavy stuffy smell inside the room, and I thought, 'Doesn't the little so-and-so put her windows up at night?' Then I saw her; she was lying on the floor with her head inside that trunk. I went over and touched her. She was cold. I didn't investigate further; I didn't want to. But now comes the hardest part of the story to tell. I walked back out of the room by the way I had come, with the key in my hand, and stood in the hall. My first impulse, naturally, was to set up an alarm; to go and wake Dan, or wake somebody. But I'll admit it: I got the wind up. My trouble is that I always want to know what's going on, and I won't act until I do. Without saying a word I went back to my room and tried to think. This was about five minutes past seven o'clock.

"At a quarter-past seven I heard the maid coming on duty; I heard her jingle. And I was still racking my brains. Somebody had killed Jenny. I knew something queer had been going on last night, but *I* wasn't going to find that body. I had been the last person alone with her, and—you know. What bothered me most, and kept on bothering me, was *how* she had been killed. I wondered why on earth I had not stopped to make sure. There had been something done to her face; that's all I could tell, because it was early morning and very nearly dark. I felt I had to know, but I couldn't screw up quite enough nerve to go back to that room.

"It was going on towards eight o'clock when I remembered something that was nearly the last devilment. *I* had Jenny's bracelet. It's a distinctive-looking thing; it undoubtedly cost a lot of money; it would be certain to be missed; and if they found it in my possession—

"Well, no frills. I felt like that, anyhow. On top of this, I heard two men coming along the corridor saying something about 707. I got my door open a crack, and saw them go round, and heard them talking about a master-key in front of the main door of 707. How the devil was I to know one of 'em was you?" he demanded, turning to Kent. "I heard the door to 707 being opened, and closed, and then dead silence. The other man—the porter—was still out in the hall talking to the maid. On top of all this, the side door of 707 opened, and the first man (you) slid out with his head tucked into his overcoat collar. He didn't give an alarm; he hurried down the hall and got away."

Dr. Fell interposed again, this time turning to Kent.

"Hold on! When you got out the side door, Mr. Kent, do you remember whether or not it was bolted on the inside?"

"It was bolted," said Kent. "I remember that quite well—drawing the bolt back."

"H'mf, yes. Go on, Mr. Wrayburn."

"I'll tell you exactly what it was like for me," said the other, who had been reflecting, and could not stop his own garrulousness. "It was like standing in the street before oncoming traffic, and wanting to get to the other side. You think you've got good clear margin to get across before the traffic bumps you; but, all the same, you hesitate. Then, when it's almost too late, you suddenly make up your mind and dash for it. And the traffic nearly bumps you to glory after all. That's what I did. I had Jenny's bracelet in one hand, and the key in the other. Just after that fellow—you—had gone, I made up my mind to do what I should have done before. If the key opened the main door of Jenny's room, I was sure it would open the side door as well: my own key did. I went across the corridor and got in there while the porter was still outside. Mind, I kept *some* sense. I touched things only with a handkerchief. All I wanted to do was dispose of that bracelet, so I simply dropped it in the bureau drawer. That took only a few seconds; and there was Jenny on the floor. I had to see her and find out what was wrong, now I'd got my courage to the sticking-point. It was broad daylight, though the blinds were drawn. I wanted to see her face, but I couldn't because her head was still inside that trunk. I dragged her out. I took one look—and then bolted. I was back in my own room again, closing the door, by the time the porter barged into 707. And, of course, I walked off with the blasted key after all. There it is.

"That's what I did, and that's all I did. Call it what you like; I claim it was only natural and human. The trouble is that I'm a ruddy rotten criminal. I once picked up a pound-note off the floor in the foyer of a theatre and kept it; and afterwards I was convinced everybody in the place had seen me, and was ready to denounce me. That's how I felt to-day. I couldn't keep it down. So I decided, in the words of your favourite film-star, to come clean. I've now come so clean that I feel I've been through a wringer. Thus spake Zarathustra."

He ended with a deep breath, and sat down on the bed with enough violence to make it creak. He had sketched out a perfect characterisation of himself, Kent thought.

Dr. Fell and Hadley looked at each other.

"Is it too early to inquire," said Wrayburn, "whether you believe me? Or is it handcuffs and bread-and-water. Arrh!"

Hadley looked hard at him. "It certainly fits all the facts," he acknowledged. "And coming clean, I don't mind telling you, was very wise. Well, Mr. Wrayburn, if your story about the telephone-call at midnight is confirmed, I don't think you've got much to worry about. One other thing. While you were in this room on any of those occasions, did you come across a silver linked bracelet set with diamonds, and belonging to a Mrs. Jopley-Dunne?"

"Eh? No. I never heard of it or her."

"For the moment, then, that's all. You might wait across the hall."

When Wrayburn had gone, Hadley whistled softly between his teeth. "So that's the story of the reappearing bracelet. Yes, I don't think we can doubt that the murderer was looking for it, and made a thorough search to find it. Only it wasn't here. And therefore, presumably—?"

"The murderer pinched Mrs. Jopley-D.'s property, wondering if it might be an old friend in disguise," said Dr. Fell. "Why not? The background of both, so to speak, is similar. Both are linked bracelets, and silver looks much like white gold. H'mf, yes. The murderer was looking for the bracelet with the black stone, all right. But that's not, I think, the really important point of the story. And, oh, Bacchus, Hadley, the real point is important! I mean the key left behind in the door."

"You think it clarifies anything?"

"I know it does. Look here!—Eh? Yes? What is it?"

A knock at the door was followed by the entrance of Sergeant Betts.

"Just finished, sir," he reported to Hadley. "And it's no go. I've been over every room, cupboard, cranny, and rat-hole in this wing; and there's no uniform hidden anywhere."

Chapter XI

THE SOLUTION ACCORDING TO FICTION

A winter evening, when there is good food behind plate glass, money in the pocket, and a warmth of light to be seen on snow from inside, may be considered the best of all times for argument. Christopher Kent, entering the Restaurant des Epicures in Lisle Street at seven o'clock that evening, was ready for all of them. It had been a long day—which, for him, only began when Hadley and Dr. Fell finished their questioning at the Royal Scarlet Hotel.

The most important business had been the establishing of his own alibi for the night before, and the cashing of a cheque to bring him to the surface again. The first was not difficult; the second enabled him to pour largesse on the clubmen at the coffee-stall who swore to it, and to redeem his suit-case from the landlady in Commercial Road, East. Once his alibi was beyond question, Superintendent Hadley became genial and almost talkative. Kent was accumulating facts, facts, facts. He felt somewhat surprised at this: facts had never before been a great concern of his. But, relaxing under the ministrations of the barber, and spending a fine hour steaming in the Turkish baths at the Imperial, he began to tabulate the discoveries for reference.

1. The writing-printing in red ink on the "quiet" sign, which might have been so promising a clue, ended in nothing. It was so much printing and so little writing that it had to be classified as the former; and could never be identified.

2. The two sets of finger-prints found in the room were his own and Jenny's. Since the room had been cleaned and dusted by the maid just before Jenny moved into it, there were few old prints beyond smudges. Wrayburn, evidently by accident the first time and design the second, had left no prints at all.

3. Wrayburn was proved to have been speaking on the phone between midnight and three minutes past. Hadley, nothing if not thorough, set half a dozen persons to speak anonymously over the wire to Billings, the night-porter, and Billings had again identified Wrayburn's voice at once.

4. There was nothing wrong with the clocks, and no possibility of tampering with them. They were all electric clocks, with glass fronts which did not come off; all were operated on Greenwich time from a central switch. If Dan had seen the figure in uniform outside Jenny's door at two minutes past twelve, the time was exactly two minutes past twelve and no other.

5. Nothing, so far as could be ascertained, was missing from Jenny's possessions. Melitta Reaper went through them and said she was certain of this. There were several good pieces of costume jewellery in Jenny's trunk, in addition to £30 in notes in her handbag and travellers' cheques for £400 on the Capital Counties bank. But there was no silver or loose change whatever in her handbag.

6. The batch of small folded cards, bearing the room-numbers of each guest, had in fact been handed to Dan. He did not definitely remember seeing the card for 707 among them, since he had not looked at them. But he confirmed Melitta's statement that he had put them down on the bureau in their bedroom.

7. A detailed deposition from each of the persons concerned, regarding where they were at about two minutes past midnight, produced the following statements: Sir Gyles Gay had been reading in bed. Melitta Reaper had been taking a bath in the private bathroom of their suite. Francine Forbes had been "doing her hair" in her own room. Wrayburn and Dan were accounted for. Kenneth Hardwick, the hotel-manager who had been questioned along with the others, provided another alibi: from midnight until ten minutes past, in his own rooms, he had been going over the next day's menus with the head-waiter of the Royal Scarlet dining-room.

Thus the facts stood; and Christopher Kent had been tinkering with them as though for a story. To be near the party, he had reserved the only vacant room in Wing A, and he wondered about a number of things. He had invited Francine, Dr. Fell, and Hadley to dinner that night. Hadley (as usual) would be detained at the Yard, but Dr. Fell accepted with heartiness and Francine after some consideration.

When he entered the Restaurant des Epicures at seven o'clock, he found Francine waiting for him. She looked rather lonely in that crowd, and he suddenly felt protective. They sat down by a shrouded window, with a yellow-shaded lamp between them, and he ordered cocktails; but, instead of taking advantage of this mood, he said, "Well?"—which was definitely the wrong thing.

"Well, what?" she said instantly, and put down her glass.

He had meant nothing by it, merely a sort of clumsy opening to start a conversation: which causes much difficulty. He admitted this.

"Look here, what's wrong between us?" he inquired in some desperation. "I'm not your worst enemy: I swear it. I'm not trying to put one over on you or do you in the eye. But—"

After a time she spoke in a reflective tone. "Oh, Chris, if you weren't so beastly intolerant!"

His own glass slid on the table as he put it down.

"Intolerant? *Me?*"

"If you could only hear yourself say that," said Francine, and was amused. "Oh, come on, let's face it. You think being intolerant merely means persecuting somebody for moral or religious reasons, or not liking lowbrows and fish-and chips, or all the rest of it. But it doesn't. It doesn't!" she said fiercely. "It means that you simply go your own sweet way, and pay absolutely no attention to anything that isn't in your ken. You're tolerant on moral grounds because you sympathise with most of the offences, you're tolerant on religious grounds because you haven't got any religion, you're tolerant of low-brows because you *like* Wild West stories and band music and merry-go-rounds. But if there's something that doesn't come into your ken, like doing some real good in the world—all right: I won't say that: I'll take something in your own province—like the work of certain great authors whose beliefs you don't agree with, then you simply don't discuss them as being beneath contempt. Grr! Your idea of being generous is merely to be ridiculously generous with money, that's all."

"Sorry," he said. "Is that really it? All right. Honestly, if it will make you any happier, I will even admit that Blank Blank or Dash Dash is a great writer; but privately—"

"There. You see?"

"And if, in the latter part of the indictment, you were referring to certain gifts which you practically threw back in my face—"

"Trust a man," said Francine icily, "to take the conversation straight to the personal. You always do, and then accuse us of doing it." She paused. "Oh, I don't mind, really!" she cried in a different tone. "But you will *not* notice things, Chris; you sail through the world in your own sweet way, and you never do! For instance—Jenny."

The evil subject was back again; they could not keep it out. Francine spoke in an off-hand tone:

"I don't suppose you even noticed she was making a play for you, did you?"

"Nonsense."

"She jolly well was!" cried Francine, firing up.

He sat back and stared at her. Into his mind, doubtfully, had come a gleam of light; and with it a feeling of uproarious happiness sang through him. They looked at each other, each knowing the other knew.

"I wish I could persuade *you*," he said, "that I am the fair-haired prize-package you seem to believe other women think. Jenny? That's impossible! I never—"

"Thought of it? Neither did poor old Harvey Wrayburn, as decent a sort as there is, until she got after him during a long sea-voyage. She really was a terror, Chris. She did it as much to amuse herself as anything else. What annoys me is that I can't see how she did it, or how she had the knack. But she was most definitely going out to make a play for you."

"But I hope you don't think I—? To begin with, she was Rod's wife—"

"Your cousin's wife. Yes. And you wouldn't think of making love to the wife of a friend of yours, would you? In fact, the idea rather shocks you, doesn't it?"

"Frankly, yes," he admitted with what he hoped was dignity. "Your friends' wives are—well, damn it, I mean—"

"Not-to-be-thought-of-like-that," said Francine. "Oh, Chris, you are an old mossback!"

"Very interesting," he said coldly. "I suppose that in Russia—"

"Don't you say anything about Russia!"

"I was merely about to point out—"

"Don't you see, Chris," she urged with great sincerity, "that the moral issue involved is precisely the same whether the woman is your friend's wife or the wife of someone you don't know? You wouldn't make love to Rod's wife; but you'd have no compunction—not you!—about making love to the wife of some poor devil who's making maybe two pounds a week, and has to stay at the factory all day, and hasn't your leisure to—"

"One moment," he said, rather dazed. "So far as I remember, I never said one word about roaring round the country after other men's wives. As a menace to the home I am practically nil. But will you explain to me how it is that we can never touch on any subject without your somehow coming round to the political and economic aspect of it? I'll swear you and the world and Davy Jones seem to have gone politics-mad—"

"Indeed," observed Francine with sweet savagery. "It must be so nice, it must be so stimulating, for you to sit on your Olympian height and watch all the little imbeciles crawl about in the valley. I was attempting to explain, in as elementary a way as I could, that it is your kind of outworn, stupid codes and shibboleths which have made such a mess of the country—"

"Well, would it please you any better if I made love *both* to my friend's wife and the factory-worker's wife? Do you think we should be happier then?"

"My God, Chris Kent, there are times when I could kill you. You go and make love to whom you like! You—"

"That's what I am trying to do, my dear. Only—"

"*Ahem,*" said Dr. Fell.

They stopped. The vast presence of Dr. Fell towered over the table, beaming down with doubtful but benevolent interest, and following the thrusts with his head as you follow strokes in a tennis match. Now he cleared his throat. Francine, radiant with cold anger, put a handkerchief to her lips; but she burst out laughing instead.

"Ah, that is better," beamed Dr. Fell. "Heh-heh-heh. I dislike to interrupt; but the waiter has been hanging about the table for the past five minutes with the *hors-d'œuvre* wagon, and hesitating to say, 'Sardine?' for fear it should seem to have a personal application."

"He's a pig-headed—" said Francine.

"I have no doubt of it, my dear," said Dr. Fell, cheerfully. "In fact, it is a very good sign. The woman who does not think her husband is pig-headed is already beginning to dominate him, and that would be bad. I beg your pardon: I do not wish to begin an argument about equality or inequality in marriage. As the Frenchman said about love-making, 'Never before the fish!' But, if I might make a suggestion here, I should suggest that you get married; then you could stop being on the defensive and begin to enjoy yourselves."

"Jenny got married," said Francine.

"Not now," interposed Dr. Fell, with sudden strong authority. "Not that—just now."

That meal was like a loosening or unbuckling of armour, while the doctor's face grew redder and redder, and his chuckles more explosive behind the wine-bottles. However unbelievable his anecdotes became, however his rapid paradoxes gave his listeners the impression that they had just been whirled round a particularly fast switchback after having drunk two Seidletz powders, it was all directed towards one thing: putting these two at their ease. What a master of ceremonies he made Kent never fully realised until afterwards. But it was not until they were padded round against night and the things of night, over the brandy, that the subject was introduced again.

"Harvey should have heard that story—" began Francine.

Dr. Fell trimmed the ash off his cigar, and blinked sideways at her.

"Yes. Now is the time," he said. "What do you think of the whole affair, Miss Forbes?"

"I can answer that. It's the idea of—someone close to you—doing all that," she told him quietly. "Someone you've known a long time, but who's got a hinge loose. I don't think I'm afraid, though. I think it's all over."

"Why?"

"Because the poker was left behind this time." She took a deep inhalation of her cigarette, and spoke in the same even tone. "It wouldn't have been left stuck in those towels if somebody had had a further use for it. Unless, of course—well, unless someone has grown too fond of blood. But I can't credit that. I was trying to tell Chris what I thought, a while ago."

She considered.

"Some people might have been able to take Jenny, and Jenny's ways, lightly. I could, for instance. Probably most people could. But the tenth person mightn't be able to see her in so light-hearted a way. I've often wondered what Rod thought of her. Oh, she managed him, and her noted devotion to him, beautifully. Do you know, it was all so skilful that it was rumoured—and many people believed, at the time—*Rod* was marrying *Jenny* for her money?"

The glasses almost dropped off Dr. Fell's nose; he gave one wheeze through that nose. Then he said:

"Repeat that, please."

"It's true! It went all round our crowd in South Africa; and it's the first thing Sir Gyles Gay joked Rod about (subtly, of course) when we came over here; so the version was pretty broad and pretty garbled. It hurt Rod a good deal, though he simply said nothing about it and never even bothered to deny it. But I think some people even in our crowd believed it."

"Was she wealthy?"

"Well-off, anyway. I think."

"From what source?"

"From her parents, we thought, though a stony veldt farm isn't usually—and then her dressmaking business must have been very profitable. She had wonderful taste in clothes, there's no getting away from that."

"But why are you so interested in that piece of gossip?" demanded Kent.

"Because it's merely the motive for your cousin Rodney's murder," groaned Dr. Fell. "Oh, Lord, what a duffer I've been! What a thundering idiot! And yet there was no hint—!" He knocked his fists against his temples. "You see, the first murder was the one which wouldn't fit into any rational scheme of things. It wasn't rational sense; it wasn't even rational insanity. But Rodney marrying the woman for her money: that provides a very deadly and sane explanation."

"How? If you know anything," urged Francine, her too-fair skin flushed with wine, and looking less poised and more beautiful than Kent had ever seen her: "if you know anything, or guess anything, *won't* you tell us? It isn't just curiosity. It's to keep the devils out."

"That's fair enough," said Kent.

It was a little time before Dr. Fell answered.

"No!" he roared. "No, by the temple of Eleusis! And there's one main reason why I don't. I think (mind you, I say I think) I know just half this affair; with luck I may be able to get the other half. But there's a strong possibility, on which I am balanced at the moment, that the explanation may be exactly opposite to what I think it is: for that reason I haven't even dared to explain fully to Hadley. And he has some new information. I don't want to raise your hopes, and put you off-guard in case—"

"Eleusis," repeated Kent, as Dr. Fell stopped in mid-sentence. "If Wrayburn were here, with his mine of good-for-nothing lore, we might get that explained. Didn't the Eleusinian mysteries celebrate the descent of Persephone into the underworld, and her return to the light of day? System of rewards and punishments?" He added, " 'To wake the dead.' "

Dr. Fell chuckled. " *Pale beyond porch and portal, Crowned with calm leaves she stands—*' It's a curious thing about Swinburne, but the more intolerably doleful the poem, the more the rich gusto with which you can recite it. *'Who gathers all things mortal, With cold immortal hands—*' "

"Who does?" inquired Francine, who had a practical mind. "What on earth are you talking about?"

"Yes, we had better stop it. But the character of Mrs. Kent fascinates me as it unfolds. If we had only seen her, if we had only known after Rodney Kent's death what we know now, we might have been able to prevent Mrs. Kent's death." Dr. Fell brooded. "Or could we? I don't know. I doubt it."

"You think there's still—danger?"

"There's no danger," said Dr. Fell, "if you keep your door locked at night. I'm sorry if I seem to act as a Job's comforter; but we have got to take care of all possibilities. Can either of you help me? You must have some ideas. Where would you look?"

Kent thought of his sheaf of notes.

"My trouble is," he replied despondently, "that even now I can't look at the thing with an eye of human reason. All I can think of is how I should make it work out if I were writing the story. That's the phobia of all fiction-writers. I tell you, according to the laws of fiction there's only one possible solution and only one possible murderer! But it's not only guessing at an artistic solution; it's a very strong case. And yet—"

Dr. Fell looked at him with interest. "I know," he said guiltily. "I thought of that, too."

"You thought of what?"

From the breast pocket of his coat Dr. Fell began to take out an enormous collection of old papers and envelopes (there were enough of them to stuff a waste-paper basket) until he found the stub of a pencil. On

one comparatively clean surface of paper he wrote a few words. Then he
turned the paper over and pushed it across to Kent.

"Write down," he suggested, "the name of the person who springs to
your mind as the murderer. That's it: thank you. Now, Miss Forbes, take
this piece of paper and look at both sides."

Francine stared at it.

"But you've both written down the same name!"

"Of course," agreed Dr. Fell gloomily. "Kenneth Hardwick, the manager of the Royal Scarlet Hotel."

Chapter XII

ABOVE SUSPICION?

Francine, it appeared, could not understand whether they were joking
or whether Dr. Fell's glum face was as serious as it looked.

"But you don't honestly mean that? Or is this another of Chris's
ridiculous— That nice quiet man?"

"You really will throw suspicion on him if you talk like that," Dr. Fell
grunted. "Let's hear the case against him."

"To begin with, it's a question of keys," said Kent. "Somebody got
into that linen-closet and took out fifteen bath-towels and one face-towel.
Therefore somebody had to open the door of the linen-closet: unless the
maid failed to lock it last night. There's no sign of burglarious entry, so
apparently the door must have been opened with a key. But, according to
this new system of locks—here I'm quoting Hardwick himself—it's
impossible for any unauthorized person to open even so much as a
linen-closet. Now I remember it, he used the word 'linen-closet.' On the
other hand, again quoting him, he alone can open any door in the whole
building. That's a short and simple point to start with."

"Good," said Dr. Fell. "Go on."

"Next, the question of disguise. There couldn't be any more admirable
disguise for him than the uniform of one of his own attendants. It's like
the story he told about the porter who dressed up in pyjamas and
pretended to be a guest. If Hardwick were seen by one of the real guests,
he wouldn't be recognised even if someone got a glimpse of his face: the
uniform would do the trick. He would know, furthermore, that he ran
very little danger of being spotted by one of his own employees: the only

employee who could come upstairs after eleven-thirty would be one of the under-porters, and on such large floors he wouldn't have much difficulty in hiding himself if he saw the under-porter coming. As two additional points, I might mention that his private rooms are on the seventh floor; and that he would have easy access to any kind of uniform he chose to wear. You notice that the mysterious costume hasn't been found. But, if it were a real uniform belonging to the hotel, why should it be found?"

"Chris, that's awfully good," said Francine. "Do you think it's true?"

He reflected.

"I don't know; I'm only saying it's the way a story should work. For the crux of it is this: the production of an alibi."

"The clocks!" said Dr. Fell with a wheeze of great pleasure.

"Yes. You think of the dozens of wall-clocks in that hotel, all worked from a central switch, and you've got it first shot. I remember we had the same sort of system at school. One day, in the Schoolroom, roars of delight were caused when the clock on the wall went crazy: its hands began to whirl round the dial and point to all hours like something in a pantomime. What had happened—a master informed us acidly—was that all the clocks in the building had stopped, and were being re-set from a controlling-station in the headmaster's study.

"Now, you can see the beauty of that device. Suppose a murderer wants fifteen minutes out for an alibi, and this person has access to the master-clock. Well, he gets hold of the dupe who is later to swear to his presence; he talks to the dupe between (let's say) 11.55 and 12.10; then he dismisses the witness. Whereupon he goes to the master-clock and sets it back to 11.55: *thereby altering every clock in the building*. Out he goes to commit his murder. He may even let himself be seen. Afterwards he returns to his office, and puts every clock right again. He has created a hiatus in time of ten to fifteen minutes; and his dupe will later swear to his alibi during the time the murder was committed. The excellence of it is that he runs no risk of being caught out, or having anybody notice a discrepancy in time; no matter who looks at no matter what clock, they will all have precisely the same time. And, at the Royal Scarlet, in whose charge would the master-clock be? I'll lay you a fiver it's the manager. Hardwick, you observe, has an alibi for just those minutes."

He stopped in some doubt, and finished his brandy with a feeling of defiance.

"It really is good," admitted Francine. "It's so horribly ingenious that I can't believe a word of it."

"I am afraid that will be the general impression," beamed Dr. Fell. "Though I like the idea very much myself. It might, you see, cause some curiosity if a chance guest glanced at one of the clocks and saw its hands suddenly jump fifteen minutes in one way or another."

"At midnight? How many people were abroad in the halls then? I'll acknowledge," said Kent, hunching his shoulders, "that it still leaves much to be explained." The grizzled, amiable figure of Hardwick rose in his mind. "Where's the motive? Unless he's somebody out of Jenny's dark past; you appear to think she has one. What's the reason for all that hocus-pocus with shoes and 'Dead Woman' signs? Why, after getting into the room, does the murderer take Jenny's own key and shove it into the lock outside the door—"

"H'mf, yes. I told you that was an intriguing point."

"—and, lastly which in sequence was firstly, why was the same uniform worn at Gay's place in Sussex? Every explanation of the case, as you said this morning, takes a violent header over the first appearance of the uniform in a country house at two o'clock in the morning. Unless—"

"Keep at it!" urged Dr. Fell. "You're going great guns. That's the point on which I very badly need help. Why?"

"Symbolic meaning in a uniform?"

"Harrumph—well. Maybe."

"I believe I've got it," said Francine, putting down her cigarette and looking at the lamp in a startled fashion. "Did Hardwick know Dan had booked rooms for all of us at the Royal Scarlet?"

"Yes, naturally. Dan arranged it a long time ago, before any of us left South Africa."

"The murderer," she told them, "was seen at Northfield in a uniform because he *wanted* to be seen. That was the reason for it! He wanted to draw attention to the uniform. If he hadn't been observed by the drunk on the sofa, he'd have said Boo to someone else. Think of him walking straight down the hall, like—like someone behind footlights, do you see? It was easy. He shook the drunk by the shoulder, and then let himself be seen much too obviously. But that must mean—no, don't say anything, Chris!—that must mean he was preparing everybody's mind for his appearance later, when he came to kill Jenny—preparing our minds to see—but where is there any indication in just a coat and a pair of trousers?" She paused. "I'm afraid that's the best I can do."

Dr. Fell studied her with an odd frown. "I should not be surprised," he commented, "if that remark came closer to the truth than anything we have heard."

"Meaning?" asked Kent.

"Meaning that Hadley and I are trying to work out a plan of campaign. To-morrow we are going down to Northfield; and we're—h'mf—well, we're going to ask all your party to go down there as well. In the first place, Sir Gyles Gay's house interests me. In the second place, I want to go to the jail and see Mr. Ritchie Bellowes; specifically, I want to find out what he was really supposed to see."

"Supposed to see?"

"Yes. Isn't it fairly obvious?" inquired Dr. Fell, opening his eyes. "I think you're quite right in one respect, Miss Forbes. There had to be a witness to see our figure in uniform walking down the hall. What do you think of the theory that Ritchie Bellowes was deliberately chosen?"

"Hold on," protested Kent; "I don't follow that. How do you mean, deliberately chosen? The murderer couldn't have known that the village toper would have come wandering in conveniently on the very night of the murder."

"Oh, yes, he could," said Dr. Fell, "if the village toper had been summoned."

For a time he remained wheezing, his eyes half-shut, and then he went on in an abstracted tone:

"Very well, I'll give you a hint; and you can see what you make of it. Not enough attention, I think, has been paid to the first murder. First tell me this: did any of your party ever meet Bellowes before he was found in the house that night?"

"No, we didn't exactly meet him," said Francine. "Our amiable host brought him in one night during the first week we were there, as a sort of hired entertainer, to show us his mental tricks. You'd riffle through a pack of cards in front of him and he'd afterwards tell you each of the cards in the order he saw them. You mix up several dozen articles on a table, and he identifies them all after one second's look; that sort of thing. Tall, hollow-eyed chap, very pleasant-spoken. He talked to us casually. Then our host took him out to the kitchen and sent him home full of whisky. I thought it was rather rotten of Sir Gyles, because that used to be Bellowes's home, you know. That was why, when Rod was killed, we thought at first—"

Dr. Fell shook his head, fiery with argumentativeness.

"Now consider the following indications! I pointed out to Hadley this morning Bellowes's importance in the case. You see, his presence there on the very night of a particularly brutal murder was a little too fortuitous. The man himself was unquestionably dead drunk and incapable of mischief. His presence there might be a coincidence, a somewhat painful tearing of coincidence; but there were certain indications against it.

"First (you recall), when he was found on the sofa at two o'clock in the morning he had a key to the house in his pocket. That meant either that someone had given him a key, or it was an old one of his own; but, in either case, it meant he had left his lodgings early that evening intending to go to his old home—and intended it before he had taken a drop to drink! What, then, becomes of the homing pigeon reeling back by instinct?

"Second, he concluded his evening at the pub, contrary to custom, by drinking whisky and going away with a pint of it. Now, I don't know whether you know anything about the habits of village pubs. I, to my joy, do. The drink there is beer, because spirits are too expensive. Whisky is a luxury reserved for rare and mystic occasions. Bellowes, we know, was almost penniless; his usual tap was beer; but on this occasion, *with* a key to the house in his pocket, he orders whisky. It looked as though someone had been supplying him with extra cash. Why?

"Third, you recall that Bellowes's finger-prints were actually found in the room where Rodney Kent was murdered—which made it look very bad for him—although Bellowes absolutely denied ever having been in that room. He had at least looked in there, since the prints were round the light-switch. But he didn't remember it.

"Suppose Bellowes had been summoned or invited to the house at a certain hour. But why? It assuredly was not to be a scapegoat for the real murderer. If this had been so, he would have been made a far more thoroughgoing scapegoat. The poker, instead of vanishing mysteriously from the house, would have been found in his hand. There would have been blood on him; and finger-prints in more damning places than merely round the light-switch. Furthermore, the real murderer would have known—stop; or would he wonder?—that Bellowes's nearly paralysed left arm would make it impossible for him to have strangled Rodney Kent in the crushing two-handed grip that was used.

"Yet, the more I turned it over, the more it seemed to me certain that Bellowes had been invited there. In short, he was to be a witness: as he was. A far from sober witness: as he was. An incurious witness: as he was. A witness with a photographic memory: as he was. And a complete witness to some skilful and evil design for strangling, planned to throw suspicion on the wrong person: as, alas, he was *not*. He got too drunk. What might he have seen when he looked into the room where Rodney Kent was killed? In other words, what lies just under the surface of this first crime, which is rather more devilish than the second? Bellowes saw part of what he was meant to see. But was there anything else? Archons of Athens! I wish I knew! And we are going down to Sussex to find out."

Ending on a note of some savagery, Dr. Fell drew out a large red bandana handkerchief, mopped his forehead with it, and blinked at the other two from under its folds. He added:

"I trust you take my meaning?"

"But if someone invited or got Bellowes to the house," muttered Kent, "it must have been the murderer. Consequently, Bellowes must know who the murderer is?"

Dr. Fell put away the bandana. "I wish it were as simple as that. But I'm afraid it's not. Bellowes, you see, could hardly have been paid to keep silent when he himself was in danger. I don't think he suspects at all;

if he did, perhaps it's just as well that he's safely in jail. What I am going to do, you perceive, is find out what he was supposed to see on the night of January 14th. I am going to dig into the subconscious; and digging into the subconscious, we are assured by the tenets of the newest science, inevitably produces a nightmare. Shall we have a final brandy?"

Their cab prowled up Piccadilly, the chains on its wheels clanking faintly. Dr. Fell had gone home, more silent than was usual with him; and Kent had told the driver to take a turn anywhere he liked. It was warm enough to be pleasant inside the cab. Pale lamps looked in on them; the street was churned to slush, but by the time they turned into the high dimness of the Park, there were lawns of snow outside the windows and the bare trees wore bonnets. Francine, a bundle of furs topped by yellow hair that fluffed out over them, leaned against his shoulder and stared straight ahead. He had just put his hand on a cold hand when she spoke.

"Chris, do you know who he suspects?"

"Who—?" For a moment Kent was puzzled; it seemed incongruous at such a time. Though she pressed his hand, she did not turn round. "I don't know," he confessed. "Harvey Wrayburn seems out of the running, and my elaborate case against Hardwick was, I admit, sheer fireworks. I don't like to think of anyone else."

"He suspects Melitta Reaper."

It was so abrupt and so startling that he dropped her hand. Of her face he could so far see only the tip of her nose; now she moved turning towards him squarely.

"Meli—rubbish!"

"It's not, Chris. I know. I can feel these things." She spoke with fierce intensity. "You think a minute and you'll realise it. Do you remember? I was maundering along, trying to find a reason for someone wearing the uniform. I hardly knew what I was saying—but I saw his eyes. I said, 'But where is there any indication in just a coat and a pair of trousers?' A pair of trousers, Chris; it was as though I had made some kind of slip of the tongue. And he didn't thunder out. He just said it was closer to the truth than anything else. It was enough to give me gooseflesh, because I saw. Why would a murderer be so horribly anxious every time to print a picture in our heads of a man, a man in an especially mannish kind of uniform? You see? Because it's a woman."

He looked at the white face over the furs, with the large, long brown eyes shifting slightly. The run and crossing of car-lamps among the trees shifted like her eyes; and the wheels seemed to hammer loudly.

"But that's crazier than any of my guesses! You don't believe it, do you?"

"No; I suppose I don't, really, but—"

"But what?"

"Chris, I've been a beast. I suppose, from now on, I'll tell you every thought that's in my head; because I'd like to; but I'm always having them." She seemed rather incoherent from the strain of the past weeks, but she spoke in a quiet voice, looking up now and again. "Suppose it's Dan himself who's been tied up with Jenny? It's quite possible, you know: living in the same house, and Jenny being what she was. To say nothing of the fact that Dan's close to being a millionaire. You saw how queer Dan was to-day when we talked about Jenny's real nature, didn't you? And didn't it strike you that Melitta was just a little too quick to defend Jenny, and say bah-bah-my-dears-there's-nothing-in-it, and act in a way that's not exactly like her? If Dan is the man in the case, the one from whom Jenny has been getting all the cheques—"

He felt cold, though he would have nothing to do with the idea.

"Well, old girl, in my opinion it's still raving lunacy. Melitta: definitely not. Why should she?"

"You say I'm mad on economics. But you know how Melitta is about plain money."

"But how does Rod fit in?"

"Jenny lived off Dan; Rod was supposed to live off Jenny—"

"Come here," he ordered. "And forget that gibberish. If we go on like this, there'll be nobody at all we can dare trust. We can't go on feeling that everybody round us is a hobgoblin. Why not Dan himself? Why not me? Why not you?"

"Why not?" she said, and plucked at a button of his overcoat. The bundle of furs stirred; the cab jolted slightly, and moved on into the darkest curve of the park. "I wonder," she added in a small voice, "just what that chap Bellowes will say?"

Chapter XIII

A WELCOME AT FOUR DOORS

"All I can say," replied Ritchie Bellowes, "is what I have said. I'm sorry I went there, but I don't see that I did any great harm."

He sat back on the bunk of the cell and regarded his visitors with an air of polite cynicism which was not even marred by the stubble on his face. He was that rare product, a gentleman; and it was all the more odd to meet him in a jail in Sussex. Tall, with dark hair in a wide parting, he looked even more hollow-eyed from his fortnight's enforced sobriety. He wore a grey shirt open at the neck, and a pair of brown braces with one button missing made him hitch his shoulder frequently.

They had gone down to Sussex early on the morning of February 1st, Christopher Kent accompanying Dr. Fell and Hadley, and the others arranging to follow on a faster train. The nine-fifteen from Charing Cross idled through the succession of tunnels which make the Kentish hills seem to shut away London as though with a wall. The flat lands beyond were stiff with snow. Dr. Fell was occupied with a vast series of notes, spreading over from one small piece of paper to the other, so Hadley gave up any attempt to talk to him and settled down glumly with a cross-word puzzle. They changed at Tonbridge; and, the nearest station to Northfield being Eglamore, a police car was waiting for them there.

Northfield, an attractive enough village in summer, now carried out its reputation sufficiently to look like something off a Christmas-card. Great pillars of yew-hedge before the church, and arching over the lychgate, were powdered with snow. The village green, hard earth, sloped down to the public-house of the Stag and Glove, as though tilting its inhabitants there; it was fronted by low houses of white weather-boarding and others of that faded half-timbering which looks brittle to the touch. The visitors, after having been inside several of the houses, thought that they had never seen so many oak beams; oak beams seemed to sprout and crowd, to the manifest pleasure of the owners; but living inside too many oak beams, Kent decided, must be like living inside the stomach of a zebra.

They did not go to Four Doors, Sir Gyles's house, since Gay himself had not arrived. After (at Dr. Fell's insistence) testing the local brew at the Stag and Glove, and finding it good, they went on to the district police-station on the road to Porting. The station consisted of two con-verted semi-detached houses, and was presided over like a householder by Inspector Tanner. Dr. Fell—one or two of whose great sheaf of notes had suffered from having fallen into the beer—was determined to conduct the examination of Bellowes. After a great unlocking of underground doors, they found Bellowes reasonably courteous, but apathetic and cynical.

"Look here, I'll be frank," said Dr. Fell, getting down to business with a directness which pained Hadley. "We're here because we're not satis-fied you told the whole truth about the night of January 14th."

"Sorry," said Bellowes. "But I've already said it a hundred times. *I—did—not—*"

"Now, steady!" urged Dr. Fell, with a redder tinge in his face. "The question is not what you did; the question is why you did it. Quick! Did someone tell you to go to Four Doors on that night?"

Bellowes had been reading a well-thumbed Wild West magazine. Now he put it down on the floor beside the bunk; and, stirred out of his apathy, regarded the doctor with what Kent could have sworn was genuine surprise.

"No," he said.

"You're sure of that, now?"

"I'm certain of it. What's all this? Why should—well, why should anybody want me there? Why should anybody want me anywhere?" he added, with a rush of bitterness which was dangerously near self-pity.

"You still maintain you wandered there of your own accord, while you were drunk, and had no intention of doing it beforehand?"

"I don't know why I went there. Yes, I suppose I do know; but you understand what I mean. But I hadn't any intention of doing that early in the evening. I honestly don't go about breaking into people's houses as a rule, and I can't understand how it happened."

"How do you explain the fact that there was a key to the house in your pocket?"

"Key? But I always carry that key; I've carried it for years," replied Bellowes, bringing his heel down with some violence on the floor. "Ask my landlady. Ask anybody. I don't suppose I'm entitled to it; but Sir Gyles knows I have it—"

"Forgive my mentioning this: but you were rather in funds on the night of the fourteenth?"

The other's face grew pinched.

"I was."

"Well?"

"You may have heard," said Bellowes gravely, "that I gave a little tame conjuring entertainment for the guests at Four Doors. As I was leaving Sir Gyles pushed an envelope in my pocket. There was more in that envelope than I deserved; and, just between ourselves, than I had—hoped for. We used to learn a lot of tosh about people being too proud to accept charity. I was not."

"Damn and blast!" said Dr. Fell. He opened and shut his hands; he would have surged up with oratorical thunder had the size of the place permitted it. After a curt remonstrance from Hadley, he subsided to mutterings, and pursued the subject with almost ghoulish hopefulness.

"Would you maintain in court that nobody prompted you to go to that house?"

"I would."

"Humph. Ha. If you don't mind, I'd like to take you over that statement of yours. But, first, as a general thing: you know Sir Gyles Gay fairly well?"

"I'm acquainted with him. That is, I've been to the house two or three times in the past year."

"When you went there to entertain the guests, I suppose you met all of them?"

Bellowes frowned. "Yes, I was introduced to all of them—I think. I didn't talk much to them, barring when they asked questions: except to Mr. Reaper. I liked him," said Bellowes, staring at the past. "He's my style, somehow. He asked me if I'd like to get a new start in South Africa, and I think he meant it."

"Did you meet Rodney Kent, who was later—"

"It's a queer thing about that. I suppose he must have been there, because he was one of the party: as I have good reason to remember, God knows. But I can't remember seeing him at all."

"Did you ever see any of the others on any subsequent occasion?"

"Yes, but not to speak to. Mr. Reaper dropped in at the pub one evening later, but he was in the private bar and I was in the public. I didn't have—have the nerve to walk in and say good evening. Then another of them was in the pub early on the night—the night it all happened; but that was very early in the evening."

"Which one was it?"

"I think the one named Wrayburn. But he was only there to order half a dozen of sherry, and didn't stay more than a minute or two."

Dr. Fell made another note. Hadley was growing restive; and Bellowes, whose long sobriety had done him no good, was beginning to twitch.

"Now, about the night of the 14th in question," rumbled the doctor. "Let's begin with the time you were in the bar of the Stag and Glove. What made you change to whisky and go away with a bottle of it?"

"Oh, I don't know. Why do you ever do anything like that? I thought of it, and so I did."

"Yes, I know," admitted Dr. Fell. "With the idea of going out to this clearing called Grinning Copse and drinking the bottle?"

"That's right. If I take a bottle home, Mrs. Witherson always starts to preach. She waits up for me. I hope you find this helpful," said Bellowes between his teeth.

"How drunk were you?" asked Dr. Fell blandly.

"I was—padded. Muzzy."

"Have you got a strong head?"

"No."

"You started for Grinning Copse, I understand, at closing-time: ten o'clock: H'mf, yes. You sat down on an iron bench or chair in the copse and began on the whisky. Never mind; I know you've made a statement; but just tell me everything that comes back to you in connection with it."

"There's nothing more I can tell," answered Bellowes, with a duller colour in his face. "Things began to run together and mix up then, but that was what I wanted them to do. I've got a hazy idea that at one point someone was talking to me; but don't take this too seriously—I was probably speaking aloud myself. Reciting or something. I'm sorry; that's everything. The next thing I knew I was sitting on some different kind of surface, which turned out to be leather; and in some different kind of place, which turned out to be the upstairs hall at Four Doors. You know what I did. I thought it was as good a place as any, so I just lay down on the sofa."

"Can you put a time to any of this; even an approximate time?"

"No."

"You say in your statement to the police—where are we?—'At this time I do not think I went to sleep immediately. While I was lying there,' and so on to describe the appearance of the figure in uniform. Are you certain you did not go to sleep?"

"No, I'm not sure."

"What I am endeavouring to establish is this," persisted Dr. Fell, with such unwonted sticking to the point that Hadley was disturbed. Every wheeze seemed to emphasise a word. "Were you conscious of an interval, any time between your lying down on the sofa and the time you saw the figure?"

"I don't know," groaned Bellowes, massaging the veins in the back of his hand. "Don't you think I've been over all that a hundred times? I think there was an interval, yes. Something to do with the light—the moonlight. But I'm not sure what." He broke off. "Are you a lawyer, by the way?"

Dr. Fell certainly sounded like one, though it was a suggestion which at any other time he would have repudiated with some heat.

"You'd call it a kind of semi-conscious state, then?"

"Yes, that's a polite way of putting it."

"While you were lying there, do you remember any sounds, anyone moving, anything like that?"

"No."

"But what roused you? I'm digging in here, you see. Something must have made you look up, or stirred you in some way?"

"I suppose it did," the other admitted doubtfully. "I have a vague impression that it may have been someone talking, or maybe whispering. But that's the closest I can get."

"Now listen. I'm going to read over a part of your statement again.

" 'I should describe him as a medium-sized man wearing a uniform such as you see in the big hotels like the Royal Scarlet or the Royal Purple. It was a dark-blue uniform with a long coat, and silver or brass buttons; I could not be sure about colours in the moonlight. I think there was a stripe round the cuffs, a dark red stripe. He was carrying a kind of tray, and at first he stood in the corner and did not move.

" '*Question:* What about his face?

" 'I could not make out his face, because there seemed to be a lot of shadow, or a hole or something, where his eyes ought to be.' "

Dr. Fell put down the sheet. In the light and warmth of a town, in a soft-carpeted hotel, such a figure had seemed merely fantastic. Here in the sealed countryside it was beginning to assume hues of something else altogether. Kent, who had not before dwelt too closely on that description of the face, felt a sensation very similar to that with which he had first seen Jenny's body.

"Have you anything to add to that, Mr. Bellowes?"

"No. I'm sorry."

"Would you recognise the face if you saw it again?"

"No, I don't think so. It was a fattish kind of face, I think; or the shadows or something gave it that effect. Man," cried Bellowes, and, to everyone's acute discomfort, the tears of raw nerves or self-pity overflowed his eyes, "what do you think I am? I wasn't in any condition to see it. If I hadn't been what they call a camera-eye observer, I shouldn't have seen anything at all, probably, and maybe I'm all out of focus as it is."

"Now, steady!" urged Dr. Fell, disturbed. He wheezed violently. "You make a reference here to the 'Blue Room.' Was that where Mr. Kent was killed?"

"So they tell me."

"And you didn't go in there?"

Bellowes grew more quiet. "I know all about those finger-prints, or alleged finger-prints. But, in spite of them, I don't honestly think I did go in there, even when I was drunk. From the time I was a kid I never liked that room. It was my grandfather's, you see, that's the reason for all the old-fashioned furniture, which went when I disposed of the house: and to keep me quiet, when I was a kid, my father turned the old man into something like an ogre."

"One last point, Mr. Bellowes. Do you remember this tray or salver?"

"I remember seeing it."

Dr. Fell leaned forward. "Was there anything on it?"

"On it?"

"Carried on it. Think! A number of small articles are put out in front of you, and you remember them all. It's your gift. You must use it. Was there anything on that tray?"

Ritchie Bellowes put up a hand and rubbed his forehead; he stared down at the Wild West magazine; he shuffled his feet; and nothing happened.

"I'm sorry," he apologised for the dozenth time. "No. There may have been. I don't remember."

"Thank you very much," Dr. Fell said in a dispirited voice. "That's all."

But even so he had not finished. When they were on their way out he went back to ask the prisoner still one more question; whatever it was, Bellowes seemed to return a decided negative, and this appeared to cheer the doctor somewhat. During this interview Hadley, who had been corking himself down, had with some effort managed to keep silent. But when they were driving back to Northfield he let himself go.

"All right," said the superintendent grimly. "Let's hear it. I asked you much the same sort of question once before. What was being carried on that salver? Somebody's head?"

"Yes," replied Dr. Fell with every evidence of seriousness. "Mine. A sheep's head, and a whacking great one, too. You know, I never realised until last night the purpose or meaning of that salver. It presented a real problem; and yet it's quite simple. I must be running on senile decay."

"Good," said Hadley. "I mean, I'm glad you find it so easy. I confess that so far it escapes me. But that's not the main point. You're not going to divert me from the solid information I got from South Africa. You were bombarding me with a hell of a lot of 'suggestive' points yesterday evening, among them your new idea that somebody invited Bellowes to the house early in the evening on the night of the murder. What becomes of that now?"

Dr. Fell made a handsome concession. "I withdraw it in the form in which it was presented. I also call your attention—"

"More suggestive points?"

"Didn't you see any?"

"As soon as I begin to hear the call of mumbo-jumbo," Hadley snapped, "I begin to have an idea (yes, I'll admit it) that you're probably on the right track. But I still don't like it. One of these days, my lad, you're going to come a cropper; and it will be the world's most outstanding cropper. Why do you want our party buried down here again? If you want a look at the house, couldn't you do it without bringing them back here? When they're in London, at least I've got an idea I could keep my eye on them. But I've got no such comfortable feeling about Northfield."

For a moment Dr. Fell did not reply. Their car circled the green at Northfield, and eased its way down a gravel road beside the church: a road dusted with snow as lightly as you might dust finger-print powder. At the end of a gradual descent the hedges curved and opened on the small grounds of Four Doors. The house was of that style of Queen Anne architecture which seems at once massive and yet squeezed together, as though the designer had tried to crowd too many arched windows into deep walls. The bricks were of a grimy colour; the front door, painted white like the window-facings, was as square as the house's heavy length;

and dead wistaria clung to its face. An abrupt little garden, with a herbaceous border and a sundial in a brick path up the centre, also clung to the front of it. The party from London had evidently arrived from the station: a big black sedan, cut ropes hanging from its luggage-grid, was slewed round in the drive. Behind the house you could see the slope of the hill, and one great elm against the sky. A wind blowing down from the east brought, very distinctly, the sound of the church clock striking noon.

They looked at it for a time; while that wind rattled in the bushes and a little dust-devil of snow danced round the sundial.

"You see what I mean?" inquired Hadley.

"I do not see what you mean," said Dr. Fell. "Will you accept my assurance that there is absolutely no danger?"

The door was opened for them by Sir Gyles Gay, before their car had even come to a stop. Gay stood on the threshold with that slightly shivering air, as of one on the edge of a pool, with which many hosts either welcome or bid good-bye. He seemed still interested, even smiling, his hands behind his back as though in meditation. But his very correct tie was rumpled, and he greeted them with a certain gravity.

"Come in, gentlemen. I was wondering how long you would be. We have been here only an hour, but even in that time there have been certain happenings. Country air seems to have a curious effect."

Hadley stopped dead on the doorstep.

"No, no," their host assured them, with wrinkled amusement. "Not what you may be thinking; nothing serious. I mean that country air seems to bring about a sense of humour. But it is an unusual and perverted sense of humour, and,"—he looked back over his shoulder into a warm, comfortable hall—"I can't say I like it."

"What's happened?"

Again Gay looked over his shoulder; but he made no move to go inside.

"You remember my telling you yesterday that we played all sorts of parlour games down here, including that of pinning a paper tail on a paper donkey?"

"Yes; well?" said Dr. Fell.

"I did not know, when you asked whether we would all come down here, whether you wanted us for the day only, or for several days. Anyhow, I set aside rooms for you gentlemen, in case you should care to honour me with a visit." He looked at Dr. Fell. "It concerns the room which is at your disposal, doctor. Within the last half-hour, someone has had the highly humorous notion of taking a paper donkey's tail and pinning it to the door of your bedroom."

They looked at each other. But nobody was amused.

"That, however, is not all," Gay went on, sticking out his neck and looking round each corner of the door. "The humorist has gone even further. Put in a highly ingenious place—where somebody was certain to find it soon, I discovered this."

He took his hands from behind his back and held out a piece of stiff paper. It was a group photograph some eight by ten inches, taken by one of those professionals who lie in wait at amusement resorts and persuade you to buy the photograph afterwards. Kent recognised it easily as being the inside of the "fun-fair" at the Luna Park outside Durban. He remembered the slope of a rafter, a lemonade-stand by a window. The picture was taken from the top of the broad platform of one of those big slides or chutes by which you sail down into darkness. All the members of Dan's crowd were standing at the top of the chute, most of them turning laughing faces towards the camera—though Melitta was looking dignified and Francine annoyed. Someone, who could not be seen because Dan's body blocked the view, appeared to be sitting on the edge of the slide and making a sudden protesting gesture against the descent.

"Now look at the other side," said Gay, turning the photograph over.

It was scrawled in exactly the same printing-handwriting they had seen before. It was in red ink, and had a sloppy look. It said:

THERE IS ONE MORE TO GO.

Chapter XIV

RED INK

"Very funny, isn't it?" asked Gay. "I was inclined to split my sides when I saw it. But you had better come inside."

Four Doors, centrally heated, was as warm as the hotel had been. Gay took them across a comfortable hall and into a lounge where an additional fire had been lighted. Though the house was of massive build, with fan-lights over the pillared doors and white woodwork round high ceilings, Gay had overlaid it with furniture of genuine comfort. There was no sight or sound of anyone else about. But Gay closed the double-doors.

"Where did you find this?" Hadley asked quietly.

"Ah, there's another piece of subtle humour," said their host. "I went into the bathroom to have a wash. Then I reached out after a towel off the rail, and this fell out from among the towels."

"When did you find it?"

"Not ten minutes ago. By the way, I have established one thing. When we arrived here at eleven o'clock, there was no such delightful piece of mummery hidden in the towels. You see, I keep a cook and two maids. When we got here Letty had just finished tidying up the bathroom and putting out fresh towels. Consequently—"

"Who knows about this, besides yourself?"

"Only the humorist who put it there. I hope you do not think I was indiscreet enough to tell Letty anything. I also pulled that donkey's tail down off the door before (I hope) anyone spotted it. I don't know when it was put up. I noticed it when I was coming out of the bathroom, on the principle that jokes never come singly."

"Yes. And what do you think this means?"

"My good friend," replied Gay, drawing himself up and looking Hadley in the eye, "you must know very well what I think it means. I am fond of good crimes in the abstract; but I do not like funerals. This has got to stop." He hesitated, after which his face altered, and he addressed Kent with great gravity. "Sir," he added, "I beg *your* pardon."

"Granted readily," said Kent, who liked him. "But why?"

"Because I was more than half inclined to suspect you. Er—you have been with Dr. Fell and the superintendent? Between eleven and twelve o'clock, I mean?"

"Yes. We were at the police-station then. But why suspect me, in particular?"

"Why, frankly," responded Gay, with an air of candour, "because your turning up at the hotel yesterday seemed almost too good to be true. Also, because there has been a persistent rumour that you were more than a little interested in Mrs. Josephine Kent—"

"That can wait," snapped Hadley. He turned to Dr. Fell and held out the photograph. "So you'll give me your assurance that there's no danger? How does this fit in with it?"

The doctor put his shovel-hat under his arm and propped his stick against his side. Settling his eyeglasses with a vaguely troubled air, he studied the photograph.

"I don't mind the donkey's tail," he said. "In fact, I think it rather moderate. There are times when I feel I deserve the fate of Bottom the Weaver. But this, honestly, is not one of them. On the other hand, it's a complication I definitely do not like. Someone is growing frightened." He looked at Gay. "To whom does this photograph belong? Did you ever see it before?"

"Yes, it's mine. That is to say, I don't know whether you're aware of Reaper's passion for having photographs taken. He sent me on a batch of them, showing his friends on aquaplanes, and his friends holding up glasses of beer, and so on."

"H'mf, so. Where did you see it last?"

"I think it was in the desk in my study, with the others."

"What is more, this isn't ordinary writing-ink," pursued Dr. Fell, scratching the nail of his little finger across the thick and flaky surface of the inscription on the back of the photograph. "It's too viscid. It looks like—"

"Drawing-ink. That is what it is," supplied Gay. "Just come with me."

He seemed much stiffer than yesterday; he retained that hard glaze like the polish on a tombstone, even to his smile. As though coming to a decision, he led them to another pair of double-doors at the end of the room, and into a room fitted up as a study at the back of the house. Its windows looked out on a back-garden raked by the wind: on a gate in the brick wall, and the elms in the churchyard. But the study also was cheerful with firelight. It was conventional enough, with its bookshelves and busts above, except for an inner staircase ascending along the end wall: a room antiquated rather than ancient. Their host glanced towards this inner staircase before he indicated an open roll-top desk.

"There are, as you can see, four or five bottles of drawing-ink. Various colours," he pointed out. "I seldom or never use them; but the winters pass slowly for me, and, one winter, my hobby was architecture. By the look of that printing, I should think the pen used was this."

He lifted the stopper out of a bottle of black ink. To the stopper, inside, was attached a broad pen-nib—a feature common to bottles of drawing-ink—for testing it before use. He waggled it at them. Kent did not like the expression of his face now.

"I suppose you can guess where that staircase leads? The door at the top of it is beside the bathroom door upstairs. This humorist, this *slim* fellow, can simply walk down here, scrawl on that photograph like a child on a wall, and walk up with it."

For the first time Hadley was indecisive. Apparently he did not like it either, and there had been a strain ever since they entered the house, but he was studying Gay in a very curious way.

"Do you keep the desk locked?"

"No; why should I? There's nothing of value in it. Half the time the top is not even closed, as it is now."

"But where are the photographs?" asked Dr. Fell. "I've come a long way to see those photographs, you know."

Gay turned round quickly. "I beg your pardon? You've what?"

"Come a long way to see the photographs. Where are they?"

Their host reached towards his trouser-pocket; then he shrugged his shoulders and pulled open a drawer in a tier at the right-hand side of the desk. "I am afraid you will not be well rewarded," he said sardonically. "There is very little to—good God!"

He had jerked back his hand quickly. What oozed out from between his fingers, what he moved back to avoid in case it should splatter on his clothes, was not blood. It looked like blood. But it was red ink. Gathering round him, they saw that the inside of the drawer was what Dr. Fell literally described as an incarnadined mess. In the drawer there had been photographs: some loose ones of all sizes, and others which had obviously been taken of or by Gay himself, for they had been pasted into an album. All were ripped and torn into many shreds, a kind of pudding, over which had been poured some half a bottle of red drawing-ink.

Dr. Fell groaned. Sir Gyles Gay did not. Standing with his hand stiffly outstretched while he swabbed at the fingers with a handkerchief, he began to curse. He cursed with such careful, cold-voiced, measured authority that it showed a new side to the man, a new use for marble teeth. He cursed in English, *Afrikaans* and Kaffir, the sort of thing which would have skinned the hide either from an offending houseboy or a Government department: yet Kent could not help feeling he had heard exactly the same tone of voice on a golf-course when someone has just foozled about the sixth easy stroke. Kent saw the veins in his neck.

"I hope," Gay continued, without changing his even tone, "I can be called a good host. I like my guests. I have enjoyed their presence immensely. But this—by God! this is going too far. That ink is still running in the drawer. It hasn't been put in for much more than half an hour. And where are my guests now? Why, I'll tell you. Without a doubt each is sitting or standing in his own room. Without a doubt nobody has ventured out, as on other occasions. It is all beautifully quiet; by the so-and-so it is."

Dr. Fell scratched his chin. "Do you mind my saying," he observed, "that you're rather a rum sort of bloke?"

"Thanks very much."

"No, I mean it. When a murder is committed—even one in your own house—you are helpful, philosophical, and all good things. It is an intellectual problem. It stimulates you. But you go off the deep end, with one majestic volplaning sweep, when someone plays a senseless practical joke that makes you mess up your hands. You don't mind a throat being cut; but you can't stand a leg being pulled."

"I can understand murder," said Gay, opening his eyes. "I cannot understand this."

"You don't see any meaning in it?"

"Ah, there I am not qualified to judge. But I want to know what has been going on. Up to this time 'somebody' has confined his or her inane scribblings to night-time. Now this humorist walks about in the light of day and writes—Chequebook!" said Gay, breaking off.

Now not minding the confusion in the drawer, he began to grub in it. With some relief he produced a leather-bound cheque-book on the Capital

Counties Bank; it was by some chance not stained at all, and he put it gingerly on the desk. Then he drew out a small leather purse, of the sort used by countrymen for carrying loose change, and snicked it open.

"Something wrong here," he added in an altered tone—a natural tone. "There's some money missing."

"Money?" said Hadley. "I thought you said you kept nothing valuable in that desk."

"Quite true, superintendent; I don't. All this purse ever contains is a little silver in case I have to pay for a parcel, or hand out a tip, or the like. There's never more than a pound here at any time."

"How much is missing?"

"Twelve shillings, I make it," said Gay with competence. "Is this some more highly subtle humour, do you think?"

Hadley took a deep breath and studied the room with a vindictiveness that equalled Gay's own. With his hand in a handkerchief, he picked up the bottle of red drawing-ink from the desk. It had undoubtedly been used to deluge the drawer; it was nearly empty.

"Yes," he growled, "yes, I'm taking precautions about finger-prints in going after a practical joker. I remember a time, Fell, in the Mad Hatter case, when the answer to a piece of tomfoolery was the answer to a murder. You know—" Hadley stopped and cooled off. "We'll settle this up right now. Will someone—will you," he looked at Kent, "go and round up all the others? No, never mind sending a servant, Sir Gyles; I want all the servants here now, if you'll send for them. We'll begin with them. If you've got two maids, I don't see how it's impossible for someone to have raised the devil like that without *anything* being seen." He added to Kent, grimly: "Yes. Tell 'em what you like. It won't do any harm."

Kent went up the inner staircase to the hall of the floor above. He went quickly, because he did not want time to think. Four Doors, according to the plan of its (would-be) period, was severely oblong, with a central hall running broadwise through the building. And he had no difficulty in finding three out of four of his quarry. Francine, Dan, and Melitta were sitting together in a sort of upstairs den whose big oriel window looked out over the main door. They sat round a gas-fire in an atmosphere of grousing.

Dan greeted him peevishly.

"I must say you're a fine sort of friend. You walked out last night with the wench here—well, that's understandable enough. But this morning you up and walked out with the police—"

It was the home atmosphere again.

"I walked out with the police," Kent said, "because Dr. Fell countenanced it, and because I wanted to see whether I could find anything to help us out of this mess. And there's a lot more to say now." He looked round; Wrayburn's absence was a noticeable gap. "Where's Harvey?"

Dan's intuition was disconcertingly keen: keener, perhaps, than Melitta's. He had been sitting with his elbows thrust out and his hands on his knees; now he got up as though he were levering up a boulder. On one side of him sat Melitta in stout discontent and a Chanel dress. On the other, Francine smoked a cigarette and looked properly attentive. He always remembered them at that moment, because of the home atmosphere which seemed to connect this with bright-hued villas in Parktown. What had happened this morning was like a home-bickering become distorted: a clash of wills or a bad joke, like breaking into somebody's liquor-cabinet or setting a booby-trap. The worst of it was that it was real. It could happen, and did happen—on a scale that ended in murder. And Dan guessed. He was standing so close to the gas-fire that you could smell the fire scorching a tweed suit.

Dan said: "Harvey? He went up to the pub after cigarettes. What's up?"

"Somebody's been acting the fool." Kent stopped. It was not actually that, in spite of every ludicrous attempt at a jeer in the actions that had been done this morning. "How long have you three been in here together?"

"Mel and I just came in. Francine has been here all the time. What's *up?*"

Kent told them.

The way in which they received it might or might not have been considered curious. They were very quiet. It was like Melitta's what-a-holiday mood, as though they had taken seaside lodgings where it rained steadily for two weeks. Only at the end did something appear to rouse Dan.

"I never heard of such tomfoolery in all my born days!" he said, looking for the perpetrator in corners of the room. "Let me see if I have this straight: somebody takes that photograph, writes on the back of it, and puts it in among the towels. Somebody tears all the other photographs to pieces and douses them with red ink. Then someone steals twelve shil—oh, here! Why steal the money?"

"You've got it," said Kent, realising. He knew at last what was wrong with the picture. "I've had a feeling that something didn't ring true, and you've got it. It's the money. The rest of it might have been perverted humour, or there might be an explanation for most of it; I think I can see one. But stealing the money doesn't fit in."

"May not have anything to do with it," Dan pointed out. "Suppose one of the maids took the money, or something like that?"

"Jenny had none, you know," interposed Melitta.

"Jenny had none of what?"

"No silver, coppers, small change of any kind," she answered obediently. "In her handbag at the hotel. I know, because they asked me to go through her things."

It was true; Kent remembered having written it down in his notes. Melitta, whose handsome nose was pink this morning, warmed up.

"Now do not tell me I don't know what I'm talking about. I thought it was awfully queer at the time, and I told Mr. Hadley so; because whoever travels you know, *always* carries some change, and I am quite sure Jenny always did. When I saw it was not there I felt somebody must have taken it, though of course I knew it was no good saying anything."

"But she had thirty pounds in notes, and that wasn't touched."

"So she had, my dear; but how did you know that?"

"Because I took charge of it," Dan returned grimly. He had evidently noticed no implication. "Somebody's got to take the responsibility here. I'm the fellow who cleans up afterwards. That's all right; I'm the executor; but I want this nonsense stopped. Do you mean that there's someone who goes around consistently stealing loose silver and coppers, and letting big banknotes alone?"

"I'm sure I don't know, my dear," said Melitta with her infuriating placidness, and smoothed her skirt. "As my grandfather used to say—"

Dan lowered his head for a moment.

"Mel," he observed, "there's something *I* want to say. And don't misunderstand me in saying it. I'm your husband. I'm fonder of you than of anyone in the world, if you'd only Snap Out Of It. What I want to say is this, man to man. Damn your grandfather, and your Uncle Lionel, and your Aunt Hester, and your Aunt Harriet, and your cousin Who-is-it, and all their garnered wisdom. There never was a man so afflicted with relatives as I am; and every single one of 'em is dead."

"Easy!" Kent urged, as Dan stalked gloomily across to the window. "This thing has got all our nerves to such a pitch—"

"I suppose so," admitted Dan. "Sorry, Mel. Only I'd give anything I've got just to hear you laugh again. Well, what do we do now?"

"If you could show, to Hadley's satisfaction, where you were between the time you arrived here at eleven o'clock and, say, a quarter to twelve—"

"Library," said Dan promptly. "I was fooling about with the books, and wondering where everybody else was and why we were here at all."

"You don't mean Gay's study?"

"No, no; the library at the other side of the house."

"And you say Harvey went to the pub after cigarettes? When did he leave?"

"Almost as soon as we got here. He walked back with the chauffeur who drove us. So he's out of it—again."

They both looked at Francine, who had been unwontedly silent. "I hope, Chris," she said, and smiled while she contemplated the fire, "you haven't got round to suspecting me. I told them all about your grand case against Hardwick, so I imagine nobody's safe."

"I didn't mean that." What he meant was that he could not straighten out last night, when each had so very nearly spoken, and then there had come between them the dead wall of her mood. But he was not speaking of what he meant. "The police are going to ask you in about one minute—"

"Oh. Yes. I was up here, between my old room and this room. I didn't go downstairs at all."

"Melitta?"

"I was having a bath."

There was a silence. "You were having a bath?" repeated Dan. "You always seem to be having baths when these things happen. When? I mean, where?"

This time she did laugh, an honest and homely sound. "Well, really, my dear, there is only one place I do, usually. Though I remember, when we were first married, you used to have them in the water-butt, and nearly drowned the parrot each time. I was in the bathroom, of course. You got us up so terribly early to come down here, and I didn't have time at the hotel. I rang for the maid—Letty or Alice; Letty, I think it was—and she drew it for me. That was just after we got here. I know, because she was just finishing tidying up the bathroom, and putting new towels there when I asked her to start the bath running."

"Then—" said Kent. "How long were you in the bathroom?"

"I'm afraid it was well over three-quarters of an hour, really." She wrinkled her forehead. "I renewed the hot water twice. And then there was that nice church clock, and I think it is so nice that you can hear it from here. It struck the half-hour after eleven, and then the quarter-hour, before I was out of the tub—"

"Did you use the towels?"

"Fiddle-dee-dee! Of course I used the towels. Two of them. And that photograph was not there."

He spoke slowly. "We got here at just noon by that clock; we heard it strike. Gay met us at the door with the photograph. He said he had found it in the bathroom—"

"You certainly got here at noon," interrupted Francine. "I was sitting up here at this window watching you; and I saw him standing down there with the photographs behind his back. But *I* wasn't going down to inquire. I didn't wish to be told to mind my own business."

"Wait!" he said, feeling as though he were half mesmerised. "Gay said he had found it in the bathroom ten minutes ago; or, in the exact words, 'not ten minutes ago.' "

Melitta smoothed her skirt again. "Well, I'm sure I don't wish to say anything against anyone's character; but you remember, Chris, and you too, Dan, I *warned* you. Of course he may have found it there, but I don't really see how he could have. Because I wasn't out of the tub until after I heard the quarter-hour strike: that was what made me get out, now I come to think of it: and then I dried myself, and tidied up the bathroom, and opened the upper part of the window to let the steam out, and actually, you see, I've only just got dressed."

Dan's face changed colour.

"You think the old devil wrote it himself?"

"I think," Kent said decisively, "we'd better go downstairs and Melitta had better tell this, before they get the idea that we're up here inventing a story to stick to. There's something damned funny about every move that's been made this morning. Gay's behaviour was odd. But so was Hadley's. He's got something on his mind. He made no objection to my coming up here and telling you everything. In fact, he practically directed me to, though I should think he'd want to spring it on you and see what happened. I tell you, there's something going on under the surface, and I wish I knew what it was."

In just two minutes he found out.

Chapter XV

DUELLO

It was Hadley's voice which made him stop with his hand on the knob of the door. The voice was not raised; it had the unimpassioned tone of one discussing a business-deal; but Kent had not heard just that different tone in it before.

The door, at the head of the private stair leading down into the study, was open some two or three inches. He could look down on them with a tilted, theatre-like view, which was yet close enough to follow every movement of a wrinkle or turn of an eye. He saw the brown carpet spread out below, its ancient pattern of roses faded. Past the chandelier he saw Superintendent Hadley's head. Hadley was sitting by the fireplace, facing outwards, his back to the watcher above. Opposite him sat Sir Gyles Gay—his hands lifted, the fingers lightly interlocked as though he were inspecting them—a business man listening to a business proposition. The firelight shone fully on Gay's face, on his alert little look. There was no

sign of Dr. Fell. Round the house the wind deepened in a winter afternoon; from the back of it drifted the smell of hot food being prepared for
lunch.

What Hadley had said was:

"—and, since we're alone, I feel inclined to tell you a little of what I
know."

It did not need Kent's fierce gesture to stop and silence the three
persons following him. They all waited, and they all listened.

Gay assented to the proposition with a slight nod.

"You have just heard the testimony of the maid, Alice Weymiss?"

Again Gay nodded.

"You heard her say that that drawer in the desk, where the photographs
were kept, is always kept locked by you?"

"I heard it."

"Was it true?"

"You see, superintendent, Alice has no business to know whether
drawers are kept locked or not. If she does know, it puts her trustworthi-
ness in doubt. You can see for yourself that the drawer is unlocked now."

Hadley leaned forward.

"Have you a key to that drawer, Sir Gyles?"

"I believe so, somewhere."

"Are you carrying that key in your right-hand trouser-pocket now?"

Gay answered neither yes nor no; he waited, and shook his head
slightly as though the question were of no consequence.

"You also heard what the other maid, Letty King, said? She said that
she prepared a bath for Mrs. Reaper at shortly after eleven o'clock: that
Mrs. Reaper remained in the bathroom until five minutes to twelve: that
she knows this because she kept an eye out in case the bathroom should
have to be tidied up afterwards."

Their host looked puzzled. "Naturally. I don't deny any of that. When I
told you I found the photograph there within the last 'ten minutes,'
perhaps I should have consulted my watch. Perhaps I should have said
five. But I did not consult my watch. I went downstairs and questioned
Letty about whether the photograph had been there when she laid out the
towels earlier."

"Therefore your position is that Mrs. Reaper put the photograph
there?"

"Come, come, man!" said Gay, as though mildly disappointed. "My
position is nothing of the kind. I don't know who put it there; I wish I did.
To put the photograph there would have taken perhaps ten seconds—after
Mrs. Reaper left, if you like. Or whenever you like."

After a pause there was a certain sort of amusement in Hadley's tone; it
was not pleasant to listen to.

"Sir Gyles, I wonder if you think everyone who opposes you is blind. I wonder if you think we've been blind from the beginning of this case. Now, I've had instructions not to trouble you more than was necessary. You know you're being favoured. So I've hesitated to come out with it until I had enough to trouble you a whole lot. But, after what you've said this morning, I've got no choice. The plain fact is that you've been telling me a pack of lies."

"Since when?" inquired the other, interested.

"Since yesterday. But we'll begin with to-day. Your story about this 'donkey's tail' on Fell's door was rubbish. Don't try to play with flourishes like that. Had you told any of your other guests that you expected to entertain either Fell or myself here overnight? Think before you answer. They will remember, you know."

"No, I suppose I didn't."

"Of course you didn't—sir. Then how could any of the others be expected to know even that he would be here at all; let alone what room you had 'set aside' for him?"

It is a sober fact that a reddish patch showed across Gay's forehead, though he kept the atmosphere of a business discussion.

"I think it was well known," he answered without hesitation, "that you both were coming down here. This house, as you know, boasts eight bedrooms. The others would have their old rooms; and I assuredly would not put anyone in the room where Mr. Kent was murdered. That leaves only two. There is not much margin for error. It is possible, you know, that the donkey's tail was meant for *you*."

"Just between ourselves, do you still stick to that flap-doodle?"

"There is nothing 'between ourselves.' You will see to that. Incidentally, I stick to the truth."

The fire was built of somewhat slaty coal; it crackled and popped, distorting the light on Gay's calm, interested face. Hadley leaned down beside his chair, picking up the photograph.

"Let's take this printing on the back. Even without calling in a handwriting man, I think we can decide that this was written by the same hand that wrote 'Dead Woman' on another card. Do you agree? Yes, so do I. Was this message written this morning between eleven and twelve?"

"Obviously."

"It was not. That's definite, Sir Gyles," Hadley returned. "Fell noticed it—maybe you saw him scrape his little finger across the ink. This thick stuff takes a very long time to dry. And this particular printing was not only dry; it was so flaky that it shredded off when he touched it. You saw that. That message has been written on the card for well over a week, if not more."

Again Gay would not be drawn. A dawning anger showed in his eyes, as (Kent remembered) he had shown before in that odd impression of a man foozling an easy golf-stroke, and knowing it. But he regarded his clasped hands from several angles.

"I gave an opinion, my friend."

"I give a fact—sir. Unless that writing was really done this morning, there seems no point at all to torn photographs and splattered ink. And it was not made this morning. So far, I understand, Fell and I disagree about this case. But we both agree about this, I think. . . . We'll go on to something else. Your maid swears that you always keep that particular drawer locked. You maintain that it is always open. Fair enough. But, when you were asked to open it and get the photographs out, you automatically reached for the key—in your right-hand pocket—before you remembered the drawer was supposed to be unlocked. You then jabbed your hand, much too ostentatiously, into the drawer, in order to get red ink on it and show how surprising the thing was. Anybody would have looked before doing that. You didn't. I know two burglars and a screw-man who made the same mistake."

After some deliberation, Gay crossed one leg over the other, shifted in his chair, and seemed to grow comfortable.

"You have talked for a while," he murmured. "Now let me talk. Do I understand that you accuse me of faking the whole thing? That I put the photograph in the towels; that I tore up the other photographs in my own drawer, and poured ink over them?"

"Yes, that ink was fresh."

"Quite so. Then am I accused of insanity? For there are two sides to your attack, and they won't fit. First you inform me that I did all this within an hour or so ago. Then you turn round and say that the printing on that photograph was made well over a week ago. Which is which and what is what? I'll try to meet your charges, Mr. Hadley, if I can understand them."

"Very well. To begin with—"

"Wait. Am I, by the way, accused of stealing twelve shillings of my own money?"

"No. You were really surprised when you discovered that: it was different from the other acting."

"Ah, then you acknowledge that someone else besides myself could have got into that drawer? So far, you've been building a good deal on the fact that I'm the only person who has a key to it. Excuse this insistence on small points," begged Gay, beginning to show his teeth; "but, since all your charges are built on nothing else, I want you at least to be consistent."

Hadley's tone changed again; Kent would not have liked to look him in the eye then.

"I'll give you a big one, Sir Gyles. You were acquainted with Mrs.

Josephine Kent, then Miss Josephine Parkes, when she was in England four years ago."

Again the fire crackled and popped in a gush of light; a grain of burning slate exploded out towards Gay, but he did not notice it. His eyes were wide open.

"That, I concede, *is* something; if you think it is true. But what makes you believe even that she had ever been in England? You heard all her friends, her relatives, everyone say that she had never been out of South Africa in her life."

"Yes," said the superintendent grimly, "I heard it. I also heard them swear she never did any travelling at all, that she hated travelling, and could not stand even a short journey in South Africa. Then, yesterday, I saw her trunk—Fell called my attention to it. Have you seen that trunk?"

"No."

"I think you have. It is an old, battered, worn one; it has seen years of good service in trains and ships, as it shows by its handling. That trunk was certainly Mrs. Kent's own: she did not, for instance, inherit it from someone else who had done the travelling. Her maiden name, Josephine Parkes, was painted in it in chipped, faded lettering that was as old as the trunk; it had certainly got its knocking-about at the same time as the trunk itself. You see what I mean. The trunk had been used by her."

At the top of the stairs Kent turned round and glanced at Dan, who was looking guilty in the gloom of the hall. He heard Dan breathe. Nobody hesitated in the ancient practice of eavesdropping; they were listening with all their ears. And Kent remembered only too well the worn lettering on the worn trunk.

"We heard also how badly she was affected by train and sea-sickness: though she was one of the few who stood up to bad weather on the voyage out. Never mind that. But we learned that she 'turned up' unexpectedly in Johannesburg three years ago: she had come, she *said,* from her old home in Rhodesia. It surprised everyone that she had a great deal of money, which she had 'inherited' from her dead parents."

"But still—"

"Just a moment, Sir Gyles. It was worth looking up. I looked it up. I had her passport: or, rather, a joint husband-and-wife passport made out to Mr. and Mrs. Rodney Kent. Last night I cabled Pretoria about it, and got an answer. In order to obtain that joint one, she had to turn in a previous passport on the Union of South Africa, Number 45695, made out in the name of Miss Josephine Parkes." Hadley again opened his brief-case, without haste, and consulted notes. "Here I've got the immigration stamps on it.

"She landed at Southampton on September 18th, 1932. She then, at various times, paid any number of visits to France: here are the dates: but she was domiciled in England. She left England on December 20th,

1933, and landed again at Capetown on January 6th, 1934. Are you satisfied?"

Gay shook his head a little, as though fascinated.

"I won't deny your facts, of course. But still what has it to do with me?"

"She came to England to see you."

"Er—can you prove that?"

"I have proved it. Here are the papers. You were then, if you recall, Under-Secretary for the Union, and you should recognise this. Mrs. Kent said that she intended to take some kind of employment. She was given a form to fill up. She rather grandly wrote on it just this—here's the form—'To see my friend Sir Gyles Gay, who will arrange it for me.' Would you like to see it? I got it from South Africa House last night."

"I wonder, my friend, if you have any idea of just how many people passed through my office, in the course of a season, while I was on executive duty?"

"She was not a friend of yours?"

"No, she was not. I never saw the woman in my life."

"Then just take a look at this. They tell me it's a very unusual thing, nearly unheard-of, and shows direct personal intervention. Across here is written, 'Personal interview; satisfactory,' written and signed by you. Will you acknowledge this as your handwriting?"

Gay did not take the paper which Hadley was holding out. Instead he got up from his chair with an abrupt movement, and began to walk up and down the room under the dead marble busts on the bookshelves. The fire was simmering now, its light not so bright. Stopping by a humidor on a side-table, Gay tapped his fingers on the lid, opened it, and took out a cigar. He did not seem so much alarmed as very thoughtful. He spoke without turning round.

"Let me see. You think I knew, before Reaper's party got here, that a certain Mrs. Josephine Kent was really a certain Miss Josephine Parkes?"

"You might or might not. She had a different surname."

"Yet I must have known who she was? I had the photographs there, which Reaper sent on recently."

Hadley allowed a pause before he answered.

"Yes, you had the photographs, Sir Gyles. That was why they all had to be torn up and made unrecognisable with red ink."

"I confess I don't follow that."

"I mean," said Hadley, raising his voice a little, "that the photographs Mr. Reaper sent weren't the only ones you had in that drawer. There were a lot of old ones belonging to you, in your album. I'm suggesting that some of them showed you and Mrs. Kent together. That's why they had to go."

Gay closed the humidor with a snap and turned round.

"Damn your ingenuity. All very clever, all very beautiful, and—basically—all wrong. Whatever I am, I'm not as much of a lunatic as all that. It won't hold water, my friend. If what you say is true, I had week upon week's time to destroy everything long beforehand. Yet you say I waited until this very morning to do it; and then I went out of my way deliberately to call attention to it. How do you explain that?"

"I'm waiting for *you* to explain it."

"You mean that you cannot? Then there is that photograph with the obvious threat written on the back of it. According to you, the ink has been dry for over a week. Yet I am supposed to make use of it this morning, for some purpose which escapes me. Have you anything else?"

Evidently he was recovering his mental wind, after a bad attack of cramp, and had begun to fight back. But, in clipping the end off the cigar, he almost got his own finger. Hadley was not impressed.

"I have. We were rather busy last night. Sergeant Betts, following this lead, went down to Dorset to see Mrs. Kent's two aunts. We can rule them out so far as suspicion goes. They really never had seen her before. She hadn't thought it necessary to visit them when she was in England before: it seems she had other business. But they were very convenient. When she wanted to avoid meeting you, and keep up her pretence that she had never been in England, she decided to stay with them—"

"Curse it all," said Gay, in such a melodramatic way that he seemed to be shaken clear through, "why should she want to pretend she had never been in England before? Answer that, if you can. Had she committed a crime? Also, I think you forget that I did meet her, on the evening before last."

"The night she was murdered," agreed Hadley, as though merely confirming the fact. "Yes. I told you we had something else. While she was with her aunts, Mrs. Kent received two letters written from here. One was from her husband—the aunts had seen that handwriting before. One was in a handwriting they did not know."

"You have the letters, of course?"

"We have the letter from Rodney Kent. The other she destroyed. Why? But she answered both of them." Hadley leaned forward. "I'm suggesting to you, Sir Gyles, that you recognised Mrs. Kent from the pictures Mr. Reaper sent on. (No wonder she objected to making the trip to England.) You then wrote to her to assure her that you would be prepared to meet her as a stranger. And, the night before last, you did."

Gay lit his cigar. He said:

"You started on me with a charge of playing senseless pranks. Somewhere along the line the gears were shifted. It's beginning to dawn on me that you're running me straight into a charge of murder." He spread out his hands, crisping the fingers, and spoke past the cigar in his mouth. "My God, man, do you really think I"—the fingers opened and shut—"I took these and killed two inoffensive—" His voice ended in a kind of deep yelp. "It's p-p-preposterous!"

"I asked you for an explanation of certain things, Sir Gyles. You haven't so far answered one straight question. If you don't give me an explanation, I shall have to ask you to come back with me to London for further questioning. And you know what that is apt to mean."

Across the room Kent saw the white-painted door leading to the lounge at the front of the house. From outside this door there abruptly began a fusillade of knocks. Kent knew why it startled him: it was the first sign of life, of bouncing movement, that had echoed up in this house. The knocks were not really loud; but they seemed to have a heavy and insistent din in the quiet afternoon. From outside the door rose up Harvey Wrayburn's hearty voice. He did not stop for replies: he asked the questions and sang out the answers himself.

"Knock, knock," said Wrayburn.

"Who's there?"

"Jack.

"Jack who?

"Jack Ketch," said Wrayburn, suddenly opening the door and grinning at them. "Sorry; I know it's a rotten one, and doesn't even keep to the rules; but I'm just back from the pub, and I thought it was applicable."

Gay's face had gone muddy pale. You could see the Adam's apple move in his neck.

The others did not wait to hear what Wrayburn, apparently in careless fettle, would say when he saw Hadley. Behind Kent's shoulder Dan whispered: "Let's get out of here," nor did any of them care for the smell of boiled lamb for lunch, coming up the back stairs across the upper hall. Melitta and Francine were the first to turn back. They all went on tiptoe like thieves: which, in fact, was what Kent felt like.

And the first thing they encountered behind them, towering up in the hall as though it would block the way, was the vast presence of Dr. Fell.

Chapter XVI

THE WOMAN ON THE SLIDE

"I have just been looking at the famous Blue Room," said Dr. Fell amiably. "And I think you're wise; you're not really wanted downstairs now, any more than I am. Why not sit down for a minute?"

He indicated the open door of the den looking out towards the front, and shepherded them in with his stick like a master of ceremonies. Kent, with a vague and warm feeling that he was being made a fool of, followed in some perplexity. For a few seconds nobody commented. Then Melitta Reaper, who had gone by instinct towards the gas-fire, turned round and summed it up (if inadequately) in one explosive word:

"*Well!*"

"You never heard Hadley run out his masked batteries before, eh?" inquired Dr. Fell, steeling his chins in his collar. "Yes, it's an improving process. And anyone who can break down Sir Gyles Gay's guard has my sincere admiration. I wonder if he's done it? I wonder if he will do it?"

Dan regarded the doctor with a wary eye. "You heard all that, did you?"

"Yes, indeed. I was as interested as you were. Of course I knew what was up his sleeve—in fact, I helped to stuff the sleeve myself—but I wasn't sure when or how he would produce it. Harrumph."

He beamed on them.

"Then Gay is guilty after all?" demanded Dan, who seemed on the edge of an explosion that never quite came off. "I never thought it. By God, I never did: down inside. And Jenny seems to have made roaring fools out of all of us with her past history. But even if he did it, why should he?"

Dr. Fell grew quiet. He lowered himself on the edge of the window-seat.

"Would it make you feel any happier if you knew he was guilty? Eh?"

"It would clear the air," said Dan, with a quick glance. "Every time I go round a corner or open a door, I've been feeling I ought to look a leedle oudt. The trouble is that it's nothing you can hit back at."

"But is he guilty?" asked Francine quietly. "You don't think so, do you?"

The doctor considered this.

"I merely wish to know more about it, you see. Being afflicted with a real scatter-brain, I am full of a hideous curiosity about very small details, and tend to let the main picture go hang. Hah!" He folded his hands over the head of his stick. "And I'll tell you the impression I got from that little episode," he added impressively. "Supposing always that things are what they seem, on every major issue Gay was floored. On every minor issue he floored Hadley. You might be able to make out a case against him as a murderer. But you cannot make out a case against him as a practical joker. You see, I am one of those people who honestly think it is funny to paint a statue red; and I can see the force of it."

"What's that got to do with it?"

"Well, look here! If that drawer full of photographs had really con-tained a picture of him with Mrs. Kent, or anything of a betraying nature, why should he have waited until this morning to destroy it? Why wasn't it destroyed quietly instead of being joyously besprinkled with red ink to call attention to it? Burning would have done it in one minute, with nobody the wiser. Gay made those points himself. And they were so pertinent that Hadley had to dodge them.

"Then there is the question of the fun-fair photograph. Hadley was quite right: the ink on the back of that picture is at least a week old, and probably a good deal more. Now, psychologically, that rather unpleasant-sounding threat, 'There is one more to go,' was inspired by precisely the same motive as a joke. But the whole point of such a trick is its immediate execution and its full, fine flavour while you are in the mood. I will give you an example. Let us suppose that I am a member of the House of Lords. One day, musing dreamily on the back benches, it occurs to me what an excellent thing it would be if I were to inscribe a piece of paper reading, 'Just call me Snookums,' or 'Ready-made, £1 3s. 6d.'; to pin this paper to the back of the unsuspecting fellow-peer in front of me; and to study the interesting effect as he stalked out afterwards.

"Now, either I decide not to do this, or (if I am made of nobler stuff) to do it. There is only one thing I assuredly do *not* do. I do not write out the sign and put it carefully away in my pocket, saying to myself: 'I will hang this paper on old Plushbottom's back exactly a week from next Thursday, the proper time for it, and meanwhile I will keep it always ready at hand, guarded against all ravages.' Why on earth should I? It takes only a second to scribble: I many have a different mood or a brighter thought: it is an utterly useless sort of thing to carry about, and may cause surprise if it falls out at the dinner-table.

"Don't think I am not serious because I use such an example. Exactly the same principle applies here. But it applies much more strongly. If I am caught, all I risk from old Plushbottom is a dirty look or a punch in the nose. The person who wrote this, and kept it about him, risked the hangman. So why should Gay do any such nonsensical thing as write it weeks ago and keep it at hand for a possible opportunity?"

There was a silence.

"I've wondered," Francine said demurely, "just where in this affair you would live up to your reputation and really begin to lecture. But, I say, I don't see that it applies only to Sir Gyles. It applies to anybody else as well, doesn't it?"

"Exactly. And therefore I have wondered why Hadley has neglected to ask the only really important, the only really significant question about that photograph."

"What question?"

"Why, the question of who is *in* the photograph, of course!" thundered Dr. Fell, and brought his hand down on the head of the stick. "Or, more properly, who isn't in it. It's not very complicated, is it? If this means a menace at all, it means a menace to someone in the group. And if it follows the distortedly jesting symbolism which is the only symbolism it can have, the victim indicated is the person who is being pushed down the slide in the picture: the one who seems to be making a protesting gesture about it. But that is the only person in the group whom you can't see. Mr. Reaper's back is in the way, and hides the view." He paused, wheezing, and added mildly: "Well, that's what I'm here to find out. Do you remember that picture being taken? And, if so, who was being pushed down the slide?"

He looked at Dan, who nodded.

"That's smart," said Dan thoughtfully. "Yes, naturally I remember it. It was Jenny. She didn't want to go down the chute; afraid she'd show her thighs or something; but I gave her a push."

"But that means—!" cried Francine, with a sort of inspiration.

Dr. Fell nodded. "It was Mrs. Kent. I thought so. And that's the whole sad, ugly story. Do you begin to see why the message, 'There is one more to go,' was written a fortnight ago? Eh? When Rodney Kent was killed, the murderer scrawled this message on the back of the photograph and intended to leave it on the scene of the crime: just as later he sardonically scrawled, 'Dead Woman' when the threat was fulfilled. 'There is one more to go' *applied to Mrs. Kent.* But the murderer changed his mind about leaving it: this murderer you see, can never seem to make up his mind about anything—that's what has betrayed him. But he was wise in not leaving it. That would have incautious. And the photograph-cum-message has been calmly reposing in this house, probably in Gay's desk, ever since: until it was hauled out for some very curious monkey-tricks this morning. Well, do these heavy cogitations lead you on to deduce anything else?"

He watched them with grim affability. Getting out his pipe, he unscrewed it and blew through the stem as though he were blowing a particularly seductive whistle. He was still whistling for something, certainly.

"In Gay's desk," muttered Christopher Kent. "The heavy cogitations show that Gay can't possibly be the murderer."

"Why not?"

"It's pretty plain. If the picture was intended to represent a threat to Jenny, the murderer knew that the person being pushed down the slide *was* Jenny. But you can't tell that just by looking at the picture. She's hidden. You can't even tell it's a woman. So the murderer must be somebody who is either in the picture or was there when it was taken; and that rules out Gay."

"Won't do," objected Dan, shaking his head with decisiveness. "I remember telling Gay who it was, or writing about it, or—here! Seems to me I've seen that picture more recently, somewhere—seen it—seen it—"

"Yes," chimed in Francine abruptly. "And so have I. We saw it—"

Their voices stopped: that mutual jump at thought seemed to defeat itself as they came into conflict, like two people trying to open a door from opposite sides. Dr. Fell's whistle piped enticingly, and piped again. Nothing happened.

"It's no good," said Dan. "I've forgotten."

"H'mf, ha! Well, never mind. But still is there anything else that strikes you?" prompted the doctor.

"But still, about Gay's innocence," persisted Kent. "I'd like to—er—yes, I'd like to think he's guilty. All the same, it comes back to what we were arguing about a while ago: the blazing fathead who would keep the thing in his possession for a couple of weeks. You say you think it was probably in Gay's desk. But, if he were the murderer, wouldn't he have destroyed it?"

"Warm," said Dr. Fell. "Unquestionably warm. Therefore?"

"The only thing I can think of was that it was planted on him." Kent started; it was as though his sight went into another focus, and he could see the other face in the moon. "I believe I've got it! Listen. Someone planted it in the desk two weeks ago. But Gay hadn't found it because he hadn't looked in that drawer in the meantime. When he came back home to-day, he did look in the drawer, and discovered it among the other photographs. Now, listen!—"

"Chris," said Francine coldly.

"He was properly scared out of his Sunday trousers, because he wondered whether it would be found or whether somebody mightn't have seen it among his things already. It was all the worse because he really had been tied up with Jenny in the old days; and, for some reason, has persistently denied it. So he pretended to 'find' the photograph-and-message somewhere else. To cover up its sudden appearance, and pretend that the murderer had been up to funny business again, he tore up the rest of the pictures and sloshed them with red ink. He invented a story about donkeys' tails and pinched some silver out of his own drawer. That's it! It would explain both his guilty and innocent actions; his behaviour to-day and the rotten badness of his acting when—"

"Warmer and warmer yet, I think," beamed Dr. Fell. "But not, I am afraid, quite on the mark. It is significant that the only picture left completely intact did not contain a likeness of Mrs. Kent. True enough, I managed to dig one out of the mess, one that had not been effaced by tearing or ink; but—"

He stopped. There were heavy footsteps outside. Hadley, with a depressed-looking Wrayburn who was not now inclined to bounce, glanced in at the door. He gave the others a perfunctory good morning.

"May I see you alone for a minute, Fell?" he said.

When Dr. Fell had lumbered out, Hadley was careful to close the door. There was an uneasy silence, while they all looked at each other. Wrayburn, jamming his hands again into the pockets of his coat, attempted a light note in speech. His face was glossy.

"It may interest you to know," he remarked, "that I've just dropped one of the world's heavier bricks. The trouble being that I haven't got the remotest idea what it is. I made quite a study of psychology once; but I still don't know. I came back from the pub enlivened with a couple of pints, and charged back to the study, and said something asinine: still, I don't see how it could have been as asinine as all that. Hadley rather prefers the measles to me. Our host, after a conference with Hadley, is sitting downstairs with his head in his hands, looking like death. Poor old cuss: I felt sorry for him. I knew a fellow once, fellow named—"

"Shut up," said Dan briefly.

"Oh, all right. But fair's fair, and somebody ought to talk to me. If I'm still in disgrace for making a fool of myself over Jen—"

"Shut *up,*" said Dan.

There was another silence.

"Yes, but all the same," argued Wrayburn, "isn't that what's making everybody so frosty? I had to get a couple of pints inside me to ask it; but what have I done that others haven't done? You know, I've been wondering about something I never thought of before. Just why did we call her *Jenny?* Is it natural? The ordinary diminutive for 'Josephine' is 'Jo' or even, save the mark, 'Josie.' But she always referred to herself as Jenny, you know. Would it be Jenny Wren? No, I've got a better idea—"

"What the devil are you burbling about?" asked Dan, out of the thick wool of reflection.

Both of them broke off when the door opened, and even as Kent remembered Dr. Fell's remark that his first interest in the case had been in names. It was Dr. Fell who opened the door. He was alone.

"I am afraid," he said gravely, "that some of us will not be staying to lunch. But—hum—before we go, will you do me one favour? Believe me, it is necessary. Will you all come up to the Blue Room with me for just a short time?"

There was a noticeable shuffling of feet when they went out. The long hall which bisected the house, of rough plastering and beamed ceiling, had a large but small-paned window at each end. The windows were of slightly crooked glass, and held a reflection of snow. Kent knew which door would be the door to the Blue Room, since the famous leather sofa stood near it. They were all awkward about getting through the doorway.

The room in which Rodney Kent had died was at the back of the house, its windows looking out over the garden wall and the elms of the churchyard. Like the other rooms it was large but narrow, papered in velvety dark-blue stuff which now merely succeeded in looking dismal. The furniture, old-fashioned without being ancient, was of the fashion of some seventy years ago: a great double bed in oak, its headboard and footboard pointed at the top but sloping down shallowly to a curve by the little posts, showed much scroll-work and aggressively dominated the room. A bureau, and a dressing-table with a very tall mirror, both had marble tops like the round table in the centre. There were two chairs trying to break their backs with straightness, and a wash-hand-stand (marble-topped) bearing blue-and-white china. Face-towels hung neatly from a rack beside it. On the dark-flowered carpet near the table there was a broad greyish mark of scrubbing. Tasselled draperies on the windows were not drawn close enough to shut out a view of a headstone or two, or of the church tower, whose clock now made the glass vibrate by striking one. Dr. Fell stopped by the table.

"Is this room," said Dr. Fell, "except for one exhibit, now just as it was when Mr. Kent was murdered?"

It was Dan who answered yes.

"There were no signs of a struggle?"

"None."

"I have seen it in the police photographs," rumbled Dr. Fell, "but they did not show what I wanted. Will you get down on the floor as nearly as you can in the position the body was lying? . . . H'mf, thank you; that's fairly clear. Right side; head almost touching the left-hand caster of the bed; feet near the table. The bruise on the back of the head was rather high up, I take it?"

"Yes."

"Where was the towel?"

"Draped over the shoulder."

"As in Mrs. Kent's case?"

"Yes."

There was a heavy finality in question and answer which was like the striking of the clock.

"All right, there's that," growled Dan. "But what does it show, now you've seen it?"

"I'm inclined to think it shows a great deal," said Dr. Fell. "You see, up until this morning I wondered if I might be wrong. Now I know I must be right. At least we know one thing that was in the dark before. We know how Rodney Kent really died."

There was not as much light as there should have been, either in the room or in their minds. They stared at him.

"This is really a lot of most unnecessary nonsense," interposed Melitta, who had been sniffing as though she were going to cry. "You are perfectly well aware we *know* how poor Rodney died."

"The murderer was talking to him amicably enough," said Dr. Fell. "Then the murderer distracted his attention to something, so that he turned his head away. The murderer struck him on the back of the head with a weapon smaller than a poker. When he was unconscious, the murderer first strangled him to death and then beat his face with the poker. Yes. But what I said before is still true: we did not know, before, how he was really killed. It is not a riddle. You see, the murderer was someone who hated Rodney Kent very much. And therefore the murder of Josephine Kent—"

"Jenny," said Wrayburn.

"*Will* you be quiet?" requested Dan, turning in exasperation.

"No, I mean it," said Wrayburn. "We all know how attractive a—a woman Jenny was. Excuse me: I was going to say 'piece of goods,' but that doesn't fit. With all the inane crookedness in the little piece of goods's heart and soul, it still doesn't fit. There are women like that. They sort of—hold on."

"You're drunk," said Dan.

"Not on two pints. No. I'm myself. I was telling them, doctor (or trying to tell them) that it occurred to me a while ago how she came to be called Jenny. Of course she liked it. But she didn't coin the name for herself. No. It was some man who did that. God knows who he is or where he is—and if I had an idea, I wouldn't tell you. But he's middle-aged, the sort Jenny liked. She was the ideal Old Man's woman; or has someone said that? And he's probably not far off now, wondering why he killed her and what life will be like now that he hasn't got anything to hate."

"Oh, brace up," growled Dan. "We're all getting soft-headed. Why don't you begin on verse?"

"I will," said Wrayburn. He nodded gravely, his hands jammed into his pockets and his eyes on the window.

> *"Jenny kissed me when we met,*
> *Jumping from the chair she sat in,*
> *Time, you thief, who love to get*
> *Sweets into your list, put that in!*
> *Say I'm weary, say I'm sad,*
> *Say that health and wealth have miss'd me,*
> *Say I'm growing old, but add—"*

Chapter XVII

THE QUESTIONS OF DR. FELL

"Murder—" began Dr. Fell affably.

"Hold on," said Hadley, putting down his tankard and giving the doctor a suspicious look. "There is something in your expression,"—it was, in fact, one of fiendish and expansive pleasure—"which tells me you're about to begin a lecture. No! We don't want to listen to any lectures now. We've got too much work to do. Furthermore, when Gay gets here—"

Dr. Fell looked pained. "I beg your pardon," he rumbled with dignity. "So far from demeaning myself to lecture to you, I was about to submit myself voluntarily to the intolerable process of listening to you lecture. I gather that for once in your life you are inclined to agree partly with me about a case. At least, you are willing to give a sporting chance to a belief. Very well. I have some questions for you."

"What questions?"

It was nearly ten o'clock, and a rush of last-minute customers at the bar penetrated through from the other side of the door. Dr. Fell, Hadley, and Kent sat alone in the comfortable, raftered bar-parlour of the Stag and Glove. There was ample living-accommodation at the pub, and they had taken rooms there for the night. This Kent knew; but it was all he knew. That day had consisted of cross-currents and mysterious conferences about whose import he had been given (and had asked for) no hint. Dr. Fell had disappeared for a long time during the afternoon. When the doctor returned, Hadley disappeared. There was also a conference with the long and saturnine Inspector Tanner. What was to be done about Sir Gyles Gay, or whether anything was to be done, Kent had not heard. He had not seen Sir Gyles after that episode of eavesdropping. To get away from the atmosphere of tension at Four Doors, he and Francine had gone for a long walk in the snow; but the tension was still there, and the silver of a winter sunset looked merely angry. The only memory he carried away from it was of Francine, in a Russian-esque kind of astrakhan cap, sitting on a stile in her fur coat, with the low grey hills beyond.

That same tension had not even disappeared in the bar-parlour of the

Stag and Glove. They were waiting for something. Yet Dr. Fell showed it much less than Hadley. It was a bitter night, though without wind. A big fire had been built in the bar-parlour, so bit that its reflections were almost wild: they flickered on Dr. Fell as he sat enthroned in the window-seat, with the leaded panes behind him and a pint tankard in front of him, beaming with pleasure.

He took a deep pull at the tankard, and assumed an argumentative air.

"Murder, I was about to say," Dr. Fell pursued, "is a subject on which my views have been somewhat misunderstood: largely, I confess, because I have muddled them in the telling or in the enthusiasm of controversy. I feel inclined to rectify this, for a very good reason.

"I have admitted to a weakness for the bizarre and the slightly fantastic. I have, in fact, worn it as a badge of pride. That affair of the Hollow Man, and Driscoll's murder at the Tower of London, and that wild business aboard the *Queen Victoria,* will always remain my favourite cases. But this does not mean that I, or any rational person, would take pleasure in a mad world. It is precisely the opposite, in fact, of what I do mean: and this is the only reason why I mention it at all.

"Now, to the quietest human being, seated in the quietest house, there will sometimes come a wish for the possibilities or impossibilities of things. He will wonder whether the teapot may not suddenly begin to pour out honey or sea-water; the clock point to all hours of the day at once; the candle begin to burn green or crimson; the door to open upon a lake or a potato-field instead of a London street. Humph, ha. So far, so good. For a reverie or a pantomime it is all very well. But, regarded as a scheme of everyday life, it is enough to make a man shiver.

"I have enough difficulty in finding my eyeglasses as it is, even when they remain where I last put them down. If they suddenly went sailing up the chimney as I reached for them, my language would be difficult to control. The precise book I am looking for on a shelf has no need of magic to elude me. A malevolent spirit already dwells in my hat. When a person goes from Charing Cross to Bernard Street by underground, he can think himself jolly lucky if he gets to Bernard Street. But if he makes the same journey—say for an urgent appointment at the British Museum—and gets out at Bernard Street, and suddenly finds himself not in Bernard Street, but in Broadway or the rue de la Paix, he would be justified in thinking that matters had become really intolerable.

"Now, this principle particularly applies to criminal cases. It would be a very dull business to have a calm, sane criminal in a mad world. The criminal would not be interesting at all. You would do much better to go and watch the nearest lamppost dance the rumba. Outside things must not act on the criminal: he must act on them. That is why the eternal fascination is to watch a slightly unbalanced criminal—usually a murderer—in a quite sane world.

"This is not, of course, to say that all murderers are mad. But they are in a fantastic state of mind, or they would not be murderers. And they do fantastic things. It would be, I think, an easy thesis to prove.

"We all know, in any murder case, the questions *who, how,* and *why.* Of those three, the most revealing, but usually by far the most puzzling, is *why.* I don't mean merely the actual motive for the crime itself. I mean the why of certain other actions, eccentricities of behaviour, which centre round the performance of the crime. They torment us at the time: a hat placed on a statue, a poker removed from the scene of the crime when by all reason it should not have been removed. More often the why torments us even when we know, or think we know, the truth. Why did Mrs. Thompson write those letters to Bywaters? Why did Mrs. Maybrick soak the fly-papers in water? Why did Thomas Bartlett drink the chloroform? Why did Julia Wallace have an enemy in the world? Why did Herbert Bennett make a sexual attack on his own wife? Sometimes they are very small points—three rings left behind, a broken medicine-bottle, an utter absence of blood on clothes. But they are fantastic, as fantastic as mad clocks or the real crimes of Landru; and, if we knew the answers to the why of them, we should probably know the truth."

"What questions?" inquired Hadley.

Dr. Fell blinked. "Why, the questions I've just been indicating to you. Any of 'em."

"No," said Hadley. "I mean what questions were you going to ask me?"

"Eh?"

"I've been patiently waiting to hear. You said you were not going to lecture; you said it was an honour you passed on to me, and that you had some questions to ask me. Very well: let's hear 'em."

Dr Fell leaned back with an evil dignity.

"I spoke," he retorted, "by way of preface to the document I am going to lay before you. I have noted down here, on various small sheets, a number of questions. They are mostly 'whys'; any of the 'what' variety are of the why nature. All of them must be answered and answered satisfactorily, before we can say we have a complete solution to this case. Look here, we'll put this up to an umpire." He turned to Kent, and went on doggedly:

"Between last night and this morning, Hadley became convinced that Gay was our man. I was not so sure. I doubted it then, and I am now certain he isn't; but I was compelled to regard it as a possibility. Gay has been given a few hours' grace to answer certain matters: he should be along any minute. We are then—um—going to test a theory of mine, which Hadley regards with at least an open mind. It is now ten o'clock. By midnight we may have the real murderer. Now, both of you, how are the following questions to be answered? How do they fit in with Gay's guilt, or anyone else's guilt? It is your last chance to have a shot at it before the gong."

He spread out his multitudinous note-sheets.

"1. Why, on both occasions, did the murderer wear the costume of a hotel-attendant? An old question, but still a stimulating one.

"2. What happened to that costume afterwards?

"3. Why, on both occasions, was a towel used in strangling the victim?

"4. Why was it necessary for the murderer to hide his face from Josephine Kent, but *not* from Rodney Kent?

"5. Why did Josephine Kent first begin to wear a curious bracelet, having a square black stone cut with a Latin inscription, only a few hours before she was murdered?

"6. Why did she pretend she had never been in England before?

"7. What is the explanation of her words to Miss Forbes, in reply to the latter's question about whether the inscription on the bracelet meant anything? Her reply, you recall, was, 'Only if you're able to read it; that's the whole secret.'

"8. How did the murderer get into a locked linen-closet at the Royal Scarlet Hotel?

"9. Similarly, how did the murderer—supposing it to be some person other than Gay—get into a locked drawer in the desk of the study at Four Doors: a drawer to which only Gay had a key? You observe that the murderer seems able to go anywhere without difficulty.

"10. Why was a small amount of loose change stolen from Mrs. Kent's handbag, and also from the desk in Gay's study?

"11. It must be presupposed, in Mrs. Kent's case, that the murderer placed a pair of odd shoes outside the door of 707, and also hung the 'quiet' sign on it. If he wished to make sure of not being disturbed, this is understandable. But he wrote 'Dead Woman' in red ink, as though to call attention to his presence while he was there. Why?

"12. Perhaps the most intriguing 'why' in the whole case. We believe (I think correctly) that the murderer, dressed as a hotel-attendant and carrying his pile of towels, was admitted to room 707 by Mrs. Kent herself. Very well. At this time, we know from another witness—Wrayburn—Mrs. Kent's key to that room was in her handbag. But the next morning this same key was found by

Wrayburn in the lock *outside* the door. You follow the fascinating double-turn of that? The murderer goes in. For some reason
he takes the key out of the handbag, having found it there in his
search of the room, and puts it in the outside of the door. Why?"

Dr. Fell put the sheaf of notes together and made a mesmeric pass over
them.

"Eh bien?" inquired the doctor. "Or which of them appears to you the
most interesting?"

"As umpire," answered Kent, "I should say the second one. In other
words, what has happened to that infernal costume? It applies to everyone
else as well as to Gay. But the uniform seems to have disappeared like
smoke. The murderer couldn't have got rid of it in any way I can follow.
He couldn't have tossed it out of the window, or burnt it, or hidden it: I
suppose you took care of that. We seem to be reduced to the logical
certainty that it must be in the hotel somewhere. Which would make it a
genuine uniform, borrowed or pinched from somebody. It's unlikely that
the murderer went roaming about looking for a uniform at random: it
looks like collusion. And so we get back to the hotel again—like my case
against the manager."

"And nothing else suggests itself to you?" inquired Dr. Fell, with a
curious look at him. "Hasn't any member of your crowd ventured on a
suggestion? Come! Surely there would be an ingenious theory somewhere. A theory from Wrayburn, for instance?"

"No, I've seen very little of him. There's been no suggestion except—"
He stopped, having made a slip.

"Except what?" asked Dr. Fell quickly.

"Nothing at all. It was only—"

"It was enough. At a conference of the powers, I think we had better
hear it."

"Some far-fetched idea about the possibility of the murderer having
been a woman. I suppose you hadn't thought of that?"

Dr. Fell and Hadley exchanged glances. The doctor chuckled.

"You wrong me," he said with offhand geniality. "It was one of the
very first thoughts that did occur to me. You mean as regards the
uniform, to make us postulate a man from the sight of it?"

"Yes. But you see the reason why it couldn't be so? I mean," said
Kent, "the suède shoes. In the first place, it's unlikely that a woman
would have taken two odd shoes; she'd have selected a pair. Second and
more important, she'd never have put out suède shoes, which can't be
polished. That means it was a man. I can realise—once I think about
it—that you don't polish suède. But, if I had been the murderer and
simply wanted to shove a pair of shoes outside the door, I question

whether I should have thought of that at the time. I'd have picked up the first shoes that came handy, as the murderer evidently did."

"Unless," Dr. Fell pointed out with relish, "it was the double-twist of subtlety. The murderer is a woman. She wants us to believe it is a man; that, I think you will acknowledge, would be the whole point of the deception. Therefore she strengthens it by deliberately choosing a pair of shoes which no woman would choose."

Kent regarded his tankard moodily.

"I know," he admitted. "It's a very useful device in fiction, because you can prove very nearly anything by it. But, deep down inside me, I've never really believed in it. You remember the famous passage in which Dupin shows how it is possible to anticipate the way a person's mind will work, and uses as an example the schoolboy's game of evens or odds. You have a marble concealed in your left or your right hand, and the other fellow gets the marble if he picks the correct hand: so on as long as your marbles last. After estimating the intelligence or stupidity of your opponent, you put yourself mentally in his place, think what he would do, and win all the marbles. Well, it won't work. I've tried it. It won't work because, even if you have two minds exactly adjusted, the one thing they will differ over is what constitutes strategy. And, if you try any such games when the other fellow is probably only leaving it to chance, you'll build up such an elaborate edifice that you can't remember where you started. . . . Don't you honestly think that most murderers are the reverse of subtle? They haven't got time to be; and I should think they would be pretty nervous about being misunderstood."

Across the room, the private door leading to the stable-yard opened, and Sir Gyles Gay came in.

By the expression on his face, it was evident that he had heard the last few words and was turning them over in his mind. Cold air blew in with him, making the firelight dance. Ten had struck loudly from the church clock. They were turning the last customers out of the bar; you could hear a noise of firm-shutting doors and final good nights. Gay wore a soft hat pulled down on his forehead, and a heavy herringbone coat. He carried a stick under his arm.

"I am a little late, gentlemen," he said formally. "You must excuse me."

"Will you drink something?" asked Dr. Fell, reaching for the bell. "We're putting up here, you know, and we can order it."

"Yes. I know," said Gay, stripping off his gloves. He studied them. "You prefer to come here rather than accept my hospitality. Does this mean that you cannot dine with a man you mean to arrest?—In any case, I cannot accept yours."

"There's no question of arrest yet, Sir Gyles," Hadley informed him sharply. "You were asked to tell us certain things. For some reason you wanted a few hours to 'think it over.' At Fell's insistence, I was willing to agree. Have you anything to tell us now?"

Gay put his hat and stick on the table, smiling at the hat. Drawing out a chair, he sat down with some care; he seemed to be listening to the chimney growl under a cold sky.

"Yes, I am prepared to tell you the whole truth." He turned round. "I warn you that you will find it disappointing. After I have told you, you will, of course, take what steps you like. What I wanted was time for reflection. I wanted to remember whether I had ever met Mrs. Kent before in my life. Wait!" He held up his hand. "I am aware what your evidence shows, superintendent. I know that I must have met her in the sense that I must have encountered her. You would not believe me this afternoon, when I assured you that a woman could have come to England claiming acquaintance with me—in fact, many people do just that—and such a staggering number of persons go through an Under-Secretary's office in the course of a year that he would require a card-index mind to remember a quarter of them. The plain truth is still this: I do not remember that woman. I have gone over very carefully in my mind everything I can remember for the year in question. I was then living in Norfolk. With the aid of my diary I can almost reconstruct the whole year. Mrs. Kent does not fit into it anywhere. I never had any 'dealings' with her, of the sort you mean; and I shared with her no secret which would have obliged me to kill her. That is my last word."

There was a silence. Hadley rapped his fingers on the table with slow indecision. Such seemed the sincerity of the man's manner that Hadley was evidently impressed.

"And that's all you have to say?"

"No, not quite all. Now comes my confession. I did put that photograph among the towels in the bathroom; or, rather, I did not put it there, since I never went into the bathroom at all and only pretended to find it. I also ruined the inside of a drawer with red ink. But that is *all* I did."

For some obscure reason, Dr. Fell was rubbing his hands with pleasure. Hadley studied Gay, who returned his look with a sardonic smile.

"Oh, yes, it was quite asinine. Was that what you were going to say?"

"No," interposed Dr. Fell. "A more important matter. Did you tear up the other photographs?"

"I did not."

"Good. In that case," said Dr. Fell, "I think you had better tell us about it."

"It is to be conceded that my first and only venture into crime was not a success," observed Gay. This seemed to sting him more than anything else. He was prepared for an attack; he did not appear to be prepared for the casualness of his hearers. "I suffered from the delusion that, if I made the thing grotesque, it would therefore be believed. It is a weakness of mine, which—"

"We can omit that," said Hadley. "Why did you do it?"

"Because I was not going to be framed," retorted Gay, with the blood now in his shrunken face, and a certain violence about his dry fingers. He leaned forward. "If you can ever believe me again, listen to the sober truth. I had not your eye or flair for detecting that the ink on the back of that picture was so old; it occurred to me afterwards, and made me curse myself. I thought it had been put there this morning.

"We returned to Four Doors at eleven o'clock. Good. That at least you don't dispute. And there is something I fear you missed, for all your deductions. I don't keep a regular chauffeur. I hire the same man when he is needed. This man—Burns—drove us back from the station this morning. Consequently, I had to pay him. I was going to pay him out of the small-change-purse in the drawer of my desk. Shortly after we arrived, and the others had gone upstairs while Burns was taking the luggage off the grid, I went back to my study—"

"Wait. Is that drawer, as the maids say, usually kept locked?"

"It always is. I was not aware, however, that my inquisitive staff knew it. I shall remember such possibilities when I commit my next crime. Very well. I went back to my study. As I passed through the lounge I heard somebody moving about in there. And, when I opened the door of the study, I was just in time to see somebody on his—or her—way out, slipping through the door at the head of the inner staircase."

"Who?"

"Ah, there we are. I honestly do not know. I want you to believe that. I was just in time to see the upper door closing."

"But noises, footsteps?"

"Yes, I believe there had been footsteps. But I can't describe them. I called out, and there was no answer. If I said I was not uneasy, I should be lying; I *was* uneasy, particularly as I had no idea what might be up. While I was thinking of this, I unlocked the drawer of the desk. I found all those photographs torn to pieces; and, on top of them, the picture announcing another—murder. Or so I interpreted it."

"How long had it been since you looked in that drawer last?"

"Probably three weeks."

"Go on," said Hadley quietly.

Gay's voice grew cold. "You are not a fool, my friend. You know what I thought and what I still think. It was a plain, barefaced attempt to saddle me with the blame for these crimes. You wish to know why I burst out against my guests this afternoon? That is the reason. Somebody had put that there. In a very short time somebody would have had it 'found.' That is how some genial friend repays hospitality." His fingers twitched, and he put them flat on his knees. "Wasn't it obvious? I am the only person with a key to that drawer. Yet someone else had got one. How, I don't know. Why, I know only too well. If you can think of any better evidence of a premeditated attempt to throw the blame elsewhere, I should be interested to hear it."

"And so—"

"Well, there is an ancient truism about beating someone to the punch. Possibly I acted like a fool. I don't know. I know that I was more furious in that moment than I can remember being since the days of my encounters with official stupidity in the Government. I compressed several years' rage into my feelings then, nor have I even yet recovered my usual child-like good temper."

He exhibited very little sign of child-like good temper. Yet it seemed evident that he sincerely believed in this quality as belonging to himself. Nobody commented; and, after a wheezy breath Gay went on:

"If I had known who put the picture in the drawer—"

"A picture," interrupted Dr. Fell dreamily, "on which the message had been printed two weeks ago."

"And a fact," replied Gay, "which I did not know. There was certainly a prowler in my study just after eleven, and up to no good. I repeat: if I had known who did it, I should have been after him with great pleasure. I should have tried my hand at counter-framing. But I did not know, and I was unwilling to make a guess which might be wrong. You see, I am more charitable in several ways than the real murderer. But above all I was exceedingly curious to mark the effect if I should fight back with a return stroke against 'somebody.' Perhaps it would have been more sensible to have got rid of the picture and the torn fragments. But I was not willing to have the matter drop altogether. Being innocent, I wanted the police to find such clues. But, by God, gentlemen, I was unwilling for the police to find such clues in my desk!"

"It didn't occur to you to come to us and tell the truth?"

"It did not," said Gay quite simply. "That was the only course which did not occur to me."

"Go on."

Gay cocked his head on one side. Amusement crept into his wizened face, the sort of amusement which had been absent from it for some hours.

"I concede that I was a trifle too spectacular. The donkey's tail, too, was an error; and I am not sure that I gained much by ruining the inside of the drawer with red ink. But I wanted to draw attention to it. Believe me, gentlemen, there was absolutely no thought in my mind of making the snapshots in the drawer unrecognisable. I admired, even when I felt my hair rise on my scalp, the ingenuity with which you dove-tailed these bits of evidence to-day. Can you understand this?—that I was stunned into a kind of detached interest, a contemplation of myself, by the way in which you spun a case out of nothing? I was Pickwick listening to Sergeant Buzfuz, and hearing my chops and tomato sauce used against me."

He paused.

"I think that's all I have to say. You understand, I did not have to create a prowler. There really was someone in my study. You have got a valuable piece of evidence, even if you got it in a way for which I am heartily sorry. I have no dark and terrible secrets connected with the past of Mrs. Kent. There is my story; you may believe it or not; and (just between ourselves) be damned to you."

Hadley and Dr. Fell looked at each other. Hunching his neck into the upturned collar of his overcoat, Gay blinked at the fire.

"You don't find the atmosphere so hostile now, do you?" asked Dr. Fell amiably.

"Well—no. To tell the truth, no."

"Just a question or two," suggested the doctor, as Hadley scowled at his note-book. "Can you think of any reason why this person should have torn up all the pictures in that drawer?"

"No, I cannot. *That* could not be for throwing suspicion on me. Or at least I don't see how."

"H'mf, no. Would it be easy to have got a duplicate key to the drawer?"

"I shouldn't have thought so. It's something of an elaborate and intricate lock, for a desk drawer. But it's quite possible, since it was done. I am not exactly aware how these things are done. From a wide acquaintance with sensational fiction, I know that it is customary to use wax or soap; but if somebody handed me a sheet of wax or a bar of soap and said, 'Get on with it,' I don't think I should know how."

"You say you heard footsteps when someone was in your study. Light or heavy footsteps?"

"The best I can do," answered Gay, after reflection, "is the old and unhelpful 'medium' of this whole affair."

"It could not have been one of the maids?"

"Why should it be? They would have told me."

"Has your staff of servants been with you for a long time?"

"Oh, yes. They came with me from Norfolk. I—er—well, yes, I trust them absolutely, in so far as I trust anybody in this world."

"I think you told us you were living in Norfolk at the time Mrs. Kent was in this country?"

"Yes, if I have the dates down right."

"H'mf. Well—just at a guess, Sir Gyles, have you any notion as to who is responsible for all this?"

Gay shook his head without taking his gaze from the fire. An odd smile twisted his mouth. "That is your business. Mine, too, I acknowledge; but in a different way. Will you answer me, truly and freely, one question?"

Hadley was cautious, and interposed before Dr. Fell could speak. "All depends on what it is, Sir Gyles. What question?"

"Why," said Gay, still without taking his eyes from the fire, "why have you two got a police-officer watching Miss Forbes?"

Chapter XVIII

HANDS ACROSS A GRAVE-STONE

Kent remembered the thump as he put his own tankard of beer down on the table. He glanced quickly round the little group; and he realised by the quiet that Hadley and Dr. Fell had taken the words with the utmost seriousness.

"What makes you think that?" Hadley asked.

"I see," said Gay, half humorously. "Don't you ever give anybody information on any subject whatever? When Miss Forbes and Mr. Kent here went for a walk this afternoon, you had a man following them. I am not certain who it was, but it was one of the sergeants I saw at the Royal Scarlet Hotel. When they came back to Four Doors, he followed Miss Forbes. I'm inclined to suspect that the reason why you—hum—lured me here to the pub to-night, instead of coming to my home, was for the purpose of getting a man inside. I don't object. But if my house is to be used for any purpose, I think I have a right to know what is going on. The place seems to be full of policemen. There was another in the bar to-night. You can't expect to disguise things like that in a village, you know; and I've been wondering what is going on."

"You'd better tell him, Hadley," said Dr. Fell. "I've been urging it all along. He could give us a lot of help; and, if things went wrong in any way, he might wreck the plan."

"Why," interposed Kent, "have you been having Miss Forbes watched?"

Hadley smiled without enthusiasm. "Not for the reason you think. Just to see that she doesn't get into any trouble. As she might." He turned to Gay. "Very well. The whole story is that, with luck, we may get the murderer to-night."

Gay whistled two notes and sat up. "Interesting—also attractive! Where and how?"

"Your house is unusual," said Hadley. "It really lives up to its name. Unlike Seaview and Parkside, it really does have four doors, one on each side of the house. All those doors must be watched. If Fell is right, we hope to meet someone coming out of the house by one of those doors in the middle of the night."

"Leaving the house? Why?"

"That," said Hadley, "is as far as the story goes now."

Gay looked puzzled. "But I still don't follow this. If you merely caught somebody sneaking out of the house in the middle of the night, would that, *per se,* prove it was the murderer? I have always thought"—he frowned in a meditative manner—"that, when these traps were laid and someone is caught suspiciously prowling, the person caught is almost too ready to break down and admit his guilt. Suppose he were to fold his arms and say, 'This is a frame-up; I refer you to my solicitors'? Where would your evidence be?"

"We've got reason to hope," said Hadley, "that it would still exist." His tone changed. "What I'd like to ask of you, Sir Gyles, is this. If you should happen to see a police-officer in the house: in fact, no matter what you do see or however suspicious it appears: do nothing and say nothing to anybody. Let the household go to bed in the ordinary way, just as usual. At some time early in the morning you may be waked up; but by that time, if we have any luck, it may be all over. Will you promise that?"

"With pleasure. I—er—take it you accept my own story as being true?"

"If I didn't accept it, would I confide this to you?"

"I don't know," said Gay, with candour. "However, you can depend on me. If I scent the presence of dirty work, I also like the presence of dirty work. Good night, gentlemen. I hope I shall see you soon."

He pulled down his soft hat on his forehead, got up, and put the stick under his arm. By the door—the same door as that by which he had entered—he studied them for a moment before he made a brief salute and slipped out. The night, which remained cold and almost absolutely still, sent in hardly a chill after him.

Hadley looked at his watch.

"I'd better see the landlord," the superintendent commented. "We want none of *that* interference."

And he reached up and switched off the electric lights.

While the uncertain firelight rose up, and they heard Hadley blundering out into the bar, Kent looked at Dr. Fell. Dr. Fell drained his tankard without comment; he seemed to be listening for the sound of the church clock, which should be close on the half-hour.

"Am I allowed to know what's up?" demanded Kent, yet speaking in little above a whisper. "What's this about Francine? I've got a right to know—"

He could not see the doctor clearly, though he heard the wheezy

breathing. "Miss Forbes," declared Dr. Fell, "is in no danger of being
hurt. Set your mind easy about that."

"But if she's in any danger I want to—"

"H'mf, yes. That, I believe, is a part of the idea."

"I mean, I want to be on the spot to—"

"No," said Dr. Fell. "Never again. I allowed it in that case of the Eight
of Swords; and I swore a mighty oath that it should never happen again. It
merely meant tragedy. It's a professional's job, my lad; and a professional's doing it. But you can make yourself useful, if you will. We
want two men on each of the four doors, and we're short-handed. If you
like, you can share the watch. Without stretching the matter in the least, I
can tell you that we may run foul of someone who is apt to turn infernally
nasty if certain schemes go wrong."

The church clock struck the half-hour.

Hadley returned with the tankards filled. Very few words were passed.
Sitting down close to the fire, so that he could keep his eyes on his
wrist-watch, Hadley bent over it. Nor were there many sounds except the
scrape of pewter on wood, the watch ticking, and the fire: which had
turned to a red-glowing bank. The quarter-hour rang, and then the hour.
Northfield was asleep.

At a few minutes past eleven Hadley, who had been going from one
window to the other to pull back the curtains, moved across to the door
opening on the stable-yard. He opened the door wide and stood peering
out. A patch of cold crept over the floor like a carpet, widening against
the walls, while the smoke of Hadley's breath blew back over his
shoulder. There was a creak in the stable-yard, and a whisper.

"Tanner!"

"Superintendent?"

"Men in position?"

"All ready, sir."

"Hold on."

Hadley moved out on to a creaking board, and there was the mutter of a
conference. When he returned he picked up his own overcoat from a
chair. He faced Kent.

"Your beat," he said, "will be with the inspector at the back door of the
house. He's got his instructions, so you just follow the leader. You're not
to go into the back garden. Miss Forbes's room overlooks the back, and
you might be seen if the moon should come out. Stay just outside the iron
gates to the back garden on the edge of the churchyard. You'll have a
clear view of the back door from there. Haven't got the wind up, have
you?"

"I don't think so."

"In any case—" Hadley bent down, picked up the poker from the hearth, and handed it to him. "In any case, just take this along. You're a private citizen, so you can be armed. All right."

Hadley went with him to the door. Inspector Tanner was waiting, his flat cap looking belligerent; but he muttered little beyond issuing directions. They moved out quietly through a gate opening on the green.

Or, at least, Kent supposed it must be the green. It was his first experience of that puzzling, disquieting phenomenon, the complete pitch-blackness and silence of an English village at night. We use terms loosely. Few urban streets, few parts of the remotest town in the deadest hour of the night, are ever without *any* light or *any* sign of movement. There is always someone awake. The African veldt is lighter and more aware than this core of a well-populated district, a village. Venture into one after nightfall, and you will never know you are there until you are in the middle of it: a house is as startling as a ghost. Your impression is that people must fall into a drugged sleep at nightfall. Even when a public-house remains open until ten o'clock, the blinds are so sealed or the lights so remote that it looks as dead as the rest; it might be a public-house in Pompeii.

Though he walked slowly beside the inspector, Kent heard his own footsteps sound with such distinctness on the frosty ground that he might have been making footprints for trackers to follow. It was a night of smoky cold, in which you could smell mist without seeing any of it. Later there might be a moon. Their own heavy footfalls went ahead of them round the green. There did not seem, Kent thought, to be any dogs in Northfield.

Instead of going down the dim road past the church Inspector Tanner softly opened the lych-gate of the church itself. Kent followed him through under the great pillars of yew. The poker had grown blistering cold in his hand; he was gripping it too tightly; so he thrust the end of it into his deep overcoat pocket and crooked his arm round it. They moved down a flagged path, still slippery with snow, and round the church. Beyond it was so dark that each of them kept a hand out in front. Then they went into the churchyard, which sloped down with some abruptness and in whose maze flat stones made obstructions.

"Which way?"

"Down here. Look sharp!"

Great elms were materialising out of the sky in front of them. Beyond ran a wall pierced by iron gates, and he could see a faint light. Evidently someone at Four Doors was still awake.

Kent, who had had it drilled into him as a boy that you must never step on a grave, had been doing some unusual walking to avoid them. He barked his chilled knuckles several times on the stones. Then, just as they stopped on the edge of the churchyard, the light at the house went out.

But his eyesight was now growing accustomed to the dark; he had lost that naked feeling such as is experienced on groping into a dark theatre, and losing the usher with the flashlight half-way down the aisle. He could see a sort of shine on the iron gates. Beyond that, the white window-frames and white back door of the house loomed up with some clarity. He could even pick out the line of the chimneys. If it were not so infernally cold—

The church clock struck the quarter-hour.

He was leaning, incongruously, against the headstone of a grave, only a few feet from the gates. Objects were now assuming a night-time clarity; he made out the steps to the back door, the dust-bin, and all white paint seemed to shine. But he wished he had brought a pair of gloves. His hands felt raw, and a shiver went through him. "Walking over some-body's grave" was the thought that occurred to him: it was the same sort of feeling.

All the same—

What was going on in that house? Who or what did they expect to slip out of a door, when only the church clock was allowed to talk? He put the poker, which was beginning to irk him, down in the rimy grass by the headstone. Bending forward, he made certain that the rear gates had been left unlocked. They creaked softly, and he drew back. It seemed to be the consensus of opinion (good old sober phrase) that there was no danger. But there must be danger inside, or they would not have surrounded the place with a ring of guards. If they had let him go in to Francine, he would have felt better. The roles (he mused) were reversed. Those inside the house, those tucked into stolid steam-heated walls, were the persons who ran a risk; the people outside, in loneliness where there was no cover, were safe.

After touching the padlock on the gates, he crouched back to the headstone. He would get a crick in the back if he stood long like this. Sit down? That would be the easiest thing. The damp headstone, worn to a wafer by time, was scrolled along the top like the bed in the room where Rodney Kent had died. His fingers brushed it as he bent down to pick up the poker. And the poker was not there.

The poker was not there. His fingers groped in sharp patches of snow. He squatted down, moving his hand wide. He remembered just where the end of it had lain, and it was not there.

"What the devil—?" he whispered to his companion beside him.

"I have it," whispered the other voice.

Kent turned round in relief. His companion was standing just where he had stood when they took up their posts, still motionless and large. Kent's eyes, accustomed to the gloom, could not pick out details. He saw the blue coat, no overcoat being worn; he saw the silver buttons shining dimly; and he saw something else.

It was not an inspector of police who had been walking through the churchyard with him.

Then it moved. The noise of the poker in the air was a kind of *whup;* it sang in brittle air, and struck the headstone as it was intended to strike a head. Kent had not dodged: he had stumbled, or so he always remembered it afterwards. He heard his own knee strike the ground. He rolled, and bounced to his feet like an india-rubber cat, as the poker rose up and fell again. Then they were standing, breathing hard, with the headstone between them.

Now it seemed a very long time, minutes by the church clock, before any other movement was made. The longest adjustment is an adjustment of thought. In front of him, at not much more than arm's length, was the person they had been looking for. How this person had come there was not the question. The question was what to do. It never once occurred to Kent to cry out and call for help. And this was not bravery, for he was frightened green and he could hear a thick beating in his ears. It is possible that he did not have time to think. He stood looking at the other through the mist of his own breath.

"Put that down," he whispered. "Who are you? Put it down."

The other did not reply. Instead he began to edge round the headstone.

"Put it dow—"

If it had been a longer weapon that his adversary carried, he might have risked a grab at it. But it was too suitable for murder at close quarters; that last blow, if it had landed, would have smashed his skull like an orange. As the indistinct figure shuffled round, Kent moved back. His adversary was moving the poker a little, like a boxer about to feint. Then he struck again—and overshot his mark.

Both were turning at the time. Kent felt no more than a faint burning sensation, as of pins-and-needles, in his thumb: which then seemed to be warm and soft and numb. It was the mound of the grave itself, wiry and slippery underfoot, which tripped the other in his forward drive. His body struck the headstone. His feet, off-balance, clawed for support. Thrown almost against Kent's chest, his neck was across the stone; and the poker rattled on stone as he tried to swing it. Kent, out of sheer fear, struck once the worst blow he knew. He struck with the closed fist, in the form of the rabbit-punch, across the back of the neck; and it caught the back of his adversary's neck on the gravestone as you might catch iron on an anvil.

Even as he heard the poker drop and roll in wiry grass, there was another and more rapid rustling. Three men came into the dimness under the bare elms; and two of them carried flashlights. He heard them breathe. And he recognised the heavy but not quite steady voice of Superintendent Hadley.

"No, don't call me anything," Hadley said. "I didn't turn him loose on you. I didn't know he was anywhere near here. The swine stole a march on us—"

He paused, drawing in his breath. Kent coughed, and kept on coughing for a moment.

"Whatever happened," he said, "*I've* probably committed the murder this time. There wasn't anything else to do. You'd better see if his neck's dislocated."

The figure had slipped down and rolled like the poker. Hadley bent over it as more heavy footsteps sounded, and Dr. Fell wheezed into the group.

"No, he's all right," said Hadley. "He'll be in proper shape to have it dislocated in another way. But he nearly got just about what he gave his victims. All right, boys. Roll him over. Make sure nothing has fallen out of his pockets."

Kent stared at his late adversary as the flashlight moved, and turned round again.

"Is that—?" he said.

Dr. Fell, who had been mopping his forehead with the bandana, got his breath. He ran the bandana through his fingers, blinked, and looked down in a disconsolate way.

"Yes," he said. "That's the real murderer, of course—Ritchie Bellowes."

Chapter XIX

THE GENTLER CRIME

"And he wore—?" asked Kent.

At the head of the lunch-table Dr. Fell leaned back expansively.

"He wore," said Dr. Fell, "for reasons which will be indicated, the spare uniform of an inspector of police; which is so exactly like that of the liftmen at the Royal Scarlet Hotel that I have sometimes been tempted to address them as 'officer.' You have not forgotten the description of the liftmen's uniform as given us by Hardwick? 'A short single-breasted blue coat high at the neck; silver buttons, shoulder epaulets.' You observe that they were the only uniformed men who wore *short* coats, like a police officer: the others had frock coats or tails. The only true and honest witness who had seen our phantom in blue (Mr. Reaper) said that he believed the phantom wore a short coat. Thus the field was tolerably narrow in drawing analogies. But all Ritchie Bellowes wanted anybody to notice (and calculated on anybody noticing) was the blue coat and silver buttons. You will see."

"But how did he get out of clink?" roared Dan. "And why—?"

To say that an atmosphere of tension had lifted from this group: to say that a hobgoblin had drifted away and a bad smell faded, would be to understate the case at Four Doors on that frosty morning of the second of February. Melitta Reaper was said to have cried all night, a proceeding which was generally thought to reflect great credit on her. A brittle sunlight showed at the windows of the dining-room, where Gay had provided a lunch that was something in the nature of a celebration. Kent's thumb, it is true, had given him a bad night after catching the weight of the poker in Ritchie Bellowes's hand; but he was too easy with wine and relief to be troubled about that. Dr. Fell presided at the head of the table like the Ghost of the Christmas Present. And Dr. Fell, wagging his cigar drowsily, said:

"Ahem. Yes, I am inclined to lecture, if only because I have so far had no opportunity satisfactorily to oil the wheels of my eloquence. But there is another and (if this can be credited) even more cogent reason. Academically, I like this case. If affords one of the better opportunities for gathering up pieces of evidence into one whole; and, to such of you as enjoy deductive orgies, it should prove of interest. The superintendent and I," he waved his cigar towards Hadley, "followed its tail together. If it is I who tell you about it, this is not because I have any great far-sightedness; it is simply that I am the more enthusiastic and inexorable talker.

"The most satisfactory way to approach it will be to outline it to you from the first as we followed it. Now, when I went to the Royal Scarlet Hotel at first, I had only one firm idea in the welter: that Mrs. Josephine Kent was not what she seemed. Hadley, in his sharp brush with our host yesterday, outlined the reasons for investigating this; they began with the scuffed condition of the lettering on the battered trunk, and they did not end with some suggestive information we received from South Africa. They woke certain doubts to ally with others.

"At the inception, again, I had little doubt of Ritchie Bellowes's story. The police were fairly sure he was not guilty; there were too many physical objections to it—notably his paralysed left arm, which would have made it impossible for him to have strangled Rodney Kent. Again, he certainly was very drunk at two o'clock when he was found. If he had committed a murder at midnight, he would not have gone to sleep on a sofa outside his victim's door and waited to be found at two o'clock. Again, the weapon was missing. Again, there was a complete lack of motive. Finally, I was inclined to credit his story of the 'man in the hotel-attendant's uniform' simply because it was too preposterous not to be true. This is not merely a congenital sympathy with the preposterous. I mean that it was not the *sort* of story which would do a deliberate liar any good. If Bellowes were the murderer, he would try to shield himself with a lie; but presumably not a lie so (apparently) meaningless and unrelated to the whole affair. At first glance the story of the hotel-attendant had no point unless it were true. If he were a liar, he might say he had seen a burglar in the hall: but not that he had seen an Arctic explorer, a ballet-dancer, or a postman.

"Thus, when we first came to the hotel, I was inclined to believe the murderer was actually in the hotel. More specifically, that it was one of the guests on the seventh floor. Then two points appeared to trouble me very badly about this.

"First, the utter disappearance of that uniform. Where in blazes had it got to? It was not hidden, burnt, or tossed out of a window; we should have found it, or traces of it. If a guest wore it, how was it conveyed into limbo afterwards? You see, it amounted to that. You might say that a guest was in collusion with an employee of the hotel, and had borrowed a real uniform for use in the masquerade, to return it later. Even if this were true, how was it spirited out of Wing A? The only entrance to that wing was watched all night, and up until the time the police arrived, by the three men working on the lift. Was it dropped out of a window by the guest, to be picked up in Piccadilly or in the air-well by an employee in the conspiracy? This seemed unlikely; and yet the uniform was gone.

"Second, a circumstance which brought much light. Musing, it occurred to me that a door had been found strangely open. This was the spring-locked door of the linen-closet. Now, we had heard much of these varied new locks, which cannot be opened from the outside by any unauthorised person. The linen-closet was locked by the maid on the night before. It was found open in the morning. Therefore (and not unnaturally) ominous sideways glances were directed towards Mr. Hardwick, the manager.

"But my own mind is of a simpler nature. Nobody could have unlocked that door from outside. But anybody on earth can open a spring-lock from *inside*. You turn the little knob on the lock; and the thing is done. It therefore interested me to glance into the linen-closet. H'mf, ha. By the way, has anybody else here done that?"

Kent nodded.

"Yes. I looked in there when the superintendent sent me down to get

Melitta," he answered, with a vivid recollection of the place. "What about it?"

"Good," said Dr. Fell. "Now, at the beginning of the whole case, we brought up the various ways by which an outsider could have got in and out of the hotel without being seen by the men working on the lifts. These were (1) climbing up and down the face of the building into Piccadilly; (2) climbing up and down the face of the building from inside the air-well; (3) by means of the fire-escape outside the window at the end of the corridor. All these were ruled out as 'so unlikely as to be very nearly impossible.' There were obvious objections to *(a)* and *(b)*. As for *(c)*, this would have been a broad highway of entrance and exit—an obvious lead, a dazzler of an easy way—but for one apparently overpowering fact. The locked window guarding the fire-escape was stuck and could not be opened; hence a sad eye passed over *(c)*. But we looked into the linen-closet and got a shock. You," he turned to Kent, "looked in there on the morning after. What did you see?"

"A window," said Kent.

"Open or shut?"

"Open."

"H'mf, exactly. Since it would be a nuisance to take you back to the hotel in order to demonstrate this," pursued Dr. Fell, "we might just glance at the plan of Wing A. You see the window in the linen-closet. You also see that the commodious fire-escape outside comes within a foot—one foot—of the same window. A man would scarcely have to be a steeple-jack in order to stand on the fire-escape and climb in through the window.

"I stared. I saw. I was uneasy.

"For values had shifted backwards. Unless Hardwick or the maid had opened it, that linen-closet door could not have been unlocked from outside in the corridor: not by a guest, that is. And, if Hardwick or the maid opened it, they must first have got upstairs past the lift-workers: which they did not do. Therefore the linen-closet door was unlocked from inside the linen-closet itself, by the simple process of turning the knob. Therefore the murderer came into the linen-closet from outside. Therefore the murderer was (not to be too painfully repetitive about it), an outsider."

Dr. Fell put his large elbows on the table, seemed in danger of scratching his head with the lighted end of the cigar, and frowned at his coffee-cup.

"I hesitated, let me confess, on the brink of the deduction. I was not amused. Cases are not solved by one flying leap. The man who says, '*Only* this can be true; there can be no other explanation,' excites my admiration as much as he inspires my regret. But of the twelve major queries to be answered—the queries I propounded last night to Hadley and Christopher Kent—this theory would take care of two. These were (7), 'How did the murderer get into a locked linen-closet at the Royal Scarlet Hotel?', and (2) 'What happened to the costume afterwards?' The answers being, 'He came in from outside,' and 'He walked away in the uniform when he left the hotel.'

"But, if it might—might, you understand—be an outsider, what outsider? Our little coterie was all under this roof. Every person who had been at Four Doors on the night of the first tragedy, the night the uniformed figure had first been seen, was in the Royal Scarlet Hotel that night; and therefore segregated. Everybody— H'mf, well, not quite. Ritchie Bellowes was missing, for instance. And this for a good reason, since he was locked up at the police-station. In any case, he had never met Mrs. Josephine Kent—for she had not come to Northfield.

"This had been a fascinating query from the first: why did she rush away to riot in the home of her aunts? Why did she refuse to go to Northfield at any time, even after her husband had been murdered? We had then reason to suspect, and shortly afterwards reason to know, that she was not what she seemed. She had been in England for well over a year; she had returned to South Africa with a packet of money; but this visit she carefully concealed, and swore she had never been here before in her life. Why? Now note: she makes no real objection to travelling: she makes no objection to coming to London: she makes no objection to meeting people (such as Sir Gyles Gay, for example); but she will not *go to Northfield*. In a woman whose real character we were already beginning to see, that attack of 'utter nervous prostration' after her husband's death seemed to be overdoing it.

"This, then, was what one part of our simple minds registered. The other part of our minds registered still another question.

"As troublesome as the uniform was the murderer's consistent weakness for towels. Why, in the case of both murders, was a towel used to strangle the victim? As I pointed out to Hadley, it is assuredly a cumbersome and clumsy kind of attack, an unnatural kind of attack. Above all, it was unnecessary. The murderer assuredly did not use it for fear of leaving finger-prints: he would know what anybody knows, that you cannot leave finger-prints on human flesh, and that the marks of hands of a throat cannot be identified. We also know, from the universal lack of finger-prints on furniture or other surfaces, that the murderer must have worn gloves. We are therefore faced with the incredible spectacle of a murderer who uses *both* gloves and a towel to avoid leaving marks. And that will not do. We must look for another reason.

"Kindly note, to begin with, that Mrs. Kent was not strangled. No. She was put into the Iron Maiden trunk, and it was closed on her throat, with the towel wrapped round her throat so that the edges should not cut: so that it should leave bruises on the throat *like* strangulation. But why again, such a clumsy device? It would have been much simpler to have strangled her in the ordinary way, as (presumably) Rodney Kent had been strangled. This unnaturalness plus the unnaturalness of the towel began to make such a tower of inconsistencies that there must be method in them. What, offhand, would that Iron Maiden device suggest to you?

"Why, it would suggest that the murderer was of too weak strength for ordinary strangulation—or a person who had the full use of only one arm.

"The full use of only one arm, the right arm.

"What else? The body is propped inside the trunk. The trunk is supported and propped against the left leg; the right hand pulls it powerfully together against that support of the murderer's left leg, and the thing is done.

"But this did not square with the murderous two-handed grip which was used on Rodney Kent. It seemed to put the matter out of court as a fantastic suggestion, until I reflected dimly on the subject of Rodney Kent's murder. Hadley had already described the furniture in the Blue Room here at Four Doors. The matter was not a certainty until I came here and saw for myself, but I could envision the scene. I have seen furniture of a much similar type. Just recall the footboard of the bed. It is a heavy piece of work, pointed at the top and sloping down shallowly to a curve or round depression by the little posts. Thus."

He took up a pencil and drew rapidly on the back of an envelope.

"Like, you might say, the neck-piece or collar of a guillotine, in which the condemned man's neck lies. Rodney Kent was lying with his head almost touching the leg of the bed. Suppose the neck of an unconscious man has been put sideways into that homely guillotine. Suppose that neck were wrapped in a face-towel: not a bath-towel, which might be too thick and woolly to leave the proper sort of marks. Suppose the murderer stands over him; and, with one hand gripping one side of the neck, lets the other side be gripped by that broad curve of the wood, the victim's windpipe being pressed against the edge. When the murderer's work is finished—the marks being neatly blurred and made unrecognisable *as fingers* by the towel—you will have bruises in evidence of a crushing two-handed grip which went round both sides of his throat.

"Once might be coincidence. Twice could not be. It would explain the use of the towels. It would indicate that the murderer was a man who had the complete use of only one arm.

"Humph, hah! Well! I began to see the indications expanding like the house that Jack built, into (*a*) the murderer came from outside the Royal Scarlet Hotel; (*b*) he wore a uniform and went away in it; (*c*) he is, to all intents and purposes, one-armed. The only person who corresponded to this description was Ritchie Bellowes. The very thing which had so operated in his favour at first—namely, the partially paralysed left arm— was the thing which now rebounded against him. Everything began to rebound against him, once you considered. For, even if you still believed him to be ruled out as a suspect because he had been locked up at the police-station, the next connection was clear to any simple straightfor- ward mind: I mean the connection between police-stations and blue uniforms.

"This point I indicated a while ago. 'A short single-breasted blue coat high at the neck, silver buttons, shoulder epaulettes.' Ladies and gentle- men, you have seen that costume on the streets every day; if the connec- tion did not occur to you, it was because the prowling intruder was without any headcovering. If I wished (as I do not) to coin a bad riddle, I should cryptically inquire: When is a policeman not a policeman? And I should answer, amid universal groans, but quite sincerely: When he is without his helmet. This astonishing difference will have been noted by anyone who has ever gone to a trial and seen the police in court without their hats. Wearing their own hair, they are a different race. They look like attendants: as a matter of fact, in that capacity they *are* attendants.

"But to return. Ritchie Bellowes was locked up at the police-station. It was not reasonable to think that he said to his jailers: 'Hoy! Let me out of here and lend me a spare uniform, will you? I've got to go to London and commit a murder; but I'll be back later to-night."

"Nevertheless, we begin to reflect on one feature of national life—the village police-station. Like the village bank, it sometimes surprises observers. It is not a great grim temple of stone, erected in some city for the especial purpose of housing a hundred drunks overnight. No; it is an ordinary converted house (like the one at Northfield) such as you and I might live in. It has been taken over for the purpose of turning it into a police-station. But somebody had to build it. And, whispering back through the halls of consciousness, we hear the information that Ritchie Bellowes's father, the grand old man and 'character,' was a builder— who, as Hadley had informed me, had put up half the modern houses in the whole district.

"We heard of old Bellowes's taste for doing the work with his own hands. We heard in particular of his very particular sense of humour, much of which has been twisted and burnt to more ugly purposes into the soul of his son. We heard of the old man's fondness for tricks and gadgets and ingenious deceptions: in particular the trick door or passage. We heard of the 'greatest joke in the world' he was going to bequeath to the village. Since I share the same liking, I can have a radiant vision of what *would* seem a private joke of this kind: a joke of the ripest vintage: a use to which such a device, so far as I know, has never before been put: I mean, ladies and gentlemen, a trick door in the cells of a police-station."

Dr. Fell sat back, musing.

"Of course we have one precedent several thousand years old. You recall Herodotus's story of the sardonic builder who did the same sort of thing in King Rhampsinitus's treasure-house? But, with regard to young Ritchie Bellowes, observe one suggestive fact. This story he told—of the hotel-attendant seen at Four Doors at the time of Rodney Kent's murder—when did he tell that story first? Did he tell it immediately after he was nabbed on the night of the murder? Not at all. He only told it late next day, when he found himself in the police-station. Eh? Not only in the police-station, but in a particular cell of that place. Suppose he knew quite well that he could get out of that cell whenever he liked? Suppose he had badly bungled and ruined the first crime, for reasons I will indicate in a moment? But, if another crime is committed, he is now safe from suspicion. And so, with a hysterical cleverness I cannot help rather admiring—for adolescent hysteria, as you may have observed when we talked to him, was the keynote of his character—he told a certain story. . . .

"A story which, as Hadley said, was either delirium tremens or prophecy or truth. And, by thunder, but it was prophecy! Calmly considered, it was too prophetic. It not only put the cart before the horse: it set the cart running uphill without any horse to push it. Not only did he describe a hotel-attendant, but he actually and barefacedly gave the name of the hotel at which the attendant was employed. You recall: 'I should describe him as a medium-sized man wearing a uniform such as you see in the big hotels like the Royal Scarlet or the Royal Purple.'

"Of course this was necessary to implant the image in our minds. If it is definite to a nearly damning extent, it had to be; and he had, fortunately, his reputation as the camera-eye observer to sustain him. He had to turn a blue coat and silver (or brass) buttons—which might have meant anything, and to an innocent observer would probably have suggested something altogether different—into a concrete figure. Hence the salver. The meaning of the salver plunged me into a spiritual abyss until I had hit on Ritchie Bellowes's guilt. Naturally, it was merely an extra flourish to limn out and establish his picture; there never had been any such salver or any such figure. But I am afraid I am running ahead of the actual evidence. Incidentally Hadley, where did you find the trick entrance in the police-station?"

Hadley glanced round the table as though reluctant to speak of matters in mixed company. But he saw only interested faces: the refreshed alertness of Gay and Harvey Wrayburn, the heavy admiration of Dan Reaper, Melitta's surprising cheerfulness, and the blank absorption of Francine.

"Find it?" growled Hadley. "We've been finding nothing else all morning. There were three of 'em; and nobody ever knew. This is going to cause a number of smart remarks in the Press when it all comes out. Of course it wasn't quite as simple as it looked for Bellowes. The trick doors to the cells, you know, connected only with the cellar of the inspector's private house next door. He didn't have the run of the station. Consequently, though he could walk through the inspector's house and out of the place, he couldn't go—"

"Go where?" asked Gay.

"Where he really wanted to go," said Dr. Fell, "and needed to go. That is, up from the cells into the charge-room and waiting-rooms of the station itself. There were several barred doors, including that of his own cell, in between. Also, there were men on duty at inconvenient hours in that part of the station. It was a nasty knock because, to a man planning what he had planned, two things are vitally necessary. He needs clothes, and he needs money.

"Bellowes, as you know, was being charged with burglarious entry. Well, there are certain formalities attached to that. They had put away his money, they had put away his tobacco, they had put away his overcoat. All these things were safely locked up upstairs in the station, where he could not get at them, and he was naked without most of them. Do you begin to see? He could not return to his own lodgings in Northfield without exciting some curiosity on the part of the landlady. He could not wake up a friend in the middle of the night and ask to borrow a mackintosh or ten shillings for train-fare. He was either in jail or he wasn't: there could be no middle course: and he must *not* be seen. The only thing he could take for the night, without being detected, was a spare uniform from the inspector's place next door. He must take it, for, oh, Bacchus, he needed that uniform! You recall, when we talked to him in his cell, he was in his shirt-sleeves on not too warm a day. There was no sign of a coat or jacket or sweater in the cell, because he hadn't been wearing one when he was arrested. Now the cells were heated and warm enough for him to stay there without discomfort. But he couldn't walk about on a snowy January night without discomfort, to say nothing of the more vital necessity to attract no attention. Hence the inception of his rather brilliant triple-barrelled scheme of the uniform; first as covering, second as an excellent disguise, third as the phantom attendant at the Royal Scarlet. Between the night of January 14th, when Rodney Kent was murdered, and the night of the 31st, he had plenty of time to explore; and to prepare the ground. He knew what everyone else knew (as you shall see) that the whole party was going to the Royal Scarlet: that Mr. Reaper had specifically insisted on booking rooms in Wing A of the new seventh floor: that Josephine Kent was joining them there on a specified date—"

"But how could he have know it?" cried Francine.

"H'mf, wait. One moment. Finally, to kill small Josephine had become the deepest and strongest obsession of his life. You can guess the reason why."

"Well?"

"She was Ritchie Bellowes's lawfully wedded wife," said Dr. Fell. "But she could hardly be very garrulous about anything without admitting that she had committed bigamy."

Chapter XX

THE END OF THE STONE

"Once that tumbler falls into place," said Dr. Fell, "the safe-door opens by itself. You understand why she was so positive in pretending she had never been in England before. You understand why she was so anxious to keep away from Northfield, where she had previously lived. You understand why, though she knew quite well that Ritchie Bellowes had killed Rodney Kent, she had no intention of denouncing him or his motive. You understand why she was not unduly apprehensive about her own safety, since she thought Bellowes was in jail. And the hub of it is this: Josephine Parkes Bellowes was supposed by everyone except her husband to be dead. But I beg your pardon. I must give you the reasons which led us to think this."

Kent, at that moment, was remembering a face. He was remembering Ritchie Bellowes sitting on the edge of the bunk in the cell, fidgeting. Tall and thin and hollow-eyed, Bellowes seemed to look back at him now as he had looked back last night across a gravestone. But most of all Kent remembered an atmosphere and two gestures. The first gesture was that of Bellowes's fingers massaging the veined hand of his withered left arm. The second was Bellowes's suddenly stamping his foot on the floor, when there was addressed to him a question he did not like: stamping his foot on the floor of the cell like a child in a tantrum. It was an oddly revealing gesture like the whole atmosphere of this man who had never quite grown up.

"I have told you," said Dr. Fell, "reasons for believing in Bellowes's guilt and Josephine Kent's past connection, in some fashion, with Northfield. If we looked for a motive, it could only be in some relationship which had existed between this woman and Bellowes in the past. What, offhand, did we know about Bellowes himself? I knew from the beginning—Hadley told me—some pertinent things about his past history, and the sudden moral collapse of this well-to-do builder's son. He had been married, and his wife had 'died of typhoid at the seaside': a term which stirred my interest when I heard it. She did not die under the eyes of the Northfield villagers, then. In any case, from this time on began the abrupt disintegration of Bellowes into a thoughtful, polite, sober-pacing toper. Beware of such, my lads: especially when they go out to wintry copses to drink alone and 'recite' in the moonlight, as Bellowes admitted he did. But you will note that Bellowes's change was not merely one of stamina: it was a crashing financial collapse as well. One moment he was tolerably well off, and the next he was stony. It surprised people. In murder trials they are fond of quoting the Latin proverb. 'No one ever became suddenly the basest of men.' I will affirm that nobody ever became suddenly the brokest of men, unless there had been a snatching away of great proportions some where.

"And 'Miss Josephine Parkes' arrived back in Johannesburg from England with—Well, let us consider her and certain of her actions. On the evening she was murdered, the first evening she had ventured out from the shelter of her aunts, she was wearing a bracelet of an extraordinary sort. Nobody had ever seen it before. It seemed unlikely that she had got it in the country. To a simple mind it seemed much more likely that the bracelet was something out of her past life: something which, up to that time, she had carefully concealed. Why? Why bring it out now? She herself throws out hints which convince Miss Forbes that it had been given to her by someone she fears. She hints that she may be in danger, and that the bracelet is a safeguard against danger, because it contains a clue to the identity of the man she fears. To Miss Forbes she says 'If anything ever happens to me, which I don't anticipate, you shall have it.' Then she changes her mind, and in a fit of night-terrors she turns it over to Mr. Wrayburn with the words: '*You keep that for always. Then nobody will try to wake the dead.*'

"To wake the dead—

"That her fears were justified, and that the murderer also thought it was a danger to him, are indicated by his frantic ransacking of her hotel-room to find the bracelet: even to the extent of stealing another linked bracelet resembling it, in the ghost of a hope that it might be the right one in disguise. But I couldn't help thinking of Bellowes's 'dead' wife at the seaside. Was she dead? Or had she quietly kissed sad fingertips and slipped away with Bellowes's money in her pocket: leaving him to explain as best he could how he had been made a laughing-stock? That also was worth investigating."

Wrayburn made a wig-wagging gesture as though he were trying to stop a bus.

"Wait!" he urged. "What's the point of that damned bracelet anyhow? What's the secret?"

"I will deal with the bracelet," said Dr. Fell, "shortly. Here I feel inclined to tell you in a few words the facts, as we have got them now, of the Bellowes-Parkes marriage. Hadley got them this morning, from Ritchie Bellowes himself. He does not deny his guilt. Considering the evidence against him, I don't see how he could.

"He met her and married her after two weeks in London in March 1933. It was, perhaps, inevitable. She had come to England looking for fresh woods and pastures new; and she had failed. Her bluff of knowing Sir Gyles Gay, and of being put on to something good in the way of employment, had succeeded only in getting her an interview with him—"

"Thank you," said Gay gravely.

"It must have been a sore setback, for I think she had great confidence in herself. A man like Ritchie Bellowes was her obvious move. He was quiet, he was obscure, he was emotionally immature, he was idealistic, he was content to worship; and he was moderately well off, which could be useful. In short, I think you will find his outward semblance much like that of Rodney Kent. She married him in her real name; but she did not tell him she came from South Africa. If she should wish to change her plans later, it would be a snag to let herself be traced. So they married, and they went to Northfield, and she made him an excellent wife (admired by all for her devotion) for eight or nine months. But she could not stifle here; and besides, being an abstemious woman, she disliked his fondness for drink. At her suggestion, and as a sound business principle in case anything should happen to the somewhat shrunken business he had inherited from his father, most of his money had been transferred into her name. She went for a seaside holiday. Just before doing so, she withdrew six thousand eight hundred pounds in cash; she left him a gentle, reproachful letter; and she disappeared. Well, you cannot do that without running a man into debts he can't pay, and nearly everything he has got must be sold to meet them. But banks, you know, don't tell.

"And there is one thing you must not do to a man of Ritchie Bellowes's type: you must not make a fool of him.

"These facts, night before last, I did not know. But, suspecting that Bellowes would do anything else in the world before letting this be known, suspecting that he had gone to some trouble and frenzy to create a mythical 'death' for the benefit of the neighbours, we had new questions ahead. How would Ritchie Bellowes learn that 'Josephine Kent'—the attractive wife of a South African who was coming to visit Sir Gyles Gay—was in reality his own nimble lady? The photographs, of course.

"You, Sir Gyles, were not living in Northfield at the time Josephine Bellowes-Kent was in England. You lived in Norfolk, as you told me, and moved here when Bellowes was compelled to sell this house. (You observe, though, how it brings our dates into line with the departure of the lady out of England?) But you were well acquainted with Bellowes. He had been several times to see you here. You were full of the subject of your visitors. You showed him all the photographs, didn't you?"

"I did," said Gay grimly. "*And* I talked. He seemed interested."

"On the other hand, it was not likely that many people from Northfield would see these photographs, and have their curiosity roused by the strange reappearance of Mrs. Bellowes. By your own confession, people are kept away from you by your manner; though Bellowes—drawn here by the fondness for his old home—you made hearty friends with as you are willing to be friends with anybody. The servants, usually local people, would not stumble on anything; you brought them from Norfolk. But Bellowes could not risk anything. Sooner or later, he had to see that those unfortunate pictures were destroyed—for when she died there must be no picture of her in a newspaper.

"Unfortunately it was you—the night before last—who threw a sizable spanner into *our* machinery. Just before I went out to dinner with those two"—he glanced sadly at Francine and Kent—"I had a conference with Hadley. He had got his cable from South Africa and his information from South Africa House. It threw light on Mrs. Kent; but, by all the top-hats of hell, it also threw suspicion on you. My stride was interrupted by you. It was possible that my idea was as wild as wind; that one Sir Gyles Gay was the man in the case and the murderer at the Royal Scarlet Hotel. Harrumph. Heh. Hah. Therefore, Miss Forbes, when you said to me, 'Won't you tell us who is guilty so that we can sleep soundly,' or words to that effect, I had to—"

Francine sat up.

"Yes," she said, "I've been waiting to ask you about that. Why did you deliberately sit there and make out (partly, anyway) a case to show that Bellowes was innocent, and had been brought as a witness to Rod's murder—?"

"I don't think you understand," said Dr. Fell humbly. "I deliberately sat there, as you put it, and tried to make out the strongest case I could in favour of Bellowes, in order to convince both myself and you that he *must* be guilty. Particularly to convince myself."

"*What?*" said Kent. "Hold on! The paradoxes are coming a bit too—"

"It's not very complicated, is it? I prayed that you would knock holes in my case. An intelligent sneer would have been manna to me. But you didn't, worse luck. You see, I was quoting all the points which in my mind told against Bellowes—(1) his having a key to this house in his pocket, with deliberate intent beforehand; (2) his whisky-drinking to screw up his courage for the murder of Rodney Kent, which drinking made him foozle the job after all; (3) the fact that his finger-prints were in the Blue Room—and I was trying to see whether innocent explanations of them could be found. If Bellowes were *not* guilty, those facts had innocent explanations. I raked my wits to find 'em. For these innocent explanations did not satisfy me. I hoped you would say, 'Bosh,' as I felt b-o-s-h. I hoped you would say, 'Gideon, *mon vieux,* all this is the merest eyewash. Your facts damn Bellowes; your explanations do not exculpate him. Witness? Do you expect us to believe that a murderer is so fond of witnesses to his crime that he pays one to come in and watch it? In all your fog of words, where is the sense?' I should then have said, radiantly, 'Good. Excellent. That is what must be so.' But you didn't. You appeared to accept it. Perhaps you noticed my strange behaviour, which caused me to mop my forehead resolutely; and I went home, a most unusual thing, before it was time for the party to break up.

"I was particularly despondent because you, Miss Forbes, had almost burnt your fingers a moment before on just what I believed to be the reason for the masquerade in the blue uniform. I can hear you yet, 'That must mean,' you were saying, 'he was preparing everybody's mind for his appearance later, when he came to kill Jenny—but where is there any indication in just a coat and a pair of trousers?' I came close to uttering a cheer; I stimulated you with my fiery glance; but the light went out.

"For this is what I thought, and know now, had really happened—beginning with the first murder:

"Bellowes coolly determined to kill Rodney, in a quiet and workmanlike manner. There was to be no flourish of hotel-attendants. Bellowes had met all of your party at his memory-entertainment; he knew Rodney; it would be easy to find out which room Rodney occupied. By the way, he made one more hideous slip when he told me an unnecessary lie at the police-station: Bellowes told me that he (the memory-expert) couldn't remember a single feature of Rodney's face. And his motive? You, Miss Forbes, told me about that at our celebrated dinner. It was believed by many people—and well known to Sir Gyles here, who liked to joke about it—that Rodney Kent had married Josephine for her money. Her money? Ritchie Bellowes's money. You must not tamper with men of Bellowes's kind. I can imagine him looking at the colourless figure of Rodney, the pleasant and colourless Rodney; and I can imagine the inside of his mind turning black with pure hate. Conjure up before you a picture of Bellowes's face, and you will see what I mean.

"But the murder was to be a workmanlike job. It was to be a murder by 'strangling,' since Bellowes's arm is paralysed and he can strangle nobody. He had had a long time to think about it, you know. Did he know about the useful furniture in the Blue Room, which would enable him to do it? Of course he knew about it; that furniture was there in his father's time, and Sir Gyles Gay must have bought it with the house; Bellowes told us so himself.

"Bellowes left the pub at ten o'clock, with just the right amount inside to steady himself, and a bottle of whisky to keep him at it. He waited until the household at Four Doors had gone to bed at about midnight. He allowed a few minutes more, and then let himself into the house with his key. He went upstairs quietly. He was then wearing gloves; he was carrying a life-preserver in his pocket, and a poker under his overcoat, supported by his more-or-less useless left arm. He went into Rodney's room. Rodney, just retiring, would be surprised to see him; but not startled or alarmed. Any excuse for his presence would suffice. He distracts Rodney's attention, and knocks him unconscious with the life-preserver. Then he does what has to be done.

"Afterwards (at, say, about twenty minutes past twelve) he slips downstairs. His work in the house is not finished. He goes to—why, the study, of course, where his father's old-fashioned furniture remains in the house exactly as it remains in the Blue Room upstairs. He opens—the locked drawer of the desk, certainly, with the paternal keys he has kept as he has kept everything else he can. Who else could have opened that (admittedly, by Gay) elaborate lock? That is where he knows he will find the photographs.

"The whole scheme is arranged. Josephine is to go next. In fact, he has already written to her, announcing coolly that he will do this; for he knows it is one letter she will never dare show to anyone. (You recall, she received two letters postmarked Northfield, one from her husband and the writer of the other unknown?) She replied to this. She replied with equal coolness that he had better not try any tricks, for if anything happens to her she still has a bracelet which will hang him. Hence the reappearance of the bracelet. Meantime, Bellowes will give a turn of the screw to her feelings by killing her bigamous husband, Rodney; still knowing that she will not dare to speak.

"After the murder of Rodney, then, Bellowes crept down to the study. He closed the curtains and turned on one small lamp. It will interest you to know what we heard this morning, the place he had chosen to hide his murder-properties—the poker, the life-preserver, the gloves, the key to the desk, and so on—until he should need them again. Well, they were actually in the desk all the time. They were in a false compartment at the back of it, another of the devices of his father. It was the best of all hiding-places for them: if by any remote chances they were found, they would only serve to incriminate Sir Gyles or some member of the party.

"After stowing them away, he proceeded systematically to tear to pieces every photograph in the desk drawer, Sir Gyles's own as well. But a new idea occurred to him. I told you this man could never be satisfied

with anything. I told you he could never let well-enough alone; and that is
what betrayed him. The only photograph he did not destroy was the big
group one, the slide at the fun-fair—"

Gay interposed.

"There is another question here," he said. "I suppose he kept that
picture because he could use it as a threat against Mrs. Kent without ever
leaving behind a view of her face. But how did he know it *was* Mrs. Kent
in the photograph? I imagine I must have shown him the picture, at one
time or another; but I didn't learn who it was until you people had actually
arrived here—"

"The memory-test!" said Francine.

"I beg your pardon?"

"That's it," agreed Dan, opening his eyes. "Damnation! I've been
trying to remember just where I'd seen that picture recently. We were
both trying to remember it yesterday. The memory-test, of course. When
Bellowes gave his demonstration, I mean. One of the inevitable tests is to
shove a photograph under somebody's nose, a group photograph with lots
of details, and ask him to quote the smallest detail after one look. We
used that picture! And somebody remarked that the unseen figure was
Jenny. All right. Go on."

"The sight of the bottles of coloured inks," resumed Dr. Fell obediently, "put into his head the idea of writing, 'There is one more to go,' and
of putting it beside his first victim. He did write it. But he rejected the
idea as much too dangerous. He wanted the woman to know she was in
danger. But he didn't want anybody else to know it. So he sat there by the
desk in the middle of the night, puzzling the matter through his little
brain—and at the same time (now his job was finished) gulping down
steady pulls at a bottle of neat whisky.

Wrayburn stared. "You mean, with a dead body upstairs, he sat as cool
as anything in somebody else's house—"

"You forget," said Dr. Fell, "that he wasn't in somebody else's house.
That's the keynote to the whole affair. He was in his own house, the only
place familiar to him. The others were interlopers, whom he hated. And,
instead of hurrying out of the house, the fool proceeded to get drunk. As
you might have guessed, the more he took the more indecisive he
became, the more uncertain; for he could *not* let well-enough alone. Was
everything all right upstairs? Was there anything he had omitted? It was
Ritchie Bellowes's form of self-torture. And, when he was three parts
gone, he had to see. He left the photograph in the desk. He went upstairs
in the dark, with no glove on his hand and hardly a thought of precaution
in his head. Scarcely in a condition to see, he opened the door of the Blue
Room wide—as it was found—and proceeded to leave finger-prints by
turning on the light. He had enough sense left to realise that he had been a

fool; but it was too late. He had no sooner turned out the light and gone out (in the moonlight) when you, Mr. Reaper, opened your own door. He couldn't run; he could barely walk. So he did the instinctive thing. He tumbled down on a sofa and pretended to a stupor which was only half pretence.

"That, in the wrecking of the plan, was the story of the first crime and the reason for the second.

"I have told you how, out of necessity and his own cunning, he got the scheme for the second. He was going to kill Josephine at the Royal Scarlet, and he was going to be an 'attendant' in uniform; hence his story. He knew you were all going to the Royal Scarlet, he knew about the new top floor, he even knew the date: heaven knows you all talked enough about it. Then you altered the date, and went one day earlier; a piece of information which was kindly passed along to him by Inspector Tanner in Tanner's daily questionings.

"They lock up the cell-row for the night at nine-thirty. Before a quarter to ten he was out of jail, dressed, in one of those pitch-black village nights where nobody would have noticed him even if he had been seen. If he were going to London, as I told you, he would need money. But nothing could be simpler. He still had his key to Four Doors. There was nobody here except servants. In the drawer of the study desk, as he knew from his visit two weeks before, there was a purse containing at least enough money to pay his bus-and-train fare to town.

"And, of course, he had to come here to get his invaluable poker as well. . . .

"Hence the mysterious theft of loose change. With good connections by train and bus, the time from here to town is an hour and ten minutes. This would get him to Charing Cross at just gone eleven. A bus to the hotel, the poker wrapped in a newspaper; now (invaluable!) the status of his police uniform, which is not only a passport anywhere, but will allow him—unsuspected—to question car-starters or outside-porters about where fire-escapes lead; and within fifteen minutes he is on the fire-escape outside the corridor of Wing A in time to see your party return from the theatre.

"He had to wait until the departure of the maid before he could get into the linen-closet through the window. But even then, he waited until midnight before he attacked: why? Because he was patiently waiting for someone to *see* him. With his cap off, he was now disguised; he was transformed into an employee. He mustn't be seen by a real employee, of course, which will blow the gaff immediately. But he wants a guest to catch a glimpse of him—and they obstinately remain in their rooms. The linen-closet will be his refuge if anyone should come too near. It was lucky for him, however, that he did not attack. Wrayburn was in the woman's room, though he couldn't tell that because Wrayburn had entered and left by the side door to 707; and, as it was, they narrowly missed each other.

"They would have missed each other by a still narrower margin if Mrs. Kent had not prudently waited a couple of minutes to make sure the coast was clear before she opened the door to the attendant, who murmured, 'Extra towels, madam.' She was not afraid then. Her attacks of tremors had passed; Bellowes was safely under lock and key; and Wrayburn was within call. In this brief interval you, Mr. Reaper, glanced out to set your watch. If you had looked a second longer, you would have seen an attendant walk into 707 with the towels—and he wouldn't have minded if you had. In fact, it was what he was hoping for. He posed for you.

"Mrs. Kent, with a comforted heart, opens the door to a mound of towels. She says, 'Yes?' He gets just across the threshold and lowers the towels, and she has one good glimpse of his face before he does what has to be done. He couldn't catch her on the back of the head as he had caught Rodney. She knew him.

"But, above all things, he must find that bracelet. It will require, as we decided before, an intensive search of the room. To keep himself secure against interruption, he hastily puts a pair of shoes (or what he thought to be one) outside, and hangs the 'quiet' notice on the door. He is wearing the same old gloves he used for Rodney's murder. But he can't find the bracelet! He comes across the key to the room, and he pockets all the loose change in her handbag; he is not (he will now point out to you, somewhat frenziedly) a thief, and he doesn't want any other money. But still he can't find any bracelet except Mrs. Jopley-Dunne's. Do you know what he did with that bracelet later, by the way? He threw it down a drain out of sheer spite, proving that there are vagaries to the character of even the most altruistic murderer.

"Next observe how the technique of this crime is exactly like the first. Again, though with better reason this time, he cannot let well-enough alone. He is convinced that the right bracelet isn't anywhere in the room. Yet he is nearly wild with indecision. Once he actually does leave the room—and takes the key to 707 with him—because he knows he's going only as far as that linen-closet; and he will come back. He wavers exactly as he wavered here. Yet he can't delay too long, or he will miss the last train back. Back he goes to that room for one last look. The little devil has tricked him, even if she's dead. Where in the name of Satan is that bracelet? In the same kind of jeer at her as he had thought of once before, he takes the 'quiet' sign off the door, he scrawls 'Dead Woman' on it with a pen he has found in the trunk. Leaving the key in the door, he goes at last."

Dr. Fell drew a deep, wheezing breath, and put down his dead cigar.

"Well, you can guess our plan of campaign. If our views about Bellowes were correct, we already had enough evidence to convict him. But he would be damned beyond excuse if we could once more entice him to come out in that uniform. I had to handle him warily when I spoke to him at the police-station; I wouldn't let Hadley get in a question edgeways. It was all the worse because Bellowes was in a bad state of nerves: he hadn't had a drink in two weeks, and he really was in a state of enforced sobriety as great as though he had been locked up there beyond any getting out. You see, he couldn't get out except at night when the watch was withdrawn; and, by the time he could reach a pub where he wouldn't be recognised, our beautiful licensing hours had closed the pubs.

"I gave him firmly to understand I believed in his innocence. I outlined to him my bogus theory of himself as a 'witness.' He was so surprised at the novel idea that for a minute he was thrown off balance, and couldn't play up to it; believe me, I cursed in my sleeve at that. By the time he was tentatively agreeing to it, it was too late. What I had to do was bring the missing bracelet into the conversation somehow, without exciting suspicion. I finally got round it by the wild expedient of suggesting that the 'phantom attendant' had been carrying something on a salver at Four Doors. I couldn't go further without making the thing apparent. When we were leaving, you recall, I went back and spoke to him. I said that we had found a piece of evidence which the late Mrs. Kent had said would be important, a bracelet: I described it: I asked him if it might have been in the possession of the blue-coated phantom. He said no. I said, with a thoughtful shrug of my shoulders (which could, I fear, only be measured with a seismograph) that we were sending it for expert inspection, and showing it about to a few persons: I said Miss Forbes was keeping it for us.

"I believed, you see, that he would be fool enough and in a bad enough state of nerves to have one more go at that bracelet, and wouldn't hesitate if he thought he was dealing with a woman. He didn't hesitate. But the plan nearly miscarried. Everything was all right—we were going to let him get into Four Doors, let him pinch the bracelet, and catch him with it coming out—as we saw it. I assure you (cease this uproar) that Miss Forbes was in no danger: there were two men in her bedroom, although she didn't know it, and would have been at him if he had come within two yards of her. Things went well until Bellowes, who knew Hadley and I were staying at the pub, came close to reconnoitre on his way down. Hadley (quite naturally, in that dead blackness) mistook him for Tanner. And Bellowes couldn't run again. From what Hadley said, he knew the game was up. The only question was what he should do about it. I think he pondered it very carefully in his usual quiet style. After reflection he decided that, since he was going to be caught, he would simply take somebody with him; and he was not particular who. When the real Tanner turned up at the pub ten minutes later, your humble undersigned turned suddenly ill. That there was no casualty was not our fault. I salute your courage, sir; I congratulate your future wife; and I think that's all."

They looked at each other, and Wrayburn smote the table.

"No, by the gods, it's not all," said Wrayburn. "What about that bracelet? Where is the secret writing on the bracelet or the acrostic or whatever it is? I've made a fairly extensive study of puzzles; but I can't make head or tail of it."

"The secret," said Dr. Fell, "is that there is no secret writing."

"But there's got to be! You've quoted what Jenny said to me. What about the things she told Francine, particularly: 'Has the inscription any meaning?' 'Only if you're able to read it; that's the whole secret.' "

Dr. Fell chuckled.

"She was quite right, correctly and literally right. I am not here referring to one fact which does not concern us: namely, that originally there was an inscription 'J.P. from R.B.' engraved on the inside, which she had had removed some time ago. Bellowes, of course, thought it was still on there, covered over in some way. The real secret is something quite different. Josephine thought it was quite sufficient to damn Bellowes, if it were found, and she was right. There were only two of those black stones—originally belonging to Bellowes's father—and set in rings. Ritchie had one of them put into a bracelet for her, keeping the other himself. Many people had seen them; and the secret was so curious that it would be remembered. Do you know what the secret was? It lies in two words, a description not of the jewel itself, but of the device which that jewel represented."

"Well, what was it?'

"It was a sober-stone," said Dr. Fell.

After a pause Wrayburn struck the table more softly. "Of course," he said. "By Xenophon's ten thousand, of course! Why didn't I ever think of it? To wear a sober-stone ring was the mark of the well-bred Roman at banquets. Suetonius is very serious about it." He grew excited. "Hang it, it's such a good and practical device that it ought to be revived to-day. The sober-stone was a semi-precious jewel of any kind on the flat surface of which could be engraved a few lines of writing. Some good text: this one was especially applicable, and in clear but small print. The noble Roman began drinking at a banquet, and from time to time he consulted his ring. Whenever he could not clearly read the text written on it, he knew he had got over the line of being sober and that it was time to stop.

'*Claudite jam rivos, pueri, sat prata biberunt.*' 'Stop singing; enjoyment has been taken.' And, 'Only if you can read it; that's the whole secret.' Oh, my *eye!*"

"Exactly," said Dr. Fell with benevolet placidness, "though the device, far from commending itself to me, is so conscientious that it makes my flesh creep. The interesting point is that Ritchie Bellowes gave it to her. They plighted their troth to each other with the stones. It was her good influence, you know, her sweetness and light, which turned Bellowes from a potentially sound and likeable man into a murderer with a fixed idea. I don't think I blame him, morally."

Dan Reaper drew a deep breath. "All I've got to say is," he declared, "that I wouldn't go through that again for—well, for a lot of money. I didn't know what to think. Half the time—"

"Whom did you suspect, my dear?" asked Melitta placidly.

They all started a little, and looked at each other. It was the letting out of a secret, a releasing of tension, which made them all sit back with a jerk. And then, gradually, a shame-faced grin appeared on several faces.

"Yes," said Wrayburn. "Let's have it. Who?"

"I suspected *you*, you cuss," Dan told him with some violence. "Maybe I had been reading too many of Chris's tomfool ideas. But, since you had a cast-iron alibi and were ruled out of it practically from the start after having been once suspected—well, it looked funny. Sorry about my rotten manners—"

"Oh, that's all right. Here, what about another glass of wine? To tell you the truth, I should have voted for our good host—"

"The notion," agreed Gay, "seems to have occurred to several persons. For myself, since frankness seems not to be resented, I first favoured Mr. Kent there. But I very quickly shifted to Miss Forbes—"

"Me?"

"Especially since," insisted Gay, "it was you who were prowling about in the study yesterday, just before I found that long-lost photograph in the desk. I saw you closing the door at the top of the stairs—"

"But I was only looking in there to see what had happened to everybody! I never even thought of it afterwards."

"—and, when I saw the police had a man following you," pursued Gay, "I was sure of it. I should have been very sorry. You observe that I shielded you. Have you any views, Mrs. Reaper?"

Melitta, almost beaming, had already wound herself up. "Well, of course, I shouldn't like to venture any opinion, but I felt sure my husband must have something to do with it. I do not say, mind you, that he is any worse than other men; but then that is what other men do, and I have felt most horribly unhappy about it. As my grandfather used—"

"So now I'm guilty," said Dan. "Well, you're luckier, old girl. With Chris's case against the hotel-manager, that makes a pretty big round, and you're the only one who has escaped suspicion."

"No, she hasn't," Kent pointed out. "Melitta has been suspected by Francine here—"

Francine looked at him sadly. She said: "Chris, you didn't really believe that?" and she stared at him in genuine perplexity.

"Believe it? Why, you told me yourself—"

"Chris, you are a blockhead! Of course I thought it was you. Why do you think I've been acting like such a harridan? I thought you were carrying on with her. I always thought so. That's why I was so terribly anxious to get that bracelet and find out if it concerned you. And at the restaurant, and afterwards much harder in the taxi, I was trying and trying to get you to tell me if you had killed her by saying it might be Melitta—"

Kent stared round.

"Let me understand this," he said. "Things have come to a fine pass. You don't know what people are thinking even when they tell you. What do you call that?"

From the head of the table Dr. Fell put down his glass and spoke.

"I call it," he said, "a detective story."

THE CROOKED HINGE

I

Wednesday,
July 29th

THE DEATH OF A MAN

The first rule to be borne in mind by the aspirant is this: Never tell your audience beforehand what you are going to do. If you do so, you at once give their vigilance the direction which it is most necessary to avoid, and increase tenfold the chances of detection. We will give an illustration.
— *PROFESSOR HOFFMANN, Modern Magic*

Chapter I

At a window overlooking a garden in Kent, Brian Page sat amid a clutter of open books at the writing-table, and felt a strong distaste for work. Through both windows the late July sunlight turned the floor of the room to gold. The somnolent heat brought out an odour of old wood and old books. A wasp hovered in from the apple-orchard behind the garden; and Page waved it out without much animation.

Beyond his garden wall, past the inn of the *Bull and Butcher,* the road wound for some quarter of a mile between orchards. It passed the gates of Farnleigh Close, whose thin clusters of chimneys Page could see above rifts in the trees, and then ascended past the wood poetically known as Hanging Chart.

The pale green and brown of the flat Kentish lands, which rarely acquired a harsh colour, now blazed. Page imagined that there was even colour in the brick chimneys of the Close. And along the road from the Close Mr. Nathaniel Burrows's car was moving with a noise audible for some distance, even if it was not moving fast.

There was, Brian Page thought lazily, almost too much excitement in Mallingford village. If the statement sounded too wild for belief, it could be proved. Only last summer there had been the murder of buxom Miss Daly, strangled by a tramp who had been dramatically killed while trying to get away across the railway-line. Then, in this last week of July, there had been two strangers putting up at the *Bull and Butcher* on successive days: one stranger who was an artist and the other who might be—nobody knew how this whisper got started—a detective.

Finally, there had been today the mysterious running to and fro of Page's friend Nathaniel Burrows, the solicitor from Maidstone. There seemed to be some general excitement or uneasiness at Farnleigh Close, though nobody knew what it meant. It was Brian Page's custom to knock off work at noon, and go over to the *Bull and Butcher* for a pint of beer before lunch; but it was an ominous sign that there had been no gossip at the inn that morning.

Yawning, Page pushed a few books aside. He wondered idly what could stir up Farnleigh Close, which had seldom been stirred up since

Inigo Jones built it for the first baronet in the reign of James the First. It had known a long line of Farnleighs: a stringy, hardy line still. Sir John Farnleigh, the present holder of the baronetcy of Mallingford and Soane, had inherited a substantial fortune as well as a sound demesne.

Page liked both the dark, rather jumpy John Farnleigh and his forthright wife, Molly. The life here suited Farnleigh well; he fitted; he was a born squire, in spite of having been so long away from his home. For Farnleigh's story was another of those romantic tales which interested Page and which now seemed so difficult to reconcile with the solid, almost common-place baronet at Farnleigh Close. From his first voyage out to his marriage to Molly Bishop little more than a year ago, it was (thought Page) another advertisement for the excitements of Mallingford village.

Grinning and yawning again, Page took up his pen. Got to get to work. Oh, Lord.

He considered the pamphlet at his elbow. His "Lives of the Chief Justices of England"—which he was trying to make both scholarly and popular—was going as well as might be expected. He was now dealing with Sir Matthew Hale. All sorts of external matters were always creeping in, because they had to creep in and because Brian Page had no wish to keep them out.

To tell the truth, he never really expected to finish the "Lives of the Chief Justices," any more than he had finished his original law-studies. He was too indolent for real scholarship, yet too restless-minded and intellectually alert to let it alone. It did not matter whether he ever finished the Chief Justices. But he could tell himself sternly that he ought to be working, and then with a sense of relief go wandering down all sorts of fascinating bypaths of the subject.

The pamphlet beside him read, *A Tryal of Witches at the Assizes Held at Bury St. Edmonds for the County of Suffolk, on the Tenth Day of March, 1664, before Sir Matthew Hale, K^t, then Lord Chief Baron of his Majesty's Court of Exchequer: printed for D. Brown, J. Walthoe, and M. Wotton, 1718.*

There was a bypath down which he had wandered before. Sir Matthew Hale's connection with witches, of course, was of the slightest. But it would not prevent Brian Page from writing a superfluous half-chapter on any subject which happened to interest him. With a breath of pleasure he took down a well-worn Glanvill from one of the shelves. He was just beginning to muse over it when he heard footsteps in the garden, and somebody "oi'd" at him from outside the window.

It was Nathaniel Burrows, swinging a brief-case with unsolicitor-like gestures.

"Busy?" demanded Burrows.

"We-el," Page admitted, and yawned. He put down Glanvill. "Come in and have a cigarette."

Burrows opened the glass door giving on the garden and stepped into the dim, comfortable room. Though he held himself well in hand, he was excited enough to look chilly and rather pale on a hot afternoon. His father, grandfather, and great-grandfather had handled the legal affairs of the Farnleighs. Sometimes it might have been doubted whether Nathaniel Burrows, with his enthusiasms and occasional explosive speech, was the proper person for a family lawyer. Also, he was young. But as a rule he had all these things under control; and managed, Page thought, to look more frozen-faced than a halibut on a slab.

Burrows's dark hair had a wide parting, and was smoothed round his head with great nicety. He wore shell-rimmed spectacles on a long nose; he was peering over the spectacles, and his face at the moment seemed to have more than the usual number of muscles. He was dressed in black with great nicety and discomfort; his gloved hands were clasped on the brief-case.

"Brian," he said, "are you dining in tonight?"

"Yes. I—"

"Don't," said Burrows abruptly.

Page blinked.

"You're dining with the Farnleighs," Burrows went on. "At least, I don't care whether you dine there; but I should prefer that you were there when a certain thing happens." Something of his official manner came back to him, and swelled his thin chest. "I am authorized to tell you what I am going to tell you. Fortunately. Tell me: did you ever have reason to think that Sir John Farnleigh was not what he seemed?"

"Not what he seemed?"

"That Sir John Farnleigh," explained Burrows carefully, "was an impostor and a masquerader, not Sir John Farnleigh at all?"

"Have you got sunstroke?" asked the other, sitting up. He felt startled and irritated and unwarrantably stirred up. It was not the sort of thing to spring on a person at the laziest period of a hot day. "Certainly I never had reason to think any such thing. Why should I? What the devil are you getting at?"

Nathaniel Burrows got up from the chair, depositing the brief-case there.

"I say that," he answered, "because a man has turned up who claims to be the real John Farnleigh. This isn't a new thing. It's been going on for several months, and now it's come to a head. Er—" He hesitated, and looked round. "Is there anybody else here? Mrs. What's-her-name—you know, the woman who does for you—or anyone?"

"No."

Burrows spoke as though entirely through the front of his mouth and teeth. "I shouldn't be telling you this. But I know I can trust you; and (between ourselves) I am in a delicate position. This is going to make trouble. The Tichborne case won't be a patch on it. Of course—er—officially, as yet, I have no reason to believe that the man whose affairs I administer isn't Sir John Farnleigh. I am supposed to serve Sir John Farnleigh: the proper one. But that is the point. Here are two men. One is the real baronet and the other is a masquerading fraud. The two men are not alike; they don't even *look* alike. And yet may I be damned if I can decide which is which." He paused, and then added: "Fortunately, though, the affair may be settled tonight."

Page had to adjust his thoughts. Pushing the cigarette-box across to his guest, he lit a cigarette for himself and studied Burrows.

"This is one clap of thunder after another," he said. "What started it, anyhow? When has there been any reason to suppose that an impostor stepped in? Has the question ever come up before now?"

"Never. And you'll see why." Burrows got out a handkerchief, mopped his face all over with great care, and settled down calmly. "I only hope it's a mare's nest. I like John and Molly—sorry, Sir John and Lady Farnleigh—I like them enormously. If this claimant is an impostor, I'll dance on the village green—well, maybe not that, perhaps—but I shall make it my business to see that he gets a prison sentence for perjury longer than Arthur Orton's was. In the meantime, since you're going to hear about it tonight, you'd better know the background of the whole thing, and why the infernal mess has come up. Do you know Sir John's story?"

"In a vague general way."

"You should know nothing in a vague general way," retorted Burrows, shaking his head disapprovingly. "Is that the way you write your history? I hope not. Listen to me; and keep these simple facts firmly fixed in your mind.

"We are going back twenty-five years, when the present Sir John Farnleigh was fifteen. He was born in 1898, the second son of old Sir Dudley and Lady Farnleigh. There was no question then of his inheriting the title: the elder son, Dudley, was his parents' pride and joy.

"And they required something noble in the way of sons. Old Sir Dudley (I knew him all my life) was a late-Victorian of the most rigid sort. He wasn't as bad as the romances paint such types nowadays; but I remember as a kid that it always surprised me when he gave me a sixpence.

"Young Dudley was a good boy. John wasn't. He was a dark, quiet, wild sort of boy, but with so much sullenness that nobody could pardon the least offensive things he did. There was no real harm in him; it was merely that he didn't fit and wanted to be treated as a grown-up before he had grown up. In nineteen-twelve, when he was fifteen, he had a fully-grown-up affair with a barmaid in Maidstone—"

Page whistled. He glanced out of the window, as though he expected to see Farnleigh himself.

"At fifteen?" Page said. "Here, he must have been a lad!"

"He was."

Page hesitated. "And yet, you know, I'd always thought from what I've seen of him that Farnleigh was—"

"A bit of a Puritan?" supplied Burrows. "Yes. Anyhow, we're talking about a boy aged fifteen. His studying occult matters, including witchcraft and Satanism, was bad enough. His being expelled from Eton was worse. But the public scandal with the barmaid, who thought she was going to have a child, finished it. Sir Dudley Farnleigh simply decided that the boy was bad clean through, some throwback to the Satanist Farnleighs: that nothing would ever change him: and that he did not care to see him again. The usual course was adopted. Lady Farnleigh had a cousin in America, who was doing well there, and John was packed off to the States.

"The only person who seemed able to manage him at all was a tutor named Kennet Murray. The tutor, then a young fellow of twenty-two or three, had come to Farnleigh Close after John left school. Kennet Murray's hobby, it is important to mention, was scientific criminology: which was what drew the boy to Murray from the beginning. It wasn't a genteel hobby in those days; but old Sir Dudley liked and approved of Murray, so not much more was said.

"Now at this time, it happened, Murray had just been offered a good position as assistant headmaster of a school in Hamilton, Bermuda—provided he cared to go so far away from home. He accepted; his services were no longer required at the Close, anyway. It was arranged that Murray should travel out with the boy to New York, to see that he kept out of trouble. He should hand over the boy to Lady Farnleigh's cousin, and then take another ship down to Bermuda."

Nathaniel Burrows paused, considering the past.

"I don't remember much about those days, speaking personally," he added. "We younger children were kept away from the wicked John. But little Molly Bishop, who was then only six or seven years old, was frantically devoted to him. She wouldn't hear a word against him; and it may be significant that she has since married him. It seems to me I vaguely remember the day John was driven to the railway-station, in a phaeton, wearing a flat straw hat, with Kennet Murray beside him. They were sailing next day, which was a gala day for more reasons than one. I don't need to tell you that the ship they took was the *Titanic*."

Both Burrows and Page now looked at the past. The latter remembered it as a confused time of shoutings, and newspaper-bills at the corners, and legends without foundation.

"The unsinkable *Titanic* rammed an iceberg and sank on the night of April 15th, nineteen-twelve," Burrows went on. "In the confusion Murray and the boy were separated. Murray drifted for eighteen hours in icy water, holding to a wooden grating with two or three others. They were presently picked up by a cargo-boat, the *Colophon*—bound for Bermuda. Murray was taken to the place he meant to go. But he did not worry any longer when he heard by wireless that John Farnleigh was safe, and later got a letter confirming it.

"John Farnleigh, or a boy purporting to be John, was picked up by the *Etrusca,* bound for New York. There Lady Farnleigh's cousin, a Westerner, met him. The situation was exactly as it had been before. Beyond making sure the boy was alive, Sir Dudley was still quit of him. And old Sir Dudley wasn't any more bitter than the boy himself.

"He grew up in America, and lived there for nearly twenty-five years. He wouldn't write a line to his people; he would see them dead before he sent a photograph or a birthday message. Fortunately he took an immediate liking to the American cousin, a man named Renwick, and that supplied the need of parents. He—er—seemed to change. He lived quietly as a farmer on broad acres, just as he might have lived here. During the latter years of the war he served with the American army, but he never once set foot in England or met any of the people he had known. He never even saw Murray again. Murray was existing, though not prospering, in Bermuda. Neither could afford a journey to visit the other, especially as John Farnleigh lived in Colorado.

"Back here at home nothing was disturbed. The boy had been practically forgotten; and, after his mother died in nineteen twenty-six, he was completely forgotten. The father followed her four years later. Young Dudley—he was not so young now—inherited the title and all the estate. He had never married; he said there was time enough for that. But there wasn't. The new Sir Dudley died of ptomaine poisoning in August, nineteen thirty-five."

Brian Page reflected.

"That was just before I came here," Page observed. "But look here! Didn't Dudley try to get in touch with his brother at any time?"

"Yes. The letters were returned unopened. Dudley had been—well, rather a prig in the old days. By this time they had grown so far apart that apparently John didn't feel any family relationship. However, when it became a question of John's inheriting the title and the estate at Dudley's death—"

"John accepted."

"He accepted. Yes. That's the point," said Burrows explosively. "You know him and you understand. Nothing seemed so *right* as his coming back here. It didn't even seem strange to him, though he'd been away for nearly twenty-five years. He didn't seem strange: he still thought and acted and to a certain extent talked like the heir of Farnleigh. He came here at the beginning of nineteen thirty-six. As an additional romantic touch, he met a grown-up Molly Bishop and married her in May of the same year. He settles in for a little over a year; and now this happens. This happens."

"I suppose the suggestion is," said Page with some uncertainty, "that there was a substitution of identities at the time of the *Titanic* disaster? That the wrong boy was picked up at sea, and for some reason pretended to be John Farnleigh?"

Burrows had been walking up and down with measured slowness, wagging his finger at any piece of furniture he passed. But he did not look comic. There was about him an intellectual strength which soothed or even hypnotized clients. He had a trick of turning his head sideways and peering at a companion past the sides of his big spectacles, as he did now.

"That's exactly it. Exactly. If the present John Farnleigh has been playing an imposture, don't you see, he has been playing it since nineteen-twelve—while the real heir lay low? He has grown into it. When he was rescued from the lifeboat after the wreck he wore Farnleigh's clothes and ring; he carried Farnleigh's diary. He has been exposed to the reminiscences of his Uncle Renwick in America. He has come back and settled into old ways. And twenty-five years! Handwritings change; faces and marks alter; even memories become uncertain. Do you see the difficulty? If sometimes he makes a slip, if there are gaps or clouds anywhere, that's only natural. Isn't it?"

Page shook his head.

"All the same, my lad, this claimant has got to have a thundering good case to gain any credence. You know what the courts are like. What sort of case *has* he got?"

"The claimant," answered Burrows, folding his arms, "offers absolute proof that he is the real Sir John Farnleigh."

"Have you seen this proof?"

"We are to see it—or not to see it—tonight. The claimant asks for an opportunity to meet the present holder. No, Brian: I am not in the least simple-minded, although I have nearly gone mad over this affair. It is not merely that the claimant's story is convincing, and that he offers all the minor proofs. It is not merely that he walked into my office (with, I regret to tell you, a bounder who is his legal representative) and told me things which only John Farnleigh could have known. *Only* John Farnleigh, I say. But he has proposed that he and the present holder shall submit to a certain test, which should be conclusive."

"What test?"

"You will see. Oh, yes. You will see." Nathaniel Burrows picked up his brief-case. "There has been only one gleam of comfort in the whole cursed mess. That is, so far there has been no publicity. The claimant is at least a gentleman—both of 'em are—bah—and he isn't anxious for a row. But there is going to be a remarkable row when I get my fingers on the truth. I'm glad my father isn't alive to see this. In the meantime, you be at Farnleigh Close at seven o'clock. Don't bother to dress for dinner. Nobody else will. It's only a pretext and there probably won't even be any dinner."

"And how is Sir John taking all this?"

"Which Sir John?"

"For the sake of clearness and convenience," retorted Page, "the man we have always known as Sir John Farnleigh. But this is interesting. Does it mean you believe the claimant is the real thing?"

"No. Not actually. Certainly not!" said Burrows. He caught himself up and spoke with dignity. "Farnleigh is only—sputtering. And I think that's a good sign."

"Does Molly know?"

"Yes; he told her today. Well, there you are. I've talked to you as no solicitor should and few ever do; but if I can't trust you I can't trust anybody, and I've been a bit uneasy about my conduct of things since my father died. Now get into the swim. Try my spiritual difficulties for yourself. Come up to Farnleigh Close at seven o'clock; we want you as a witness. Inspect the two candidates. Exercise your intelligence. And then, before we get down to business," said Burrows, banging the edge of his brief-case on the desk, "kindly tell me which is which."

Chapter II

Shadows were gathering on the lower slopes of the wood called Hanging Chart, but the flat lands to the left of it were still clear and warm. Set back from the road behind a wall and a screen of trees, the house had those colours of dark-red brick which seem to come from an old painting. It was as smoothed, as arranged, as its own clipped lawns. The windows were tall and narrow, with panes set into a pattern of stone oblongs; and a straight gravel drive led up to the door. Its chimneys stood up thin and close-set against the last light.

No ivy had been allowed to grow against its face. But there was a line of beech-trees set close against the house at the rear. Here a newer wing had been built out from the centre—like the body of an inverted letter

T—and it divided the Dutch garden into two gardens. On one side of the house the garden was overlooked by the back windows of the library; on the other by the windows of the room in which Sir John Farnleigh and Molly Farnleigh were waiting now.

A clock ticked in this room. It was what might have been called in the eighteenth century a Music Room or Ladies' Withdrawing Room, and it seemed to indicate the place of the house in this world. A pianoforte stood here, of that wood which in old age seems to resemble polished tortoise-shell. There was silver of age and grace, and a view of the Hanging Chart from its north windows; Molly Farnleigh used it as a sitting-room. It was very warm and quiet here, except for the ticking of the clock.

Molly Farnleigh sat by the window in the shadow of a great "octopus" beech-tree. She was what is called an outdoor girl, with a sturdy and well-shaped body, and a square but very attractive face. Her dark brown hair was uncompromisingly bobbed. She had light hazel eyes in a tanned, earnest face; and a directness of look which was as good as a handclasp. Her mouth might have been too broad, but she showed fine teeth when she laughed. If she was not exactly pretty, health and vigour gave her a strong attractiveness which was better than that.

But she was not laughing now. Her eyes never left her husband, who was pacing the room with short, sharp steps.

"You're not worried?" she asked.

Sir John Farnleigh stopped short. Then he fiddled with his dark wrists, and resumed his pacing.

"Worried? No. Oh, no. It's not that. It's only—oh, damn it all!"

He seemed an ideal partner for her. It would convey the wrong impression to say that he looked in his element as a country squire, for the word has come to be associated with beefy roisterers of a hundred years ago. Yet there is a truer type. Farnleigh was of middle height, of a stringy, active leanness which somehow suggested the lines of a plough: the bright metal, the compactness, the crisp blade that cuts the furrow.

His age might have been forty. He was of darkish complexion, with a thick but close-cropped moustache. He had dark hair in which there were thin lines of grey, and sharp dark eyes with growing wrinkles at the corners. You would have said that at the moment he as at the top of his mental and physical form, a man of enormous repressed energies. Strid-ing back and forth in the little room, he seemed less angry or upset than uncomfortable and embarrassed.

Molly started to rise. She cried:

"Oh, my dear, why didn't you *tell* me?"

"No use worrying you with it," the other said. "It's my affair. I'll manage."

"How long have you known about it?"

"A month or so. Thereabouts."

"And that's what's been worrying you all this time?" she asked, with a shade of different worry in her eyes.

"Partly," he grunted, and looked at her quickly.

"Partly? What do you mean by that?"

"What I say, my dear: partly."

"John . . . it hasn't got anything to do with Madeline Dane, has it?"

He stopped. "Good God, no! Certainly not. I don't know why you ask questions like that. You don't like Madeline, really, do you?"

"I don't like her eyes. They're queer eyes," said Molly, and checked herself out of a certain pride or another feeling she refused to name. "I'm sorry. I shouldn't have said anything like that, with all these other things coming up. It's not very pleasant; but there's nothing to it, is there? Of course the man hasn't got a case?"

"He hasn't got a right. I don't know whether he's got a case."

He spoke brusquely, and she studied him.

"But why is there so much fuss and mystery? If he's an impostor, couldn't you sling him out and let the matter drop?"

"Burrows says it wouldn't be wise. Not yet, anyway, until we've— er—heard what he has to say. Then we can take action. And real action. Besides——"

Molly Farnleigh's face grew expressionless.

"I wish you'd let me help you," she said. "Not that I could do anything, I suppose, but I should just like to know what it's all *about*. I know this man challenges you to let him prove he's really you. Of course that's all nonsense. I knew you years ago; and I knew you when I saw you again; you would be surprised how easily I knew. But I know you're having this fellow here at the house, with Nat Burrows and another solicitor, and being horribly mysterious. What are you going to do?"

"Do you remember my old tutor, Kennet Murray?"

"Faintly," said Molly, wrinkling her forehead. "Largish, pleasant man with a little cropped beard like a naval man or an artist. I suppose he was really young then, but he seemed ages old. Told wonderful stories——"

"His ambition was always to be a great detective," answered the other curtly. "Well, the Opposition have brought him from Bermuda. He says he can absolutely identify the real John Farnleigh. He's at the *Bull and Butcher* now."

"Wait a bit!" said Molly. "There's a man staying there who 'looks like an artist.' The village is full of it. Is that Murray?"

"That's old Murray. I wanted to go down and see him; but it wouldn't be—well, it wouldn't be sporting," said her husband, with a kind of inner struggle and writhing. "It might look as though I were trying to influence him. Or something. He's coming up here to see us both, and identify— me."

"How?"

"He's the one person in the world who really knew me well. The family has pretty well died out; you know that. The old servants have died out with my parents: except Nannie, and she's in New Zealand. Even Knowles has been here for only ten years. There are plenty of people that I knew vaguely, but you know I was an unsociable cuss and I didn't make friends. Poor old criminal-investigating Murray is undoubtedly it. He's remaining neutral and not having anything to do with either side; but, if he wants to have the one shot of his life at playing the great detective——"

Molly drew a deep breath. The health of her tanned face, the health of her whole body, animated the directness with which she spoke.

"John, I don't understand this. I do not understand it. You talk as though this were a wager or a game of some kind. 'Wouldn't be sporting.' 'Not having anything to do with either side.' Do you realize that this man—whoever he is—has coolly announced that he owns everything you own? That he's John Farnleigh? That he's the heir to a baronetcy and thirty thousand pounds a year? And that he means to have it from you?"

"Yes, I realize that."

"But doesn't it mean anything to you?" cried Molly. "You're treating him with as great care and consideration as though it didn't."

"It means everything to me."

"Well, then! If anybody had come to you and said, 'I am John Farnleigh,' I should have thought you would have said, 'Oh, really?' and merely kicked him out without thinking anything more about it, unless you sent for the police. That's what I should have done."

"You don't understand these things, my dear. And Burrows says——"

He looked slowly round the room. He seemed to be listening to the quiet ticking of the clock, to be savouring the odours of scrubbed floors and fresh curtains, to be reaching out in the sunlight over all the rich and quiet acres he now owned. At that moment, oddly enough, he looked most like a Puritan; and also he looked dangerous.

"It would be rather rotten," he said slowly, "to lose all this now."

He caught himself up, altering the quiet violence of his manner, as the door opened. Knowles, the old and bald-headed butler, ushered in Nathaniel Burrows and Brian Page.

Burrows, as Page had observed during their walk up here, wore now his most buttoned-up and halibut-like look. Page would not have known him for the human being of that afternoon. But Page supposed it was necessary because of the awkward atmosphere: he felt it at its worst. Glancing at his host and hostess, he began to wish he hadn't come.

The solicitor greeted his host and hostess with almost painful formality; and Farnleigh had drawn himself up stiffly, as though he were going to fight a duel.

"I think," Burrows added, "we shall be able to proceed to business soon. Mr. Page has kindly consented to act as the witness we desired——"

"Oh, look here," protested Page, with an effort. "We're not being besieged in a citadel, you know. You're one of the largest and most respected landowners in Kent. To hear what I've just heard from Burrows," he looked at Farnleigh, and could not discuss the matter, "is like hearing that grass is red or water runs uphill. It's about as reasonable, in the eyes of most people. Have you got to be so much on the defensive?"

Farnleigh spoke slowly.

"That's true," he admitted. "I suppose I'm being a fool."

"You are," agreed Molly. "Thanks, Brian."

"Old Murray——" said Farnleigh, with a far-away look. "Have you seen him, Burrows?"

"Only for a short time, Sir John. Not officially. Neither have the Other Side. His position is, plainly, that he has a test to apply; and in the meantime he says nothing."

"Has he changed much?"

Burrows became more human. "Not much. He's older and stiffer and sourer, and his beard is grey. Old days——"

"Old days," said Farnleigh. "My God, yes!" He turned something over in his mind. "There's just one question I want to ask you. Have you got any reason to suspect that Murray isn't straight? Wait! I know it's a rotten thing to say. Old Murray always was too honest: transparently. But we haven't seen him for twenty-five years. It's a long time. *I've* changed. No possibility of crooked work, is there?"

"You can rest assured there is not," said Burrows grimly. "I think we have discussed that before. It was the first thing that occurred to me, of course; and, considering the steps we have taken, you yourself have been satisfied of Mr. Murray's *bona fides*. Have you not?"*

"Yes, I suppose so."

"Then may I ask why you bring it up now?"

"You will oblige me," retorted Farnleigh, suddenly freezing up in a very passable imitation of Burrows's own manner, "by not looking as though you thought I were the impostor and the crook. You're all doing it. Don't deny it! That's exactly what you're doing. Peace, peace, peace: I've been looking all over the world for peace, and where am I going to get it? But I'll tell you why I ask about Murray. If you don't think there is

*Newspaper-readers may remember, in the bitter debate which followed tragedy in the Farnleigh case, that this point was often brought up by amateurs. Having myself once wasted time on many futile theories in an attempt to solve the mystery, I feel that I had better clear it up here. The honesty and good faith of Kennet Murray may be accepted as a fact. The evidence he possessed, with regard to establishing the identity of the real heir, was genuine evidence; and, it may be recalled, was later used to establish the truth.—J. D. C.

anything crooked about Murray, why have you got a private detective watching him?"

Behind the big spectacles Burrows's eyes opened in obvious astonishment.

"I beg your pardon, Sir John. I have had no private detective watching Mr. Murray or anybody else."

Farnleigh pulled himself up. "Then who's the other fellow down at the *Bull and Butcher?* You know: youngish, hard-faced chap with all the sly asides and questions? Everybody in the village says he's a private detective. He says he's interested in 'folklore,' and writing a book. Folklore my foot. He's sticking to Murray like a limpet."

They all looked at each other.

"Yes," Burrows observed thoughtfully. "I have heard of the folklorist and his interest in people. He may have been sent by Welkyn——"

"Welkyn?"

"The claimant's solicitor. Or he may have nothing to do with the case, as is most probable."

"I doubt it," said Farnleigh, and the blood seemed to come up under his eyes, making his face darker. "Not all he's interested in. The private detective chap, I mean. He's been asking all kinds of questions, from what I hear, about poor Victoria Daly."

To Brian Page it seemed that values had shifted slightly, and all familiar things were becoming unfamiliar. In the midst of a debate about his right to an estate worth thirty thousand pounds a year, Farnleigh seemed more preoccupied with the commonplace—if sordid—tragedy of the previous summer. Well? Victoria Daly, an inoffensive spinster of thirty-five, strangled in her cottage by a tramp who professed to sell boot-laces and collar-studs? Strangled, curiously enough, with a boot-lace; and her purse found in the tramp's pocket when he was killed on the railway line?

In the midst of a silence, while Page and Molly Farnleigh looked at each other, the door of the room opened. Knowles came in with an air of equal uncertainty.

"There are two gentlemen to see you, sir," Knowles said. "One is a Mr. Welkyn, a solicitor. The other——"

"Well? The other?"

"The other asks me to say that he is Sir John Farnleigh."

"Does he? Oh. Well——"

Molly got up quietly, but muscles had tightened at the corners of her jaws.

"Take back this message from Sir John Farnleigh," she instructed Knowles. "Sir John Farnleigh presents his compliments; and, if the caller has no name to give other than that, he may go round and wait in the servants' hall until Sir John finds time to see him."

"No, come, come!" stuttered Burrows, in a kind of legal agony. "Trying circumstances—necessary to be tactful—freeze him all you like, but don't——"

The shadow of a smile crossed Farnleigh's dark face.

"Very well, Knowles. Take that message."

"Impudence," said Molly, breathing hard.

When Knowles returned he had less the air of a courier than of a sensitive tennis-ball being driven to different corners of the court.

"The gentlemen says, sir, that he deeply apologizes for his message, which was premature, and hopes there will be no ill-feeling in the matter. He says he has chosen for some years to be known as Mr. Patrick Gore."

"I see," said Farnleigh. "Show Mr. Gore and Mr. Welkyn into the library."

Chapter III

The claimant got up from his chair. Despite the fact that one wall of the library was built of windows, multitudinous panes set in a pattern of stone oblongs, the daylight was going; and the trees threw heavy shadows. On the stone-flagged floor there was insufficient carpeting. The heavy bookshelves were built up like tiers in a crypt, scrolled along the top. Green-shadowed light through the windows drew across the floor a silhouette of a hundred panes, stretching almost to the man who rose to his feet beside the table.

Molly has since confessed that her heart was in her mouth when the door opened, and that she wondered whether a living counterpart of her husband might not appear from behind it, as in a mirror. Yet there was no great resemblance between these two.

The man in the library was no heavier than Farnleigh, yet less wiry. His dark, fine hair had no grey in it, but he was going a little thin on top. Though dark of complexion, he was clean-shaven and his face was comparatively unfurrowed. Any wrinkles in his forehead or round his eyes were those of amusement rather than doggedness. For the claimant's whole expression was one of ease, irony, and amusement, with very dark grey eyes, and eyebrows wisped up a little at the outer corners. He was well dressed, in town clothes as opposed to Farnleigh's old tweeds.

"I beg your pardon," he said.

Even his voice was a baritone, in contrast to Farnleigh's harsh and rasping tenor. His walk was not exactly limping, but a bit clumsy.

"I beg your pardon," he said with grave courtesy, but with a certain oblique look of amusement, "for seeming so insistent about returning to my old home. But you will, I hope, appreciate my motives. Er—let me present my legal representative, Mr. Welkyn."

A fat man with somewhat protuberant eyes had got up from a chair at the other side of the table. But they hardly saw him. The claimant was not only studying them with interest; he was glancing round the room as though he were recognizing and drinking in every detail.

"Let's get down to business," said Farnleigh abruptly. "I think you've met Burrows. This is Mr. Page. This is my wife."

"I have met—" said the claimant, hesitating and then looking full at Molly—"your wife. Forgive me if I do not know quite how to address her. I can't call her Lady Farnleigh. And I can't call her Molly, as I used to do when she wore hair-ribbons."

Neither of the Farnleighs commented. Molly was calm but flushed, and there was a dry strain about her eyes.

"Also," went on the claimant, "I should like to thank you for taking this very awkward and unpleasant business in such good part——"

"I don't," snapped Farnleigh. "I take it in devilish damned bad part, and you might as well understand that. The only reason why I don't throw you out of the house is because my own solicitor seems to think we ought to be tactful. All right: speak up. What have you got to say?"

Mr. Welkyn moved out from the table, clearing his throat.

"My client, Sir John Farnleigh—" he began.

"One moment," interposed Burrows, with equal suavity. Page seemed to hear a faint hiss as legal axes began to grind; as forensic sleeves were rolled up; as the conversation was being geared to the pace these gentlemen would have it take. "May I request, for the sake of convenience, that we refer to your client by some other name? He chose to give the name of 'Patrick Gore.' "

"I should prefer," said Welkyn, "to refer to him simply as 'my client.' Will that be satisfactory?"

"Perfectly."

"Thank you. I have here," pursued Welkyn, opening his brief-case, "a proposal which my client is prepared to submit. My client wishes to be fair. While under the necessity of pointing out that the present holder has no claim to the title and estates, nevertheless my client remembers the circumstances under which the imposture was begun. He also recognizes the present holder's able stewardship and the fact that nothing but credit has been reflected on the family name.

"Therefore, if the present holder will at once withdraw without making it necessary to take the matter into the courts, there will be, of course, no question of prosecution. To the contrary, my client is willing to make some financial compensation to the present holder: let us say an annuity of one thousand pounds a year for life. My client has ascertained that the present holder's wife—*née* Miss Mary Bishop—has inherited a fortune in her own right; and the question of straitened finances should not, therefore, arise. Of course, I confess that should the present holder's wife care to question the validity of the marriage on the grounds of fraudulent——"

Again the blood had come up under Farnleigh's eyes.

"God!" he said. "Of all the brazen, bare-faced——"

Nathaniel Burrows made a noise which was too polite to be called shushing, but it restrained Farnleigh.

"May I suggest, Mr. Welkyn," Burrows replied, "that we are here at the moment to determine whether your client has a claim? Until that is determined, any other considerations do not arise."

"As you please. My client," said Welkyn, with a disdainful movement of his shoulders, "merely wished to avoid unpleasantness. Mr. Kennet Murray should be with us in a few minutes. After that I fear the result will be no longer in doubt. If the present holder persists in his attitude, then I am afraid the consequences will be——"

"Look here," Farnleigh interposed again, "let's cut the cackle and get down to the horses."

The claimant smiled, which seemed to turn his eyes inwards with some secret joke. "You see?" he remarked. "His pseudo-gentility is so grafted on him that he cannot bring himself to say 'osses."

"It doesn't bring him to giving cheap insults, in any case," said Molly; and now it was the claimant who showed a slight flush.

"I beg your pardon. I should not have said that. But you must remember," said the claimant, his tone again changing a little, "that I have dwelt among wicked ways, and hardly by the springs of Dove. Have I leave to present my own case in my own way?"

"Yes," said Farnleigh. "Shut up," he added to both lawyers. "This is a personal matter now."

As though by common consent they all moved towards the table and took chairs. The claimant sat with his back to the great window. For a time he remained thoughtful, absently patting the slight thinning patch that showed in the crown of his dark hair. Then he looked up, with the edge of mockery showing in the wrinkles round his eyes.

"I am John Farnleigh," he began with great simplicity and apparent earnestness. "Kindly do not interrupt me with legal quibbles at this time; I am presenting my case, and am entitled to call myself the Cham of Tartary if I feel so inclined. However, I really do happen to be John Farnleigh, and I will tell you what happened to me.

"As a boy I may have been something of a young swine; though even now I am not certain I did not have the right attitude. My late father, Dudley Farnleigh, would put up my hackles just as much if he were alive now. No, I cannot say I was wrong, except that I should have learned more give-and-take. I quarreled with my elders for pointing out that I was young, I quarreled with my tutors because I despised every subject in which I was not interested.

"To get down to business, you know why I left here. I sailed with Murray in the *Titanic*. And, from the first, I spent as much time as I could with the steerage passengers. Not, you understand, because I felt any particular liking for the steerage passengers, but simply because I hated my own crowd in first-class. This is not a defence, you know: it is a psychological account which I think you will find convincing.

"In the steerage I met a Rumanian-English boy, about my own age, who was going out alone to the States. He interested me. His father—who could never afterwards be found—he said was an English gentleman. His mother was a Rumanian girl, a snake-dancer at a travelling circus in England during the times when she was not drinking. There came a time when real snakes would not mix with imaginary ones, and the woman was reduced to the position of part-time cook in the circus mess-tent. The boy became a nuisance. An old admirer of hers was doing well in a small way with a circus in America, and so she was sending the boy out to him.

"He would be taught to ride a bicycle on the tight-rope, he would be taught—and how I envied him. Lord of saints and snakes, HOW I envied him! Will any right-minded boy or man blame me?"

The claimant shifted a little in his chair. He seemed to be looking back cynically, yet with a certain satisfaction; and none of the others moved. The suave Mr. Welkyn, who seemed about to interpose with a comment or suggestion, looked quickly round at the group of faces and remained silent.

"The odd part of it," continued the speaker, examining his fingernails, "was that this boy envied me. His name (which was something unpronounceable) he had changed to 'Patrick Gore' because he liked the sound of it. He disliked circus life. He disliked the movement and the change and the din and the upset. He hated stakes driven in overnight to be pulled up in the morning, and elbows in your face at the soup-kitchen. I don't know where he got it: he was a reserved, cold-faced, well-mannered little bounder. The first time we met we flew at each other and fought until half the steerage had to drag us apart. I am afraid that I was so enraged I wanted to go at him afterwards with my clasp-knife. He simply bowed to me and walked away; I can see him yet.—I am referring, my friend, to you."

He glanced up at Farnleigh.

"This can't be real," Farnleigh said suddenly, and passed his hand across his forehead, "I don't believe it. It's a nightmare. Are you seriously suggesting——?"

"Yes," agreed the other, with a decisive snap. "We discussed how pleasant it would be if we could swap identities. Only as a wild dream of let's pretend, of course: at that moment. You said it would never work, though you looked as though you would like to murder me to get it. I don't suppose I ever really meant to carry out any such thing; the interesting point is that you did mean it. I used to give you information about myself. I used to tell you, 'Now if you met my Aunt So-and-So or my Cousin This-and-that, this is what you must say to them,' and lord it over you in a way that I do not like to remember: for this is no justification of my behaviour there. I thought you were a prig and I still think so. I also showed you my diary. I always kept a diary, for the simple reason that there was nobody on earth I could talk to. I still keep one." Here the claimant glanced up almost whimsically. "Do you remember me, Patrick? Do you remember the night the *Titanic* went down?"

There was a pause.

On Farnleigh's face there was no expression of anger: only of bewilderment.

"I keep telling you," he said, "that you're mad."

"When we struck that iceberg," the other went on carefully, "I will tell you exactly what I was doing. I was down in the cabin I shared with poor old Murray, while he was in the smoking-room playing bridge. Murray kept a flask of brandy in one of his coats; and I was sampling it because they would not serve me in the bar.

"I scarcely felt it when we struck; I question if anybody did. There was a very slight bump, hardly enough to spill a filled cocktail-glass on a table; and then the stopping of the engines. I only went out into the alleyway because I wondered why the engines had stopped. The first I knew of it came from the noise of voices getting louder and closer; and then a woman suddenly running past screaming with a blue quilt wrapped round her shoulders."

For the first time the claimant hesitated.

"I am not going to bring back old tragedies by saying anything more about that part of it," he said, opening and shutting his hands. "I will say only this, for which God forgive me, even as a boy: I rather enjoyed it. I was not in the least frightened. I was exhilarated. It was something out of the common, something to take away the ordinary sameness of everyday life; and I had always been looking for things like that. And I was so wild with excitement that I agreed to change identities with Patrick Gore. The determination seemed to come to me all at once, though I am wondering if he had thought about it for a long time.

"I met Gore—I met you," amplified the speaker, looking at his host steadily, "on B Deck. You had all your possessions in a little straw suitcase. You told me quite coolly that the ship was going down, and going down fast: if I really wanted to change identities, it might be managed in the confusion, or if either of us survived. I said, what about Murray? You lied, saying that Murray was overboard and dead already. And I was willing enough to become a great circus-performer, so we changed: clothes, papers, rings, everything. You even got my diary."

Farnleigh said nothing.

"Afterwards," added the claimant, without altering the tone of his voice, "you were very neat. We were ready to run for the boats. You waited until my back was turned; then you fished out the steward's wooden mallet you had stolen, you caught me on the back of the skull with it, and you tried with three blows to finish the work."

Farnleigh still said nothing. Molly got up from her chair; but, at a gesture from him, she sat down again.

"Mind you," insisted the claimant, with a movement as though he were flicking dust from the table, "I am not here to bring that up against you. Twenty-five years is a long time, and you were a boy then, though I am wondering into what sort of man you have grown. I was considered a bad lot myself. It is possible that you despised me and believed you had justification. You need not have been so thorough, because I should have assumed your identity in any case. Still—even if I was the black sheep of the family, I was never quite so black as that.

"The rest of it will be clear to you. By what I must insist was a stroke of luck I was found, damaged but alive, and pushed into the last surviving boat. The casualty lists were at first uncertain, and America is a large country, and I was for some time in the world of shadows. Both the names of John Farnleigh and Patrick Gore appeared as missing. I thought you were dead, as you thought I was. When my possessions and papers identified me as Patrick Gore to Mr. Boris Yeldritch, the circus-proprietor—who had never seen you—I was entirely content.

"If I did not like the life, I thought, I could always reveal myself. Perhaps I should have better treatment, I thought, if I miraculously returned from the dead. The prospect pleased me; it was a dramatic card in reserve; and, believe me, it gave me many comforting nights."

"And," said Molly as though with elaborate interest, "did you become the trick bicycle-rider of the circus?"

The claimant turned his head sideways. His dark grey eye was kindled with such strong inner amusement that he resembled a crafty small boy. Again he lifted his hand and rubbed the thinning patch on the crown of his head.

"No. No, although I had my first sensational success with the circus, I became something else. For the moment I should prefer not to tell you what it was. In addition to the fact that it is an excellent secret, I do not wish to bore you with details of my subsequent life.

"Believe me, I had always intended one day to return to my old home and astonish them with the baaing of a black sheep from the grave. For I *have* been successful; by all the prophets I have!—and I felt that this would make my brother Dudley writhe. But this dramatic plum I reserved. I even visited England without being too much tempted. For, mind you, I had no reason to suspect that 'John Farnleigh' was alive. I thought he was supposed to be dead, instead of flourishing in Colorado.

"You will therefore understand my surprise, some six months ago, when quite by chance I picked up an illustrated paper and saw the picture of Sir John and Lady Farnleigh. My brother Dudley, I noted, was dead of a surfeit of lampreys. His 'younger brother' had inherited. At first I thought this must be the mistake of the paper for some distant connection. But a few inquiries uncovered the truth; and after all, you know, I *am* the heir. Still a young man—still vigorous—but not revengeful.

"Such things grow exceedingly dim. A generation has grown up; there are a thousand good memories between me and the small whelp who tried to alter the succession with a seaman's mallet and who, I hear, has become a useful citizen since. All the trees look the same; but my eyes have changed. I feel strange and raw in my own home. I am not sure that I shall make the best possible patron for the local cricket-club or the local Boy Scouts. But I have (as you observe) a strong weakness for making speeches, and I daresay I shall get on well enough. Now, Patrick Gore, you have heard my proposal. It is generous enough. If I take you to court, I warn you I will have your hide. In the meantime, gentlemen, I am open to answer questions from anyone who has ever known me. I have a few questions to put myself, and I will defy Gore to answer them."

For a time after he had spoken, it was quiet in the darkening room. He had an almost hypnotic voice. But they were looking at Farnleigh, who had risen and stood with his knuckles on the table. In Farnleigh's dark face there was quiet, and relief, and a certain curiosity as he examined his guest. He brushed a hand under his cropped moustache; he almost smiled.

Molly saw that smile, and drew a deep breath.

"You have something to say, John?" she prompted.

"Yes. I don't know why he's come here with this story, or what he hopes to get out of it. But what this man says is absolutely false from beginning to end."

"You intend to fight?" asked the claimant with interest.

"Of course I mean to fight, you ass. Or, rather, I'll let you do the fighting."

Mr. Welkyn seemed about to intervene, with a vast throat-clearing, but the claimant stopped him.

"No, no," he said comfortably. "Please stay out of this, Welkyn. You brethren of the law are all very well to put in the 'whereases' and the 'proceed with caution,' but you are out of place in a personal skirmish like this. To tell the truth, I shall enjoy this. Well, let us apply a few tests. I wonder if you would mind calling your butler in here?"

Farnleigh frowned. "But look here: Knowles wasn't——"

"Why not do as he asks, John?" suggested Molly sweetly.

Farnleigh caught her look; and, if there is a paradox which can be called humourless humour, his sharp features showed it. He rang for Knowles, who entered in the same uncertain way. The claimant regarded him musingly.

"I thought I recognized you when we came in here," the claimant said. "You were here in my father's time, were you not?"

"Sir?"

"You were here in my father's, Sir Dudley Farnleigh's time. Weren't you?"

An expression of disgust went over Farnleigh's face.

"You will do your case no good by this," interposed Nathaniel Burrows sharply. "The butler in Sir Dudley Farnleigh's time was Stenson, who has been dead——"

"Yes. I was aware of that," said the claimant, turning his eyes sideways. Then he contemplated the butler, sitting back and crossing his legs with some effort. "Your name is Knowles. In my father's time you were the butler at old Colonel Mardale's place, over in Frettenden. You used to keep two rabbits that the colonel knew nothing about. You kept them in a corner of the coach-house nearest the orchard. One of the rabbits was named Billy." He looked up. "Ask this gentleman the name of the other."

Knowles had gone slightly pink.

"Ask him, will you?"

"Rot!" snapped Farnleigh, and drew himself back into his dignity again.

"Oh," said the claimant. "You mean you cannot answer?"

"I mean I don't choose to answer." Yet six pairs of eyes were fastened on him, and he seemed to feel the pressure; he shifted and almost stuttered. "Who can be expected to remember the name of a rabbit after twenty-five years? All right, all right: stop a bit! There was some nonsense about their names, I remember. Let me think. Billy and W—no, that's not it. Billy and Silly, that's it? Or was it? I'm not sure."

"That is correct sir," Knowles told him with an air of relief.

The claimant was not out of countenance.

"Well, let us try again. Now, Knowles. One evening in summer—it was the year before I went away—you were going through that same orchard to take a message to a certain neighbour. You were surprised and rather shocked to find me making love to a certain young lady of twelve or thirteen. Ask your employer the name of that young lady."

Farnleigh was dark and heavy-looking.

"I don't remember any such incident."

"Are you trying to convey the impression," said the claimant, "that your natural chivalry restrains you? No, my friend, that will not do. It was a long time ago and I give you my solemn word that nothing of a compromising nature passed. Knowles, *you* remember what went on in the apple-orchard, don't you?"

"Sir," said the bedevilled butler, "I——"

"You do. But I thought this man would not remember it, because I do not think I entered the fact in my valuable diary. What was the name of the young lady?"

Farnleigh nodded. "All right," he answered with an attempt at lightness. "It was Miss Dane, Madeline Dane."

"Madeline Dane—" began Molly.

For the first time the claimant seemed a little taken aback. His quick eyes moved round the group, and his quick intuition seemed to move too.

"She must have written to you in America," returned the claimant. "We shall have to cut deeper. But I beg your pardon: I hope I have committed no blunder? I hope the young lady is not still living in the district at a more mature age, and that I have not touched on any inconvenient subject?"

"Damn you," said Farnleigh suddenly, "I've stood about enough of this. I can't keep my temper much longer. Will you kindly get out of here?"

"No," said the other. "I mean to break down your bluff. For it is a bluff, my boy, and you know it. Besides, I think it was agreed that we should wait for Kennet Murray."

"Suppose we do wait for Murray?" Farnleigh spoke with toiling lucidity. "Where will it get us? What will it prove, beyond this fiddle-faddle of questions to which we both apparently know the answers? And yet you don't know the answers, because you're the one who is bluffing. I could ask some myself, just as nonsensical as yours. But that's nothing. How did you ever expect to prove a thing like this. How do you still think you can prove it?"

The claimant sat back, richly enjoying his position.

"By the incontrovertible evidence of fingerprints," he said.

Chapter IV

It was as though the man had been keeping this in reserve, waiting for the proper moment to say it and savouring triumph in advance. He seemed a little disappointed that he had to produce the trump so early, and under circumstances less dramatic than he might have wished. But the others were not thinking in terms of drama.

Brian Page heard Burrows breathe in with a shaky kind of noise. Burrows got to his feet.

"I was not informed of this," the solicitor said fiercely.

"But you guessed it?" smiled fat Mr. Welkyn.

"It is not my business to guess at anything," returned Burrows. "I repeat, sir, I have not been informed of this. I have heard nothing about fingerprints."

"Nor have we, officially. Mr. Murray has kept his own counsel. But," inquired Welkyn, with rich suavity, "does the present holder *need* to be told? If he is the real Sir John Farnleigh, surely he remembers that Mr. Murray took the fingerprints of the boy as long ago as the year nineteen ten or eleven."

"I repeat, sir——"

"Let *me* repeat, Mr. Burrows: did you need to be informed of it? What does the present holder himself have to say?"

Farnleigh's expression seemed to have retreated, to have become locked up. As usual when he was among mental brambles, he did two things. He began to walk round the room with short, quick steps; and he took a key-ring out of his pocket and twirled it round his fore-finger.

"Sir John!"

"Eh?"

"Do you remember," asked Burrows, "any such circumstances as Mr. Welkyn mentions? Did Mr. Murray ever take your fingerprints?"

"Oh, that," said Farnleigh, as though it were of no importance. "Yes, I remember it now. I'd forgotten it. But it occurred to me when I was talking to you and my wife a while ago—you know. I wondered if that could be it, and it made me a whole lot easier in my mind. Yes, old Murray got my fingerprints right enough."

The claimant turned round. He wore an expression not only of mild astonishment, but of sudden and wondering suspicion as well.

"This will not do, you know," the claimant said. "You don't maintain that you will face the test of fingerprints?"

"Face it? Face it?" repeated Farnleigh, with grim pleasure. "Man, it's the best thing that could have happened. You're the impostor, and you know it. Murray's old fingerprint test—by George, now I come to think of it, I can remember every detail of that business!—will settle matters. Then I can throw you out."

And the two rivals looked at each other.

For some time Brian Page had been trying to put weights into a scales which would not remain still. He had been trying, without friendship or prejudice, to see where the imposture lay. This issue was simple. If Patrick Gore (to give him the name by which he had been announced) were the impostor, he was one of the coolest and most smooth-faced crooks who ever walked into another man's house. If the present John

Farnleigh were the impostor, he was not only a slippery criminal behind that naive, straightforward mask: he was a would-be murderer as well.

There was a pause.

"You know, my friend," observed the claimant, as though with refreshed interest, "I admire your cheek. One moment, please. I do not say that as a baiting jeer or to start a row. I state, as a matter of simple fact, that I admire an *aes-triplex* cheek which Casanova himself could not have equalled. Now, I am not surprised that you 'forgot' the fingerprints. They were taken at a time before I began to keep my diary. But to say you forgot them: to SAY you forgot them——"

"Well, what's wrong with that?"

"John Farnleigh wouldn't or couldn't have forgotten a detail of that. I, being John Farnleigh, certainly didn't. That is why Kennet Murray was the only person in the world who had any influence with me. Murray on Footprints. Murray on Disguises. Murray on the Disposal of the Body. Wough! And particularly Murray on Fingerprints, which were then the newest scientific craze. I am aware,"—he interrupted himself, raising his voice and looking round the group,—"that fingerprints were discovered by Sir William Herschel in the eighteen-fifties, and re-discovered by Dr. Faulds in the late seventies. But they were not admitted as legal evidence in an English court until nineteen-five, and even then the judge was dubious. It took years of argument to establish them. Yet, as a possible 'test' of Murray's, you say you never thought of fingerprints."

"You're doing a hell of a lot of talking," said Farnleigh, who again looked swollen and dangerous.

"Naturally. Though you never once thought of fingerprints before, it all comes back to you now. Tell me this. When the prints were taken, how were they taken?"

"How?"

"In what form?"

Farnleigh pondered. "On a sheet of glass," he said.

"Nonsense. They were taken in a 'Thumbograph,' a little book which was quite a popular game or toy at the time. A little grey book. Murray had a lot of others, my father's and my mother's and anybody else's he could get."

"Stop a bit. Hold on. I believe there was a book—we sat over in that window——"

"So you profess to remember now."

"Look here," said Farnleigh quietly, "who do you think I am? Do you think I'm that fellow in the music-halls, the one you shoot questions at and he instantly tells you the number of clauses in the Magna Charta or what horse ran second in the Derby in 1882? That's what *you* sound like. There's a lot of rubbish that's better forgotten. People change. They change, I tell you."

"But not their basic characters, as you profess to have changed. That is the point I am making. You cannot turn your whole soul inside out, you know."

During this controversy Mr. Welkyn had been sitting back with a massive gravity but with a certain complacence which beamed forth from his protuberant blue eyes. Now he lifted his hand.

"Gentlemen, gentlemen. Surely this wrangling is not—er—seemly, if you will allow me to say so? The matter, I am glad to say, can be settled within a very short time——"

"I still insist," snapped Nathaniel Burrows, "that, not having been instructed about this matter of the fingerprints, I may, in the interests of Sir John Farnleigh—"

"Mr. Burrows," said the claimant calmly, "you must have guessed it, even if we did not choose to tell you. I suspect you guessed it from the first, and that is why you tolerated this claim. You are trying to save your face on both sides, whether your man should turn out to be a fraud or whether he should not. Well, you had better come over to our side soon."

Farnleigh stopped pacing. He tossed up the key-ring, caught it with a flat smack against his palm, and closed his long fingers round it.

"Is that true?" he asked Burrows.

"If it were true, Sir John, I should have been compelled to take other steps. At the same time, it is my duty to investigate——"

"That's all right," said Farnleigh. "I only wanted to know where my friends stand. I'm not saying much. My memories, pleasant or unpleasant: and some of them have kept me awake at nights: I'll keep to myself. Just bring on your fingerprints, and then we shall see. The point is, where is Murray? Why isn't he here?"

The claimant wore a look of Mephistophelian pleasure, in which he contrived to suggest a sinister frown.

"If events ran according to form," he answered with relish, "Murray would already have been murdered and his body hidden in the pond in the garden. (There is still a pond there, isn't there? I thought so.) As a matter of sober fact, I believe he is on his way here now. Besides, I do not wish to put ideas into anybody's head."

"Ideas?" said Farnleigh.

"Yes. Like your old one. A quick cosh and an easy life."

The way he spoke seemed to put an unpleasant chill in the air. Farnleigh's voice went high and rasping. He lifted his hand, and then rubbed it down the side of his old tweed coat, as though in a nervous gesture of controlling himself. With uncanny skill his opponent seemed to pick out exactly the sentences that would sting him. Farnleigh had rather a long neck, which was now much in evidence.

"Does anybody believe that?" he got out. "Molly—Page—Burrows—do you believe that?"

"Nobody believes it," answered Molly, with level eyes. "You're being foolish to let him put you off balance, which is exactly what he's trying to do."

The claimant turned an interested look on her.

"You too, madam?"

"Me too, what?" asked Molly, and then grew furiously annoyed with herself. "Sorry to sound like a musical scale, but you know what I mean."

"You believe your husband is John Farnleigh?"

"I know it."

"How?"

"I'm afraid I must answer woman's intuition," said Molly coolly. "But I mean something sensible by it: something that in its own way, and within its own limits, is always right. I knew it the moment I saw him again. Of course I am willing to listen to reasons, but they have got to be the right sort of reasons."

"Are you in love with him, may I ask?"

This time Molly flushed under her tan, but she treated the question in her usual way. "Well, let's say that I am rather fond of him, if you like."

"Exactly. Ex-actly. You are 'fond' of him; you will always be 'fond' of him, I think. You get on and you will get on very well together. But you are not in love with him and you did not fall in love with him. You fell in love with me. That is to say, you fell in love with an imaginary projection of me from your childhood, which surrounded the impostor when 'I' returned home——"

"Gentlemen, gentlemen!" said Mr. Welkyn, like a master of ceremonies to a rowdy banquet. He seemed rather shocked.

Brian Page entered the conversation: with broad amusement, to steady their host.

"Now we're being psychoanalytic," Page said. "Look here, Burrows, what are we to do with this flower of something-or-other?"

"I only know that we are putting in an awkward half-hour," returned Burrows coldly. "Also, we are straying from the point again."

"Not at all," the claimant assured him. The claimant seemed genuinely anxious to please. "I hope I haven't said anything to offend anybody again? You should live with a circus; your skins would grow tougher. However. I appeal to you, sir," he looked at Page. "Don't I state a reasonable proposition with regard to this lady? You may make an objection. You may say that, in order to fix her affections on me as a child, she must have been somewhat older—the age, say, of Miss Madeline Dane? Was that your objection?"

Molly laughed.

"No," said Page. "I wasn't thinking of either a support or an objection. I was thinking of your mysterious profession."

"My profession?"

"The unspecified profession you mentioned, the one you first made a success of at the circus. I can't decide whether you are (1) a fortune-teller, (2) a psychoanalyst, (3) a memory-expert, (4) a conjuror, or even a combination of them. There are mannerisms of them all about you, and much more besides. You are a little too suggestive of Mephistopheles in Kent. You don't belong here. You disturb things, somehow, and you give me a pain in the neck."

The claimant seemed pleased.

"Do I? You all need to be stirred up a bit," he declared. "Regarding my profession, I am perhaps a little of all those things. But there is one person I certainly am: I am John Farnleigh."

Across the room the door opened, and Knowles entered.

"Mr. Kennet Murray to see you, sir," he said.

There was a pause. By a trick of the fading light, a last fiery glow of sunset shifted in through the trees and the high window-panes. It kindled the heavy room; then it subsided to a steady, warm light which was just bright enough to make faces and figures a little more than visible.

Kennet Murray himself had been remembering many things in that mid-summer dusk. He was a tall, lean, rather shambling man, who, in spite of a first-rate intelligence, had never been cut out to be a particular success at anything. Though he was hardly fifty, his fair moustache and fair beard, so closely cropped that they looked like stubble, were greyish. He had aged, as Burrows had said; he had grown leaner and more sour out of his former easy good-nature. But there was much of that good-nature remaining, and his look showed it as he ambled into the library. His eyes had the slightly squinted-up look of one who lives under hot suns.

Then he stopped, frowning as though at a book, and drawing himself up. And, to one of the contestants for the estate, old days returned with old memories and fierce bitterness against dead people; yet Murray himself did not look a day older.

Murray stood studying the persons before him. He frowned, then he looked quizzical—the eternal tutor—and then grim. He fixed his eyes at a point midway between the holder and the claimant.

"Well, young Johnny?" he said.

Chapter V

For a second or two neither of the contestants moved or spoke. First it seemed that each was waiting to see what the other would do; and then each went his separate way. Farnleigh moved his shoulder slightly, as though he would not enter this as a debate, but he consented to nod and gesture and even smile stiffly. There had been authority in Murray's voice. But the claimant, after a slight hesitation, showed no such views. He spoke with quiet affability.

"Good evening, Murray," he said; and Brian Page, who knew the ways of students towards their former schoolmasters, suddenly felt the scale-pans dip towards Farnleigh.

Murray looked round.

"Someone—er—had better present me," he said in a pleasant voice.

It was Farnleigh, stung out of apathy, who did this. By tacit consent Murray was the "old man" of the group, though he was a good deal younger than Welkyn; there was something of the "old man's" manner about him: something brisk and assured, yet wandering. He sat down at the head of the table, with the light behind his back. Then he gravely fitted on a pair of owlish shell-rimmed reading glasses, and surveyed them.

"I should never have recognized Miss Bishop or Mr. Burrows," he went on. "Mr. Welkyn I know slightly. It was through his generosity that I was able to take my first real holiday in a long time."

Welkyn, evidently well satisfied, thought that the time had now come for him to take charge and get down to real business.

"Exactly. Now, Mr. Murray, my client——"

"Oh, tut, tut, tut!" said Murray, rather testily. "Let me get my breath and talk a moment, as old Sir Dudley used to say." It was as though he wanted to get his breath literally, for he breathed deeply several times, looked round the room, and then at the two opponents. "However, I must say you seem to have landed yourself in the middle of a very bad mess. The affair has not become public property, has it?"

"No," said Burrows. "And you, of course, have not said anything about it?"

Murray frowned.

"There I must plead guilty. I have mentioned it to one person. But, when you hear the name of the person, I don't think you will object. It was my old friend Dr. Gideon Fell, a former schoolmaster like myself, of whose connection with detective work you may have heard. I saw him as I was passing through London. And I—er—mention this to give you a word of warning." Despite Murray's benevolence, his squinted grey eyes became bright and hard and interested. "It is possible that Dr. Fell himself may soon be in this part of the world. You know that there is another man staying at the *Bull and Butcher* besides myself, a man of inquisitive habits?"

"The private detective?" Farnleigh asked sharply, and to the ostensible surprise of the claimant.

"So it took you in?" said Murray. "He is an official detective from Scotland Yard. It was Dr. Fell's idea. Dr. Fell maintained that the best way to conceal your identity as an official detective is to act like a private detective." Though Murray seemed hugely delighted, his eyes remained watchful. "Scotland Yard, on the advice of the Chief Constable of Kent, seem to be curious about the death of Miss Victoria Daly here last summer."

Sensation.

Nathaniel Burrows, who looked fussed, made a vague gesture.

"Miss Daly was killed by a tramp," Burrows said, "later killed himself in escaping the police."

"I hope so. However, I heard it in passing when I mentioned my own little problem in mixed identities to Dr. Fell. He was interested." Again Murray's voice became sharp; and, if the word can be used, opaque. "Now, young Johnny——"

Even the air of the room seemed to be waiting. The claimant nodded. The host also nodded, but Page thought that there was a faint glitter of sweat on his forehead.

"Can't we get on with this?" Farnleigh demanded. "It's no good playing cat and mouse, Mr.—it's no good playing cat and mouse, Murray. It's not decent, and it's not like you. If you've got those fingerprints, trot 'em out and then we shall see."

Murray's eyes opened, and then narrowed. He sounded annoyed.

"So you know about that. I was reserving it. And may I ask," his voice grew professionally poised and sarcastic, "which of you thought that the final test would be fingerprints?"

"I think I can establish that honour," answered the claimant, looking round as though inquiringly. "My friend Patrick Gore here claims to have remembered it afterwards. But he seems to have been under the impression that you took fingerprints on a sheet of glass."

"And so I did," said Murray.

"That's a lie," said the claimant.

It was an unexpected change of voice. Brian Page suddenly realized that, under his mild and Mephistophelian airs, the claimant concealed a violent temper.

"Sir," said Murray, looking him up and down, "I am not in the habit——"

Then it was as though old days returned; the claimant seemed involuntarily about to move back and beg Murray's pardon. But he conquered this. His face smoothed itself out, and the usual mocking expression reappeared.

"Let us say, then, that I have an alternative suggestion. You took my fingerprints in a 'Thumbograph.' You had several such Thumbographs; you bought them in Tunbridge Wells. And you took the fingerprints of myself and my brother Dudley on the same day."

"That," agreed Murray, "is quite true. The Thumbograph with the fingerprints I have here." He touched the inside breast pocket of his sports-coat.

"I smell blood," said the claimant.

It was true that a different atmosphere seemed to surround the group at the table.

"At the same time," Murray went on, as though he had not heard this, "the first experiments I made with fingerprints were on small glass slides." He grew even more inscrutable and sharp. "Now, sir, as the claimant or plaintiff here, you must tell me a few things. If you are Sir John Farnleigh, certain things are known to me which are known to nobody else. In those days you were an omnivorous reader. Sir Dudley, who you will admit was an enlightened man, made out a list of books which you were permitted to read. You never spoke your views on these books to anyone else: Sir Dudley once spoke a word of harmless ridicule to you about your notions, and tortures would not have opened your mouth afterwards. But you expressed yourself to me in no uncertain terms. Do you remember all that?"

"Very well indeed," said the claimant.

"Then kindly tell me which of those books you liked best, and which made the most impression on you."

"With pleasure," answered the claimant, casting up his eyes. "All of Sherlock Holmes. All of Poe. *The Cloister and the Hearth. The Count of Monte Cristo. Kidnapped. A Tale of Two Cities.* All ghost stories. All stories dealing with pirates, murders, ruined castles, or——"

"That will do," said Murray noncommittally. "And the books you intensely disliked?"

"Every deadly line of Jane Austen and George Eliot. All snivelling school-stories about 'the honour of the school' and so on. All 'useful' books telling you how to make mechanical things or run them. All animal-stories. I may add that these, in general, are still my views."

Brian Page was beginning to like the claimant.

"Let us take the younger children who were hereabouts," Murray continued. "For instance, the present Lady Farnleigh, whom I used to know as little Molly Bishop. If you are John Farnleigh, what was your private nickname for her?"

" 'The gipsy,' " answered the claimant instantly.

"Why?"

"Because she was always tanned, and was always playing with the children in the gipsy tribe that used to camp at the other side of the Chart."

He glanced at a furious Molly, smiling a little.

"And Mr. Burrows, there—what was your nickname for *him*?"

"Uncas."

"The reason for that?"

"At any I-Spy games, or things like that, he could slide through the shrubbery without making a sound."

"Thank you. And now for you, sir." Murray turned to Farnleigh, and eyed him as though he were about to tell him to straighten his tie. "I do not wish to convey the impression that I am playing cat-and-mouse. So I have only one question for you before I proceed to take the fingerprints. On this question, actually, will depend my private judgment before I see the proof in the prints. The question is this. What is the Red Book of Appin?"

It was almost dark in the library. The heat was still strong, but a small breeze had begun to stir with sundown. It moved through the one or two opened panes of the windows; and the trees stirred with it. A grim—a rather unpleasant—smile moved across Farnleigh's face. He nodded. Taking a notebook and a little gold pencil from his pocket, he tore out a sheet and wrote some words on it. This he folded up and pushed across to Murray.

"It has never caught *me*," Farnleigh said. And then: "Is that the right answer?"

"That is the right answer," agreed Murray. He looked at the claimant. "You, sir: will you answer the same question?"

For the first time the claimant seemed uncertain. His gaze flashed from Farnleigh to Murray with an expression which Page could not read. Without a word he beckoned flatly for the notebook and pencil, which Farnleigh handed over. The claimant wrote only two or three words before he ripped out the sheet and gave it to Murray.

"And now, gentlemen," said Murray, rising. "I think we can take the fingerprints. Here I have the original Thumbograph: much aged, you see. Here is an ink-pad, and here are two white cards. If you will just—may I have some light, please?"

It was Molly who went across and touched the electric switch beside the door. In the library there was a chandelier in tiers of wrought iron which had once supported crowns of candles; now there were small electric bulbs, not all of which worked, so that the light was not overly bright. But it pushed back the summer night; a hundred little reflections of bulbs were thrown back from the window-panes; and the books on the tall shelves looked more grimy still. On the table Murray had spread out his paraphernalia. The Thumbograph, at which they all looked first, was a rickety little book with grey paper covers grown thin from use: the title in red letters, and a large red print of a thumb underneath.

"An old friend," said Murray, patting it. "Now, gentlemen. 'Rolled' prints are better than flat ones; but I did not bring a roller because I wished to reproduce the original conditions. I want only your left thumb-print; there is only one print to compare. Here is a handkerchief with an end doused in benzoline: it will take away the perspiration. Use it. Next——"

It was done.

During that time Page's heart was in his mouth; he could not have said why. But they were all in unnatural states of agitation. For some reason Farnleigh insisted on rolling up his sleeve before making the print, as though he were going to have a blood-transfusion. The mouths of both solicitors, Page was glad to observe, were open. Even the claimant used the handkerchief briskly before he leaned against the table. But what impressed Page most was the confidence of both contestants. The wild thought occurred to Page: suppose those two thumbprints turn out to be exactly alike?

The chances of this happening, he recalled, were just one in sixty-four thousand millions. All the same, nobody faltered or cried off before the test. Nobody——

Murray had a bad fountain-pen. It scratched as he wrote names and markings at the foot of each white (unglazed) card. Then he blotted them carefully, while the contestants wiped their fingers.

"Well?" demanded Farnleigh.

"Well! Now if you will be good enough to give me a quarter of an hour to myself, I can get down to work. Forgive my unsociability; but I realize the importance of this as much as you do."

Burrows blinked. "But can't you—that is, aren't you going to tell us——?"

"My good sir," said Murray, whose own nerves appeared to be feeling the strain, "are you under the impression that a glance at these prints will be enough to compare them? Especially with the print of a boy done in faded ink twenty-five years ago? They will require many points of agreement. It can be done, but a quarter of an hour is an unnaturally modest estimate. Double that: you will be nearer the truth. Now may I settle down?"

From the claimant came a low chuckle.

"I expected that," he said. "But I warn you, it is unwise. I smell blood. You will have to be murdered. No, don't scowl; twenty-five years ago you would have relished the position and revelled in your own importance."

"I see nothing funny in the matter."

"In point of fact, there is nothing funny in it. Here you sit in a lighted room, with a wall of windows giving on a dark garden and a screen of trees and the devil whispering behind every leaf. Be careful."

"Well," returned Murray, with a faint smile creeping round his moustache and into his beard, "in that case I shall take all care. The more nervous of you can keep an eye on me through the window. Now you must excuse me.''

They went out into the hall, and he closed the door on them. Then six persons stood and looked at each other. Lights had already been turned on in the long, pleasant hall; Knowles stood at the door of the dining-room, in the "new" wing which had been built out at the back from the centre of the house, like the body of the letter T with its head as the front. Molly Farnleigh, though flushed and strained, tried to speak coolly.

"Don't you think we had better have something to eat?" she said. "I've ordered a cold buffet prepared. After all, there's no reason why we shouldn't carry on as usual.''

"Thank you," said Welkyn, relieved; "I should like a sandwich."

"Thank you," said Burrows; "I am not hungry."

"Thank you," said the claimant, to swell the chorus. "Whether I accepted or refused, it would sound equally bad. I am going somewhere to smoke a long, strong, black cigar; and then I am going to see that no harm comes to Murray in there.''

Farnleigh said nothing. Just behind him in the hall there was a door giving on that part of the garden overlooked by the library windows. He studied his guests with a long, careful scrutiny; then he opened the glass door and went out into the garden.

In the same way Page presently found himself deserted. The only person in sight was Welkyn, who stood in the dimly lighted dining-room and ate fish-paste sandwiches with great steadiness. Page's watch said that it was twenty minutes past nine o'clock. He hesitated, and then followed Farnleigh out into the cool dimness of the garden.

This side of the garden seemed shut off from the world, and formed an oblong some eighty feet long by forty feet broad. On one side it was closed in by the new wing; on the other by a stretch of high yew hedge. Through the beech trees the library windows spread out a faint and broken wall of light from the narrow side of the oblong. In the new wing, too, the dining-room had glass doors opening out into it, with a balcony overlooking it from the bedroom windows above.

Inspired by King William the Third at Hampton Court, a seventeenth-century Farnleigh had laid out the garden in severe curves and angles of yew hedge, with broad sanded walks between. The hedges were built waist-high; it was, in fact, very much like the foundation of a maze. Though you had no actual difficulty in finding your way about the garden, it would be (Page had always thought) a rare place for hiding-games if you kept down below the line of the hedges. In the centre was a large round open space, buttressed with rose-trees; and this space in turn enclosed an ornamental pool some ten feet in diameter, with a very low coping. In the uncertainty between the lights, with faint gleams from the house meeting a faint afterglow from the west, it was a secret and fragrant place. Yet for some reason Page had never liked the *feel* of that garden.

With this thought came another, a more unpleasant one. There was nothing about a mere garden, a handful of hedges, shrubs, flowers, and soil, which could inspire disquiet. It may have been that the minds and thoughts of everyone here were concentrated so fiercely on the library, moving against that lighted box like moths on the glass. Of course, it was absurd to suppose that anything could happen to Murray. Things are not managed like that; they are not so convenient; it was only the claimant's hypnotic personality which had been able to worm in the suggestion.

"However," Page almost said aloud, "I think I might just stroll past the window and have a look."

He did so, and jerked back with muttered profanity, for someone else had been having a look as well. He did not see who the other person was, because the other person drew away from the screen of beeches against the library windows. But Page saw Kennet Murray inside, sitting at the library table with his back to the windows, and Murray seemed to be just opening a greyish book.

Nonsense.

Page moved away, and walked quickly out into the cool garden. He skirted the round pool, looking up at a single clear star (Madeline Dane had a poetic name for it) which you could see just above a cluster of chimneys in the new wing. Working his way through the low labyrinth, he reached the far end in labyrinthine thought.

Well, was Farnleigh the impostor, or the other fellow? Page did not know; and he had changed his mind so many times in the past two hours that he did not like to guess. Then, too, there had been the persistent, accidental introduction at every turn of the name of Madeline Dane——

At the end of this side of the garden there was a laurel hedge which screened a stone bench from the house. He sat down and lighted a cigarette. Tracing his thoughts back as honestly as he could, he admitted to himself that a part of his grouse at the universe was the persistent recurrence of Madeline Dane's name. Madeline Dane, whose blonde and slender good looks suggested the origin of her surname, was the person who mixed up the "Lives of the Chief Justices" and everything else in Page's thoughts. He was thinking more about her than was good for him. For here he was, getting on towards being a crusty bachelor——

Then Brian Page jumped up from the stone bench, thinking neither of Madeline nor of marriage: only of the sounds he had heard from the garden behind. They were not loud sounds, but they came with terrifying clarity out of the dim, low hedges. The choking noise was the worst: then the shuffle and scrape of feet: then the splash and thrashings.

For a moment he did not want to turn round.

He did not really believe that anything had happened. He never believed that. But he dropped his cigarette on the grass, set his heel on it, and walked back towards the house at a pace that was almost a run. He was some distance away from the house; and in the hide-and-seek paths he took two wrong turnings. At first the uncertain place seemed deserted; next he saw Burrows's tall figure pounding towards him, and the beam of a flashlight flickered over the hedges into his face. When he came close enough to see Burrows's face behind the light, the coolness and fragrance of the garden were lost.

"Well, it's happened," said Burrows.

What Page felt at that moment was a slight physical nausea.

"I don't know what you mean," he lied, "except that it can't have happened."

"I'm simply telling you, that's all," returned a white-faced Burrows, with patient insistence. "Come along quick and help me haul him out. I can't swear he's dead, but he's lying on his face in that pond and I'm pretty sure he's dead."

Page stared in the direction he indicated. He could not see the pool, which was hidden by the hedges; but he now had a good view of the back of the house. From one window of a lighted room over the library, old Knowles the butler was leaning out; and Molly Farnleigh was on the balcony outside her bedroom windows.

"I tell you," Page insisted, "nobody would dare have a go at Murray! It's impossible. It's nonsensical to—and, anyway, what's Murray doing at the pond?"

"Murray?" said the other, staring at him. "Why Murray? Who said anything about Murray? It's *Farnleigh*, man: John Farnleigh. It was all over before I could get there; and I'm afraid it's too late now."

Chapter VI

"But who the devil," Page asked, "would want to kill Farnleigh?" He had to adjust his thoughts. Afterwards he has acknowledged that his original notion of murder had been mere suggestion. Yet, even when another suggestion replaced it, he remembered his first thought: *if* this were murder, it had been ingeniously conceived. As though by an effect of sleight-of-hand, every eye and ear had been concentrated on Kennet Murray. No person in the house had a thought in his head for anybody but Murray. No one would know where anybody had been, anybody but Murray. A person who acted in that vacuum could attack unseen, so long as he did not attack Murray.

"Kill Farnleigh?" repeated Burrows in a queer voice. "Here, this won't do. Wake up. Stop. Steady. Come on."

Still talking like a man giving directions for backing a car, he led the way with his lanky stride. The beam from the flashlight was steady. But he switched it off before they reached the pond, either because there was still enough light from the sky or because he did not wish to see things too clearly just then.

Round the pool there was a border of packed sand some five feet wide. Forms, even faces, were still dimly visible. Farnleigh lay prone in the pool, turned a little towards the right as you faced the rear of the garden. The pool was just deep enough so that his body rocked with the water, which still slopped and splashed over the low round edge of the coping, running across packed sand. They also saw a darker dye in the water, curling upwards and spreading round him; but they did not see the full colour of this dye until it touched a patch of white water-lilies close to the body.

The slopping agitation of the water began again when Page started to haul him out; Farnleigh's heel just touched the edge of the low coping. But, after one minute which Page never wished to remember afterwards, Page got up.

"We can't do him any good," Page said. "His throat's been cut."

The shock had not worn off yet, and they both spoke calmly.

"Yes. I was afraid of that. It's——"

"It's murder. Or," said Page abruptly, "suicide."

They looked at each other in the dusk.

"All the same," argued Burrows, trying to be official-mannered and human at the same time, "we've got to get him out of there. That rule about touching nothing and waiting for the police is all very well, but we can't let him lie there. It's not decent. Besides, his position has been disturbed as it is. Shall we——?"

"Yes."

The tweed suit, now black and bulging, seemed to have accumulated a ton of water. With difficulty they rolled Farnleigh over the edge, sending a minor tidal wave across themselves. The peaceful evening scent of the garden, especially the roses, had never seemed more theatrically romantic than in the midst of this reality. Page kept thinking: this is John Farnleigh, and he's dead. This is impossible. And it was impossible, except for one thought which grew clearer every second.

"You mean suicide," said Burrows, wiping his hands. "We've had a hallucination of murder put on us, but I don't like this any better. You see what it means? It means he was the impostor after all. He bluffed it out as long as he could, and hoped against hope that Murray might not have the fingerprints. When the test was over he couldn't face the consequences. So he came out here, stood on the edge of the pool, and—" Burrows put up a hand to his throat.

It all fitted very well.

"I'm afraid so," admitted Page. Afraid? Afraid? Yes: wasn't that the worst charge you could make against a dead friend, pile the whole burden on him now that he couldn't speak? Resentment rose up in a dull ache, for John Farnleigh had been his friend. "But it's the only thing we can think. For God's sake what happened here? Did you see him do it? What did he do it with?"

"No. That is, I didn't exactly see him. I was just coming out of the door from the hall back there. I'd got this torch,"—Burrows snapped the button on and off, and then held it up,—"out of the drawer of the table in the hall. You know how weak my eyes are when I go out in the dark. Just as I was opening the door, I saw Farnleigh standing out here—very dimly, you know—on the edge of the pool, with his back towards me. Then he seemed to be doing something, or moving about a bit: with my eyesight, it's very difficult to tell. You must have heard the noises. After I heard that splash—and the thrashing round, you know, which was worse. There never was a balder, worse story."

"But there wasn't anybody with him?"

"No," said Burrows, spreading out his fingers against his forehead and pressing the tips of them there. "Or at least—not exactly. These hedges are waist-high, and——"

The meaning of the words "not exactly," spoken by the meticulously careful Nathaniel Burrows, Page did not have time to inquire. Voices and footsteps were stirring from the direction of the house, and he spoke quickly.

"You're the one with authority. They're all coming. Molly mustn't see this. Can't you use your authority and head 'em off?"

Burrows cleared his throat two or three times, like a nervous orator about to begin, and his shoulders straightened. Switching on the flash-light, he walked towards the house with the light pointing in that direction. Its beam picked out Molly, with Kennet Murray following; but it did not shine on their faces.

"I am sorry," began Burrows, in tones of high and unnatural sharpness. "But there has been an accident to Sir John, and you had better not go out there——"

"Don't be a fool," said Molly in a hard voice. With deliberate strength she pushed past him, and came into the gloom beside the pool. Fortunately she could not see the extent of what had been done. Though she tried to give the impression of calmness, Page heard her heel turn in the path. He put an arm round her shoulder to steady her; she leaned against it, and he felt unsteady breathing. But what she said, flung out in a sob, seemed merely cryptic. Molly said:

"D-damn him for being *right!*"

By something in the tone Page knew that she could not be referring to her husband. But for a moment it so startled him that he could not take it in. Then, hiding her face even from the dark, she started in a hurried walk for the house.

"Let her go," said Murray. "It will be better for her."

But Murray did not appear as capable as you might have thought, faced with a thing of this sort. He hesitated. Taking the flashlight from Burrows's hand, he directed its beam on the body beside the pool. Then he let out a whistle, his teeth showing between cropped moustache and beard.

"Did you prove," asked Page, "that Sir John Farnleigh was not Sir John Farnleigh?"

"Eh? I beg your pardon?"

Page repeated his question.

"I have proved," said Murray with heavy gravity, "absolutely nothing. I mean that I had not completed my comparison of the prints; I had barely begun it."

"It would appear,"—Burrows spoke rather weakly,—"that you would not need to finish."

And so it would. There could not be, in all truth and reason, much doubt of Farnleigh's suicide. Page saw that Murray was nodding, in his sometimes vague manner: nodding as though he were not thinking of the matter at all: and stroking the cheek of his beard like a man who tries to place an old memory. It was not a physical wriggling, yet it gave that impression.

"But you can't have much doubt, can you?" Page was prompted to ask. "Which one of them did you think was the fake?"

"I have already informed you—" Murray snapped.

"Yes, I know, but look here. I was only asking, which one of them did you *think* was the impostor? You surely must have had some notion after you'd talked to them. After all, it's the only really important thing either about the imposture or about this; and you can't have any doubt about it? If Farnleigh is the impostor, he had good reason to kill himself and we can certainly agree that he did. But if by any inconceivable chance he were not the impostor——"

"You are assuming——?"

"No, no, only asking. If he were the real Sir John Farnleigh, there would be no reason for him to cut his throat. So he must be the impostor. Isn't he?"

"The tendency to leap to conclusions without even examining the data," began Murray, in a tone between asperity and comfortable discussion, "is one to which the unacademic mind is strongly——"

"Right you are; question withdrawn," said Page.

"No, no, you misunderstand." Here Murray waved his hand like a hypnotist; he seemed uncomfortable and flustered that the balance of argument had been disturbed. "You intimate that this might be murder on the grounds that, if the—er—unfortunate gentleman before us were the real John Farnleigh, he would not kill himself. But, whether he is or is not the real Johnny, why should anyone kill him? If he is a fraud, why murder him? The law will attend to him. If he is real, why murder him? He has done no harm to anyone. You see, I am only taking both sides of it."

Burrows spoke gloomily. "It's all this talk, suddenly produced, about Scotland Yard and poor Victoria Daly. I've always thought I was a sensible sort of fellow; but it's given me all sorts of ideas that I've got to root out of my head. And then I've never liked the feel of this blasted garden."

"You felt that too?" demanded Page.

Murray was regarding them with a blaze of interest.

"Stop," he said. "About the garden: why don't you like it, Mr. Burrows? Have you any memories connected with it?"

"Not exactly memories." The other considered; he seemed uncomfortable. "It was only that, when anyone used to tell a ghost-story, it was twice as effective here as anywhere else. I remember one about—but that doesn't matter. I used to think it would be very easy to raise the devil here; and I don't mean cut up a row, either. However, this is still beside the point. We've got work to do. We can't stand here talking——"

Murray roused himself; he grew almost excited. "Ah, yes. The police," he said. "Yes, there is a great deal to be done, in the—er—practical world. You will, I think, allow me to take charge. Will you come with me, Mr. Burrows? Mr. Page, will you oblige us by remaining with the—er—body until we return?"

"Why?" asked the practical Page.

"It is customary. Oh, yes. Indeed, it is absolutely necessary. Kindly give Mr. Page your flashlight, my friend. And now this way. There was no telephone at the Close when I lived here; but I presume there is one now? Good, good, good. We must also have a doctor."

He bustled off, shepherding Burrows, and Page was left beside the pool with what remained of John Farnleigh.

With the shock wearing off, Page stood in the dark and reflected on the increasing uselessness and complexity of this tragedy. Yet the suicide of an impostor was simple enough. What disturbed him was the realization that he had got absolutely no change out of Murray. It would also have been simple enough for Murray to have said, "Yes, that is undoubtedly the impostor: I knew it from the beginning"; and, in fact, Murray's whole atmosphere had conveyed that this was what he thought. But he had said nothing. Was it, then, merely his own love of mystery?

"Farnleigh!" Page said aloud. "Farnleigh!"

"Did you call me?" asked a voice almost at his elbow.

The effect of that voice in the dark was to make Page jump back so that he almost stumbled over the body. Forms and outlines were now completely lost in night. The stir of a footstep on a sanded path was followed by the rasping of a match. The flame of the match sprang up over its box, cupped in two hands; and showed, in one opening of the yew hedge, the face of the claimant—Patrick Gore, John Farnleigh—looking into the space beside the pool. He came forward at his slightly clumsy walk.

The claimant was carrying a thin black cigar, half-smoked and gone out. He put it into his mouth, lit it carefully, and then peered up.

"Did you call me?" he repeated.

"I didn't," Page said grimly. "But it's a good thing you answered. Do you know what's happened?"

"Yes."

"Where have you been?"

"Wandering."

The match went out; but Page could hear him breathing faintly. That the man was shaken there could be little doubt. He came closer, his fists on his hips and the cigar glowing in a corner of his mouth.

"Poor crook," said the claimant, looking down. "And something about him a good deal to be respected, too. I'm rather sorry I did this. I've no doubt he reverted to the Puritan faith of his fathers and spent a good many years repenting at the same time he kept fast hold on the estate. After all, he could have continued posing and made a better squire than I ever shall. But the wrong Farnleigh stuff was missing, and so he did this."

"Suicide."

"Without a doubt." The claimant took the cigar out of his mouth and blew out a cloud of smoke, which curled in the darkness with the odd effect of a ghost taking form. "I suppose Murray has finished comparing the prints. You were present at that little inquisition by Murray. Tell me: did you notice the exact point at which our—late friend slipped and gave away the fact that he was not John Farnleigh?"

"No."

Then Page suddenly realized that the claimant's shaken air was due as much to relief as to any other emotion.

"Murray would not be Murray," he said with a certain dryness, "if he had not included a catch question. That always was his nature. I was expecting it and even dreading it: in case it should not really be a catch question, but something I had forgotten. But it was a fairly obvious catch when it came. You remember. 'What is the Red Book of Appin?' "

"Yes. Both of you wrote down something——"

"Of course there is no such thing. I should be interested to see what gibberish my late rival wrote down in order to explain it. It was all the more intriguing when Murray, with a face as solemn as an owl, assured him he had written the correct answer; but you observed that the very assurance almost finished my rival. Oh, curse it all," he broke off, and made a gesture with the lighted end of his cigar which was curiously like a question-mark. "Well, let us see what the poor devil did to himself. May I have that electric torch?"

Page handed it over, and moved away while the other squatted down with the light. There was a long silence, with an occasional muttering. Then the claimant got up. Though he moved slowly, he snapped the button of the electric torch on and off.

"My friend," he said in a different voice, "this won't do."

"What won't do?"

"This. I hate what I am going to say. But I will take my oath this man did not kill himself."

(Score one for suggestion, intuition, or the influence of a certain garden at twilight.)

"Why?" said Page.

"Have you looked at him closely? Then come and do it now. Does a man cut his own throat with three separate slashes, all of which sever the jugular vein, and any one of which would have caused death? Can he do it? I don't know, but I doubt it. Remember, I began my self-made career in a circus. I never saw anything like this since Barney Poole, the best animal-trainer west of the Mississippi, was killed by a leopard."

A night breeze moved in the labyrinth, and stirred the roses.

"Where, I wonder, is the weapon?" he went on. He played the beam of his torch over the misted water. "Probably in the pool here, but I don't think we had better go after it. The police may be more necessary in this business than we think. This alters matters in a way that—that worries me," said the claiment, as though making a concession. "Why kill an impostor?"

"Or a real heir, for that matter," said Page.

Then Page could sense that the other was eyeing him sharply. "You do not still believe——?"

They were interrupted by footsteps coming rapidly if pontifically from the direction of the house. The claimant turned the beam of light on Welkyn, the solicitor, whom Page last remembered eating fish-paste sandwiches in the dining-room. Welkyn, now evidently a very scared man, gripped the edge of the white slip inside his waistcoat as though he were going to make a speech. Then he changed his mind.

"You'd better get back to the house, gentlemen," he said. "Mr. Murray would like to see you. I *hope*," he gave the word a sinister emphasis, and looked hard at the claimant, "I hope neither of you gentlemen has been in the house since this thing happened."

"Patrick Gore" whipped round. "Don't tell me anything else has happened?"

"It has," said Welkyn snappishly. "It appears that someone has taken advantage of this confusion. In Mr. Murray's absence, someone went into the library and stole the Thumbograph containing our only evidence."

II

Thursday, July 30th

THE LIFE OF AN AUTOMATON

Then all was silent, and presently Moxon reappeared and said, with a rather sorry smile:

"Pardon me for leaving you so abruptly. I have a machine in there that lost its temper and cut up rough."

Fixing my eyes steadily upon his left cheek, which was traversed by four parallel excoriations showing blood, I said:

"How would it do to trim its nails?"

—AMBROSE BIERCE, Moxon's Master

Chapter VII

In early afternoon of the following day, while grey, warm rain darkened the countryside, Page sat again at the desk in his study; but this time with very different thoughts.

Up and down the room, in a way as monotonous as the sound of the rain itself, paced Detective-Inspector Elliot.

And throned in the largest chair sat Dr. Gideon Fell.

The doctor's thunderous chuckles were today subdued. He had arrived in Mallingford that morning, and he did not seem to like the situation he found. Sitting back in the big chair, he wheezed gently. His eyes, behind the eyeglasses on the broad black ribbon, were fixed with singular concentration on a corner of the desk; his bandit's moustache bristled as though ready for argument, and his big mop of grey-streaked hair had fallen over one ear. On a chair beside him lay his shovel-hat and his stick with the ivory crutch-handle. Though there was a pint tankard of beer at his elbow, he did not seem interested even in this. And, though his red face was even more red in the July heat, it hardly expressed his customary joviality. Page found him even larger, both in height and circumference, than he had been described; when he first came into the cottage, wearing his box-pleated cape, he seemed to fill the place and crowd out even the furniture.

Nor did anybody like the situation within the district of Mallingford and Soane. The district retreated within itself; it was not even eloquently silent. Everybody now knew that the stranger known as a "folklore authority" at the *Bull and Butcher* was an inspector of the Criminal Investigation Department. But not a word was said of it. In the taproom of the *Bull and Butcher,* those who came in for their morning pint spoke in a little lower tone, and drifted away sooner; that was all. Dr. Fell had been unable to get accommodations at the pub—inn by courtesy—since both guest rooms were occupied; and Page had been only too glad to offer the hospitality of his cottage.

Page liked Inspector Elliot as well. Andrew MacAndrew Elliot looked out of place neither as folklore authority nor as Scotland Yard man. He was youngish, raw-boned, sandy-haired, and serious-minded. He liked argument, and he liked subtleties in a way that would have displeased Superintendent Hadley. His education had been that thorough Scots one which deals with the minutest details of the minutest subject. Now, pacing the floor of Page's study while the grey rain fell, he tried to make his position clear.

"H'mf, yes," grunted Dr. Fell. "But exactly what has been done so far?"

Elliot considered. "Captain Marchbanks, the Chief Constable, telephoned to the Yard this morning and washed his hands of the business," he said. "Ordinarily, of course, they'd have sent a chief inspector. But, since I happened to be on the spot and already investigating something that may be connected with this——"

(The murder of Victoria Daly, thought Page. But how connected?)

"You got your chance," said Dr. Fell. "Excellent."

"Yes, sir, I got my chance," agreed Elliot, placing a freckled fist carefully on the table and bracing himself over it. "And I mean to make something of it, if I can. It's opportunity. It's—you know all that." He expelled his breath. "But you know the difficulties I'm going to find. People hereabouts have shut up tighter than windows. You try to see inside, but they won't let you inside. They'll drink a glass of beer and talk just as usual; but they fall away as soon as you say anything about it. With what we'll call the gentry of the whole district"—his tone showed a certain faint contempt for the word—"it's been even more difficult, even before this thing happened."

"About the other affair, you mean?" inquired Dr. Fell, opening one eye.

"About the other affair. The only one who's been at all helpful is a Miss Dane, Madeline Dane. There," declared Inspector Elliot, with measured carefulness and emphasis, "is a real woman. It's a pleasure to talk to her. *Not* one of your hard-boiled misses who blow smoke in your eye and ring up their lawyers as soon as you send in a card. No. A real woman; reminds me of a girl I used to know at home."

Dr. Fell opened both eyes, while Inspector Elliot (so to speak) fidgeted under his freckles for having said this. But Brian Page understood and approved. He was even conscious of a twinge of nonsensical jealousy.

"However," the inspector resumed, "you'll want to know about Farnleigh Close. I've taken a statement from everybody who was there last night: exclusive of servants, as yet. A brief statement. I had to round some of them up. Mr. Burrows stayed at the Close last night, to be ready for us today. But the claimant, this Mr. Patrick Gore, and his solicitor (name of Welkyn) both went back to Maidstone." He looked round at Page. "I gather, sir, there was a bit of a row—or, well, say that things got pretty strained after this Thumbograph had been stolen?"

Page admitted it with some fervour.

"Especially after the Thumbograph was stolen," he replied. "The odd part of it was that to everybody except Molly Farnleigh it seemed more important that the evidence had been stolen than that Farnleigh had been murdered—if he was murdered."

A gleam of interest stirred in Dr. Fell's eye. "By the way, what was the general attitude in the question of suicide *v.* murder?"

"Very cautious. A great lack of attitude, which is surprising. The only one who definitely said he'd been murdered (screamed it, in fact) was Molly—Lady Farnleigh, I mean. Otherwise accusations of crookedness hurtled about in a way I hope won't be remembered today. I'm glad to say I don't remember half of it. I suppose it was only natural. Beforehand we had all been so strainedly and unnaturally on our best behaviour that the reaction was a little too much. Even solicitors, it appears, are human. Murray tried to take charge, and was swept under. Our local police-sergeant wasn't much better."

"I am endeavouring," said Dr. Fell, making a hideous face of emphasis, "to clear the way to the problem. You say, inspector, you don't have much doubt that it is murder?"

Elliot was firm.

"No, sir, I haven't. There were three gashes across the throat, *and* no weapon I've been able to find so far, either in the pool or anywhere at hand. Mind," he said cautiously, "I haven't had the medical report. I don't say it's impossible for a man to inflict three such wounds on himself. But the absence of a weapon seems to decide it."

For a moment they listened to the rain, and to the doubtful wheezing of Dr. Fell's breath.

"You don't think," suggested the doctor, "I only—harrumph—put it forward as a suggestion: you don't think he might have killed himself and, in the convulsion, flung the weapon away from him, so that you haven't found it? That has happened before, I think."

"It's remotely possible. But he can't have thrown it clear out of the garden; and, if it's there anywhere, Sergeant Burton will find it." There was a curious look on Elliot's hard face. "Look here, sir: do *you* think this is suicide?"

"No, no, no," said Dr. Fell earnestly, as though this rather shocked him. "But, even believing that this is murder, I still want to know what our problem is."

"Our problem is who killed Sir John Farnleigh."

"Quite. You still don't perceive the double-alley of hell into which that leads us. I am worried about this case, because all rules have been violated. All rules have been violated because the wrong man had been chosen for a victim. If only Murray had been murdered! (I speak academically, you understand.) Hang it all, Murray should have been murdered! In any well-constituted plot he would have been murdered. His presence cries out for it. Here is a man possessing evidence which will decide a vital problem at the outset: here is a man who probably can solve the puzzle of identities even without that evidence: well, he is the certain candidate for the death-blow. Yet he remains untouched, and the problem of identities is merely made more inexplicable by the death of one of the claimants. You follow that?"

"I do," said Inspector Elliot grimly.

"Let's clear away some of the underbrush," insisted Dr. Fell. "Is the whole thing, for instance, an error on the part of the murderer? Was Sir John Farnleigh (to give him his present name) not intended to be the victim at all? Did the murderer kill him in mistake for somebody else?"

"It seems doubtful," said Elliot, and looked at Page.

"It's impossible," said Page. "I'd thought of that too. Well, I repeat: it's impossible. The light was too good. Farnleigh didn't look like anybody else, and wasn't dressed like anybody else. Even from some distance away you could never have mistaken him, let alone at the close quarters of someone who cuts his throat. It was that queerish watery light where details are blurred but all outlines are clear."

"Then Farnleigh was the intended victim," said Dr. Fell, clearing his throat with a long rumbling noise. "Very well. What other possible undergrowths or verbiage can we rake away? For instance, is it possible that this murder has no connection whatever with the battle over the title and estates? Did some person unaffected by this debate—some person who didn't care whether he was John Farnleigh or Patrick Gore—choose just this moment to slide through the screen and kill him for some outside motive we don't know? It is possible. It is possible if the Powers are being coy. But I for one am not going to worry about it. These things are cohesive; they depend on each other. For, you notice, the Thumbograph-evidence was stolen at the same time Farnleigh was murdered.

"Very well. Farnleigh was deliberately murdered, and murdered for some reason connected with the question of the right heir to the estates. But we still haven't decided what our real problem is. The problem is still double-headed, not to say double-faced. Thus. If the murdered man was an impostor, he might have been killed for any one of two or three reasons. You can imagine them. But, if the murdered man was the real heir, he might have been killed for any one of two or three totally different reasons. You can imagine those too. They entail different sides, different eyes, different motives. Therefore, which of those two is the impostor? We have got to know that before we have the remotest idea in which direction we've got to look. Harrumph."

Inspector Elliot's face hardened.

"You mean that the key is this Mr. Murray?"

"I do. I mean my old, enigmatic acquaintance, Kennet Murray."

"You think he knows which is which?"

"I've got no doubt of it," growled Dr. Fell.

"Nor I," said the inspector dryly. "Let's see, now." He got out his notebook and opened it. "Everyone seems to be agreed—remarkable what a lot of agreement there is—that Mr. Murray was left alone in the study at about twenty minutes past nine o'clock. Correct, Mr. Page?"

"Correct."

"The murder (we'll call it that) was committed at about half-past nine. Two persons give a definite time about this: Murray and the solicitor, Harold Welkyn. Now ten minutes may not be a long time. But the comparison of fingerprints, though you've got to be careful about it, isn't the all-night job Murray gave you to understand. You can't tell me he didn't have *some* idea—Do you think he's a wrong 'un, sir?"

"No," said Dr. Fell, frowning heavily at the tankard of ale. "I think he's trying to do a spot of sensational detection. And in just a minute I'll tell you what I think this case is. You say you got a statement from each of them as to what each was doing during that ten minutes?"

"Bald few lines from everybody," said Elliot, suddenly angry. "No comments. They asked what comments they could make. Well, I mean to ask again, and comment too. Queerish crowd, if you ask me. I know things sound pretty shorn in a policeman's report, because you've got to stick little bits of facts together without anything between: and thankful to get what you do. But there's black murder and plain hell in the midst of them, and this is what they say. Listen."

He opened his notebook.

"*Statement of Lady Farnleigh:* When we left the library I was upset, so I went upstairs to my bedroom. My husband and I have adjoining bedrooms on the first floor of the new wing, over the dining-room. I washed my face and hands. I told my maid to lay out another frock, because I felt grubby. I lay down on the bed. There was only a very small light from the bedside lamp. The windows were open on the balcony of my room overlooking the garden. I heard noises like a fight and a scuffling and a kind of cry, and then a splash. I ran to the balcony and saw my husband. He seemed to be lying in the pool and fighting. He was alone then. I could see this clearly. I ran downstairs by the main staircase, and out to him. I did not see or hear anything suspicious in the garden.

"Next we have:

"*Statement of Kennet Murray:* I remained in the library between nine-twenty and nine-thirty. No one entered the room, and I saw no one else. My back was to the window. I heard the sounds (similarly described). I did not think anything serious had happened until I heard someone run downstairs in the hall. I heard Lady Farnleigh's voice calling out to the butler that she was afraid something had happened to Sir John. I looked at my watch; it was then just nine-thirty. I joined Lady Farnleigh in the hall, and we went out into the garden, where we found a man with his throat cut. I have no comment to make at this time on the fingerprints or my comparisons of them.

"Fine and helpful, isn't it? Then we have:

"*Statement of Patrick Gore, claimant:* I wandered. I was out on the front lawn first, smoking. Then I wandered round the south side of the house to this garden. I did not hear any sounds except a splash, and I heard that very faintly. I think I heard this when I had just started round the side of the house. I did not think anything was wrong. When I came into the garden I heard loud voices talking. I did not want any company, so I kept to the side path along the high yew hedge bounding the garden. Then I heard what they were talking about. I listened. I did not go to the pool until all of them except a man named Page had gone back to the house.

"Finally, we come to:

"*Statement of Harold Welkyn:* I remained in the dining-room and did not leave it at any time. I ate five small sandwiches and drank a glass of port. I agree that the dining-room has glass doors opening out into the garden, and that one of these doors is not far from the pool in a straight line. But the lights were full on in the dining-room, and I could not see anything in the garden because of the contrasting lights——

"A witness dead on the scene. Ground floor: hedges only waist-high: not more than twenty feet from where Farnleigh must have been standing," said Elliot, flicking his notebook with finger and thumb. "But he's deaf and blind in his 'contrasting lights.' He concludes:

"At nine thirty-one by the grandfather clock in the dining-room I heard certain noises resembling a scuffle and a stopped cry. This was followed by a series of loud splashings. I also heard a kind of rustling noise in the hedges or shrubbery, and I thought I saw something looking at me through one of the glass panels of the door, one of the panels down nearest the ground. I was afraid that certain things might have happened which were no affair of mine. I sat down and waited until Mr. Burrows came in and told me the fraudulent Sir John Farnleigh had committed suicide. During this time I did not do anything except eat another sandwich."

Dr. Fell, wheezing into a more upright position, reached out after the tankard of ale and took a deep pull. There was a steady, gleaming excitement behind his eyeglasses, a sort of astonished pleasure.

"Oh, Bacchus!" he said in a hollow voice. " 'Shorn' statements, hey? Is that your considered opinion? There is something in our Mr. Welkyn's statement which tends to give me a cauld grue. H'mf, ha, stop a bit. Welkyn! Welkyn! Haven't I heard that name somewhere before? I'm certain of it, because it cries aloud for bad puns, and therefore it would stick in my—'What is mind?' 'No matter.' 'What is matter?' 'Never mind.' I beg your pardon; I was scatter-braining again. Have you got anything else?"

"Well, there were two other guests, Mr. Page here and Mr. Burrows. You've heard Mr. Page's statement, and you've had the gist of Mr. Burrows's."

"Never mind. Read it again, will you?"

Inspector Elliot frowned.

"*Statement of Nathaniel Burrows:* I could have eaten something, but Welkyn was in the dining-room and I did not think it proper for me to talk to him then. I went to the drawing-room at the other side of the house and waited. Then I thought that my proper place was with Sir John Farnleigh, who had gone out into the south garden. I took an electric torch out of the table in the hall. I did this because my eyesight is not good. As I was starting to open the door to the garden I saw Sir John. He was standing on the edge of the pool. He seemed to be doing something, or moving about a little. From the door to the nearer edge of the pool is about thirty-five feet. I heard the scuffling sounds, and then the splash and the churnings in water. I ran down there and found him. I am not able to swear whether or not there was anybody with him. I cannot give an exact description of the movements he made. It was as though something had got hold of his feet.

"And there we are, sir. You notice certain things. Except Mr. Burrows, nobody ever actually saw the victim before he was attacked and fell or was thrown into the pool. Lady Farnleigh didn't see him until he was in the pool; Mr. Gore, Mr. Murray, Mr. Welkyn, and Mr. Page didn't see him until afterwards—or so they say. There are other things," he prodded, "which you'll have noticed?"

"Eh?" said Dr. Fell vaguely.

"I asked what you made of it."

"Why, I'll tell you what I was thinking. 'A garden is a lovesome thing, God wot,' " said Dr. Fell. "But what about the sequel? After the murder, I gather, the Thumbograph was pinched from the library when Murray came out to see what was up. Did you get a statement from the various persons about what they were doing then, or who might have pinched it?"

"I did," said Elliot. "But I won't read it to you, sir. And why? Because it's one great, serene blank. Analyzed and boiled down, it amounts to this: that anybody might have stolen the Thumbograph, and that in the general confusion nobody would have noticed who did."

"Oh, Lord!" Dr. Fell groaned, after a pause. "We've got it at last."

"Got what?"

"What I've been half-dreading for a long time—an almost purely psychological puzzle. There are no discrepancies in the various stories, in the various times given, even in the various possiblities. There are no incongruities to explain, except the thundering psychological incongruity of why the wrong man should have been so carefully murdered. Above all, there is an almost complete absence of material clues: no cuff-links, cigarette-ends, theatre-ticket-stubs, pens, ink, or paper. H'mf. Unless we get our claws into something more tangible, we shall merely fumble with the greased pig called human behaviour. Which person, then, would be most likely to kill the man who was killed? And why? And which person fits best, psychologically, into the pattern of devilry you've drawn round Victoria Daly's murder?"

Elliot began to whistle through his teeth. He said: "Any ideas, sir?"

"Let me see," muttered Dr. Fell, "if I have mastered the essential facts in the case of Victoria Daly. Age 35, spinster, pleasant, not intelligent, lived alone. H'mf. Ha. Yes. Murdered about 11.45 P.M. on July 31st, last. Right, my lad?"

"Right."

"Alarm given by farmer driving home past her cottage. Screams coming from there. Village policeman, passing on bicycle, follows farmer. Both see a man—tramp known in district—climbing out of window, ground-floor, rear. Both follow in quarter-mile chase. Tramp, trying to cut off pursuit by getting over gates and across tracks ahead of Southern Railway goods-train, is eliminated quickly if not neatly. Right?"

"Right."

"Miss Daly found in ground-floor room of cottage: her bedroom. Strangled with bootlace. When attacked, was retiring but had not yet gone to bed. Wore night-dress, quilted dressing-gown, and slippers. Apparently clear case—money and valuables found on tramp—except for one fact. On examination by doctor, body found smeared with dark sooty compound; same compound also found under all finger-nails. Eh? This substance, analyzed by Home Office man, proved to be composed of juice of water parsnip, aconite, cinquefoil, deadly nightshade, and soot."

Page sat up, mentally stuttering. Until the last part of Dr. Fell's statement, he had heard it all a thousand times before.

"Here!" he protested. "That's the first time anybody's mentioned a thing like that. You found smeared on the body a substance containing two deadly poisons?"

"Yes," said Elliot, with a broad and sardonic grin. "The local doctor didn't have it analyzed, of course. The coroner didn't think it was important and didn't even bring it up at the inquest. He probably thought it was some kind of beauty-preparation, which it would be indelicate to mention. But the doctor later passed on a quiet word, and——"

Page was troubled. "Aconite and deadly nightshade! All the same, they weren't swallowed, were they? They wouldn't have killed her if they only touched her externally, would they?"

"Oh, no. All the same, it's a fairly clear case. Don't you think so, sir?"

"An unfortunately clear case," admitted Dr. Fell.

Above the noise of the rain Page heard a rapping at the front door of the cottage. Trying to place an elusive memory, he went out through the short passage and opened the door. It was Sergeant Burton of the local police, wearing a rubber hood and coat, under which he was shielding something wrapped in newspapers. What he said brought Page's thoughts back from Victoria Daly to the closer problem of Farnleigh.

"Might I see Inspector Elliot and Dr. Fell, sir?" Burton said. "I've got the weapon, right enough. And——"

He gestured with his head. Beyond a muddy front garden pricked up into puddles by the rain, a familiar car stood by the front gate. It was an ancient Morris, and there seemed to be two persons behind the side-curtains. Inspector Elliot came to the door hurriedly.

"You said——?"

"I've got the weapon that killed Sir John, Inspector. And something else too." Again Sergeant Burton moved his head in the direction of the car. "It's Miss Madeline Dane and old Mr. Knowles, who works up at the Close. He used to work for Miss Dane's father's best friend. When he wasn't sure what to do he went to Miss Dane, and she sent him to me. He's got something to tell you that'll probably straighten out the whole case."

Chapter VIII

They put down the newspaper-parcel on Page's writing-table, and unfolded it to reveal the weapon. It was a pocket-knife; a boy's pocket-knife of old-fashioned design; and, under the present circumstances, a heavy and murderous-looking pocket-knife.

In addition to the main blade—which was open now—its wooden handle contained two smaller blades, a corkscrew, and an implement once alleged to be useful for removing stones from horses' hoofs. To Page it brought back the days when to possess such a fine knife was the proud mark of almost-manhood: when you were an adventurer, almost a red Indian. It was an old knife. The main blade, well over four inches long, bore two deep triangular nicks, and the steel was ragged in places; but it was not rusty, and it had been kept razor-sharp. There was about it now no suggestion of playing at Indians. From point to handle the heavy blade was discoloured with bloodstains which had recently dried.

A feeling of uneasiness touched them all as they looked at it. Inspector Elliot straightened up.

"Where did you find this?"

"Stuck down deep inside one of those low hedges; about," said Sergeant Burton, half-closing one eye to estimate, "about ten feet away from the lily-pond."

"Away from the pool in which direction?"

"Towards the left, standing with your back to the house. Towards that high hedge that's the south boundary. A bit nearer in to the house than the lily-pond is. You see, sir," explained the sergeant carefully, "it was luck—me finding it. We might have searched for a month and never found it. No more we mightn't, unless we pulled all the hedges to bits. That yew's as thick as sin. It was the rain that did it. I was running my hand along the top of one hedge; not meaning anything, you understand; just wondering where to look. The hedge was wet, and my hand came away with a bit of reddy-brown colour on it. That was where it'd left a bit of blood on the flat top of the hedge when it went through. You couldn't even see the cut in the top where she'd gone through. I dug her out. The hedge kept the rain off, as you see."

"Somebody'd pushed it straight down through the hedge, you think?"

Sergeant Burton considered.

"Yes, it'd be that. I think. She was stuck in there straight, point downwards. Or else—that's a good heavy knife, sir. Blade's as heavy as the handle. If somebody threw her away, or up into the air, she'd have come down blade first and gone through just like that."

There was a certain look on Sergeant Burton's face which no one there failed to interpret. Dr. Fell, who had been sunk in some obscure musing, rolled up his head; Dr. Fell's large under-lip came out in a mutinous way.

"H'm," he said. " 'Threw her away?' After suicide, you mean?"

Burton's forehead altered slightly; he said nothing.

"It's the knife we want, right enough," Inspector Elliot conceded. "I didn't like the jagged, crooked look of two of the three wounds on that fellow. They looked more like mauling or tearing. But look here!—look at the notches in this blade. They'll fit or I'm a Dutchman. What do you say?"

"About Miss Dane and old Mr. Knowles, sir——?"

"Yes; ask them if they'll come in. That's good work, sergeant; damned good work. You might go and see whether the doctor has any news for me."

Dr. Fell and the inspector were beginning to argue as Page picked up an umbrella from the passage and went out to bring Madeline in.

Not rain or mud could alter Madeline's trimness, or ruffle her quiet good-temper. She was wearing one of those transparent oilskin water-proofs, with a hood, which made her look as though she were wrapped in cellophane. Her blonde hair was done into something like curls above the ears; she had a pale, healthy face, the nose and mouth a little broad, the eyes a little long; yet the whole of a beauty which grew on you the more you noticed it. For she never gave the impression of wanting to be noticed; she was one of those persons who seem cut out to be good listeners. Her eyes were very dark blue, with a deep glance of sincerity. Though her figure was good—Page always damned himself for noticing her figure—she conveyed an impression of fragility. She put her hand on his arm, and gave him an uncertain smile, as he helped her out of the car under the umbrella.

"I'm terribly glad it's at your house," she said in her soft voice. "It makes things easier, somehow. But I really didn't know what to do, and it seemed the best way——"

She glanced back at stout Knowles, who was getting out of the car. Knowles carried his bowler hat even in the rain, and he was picking his way in a pigeon-toed waddle through the mud.

Page took Madeline into the study, and introduced her proudly. He wanted to show her off to Dr. Fell. Certainly the doctor's response was everything that could be wished. He beamed down on her in a way that threatened to split several waistcoat-buttons, and seemed to turn on lights behind his eyeglasses; he towered up, chuckling, and it was the doctor himself who took her waterproof when she sat down.

Inspector Elliot was at his most brisk and official. He spoke like a shop-assistant behind a counter.

"Yes, Miss Dane? And what can I do for you?"

Madeline regarded her clasped hands, and looked round with a pleasant frown before her candid gaze met the inspector's.

"You see, it's very difficult to explain," she said. "I know I must do it. Someone must do it, after that terrible affair last night. And yet I don't want Knowles to get into trouble. He mustn't, Mr. Elliott——!"

"If anything's bothering you, Miss Dane, just tell me," said Elliot briskly; "and nobody will get into trouble."

She gave him a grateful look.

"Then perhaps—You'd better tell them, Knowles. What you told me."

"Heh-heh-heh," said Dr. Fell. "Sit down, man!"

"No, sir; thank you; I——"

"Sit down!" thundered Dr. Fell.

As an alternative to being pushed down, which from the doctor's gesture seemed imminent, Knowles obeyed. Knowles was an honest man: sometimes a dangerously honest man. He had one of those faces which in moments of mental stress go transparently pink, as though you could see through the face like a shell. He sat on the edge of the chair, turning his bowler hat round in his hands. Dr. Fell tried to give him a cigar, but he declined this.

"I wonder, sir, if I may speak frankly?"

"I should advise it," said Elliot dryly. "Well?"

"Of course, sir, I know I should have gone to Lady Farnleigh straight-away. But I couldn't tell her. I mean quite sincerely that I couldn't make myself do it. You see, it was through Lady Farnleigh that I came to the Close when Colonel Mardale died. I think I can say honestly that I think more of her than anyone else I know. Honest to God," added Knowles, with a sudden and unexpected descent into the human, and a slight surge up out of his chair. Then he relapsed. "She was Miss Molly, the doctor's daughter, from Sutton Chart. I knew——"

Elliot was patient.

"Yes, we appreciate that. But this information you were going to give us?"

"It's about the late Sir John Farnleigh, sir," said Knowles. "He committed suicide. I saw him do it."

The long silence was broken only by the diminishing noise of the rain. Page heard the rustle of his own sleeve as he looked round to see whether they had hidden the stained clasp-knife; he did not want Madeline to see it. It was now concealed under the newspapers on the table. Inspector Elliot, seeming even more hard-boned, was staring steadily at the butler. From Dr. Fell's direction there issued a faint ghost of a noise, like half-humming or half-whistling behind closed teeth; he has a habit of whistling thus at times, to the tune of 'Auprès de ma Blonde,' though he looked half asleep.

"You—saw—him—do it?"

"Yes, sir. I could have told you this morning; only you didn't question me; and, frankly, I'm not sure I should have told you even then. It's like this. I was standing at the window of the Green Room last night, the room just over the library, looking out into the garden, when it all happened. I saw everything."

(This, Page remembered, was true. When he had gone with Burrows to look at the body first, he had seen Knowles standing at the window of the room above the library.)

"Anybody will tell you about my eyesight," Knowles said warmly. Even his shoes squeaked with vehemence. "I'm seventy-four years old, and I can read a motor-car number plate at sixty yards. You just go out in the garden there, and you take a box or a sign or something with small letters—" He corrected himself, and sat back.

"You saw Sir John Farnleigh cut his own throat?"

"Yes, sir. As good as."

" 'As good as?' What do you mean by that?"

"I mean this, sir. I didn't actually see him draw the—you know—because his back was towards me. But I saw him put his hands up. And there wasn't a living soul near him. Remember, I was looking straight down on him and into the garden. I could see into that circular open space all round the pool; and there's a good five-foot border of sand between the pool and the nearest hedge all round. Nobody could have come near him without my seeing. And he was all alone in that open space, I'll tell you to my dying day."

Still the sleepy and tuneless whistling wheezed from Dr. Fell's direction.

" 'Tous les oiseaux du monde,' " muttered the doctor, " 'viennent y faire leurs nids—' " Then he spoke out. "Why should Sir John Farnleigh kill himself?"

Knowles braced himself.

"Because he wasn't Sir John Farnleigh, sir. The other gentleman is. I knew it as soon as I clapped eyes on him last night."

Inspector Elliot remained impassive.

"What reason have you for saying that?"

"It's hard to tell you so you'll understand, sir," Knowles complained. (For the first time in his life he showed a lack of tact.) "Now, I'm seventy-four. I wasn't any chicken, if you'll excuse me for saying so, when young Mr. Johnny went away from home in nineteen-twelve. You see, to old people like myself the younger ones never change. They always seem just the same, whether they're fifteen or thirty or forty-five. Lord bless you, do you think I wouldn't have recognized the real Mr. Johnny whenever I met him? Mind!" said Knowles, again forgetting himself and raising his finger. "I don't say that when the late gentleman came here and pretended to be the new Sir John—I don't say I twigged it. No. Not at all. I thought, Well, he's different; he's been to America, and you never know them after that; it's only natural, and I'm getting old. So I never really suspected him of not being the right master, though I'm bound to admit that now and again he did say things that———"

"But———"

"Now, you'll say," continued Knowles, in real and blinding earnest, "I wasn't at the Close in the old days. That's true. I've been here only ten years, since Miss Molly asked the late Sir Dudley to offer me the honour. But, when I served Colonel Mardale, young Mr. Johnny used to spend a lot of time in the big orchard between the colonel's and the major's——"

"The major's?"

"Major Dane, sir, Miss Madeline's father; he was the colonel's great friend. Well, young Mr. Johnny liked that orchard, with the wood behind it. That orchard is close to the Hanging Chart, you know—leads into it. He pretended he was a wizard, and a mediaeval knight, and I don't know what; but some things I didn't like at all. Anyway, I knew last night, even before he started asking me about rabbits and the like, that this new gentleman was the real Mr. Johnny. He knew I knew it. That's why he had me called in. But what could I *say*?"

Page remembered that interview only too well. But he remembered other things too, and wondered if Elliot had learned them. He glanced across at Madeline.

Inspector Elliot opened his notebook.

"So he killed himself. Eh?"

"Yes, sir."

"Did you see the weapon he used?"

"No, not properly, I'm afraid."

"I want you to tell me just exactly what you did see. For instance, you say you were in the 'Green Room' when it happened. When and why did you go there?"

Knowles got his wits together.

"Well, sir, it might have been two or three minutes before it happened——"

"Twenty-seven or twenty-eight minutes past nine. Which?" asked Inspector Elliot, with a hard passion for accuracy.

"I can't say, sir. I didn't take any account of the time. One of them. I was in the hall near the dining-room, in case I should be wanted, though there was nobody in the dining-room except Mr. Welkyn. Then Mr. Nathaniel Burrows came out of the drawing-room, and asked me where he could find an electric torch. I said I thought there was one in the Green Room upstairs, which the late—gentleman used as a kind of study, and I said I would go and fetch it for him. I have since learned," Knowles was now giving evidence, as his diction showed, "that Mr. Burrows found one in the drawer of the table in the hall; but I had not known there was one there."

"Go on."

"I went upstairs and I went into the Green Room——"

"Did you turn on the light?"

"Not then," said Knowles, a little flustered. "Not just at that moment.

There is no wall-switch in the room. You must turn on the light from the ceiling-fixture. The table where I thought I had seen the electric torch is between the windows. I went towards that table, and when I went past I glanced out of the window."

"Which window?"

"The right-hand one, facing out on the garden."

"Was the window open?"

"Yes, sir. Now, here's how it was. You must have noticed. There are trees all along the back of the library; but they've been pruned down so that they don't cut off the view from the windows of the floor above. The ceilings at the Close are eighteen feet high, most of them—except the new wing, which is a little low doll's house of a place—and that gives you a good height of tree without having them stretch up past the windows of the Green Room. That's why it's called the Green Room, because you look out over tree-tops. So you see I was high over the garden, looking down into it."

Here Knowles got up from his chair and craned himself forward. He had seldom executed this movement before, and it evidently gave him a twinge, but his grimness was such that he held the position while he talked.

"Here I was, you see. Then there were the green leaves, lit up from underneath by the library windows." He moved his hand. "Then there was the garden, with every hedge and path distinct, and the pool in the centre. The light wasn't bad, sir. I've seen them play tennis in worse. Then there was Sir John—or the gentleman who called himself that—standing by it with his hands in his pockets."

At this point Knowles had to leave off play-acting and sit down.

"That's all," he said, with a slightly quicker breath.

"That's *all?*" repeated Inspector Elliot.

"Yes, sir."

Elliot, pulled up at this unexpected conclusion, stared at him.

"But what happened, man? That's what I'm trying to get you to tell me!"

"Just that. I thought I heard a movement down in the trees under me, and I glanced down. When I looked up again——"

"Are you going to tell me," said Elliot very calmly and carefully, "that YOU didn't see what happened either?"

"No, sir. I saw him fall forward in the pool."

"Yes; but what else?"

"Well, sir, there certainly wasn't time for someone—you know what I mean, sir—to cut his throat three times and then run away. There couldn't 'a' been. He was alone every bit of the time, before and after. So he must have killed himself."

"What did he use to kill himself?"

"A kind of knife, I think."

"You think. Did you see the knife?"

"Not properly, no."

"Did you see it in his hand?"

"Not properly. It was too far away to see that plain. Sir," replied Knowles, remembering that he had a position in the world and drawing himself up with dignity, "I am trying to give you a true, so-help-me-God story of what I saw——"

"Well, what did he do with the knife afterwards? Did he drop it? What happened to it?"

"I didn't notice, sir. I honestly didn't. I was paying attention to him; and something seemed to be happening to the front of him."

"Could he have thrown the knife from him?"

"He might. I don't know."

"Would you have seen it if he had thrown it?"

Knowles considered long. "That would depend on the size of the knife. And there are bats in that garden. And sometimes, sir, you can't see a tennis-ball until it's—" He was a very old man. His face grew clouded, and for a moment they were afraid he was going to cry. But he spoke again with dignity. "I am sorry, sir. If you don't believe me, have I your permission to go?"

"Oh, hang it all, it isn't that—!" said Elliot, stung to youthful naturalness, and his ears grew slightly red. Madeline Dane, who had said not a word the whole time, was watching him with a faint smile.

"Just one other point, for the time being," Elliot went on stiffly. "If you had a good view of the whole garden, did you see anybody else in the garden at the time of the—attack?"

"At the time it happened, sir? No. Immediately afterwards, though, I turned on the lights in the Green Room, and by that time there were a number of persons in the garden. But beforehand, at the time of the— *excuse* me, sir; yes, there was!" Again Knowles raised his finger and frowned. "There was somebody there when it happened. I saw him! You remember, I said I heard a noise down in the trees round the library windows?"

"Yes; well?"

"I looked down. That was what took away my attention. There was a gentleman down there, looking into the library windows. I could see plainly; because the branches of the trees, of course, don't quite reach to the windows, and everything was all lighted up between, like a little alley between the trees and the windows. He was standing there looking into the library."

"Who was?"

"The new gentleman, sir. The real Mr. Johnny that I used to know. The one who now calls himself Mr. Patrick Gore."

There was a silence.

Elliot very carefully put down his pencil, and glanced across at Dr. Fell. The doctor had not moved; he would have seemed asleep if one little eye had not gleamed half-open.

"Have I got this clear?" Elliot demanded. "At the same time as the attack, or suicide, or murder, or whatever-we-call-it, Mr. Patrick Gore was standing down there in your sight by the library windows?"

"Yes, sir. Over to the left he stood, towards the south. That's how I could see his face."

"Now, you'll swear to that?"

"Yes, sir, of course," said Knowles, opening his eyes.

"This was at the time of the various scuffling sounds, the splash, the fall, and so on?"

"Yes, sir."

Elliot nodded in a colourless way and leafed back through his note-book. "I should like to read you a part of Mr. Gore's testimony dealing with that same time. Listen. *'I was out on the front lawn first, smoking. Then I wandered round the side of the house to this garden. I did not hear any sounds except a splash, and I heard that very faintly. I think I heard this when I had just started round the side of the house.'* He goes on to say that he kept to the side paths along the south boundary.—Now, you tell us that, when the splash occurred, he was standing down underneath you looking into the library. His statement contradicts it."

"I can't help what he says, sir," answered Knowles helplessly. "I'm sorry, but I can't. That's what he was doing."

"But what did he do after you saw Sir John go into the pool?"

"I can't say that. I was looking towards the pool then."

Elliot hesitated, muttering to himself, and then glanced at Dr. Fell. "Any questions you'd like to ask, doctor?"

"Yes," said Dr. Fell.

He bestirred himself, beaming on Madeline, who smiled back. Then he assumed an argumentative air as he beamed on Knowles.

"There are several troublesome queries following your theory, my boy. Among them, if Patrick Gore is the real heir, the question of who stole the Thumbograph, and why. But let's stick first to the vexed business of suicide *v.* murder." He reflected. "Sir John Farnleigh—the dead man, I mean—he was right-handed, was he?"

"Right-handed? Yes, sir."

"It was your impression that he had this knife in his right hand when he killed himself?"

"Oh, yes, sir."

"H'mf, yes. Now I want you to tell me what he did with his hands after this curious seizure by the pool. Never mind the knife! We'll admit you didn't properly see the knife. Just tell me what he did with his hands."

"Well, sir, he put them up to his throat—like this," said Knowles, illustrating. "Then he moved a little, and then he lifted them up over his head and threw them out, like this." Knowles made a large gesture, spreading his arms wide. "That was just before he went forward into the pool and began to writhe there."

"He didn't cross his arms? He simply lifted them and threw them out one to each side? Is that it?"

"That's right, sir."

Dr. Fell took his crutch-handled stick from the table and hoisted himself to his feet. Lumbering over to the table, he took up the newspaper packet, unfolded it, and showed Knowles the bloodstained clasp-knife inside.

"The point is this," he argued. "Farnleigh has the knife in his right hand, supposing this to be suicide. He makes no gestures except to fling both arms wide. Even if he were helping support the knife with his left hand, his right would have the grip on it. The knife flies from his right hand as the arm is thrown wide. Excellent well. But will someone explain how in blazes that knife completely altered its flight in the air, passed high over the pool, and dropped into the hedge some ten feet to the *left?* And all this, mind you, after he has just inflicted not one, but three fatal wounds on himself? It won't do, you know."

Apparently oblivious to the fact that he was holding the newspaper with its grisly exhibit almost against Madeline's cheek, Dr. Fell frowned at it. Then he looked at the butler.

"On the other hand, how can we doubt this chap's eyesight? He says Farnleigh was alone by the pool; and there is some confirmation. Nathaniel Burrows is inclined to agree that he was alone. Lady Farnleigh, who ran out on the balcony immediately after the splash, saw nobody by the pool or within reach of it. We shall have to take our choice. On the one hand we have a somewhat preposterous suicide; but on the other hand, unfortunately, we have a more than somewhat impossible murder. Will someone kindly oblige me with an idea?"

Chapter IX

A s vigorously and even violently as he had spoken, Dr. Fell had been talking to himself. He had not expected an answer, nor did he get one. For a time he remained blinking at the bookshelves. He appeared to wake up when Knowles ventured a frightened cough.

"I beg your pardon, sir; is that *the*—?" He nodded towards the knife.

"We think so. It was found in a hedge to the left of the pool. How do you think it squares with suicide?"

"I don't know, sir."

"Did you ever see this knife before?"

"Not to my knowledge, sir."

"Or you, Miss Dane?"

Though Madeline seemed startled and a little shocked, she shook her head quietly. Then she leaned forward. Page noted again how the breadth of her face, the slight breadth and bluntness of her nose, did not in the least detract from her beauty, but seemed to add to it. His mind was always searching for comparisons or images when he saw her; and he found in her something mediaeval, something in length of eye or fulness of lip, some inner spring of quietness, which suggested the rose-garden or the turret window. The sentimentality of the comparison must be excused, for he felt it and believed it.

"I'm afraid, you know," Madeline said almost pleadingly, "that I've no right to be here at all, and that I'm talking about things which do not concern me. And yet—well, I suppose I must." She smiled at Knowles. "I wonder if you will wait for me in my car?"

Knowles bowed and was gone—vague and troubled; and still the grey rain fell.

"Yes," said Dr. Fell, sitting down again and folding his hands over the top of his stick. "You were the one I wanted to ask the questions, Miss Dane. What do *you* think of Knowles's views? About the real heir, I mean?"

"Only that it's much more difficult than you think."

"Do you believe what he says?"

"Oh, he's absolutely and completely sincere; you must have seen that. But he's an old man. And, among the children, he was always most fanatically devoted first to Molly (her father, you know, saved Knowles's mother's life once), and next to young John Farnleigh. I remember he once made a conical wizard's hat for John, out of cardboard painted blue, with silver-paper stars and whatnots. When this affair came up, he simply couldn't tell Molly; he couldn't. So he came to me. They all do—come to me, that is. And I try to do them what good I can."

Dr. Fell's forehead was wrinkled. "Still, I was wondering . . . h'mf . . . you knew John Farnleigh pretty well in the old days? I understand," here he beamed, "that there was a kind of boy-and-girl romance between you?"

She made a wry face.

"You remind me that I'm past my youth. I'm thirty-five. Or thereabouts; you mustn't ask me to be too precise. No, there never was even a boy-and-girl romance between us, really. Not that I should have minded, but it didn't interest him. He—he kissed me once or twice, in the orchard and in the wood. But he used to say that I didn't have enough of the Old Adam—or do I mean Old Eve?—in me. Not enough of the devil, anyhow."

"But you never married?"

"Oh, that's unfair!" cried Madeline, flushing and then laughing. "You talk as though I were sitting with my dim spectacled eyes over a piece of knitting in the chimmney-corner——"

"Miss Dane," said Dr. Fell, with thunderous solemnity, "I don't. I mean that I can see suitors standing in droves at your door, stretching away like the Great Wall of China; I can see Nubian slaves bowed down by the weight of great chocolate-boxes; I can—ahem. Let us omit that."

It was a long time since Page had seen a genuine blush; he believed, nowadays, that such mainsprings were dried up and with the dodo; but, all the same, he did not mind seeing Madeline blush. For what she said was:

"If you're thinking that I cherished a romantic passion for John Farnleigh all these years, I'm afraid you're hopelessly wrong." There was a twinkle in her eye. "I was always a little frightened of him, and I'm not even sure I liked him—then."

"Then?"

"Yes. I liked him later, but only liked."

"Miss Dane," said Dr. Fell, growling out of his several chins and moving his head curiously, "some inner Little Bird seems to tell me that you're trying to convey something to me. You still haven't answered my question. Do you think Farnleigh was an impostor?"

She made a slight gesture.

"Dr. Fell, I am not trying to be mysterious. Really and truly I'm not; and I think I can tell you something. But, before I do, will you—or somebody—tell me just what did happen at the Close last night? I mean, before the last horrible business happened? I mean, what those two said and did while each was claiming to be the real one?"

"We might as well have the story again, Mr. Page," said Elliot.

Page told it, with as many shadings and impressions as he could remember. Madeline nodded her head several times in the course of it; she was breathing rapidly.

"Tell me, Brian: what struck you most about the whole interview?"

"The absolute assurance of both claimants," said Page. "Farnleigh faltered once or twice, but over what seemed unimportant points; when any real test was mentioned, he was eager. I only saw him smile and look relieved once. That was when Gore was accusing him of attempted murder with a seaman's mallet aboard the *Titanic*."

"Just one other thing, please," Madeline requested, breathing still more rapidly. "Did either of them say anything about the dummy?"

There was a pause. Dr. Fell, Inspector Elliot, and Brian Page looked at each other blankly.

"The dummy?" repeated Elliot, clearing his throat. "What dummy?"

"Or about bringing it to life? Or anything about the 'Book'?" Then a mask seemed to close over her face. "I'm sorry. I shouldn't have mentioned that, only I should have thought it would be the first thing to be brought up. Please forget it."

An expression of refreshed pleasure animated Dr. Fell's large face.

"My dear Miss Dane," he rumbled, "you demand a miracle. You demand a miracle greater than any that could have happened in that garden. Consider what you demand. You refer to a certain dummy, to the possibility of its being brought to life, and to something you call the 'Book,' all presumably in connection with this mystery. You acknowledge that it is the first thing you would have thought should be brought up. And then you ask us to forget it. Do you think that ordinary human beings of feverish curiosity could——"

Madeline looked stubborn.

"But you ought not to have asked me about it," she protested. "Not that I know anything, really. You ought to have asked them."

" 'The Book,' " mused Dr. Fell. "You don't mean, I suppose, the Red Book of Appin?"

"Yes, I believe I later heard it called that. I read about it somewhere. It's not a book, really; it's a manuscript, or so John once told me."

"Wait a bit," interposed Page. "Murray asked that question, and both of them wrote down answers for it. Gore later told me that it was a catch question, and there was no such thing as 'the Red Book of Appin.' If there is such a thing, it makes Gore out the impostor, doesn't it?"

Dr. Fell seemed about to speak, with some excitement and vehemence; but he drew a long breath through his nose and restrained himself.

"I wish I knew," said Elliot. "I never thought there could be so much doubt and confusion caused by only two persons. Now you're certain it's one of them, again you're just as certain it's the other. And—as Dr. Fell says—we can't get much further until we establish that. I hope, Miss Dane, you're not trying to evade the question. You still haven't answered: do you think the late Farnleigh was an impostor?"

Madeline threw her head back against the back of the chair. It was the greatest sign of animation, the only sign of spasmodic action, Page had ever seen her give. She opened and shut her right hand.

"I can't tell you," she said helplessly. "I *can't*. Not until I've seen Molly, anyhow."

"But what has Lady Farnleigh got to do with us?"

"Only that he—told me things. Things he didn't even confide to her. Oh, please don't look shocked!" (As a matter of fact, Elliot did not; but he looked interested.) "Or believe a lot of gossip you may have heard. But I've got to tell Molly first. You see, she believed in him. Of course, Molly was only seven years old when he left home. All she hazily remembers is a boy who took her to a gipsy camp, where they taught her to ride a pony and throw stones better than any man. Besides, any dispute over the Farnleigh name or estates wouldn't trouble her at all. Dr. Bishop wasn't a country G.P.; he died worth nearly half a million, and Molly inherited it all in her own right. Also, sometimes I've thought she never really liked being mistress of that house; she doesn't seem to *care* for responsibilities of that sort. She didn't marry him because of his position or income, and she wouldn't really have cared—and won't now—whether his name is Farnleigh or Gore or whatever you like. So why should he have told her?"

Elliot looked rather dazed, as he had reason to do.

"Just a moment, Miss Dane. What are you trying to tell us: that he was or was not an impostor?"

"But I don't know! I don't know which he was!"

"The startling lack of information with which we are provided," said Dr. Fell sadly, "proceeds from all sources and o'erflows its basin. Well, let's leave that for the moment. But on one point I insist on having my curiosity satisfied. What's all this about a dummy?"

Madeline hesitated.

"I don't know whether they've still got it," she answered, staring at the window in a fascinated way. "John's father kept it locked up in an attic room, along with the—books he didn't like. The old-time Farnleighs were an unpleasant lot, as you may know, and Sir Dudley was always afraid John had taken after them. Though there certainly didn't seem to have been anything wrong or unpleasant about this figure.

"I—I only saw it once. John stole the key from his father, and took me up all those stairs to see it, with a candle in a dark-lantern. He said the door hadn't been opened for generations. When it was new, they say the figure was as absolutely lifelike and beautiful as a real woman, sitting on a kind of padded box in Restoration costume. But when I saw it, it was only old and black and withered-looking, and it frightened me horribly. I suppose it hadn't been touched for well over a hundred years. But I don't know what the story was that made people afraid of it."

There was something about her tone which made Page vaguely uneasy, because he could not place the inflection: he had never heard Madeline speak quite like that before. And he had never, certainly, heard of this "figure" or "dummy," whatever it was.

"It may have been very ingenious," Madeline explained, "yet I can't understand why there should have been anything bad about it. Did you ever hear of Kempelen's and Maelzel's mechanical chess-player, or Maskelyne's 'Zoe' or 'Psycho,' the whist-playing figure?"

Elliot shook his head, though he looked interested; and Dr. Fell was so interested that the eyeglasses tumbled off his nose.

"You don't mean—?" he said. "Archons of Athens, this is better than anything I had hoped for! They were among the best of a series of nearly life-size automatons which puzzled Europe for two hundred years. Didn't you ever read of the harpsichord, exhibited before Louis XIV, which played by itself? Or the dummy invented by Kempelen, shown by Maelzel, which was owned by Napoleon and later lost in the museum fire at Philadelphia? For all practical purposes, Maelzel's automaton was alive. It played chess with you; and usually won. There have been several explanations of how it worked—Poe wrote one—but to my own simple mind it still isn't satisfactorily explained. You can see 'Psycho' in the London Museum today. You don't mean there's one at Farnleigh Close?"

"Yes. That's why I should have thought this Mr. Murray would have *asked* about it," said Madeline. "As I say, I don't know the story. This automaton was exhibited in England during the rein of Charles II, and bought by a Farnleigh then. I don't know whether it played cards or chess, but it moved and spoke. When I saw it, as I say, it was old and black and withered-looking."

"But this—harrumph—this business of bringing it alive?"

"Oh, that was only the nonsense John used to talk when he was a silly child. I wasn't trying to talk seriously about that, don't you see? I was only trying to go back and test what could be remembered of him in the old days. The room where they used to keep the figure was full of books with—well, with downright evil in them," again she flushed, "and that was what attracted John. The secret of how to make the figure work had been forgotten; I daresay that was what he meant."

On Page's desk the telephone-bell rang. He had been so engrossed in watching Madeline, the slight turns of her head, the intentness of her dark-blue eyes, that he groped after the 'phone before finding it. But at the sound of Burrows's voice on the wire he became very much alert.

"For God's sake," said Burrows, "come up to the Close straightaway, and bring the inspector and Dr. Fell."

"Steady!" said Page, feeling a certain unpleasant warmth creep round his chest. "What's up?"

"For one thing, we've found the Thumbograph—"

"What! Where?"

They were all looking at him now.

"One of the maids: Betty: do you know her—?" Burrows hesitated.

"Yes; go on."

"Betty disappeared, and nobody knew what had become of her. They looked all over the place for her: that is, they looked in the only places she was likely to be found. No Betty. Everything was a bit disorganized, because for some reason Knowles wasn't here either. Finally Molly's maid found her in the Green Room, where it wasn't Betty's business to go. Betty was lying on the floor with the Thumbograph in her hand. But that isn't all. Her face was such a queer colour, and she was breathing so queerly, that we sent for the doctor. Old King is worried. Betty's still unconscious, and she won't be in any condition to tell us anything for a long time. She's not physically hurt, but King says there's not much doubt about what caused it."

"Well?"

Again Burrows hesitated.

"Fright," he said.

Chapter X

In the library at Farnleigh Close, Patrick Gore sat back in the embrasure of the windows and smoked a black cigar. Ranged near him were Burrows, Welkyn, and a sleepy-looking Kennet Murray. Inspector Elliot, Dr. Fell, and Brian Page sat by the table.

At the Close they had found a frightened and disorganized household, the more frightened because of a completely pointless upset in the middle of an ordinary afternoon, and the more disorganized because of the absence of the butler.

Facts? What did you mean, facts? The group of domestics whom Elliot questioned did not know what he meant. It was only this maid, Betty Harbottle; a nice girl; ordinary. She had not been seen since midday dinner. When it came time for her to wash the windows of two of the upstairs bedrooms with Agnes, another maid, Agnes had gone to look for her. She was not found until four o'clock. At this time Teresa—Lady Farnleigh's maid—had gone into the Green Room, the late Sir John's study, and found her lying on the floor by a window overlooking the garden. She was lying on her side, with the paper-covered book in her hand. Dr. King had been summoned from Mallingford; and neither the expression of his face nor Betty's did anything to reassure the household. Dr. King was with the patient still.

This thing was wrong. Terrors should not be domestic terrors. It was like being told that in your own home you may completely disappear for four hours. It was like being told that in your own home you may open a familiar door, and enter not your own room, but a room you have never seen before, where something is waiting. From the housekeeper, the cook, and the other maids he learned little except domestic details; about Betty he learned little except that she liked apples and wrote letters to Gary Cooper.

Knowles's arrival soothed the staff; and Madeline's arrival, Page hoped, would have a good effect on Molly Farnleigh. Madeline had accompanied her to her sitting-room while the men glared at one another in the library. Page had wondered what would happen at a meeting between Madeline and Patrick Gore; yet there was little on which even the imagination could fasten. They were not introduced. Madeline moved past, softly, with her arm round Molly; she and the claimant looked at each other; and Page thought that an amused look of recognition opened Gore's eyes; but neither spoke.

And it was Gore who put the case to the inspector when the others were gathered in the library, just before Dr. Fell flung a hand-grenade of remarkable explosive power.

"It's no good, inspector," said Gore, re-lighting a black cigar which would not remain lit. "You asked the same kind of questions this morning, and this time I assure you it's no good. This time it is, where were you when the girl was—well, whatever happened to her—and the Thumbograph was put in her hand? I have replied quite simply that I am damned if I know. So have all the others. We were here. You ordered us to be here. But you may be sure we were not courting each other's society, and we have not the remotest idea when the girl collapsed."

"Look here, you know," said Dr. Fell abruptly, "a part of this had better be settled."

"I only hope you can settle it, my friend," answered Gore, who seemed to have taken a sincere liking to him. "But, inspector, you have already had our statements with the servants. We have been over that again and—"

Inspector Elliot was cheerful.

"That's right, sir," he said. "And, if it's necessary, we shall have to go over them again. And again."

"Really—" interposed Welkyn.

The claimant sat on him again. "But, if you're so interested in the wanderings of that Thumbograph, why not pay some slight attention to what is *in* the Thumbograph?" He glanced at the tattered grey book, which now lay on the table between Elliot and Dr. Fell. "Why in the name of sense and sanity don't you settle the matter now? Why don't you decide, between a dead man and myself, which is the real heir?"

"Oh, I can tell you that," said Dr. Fell affably.

There was an abrupt silence, broken only by the scrape of the claimant's foot on the stone floor. Kennet Murray took away the hand with which he had been shading his eyes. The expression of cynicism remained on his ageing face; but his eyes were bright and hard and indulgent, and he used one finger to stroke his beard, as though he were listening to a recitation.

"Yes, doctor?" he prompted, in that tone used exclusively among schoolmasters.

"Furthermore," continued Dr. Fell, tapping the book on the table, "it's no good getting down to business with *this* Thumbograph. It's a fake. No, no, I don't mean that you haven't got the evidence. I merely say that THIS Thumbograph, the one that was stolen, is a fake. Mr. Gore pointed out last night, they tell me, that you had several Thumbographs in the old days." He beamed on Murray. "My boy, you retain your melodramatic soul of old, for which I am glad. You believed that there might be some attempt to pinch the Thumbograph. So you came to the house last night equipped with two of them—"

"Is that true?" demanded Gore.

Murray seemed at once pleased and annoyed; but he nodded, as though he were following the matter carefully.

"—and," continued Dr. Fell, "the one you showed to these people in the library was bogus. That was why you were so long in getting down to business. Hey? After you have shoved everybody out of the library, you had to get the real Thumbograph (a clumsy kind of book, apt to tear) out of your pocket, and put the valueless one in. But they had said they were going to keep a close watch on you. And, with a wall of windows stretching across the room, you were afraid somebody might see you and cry trickery if you were seen fooling about with the evidence. So you had to make sure there was nobody watching—"

"I was finally obliged," said Murray gravely, "to get into that cupboard and do it." His nod indicated an old book-closet built into the wall on the same side as the windows. "It is somewhat late in life to feel as though I were cheating at an examination."

Inspector Elliot did not say anything. After glancing sharply from one to the other of them, he began to write in his notebook.

"H'mf, yes. You were delayed," said Dr. Fell. "Mr. Page here, passing the windows only a few minutes before the murder, on his way out to the back of the garden, saw that you were just 'opening' the Thumbograph. So you hardly had time to get down to real work—"

"Three or four minutes," corrected Murray.

"Very well. You hardly had time to get down to real work before there were alarums of bloodshed." Dr. Fell looked pained. "My dear young Murray, you are not simple-minded. Such an alarm might be a trick, especially a trick *you* would suspect. You would never on earth have gone thundering out, leaving the Thumbograph open and inviting on that table. I couldn't believe that when I heard it. No, no, no. Back went the real one into your pocket, and out came the dummy one for a honeyed lure. Hey?"

"Confound you," said Murray without heat.

"You therefore decided to lie doggo and exultantly apply your detective faculties when the dummy was stolen. You have probably been sitting up all night writing out a statement about the prints, with the real Thumbograph in front of you, together with your affidavit that the real heir—"

"The real heir is who?" asked Patrick Gore coolly.

"Is *you*, of course," growled Dr. Fell.

Then he looked at Murray.

"Hang it all," he added plaintively, "you must have known that! He was your pupil. You must have known it. I knew it as soon as I heard him open his mouth—"

The claimant, who had got to his feet, now sat down rather awkwardly. The claimant's face expressed an almost simian pleasure; his bright grey eye and even his bald-spot seemed to twinkle.

"Dr. Fell, I thank you," Gore said, with his hand on his heart. "But I most point out that you have asked me not a single question."

"Look here, you fellows," said Dr. Fell. "You had the opportunity to listen to him all last evening. Look at him now. Listen to him. Does he remind you of anybody? I don't mean in appearance; I mean in turn of phrase, in shaping of ideas, in way of expressing himself. Well, of whom does he remind you? Hey?"

And at last the troublesome sense of familiarity fitted into place in Page's mind, while the doctor blinked round at them.

"Of Murray," replied Page, in the midst of a silence.

"Of Murray. Got it in one. Misted by time, of course; pulled round a bit by character; but there and unmistakable. Of Murray, who had him in sole charge during the formative years of his life, and was the only one with influence over him. Study his bearing. Listen to the smooth turn of those sentences, rolling like the Odyssey. It's only superficial, I cheerfully acknowledge; they are no more alike in their natures than I am like Elliot or Hadley. But the echo lingers on. I tell you, the only important question Murray asked last night was what books the real John Farnleigh had enjoyed as a boy, and what books he hated. Look at this fellow!"—he pointed to Gore. "Didn't I hear how his dead eye glowed when he talked about *The Count of Monte Cristo* and *The Cloister and the Hearth*? And of what books he hated and still hates? No impostor would have dared to talk like that before the person to whom he'd poured out his soul years ago. In a case like this, facts are piffle. Anybody can learn facts. You want the inner boy. I say, Murray: honestly, you'd better come off it and give us the truth. It's all very well to be the Great Detective and play 'possum, but this has gone far enough."

A red bar showed across Murray's forehead. He looked snappish and a trifle shamefaced. But his far-away mind caught at something out of this.

"Facts are not piffle," Murray said.

"I tell you," roared Dr. Fell, "that facts are—" He caught himself up. "Harrumph, well. No. Perhaps not. Altogether. But am I correct?"

"He did not recognize the Red Book of Appin. He wrote down that there was no such thing."

"Which he knew only as a manuscript. Oh, I am not his champion. I'm only trying to establish something. And I repeat: am I correct?"

"Confound you, Fell, you do spoil a fellow's pleasure," complained Murray, in a slightly different tone. He glanced across at Gore. "Yes, he's the real Johnny Farnleigh. Hullo, Johnny."

"Hullo," said Gore. And, for the first time since Page had met him, his face did not look hard.

The quiet in that room was of a dwindling and shrinking sort, as though values were being restored and a blurred image had come into focus. Both Gore and Murray looked at the floor, but they looked vaguely, uncomfortably amused. It was Welkyn's rich voice which now arose with authority.

"You are prepared to prove all this, sir?" he asked briskly.

"There goes my holiday," said Murray. He reached into his stuffed inside pocket, and became austere again. "Yes. Here you are. Original Thumbograph, and print—*with* signature of John Newnham Farnleigh as a boy, and date. In case there should be any doubt this is the original one I brought with me, I had photographs of it taken and deposited with the Commissioner of Police at Hamilton. Two letters from John Farnleigh, written to me in 1911: compare signatures with the signature on the thumb-print. Present thumb-print, taken last night, and my analysis of their points of agreement—"

"Good. Good, very good," said Welkyn.

Page looked at Burrows, and he noticed that Burrows's face was white. Nor had Page realized that the breaking of the long tension would have such an effect on their nerves.

But he realized it when he looked round, and saw that Molly Farnleigh was in the room.

She had come in unobserved, with Madeline Dane just behind her; she must have heard all of it. They all got up, with an awkward scraping of chairs.

"They say you're honest," she said to Murray. "Is this true?"

Murray bowed. "Madam, I am sorry."

"He was a cheat?"

"He was a cheat who could have deceived nobody who had really known him."

"And now," interposed Welkyn suavely, "perhaps it would be as well if Mr. Burrows and I were to have a talk—without prejudice, of course—"

"One moment," said Burrows with equal suavity. "This is still most irregular; and I may point out that I have seen nothing yet in the nature of proof. May I be allowed to examine those documents? Thank you. Next, Lady Farnleigh, I should like to speak with you alone."

Molly had a glazed, strained, puzzled look in her eyes.

"Yes, that would be best," she agreed. "Madeline has been telling me things."

Madeline put a hand soothingly on her arm, but she threw it off with a shake of her sturdy body. Madeline's self-effacing blonde beauty was in contrast to the anger which blazed round Molly and seemed to darken everything away from her. Then, between Madeline and Burrows, Molly went out of the room. They heard Burrows's shoes squeak.

"God!" said Patrick Gore. "And now what have we got?"

"If you'll take it easy and listen to me, sir," Elliot suggested grimly, "I'll tell you." His tone made both Gore and Welkyn look at him. "We've got an impostor who was somehow killed by that pool. Why or by whom we don't know. We've got someone who stole a valueless Thumbo-graph,"—he held up the little book—"and later returned it. Presumably because the person knew it was valueless. We've got a housemaid, Betty, whom nobody had seen since noon; but who was found at four o'clock in the afternoon, half dead of fright, in the room above this library. Who or what frightened her we don't know, or how the Thumbograph got into her hand. By the way, where is Dr. King now?"

"Still with the unfortunate Betty, I believe," said Gore. "But what then?"

"Finally, we have some new evidence," Elliot told him. He paused. "As you say, you have all been patiently repeating the stories you told last night. Now, Mr. Gore. In the account you gave of your movements at the time of the murder, were you telling the truth? Think before you answer. There is someone who contradicts your story."

Page had been waiting for it, wondering how long it would be before Elliot would bring it up.

"Contradicts my story? Who contradicts it?" asked Gore sharply, and took the dead cigar out of his mouth.

"Never mind that, if you please. Where were you when you heard the victim fall into the pool?"

The other contemplated him with amusement. "I suppose you've got a witness. I was watching this ancient," he indicated Murray, "through the

window. It suddenly occurs to me that I have now no reason for keeping
back the information any longer. Who saw me?"

"You realize, sir, that if what you say is true this provides you with an
alibi?"

"Unfortunately as regards clearing me from suspicion, yes."

"Unfortunately?" Elliot froze up.

"A bad joke, inspector. I beg your pardon."

"May I ask why you didn't tell me this at first?"

"You may. And in doing so you might ask what I saw through the
window."

"I don't follow you."

Elliot was always careful to conceal his intelligence. A shade of
exasperation passed over Gore's face. "In words of one syllable, inspector, ever since I came into this house last night I suspected the
presence of dirty work. This gentleman walked in." He looked at Murray,
and did not seem to know how to treat him. "He knew me. I knew he
knew me. But he never spoke out."

"Well?"

"What happened? I came round the side of the house—as you have so
shrewdly discovered—possibly a minute or so before the murder." He
broke off. "By the way, *have* you determined that it was murder?"

"Just one moment, please. Go on."

"I looked in here, and I saw Murray sitting with his back to me like a
stuffed dummy, not even moving. Immediately afterwards I heard all the
sounds we have so often heard, beginning with the choking noise and
ending with the thrashings in water. I moved away from the window,
over towards the left, and looked out to see what was happening in the
garden. But I did not go nearer. At this time Burrows ran out from the
house towards the pool. So I withdrew again, back towards the library
windows. The alarm seemed to have gone up inside the house. And this
time what did I see? I saw this distinguished, venerable gentleman,"
again his curt nod indicated Murray, "carefully juggling *two* Thumbographs, guiltily putting one in his pocket and hastily putting the other on
the table. . . ."

Murray had been listening with critical interest.

"So, so?" he observed, with an almost Teutonic inflection. "You
thought I was working against you?" He seemed pleased.

"Naturally. Working against me! As usual, you understate the case,"
returned Gore. His face darkened. "So I did not care to tell where I had
been. I reserved the knowledge of what I had seen for a shot in the locker
in case dirty work had been attempted."

"Have you anything more to add to that?"

"No, inspector, I think not. The rest of what I said was true. But may I ask who saw me?"

"Knowles was standing at the window of the Green Room," said Elliot, and the other began to whistle through his teeth. Then Elliot's gaze moved from Gore to Murray to Welkyn. "Has any of you ever seen this before?"

From his pocket he took a smaller section of newspaper, in which the stained clasp-knife had been carefully wrapped. He opened it and exhibited the knife.

The expressions of Gore and Welkyn showed a general blankness. But Murray sucked in his bearded cheeks; he blinked at the exhibit and hitched his chair closer.

"Where did you find this?" Murray asked briskly.

"Near the scene of the crime. Do you recognize it?"

"H'm. You have tested it for fingerprints? No. Ah, a pity," said Murray, growing brisker and brisker. "Will you allow me to touch it if I handle it with the greatest circumspection? Correct me if I am wrong. But didn't you, young Johnny"—he glanced at Gore—"use to have a knife exactly like this? Didn't I present it to you, in fact? Didn't you carry it for years?"

"I certainly did. I always carry a pocket-knife," admitted Gore, reaching into his pocket and producing an old knife only slightly smaller and lighter than the one before them. "But—"

"For once," interposed Welkyn, slapping his hand on the table, "for once and all I must insist on exercising the rights with which you, sir, have seen fit to endow me. Such questions are absurd and improper; and as your legal adviser I must tell you to disregard them. Such knives are as common as blackberries. I once had one myself."

"But what is wrong with the question?" asked Gore, puzzled. "I owned a knife like that. It went with the rest of my clothes and effects in the *Titanic*. But it seems absurd to suppose that the one here could be—"

Before anybody could stop him, Murray had whipped a handkerchief out of his pocket, moistened it at his lips (a handkerchief in the mouth is one of the things which always set Page's teeth on edge), and wiped clean a small section of the blade about halfway down. Into the cleared steel had been roughly cut letters forming the word

Madeline.

"It is yours, Johnny," said Murray comfortably. "You put this name there one day when I took you through the stone-cutting works at Ilford."

"Madeline," repeated Gore.

Opening a pane of the window behind him, he threw out his cigar into the sodden trees. But Page saw his face reflected momentarily in the gloomy glass: it was a curious, set, indecipherable face, unlike the one of mockery with which Gore usually pointed out the difference between his moods and the world's. He turned back.

"But what about the knife? Are you suggesting that that poor, tortured, would-be-honest crook kept it about him all these years, and finally cut his throat with it by the pool? You seem to have determined that this is a case of murder; and yet—and yet—"

He beat the flat of his hand slowly on his knee.

"I'll tell you what it is, gentlemen," said Elliot, "it's an absolutely impossible crime."

He detailed to them Knowles's story. The interest exhibited by both Gore and Murray was in contrast to the evident disgust and bewilderment of Welkyn. When Elliot described the finding of the knife there was an uneasy movement through the group.

"Alone, and yet murdered," said Gore reflectively. He looked at Murray. "Magister, this is a matter after your own heart. I don't seem to know you. Perhaps we have grown too far apart; but in the old days you would haved hopped round the inspector, full of strange theories and bearded like the pard—"

"I am no longer a fool, Johnny."

"Still, let us hear a theory. Any theory. So far, you are the only one who has been reticent about the whole affair."

"I second that motion," observed Dr. Fell.

Murray settled himself more comfortably, and began to wag his finger.

"The exercise of pure logic," he began, "is often comparable to working out immense sums in arithmetic and finding at the end that we have somewhere forgotten to carry one or multiply by two. Every one of a thousand figures and factors may be correct except that one; but the difference in the answer to the sum may be disconcerting. Therefore I do not put this forward as pure logic. I make a suggestion.—You know, inspector, that the coroner's inquest is almost certainly going to call this suicide?"

"Can't say that, sir. Not necessarily," declared Elliot. "A Thumbograph was stolen and then returned; a girl was nearly frightened to death—"

"You know as well as I do," said Murray, opening his eyes, "what verdict a coroner's jury will return. It is remotely possible that the victim might have killed himself and flung the knife away; it is impossible that he should have been murdered. But I assume that it is murder."

"Heh," said Dr. Fell, rubbing his hands. "Heh-heh-heh. And the suggestion?"

"Assuming that it is murder," said Murray, "I suggest that the victim was not, in fact, killed with the knife you have there. I suggest that the marks on his throat are more like the marks of fangs or claws."

Chapter XI

"**C**laws?" repeated Elliot.

"The term was fanciful," said Murray, now so didactic that Page longed to administer a swift kick. "I do not necessarily mean literal claws. Shall I argue out my suggestion for you?"

Elliot smiled. "Go right ahead. I don't mind. And you may be surprised how much there is to argue."

"Put it like this," said Murray in a startlingly ordinary tone. "Assuming that it was murder, and assuming that this knife was used to do it, one question bothers me badly. It is this. *Why didn't the murderer drop the knife into the pool afterwards?*"

The inspector still looked at him inquiringly.

"Consider the circumstances. The person who killed this man had an almost perfect—er—"

"Set-up?" suggested Gore, as the other groped.

"It is a rotten word, Johnny; but it will do. Well. The murderer had an almost perfect set-up for suicide. Suppose he had cut this man's throat and dropped the knife into the pool? Not one person would afterwards have doubted that it was suicide. This man, an impostor, was about to be unmasked: here would have seemed his way out. Even as things are you have difficulty in believing it was not suicide. With the knife in the pool it would have been a clear case. It would even take care of the matter of fingerprints: the water would have washed away any fingerprints which the dead man might have been assumed to have left on the knife.

"Now, gentlemen, you can't tell me that the murderer did not *want* this to be thought suicide. You can't tell me any murderer ever wants that. If it can be managed, a fraudulent suicide is the best possible way out. Why wasn't that knife dropped in the pool? The knife incriminates nobody—except the dead man, another indication of suicide and probably the reason why the murderer chose it. Yet instead the murderer takes it away and (if I follow you) thrusts it deep down into a hedge ten feet away from the pool."

"Proving?" said Elliot.

"No, no. Proving nothing." Murray lifted his finger. "But suggesting a great deal. Now consider this behaviour in relation to the crime. Do you believe old Knowles's story?"

"You're giving the theories, sir."

"No, that is a fair question," said Murray rather sharply. Page felt that he only just checked himself from adding, "Come, come, sir!" "Otherwise we shall get nowhere."

"We shall get nowhere if I say I believe an impossibility, Mr. Murray."

"Then you do believe in suicide?"

"I didn't say that."

"Which do you believe in, then?"

Elliot grinned faintly. "If you get the bit in your teeth, sir, you'll convince me that I ought to answer you. Knowles's story is supported by—um—contributory evidence. For the sake of argument let's say I believe he was telling the truth, or thought he was telling the truth. What happens then?"

"Why, it follows that he did not see anything because there was nothing to see. That can hardly be doubted. This man was alone in the middle of a circle of sand. Therefore no murderer went near him. Therefore the murderer did not use that notched and suggestively stained knife you have there; and the knife was, in fact, 'planted' in the hedge afterwards to make you think it was used for the crime. You follow that? Since the knife could not have flown out of the air, cut his throat three times, and dropped into the hedge, it is evident that the knife could not have been used at all. That argument is plain?"

"Not exactly plain," objected the inspector. "You say it was some other weapon? Then some other weapon hung in the air, cut his throat three times, and disappeared? No, sir. I don't believe that. Definitely not. That's worse than believing in the knife."

"I appeal to Dr. Fell," said Murray, evidently stung. "What do you say, doctor?"

Dr. Fell sniffed. Mysterious wheezes and noises of internal combustion suggested argument; but he spoke mildly.

"I abide by the knife. Besides, you know, there certainly was something moving in that garden; something of damned bluish cast of countenance, if you'allow me. I say, inspector. You've taken the statements. But d'you mind if I probe and pry into them a bit? I should very much like to ask a few questions of the most interesting person here."

"The most interesting person here?" repeated Gore, and prepared himself.

"H'mf, yes. I refer, of course," said Dr. Fell, lifting his stick and pointing, "to Mr. Welkyn."

Superintendent Hadley has often wished that he would not do this. Dr.

Fell is, possibly, too much concerned with proving that the right thing is always the wrong thing, or at least the unexpected thing; and waving flags with both hands above the ruin of logic. Certainly Page would never have taken Harold Welkyn for the most interesting person there. The fat solicitor, with his long disapproving chin, evidently did not think so either. But, as even Hadley admits, the old beggar is often unfortunately right.

"You spoke to me, sir?" inquired Welkyn.

"I was telling the inspector a while ago," said Dr. Fell, "that your name seemed very familiar. I remember now. Is it a general interest in the occult? Or are you a collector of curious clients? I rather imagine you collected our friend here," he nodded towards Gore, "in the same way you collected that Egyptian some time ago."

"Egyptian?" asked Elliot. "What Egyptian?"

"Think! You'll remember the case. Ledwidge v. Ahriman, before Mr. Justice Rankin. Libel. Mr. Welkyn here was instructed for the defence."

"You mean that ghost-seer or whatever he was?"

"Yes," said Dr. Fell, with great pleasure. "Little bit of a chap; hardly more than a dwarf. But he didn't see ghosts: he saw through people, or so he said. He was the fashion of London; all the women flocked to him. Of course, he could have been prosecuted under the old Witchcraft Act, still in force—"

"A most infamous act, sir," declared Welkyn, slapping the table.

"—but it was a question of a libel suit, and Mr. Welkyn's ingenious defence, combined with Gordon-Bates as counsel, got him off. Then there was Madame Duquesne, the medium, who was up for manslaughter because one of her clients died of fright in her house. (Fascinating point of law, eh?) Mr. Welkyn was also instructed for the defence there. The trial, as I remember it, was rather grisly. Oh, yes! And another one: a girl, good-looking blonde as I remember her. The charges against her never got past the Grand Jury, because Mr. Welkyn—"

Patrick Gore was looking at his solicitor with quick interest. "Is this true?" he demanded. "Believe me, gentlemen, I did not know it."

"It is true, isn't it?" inquired Dr. Fell. "You're the same chap?"

Welkyn's face was full of cold wonder.

"Of course it is true," he answered. "But what of it? What has it to do with the present case?"

Page could not have said why it seemed so incongruous. Harold Welkyn, examining his pink finger-nails, then glancing up sharply from little eyes, was a model of business decorum; and yet why not? The white slip inside his waistcoat, the glossy wings of his collar, had no connection with the clients he sought or the beliefs he held.

"You see, Mr. Welkyn," rumbled Dr. Fell, "I had another reason for asking. You were the only one who saw or heard anything queer in the garden last night. Will you read out the part of Mr. Welkyn's statement I mean, inspector?"

Elliot nodded, not taking his eyes from Welkyn until he opened the notebook.

" *'I heard a kind of rustling noise in the hedges or shrubbery, and I thought I saw something looking at me through one of the glass panels of the door, one of the panels down nearest the ground. I was afraid that certain things might be happening which were no affair of mine.'* "

"Exactly," said Dr. Fell, and closed his eyes.

Elliot hesitated, debating two courses; but Page had a feeling that the matter was out in the open now, and that both Dr. Fell and the inspector thought it was better so. Elliot's hard, sandy-haired head bent forward a little.

"Now, sir," he said. "I didn't want to ask you too much this morning, until we—knew more. What does that statement mean?"

"What it says."

"You were in the dining-room, only fifteen feet or so away from the pool, yet you didn't once open one of those doors and look out? Even when you heard the sounds you describe?"

"No."

" 'I was afraid that certain things might be happening that were no affair of mine,' " read Elliot. "Does this refer to the murder? Did you think that a murder was being committed?"

"No, certainly not," said Welkyn, with a slight jump. "And I still have no reason to suspect that one was committed. Inspector, are you mad? Clear evidence of suicide is brought to you; and you all go star-gazing after something else—"

"Did you think that suicide was being committed last night, then?"

"No, I had no reason to suspect it."

"Then what were you referring to?" asked Elliot practically.

Welkyn had the palms of his hands flat on the table. By lifting his fingers slightly he conveyed the effect of a shrug; but his bland dumpling countenance betrayed nothing else.

"I'll try to put it in another way. Mr. Welkyn, do you believe in the supernatural?"

"Yes," said Welkyn briefly.

"Do you believe that someone is attempting to produce supernatural phenomena here?"

Welkyn looked at him. "And you from Scotland Yard! *You* say that!"

"Oh, it's not as bad as all that," said Elliot; and he wore a curious, dark expression which his countrymen have understood for centuries. "I said

'attempting,' and there are various ways of doing that. Real and unreal.
Believe me, sir, there may be queer doings here—implanted here—
growing from one ancestor to another—queerer doings than you think. I
came down here because Miss Daly had been murdered; and there may be
more behind that than a purse of money stolen by a tramp. All the same, I
wasn't the one who suggested there might be something supernatural
here. You suggested it."

"I did?"

"Yes. 'I thought I saw something looking at me through one of the
glass panels of the door, one of the panels down nearest the ground.' You
said 'something.' Why didn't you say 'someone'?"

A small bead of sweat appeared on Welkyn's forehead, up near the
large vein by the temple. It was his only change of expression, if it can be
called that; at least it was the only moving thing on his face.

"I did not recognize who it was. Had I recognized the person, I should
have said 'someone.' I was merely attempting to be accurate."

"It was a person, then? A 'someone'?"

The other nodded.

"But, in order to peep at you through one of the lower panels, this
person must have been crouched down to the ground or lying on the
ground?"

"Not exactly."

"Not exactly? What do you mean by that, sir?"

"It was moving too quickly—and jumpily. I hardly know how to
express what I mean."

"Can't you describe it?"

"No. I only received the impression that it was dead."

Something like horror had got into Brian Page's bones; how it had
come there, even when it had come, he could not tell. Almost impercepti-
bly the conversation had moved into a new element, yet he felt that this
had always been in the background of the case, waiting for a touch to be
wakened. Harold Welkyn then made a very quick movement. He took a
handkerchief out of his breast pocket, wiped the palms of his hands
quickly on it, and replaced it. When he spoke again he had recovered
something of his old solemn, careful manner.

"One moment, inspector," he put in before Elliot could speak. "I have
been trying to tell you truthfully and literally what I saw and felt. You ask
me whether I believe in—such things. I do. I tell you frankly I wouldn't
go into that garden after dark for a thousand pounds. It seems to surprise
you that a man of my profession should have such ideas."

Elliot pondered. "To tell you the truth, it does, somehow. I don't know
why it should. After all, I suppose even a lawyer may believe in the
supernatural."

The other's tone was dry.

"Even a lawyer may," he agreed; "and be none the worse man of business for doing so."

Madeline had come into the room. Only Page noticed her, for the others were too intent on Welkyn; she was walking on tiptoe, and he wondered whether she had heard what had gone before. Though he tried to give her his chair, she sat down on the arm of it. He could not see her face: only the soft line of chin and cheek: but he saw that the breast of her white silk blouse was rising and falling rapidly.

Kennet Murray's eyebrows were pinched together. He was very polite, but he had the air of a customs-officer about to examine luggage.

"I presume, Mr. Welkyn," Murray said, "you are—er—honest about this. It is certainly extraordinary. That garden has a bad reputation. It has had a bad reputation for centuries. In fact, it was remodelled in the late seventeenth century in the hope of exorcising the shadow by fresh prospects. You remember, young Johnny, how your demonological studies tried to raise up things there?"

"Yes," answered Gore. He was about to add something, but he checked himself.

"And on your homecoming," said Murray, "you are greeted by a crawling legless something in the garden, and a housemaid frightened into a fit. Look here, young Johnny: you're not up to your old tricks of frightening people, are you?"

To Page's surprise, Gore's dusky face had gone pale. Murray, it appeared, was the only person who could sting him or rouse him out of his urbanity.

"No," Gore said. "You know where I was. I was keeping an eye on you in the library. And just one thing more. Just who the hell do you think you are, to talk to me as though I were still a fifteen-year-old child? You kowtowed to my father; and, by God, I'll have decent respect from you or I'll take a cane to you as you used to do to me."

The outburst was so unexpected that even Dr. Fell grunted. Murray got to his feet.

"Is it going to your head already?" he said. "Just as you like. My usefulness is over. You have your proofs. If I am wanted for anything more, inspector, I shall be at the inn."

"That, John," interposed Madeline softly, "was rather a rotten thing to say, don't you think? Forgive me for interrupting."

For the first time both Murray and Gore looked at her fully, and she at them. The latter smiled.

"You are Madeline," he said.

"I am Madeline."

"My old, cold light-of-love," said Gore. The wrinkles deepened round his eyes. He detained Murray, and there was apology in his voice. "It's no good, magister. We can't pick up the past, and now I am quite certain I don't care to. It seems to me that for twenty-five years I have been moving forward, mentally, while you have been standing still. I used to imagine what would happen when I returned to what are poetically known as the halls of my fathers. I used to imagine myself moved by the sight of a picture on a wall or letters cut with a pen-knife into the back of a bench. What I find is a group of alien sticks and stones; I begin to wish I had not intruded. But that is not the point now. Something seems to have gone out of line. Inspector Elliot! Didn't you say a minute ago that you had come down here because 'Miss Daly had been murdered'?"

"That's right, sir."

Murray had sat down again, evidently curious, while Gore turned to the inspector.

"Victoria Daly. That's not by any chance the little girl who used to live with her aunt—Ernestine Daly, was it?—at Rose-Bower Cottage on the other side of the Hanging Chart?"

"I don't know about her aunt," returned Elliot, "but that's where she lived. She was strangled on the night of July 31st, last year."

The claimant was grim. "Then I can at least produce an alibi there. I was happily in America then. All the same, will somebody take us out of this fen? What has the murder of Victoria Daly got to do with this business here?"

Elliot gave an inquiring glance towards Dr. Fell. The doctor nodded sleepily but violently; his great bulk hardly seemed to breathe, and he was watching. Taking up the brief-case from beside his chair, Elliot opened it and drew out a book. It was of quarto size, bound in dark calf-skin at some comparatively recent date (say a hundred years ago), and had on its back the somewhat unexhilarating title of *Admirable History*. The inspector pushed it across to Dr. Fell, who opened it. Then Page saw that it was a much older volume, a translation from the French of Sébastien Michaëlis, published at London in 1613. The paper was brownish and ridged, and across from the title-page there was a very curious book-plate.

"H'mf," said Dr. Fell. "Has anybody here ever seen this book before?"

"Yes," said Gore quietly.

"And this book-plate?"

"Yes. That book-plate has not been used in the family since the eighteenth century."

Dr. Fell's finger traced out the motto. " '*Sanguis eius super nos et super filios nostros,*' Thos. Farnleigh, 1675. 'His blood be upon us and upon our children.'—Was this book ever in the library here at the Close?"

Gore's eye quickened and gleamed as he looked at the book; but he remained puzzled. He spoke sardonically.

"No, it certainly was not. That's one of the books of darkness which my father, and his father before him, kept locked in the little room in the attic. I stole his key once, and had some duplicates made, so that I could go up there and read. Lord, the time I spent there—under pretext, if anyone should find me, of getting an apple from the apple-room next door." He looked round. "Do you remember, Madeline? I took you up there once to give you a glimpse of the Golden Hag? I even gave you a key. But I am afraid you never liked it.—Doctor, where did you get that book? How did it get out of captivity?"

Inspector Elliot got up and rang the bell for Knowles.

"Will you find Lady Farnleigh," he said to a scared butler, "and ask her if she will come in here?"

With great leisureliness Dr. Fell took out pipe and pouch. He filled the pipe, lit it, and inhaled with deep satisfaction before he spoke. Then he made a flourishing gesture and pointed.

"That book? Because of the innocuous title, nobody at the time even glanced into it or thought twice about it. Actually, it contains one of the most unnerving documents in recorded history: the confession of Madeleine de la Palud, at Aix in 1611, of her participation in ceremonies of witchcraft and the worship of Satan. It was found on the table by Miss Daly's bed. She had been reading it not long before she was murdered."

Chapter XII

In the quiet of the library, Page heard very distinctly the footsteps of Molly Farnleigh and Burrows as they came in.

Murray cleared his throat. "Meaning—?" he prompted. "Didn't I understand that Miss Daly was killed by a tramp?"

"Quite possibly she was."

"Well, then?"

It was Molly Farnleigh who spoke. "I came in here to tell you," she said, "that I am going to fight this ridiculous claim, *your* claim," her whole vigorous nature went into the glance of cold dislike she gave Gore, "to the end. Nat Burrows says it will probably take years and we shall all lose our shirts, but I can afford that. In the meantime, the important thing is who killed John. I'll call a truce for the time being, if you will. What did I hear you all talking about when we came in here?"

A certain sense of relief went through the group. But one man was instantly on guard.

"You think you have a case, Lady Farnleigh?" asked Welkyn, all solicitor again. "I am bound to warn you—"

"A better case than you may have any idea of," retorted Molly, with a curious significant look at Madeline. "What did I hear you talking about when we came in?"

Dr. Fell, fiery with interest now, spoke in a kind of apologetic thunder.

"We're on rather an important aspect of it just now, ma'am," he said, "and we should very much appreciate your help. Is there still, in the attic of this house, a little room containing a collection of books on witchcraft and kindred subjects? Eh?"

"Yes, of course. But what has that to do with it?"

"Look at this book, ma'am. Can you tell us positively whether it comes from the collection?"

Molly approached the table. They had all risen, but she made a gesture of impatience at the formality.

"I think so. Yes, I'm almost sure of it. All of them had that book-plate, and none of the other books have: it's a kind of badge. Where on earth did you get the book?"

Dr. Fell told her.

"But that's impossible!"

"Why?"

"Because there was such a terrible fuss and bother and to-do about those books. My husband caused it; I never knew why. We had only been married a little over a year, you know." Her quiet brown eyes looked at the past. She took the chair Burrows set out for her. "When I came here as a—as a bride, he gave me all the household keys except the key to that room. Of course I handed them straight over to Mrs. Apps, the house-keeper; but you know the principle of the thing. It interested me, rather."

"Like Bluebeard?" suggested Gore.

"No controversy, please," said Dr. Fell sharply, as she turned to the claimant in a cold fury.

"Very well," said Molly. "Anyhow, I heard about it. My husband wanted to burn it—the collection, I mean. It seems that when they were valuing the property just before he came into it, they had a man down from London to look at the books. He said that little collection in the attic was worth thousands and thousands of pounds and almost danced with delight, the silly ass. He said there were all kinds of rarities in it, including something unique. I do remember what that was. It was a manuscript book which was supposed to have been lost since the beginning of the nineteenth century. Nobody knew where it had gone, and there it was right in our attic. They called it the Red Book of Appin. He said it was supposed to be the big harum-scarum hocus-pocus of magic, and it was so magical that anybody who read it had to wear a hoop of iron round his head. I jolly well do remember that, because you were all arguing about it last night, and this man"—she looked at Gore—"didn't even know what it was."

"As Dr. Fell suggests, no controversy," said Gore pleasantly. But he addressed Murray. "Fair play, magister. I never knew the sacred volume under that name, you know. But I can tell you what it is, and I can even identify it if it is still upstairs. I'll give you one of its qualities. Anyone who possessed it was said to know what any inquiry would be before the inquirer opened his lips."

"That must have been very useful to you," Molly said sweetly, "last night."

"As proving that I had read the book, yes. It was also said to confer the power of giving life to inanimate objects, which almost suggests that Lady Farnleigh must have read it herself."

Dr. Fell hammered the ferrule of his stick on the floor to call for attention. When the threatened storm had been hammered away, he looked at Molly benevolently.

"Heh," said Dr. Fell. "Heh-heh-heh. I gather, ma'am, that you don't believe in the magical properties of the Red Book of Appin or anything else?"

"Oh, so-and-so!" said Molly, using a short Anglo-Saxon word which made Madeline colour.

"H'mf, yes. Exactly. But you were telling us?"

"Well, anyway, my husband was frightfully upset and concerned about those books. He wanted to burn them. I said not to be absolutely silly: if he had to get rid of them, why not sell them, and in any case what harm were they doing? He said they were full of eroticism and wickedness." Molly hesitated, but she went on in her candid way. "That did interest me a bit, if you must know. I peeped into one or two of them—when he showed me the room—but it certainly wasn't anything like that. You never read such horribly dull stuff in your life. There was nothing low about it. It was a lot of long-winded rubbish about the twin life-lines or something, and all done with those funny 'f's' for 's's' that make it look as though the writer lisped. I couldn't get up *any* interest in it. So, when my husband insisted on keeping the place locked, I never bothered any more about it and I'm sure it hasn't been opened since."

"But this book," Dr. Fell tapped it, "came from there?"

"Ye-es, I'm sure of it."

"And your husband always kept the key to that locked room. Yet somehow it got out of there and into Miss Daly's possession. H'm." Dr. Fell was smoking in short puffs; now he took the pipe out of his mouth and sniffed massively. "Consequently, we have a connection—on a thread like this—through Miss Daly's death to your husband's death. Eh?"

"But what connection?"

"For instance, ma'am, could he have given Miss Daly the book himself?"

"But I've already told you what he thought about those books!"

"That, you know, ma'am," said Dr. Fell apologetically, "was not the question. Could he? After all, we've heard then when he was a boy—if he was the real John Farnleigh, as you claim—he thought very highly of those books."

Molly faced it out.

"You've got me in a cleft stick. If I say he hated such things out of all reason, you can answer that it's too much of a change and proves he wasn't John Farnleigh. If I say he could have given the book to Victoria—well, I don't know what you'll say."

"All we want is an honest answer, ma'am," said Dr. Fell. "Or, rather, an honest impression. Heaven pity the person who tries to tell all the truth. But look here: did you know Victoria Daly well?"

"Pretty well. Poor Victoria was the sort who exulted in Good Works."

"Should you have said," Dr. Fell made a vague gesture with his pipe, "should you have said she was the sort to be deeply interested in the subject of witchcraft?"

Molly clenched her hands.

"But will you tell me, please, how on earth this witchcraft talk comes into it? Granting that's what this book is about—if it comes from the attic it must be—does it prove anything just because she was reading it?"

"There is other evidence, believe me," said Dr. Fell gently. "Your own native intelligence, ma'am, will show you that the important thing is the connection of Miss Daly + a locked library + that book. For instance: did your husband know her well?"

"H'm. I don't know. Not very well, I should have thought."

Dr. Fell's forehead was wrinkled. "And yet consider his behaviour last night, as it has been described to me. Confirm this. A claimant to his estate appears. The possession of this estate, rightfully or wrongfully, is the most important driving force in his life. And now the citadel is attacked. Mr. Gore, Mr. Welkyn, with their convincing stories and their deadly proof of fingerprints, are closing in on him. It is true that he paces the floor; yet, at the very moment the attack is launched, he seems more concerned over the fact that there is a detective in the village investigating the death of Victoria Daly. Is that true?"

It was true. Page remembered it only too well. And Molly was forced to admit it.

"So, we perceive, the thread spins out. Let's try to follow that thread wherever it leads. I am more and more interested in that locked attic room. Is there anything else up there besides books?"

Molly reflected.

"Only that mechanical robot thing. I saw it once when I was a little girl, and I rather loved it. I asked my husband why we couldn't have it down and see whether we couldn't find a way to make it work: I love things that work: but *it* stayed there too."

"Ah, the mechanical robot thing," repeated Dr. Fell, hauling himself up with a wheeze and a flash of interest. "What can you tell us about that?

It was Kennet Murray who answered, when Molly shook her head.

"Now there is a matter, doctor," Murray said comfortably, settling himself in the chair, "you would do well to investigate. *I* tried to investigate it years ago, and so did young Johnny."

"Well?"

"Here are all the *facts* I could unearth." Murray spoke with emphasis. "Sir Dudley never allowed me to look at the figure, and I had to work from outside. It was constructed by M. Raisin, the organist of Troyes, who made the self-playing harpsichord for Louis XIV; and it was exhibited with great success at the court of Charles II in 1676-77. It was a nearly life-sized figure, sitting on a kind of small couch, and it was said to represent one of the king's ladies: there is argument about which one. Its actions delighted the people of that time. It played two or three tunes on a cittern (what we nowadays call a zither); it thumbed its nose at the spectators, and went through a variety of gestures, some undoubtedly indecorous."

There was no doubt that he had caught the immediate interest of his audience.

"It was bought by Sir Thomas Farnleigh, whose book-plate you have there," said Murray. "Whether it was the immodesty of the automaton that later caused a blight to fall on it, or some other cause, I have never been able to find out. But something happened—dead silence of all records as to what. That seems no reason for the horror it inspired in the eighteenth century, though such a contraption wouldn't have recommended itself to Sir Dudley or his father or grandfather. Presumably old Thomas learned the secret of how to make it work; but that secret has never been passed on. Eh, young Jo . . . I beg your pardon. Sir John?"

At the thick and exaggerated courtesy of his tone, Gore showed some contempt. But he was interested in other matters.

"No, it was not passed on," Gore admitted. "And it will never be learned. I know, gentlemen. In my younger days I racked my brains over the secret of the Golden Hag. I could easily show you why none of the obvious explanations would work. If we—" He looked startled. "By all the gods, why shouldn't we go up and have a look at her? I only just thought of it. I'm inhibited. I was thinking of all sorts of excuses and crooked ways by which I could sneak up there as I used to do. But why not? Why not, in the open light of day?"

He thumped his fist down on the arm of the chair, blinking a little as though he himself had just come into light. Inspector Elliot interposed rather sharply.

"Just one moment, sir," Elliot said. "This is all very interesting; and we can go into it another time; but I don't see that it has any bearing on—"

"Are you sure?" asked Dr. Fell.

"Sir?"

"Are you sure?" repeated the doctor with great intensity. "I say, somebody! What does this automaton look like?"

"It's a good deal decayed, of course; at least, it was twenty-five years ago—"

"It was," agreed Madeline Dane, and shuddered. "Don't go up there. Please say you won't!"

"But why on earth not?" cried Molly.

"I don't know. I'm afraid."

Gore regarded her with indulgence.

"Yes, I hazily remember that it had a powerful effect on you. But you were asking what it looked like, doctor. It must have been uncannily life-like when it was new. The framework is of jointed iron, of course; but the 'flesh' is wax, with glass eyes—one missing—and real hair. The decay has not improved it; it is rather fat, and used to look somewhat unpleasant when you imagined things. It wears, or used to wear, a brocaded gown. The hands and fingers are of painted iron. In order to play the zither and make gestures, the fingers are long and jointed and sharp, almost like . . . It used to smile, but the smile had rotted away when I saw it last."

"And Betty Harbottle," said Dr. Fell abruptly, "Betty Harbottle, like Eve, has a strong fondness for apples."

"I beg your pardon?"

"She has, you know," urged Dr. Fell. "Betty Harbottle, the frightened maid, is fond of apples. That was the first thing which was pointed out to us when we questioned the servants. I suspect our good housekeeper, Mrs. Apps, of conveying a hint. By the darkness of Eleusis, that's exactly what it was! And you"—the doctor's red face shone with concentration as he blinked at Gore—"you told me a minute ago that you used to have a pretext when you wanted to visit the den of the books and the Golden Hag. You went to the apple room, next door to it in the attic. Will somebody offer me odds as to where Betty Harbottle was when she was frightened, and where the Thumbograph was hidden last night?"

Harold Welkyn got up and began to walk round the table; but he was the only one who moved. Afterwards Page was to remember that circle of faces in the gloom of the library, and the brief expression he surprised on one of them.

It was Murray who spoke, smoothing his moustache.

"Ah. Yes. Yes, it is undoubtedly interesting. If I still have my geography straight, the stairs to the attic are at the back of the passage beside the Green Room. You suggest that the girl was carried downstairs and put in the Green Room?"

Dr. Fell wagged his head. "I only suggest that we have got to follow our dim intelligences or go home to bed. Every thread leads back to that little den. It's the core of the labyrinth and the heart of every disturbance, like the little bowl of fluid in *The House and the Brain:* which is an apter title than we may think. We had better pay a visit there."

Inspector Elliot spoke slowly.

"I think we had. Now. Do you mind, Lady Farnleigh?"

"No, not at all, except that I don't know where the key is. Oh, bother that! Break the lock. It's a new padlock my husband had put on; and if you think it will help you can tear—you can t-tear—" Molly brushed her hand across her eyes, held tight to her feelings, and regained control again. "Shall I lead the way?"

"Thank you." Elliot was brisk. "How many of the rest of you have ever been in that room? Only Miss Dane and Mr. Gore? Will you two come with Dr. Fell and me, please? And Mr. Page. The others please remain here."

Elliot and the doctor went ahead, talking in low tones. Molly then put herself in front of them, as though discreetly deaf, placing them between herself and the claimant. Page followed with Madeline.

"If you'd rather not go up—?" he said to Madeline.

She pressed his arm. "No, please. I *want* to go up. I do, really, to see if I can understand what is going on. You know, I'm afraid something I said has upset Molly terribly, but I had to tell her: there was no other way out. Brian. You don't think I'm a cat, do you?"

He was startled. Though her half-smiling mouth made fun of this suggestion, the long eyes had a look of great intensity.

"Good Lord, no! What put that idea into your head?"

"Oh, nothing. But she didn't love him, really. She's only doing all this because she thinks she ought to. In spite of all appearances, I tell you they weren't suited to each other. He was idealistic and she is practical. Wait: I know he was an impostor, but you don't know all the circumstances or you'd understand—"

"Then give me the practical," Page snapped.

"Brian!"

"I mean it. Idealistic my eye! If he did what they say he did, and what you yourself admit he did, our late dead friend was a hundred-carat swine and you know it. Were you by any chance in love with him yourself?"

"Brian! You have no right to say that!"

"I know I haven't; but were you?"

"I was not," said Madeline quietly, and looked at the floor. "If you had better eyes, or understood things better, you would know enough not to ask that." She hesitated; it was clear that she wanted to change the subject. "What do Dr. Fell and the inspector think of—all this?"

He opened his mouth to answer, and realized that he had no idea.

He had no idea. Their group had gone up the broad, shallow oak staircase to the floor above, along the gallery, and round the turning of a passage to the left. On the left was the Green Room, its open door showing heavy study-furniture of the last century and walls biliously patterned. On the right were two bedroom doors. The passage ran straight down to a window at the end, overlooking the garden. The stairs up to the attic—Page vaguely remembered—were in the outer thickness of the wall at the end of the passage, the door to them being in the left-hand wall.

But he was not thinking of this. Despite Dr. Fell's thunderous geniality, and the easy-talking frankness of Inspector Elliot, he realized that he knew nothing whatever. Both of them would talk until Doomsday, of course. But what about routine police-work: a fingerprint here, a footprint there, a searching of the garden by Elliot or a clue sealed into an envelope? The finding of the knife, yes; he knew of that because under the circumstances it could hardly have been avoided. What else, even as regarded theories? Certain statements had been taken from certain persons; what were we to think of those statements?

After all, it was their business. Yet it disquieted him. New discoveries were being turned up out of what he had thought was old ground, like skulls at Blenheim, and you had no warning of the skull until it rolled across the table. No, better change the simile. Up ahead towered Dr. Fell's huge back, seeming to fill the passage.

"Which room is she in?" Elliot asked in a low voice.

Molly indicated the farther bedroom door, across the passage from the door to the attic. Elliot knocked very lightly at the door; but from inside came a faint muttered cry.

"Betty," whispered Madeline.

"In there?"

"Yes. They put her in the nearest bedroom. She's not," said Madeline, "she's not in very good shape."

The full implications of this were beginning to creep into Page's mind. Dr. King opened the bedroom door, glanced behind him, and eased it softly shut as he slipped out into the passage.

"No," he said. "You can't see her yet. Tonight, maybe; tomorrow or next day more likely. I wish the sedatives would take hold. They won't, properly."

Elliot looked puzzled and worried. "Yes, but, doctor, surely it's not—not—?"

"Serious, were you going to say?" asked King, lowering his grizzled head as though he were about to butt with it. "My God! Excuse me."

He opened the door again.

"Has she said anything?"

"Nothing for your notebook, inspector. Delirium, more than half of it. I wish I could find out what she saw."

He was speaking to a very quiet group. Molly, whose expression had altered, seemed to be trying to hold fiercely to accepted rules. Dr. King had been a lifelong friend of her father, and they stood on no ceremony with each other.

"Uncle Ned, I want to know. I'd do anything for Betty, and you know it. But I never realized—that is, it's not really what we can call *serious,* is it? It can't be. People get frightened, but it's not the same thing as being actually ill? It's not dangerous?"

"Oh," said the other, "it's not dangerous. Fine, lusty wench you are; no nerves; surplus energy; see something and biff it one. Yes, you would. Well, maybe it takes people differently. Maybe it was a mouse or wind in the chimney. Only I hope I don't run across it, whatever it was." His tone softened. "No, it'll be all right. No help, thanks; Mrs. Apps and I can manage. But you might have some tea sent up."

The door closed.

"Yes, my good friends," observed Patrick Gore, with his hands deep in his pockets, "I think I am safe in saying that something has happened. Shall we go upstairs?"

He went over and opened the door opposite.

The staircase inside was steep-pitched and had that faint, sour smell which comes from old stone enclosed within walls. It was as though you saw the ribs and bones inside the house, unsmoothed by modern crafts. The servant's quarters, Page knew, were at the other side of the house. There was no window here; and Elliot, who went ahead, had to use an electric torch. Gore followed him, then Dr. Fell, then Molly, with Madeline and Page in the rear.

Nor had any of this part of the attic been altered since Inigo Jones sketched out his small windows and backed his brick with stone. On the landing the floor sloped in such humped fashion towards the stairs that an unwary footstep might send you down. There was a mighty strength of oak beams, too huge for the picturesque, conveying only power to uphold or crush. Faint grey light entered; the air was thick, damp, and hot.

They found the door they wanted at the far end. It was a heavy door, black, suggesting a cellar rather than an attic. The hinges were of the eighteenth century; the knob was gone and a more modern lock disused; a tight chain and padlock now secured it. But it was not at the lock that Elliot first directed his light.

Something had been flung down and partly crushed by the closing of the door.

It was a half-eaten apple.

Chapter XIII

With the edge of a sixpence as a screw-driver, Elliot carefully unscrewed the staple which held the chain of the padlock. It took a long time, but the inspector worked carefully, like a carpenter. When the chain had fallen the door swung open of its own accord.

"The lair of the Golden Hag," said Gore with gusto, and kicked the half-eaten apple out of the way.

"Steady on, sir!" said Elliot sharply.

"What? Do you think the apple is evidence?"

"You never know. When we go in here, please don't touch anything unless I tell you to."

"When we go in" was an optimistic phrase. Page had expected to see a room. What he found was a kind of book-closet hardly six feet square, with a sloping roof in which a small and thick-grimed pane of glass showed opaque. There were many gaps in the shelves, where ragged calfskin mingled with more modern bindings. Over everything was a film of dust; but it was that thin, blackish, gritty dust of attics, in which few decipherable marks are left. An early Victorian armchair was pushed into it—and the hag herself seemed to jump out at them when the light of Elliot's torch fell inside.

Even Elliot jumped back a little. The hag was not a beauty. She might once have been an alluring charmer, but now only one eye looked out of half a face: the other side of the head was ruined, like the remnants of the velvet brocaded gown which might once have been yellow. Her appearance was not improved by the cracks opening out across her face.

Had she been standing up, she would have been something under life-size. She sat on an oblong box, once gilded and painted to resemble a couch, but not much broader or deeper than she was, and set up off the floor on wheels which were evidently of later date than the automaton itself. The hands were partly lifted with burlesque and rather horrible coquetry. The whole squat, ponderous machine must have weighed two or three hundredweight.

Madeline uttered a kind of giggle, as of nerves or relief. Elliot growled, and Dr. Fell swore. The doctor said:

"Shades of *Udolpho!* Is this anti-climax?"

"Sir?"

"You know what I mean. Did that girl try to get into Bluebeard's room, see this thing for the first time, and—" He paused, blowing out the ends of his moustache. "No. No, that won't do."

"I'm afraid it won't," agreed Elliot soberly. "*If* something happened to her here, that is. How did she get in? And who carried her downstairs? And where did she get the Thumbograph? You can't tell me that the mere sight of this thing would affect her as badly as she seems to have been affected. She might scream, or something of the sort. It might give her a turn. But nothing like this, unless she's a hysterical case. Lady Farnleigh, did the servants know about this dummy?"

"Of course," said Molly. "Nobody has seen it, except Knowles or possibly Mrs. Apps, but they all knew about it."

"Then it wouldn't even come as a surprise?"

"No."

"If, as I say, she was frightened by something in this little two-by-four place—of which we haven't any evidence—"

"Look there," said Dr. Fell, pointing with his stick.

The beam of the torch played on the floor by the base of the automaton. It found a heap of crumpled linen which, when Elliot picked it up, proved to be a maid's frilled apron. Though it had recently been freshly laundered, it was stained with patches of dust and dirt; and, in one place, there were two short jagged rents in it. Dr. Fell took it from the inspector and handed it to Molly.

"Betty's?" he said.

Molly examined a minute tab, with an even more minute name in ink, sewn to the hem of the apron; and Molly nodded.

"Stop a bit!" urged Dr. Fell, shutting his eyes. He began to lumber back and forth by the door, pressing on his eyeglasses as though to keep them from falling off. When he took his hand away again, his face was lowering and grave. "All right. I'll tell you, my lad. I can't prove it, any more than I could prove the part about the apple and the appleroom. But I can tell you what happened in that book-closet as certainly as though I had seen it. It's no longer mere routine: it's the most vital thing in the case that we should know just when, between lunch-time and four o'clock in the afternoon, that girl was frightened, and what the various people here were doing at that time.

"Because, my lad, the murderer was here—in this book-closet. Betty Harbottle found him here. I don't know what the murderer was doing; but it was vital that nobody should know he had been here at all. Something happened. Afterwards he used the girl's apron to remove possible footprints, fingerprints, marks of any kind in this dust. He carried or dragged her downstairs. He put into her hand the useless Thumbograph he had stolen the night before. And then he went away, as they all do, and left the apron lying neatly in the middle of the floor. Eh?"

Elliot raised his hand.

"Steady on, sir. Not so fast." He thought it over. "There are two bad objections to that, I'm afraid."

"Which are?"

"One. If it was so vital to conceal the fact that he'd been in this little room, doing whatever he was doing, how was he covering his tracks just by moving the unconscious girl from one place to another? He wasn't preventing disclosure; he was only postponing it. The girl's alive. She will recover. And she'll tell who was here, and what he was doing—if anything."

"Apparently a poser," said Dr. Fell. "Apparently a stinger whang in the gold. And yet, do you know," he spoke with some violence, "I should not be surprised if the answer to that seeming contradiction is the answer to our problem. What's the other objection?"

"Betty Harbottle wasn't hurt. Physically, she wasn't touched. She was put into the shape she was in by plain old-fashioned fright at something she saw. Yet all she could have seen was an ordinary human being doing something he shouldn't. It's not reasonable, sir; girls are pretty tough these days.—What could have put her into that state, then?"

Dr. Fell looked at him.

"Something that the automaton did," he answered. "Suppose it reached out now and took your hand?"

Such is the power of suggestion that every person in the group shied back. Six pairs of eyes turned to the ruined head and the curious hands of the dummy. They would not be pleasant hands to take or touch. Nothing about that figure, from the mildewed gown to the cracked-open wax of the face, would be good to the touch.

Elliot cleared his throat.

"You mean he made the dummy work?"

"He did not make it work," interposed Gore. "I thought of that years ago. That is, he did not make it work unless some electrical system or other trickery has been shoved into it since my time. Damn it all, gentlemen, nine generations of Farnleighs have tried to discover what made it work. And I'll make you a flat offer. I will pay a thousand pounds to the man who can show me how it does work."

"Man or woman?" said Madeline. Page could see that she was forcing a laugh, but Gore spoke in very desperate earnest.

"Man or woman or child or anybody else. To the man or woman who can make it work without modern hocus-pocus, and under the same conditions as it was exhibited two hundred and fifty years ago."

"The offer's generous enough," said Dr. Fell cheerfully. "Well, wheel her out and let's have a look at her."

With some effort Elliot and Page, laying hold of the iron box on which the dummy sat, pulled it out of the book-closet with a bump over the sill. She jerked her head and quivered; Page wondered whether the hair would come off. Yet the wheels moved with surprising ease. With a heavy creaking and a faint rattling noise, they pushed her over into the light from the window near the head of the stairs.

"Go on. Demonstrate," said Dr. Fell.

Gore made a careful examination. "To begin with, you will find that the body of the thing is full of clockwork. I am no mechanical expert, and I can't tell you whether all the wheels and whatnots are genuine, or whether they were put there for effect. I suspect that most of them are dummies even if some are genuine. Anyhow, the point is that the body is completely filled. There's a long window at the back. If it still opens, put you hand through, and—oh, you scratch, do you?"

Gore's face darkened, and he jerked his own hand back. In his absorption he made a gesture too close to the sharp fingers of the automaton; a crooked scratch drew blood on the back of his hand. He put it to his mouth.

"My good old clock-guts!" he said. "My faithful old clock-guts! I ought to knock the rest of your face off."

"Don't!" cried Madeline.

He was amused. "As you wish, little one. In any case, inspector—will you poke about among the works? What I want to establish is that the body is full of them and that nobody could hide in there."

Elliot was as serious as ever. The glass had long gone from the window at the back; with the aid of his flashlight he examined the mechanism and groped inside. Something seemed to startle him, but he only said:

"Yes, that's right, sir. No room for anything here. You mean it was suggested that somebody was hiding in the thing and working it?"

"The only suggestion anybody could hazard. Now, then. That takes care of the automaton itself. The only other part of it, as you can see for yourself, is the couch on which she sits. Watch."

This time he had more difficulty. At the left of the couch's front there was a small knob; Page could see that the whole front opened out like a little door on a hinge. With some manipulation he managed to get the door open. The interior of the box, bare iron badly corroded with rust, was well under three feet long and not more than eighteen inches high.

Gore beamed with pleasure.

"You remember," he said, "the explanation that was advanced for the chess-playing automaton of Maelzel? The figure sat on a series of large boxes, each with its own little door. Before the demonstration, the showman opened these doors to show that there was no hoax. It was said, however, that inside lurked a *small child,* who deftly contorted himself from one compartment to another; and these movements were so synchronized with the shrewd manipulation of doors that the spectators believed they had seen all of an empty inside.

"Something like that was said about the hag here. But spectators have written that this could not be the case. I don't need to point out that, first, it would have to be a very small child; and, second, no exhibitor could possibly travel all over Europe with a child and have nobody aware of that fact.

"But in the hag there is only one small space and one door. Spectators were invited to feel inside the space and make sure there was no deception. Most of them did so. The figure stood by itself, raised well off the ground and on a carpet provided by the host. Yet, in spite of there being no means by which she could come alive, at the word of command our lively lady received a cittern—played any tune whose name was called out by the spectators—returned the cittern—conversed with the spectators by dumb-show, and performed other antics of a nature suited to the time. Do you wonder that my respected ancestor was delighted? But I have always wondered what made him change his mind when he learned the secret."

Gore dropped his lofty manner.

"Now tell me how it worked," he added.

"You little—ape!" said Molly Farnleigh. She spoke in her sweetest manner, but her hands were clenched at her sides. "Will you always prance, no matter what happens? Aren't you satisfied? Would you like to play trains or toy soldiers? My God, Brian, come here; I can't stick this. And you too—and you, a police-officer—fiddling with a dummy—crawling round it like a lot of children, when—don't you realize a man was killed last night?"

"Very well," said Gore. "Let us change the subject. Then, for a change, tell me how *that* was worked."

"I suppose you will say it was suicide, of course."

"Madam," said Gore, with a gesture of despair, "it makes no difference what I say. Somebody invariably jumps down my throat in any case. If I say it was suicide, I am assaulted by A, B, and C. If I say it was murder, I am assaulted by D, E, and F. I have not suggested that it was accident, if only to avoid incurring the wrath of G, H, and I."

"That's very clever, no doubt. What do you say, Mr. Elliot?"

Elliot spoke out of a personal honesty.

"Lady Farnleigh, I'm only trying to do the best I can in the most difficult business I was ever put into, which isn't helped by the attitude of any of you. You must see that. If you'll think for just a minute, you must see this machine has something very much to do with the case. I only ask you not to talk out of plain temper. For there's something else to do with the machine as well."

He put his hand on its shoulder.

"I don't know whether the clockwork inside this is dummy clockwork or not, as Mr. Gore says. I'd like to have a go at it in my workshop and find out. I don't know whether the mechanism might still be expected to work after two hundred years; though, if clocks still go after that time, why shouldn't it? But this much I did find out when I looked into the back. The mechanism in this has been recently oiled."

Molly frowned.

"Well?"

"I was wondering, Dr. Fell, whether you—" Elliot turned round. "Here! Where are you, sir?"

Page's conviction that anything might happen was strengthened by the disappearance of so very tangible a bulk as the doctor. He was not yet used to Dr. Fell's trick of fading from the scene and reappearing somewhere else, usually engaged in some meaningless occupation. This time Elliot was answered by a flicker of light from the book-closet. Dr. Fell had been striking a series of matches and blinking with fierce absorption at the lower shelves.

"Eh? I beg your pardon?"

"Haven't you been listening to this demonstration?"

"Oh, that? Harrumph, yes. I can hardly claim to succeed off-hand where so many generations of the family have failed, but I should rather like to know how the original exhibitor was dressed."

"Dressed?"

"Yes. The traditional magician's costume, I daresay, which has always seemed to me singularly unimpressive but suggestive of possibilities. However, I have been pouncing and poking in that cupboard, with or without results—"

"The books?"

"The books are the usual orthodox collection of the unorthodox though there are several witch-trials that are new to me. I did find what seems to be an account of how the automaton was exhibited, which I hope I may borrow? Thank you. But particularly there's this."

While Gore watched him with bright, wicked eyes of amusement, he lumbered out of the closet carrying a decrepit wooden box. And at the same time it seemed to Page that the attic was filling with people.

It was only that Kennet Murray and Nathaniel Burrows, evidently having grown restive, had insisted on following them upstairs. Burrows's big spectacles, and Murray's towering calm face, appeared over the attic stairs as though out of a trap-door. For the moment they did not come nearer. Dr. Fell rattled the wooden box. He balanced it as well as he could on the narrow ledge of couch round the automaton.

"Here, steady the machine!" said the doctor sharply. "This floor's got a bad canter, and we don't want her rolling downstairs on us. Now have a look. An odd collection of the dust of years, don't you think?"

In the box they saw a number of child's glass marbles, a rusty knife with a painted handle, some fishing-flies, a small heavy ball of lead into which four large hooks had been welded like a bouquet, and (incongruously) a woman's garter of many years ago. But they did not look at these things. They looked at what lay on top: a double false-face or mask made of parchment on wire, and forming a kind of head with a face back and front like the images of Janus. It was blackish, shrivelled, and without features. Dr. Fell did not touch it.

"It's beastly to look at," whispered Madeline. "But what on earth is it?"

"The mask of the god," said Dr. Fell.

"The what?"

"The mask worn by the master of ceremonies presiding at witch-gatherings. Most of those who read about it, and even some of those who write about it, have no idea what witchcraft really was. I firmly do not mean to lecture. But we have an example here. Satanism was an unholy parody of Christian ritual; but it had its old roots in Paganism. Two of its deities were Janus the double-headed, patron of fertility and of the cross-roads; and Diana, patron both of fertility and virginity. The master (or mistress) wore either the goat-mask of Satan or a mask such as we have here. Bah!"

He ticked his forefinger and thumb against the mask.

"You have been hinting at something like that for a long time," said Madeline quietly. "Perhaps I shouldn't ask, but will you please answer a straight question? It seems ridiculous even to ask it. Are you saying that there is a Satanist group somewhere hereabouts?"

"That's the joke," declared Dr. Fell, with an expression of heavy enlightenment. "The answer is, NO."

There was a pause. Inspector Elliot turned round. He was so surprised that he forgot they were talking in front of witnesses.

"Steady on, sir! You can't mean that. Our evidence—"

"I do mean it. Our evidence isn't worth *that*."

"But—"

"Oh, Lord, why didn't I think of it before!" said Dr. Fell vehemently. "A case after my own heart, and I have only just thought of the solution.

Elliot, my boy: there have been no sinister gatherings in the Hanging Chart. There have been no goat-pipes or revels by night. A whole group of solid Kentish people have not been snared into any such mad tomfoolery. It was one of the things that stuck in my gullet when you began collecting your evidence, and I see the grimy truth now. Elliot, there is one crooked soul in this whole affair, and only one. Everything, from mental cruelty to murder, is the work of one person. I give you all the truth gratis."

Murray and Burrows joined the group, their footsteps creaking.

"You seem excited," Murray said dryly.

The doctor looked apologetic.

"Well, I am, a bit. I haven't got it all worked out yet. But I see the beginnings of it, and I shall have something to say presently. It's—er—a matter of motives." He stared far off, and a faint twinkle appeared in his eye. "Besides, it's rather novel. I never heard of the trick before. I tell you frankly, Satanism itself is an honest and straightforward business compared to the intellectual pleasures a certain person has invented. Excuse me, gents—and ladies. There's something I should rather like to look at in the garden. Carry on, inspector."

He had stumped towards the stairs before Elliot woke up. Elliot ignored everything, and became brisk.

"Now, then.—Yes? You wanted something, Mr. Murray?"

"I wanted to see the automaton," returned the other with asperity. "I've been rather left out of it, I notice, since I produced my proofs-of-identity and ceased to be of any value. So this is the hag. And this: do you mind if I look at it?"

He picked up the wooden box, rattling it, and moved it closer to the faint dust-grimed light from the window. Elliot studied him.

"Have you ever seen any of those things before, sir?"

Murray shook his head. "I have heard of this parchment-mask. But I have never seen it. I was wondering—"

And that was when the automaton moved.

To this day Page swears that nobody pushed it. This may or may not be true. Seven persons were jostling round it on a creaking, crackling floor which ran down in a smooth hump towards the stairs. But the light from the window was very uncertain, and Murray, his back to the hag, was fixing their attention with the exhibit he held in his right hand. If a hand moved, if a foot moved, if a shoulder moved, nobody knew. What they did not see was the rotted dummy jerking forward with the stealthy suddenness of a motor-car slipping its brakes. What they did see was three-hundredweight of rattling iron darting out of reach and driving like a gun-carriage for the well of the stairs. What they heard was the screech of the wheels, the tap of Dr. Fell's stick on the stairs, and Elliot's scream:

"For God's sake, look out below!"

Then the crash as it went over.

Page reached it. He had his fingers round the iron box, and he might just as well have tried to stop a runaway gun; but he kept it upright when it might have gone head-over-heels-side-to-side, sweeping the whole staircase in crazy descent and crushing anything in its way. The black weight kept to its wheels. Sprawling down the first steps, Page saw Dr. Fell peering upwards—half-way down. He saw the daylight from the open door at the foot of the stairs. He saw Dr. Fell, unable to move an inch in that enclosed space, throw up one hand as though to ward off a blow. He saw, out of an inferno of crashings, the black shape plunge past within a hair's clearance.

But he saw more; more which no one could have foreseen. He saw the automaton clear the open door, and land in the passage below. One of its wheels snapped off as it struck, but its momentum was too great. Lurching once, it hurtled against the door directly opposite across the passage; and the door came open.

Page stumbled down the stairs. He did not need to hear the cry from the room across that passage. He remembered who was in that room, and why Betty Harbottle was there, and what had just gone in to visit her now. In the cessation of noise after the automaton had been stopped, small sounds crept out. After a time he heard distinctly the squeak of the hinges as Dr. King opened the bedroom door, and the physician had a face like white paper. He said:

"You devil up there, what have you done?"

III

Friday,
July 31st

THE RISE OF A WITCH

*Car, au fond, c'est cela le Satanisme, se disait-il; la
question agitée depuis que le monde existe, des visions
extérieures, est subsidiare, quand on y songe; le Dé-
mon n'a pas besoin de s'exhiber sous des traits hu-
mains ou bestiaux afin d'attester sa présence; il suffit,
pour qu'il s'affirme, qu'il élise domicile en des âmes
qu'il exulcère et incite à d'inexplicables crimes.*
—*J.-K. HUYSMANS, Là-Bas*

Chapter XIV

The coroner's inquest on Sir John Farnleigh was held the following day, and produced a sensation that blew off every journalistic roof in Great Britain.

Inspector Elliot, like most policemen, is not fond of inquests. This is for practical reasons. Brian Page is not fond of them for artistic reasons: because you never learn anything you did not know before, because there is seldom anything of a sensational nature, and because the verdict, whatever it is, brings you no nearer to a solution than before.

But this inquest—held on the morning of Friday, July 31st—he admitted did not go according to pattern. A suicide verdict, of course, was a foregone conclusion. Yet it was spectacular enough to produce a first-class row before the first witness had said ten words, and it ended in a way that left Inspector Elliot dazed.

Page, drinking very black coffee at breakfast, offered up profane thanks that they had not another inquest on their hands from the business of the previous afternoon. Betty Harbottle was not dead. But she had gone through a narrow graze of it after seeing the hag for the second time, and she was still in no condition to speak. Afterwards Elliot's endless questioning ran in a dismal circle. "Did you push it?" "I swear I didn't; I don't know who did; we were tramping on an uneven floor and maybe nobody did."

Elliot summed it up when he and Dr. Fell talked late over pipes and beer. Page, after taking Madeline home, forcing her to have something to eat, quieting threatened hysterics, and trying to think of a thousand things at once, heard the conclusion of the inspector's views.

"We're licked," he said briefly. "Not a single ruddy thing we can prove, and yet look at the string of events we've got! Victoria Daly is murdered: maybe by a tramp, maybe not: but with the indications of other dirty work that we needn't discuss now. That's a year ago. Sir John Farnleigh dies with his throat cut. Betty Harbottle is in some way 'attacked' and brought down from the attic; and her torn apron is found in the book-closet upstairs. The Thumbograph disappears and returns. Finally, a deliberate attempt is made to kill you by pushing that machinery downstairs, an attempt which you only escaped by one whistle and the grace of God."

"Believe me, I appreciate that," muttered Dr. Fell uncomfortably. "It was one of the worst moments of my life when I looked round and saw that juggernaut coming down. It was my own fault. I talked too much. And yet—"

Elliot regarded him with sharp inquiry.

"All the same, sir, it showed you were on the right track. The murderer knew you knew too much. As to just what that track is, if you've got any ideas now is the time to tell me. I shall be recalled to town, you know, unless something is done."

"Oh, I'll tell you fast enough," growled Dr. Fell. "I'm not making mysteries. Even when I do tell you, though, and even in the event I happen to be right, it still doesn't prove anything. Besides, I'm not sure about another thing. I am very flattered, of course. But I'm not sure the automaton was pushed downstairs with the purpose of what is poetically known as rubbing me out."

"For what purpose, then? It couldn't be just to frighten the girl again, sir. The murderer couldn't have known it would land smack against that bedroom door."

"I know," said Dr. Fell stubbornly, and ruffled his hands through his big mop of grey-streaked hair. "And yet—and yet—proof—"

"That's exactly what I mean. Here are all these points, a connected series of events, and not one blasted one of 'em I can prove! Not one thing I can take to my superintendent and say, 'Here; grab this.' Not one bit of evidence that isn't capable of another interpretation. I can't even show that the events are in any way connected, which is the real snag. Now take this inquest tomorrow. Even the police evidence must plump for a suicide verdict—"

"Can't you get the inquest adjourned?"

"Of course. Ordinarily that's what I should do, and keep on adjourning it until we either had evidence of murder or had to drop the case altogether. But there's the last and greatest snag. What have I got to hope for by more investigation, as matters stand? My superintendent is just about convinced that Sir John Farnleigh's death is suicide, and so is the A.C. When they learned that there are traces of the dead man's fingerprints on that clasp-knife Sergeant Burton found in the hedge—"

(Here was news to Page, the final nail in a suicide's coffin.)

"—that finished it," Elliot corroborated him. "What else can I look for?"

"Betty Harbottle?" suggested Page.

"All right: suppose she does recover and tell her story? Suppose she says she saw somebody in the book-closet? Doing what? And what of it?

What connection has it got with a suicide in the garden? Where's your proof, laddie? Anything about the Thumbograph? Well, it's never been suggested that the Thumbograph was in the possession of the dead man, so where do you get with that line of argument? No. Don't look at it sensibly, sir; look at it legally. It's a hundred to one they'll recall me at the end of today, and the case will be shelved. You and I know that there's a murderer here, worming so neatly that he or she can keep right on in the same old way unless somebody stops it. And apparently nobody can stop it."

"What are you going to do?"

Elliot gulped down half a pint of beer before he answered.

"There's just one chance, as I say: a full-dress inquest. Most of our suspects will give evidence. It's remotely possible that somebody, under oath, will make a slip. Not much hope, I admit—but it's happened before (remember the Nurse Waddington case?), and it may happen again. It's the last hope of the police when nothing else works."

"Will the coroner play your game?"

"I wonder," said Elliot thoughtfully. "This chap Burrows is up to something; I know that. But he won't come to me and I can't get any change out of him. He's gone to the coroner about something. I gather that the coroner doesn't particularly like Burrows, didn't particularly like the late alleged 'Farnleigh,' and himself thinks it's suicide. But he'll play fair, and they'll all stand together against the outsider—meaning me. The ironical part is that Burrows himself would like to prove murder, because a suicide verdict more or less proves his client was an impostor. The whole thing is going to be just one hilarious field-day about lost heirs, with only one possible verdict: suicide, my recall, and the end of the case."

"Now, now," said Dr. Fell soothingly. "By the way, where is the automaton now?"

"Sir?"

Elliot roused himself out of grievances and stared at the other.

"The automaton?" he repeated. "I pushed it into a cupboard. After the whacking it took, it's not good for much now except scrap-iron. I was going to have a look at it, but I doubt if a master-mechanic could make sense of the works now."

"Yes," said Dr. Fell, taking up his bedroom candle with a sigh. "That, you see, was why the murderer pushed it downstairs."

Page spent a troubled night. There were many things for the next day besides the inquest. Nat Burrows, he reflected, was not the man his father had been; even matters like funeral arrangements had to be turned over to Page. It appeared that Burrows was busying himself over some other aspect of the difficulty. There was also the question of leaving Molly "alone" in a house of questionable atmosphere, and the disquieting news that the servants were threatening to leave almost in a body.

These things churned through sleep into a day of brilliant sunshine and heat. The riot of motor-cars began by nine o'clock. He had never seen so many cars in Mallingford; the Press and the outside world poured in to an extent that made him realize the immense noise this case was making outside their gates. It angered him. It was, he thought, nobody else's damned business. Why didn't they put up swings and round-abouts, and sell hot dogs? They swamped the *Bull and Butcher*, in whose "hall"—a sort of long shed built for the jollifications of hop-pickers—the inquest was to be held. Sunlight winked on many camera-lenses in the road. There were women. Old Mr. Rowntree's dog chased somebody clear up the road to Major Chambers's, and had a hysteria of barking all morning, and couldn't be quieted.

In this the people of the district moved without comment. They did not take sides. In country life each person depends on the other for something, giving and receiving; in a case like this you had to wait and see what happened, so that matters could be reasonably comfortable whichever way verdicts went. But from the outside world came the tumult of LOST HEIR SLAIN OR LOST HEIR FRAUD?; and at eleven o'clock in the hot morning they opened the inquest.

The long, low, gloomy shed was packed. Page felt the appropriateness of a starched collar. The coroner, a forthright solicitor who was determined to stand no nonsense from the Farnleighs, sat behind a heap of papers at a broad table, with a witness-chair at his left.

First of all, evidence of identification of the body was given by Lady Farnleigh, the widow. Even this—as a rule the merest of formalities—was questioned. Molly had hardly begun to speak when up rose Mr. Harold Welkyn, in frockcoat and gardenia, on behalf of his client. Mr. Welkyn said that he must protest against this identification in the matter of a technicality, since the dead man was not, in fact, Sir John Farnleigh; and, since the matter was of the utmost importance in determining whether the deceased took his own life or was murdered, he respectfully begged leave to bring it to the coroner's attention.

There ensued a long argument in which the coroner, aided by a frigid and indignant Burrows, quite properly sat on Mr. Welkyn. But Welkyn, relapsing, perspired with satisfaction. He had made the point. He had set the pace. He had outlined the real terms of the battle, and everybody knew it.

It also compelled Molly to discuss the matter in reply to the coroner's questions as to the deceased's state of mind. He treated her well, but he was determined to thrash the matter out and Molly looked badly rattled. Page began to realize the state of affairs when the coroner, instead of next calling evidence as to the finding of the body, called Kennet Murray. The whole story came out; and, under Murray's gentle firmness, the imposture of the deceased stood out as clear and black as a fingerprint. Burrows fought every step of the way, but only succeeded in angering the coroner.

Evidence of finding the body was given by Burrows and Page. (The latter's own voice sounded wrong to him.) Then the medical testimony was called. Dr. Theophilus King testified that on the night of Wednesday, July 29th, he had gone to Farnleigh Close in response to a telephone-call from Detective-Sergeant Burton. He had made a preliminary examination and ascertained that the man was dead. The next day, the body having been removed to the mortuary, he had on the instructions of the coroner performed a post-mortem examination, verifying the cause of death.

> *The coroner:* Now, Dr. King, will you describe the wounds on the throat of the deceased?
> *The doctor:* There were three fairly shallow wounds, beginning at the left side of the throat and ending under the angle of the right jaw in a slightly upward direction. Two of the wounds crossed each other.
> *Q:* The weapon was passed across the throat from left to right?
> *A:* That is so.
> *Q:* Would this have been the course taken by a weapon held in the hand of a man taking his own life?
> *A:* If the man were right-handed, yes.
> *Q:* Was the deceased right-handed?
> *A:* To the best of my knowledge, he was.
> *Q:* Should you say it was impossible for the deceased to have inflicted such wounds on himself?
> *A:* Not at all.
> *Q:* From the nature of the wounds, doctor, what sort of weapon should you say had been used to inflict them?
> *A:* I should say a ragged or uneven blade some four or five inches long. There was much laceration of tissue. It is a matter in which it is difficult to speak precisely.
> *Q:* We quite appreciate that, doctor. I shall presently call evidence to show that there was found in a hedge some ten feet to the left of the deceased a knife with a blade such as you describe. Have you seen the knife to which I refer?
> *A:* I have.
> *Q:* In your opinion, could the knife in question have inflicted wounds such as you describe on the throat of the deceased?
> *A:* In my opinion, it could.

Q: Finally, doctor, I come to a point which must be put with some care.
Mr. Nathaniel Burrows has testified that a moment before the deceased's fall the deceased was standing at the edge of the pool with
his back to the house. Mr. Burrows is unable to say definitely
whether or not the deceased was alone at this time, though I have
pressed him to do so. Now, in the event—I say in the event—that the
deceased was alone, could he have flung a weapon away from him to
a distance of say ten feet?

A: It is well within the physical possibilities.

Q: Let us suppose that he had a weapon in his right hand. Could this
weapon instead have been thrown towards the left?

A: I cannot venture on a guess as to the convulsions of a dying man. I
can only say that such a thing is physically possible.

After this high-handed carrying of matters, the story of Ernest Wilbert-
son Knowles left no doubt. Everybody knew Knowles. Everybody knew
his likes, his dislikes, his nature. Everybody had seen for decades that
there was no guile in him. He told of the view from the window, the man
alone in a closed circle of sand, the impossibility of murder.

Q: But are you satisfied in your own mind that what you saw was the
deceased taking his own life?

A: I am afraid so, sir.

Q: Then how do you account for the fact that a knife held in the right
hand was thrown to the left rather than the right?

A: I am not sure I can properly describe the gestures the late gentleman
made, sir. I thought I could at first, but I have been thinking it over
and I am not sure. It was all so rapid that his gestures might have been
anything.

Q: But you did not actually see the knife thrown from him?

A: Yes, sir, I am under the impression that I did.

"WOW!" said a voice among the spectators. It sounded rather like
Tony Weller speaking out from the gallery. And it was, in fact, Dr. Fell,
who throughout the proceedings had remained wheezily asleep with his
red face smoking in the heat.

"I will have silence in this room," shouted the coroner.

Cross-examined by Burrows as counsel for the widow, Knowles said
that he would not swear to having seen the deceased throw the knife. He
had good eyesight, but not such good eyesight as that. And his patent
sincerity of manner kept the sympathies of the jury. Knowles admitted
that he spoke only from an impression and admitted the (remote) possibility of an error, with which Burrows had to be content.

There followed to an inevitable end the police evidence, the evidence of the deceased's movements, to a rounding-up. In that hot shed, with rows of pencils going like spiders' legs, there was determined for practical purposes the imposture of the dead man. Glances were being cast at Patrick Gore, the real heir. Quick glances. Appraising glances. Hesitant glances. Even friendly glances, under which he remained bland and impassive.

"Members of the jury," said the coroner, "there is one more witness to whom I shall ask you to listen, though I am unacquainted with the nature of the witness's testimony. At the request of Mr. Burrows and at her own request, the witness comes here to make a statement of importance, which I trust will be of assistance to you in your painful duty. I therefore call Miss Madeline Dane."

Page sat up.

There was a puzzled stir in the court, the reporters quickening with interest at Madeline's very real beauty. What she was doing here Page himself had no idea, but it disturbed him. Way was made for her to come to the witness-chair, where the coroner handed her the Book and she took the oath in a nervous but clear voice. As though for a kind of distant-mourning, she wore dark blue, with a dark blue hat the colour of her eyes. Something of the corrugated-iron feeling was removed. The corrugated-iron self-consciousness of the men on the jury relaxed. They did not actually beam on her, but Page felt it was not far off. Even the coroner fussed with consideration. Among the males of the population Madeline was a favorite who had few competitors. A handsome feeling went through the inquest.

"Again I must insist on silence in this room!" said the coroner. "Now will you give your name, please?"

"Madeline Elspeth Dane."

"Your age?"

"Th-thirty-five."

"Your address, Miss Dane?"

"Monplaisir, near Frettenden."

"Now, Miss Dane," said the coroner, brisk but gentle, "I believe you wished to make a statement regarding the deceased? What is the nature of the evidence you wish to give?"

"Yes, I must tell you. Only it's so difficult to know where to begin."

"Perhaps I can help Miss Dane out," said Burrows, on his feet with perspiring dignity. "Miss Dane, was it—"

"Mr. Burrows," snapped the coroner, losing all control of his temper, "you have constantly interrupted these proceedings with a lack of respect for your rights and mine which I cannot and will not tolerate. You are entitled to question the witness when I have done questioning her, and not until then. In the meantime you will remain silent or leave this court. Hrrrr! Ahem. Now, Miss Dane?"

"Please don't quarrel."

"We are not quarrelling, madam. I am indicating the respect due to this court, a court gathered to determine how the deceased met his death, and a respect which, whatever may be said of it from some sources"—here his eye sought out the reporters—"I have every intention of upholding. Now, Miss Dane?"

"It's about Sir John Farnleigh," said Madeline earnestly, "and whether he was or was not Sir John Farnleigh. I want to explain why he was so anxious to receive the claimant and the claimant's solicitor; and why he didn't show them out of the house; and why he was so eager to have the fingerprint taken; oh, and all the things that may help you decide about his death."

"Miss Dane, if you merely wish to give an opinion as to whether the deceased was Sir John Farnleigh, I am afraid I must inform you—"

"No, no, no. I don't know whether he was. But that's the whole dreadful thing. You see, *he didn't know himself.*"

Chapter XV

B y the stir in the dim shed, it was beginning to be felt that this might be the sensation of the day, even if nobody knew what it meant. The coroner cleared his throat, his head turning like an alert marionette's.

"Miss Dane, this is not a court of law; it is an inquiry; and therefore I can allow you to give what testimony you like, provided only it has some bearing which will help us. Will you be so good as to explain what you mean?"

Madeline drew a deep breath.

"Yes, if you let me explain you'll see how important it is, Mr. Whitehouse. What is hard to say in front of all of you is how he came to tell me about it. But he had to confide in somebody, you know. He was too fond of Lady Farnleigh to tell *her;* that was a part of the trouble; and sometimes it worried him so horribly that you may have noticed how ill he looked. And I suppose I'm a safe person to confide in"—she wrinkled her forehead half wryly and half smilingly—"so that's how it was."

"Yes, yes? How what was, Miss Dane?"

"You've let them tell all about the meeting the night before last, to argue over the estate and take the fingerprints," resumed Madeline, with a probably unconscious thrust. "I was not there, but I heard all about it from a friend of mine who was there. He said what impressed him most was the absolute assurance of both claimants, right up to the taking of the fingerprints and afterwards. He said that the only time poor John—I beg your pardon: Sir John—smiled at all or looked relieved was when the claimant was talking about that terrible affair on the *Titanic,* and about being hit with a seaman's mallet."

"Yes; well?"

"Here is what Sir John told me months ago. After the wreck of the *Titanic,* as a boy, he woke up in a hospital in New York. But he didn't know it was New York or about the *Titanic.* He didn't know where he was, or how he had got there, or even who he was. He had had concussion of the brain, after getting some knocks on the head accidentally or deliberately in the wreck of the ship, and he was suffering from what they call amnesia. Do you understand what I mean?"

"Perfectly, Miss Dane. Continue."

"They told him his clothes and papers had identified him as John Farnleigh. There was a man standing over the bed in the hospital, a man who said he was his mother's cousin—oh, that's badly put, but you know what I mean—and told him to go to sleep and get well.

"But you know what boys of that age are. He was very frightened and horribly worried. For he didn't know anything about himself. And worst of all, like boys of that age, he didn't dare tell anybody for fear he might be mad or there might be something wrong with him or they might put him in gaol.

"That's how it seemed to him. He hadn't any reason to think he *wasn't* this John Farnleigh. He hadn't any reason to believe they weren't telling the truth in all they told him about himself. He had a hazy recollection of shouting or confusion, something to do with open air or cold; but that was all he could remember. So he never spoke a work about it to anybody. He pretended to his cousin—a Mr. Renwick from Colorado—that he remembered everything. Mr. Renwick never suspected.

"He nursed that little secret for years. He kept reading his diary, and trying to bring things back. He told me that sometimes he would sit for hours with his hands pressed to his head, concentrating. Sometimes he would think he remembered a face or an event faintly, like something you see under water. Then again it would seem to him that there was something wrong. The only thing he ever brought out of it, as a phrase rather than an image, had to do with a hinge: a crooked hinge."

Under the iron roof the spectators sat like dummies. No papers rustled. Nobody whispered. Page felt his collar damp and his heart ticking like a watch. Smoky sunlight came through the windows, and Madeline winked the corner of her eye in it.

"A crooked hinge, Miss Dane?"

"Yes. I don't know what he meant. Neither did he."

"Go on, please."

"In those early years in Colorado he was afraid they would put him in gaol if there should be anything wrong and they found out about it. Handwriting was no good, because two of his fingers were nearly crushed in the wreck and he could never hold a pen properly. He was afraid to write home; that's why he never did. He was even afraid to go to a doctor and ask if he might be mad, for fear the doctor should tell on him.

"Of course, in time it got fainter. He convinced himself that it was an unfortunate thing which happens to some people, and so on. There was the War and all that. He consulted a mental specialist who told him after a lot of psychological tests that he really was John Farnleigh, and that he had nothing to worry about. But he never lost the horror of those years, and even when he thought he had forgotten it he dreamed about it.

"Then it was all revived when poor Dudley died and he inherited the title and estate. He had to come to England. He was—how can I say this?—academically interested. He thought at long last he *must* remember. And he didn't. You all know how he used to go wandering round like a ghost, a poor old ghost who didn't even know whether he was a ghost. You know how jumpy he was. He loved it here. He loved every acre and yard of it. Mind you, he didn't honestly doubt he was John Farnleigh. But he had to KNOW."

Madeline bit her lip.

Her luminous, now rather hard eyes wandered among the spectators.

"I used to talk to him and try to make him quiet. I would ask him not to think too much; then perhaps he would remember. I used to arrange it so that I reminded him of things, and made him think he had remembered them for himself. Maybe it would be a gramophone playing, 'To thee, beautiful lady,' far away in the evening; and he would remember how we danced to it as children. Maybe it would be a detail of the house. In the library there's a kind of cupboard with shelves of books—built into the wall by the windows, you know—and instead of being just a cupboard, it's got a door that used to open out into the garden. It still will open if you find the right catch. I persuaded him to find the right catch. He said he slept well for nights after that.

"But he still had to know. He said he wouldn't mind so much if he could only know, even if it turned out he was not John Farnleigh. He said he wasn't a wild adolescent boy any longer. He said he could face it quietly; and it would be the greatest thing in the world just to know the truth.

"He went to London and saw two more doctors; I know that. You can see how worried he was when he even went to a person who was supposed to have psychic powers—a horrible little man called Ahriman, in Half-Moon Street—who was all the rage then. He took a crowd of us along under pretext of having our fortunes told, and pretended to laugh at it. But he told this fortune-teller all about himself.

"Still he kept wandering about the place. He used to say, 'Well, I am a good steward'; and you know he was. He used to go into the church a lot, too; he liked the hymns best; and sometimes, when they played, 'Abide with Me'—anyway, when he was near the church, and looking up at the walls, he used to say that if ever he were in a position to—"

Madeline paused.

Her breast rose with a deep breath. Her eyes were fixed on the front rows, and her fingers opened wide on the arms of the chair. All passion and mysticism seemed in her then, as deep as roots and as strong as hearts; yet she was, after all, only a woman making what defence she could in a hot and stuffy shed.

"I'm so sorry," she blurted. "Perhaps it is better not to talk about that; it does not concern us, anyhow. I'm sorry if I'm taking up your time with things that don't matter—"

"I will have silence in here," said the coroner, flinging round his head at the rustle that grew. "I am not sure I think you are taking up our time with things that do not matter. Have you anything else to tell the jury?"

"Yes," said Madeline, turning and looking at them. "One other thing."

"Which is?"

"When I heard about the claimant to the estate and his lawyer, I knew what John had been thinking. You know now what was in his mind all along. You can follow every step of his thoughts and every word he said. You now know why he smiled, and why the relief was almost too much, when he heard the claimant's story about the seaman's mallet and the blows on the head in the wreck of the *Titanic*. For *he* was the one who suffered from concussion of the brain and a loss of memory that lasted for twenty-five years.

"Please wait! I don't say the claimant's story isn't true. I don't know, or profess to decide. But Sir John—the one you call the deceased as though he had never been alive—must have felt a mighty relief when he heard something that in his eyes couldn't possibly have been true. He saw his dream being fulfilled at last, that his identity should be proved. You know now why he welcomed that fingerprint test. You know why he was the most eager of all. You know why he could hardly wait, why he was all wire and nerves, to learn the result."

Madeline grasped the arms of the chair.

"Please. Perhaps I'm putting all this stupidly, but I hope you understand me. To prove things one way or the other was the one end of his life. If he were Sir John Farnleigh, he would be happy to the end of his life. If he were not, it wouldn't matter so much once he really knew. Like winning a football pool, you know. You put your sixpence on it. You think perhaps you've won thousands and thousands of pounds. You're almost sure of it, you could swear it's true. But you can't be sure until the telegram comes. If it doesn't come, you think, 'Well, that's that,' and let it go. Well, that's John Farnleigh. This was his football pool. Acres and acres of things he loved: they were his football pool. Respect and honour and sound sleep at night forever: they were his football pool. The end of torture and the beginning of the future: they were his football pool. He believed now that he had won it. And now people are trying to tell you he killed himself. Don't you think it for a minute. You know better. Can you believe, dare you believe, that he'd have deliberately cut his throat half an hour before he could learn the result?"

She put her hand over her eyes.

There was a genuine uproar, which the coroner put down. Mr. Harold Welkyn was on his feet. Page saw that his shiny face was slightly pale, and he spoke as though he had been running.

"Mr. Coroner. As a piece of special pleading, all this is no doubt very interesting," he said acidly. "I shall not be impertinent enough to remind you of your duties. I shall not be impertinent enough to point out that no question has been asked in the last ten minutes. But if this lady has completely finished her remarkable statement, which if true tends to show that the deceased was an even greater impostor than we believed, I shall ask leave, as counsel for the real Sir John Farnleigh, to cross-examine."

"Mr. Welkyn," said the coroner, flinging round his head again, "you will ask questions when I give you leave and you will remain silent until then. Now, Miss Dane—"

"Please let him ask questions," said Madeline. "I remember seeing him at the house of that horrible little Egyptian, Ahriman, in Half-Moon Street."

Mr. Welkyn got out a handkerchief and mopped his forehead.

And the questions were asked. And the coroner summed up. And Inspector Elliot went into another room and privately danced the saraband. And the jury, throwing the case straight to the police to handle, brought in a verdict of murder by a person or persons unknown.

Chapter XVI

A ndrew MacAndrew Elliot lifted a glass of very passable hock and inspected that.

"Miss Dane," he declared, "you're a born politician. No, I'll say diplomat; it sounds better; I don't know why. That touch about the football pools was sheer genius. It brought things home to the jury as certainly as sixpence and two wrong. How did you come to think of it?"

In the long, warm afterglow of sunset, Elliot, Dr. Fell, and Page were having dinner with Madeline at the unfortunately named but comfortable Monplaisir. The table stood by the French windows of the dining-room, and the French windows opened on a deep garden of laurels. At the end of it were two acres of apple-orchard. In one direction a footpath went through the orchard to what used to be Colonel Mardale's. In another it wound across a brook and up through the Hanging Chart, whose slope of trees showed dark against the evening sky to the left of the orchard. If you followed the latter path up through the chart, over its shoulder, and down again, you came to the back gardens of Farnleigh Close.

Madeline lived alone, having a woman who came in by day to cook and "do." It was a trim little house, bright with military prints that were a heritage from her father, full of brass and bustling clocks. It stood rather isolated, the nearest house being that of the unfortunate Victoria Daly; but Madeline had never minded the isolation.

She sat now at the head of the table beside the open windows, beyond polished wood and silver in a dusk which was not quite dark enough for the lighting of the dinner-table candles. She wore white. The great, low oak beams of the dining-room, the pewter and the busy clocks, all were a background for her. Dinner over, Dr. Fell had lit a Gargantuan cigar; Page had lit a cigarette for Madeline; and, at Elliot's question, Madeline laughed in the light of the match.

"About the football pools?" she repeated. She flushed a little as well. "As a matter of fact, I didn't think of it. It was Nat Burrows. He wrote it out and made me get it word-perfect like a recitation. Oh, every word I said was true. I felt it terribly. It was the most awful cheek of me to carry on like that before all those people; and every second I was afraid poor Mr. Whitehouse was going to stop me; but Nat said it was absolutely the only way. Afterwards I went upstairs at the *Bull and Butcher* and had hysterics and cried and felt better. Was it very awful of me?"

They were certainly staring at her.

"No," said Dr. Fell quite seriously, "it was a remarkable performance. But, oh, Lord! Burrows coached you? Wow!"

"Yes, he was here half of last night doing it."

"Burrows? But when was he here?" asked Page, surprised. "I brought you home."

"He came here after you left. He was full of what I had just told Molly, and terribly excited."

"You know, gents," rumbled Dr. Fell, taking a meditative pull at the large cigar, "we mustn't underestimate our friend Burrows. Page here told us long ago that he was an unco' intelligent chap. Welkyn seemed to run rings round him at the beginning of this circus; but all the time, psychologically—confound that word—he had the inquest exactly where he wanted it. He'll be fighting, naturally. It will naturally make a big difference to the firm of Burrows & Burrows whether they keep the management of the Farnleigh estate. And he's a fighter. When, as, and if the case of Farnleigh *v.* Gore ever comes to trial, it ought to be a sizzler."

Elliot faced something else.

"Look here, Miss Dane," he said stubbornly. "I'm not denying you did us a good turn. It's a victory, if only an outward and newspaper victory. Now the case won't be closed officially, even if the A.C. tears his hair and swears the jury were a pack of thick-witted yokels under the spell of a good-looking—er—female. But what I want to know is why you didn't come to *me* with all this information in the first place. I'm not a twister. I'm not—er—a half bad fellow, if you can put it like that. Why didn't you tell me?"

The odd and almost comic part of it was, Page thought, that he sounded personally hurt.

"I wanted to," said Madeline. "Honestly I did. But I had to tell Molly first. Then Nat Burrows made me swear all kinds of horrid oaths I wouldn't breathe a word of it to the police until after the inquest. He says he doesn't trust the police. Also, he's working on a theory to prove—" She checked herself, biting her lip, and made an apologetic gesture with her cigarette. "You know how some people are."

"Still, where do we stand?" asked Page. "After this morning, have we gone round in the old circle to wondering which of them is the real heir? If Murray swears Gore is, and if they don't upset that fingerprint evidence, that seems to end it. Or so I thought. This morning, once or twice, I wasn't quite so sure. Certain hints and innuendoes—you made them yourself—seemed to centre round good old Welkyn."

"Really, Brian! I only said what Nat told me to say. What do you mean?"

"Well, possibly that the whole claim to the estate might have been engineered by Welkyn himself. Welkyn, the spooks' solicitor and spir- itualists' advocate. Welkyn, who collects some rather rummy friends, and may have collected Gore as he collected Ahriman and Madame Duquesne and the rest of them. I said when we met Gore he was some kind of showman. Welkyn, who said he saw a ghost in the garden at the time of the murder. Welkyn, who at the time of the murder was only fifteen feet away from the victim and with only a sheet of glass between. Welkyn—"

"But surely, Brian, you don't suspect Mr. Welkyn of the murder?"

"Why not? Dr. Fell said—"

"I said," interposed the doctor, frowning at his cigar, "that he was the most interesting person in the group."

"It usually amounts to the same thing," said Page gloomily. "What's your real opinion, Madeline, about the real heir? You told me yesterday you thought the late Farnleigh was an impostor. Do you?"

"Yes, I do. But I don't see how anybody could keep from feeling sorry for him. He didn't want to be an impostor, don't you see? He only wanted to know who he was. As for Mr. Welkyn, he couldn't possibly be the murderer. He was the only one of us who wasn't in the attic when—well, it seems horrible to talk about after dinner and on a nice evening, but who wasn't in the attic when that machine fell."

"Sinister," said the doctor. "Very sinister."

"You must be terribly brave," said Madeline with the utmost seriousness, "to laugh about that iron idol tumbling down—"

"My dear young lady, I am not brave. The wind was blowing violently and I felt ill. Afterwards I began, like St. Peter, to curse and swear. Then I made jokes. Harrumph. Fortunately I began thinking about that girl in the other room, who hasn't my padding to sustain her. And I swore a mighty oath myself—" His fist hovered over the table, huge in the twilight. They had the impression of a dangerous force behind jokes and absence of mind, a force that could fall and bind. But he did not bring the fist down. He looked out into the darkening garden, and continued to smoke mildly.

"Then where do we stand, sir?" asked Page. "Have you found you can trust us by now?"

It was Elliot who answered him. Elliot took a cigarette out of the box on the table. He lit it with careful movings of the match. In the light of the match his expression was again brisk, impassive, but as though conveying a hint Page could not interpret.

"We must be moving along soon," the inspector said. "Burton is driving us to Paddock Wood, and Dr. Fell and I are catching the ten o'clock train for town. We have a conference with Mr. Bellchester at the Yard. Dr. Fell has an idea."

"About—what to do here?" Madeline asked eagerly.

"Yes," said Dr. Fell. For a time he continued to smoke with a sleepy air. "I was wondering. Perhaps it would be as well if I gave a few hollow subterranean whispers. For example, that inquest today served a double-barrelled purpose. We hoped for a murder verdict and we hoped that one of the witnesses would make a slip. We got the murder verdict; and somebody blundered."

"Was that where you said 'wow' out loud?"

"I said 'wow' many times," answered the doctor gravely. "To myself. At a price, the inspector and I will tell you what caused both of us to say 'wow,' or at least a hint of it. I say: at a price. After all, you ought to do for us what you did for Mr. Burrows, and under the same pledge of secrecy. A minute ago you said he was working on a theory to prove something. What theory? And what does he want to prove?"

Madeline stirred, and crushed out her cigarette. In the semi-darkness she looked cool and clean in white, her short throat swelling above the low-necked dress. Page always remembered her at that moment: the blonde hair done into something like curls above the ears, the broad face even more softened and etherealized by twilight, the slow closing of her eyes. Outside a faint wind stirred in the laurels. Towards the west over the garden the low sky was thin yellow-orange, like brittle glass; but over the mass of the Hanging Chart there was a star. The room seemed to have retreated, as though it were waiting. Madeline put her hands on the table and seemed to push herself back.

"I don't know," she said. "People come and tell me these things. They think I can keep a secret; I look the sort of person who can keep a secret; and I can. Now it seems as though all the secrets were being dragged out of me, and I feel as though I had done something indecent by all that talking today."

"And?" prompted Dr. Fell.

"All the same, you ought to know this. You really and truly ought to know it. Nat Burrows suspects someone of the murder, and hopes he can prove it."

"And he suspects—?"

"He suspects Kennet Murray," said Madeline.

The glowing end of Elliot's cigarette stopped in the air. Then Elliot struck the table with the flat of his hand.

"Murray! Murray?"

"Why, Mr. Elliot?" asked Madeline, opening her eyes. "Does it surprise you?"

The inspector's voice remained impersonal. "Murray is the last person who should be suspected, both in the real sense and in what the doctor here calls the detective-story sense. He was the person everyone was watching. Even if it might have been only a joke, he was the person they were all thinking of as the victim. Burrows is a damned sight too clever by half!—I beg your pardon, Miss Dane: 'ware language. No. And again no. Has Burrows got any reason to think this, except the idea of being clever? Why, the man's got an alibi as big as a house!"

"I don't understand part of it," said Madeline, wrinkling her forehead, "because he didn't tell me. But that's the point. Has he got an alibi, really? I'm only telling you what Nat told me. Nat says that if you go by the evidence there wasn't anybody actually watching him except this Mr. Gore, standing down by the library windows."

The inspector and Dr. Fell exchanged a glance. They did not comment.

"Go on, please."

"You remember my mentioning at the inquest today the little cupboard or book-closet built into the wall of the library—like the one in the attic? That one that's got a door opening into the garden if you find the spring?"

"I do," said Dr. Fell rather grimly. "Humph. Murray mentioned that place to us himself, when he said he went in there during his vigil to change the bogus Thumbograph for the real one so that he shouldn't be seen from the windows. I begin to understand."

"Yes. I told that to Nat, and he was terribly interested. He said to be sure to mention it so that it could go into the records. If I understood him at all, he says you're concentrating your attention on the wrong man. He says all this is a trumped-up conspiracy against poor John. He says that because this 'Patrick Gore' has a clever tongue and an interesting way with him, you've mistaken him for the leader of the group. But Nat maintains that Mr. Murray is the real—what's that horrid word they use in thrillers—?"

"Master-mind?"

"That's it. Of the gang. Of a gang composed of Gore and Welkyn and Murray; Gore and Welkyn being puppets who wouldn't have the courage for any real crime."

"Go on," said Dr. Fell in a curious voice.

"Nat was wildly excited when he explained it. He points to the rather odd behavior of Mr. Murray all through this. Well, of course I—I wouldn't know about that. I haven't seen enough of him. He does seem a bit different from the old days, but then I know we all must be.

"Poor Nat has even got a theory of how the scheme might have been worked. Mr. Murray was in touch with a shady lawyer (Mr. Welkyn). Mr. Welkyn was in a position to tell him, through one of the fortune-tellers of his clientele, that Sir John Farnleigh was suffering from loss of memory and mental trouble over you know what. So Murray, the old tutor, thought of presenting an impostor with forged credentials. Through Welkyn he found a suitable impostor (Gore) among Welkyn's clients. Murray drilled him for six months in every particular. Nat says that's why Gore's way of speaking and conducting himself is so much like Murray's: the thing Nat says you noticed, Dr. Fell."

The doctor stared across the table at her.

He put his elbows on the table and his head in his hands, so that Page could not tell what he was thinking. The air stirring through the open windows was very warm and full of fragrance; yet it is a fact that Dr. Fell shivered.

"Go on," Elliot prompted again.

"Nat's idea of what happened is—is horrible," replied Madeline, closing her eyes again. "I could see it, even if I didn't want to see it. Poor John, who had never done anybody any harm, had to be killed so that there would be nobody to fight their claim, and so that it should be believed he had killed himself. Just as most people do believe, you know."

"Yes," said Elliot. "Just as most people do believe."

"Welkyn and Gore, the sawdust-men without the courage, had their parts to play. They had the two sides of the house guarded, you see. Welkyn was in the dining-room. Gore was to watch the library windows for two reasons: first, to swear to Mr. Murray's alibi; and, second, to keep any other person away from looking in the window while Mr. Murray was out of the library.

"They stalked poor John like a—oh, you know. He never had a chance. When they knew he was in the garden, Mr. Murray came out ever so softly. He's big man. He caught John and killed him. He didn't do it until the last moment. That is, they hoped that John might break down and confess he had lost his memory and might *not* be the real heir. Then they mightn't have had to kill him. But he didn't. And so they did. But Mr. Murray had to explain why he had been so unnecessarily long in 'comparing fingerprints.' So he invented the story of juggling with Thumbographs, and stole one and later returned it. And Nat says"—she concluded rather breathlessly, looking at Dr. Fell—"he says you tumbled straight into their trap, as Mr. Murray planned you should."

Inspector Elliot carefully put out his cigarette.

"That's it, eh? Does this Mr. Burrows explain how Murray committed a murder unseen under the eyes of Knowles and practically under the eyes of Burrows himself?"

She shook her head.

"He wouldn't tell me that. Either he didn't want to, or he hasn't got it worked out yet."

"He hasn't got it worked out yet," said Dr. Fell in a hollow voice. "A slight slowness of cerebral activity. A little late with the homework. Oh, my ancient hat. This is awful."

Once again that day Madeline had talked herself into a state of quickened breathing. It was as though she herself, at the end of a great nervous strain, had been touched by that wind from the garden or the sense of expectancy and waiting from the house.

"What do you think of it?" she asked.

Dr. Fell reflected.

"There are flaws in it. Bad flaws."

"That doesn't matter," said Madeline, looking straight at him. "I don't think I believe it myself. But I've told you what you wanted to know. What were the hints you were going to give us, about what really happened?"

He regarded her in a curious way, as though he wondered.

"Have you told us everything, ma'am?"

"Everything I—I can or dare to. Don't ask me any more. Please."

"Still," argued Dr. Fell, "at risk of seeming to make more mysteries,

I'm going to ask you another question. You knew the late Farnleigh very well. Now, the point is nebulous and psychological again; but find the answer to the following question and you come near the truth. Why did Farnleigh worry for twenty-five years? Why was he weighed down and oppressed in the blindness of his memory? Most men would have been troubled for a while; yet it should not have left such a terrifying scar in his mind. Was he, for instance, tortured by a memory of crime or evil?"

She nodded. "Yes, I believe he was. I've always thought of him as being like those old Puritans in books, brought up to date."

"But he couldn't remember what it concerned?"

"No—except this image of the crooked hinge."

Page found the words themselves disturbing and bothersome. It seemed as though they ought to convey something or suggest something. What was a crooked hinge? Or, for that matter, a straight hinge?

"Sort of polite version of a screw loose?" he asked.

"N-no, I don't think so. I mean, it wasn't a figure of speech. Sometimes he seemed to see a hinge; a hinge on a door; a *white* hinge. It would become crooked as he looked, and droop or crack somehow. He said it stuck in his mind in the way you notice the pattern of a wall-paper when you are ill."

"A white hinge," said Dr. Fell. He looked at Elliot. "That rather tears it, my lad. Eh?"

"Yes, sir."

A long sniff rumbled in the doctor's nose.

"Very well. Now let's see if there are any suggestions of the truth in all this. I will give you a few.

"First. There has been much talk from the beginning about who was or wasn't battered on the head with what has been described as a 'seaman's wooden mallet.' There has been a great amount of curiosity about the fact, but very little about the mallet. Where did anybody get such an implement? How was it obtainable at all? Such an article wouldn't be of much use to sailors aboard modern mechanized ships. I can think of only one thing answering the description.

"You have probably seen such mallets if you have crossed the Atlantic. One of them hangs by each of the steel doors which are set at intervals along the passages below decks in a modern liner. These steel doors are, or are supposed to be, water-tight. In the event of disaster they can be closed, to form a series of bulkheads, or compartments against water flooding in. And the mallet by each door—a sombre reminder—is for use as a weapon by the steward in case of panic and a stampede on the part of passengers. The *Titanic,* you remember, was famous for its water-tight compartments."

"Well?" prompted Page, as the doctor paused. "What of it?"

"It doesn't suggest anything to you?"

"No."

"Second point," said Dr. Fell. "That interesting automaton, the Golden Hag. Find out what made the automaton work in the seventeenth century, and you will have the essential secret of this case."

"But it doesn't make *any* sense!" cried Madeline. "At least, I mean, it doesn't have any connection with what I was thinking. I thought you were thinking just the same things as I was, and now—"

Inspector Elliot looked at his watch. "We shall have to be moving, sir," he said in a flat voice, "if we want to catch that train and still stop in at the Close on our way."

"Don't go," said Madeline abruptly. "Don't go. Please. You won't, will you, Brian?"

"I thought we should come to it, ma'am," Dr. Fell told her in a very quiet voice. "Just what is wrong?"

"I'm afraid," said Madeline. "I suppose that's why I've been talking so much, really."

The realization of something different about her, and the reason for it, came to Brian Page with a kind of shock.

Dr. Fell laid his cigar in the saucer of his coffee-cup. Striking a match with great care, he leaned across and lit the candles on the table. Four golden flames curled and then drew up steadily in the warm, still air; they seemed to hover as though disembodied above the candles. The twilight was pushed back into the garden. In the snug little nook on the edge of it, Madeline's eyes reflected the candlelight; they were steady but dilated. It was as though in the fear there showed a measure of expectancy.

The doctor seemed uneasy. "I'm afraid we can't stay, Miss Dane. We shall be back tomorrow, but there are some ends of the case we've got to gather up in town. All the same, if Page could—?"

"You won't leave me, will you, Brian? I'm sorry to be such a fool and to bother you—"

"Good Lord, of course I won't leave you!" roared Page, feeling such a fierce protectiveness as he had never known before. "I'll cause a scandal. I won't let you beyond arm's length until morning. Not that there's anything to be afraid of."

"Aren't you forgetting the date?"

"The date?"

"The anniversary. July 31st. Victoria Daly died a year ago tonight."

"It is also," supplied Dr. Fell, looking curiously at both of them, "it is also Lammas Eve. A good Scot like Elliot will tell you what that is. It's the night of one of the Great Sabbaths and the powers from down under are exalted. H'mf. Hah. Well. I'm a cheerful blighter, eh?"

Page found himself puzzled and nervy and angry.

"You are," he said. "What's the good of putting nonsense into people's heads? Madeline is upset enough as it is. She's played other people's games and done things for other people until she's worn out. What the devil do you mean by trying to make it worse? There's no danger here. If I see anything hanging about I'll wring its ruddy neck and ask permission from the police afterwards."

"Sorry," said Dr. Fell. For a moment he stood looking down from his great height with tired, kindly, vaguely troubled eyes. Then he took his cloak, his shovel-hat, and his crutch-handled stick from a chair.

"Good night, sir," said Elliot. "If I've got the geography of the neighbourhood right, we can go up that path to the left from the garden here, and through the wood, and down to Farnleigh Close on the other side? Is that right?"

"Yes."

"Well—er—good night, then. Thank you again for everything, Miss Dane, for a very pleasant and instructive evening. And just—keep your eye out, you know, Mr. Page."

"Yes. And watch out for bogles in the wood," Page shouted after them.

He stood in the French window and watched them go down the garden among the laurels. It was a very warm night, and the scents of the garden were thick and enervating. In the east stars were brightening against a slope of sky, but they winked dimly as though distorted by heat-waves. Page's irrational anger grew.

"Bunch of old women," he said. "Trying to—"

He turned round and saw the fleeting of Madeline's smile. She was calm again; but she looked flushed.

"I'm sorry to make such an exhibition of myself, Brian," she said gently. "I know there's no danger of any kind." She got up. "Will you excuse me for a moment? I want to go upstairs and powder my nose. Shan't be a second."

"Bunch of old women. Trying to—"

Alone, he lit a cigarette with care. After a very brief time he was able to laugh at his own annoyance, and he felt better. On the contrary, an evening alone with Madeline was one of the pleasantest things he could imagine. A brown moth flashed through the window and dived in a long sweep towards one flame; he brushed it away, and shifted as it passed his face.

This little core of candlelight was very soothing and pleasant, but they might as well have more light. He went to the electric switch. Subdued wall-lamps brought out the grace of the room and the pattern of chintzes. It was odd, he thought, how clear and sharply defined the ticking of a clock could be. There were two of them in the room; they did not vie with each other, but each filled up the beats the other lacked, and produced a kind of quick rustling. The tiny pendulum of one switched backwards and forwards in a way that drew the eye.

He went back to the table, where he poured himself some almost cold coffee. The noise of his own footsteps on the floor, the rattle of the cup in the saucer, the clink of the china coffee-pot on the edge of the cup: all these made sounds as clearly defined as those of the clocks. For the first time he became aware of mere emptiness as a positive quality. His thoughts ran progressively: this room is absolutely empty: I am alone: what of it?

The emptiness of the place was emphasized by the clearness of the lights. To one subject he kept his mind closed, though he had guessed a certain secret that afternoon and confirmed it from a book in his library. Something cheerful was indicated—for Madeline, of course. This house, neat as it might be, was too isolated. Round it was a wall of darkness stretching for half a mile.

Madeline was taking rather a long time to powder her nose. Another moth zig-zagged through the open window and flapped on the table. Curtains and candle-flames stirred a little. Better close the windows. He went across the bright, hard room, stood in one French window looking out into the garden, and then stood very still.

In the garden, in the darkness just beyond the thin edge of light from the windows, sat the automaton from Farnleigh Close.

Chapter XVII

For the space of perhaps eight seconds he stood looking at it, as motionless as the automaton itself.

The light from the windows was faint yellow. It stretched out ten or a dozen feet across the grass, just touching the once-painted base of the figure. Even wider cracks gaped across her wax face; she leaned a little sideways from her fall downstairs, and half of her clockwork insides were gone. Some effort had been made to mend this by pulling the decayed gown across the wounds. Old and smashed and half-blind, she looked at him malignantly from the shadow of the laurels.

He had to force himself to do what he did. He walked out slowly towards her, feeling that his steps took him farther than need be from the lighted windows. She was alone, or seemed alone. Her wheels had been mended, he noticed. But the ground was so baked from long July drought that the wheels left hardly a trace in the grass. Not far to the left was a gravel drive which would leave no traces.

Then he hurried back to the house, for he heard Madeline coming downstairs.

Carefully he closed all the French windows. Then he picked up the heavy oak table and carried it to the middle of the room. Two of the candlesticks rocked. Madeline, appearing in the doorway, found him steadying one of them as he set down the table.

"Moths getting in," he explained.

"But won't it be awfully stuffy? Hadn't you better leave one—"

"I'll do it." He set the middle window open about a foot.

"Brian! There's nothing wrong, is there?"

Again he became aware, with intense clarity, of the ticking of the clocks; but most of all of the sympathetic presence of Madeline, exuding the wish to be protected. Uneasiness takes people in strange ways. She did not now seem so remote or self-effacing. The aura of her—there is no other word for it—filled the room.

He said:

"Good Lord, no; of course there's nothing wrong. It's just that moths are a nuisance, that's all. That's why I closed the windows."

"Shall we go into the other room?"

Better not be out of touch with it. Better not have it free to go where it liked.

"Oh, let's stay here and smoke another cigarette."

"Of course. What about some more coffee?"

"Don't trouble."

"It's no trouble. It's all prepared on the stove."

She smiled, the bright smile of one strung up by nerves, and went across to the kitchen. While she was gone he did not look out of the window. She seemed to be in the kitchen a long time, and he went in search of her. He met her in the doorway, carrying a fresh pot of coffee. She spoke quietly.

"Brian, there *is* something wrong. The back door is open. I know I left it shut, and Maria always closes it when she goes home."

"Maria forgot it."

"Yes. If you say so. Oh, I'm being silly. I know I am. Let's have something cheerful."

She seemed to wake up, with an apologetic and yet defiant laugh, and a brighter complexion. In one corner of the room, unobtrusive like Madeline herself, there was a radio. She switched it on. It took a few seconds to grow warm; then the resulting volume of noise startled them both.

She toned it down, but the flooding jingles of a dance-orchestra filled the rooms like surf on a beach. The tunes seemed as usual; the words rather worse than usual. Madeline listened to it for a moment. Then she returned to the table, sat down, and poured out their coffee. They were sitting at right angles to each other, so close he could have touched her hand. Her back was to the windows. All the while he was conscious of something outside, waiting. He wondered what his feelings would be if a cracked face were poked against the glass.

Yet, at the same time his nerves were touched, his brain stirred as well. It seemed to him that he woke up. It seemed to him that he was rationally reasoning for the first time; that bonds fell apart and the brain emerged from iron bands.

Now what were the facts about that dummy? It was dead iron and wheels and wax. It was no more dangerous of itself than a kitchen boiler. They had examined it, and they knew. Its only purpose was to *terrify*, a human purpose managed by a solid hand.

It had not pushed itself across the path from Farnleigh Close, like a malignant old woman in a wheel-chair. It had been brought here to terrify, again the solid purpose managed by the solid hand. And it seemed to him that this automaton was fitting itself into a pattern which the case had taken since the beginning, and which from the beginning he should have seen. . . .

"Yes," said Madeline, into his thoughts. "Let's talk about it. That would be better, really."

"It?"

"This whole thing," said Madeline, clenching her hands. "I—I may know rather more about it than you think."

She swam into his vision again. Again she had put the palms of her hands flat on the table, as though she were going to push herself back. The faint, frightened smile still lingered about her eyes and mouth. But she was quiet, almost coquettish; and she had never been more persuasive.

"I wonder if you know," he said, "what I've guessed?"

"*I* wonder."

He kept his eyes fixed on the partly open window. It seemed to him that he was talking less to Madeline than to something out there, something waiting, whose presence surrounded the house.

"It'll probably be best to get this out of my system," he went on with his eye still on the window. "Let me ask you something. Had *you* ever heard of a—a witch-cult hereabouts?"

Hesitation.

"Yes. I've heard rumours. Why?"

"It's about Victoria Daly. I had the essential facts yesterday from Dr. Fell and Inspector Elliot; I even had the information to interpret them; but I hadn't the wits to put the whole thing together. It's come to daylight now. Did you know that after Victoria's murder her body was found smeared with a substance composed of the juice of water parsnip, aconite, cinquefoil, deadly nightshade, and soot?"

"But whatever for? What have all those beastly things got to do with it?"

"A great deal. That is one of the formulas for the famous ointment—you've heard of it right enough—with which Satanists bedaubed themselves before going off to the Sabbath.* It lacks one of the original ingredients: the flesh of a child: but I suppose there are limits even to a murderer's efforts at realism."

"Brian!"

For it seemed to him that the picture which was emerging from these sly and tangled events was less that of a Satanist than that of a murderer.

"Oh, yes, it's true. I know something about that subject, and I can't imagine why I didn't remember it from the first. Now, I want you to think of the obvious deductions we can draw from that fact, the deductions Dr. Fell and the inspector made long ago. I don't mean about Victoria's indulgence, or pretended indulgence, in Satanist practices. That's clear enough without any deduction."

"Why?"

"Follow it out. She uses this ointment on Lammas Eve, the night of one of the great Satanist meetings. She is murdered at 11:45, and the Sabbath begins at midnight. It's clear that she had applied this ointment some minutes before the murderer caught her. She is murdered in her ground-floor bedroom, the window of which is set wide open: traditionally the way in which Satanists left, or thought they left, for their gatherings."

Though he was not looking directly at her, he thought that a slight frown had gathered on Madeline's forehead.

"I think I see what you're getting at Brian. You say 'thought they left' because—"

"I'm coming to that. But, first, what deductions can we make about her murderer? Most important, this: Whether or not the tramp killed Victoria Daly, *there was a third person in that house at the time of the murder or just afterwards.*"

Madeline sprang to her feet. He was not looking at her, yet he felt that her large blue eyes were fixed on his face.

"How so, Brian? I still don't follow that."

"Because of the nature of the ointment. Do you realize what a substance like that would do?"

"Yes, I think I see that. But tell me."

*For a medical analysis of these ointments, see Margaret Alice Murray, *The Witch-Cult in Western Europe* (Oxford University Press, 1921), Appendix V, 279–280; and J. W. Wickwar, *Witchcraft and the Black Art* (Herbert Jenkins, 1925), 36–40. See also Montague Summers, *History of Witchcraft and Demonology* (Kegan Paul, 1926).

"For six hundred years," he went on, "there's been a vast mass of testimony from those who claim to have gone to Witches' Sabbaths and seen the presence of Satan. What impresses you as you read it is the absolute sincerity, the careful detail, with which people have described things that couldn't possibly be true. We can't deny, as a matter of history, that the Satanist cult really existed and was a powerful force from the Middle Ages to the seventeenth century. It had an organization as carefully arranged and managed as the Church itself. But what about these miraculous journeys in the air, these wonders and ghosts, these demons and familiars, these incubi and succubi? They can't be accepted as facts (not by my practical mind, anyhow); and yet they are firmly presented as facts by a great number of people who weren't demented and weren't hysterical and weren't tortured.—Well, what would make a person believe them to be facts?"

Madeline said quietly: "Aconite and belladonna, or deadly night-shade."

They looked at each other.

"I believe that's the explanation," he told her, still with his attention on the window. "It's been argued, and I think reasonably, that in a great number of cases the 'witch' never left her own house or even her own room. She thought she had attended the Sabbath in the grove. She thought she had been conveyed by magic to the defiled altar and found a demon lover there. She thought so because the two chief ingredients of the ointment were aconite and belladonna. Do you know anything about the effects of poisons like that, rubbed into the skin externally?"

"My father had a *Medical Jurisprudence* here," said Madeline. "I was wondering—"

"Belladonna, absorbed through the pores of the skin—and under the quicks of the nails—would rapidly produce excitement, then violent hallucinations and delirium, and finally unconsciousness. Add to this the symptoms produced by aconite: mental confusion, dizziness, impaired movement, irregular heart-action, and an end in unconsciousness. A mind steeped in descriptions of Satanist revels (there was a book dealing with them on the table by Victoria Daly's bed) would do the rest. Yes, that's it. I think we know now how she 'attended the Sabbath' on Lammas Eve."

Madeline walked her fingers along the edge of the table. She studied them. Then she nodded.

"Ye-es. But even suppose that were true, Brian? How does it prove there was anybody else in the house the night she died? Anybody, I mean, aside from Victoria and the vagabond who killed her?"

"Do you remember how she was dressed when the body was found?"

"Of course. Night-gown, dressing-gown, and slippers."

"Yes—when the body was found. That's the point. A careful new night-gown, to say nothing of the extra flourish of a dressing-gown, over that sticky, oily, soot-coloured ointment? Acute discomfort and unusual marks afterwards? A dressing-gown for the Sabbath? The costume for the Sabbath consisted of the merest rags, which would not impede movement or get in the way of the ointment, when it consisted of any costume at all.

"Don't you see what happened? The woman was falling from delirium into unconsciousness in a dark house. A poor devil of a derelict, seeing a dark house and an open window, thought he had found an easy crib to crack. What he met was a woman roused and screaming in delirium: and it must have been rather an unnerving apparition which rose up at him from the bed or the floor. He lost his head and killed her.

"Anyone suffering delirium from that ointment couldn't have and wouldn't have put on the night-dress, dressing-gown, and slippers. The murderer wouldn't have put them on her. He was interrupted and chased before he had finished his work.

"But there was somebody else in the dark house. Victoria Daly was lying there dead with the ointment on her body and in a queer kind of costume which would cause a furious scandal when her body was found. Some wiseacre might even guess what had happened. To avert discovery, this third person crept into the bedroom before the body had been seen by anybody. (Remember? The two men who heard the screams saw the murderer escaping from the window, and gave chase; they didn't return until some time afterwards.) This third person then removed whatever 'witch's' clothes Victoria wore, and decorously dressed the body in night-gown, dressing-gown, and slippers. That's it. That's got it. That's what really happened."

His heart was thumping. The mental images, hidden for so long, were of such clarity that he knew he was right. He nodded towards Madeline.

"You know that's true, don't you?"

"Brian! How could I know it?"

"No, no, you don't understand. I mean you're as certain as I am, aren't you? That's the assumption on which Elliot has been working all this time."

She took a long time before she replied.

"Yes," she admitted, "I'd thought that. At least, I'd thought so until tonight, when those hints Dr. Fell gave didn't seem in the least to square with my ideas—and I told him so. Besides, it doesn't even seem to fit in with what they think either. You remember, he said yesterday there was no witch cult hereabouts?"

"And so there isn't."

"But you've just explained—"

"I've explained what one person did. One person, and only one.

Remember, Dr. Fell told us that yesterday. 'Everything, from mental cruelty to murder, is the work of one person.' And, 'I tell you frankly, Satanism itself is an honest and straightforward business compared to the intellectual pleasures a certain person has invented.' Put all these words together; put them into a pattern. Mental cruelty, plus intellectual pleasures, plus the death of Victoria Daly, plus a vague and undefined rumour of witchcraft among—what did Elliot tell me?—the gentry of the neighbourhood.

"I wonder what prompted this person to take it up? Pure boredom? Boredom with life, utter and simple, coming from an inability to take an interest in ordinary things? Or a tendency inherited from childhood, under the surface, but always growing up and feeding on secret things?"

"To take what up?" cried Madeline. "That's what I'm trying to get at. To take what up?"

Behind her a hand rapped on the glass of the window, with a malevolent tearing sound like a scratch.

Madeline screamed. That knock or blow had almost closed the partly open window, which rattled with a small noise against the frame. Page hesitated. The jingle of the dance-orchestra still filled the room. Then he went to the window and pushed it open.

Chapter XVIII

D r. Fell and Inspector Elliot did not catch the train. They did not catch it because, when they arrived at Farnleigh Close, they were told that Betty Harbottle was awake and could speak to them.

They did not talk much on their way through the orchard and up through the wood. What they said, too, might have seemed cryptic to a listener. But it had a very deadly bearing on events which were to take place only an hour or two later, when one of the most cunning murderers in Dr. Fell's experience was (perhaps prematurely) snared into the open.

It was close and dark in the wood. Leaves made a heavy pattern against the starlight; Elliot's flashlight threw a beam ahead on a path of bare earth, making the green spectral. From the gloom behind it sounded two voices, the harsh tenor of the inspector and the wheezing bass of Dr. Fell.

"Still, sir, are we any nearer to proving it?"

"I think so, I hope so. If I've read one person's character correctly, he'll give us all the proof we need."

"And if your explanation works?"

"H'mf, yes. If it works. Of sticks and stones and rags and bones I made it; but it ought to serve."

"Do you think there's any danger," Elliot seemed to jerk his head over his shoulder in the direction of Madeline's house, "back there?"

There was a pause before Dr. Fell answered, while their footsteps swished among ferns.

"Dammit, I wish I knew! I hardly think so, though. Consider the character of the murderer. A sly, cracked head—like the dummy's; under that pleasant exterior—just as the dummy used to have. But emphatically not a fabled monster, intent on strewing the place with corpses. Not a monster at all. A moderate murderer, my lad. When I think of the number of persons who, by all the laws of progressive homicide, SHOULD have been murdered in this case, I have a tendency towards goose-flesh.

"We've known cases in which the murderer, after taking careful pains about his original crime, then goes berserk and begins to eliminate people all over the place. It seems to be like getting olives out of a bottle: you have infinite trouble with the first one, and the rest roll out all over the table. Without, indeed, anybody seeming to pay much attention to them. This murder is human, my lad. I'm not, you understand, praising the murderer for this sporting restraint and good manners in refraining from killing people. But, my God, Elliot, the people who have gone in danger from the first! Betty Harbottle might have been killed. A certain lady we know of might have been killed. For a certain man's safety I've had apprehensions from the start. And not one of 'em has been touched. Is it vanity? Or what?"

In silence they came out of the wood and down the hill. Only a few lights burned at Farnleigh Close. They went through the part of the garden on the opposite side from the place where the murder had been committed, and round to the front door. A subdued Knowles admitted them.

"Lady Farnleigh has retired, sir," he said. "But Dr. King asks me to say that he wishes you gentlemen would join him upstairs, if you will."

"Is Betty Harbottle—?" Elliot stopped.

"Yes, sir. I think so."

Elliot whistled through his teeth as they went upstairs and into the dimly lighted passage between the Green Room and the bedroom where the girl lay. Dr. King held them off a moment before they entered.

"Now, look here," King said in his abrupt fashion. "Five minutes, ten minutes maybe: no more. I want to warn you. You'll find her as quiet and easy-spoken as though she were talking about a bus-ride. But don't let that deceive you. It's a part of the reaction, and she's got a dose of morphia in her. You'll also find her quick with her eyes and tolerably intelligent—curiosity was always Betty's chief feature—so don't start her going with too many suggestions and general fol-de-rol. Is that understood? Right, then. In you go."

Mrs. Apps, the housekeeper, slipped out as they entered. It was a large room in which every globe was illuminated in the old-fashioned chandelier. Not an impressive room: large old-fashioned photographs of Farn-leighs were framed on the walls, and the dressing-table held a menagerie of china animals. The bed was black, square, and uncompromising. From it Betty regarded them with vague interest.

She had one of those faces called "bright," with very straight bobbed hair. Her pallor, and the slightly sunken look of the eyes, were the only signs of illness. She seemed pleased to see them rather than otherwise; and the only thing or person that seemed to make her uncomfortable was Dr. King. Her hands slowly smoothed the counterpane.

Dr. Fell beamed on her. His vast presence made the whole room comfortable.

"Hullo,"̣ he said.

"Hullo, sir," said Betty with an effort at brightness.

"Do you know who we are, my dear? And why we're here?"

"Oh, yes. You want me to tell you what happened to me."

"And can you?"

"I don't mind," she conceded.

She fixed her eyes on the foot of the bed. Dr. King took out his watch and put it on the dressing-table.

"Well—I don't know how to tell you, hardly. I went upstairs there to get an apple—" Betty abruptly seemed to change her mind. She shifted in bed. "No, I didn't!" she added.

"You didn't?"

"I didn't go up to get an apple. When I get well my sister's taking me away from here (I'm going to have a holiday at Hastings, too), so that's why I'll tell you. I *didn't* go up there to get an apple. I went up often to see if I could get a peep at what's in the cupboard there, the locked cupboard."

Her tone was not in the least defiant: she was too listless to be defiant: she was merely speaking out truth as though she were under the influence less of morphia than of scopolamine.

Dr. Fell looked heavily puzzled. "But why should you be interested in the locked cupboard?"

"Oh, everybody knows about it, sir. Somebody'd been using it."

"Using it?"

"Sitting up there with a light. There's a little window in the roof, like a skylight. At night, if you're a little way off from the house, and there's a light inside, you can see it against the roof. Everybody knows about it, though we're not supposed to. Even Miss Dane knows about it. I was over at Miss Dane's house one evening, taking her a parcel from Sir John, and I was going back through the Chart. Miss Dane asked me whether I wasn't afraid to go through the Chart after dark. I said, Oh, no; perhaps I should see the light in the roof, and that would be worth it. I only said it as a joke, because the light was always on the south side, and the path through the Chart takes you to the north side. Miss Dane laughed and put her arm round my shoulder and asked whether I was the only one who had seen it. I said, Oh, no, everybody had; because we had. Besides, we were all interested about that machine like a gramophone, that dummy—"

The look in her eyes altered slightly.

There was a pause.

"But who was 'using' the room?"

"Well, mostly they said it was Sir John. Agnes saw him come down from the attic one afternoon, with his face all perspiring and something like a dog-whip in his hand. I said, So would you be perspiring, too, if you sat in a little bit of a place like that with the door shut. But Agnes said he didn't look quite like that."

"Anyway, my dear, will you tell us what happened yesterday? Hey?"

Dr. King interposed sharply. "Two minutes, my lads."

Betty looked surprised.

"I don't mind," she responded. "I went up there to get an apple. But this time, when I went past the door of the little room, I saw the padlock wasn't fastened. The padlock was open, hanging on the staple. The door was closed, but with something stuck in between the door and the frame to hold it shut."

"What did you do?"

"I went and got an apple. After that I came back and looked at the door and started to eat the apple. Then I went to the apple-room again, and finally I came back and thought I would see what was inside after all. But I didn't want to, as much as usually."

"Why not?"

"Because there was a noise in there, or I thought so. A rattly kind of noise, like winding a grandfather clock; but not very loud."

"Do you remember what time this was, Betty?"

"No, sir. Not properly. It was past one o'clock, maybe a quarter past or more than that."

"What did you do then?"

"I went over ever so quickly, before I should decide not to do it, and opened the door. The thing that was keeping it shut was a glove. Stuck into the door, you know, sir."

"A man's glove or a woman's glove?"

"A man's, I think. It had oil on it; or it smelt like oil. It dropped on the floor. I went inside. I could see the old machine-thing there, a bit

sideways to me, like. I didn't want one more look at it: not that you could
see very well in there. But I no sooner stepped inside than the door closed
ever so softly; and somebody put up the chain across the door and I heard
the padlock close together outside; so I was locked in, you see."

"Steady!" said the physician sharply. He took up his watch from the
dressing-table.

Betty was twisting the fringe of the counterpane. Dr. Fell and the
inspector looked at each other; Dr. Fell's red face was heavy and grave.

"But—are you still all right, Betty?—who was in there? Who was in
the little room?"

"Nobody. Nobody except the old machine-thing. Nobody at all."

"You're sure of that?"

"Oh, yes."

"What did you do?"

"I didn't do anything. I was afraid to call out and ask to be let out. I
was afraid I should get the sack. It wasn't quite dark. I stood there and
didn't do anything for, oh, maybe it was a quarter of an hour. And
nobody else did anything either: I mean the machine-thing didn't. Presently I started to move away from it, and got back as far as I could,
because it started to put its arms around me."

If, at that moment, so much as the ash of a cigar had fallen into an
ash-tray, Dr. Fell swears it would have been heard. Elliot heard the breath
drawn through his own nostrils. Elliot said:

"It moved, Betty? The machine moved?"

"Yes, sir. It moved its arms. They didn't move fast, and neither did the
body, the way it sort of ducked forward towards me; and it made a noise
when it moved. But that wasn't what I minded so much. I didn't seem to
feel anything, because I had been standing in there with it for a quarter of
an hour already. What I minded was the eyes it had. It didn't have eyes in
the proper place. It had eyes in the skirt, right by the knees of the old
dummy thing; and they looked up at me. I could see them move round. I
don't mind even them so much. I expect I shall get used to them. At that
time I don't remember anything more about it; I must have fainted or
something; but it's outside the door now," continued Betty, with absolutely no change of expression or tone while she nodded at the door.

"I should like to go to sleep," she added in a plaintive tone.

Dr. King swore under his breath.

"That's done it," he said. "Out you go, now. No, she'll be all right;
but—out you go."

"Yes," agreed Elliot, looking at Betty's closed eyes, "I think we had
better."

They went out with guilty quietness, and King made a pantomime of
slamming the door after them. "I hope," he muttered, "hearing common

delirium helps you." Still without speaking, Dr. Fell and the inspector went across to the dark Green Room. It was furnished as a study in heavy antique style; and the windows were rectangles of starlight. They went across and stood by one window.

"That settles it, sir? Even aside from the—er—answer to the in-quiries—?"

"Yes. That settles it."

"Then we'd better get on to town, and—"

"No," said Dr. Fell after a long pause. "I don't think it'll be necessary. I think we'd better try the experiment now, while the metal is hot. Look there!"

The garden below showed in clear etching-lines against the dark. They saw the maze of hedges veined with whitish paths, the clear space round the pool, and the white smears of the water-lilies. But they were not looking at this. Someone, carrying an object recognizable even in that light, slipped past under the library windows and round the south corner of the house.

Dr. Fell expelled his breath. Lumbering across the room to the central light-fixture, he turned on the lamp and swung round with a vast billow of his cape.

"Psychologically, as we've come to say," he told Elliot with sardonic dryness, "tonight is the night. Now's the time, man. Now, or we may lose the whole advantage. Get 'em together, I tell you! I should like to do a little explaining as to how a man can be murdered when alone in the circle of sand; and then we can pray Old Nick will come and get his own. Hey?"

A small cough interrupted them as Knowles came into the room.

"I beg your pardon, sir," he said to Dr. Fell. "Mr. Murray is here, and asking to see you gentlemen. He says he's been looking for you for some time."

"Has he, now?" inquired Dr. Fell, with ferocious affability. The doctor beamed and shook his cape. "Did he say what he wanted?"

Knowles hesitated. "No, sir. That is—" Knowles hesitated again. "He says he's disturbed about something, sir. He also wishes to see Mr. Burrows. And, as regards that—"

"Speak up, man! What's on your mind?"

"Well, sir, may I ask whether Miss Dane received the automaton?"

Inspector Elliot whirled round from the window.

"Whether Miss Dane received the automaton? What automaton? What about it?"

"You know the one, sir," returned Knowles, with a guilty expression which (less smoothly done) might have been a leer. "Miss Dane rang up this afternoon, and asked whether she might have the automaton sent over to her home this evening. We—er—we thought it was an odd request; but Miss Dane said a gentleman was coming there, an expert on such things, and she wished him to have a good look at it."

"So," observed Dr. Fell without inflection. "She wished him to have a good look at it."

"Yes, sir. Macneile (that's the gardener) mended the wheel, and I had it sent over in a cart. Macneile and Parsons said there was nobody at home at Miss Dane's at the time, so they put it into the coal-house. Then—er—Mr. Burrows arrived here, and expressed annoyance that it had gone. He also knows of a gentleman who is an expert on such things."

"How popular the hag is becoming in her old age," rumbled Dr. Fell, with a wheeze of what might or might not have been pleasure. "How excellent to eke out her days among throngs of admirers. By thunder, how excellent! A perfect woman, nobly planned, to warn, to comfort, and command. Cold eyelids that hide like a jewel hard eyes that grow soft for an hour—waugh!" He stopped. "And is Mr. Murray also interested in the automaton?"

"No, sir. Not that I know of."

"A pity. Well, shoot him into the library. He is remarkably at home there. One of us will be down in a moment. And what," he added to Elliot, when Knowles had gone, "do you make of this little move?"

Elliot rubbed his chin. "I don't know. But it doesn't seem to fit in with what we saw. In any case, it mightn't be a bad idea for me to get back to Monplaisir as fast as I can."

"I agree. Profoundly."

"Burton ought to be here with the car. If he is, I can make it by the road in three minutes. If he isn't—"

He wasn't. What adjustment had gone wrong with the scales or the night Elliot did not know. Nor could he get a car from the garage at the Close, whose doors were (revealingly) locked. Elliot set off for Monplaisir by the path through the wood. The last thing he saw before he left the house was Dr. Fell descending the main staircase, lowering himself step by step on his crutch-handled stick; and on Dr. Fell's face was an expression that is very seldom seen there.

Inspector Elliot told himself that he had no reason to hurry. But, as he mounted the hill through the Hanging Chart, he found himself walking fast. Nor did he particularly like his surroundings. He knew that they were the victims, no longer gullible, of a series of ingenious hoaxes no more to be feared than the black Janus-face in the attic. The hoax at best was unpleasant and at worst was murderous; but it was no more than a hoax.

And yet, even as he increased his step, he kept the beam of his electric torch playing from side to side. Something stirred in him that was rooted in his blood and race. Out of his boyhood he sought a word to describe the present doings, and found it. The word was "heathenish."

He did not expect anything to happen. He knew that he would not be needed.

It was not until he was almost out of the wood that he heard a shot fired.

Chapter XIX

B rian Page stood in the open French window and looked out into the garden. After that knock he had been prepared, in the usual fashion, for anything except nothing. And there was nothing—or so it seemed.

The automaton had gone. The quiet light, almost draining the grass of its colour, barely showed the wheel-marks where iron had rested. But the presence or absence of that dead metal meant nothing; someone or something had rapped on the window. He took one step across the sill.

"Brian," said Madeline quietly, "where are you going?"

"Just to see who called on us, or started to call on us."

"Brian, don't go out there. Please." She came closer, and her voice was full of urgency. "I've never asked you to do anything for me before, have I? Well, I ask you to do something now. Don't go out there. If you do I'll—well, I don't know what I will do, exactly, except that it will be something you won't like. Please! Come in and close the window, won't you? You see, I know."

"Know?"

She nodded towards the garden. "What was sitting out there a moment ago, and isn't there now. I saw it from the back door when I was in the kitchen. I didn't want to worry you in case you hadn't seen it, though I—I was pretty sure you had." She slid her hands up the lapels of his coat. "Don't go out there. Don't go after it. That's what it wants you to do."

He looked down at her, at the pleading eyes and the curve of the short throat upturned. In spite of what he was thinking and feeling just then, he spoke with a kind of impassioned detachment.

He said:

"Of all the extraordinary places to say what I am going to say, this is the most extraordinary. Of all the inappropriate times to say what I am going to say, this is the most inappropriate. I maintain this because I have got to use superlatives somehow in getting my feelings off my chest, and what I mean is that I love you."

"Then there's some good in Lammas Eve," said Madeline, and lifted her mouth.

It is a problem how far, in accounts of violence, there may be expressed the things he thought and said then. Yet, without a violence that moved round the edges of a lighted window, it is possible that he would never have learned or heard the things he learned and heard then. He was not concerned with this. He was concerned with other matters: the paradox of how remote and mysterious a loved face looks by very reason of being closer: the strange chemistry of kissing Madeline, which altered his life and in whose actuality he could not even yet believe. He wanted to utter a mighty shout of pure joy; and, after many minutes at the window, he did.

"Oh, God, Brian, why didn't you ever tell me so before?" said Madeline, who was half-laughing and half-crying. "I mustn't swear! My moral character is falling deplorably. But why didn't you ever tell me so before?"

"Because I didn't see how you could possibly be interested in me. I didn't want you to laugh."

"Did you think I would laugh?"

"Frankly—yes."

She held to his shoulders and studied him with her face upturned. Her eyes were shining curiously.

"Brian, you do love me, don't you?"

"For some minutes I have been trying to make that clear. But I haven't got the slightest objection to beginning all over again. If—"

"A spinster like me—"

"Madeline," he said, "whatever else you do, don't use that word 'spinster.' It is one of the ugliest-sounding words in the language. It suggests something between 'spindle' and 'vinegar.' To describe you properly, it is necessary to—"

Again he noticed the curious shining in her eyes.

"Brian, if you really do love me (you do?) then I may show you something, mayn't I?"

Out in the garden there was a noise of a footstep in the grass. Her tone had been odd, so odd as to make him wonder; but there was no time to reflect on this. At that swishing of the footstep they stood apart quickly. Among the laurels a figure was taking shape and coming closer. It was a lean, narrow-shouldered figure, with a walk between a brisk stride and a shamble; after which Page saw, with relief, that it was only Nathaniel Burrows.

Burrows did not seem to know whether to keep his halibut-faced expression or to smile. Between the two he appeared to struggle: producing something of an amiable contortion. His large shell-rimmed spectacles were grave. His long face, which had a very genuine charm when he chose to exercise it, now showed only a part of that charm. His very correct bowler hat was set at a somewhat rakish angle.

"Tsk! Tsk!" was his only comment, with a smile. "I've come," he added pleasantly, "for the automaton."

"The—?" Madeline blinked at him. "The automaton?"

"You should not stand in windows," said Burrows severely. "It upsets your mental equilibrium when you have visitors afterwards. You shouldn't stand in windows either," he added, looking at Page. "The dummy, Madeline. The dummy you borrowed from Farnleigh Close this afternoon."

Page turned to look at her. She was staring at Burrows, her colour heightening.

"Nat, what on earth are you talking about? The dummy *I* borrowed? I never did any such thing."

"My dear Madeline," returned Burrows, putting his gloved hands wide apart and bringing them together again. "I've not yet properly thanked you for all the good work you have done for me—at the inquest. But hang it!" Here he looked at her sideways past his spectacles. "You rang up and asked for that dummy this afternoon. Macneile and Parsons brought it over. It's in the coal-house now."

"You must be absolutely mad," said Madeline, in a high and wondering voice.

Burrows, as usual, was reasonable. "Well, it's there. That's the supreme answer. I couldn't make anyone hear at the front of the house. I came round here, and I—er—still couldn't make anyone hear. My car's out in the main road. I drove over to get the automaton. Why you should want it I can't imagine; but would you mind very much if I took it along? I can't quite see, as yet, how it fits into the picture. However, after my expert has a look at it, it may give me an idea."

The coal-house was built into the wall a little to the left of the kitchen. Page went over and opened the door. The automaton was there. He could make out its outlines faintly.

"You see?" said Burrows.

"Brian," said Madeline rather frantically, "will you believe I never did anything of the kind? I never asked for the thing to be sent here, or thought of it, or anything of the sort. Why on earth should I?"

"Of course I know you didn't," Page told her. "Somebody seems to gave gone completely mad."

"Why not go inside?" suggested Burrows. "I should like to have a little talk with both of you about this. Just wait a moment until I put on the side-lights of my car."

The other two went inside, where they looked at each other. The music from the radio had stopped; somebody was talking instead, about a subject Page does not remember, and Madeline shut off the set. Madeline seemed to be in the grip of a reaction.

"This isn't real," she said. "It's all illusion. We're dreaming it. At least—all but a part of it, I hope." And she smiled at him. "Have you any idea what's happening?"

As for what happened in the few seconds after that, Page is still confused in his mind. He remembers that he had taken her hand, and opened his mouth to assure her that he did not particularly give a curse what had happened, provided those minutes by the window were not illusion. They both heard the detonation from the direction of the garden or the orchard behind. It had a flat and bursting noise. It was loud enough to make them jump. Yet it seemed to have no connection with them, to be remote from them, in spite of the fact that a wiry sound sang close to their ears—and one of the clocks stopped.

One of the clocks stopped. Page's ears took note of that at the same time his eyes noted the small round hole, starred with a faint web of cracks, in the glass of the window. It then became clear that the clock had stopped because there was a bullet buried in it.

The other clock ticked on.

"Get back from the window," Page said. "This can't be: I don't believe it: but there's somebody firing at us from the garden. Where the devil has Nat got to?"

He went over and switched out the lights. The candles remained; and he blew them out just as a sweating Burrows, his hat crushed down on his head, ducked low through the window as though for safety.

"There's somebody—" Burrows began in a strange voice.

"Yes. We had noticed that."

Page moved Madeline across the room. He was calculating, by the position of the bullet in the clock, that two inches to the left would have sent it through Madeline's head, just above the small curls there.

No other shot was fired. He heard Madeline's frightened breathing, and the slow, sharp breathing of Burrows from across the room. Burrows stood inside the last of the windows: only his polished shoe was visible as he braced himself there.

"Do you know what I think happened?" Burrows asked.

"Well?"

"Do you want me to show you what I think happened?"

"Go on!"

"Wait," whispered Madeline. "Whoever it is—listen!"

Burrows, startled, poked his head out like a turtle's past the line of the window. Page heard the hail from the garden and answered it. It was Elliot's voice. He hurried out and met the inspector, whose run through the grass from the orchard was easy to follow. Elliot's face was inscrutable in the gloom as he listened to Page's story; also, his manner was at its most heavily official.

"Yes, sir," he said. "But I think you can put on those lights now. I don't think you will be troubled again."

"Inspector, are *you* going to do nothing?" demanded Burrows in a wiry voice of remonstrance. "Or are you accustomed to this sort of thing in London? I assure you we're not." He mopped his forehead with the back of a gloved hand. "Aren't you going to search the garden? Or the orchard? Or wherever the shot was fired from?"

"I said, sir," repeated Elliot woodenly, "that I don't think you will be troubled again."

"But who did it? What was the point of it?"

"The point is, sir," said Elliot, "that this nonsense is going to stop. For good. We've had a bit of a change in plans. I think, if you don't mind, I'd like to have you all come back to the Close with me—just in case, you understand. I'm afraid I've got to make the request something like an order."

"Oh, nobody's got any objection," said Page cheerfully; "though it would almost seem that we'd had enough excitement for one evening."

The inspector smiled in a way that was not reassuring.

"I think you're wrong," he said. "You haven't seen anything like excitement tonight. But you will, Mr. Page. I promise you you will. Has anybody got a car?"

That uneasy suggestion remained with them while Burrows drove them all to Farnleigh Close. All efforts to question the inspector were useless. To Burrows's insistence that the automaton should be removed with them, Elliot only answered that there was not time and that it was not necessary.

A worried-looking Knowles admitted them to the Close. The centre of tension was in the library. There, as two nights ago, the gaping crown of electric-bulbs from the ceiling was reflected in a wall of windows. In the chair formerly occupied by Murray sat Dr. Fell, with Murray across from him. Dr. Fell's hand was supported on his stick, and his lower lip outthrust above the chins. The echo of emotion came to them as soon as the library door was opened. For Dr. Fell had just finished talking, and Murray shaded his eyes with an unsteady hand.

"Ah," said the doctor with dubious affability. "Good evening, good evening, good evening! Miss Dane. Mr. Burrows. Mr. Page. Good. I'm afraid we have commandeered the house in a reprehensible way; but something has made it necessary. It is very necessary to have a gathering for a little conference. Couriers have been despatched for Mr. Welkyn and Mr. Gore. Knowles: will you ask Lady Farnleigh to join us? No: don't go yourself; send a maid; I should prefer that you remain here. In the meantime, certain matters can be discussed."

The tone of his voice was such that Nathaniel Burrows hesitated before sitting down. Burrows raised a hand sharply. He did not look at Murray.

"We cannot go as fast as that," Burrows returned. "Stop! Is there anything in this discussion that is likely to be of a—er—a controversial nature?"

"There is."

Again Burrows hesitated. He had not glanced in Murray's direction; but Page, studying them, felt a twinge of pity for Murray without knowing why. The tutor looked worn and old.

"Oh! And what are we going to discuss, doctor?"

"The character of a certain person," said Dr. Fell. "You will guess who it is."

"Yes," agreed Page, hardly conscious that he had spoken aloud. "The person who initiated Victoria Daly into the pleasantries of witchcraft."

It was remarkable, he thought, the effect that name had. You had only to introduce the words "Victoria Daly," like a talisman, and everybody shied away from it; the prospect seemed to open into new vistas which were not liked. Dr. Fell, vaguely surprised but interested, turned round and blinked at him.

"Ah!" said the doctor, wheezing with approval. "So you guessed that."

"I tried to work it out. Is that person the murderer?"

"That person is the murderer." Dr. Fell pointed his stick. "It will help us, you know, if the view is also shared by you. Let's hear what you think. And speak out, my lad. There will be worse things said in this room before any of us leaves it."

With some care, and a vividness of image which he hardly sought to use, Page repeated the story he had already told to Madeline. Dr. Fell's sharp little eyes never left his face, nor did Inspector Elliot miss a word. The body smeared with ointment, the dark house with the open window, the panic-mad vagabond, the third person waiting: these images seemed to be enacted in the library like pictures on a screen.

At the end of it Madeline spoke. "Is this true? Is it what you and the inspector think?"

Dr. Fell merely nodded.

"Then I ask you what I was trying to ask Brian. If there is no witch-cult—as he says—if the whole affair was a dream, what was this 'third person' doing or trying to do? What about the *evidences* of witch-craft?"

"Ah, the evidences," said Dr. Fell.

After a pause he went on:

"I will try to explain. You have among you somebody whose mind and heart have been steeped for years in a secret love of these things and what they stand for. Not a belief in them! That I hasten to point out. That I emphasize. Nobody could be more cynical as regards the powers of darkness and the lords of the four-went-ways. But a surpassing love of them, made all the more powerful and urgent by an (altogether prudish) necessity for never letting it show. This person, you understand, figures before you in a very different character. This person will never admit before you to even an interest in such matters, an interest such as you and I might have. So that secret interest—the desire to share it—the desire, above all, to experiment on other people—grew so strong that it had to burst its bonds somehow.

"Now what was this person's position? What could this person do? Found a new witch-cult in Kent, such as existed here in previous centuries? It must have been a fascinating idea; but this person knew that it was as wild as wind. This person is, essentially, very practical.

"The smallest group in the organization for the worship of Satan was (may I say?) the coven. The coven consisted of thirteen persons, twelve members and a masked leader. To be the Janus-masked leader of such a cotillion must have appealed to our person as a fine dream; but no more than a dream. It was not only that the practical difficulties were too great to be overcome. It was also that for the thing to be interesting—to be shared with a few others—the number of persons concerned must be very small. As the interest was secret, so it must be narrow and personal and individual.

"This, I emphasize, was no measured affiliation with the powers of evil, supposing any such powers to exist. It had no such high ambition; or, to put it more properly, no such high-falutin. It was not carefully planned. It was not managed by a person of any great intelligence. It was not a cult as we know cults seriously developed. It was simply an idle and greedy liking for such things, a kind of hobby. Lord love you, I don't suppose any great harm would have been done—if the person had kept away from poisonous drugs to produce hallucinations. If people choose merely to act the fool, if they don't violate any laws or even any conventions, then it's no concern of the police. But, when a woman just outside Tunbridge Wells dies from the application of belladonna to the skin (which is exactly what happened eighteen months ago, though we've never been able to prove it), then, by thunder, it *is* a concern of the police! Why do you think Elliot was sent here to begin with? Why do you think he's been so much concerned with the story of Victoria Daly? Hey?

"Do you begin to see what somebody has been doing?

"This person chose a few suitable and sympathetic friends to confide in. There were not many: two or three or four, perhaps. We shall probably never know who they are. This person had many talks with them. Many books were given or loaned. Then, when the friend's mind was sufficiently stuffed and excited with wild lore, it was time. It was time to inform the friend that there really was a Satanist cult hereabouts, to which the candidate could now be admitted."

There was a sharp noise as Dr. Fell struck the ferrule of his stick on the floor. He was impatient and he was annoyed.

"Of course there never was any such thing. Of course the neophyte never left the house or stirred from one room on the night of the gatherings. Of course it was all a matter of an ointment whose two chief ingredients were aconite and belladonna.

"And of course, as a rule, the person who instigated this never went near the friend, much less joined any gathering, on the night of an alleged 'meeting.' That might have been too dangerous, if the poisonous effects of the ointment were too great. The pleasure lay in spreading this gospel: in sharing accounts of (mythical) adventures: in watching the decay of minds under the effects of the drug and under the effects of what they thought they had seen at the Sabbaths: in short, of combining a degree of rather heavy-witted mental cruelty with the pleasure of letting loose this interest in a safe and narrow circle."

Dr. Fell paused. And in the silence that followed Kennet Murray spoke thoughtfully.

"It reminds me," he said, "of the mentality which writes poison-pen letters."

"You've got it," said Dr. Fell, nodding. "It is almost exactly the same, turned to different and more harmful outlets."

"But if you can't prove the other woman died of poison—the one near Tunbridge Wells, whom I hadn't heard of—where are you? Has the 'person' done anything which is concretely illegal? Victoria Daly didn't die of poison."

"That depends, sir," observed Inspector Elliot suavely. "You seem to think that poisons aren't poisons unless they are taken internally. I can tell you different. But that's not the point now. Dr. Fell was only telling you the secret."

"The secret?"

"This person's secret," said Dr. Fell. "In order to preserve that secret, a man was murdered beside the pool in the garden two nights ago."

There was another silence, this time of an eerie quality as though everyone had drawn back a little.

Nathaniel Burrows put one finger inside his collar.

"This is interesting," he said. "Very interesting. But at the same time I feel I've been brought here under false pretenses. I'm a solicitor, not a student of heathen religions. I don't see that the heathen religions have anything to do with the only thing that matters to me. In the story you outline, there is no connection whatever with the proper succession to the Farnleigh estates—"

"Oh, yes, there is," said Dr. Fell.

He went on:

"It is, in fact, at the root of the whole matter, as I hope to make you understand in about two seconds.

"But you," he looked argumentatively at Page, "you, my friend, asked a little while ago what caused this person to take up such practices. Was it sheer boredom? Was it a kink inherited from childhood, never lost, and increasing from year to year? I'm inclined to suspect that it was a little of both. In this case all things grow up together, like the poison *Atropa belladonna* plant in the hedgerow. They are entwined and inseparable.

"Who might be a person with these instincts, always obliged to repress them? Who is there in whom we can trace the kink, with all the evidence before us? Who can be shown to be the one person, and the only one, with direct access to the toys of both witchcraft and murder? Who did undoubtedly suffer from the boredom of a loveless and miserable marriage, and at the same time suffered from the super-abundant vitality which—"

Burrows sprang to his feet with a ringing oath of enlightenment.

And at the same time, in the open door of the library, there was a whispered conference between Knowles and someone outside.

Knowles's face was white when he spoke.

"Excuse me, sir, but they—they tell me her ladyship is not in her room. They say she packed a bag some time ago, and took a car from the garage, and—"

Dr. Fell nodded.

"Exactly," he said. "That's why we don't have to hurry to London. Her flight has blown the gaff. And we shall have no difficulty now in obtaining a warrant for the arrest of Lady Farnleigh on a charge of murder."

Chapter XX

"Oh, come!" said Dr. Fell, rapping his stick on the floor and peering round the group with an air of benevolent expostulation. He was both amused and exasperated. "Don't tell me it surprises you. Don't tell me it shocks you. You, Miss Dane! Didn't you know about her all along? Didn't you know how she hated you?"

Madeline passed the back of her hand across her forehead. Then she reached out and took Page's arm.

"I didn't know about her," Madeline said. "I guessed. But I could hardly tell you that outright, could I? I'm afraid you've thought me enough of a cat as it is."

For Page some readjustment of thought was necessary. So, it appeared, was it necessary for the others. Yet a new notion caught and held in Page's brain even as he tried to assimilate the first. The thought was: This case is not finished.

Whether it was a slight expression flickering in Dr. Fell's eyes, a turn of his hand on the stick, a slight quiver even in that mountain, he could not tell. But the impression was there, and Dr. Fell still held the room as though he had not ended with revelation. Somewhere there was an ambush. Somewhere there were guns to be fired on the brain.

"Go on," said Murray quietly. "I don't doubt you; but go on."

"Yes," said Burrows in a vacant way—and sat down.

The doctor's big voice sounded sleepily in the quiet library.

"From the physical evidences," he continued, "there could hardly have been much doubt about it from the first. The centre of all disturbances, psychic and otherwise, was always *here*. The centre of all disturbances was that locked book-closet in the attic. Somebody had been haunting it. Somebody had been juggling with its contents, removing and replacing its books, playing with its trinkets. Somebody, always distinguished for exuberance of action, had made it into a kind of lair.

"Now, the notion that some outsider had done this—that some neighbour had crept into the nest—was so fantastic as not to be worth serious consideration. Such a course of action would have been impossible, both psychologically and practically. You do not make a sort of one-man club in the attic of someone else's house, particularly under the eyes of a staff of curious servants. You do not come and go through that house at night, unseen by servants or anybody else. You do not so casually treat a new padlock watched by the master of the house. For it will be observed that though Miss Dane, for instance"—here there was a broad and cherubic beam on Dr. Fell's face—"though Miss Dane had once possessed a key to that little room, it was the key to a lock no longer in use.

"Next question: what ailed Sir John Farnleigh?

"Just reflect on that, ladies and gentlemen.

"Why did that restless Puritan, already be-dazed with troubles of his own, never find any solace at home? What else was on his mind? Why does he, on the very night his great inheritance is to be challenged, do nothing but pace the floor and talk of Victoria Daly? Why is he so uneasily concerned with detectives asking 'folklore' questions in the vicinity? What is the meaning of his cryptic hints to Miss Dane? In moments of emotion he used to 'look up at the church, and say that if he were in a position to—'

"To do what? Speak out against the defamers of the church? Why does he once visit that attic with a dog-whip in his hand; but come down white and sweating, unable to use the whip on the person he finds there?

"The points in this case are mental ones, as revealing as the physical clues with which I shall deal in a moment; and I can't do better than to trace them."

Dr. Fell paused. He stared heavily and rather sadly at the table. Then he got out his pipe.

"Let's take the history of this girl, Molly Bishop: a resolute woman and a fine actress. Patrick Gore said one true thing about her two nights ago. He appears to have shocked most of you by saying that she had never fallen in love with the Farnleigh you knew. He said that she had seized upon and married a 'projected image' of the boy she had known all those years before. And so she had. Whereupon she discovered, with what fury we may never know, that it was not the same boy or even the same person.

"What was the origin of that obsession or kink, even in the brain of a child of seven?

"It's not difficult. That's the age at which our essential tastes begin to be stamped on us by outside impressions. They are never eradicated, even when we think we have forgotten them. To my dying day I shall like pictures of fat old Dutchmen playing chess and smoking church-warden pipes, because I remember one hanging on the wall of my father's study when I was a small child. You may like ducks or ghost-stories or motor-mechanisms for the same reason.

"Well, who was the only person who had idolized the boy John Farnleigh? Who was the only one to defend him? Whom did John Farnleigh take to gipsy-camps (I call the gipsy-camps to your attention as significant), and take with him into the wood? What manner of Satanist lessons did she hear him recite, before she understood them or even before she understood the lessons she learned at Sunday School?

"And the intervening years? We don't know how the taste grew and developed in her brain. Except this: that she spent much time among the Farnleighs, for she had enough influence with old and young Sir Dudley to get Knowles his position as butler here.—Didn't she, Knowles?"

He peered round.

From the moment he had made that announcement Knowles had not moved. He was seventy-four. The transparent colour of his face, which seemed to show every emotion there, now showed nothing at all. He opened and shut his mouth and nodded in pantomime of reply; but he did not say anything. About him there was only a look of horror.

"It is probable," continued Dr. Fell, "that she was borrowing books from that sealed library a long time ago. When she first instituted her private Satanist-cult Elliot has not been able to trace; but it was several years before her marriage. The number of men in the district who have been her lovers is large enough to surprise you. But they cannot or will not say anything about the Satanist business. And that, after all, is the only thing with which we are concerned. It is the thing with which *she* was most concerned, and it brought about the tragedy. For what happened?

"After a long and romantic absence, the supposed 'John Farnleigh' returned to the supposed home of his fathers. For a short time Molly Bishop was transfigured. Here was her ideal. Here was her preceptor. Him she was determined to marry in spite of hell and himself. And something over a year ago—to be exact, a year and three months—they were married.

"Oh, Lord, was there ever a worse match?

"I ask that quite solemnly. You know who and what she thought she was marrying. You know instead the sort of person she did marry. You can guess the silent, cold contempt he had for her; and the frigid politeness he had for her when he learned. You can imagine what she felt for him, and the mask of concerned wifeliness she had to adopt, knowing always that he knew. And between them lay always the polite fiction that neither was aware of the other's knowledge. For, just as he knew about her, so she as certainly knew after a very short time that he was not the real John Farnleigh. So there together they shared each other's secret, in unadmitted hate.

"Why didn't he ever give her away? It wasn't merely that she was what he in his Puritan soul condemned first to the pit. It wasn't merely that he would have taken a whip to her if he had dared. But she was a criminal (make no mistake about that, gentlemen) as well. She was a supplier of more dangerous drugs than heroin or cocaine; and he knew it. She was accessory after the fact in Victoria Daly's murder; and he knew it. You have heard of his outbursts. You know his thoughts. Why, then, didn't he ever give her away as he longed to do?

"Because he was not in a position to do so. Because they held each other's secret. He didn't *know* he was not Sir John Farnleigh; but he feared it. He didn't *know* she could prove he was not, and might do so if he provoked her; but he feared it. He didn't *know* whether she might suspect; but he feared it. He had not quite the character of sweetness and light which Miss Dane gave him. No, he was not a conscious impostor. His memory was blind and he groped there. Very often he was sure he must be the real Farnleigh. But he would not, in the depths of a natural human soul, challenge fate too far, unless it pinned him in a corner and he had to face it out. For he might be a criminal as well."

Nathaniel Burrows jumped to his feet.

"I cannot put up with this," he said in a shrill voice. "I refuse to put up with this. Inspector, I call on you to stop this man! He has no right to prejudice an issue not yet decided. As a representative of the law, you have no right to say that my client—"

"Better sit down, sir," said Elliot quietly.

"But—"

"I said sit down, sir."

Madeline was speaking to Dr. Fell.

"You said something like that earlier tonight," she reminded him. "Something about his 'labouring under a sense of crime,' even though he did not know what it was. His 'sense of crime,' that made him a worse Puritan, seems to run all through this; and yet, really and truly, I can't see what that has to do with it. What's the explanation?"

Dr. Fell put the empty pipe in his mouth and drew at it.

"The explanation," he answered, "is a crooked hinge, and the white door the hinge supported. It's the secret of this case. We shall come to it presently.

"So these two, each having a secret like a dagger in the sleeve, mopped and mowed and pretended in front of the world: even in front of themselves. Victoria Daly died, a victim of the secret witch-cult, only three months after they had been married. We know what Farnleigh must have felt by that time. *If I were ever in a position to*—had become with him a fetish and a refrain. So long as he was never in a position to speak out, she was safe. For over a year she was safe.

"But then occurred the thunderclap that a claimant to the estate had appeared. Whereupon certain eventualities presented themselves to her as flat and clear and inevitable as a,b,c. Thus:

"He was not the real heir, as she knew.

"It seemed probable that the claimant would prove to be the real heir.

"If the claimant were proved to be the real heir, her husband would be dispossessed.

"If he were dispossessed, he would no longer have a reason for not speaking out about her, and he would speak out.

"Therefore he had to die.

"As simple and certain as that, ladies and gentlemen."

Kennet Murray shifted in his chair, taking away the hand with which he had been shading his eyes.

"One moment, doctor. This was a long-planned crime, then?"

"No!" said Dr. Fell with great earnestness. "No, no, no! That's what I want to stress. It was brilliantly planned and executed in desperation on the spur of the moment two nights ago. It was as quickly flung out as the automaton was pushed downstairs.

"Let me explain. As she believed from the time she had first heard of the claimant (farther back, I suspect, than she would admit), she had nothing to fear *just yet*. Her husband would fight the claim; she must make him fight, and, ironically, fight for him. Far from wishing to see the hated one ousted, she must clasp him even more tightly than before. It was quite possible that he would win his claim, the law being what it is and the courts being very wary of claimants to an established estate. At all events the law's delays would give her breathing-space to think.

"What she did not know, what had been carefully concealed by the other side until two nights ago, was the existence of the fingerprints. Here was solid proof. Here was certainty. With that deadly fingerprint, the whole question could be settled in half an hour. Knowing her husband's mind, she knew he was coldly honest enough to admit the imposture as soon as it had been proved to him: as soon as he knew in his own soul that he was not John Farnleigh.

"When this hand-grenade exploded, she saw imminent peril. You recall Farnleigh's mood that night? If you have described it correctly to me, through every word he said and every move he made runs one strong and reckless flavour: 'Well, here's the test. If I survive it, well and good. If I don't, there is one compensation which almost reconciles me to everything else: I can speak out about the woman to whom I am married.'—Harrumph, yes. Have I interpreted the mood correctly?"

"Yes," admitted Page.

"So she took desperate measures. She must act at once. At once, at once! She must act before the fingerprint-comparison had been completed. She took these measures—just as yesterday, in the attic, she struck back at me before the words were out of my mouth—she acted magnificently; and she killed her husband."

Burrows, white-faced and sweating, had been vainly hammering on the table to call for order. Now there was a gleam of hope in his manner.

"There seems to be no way of stopping you," Burrows said. "If the police won't do it, I can't do more than protest. But now, I think, you are at a place where these glib theories won't do. I say nothing of the fact that you have no evidence. But until you can show how Sir John was murdered—alone, mind you, with nobody near him—until you can show that—" His words choked him; he only stuttered, and made a broad gesture. "And that, doctor, that you cannot show."

"Oh, yes, I can," said Dr. Fell.

"Our first real lead came at the inquest yesterday," he went on reflectively. "It's good that the testimony is in the records. After that we had only to pick up certain pieces of evidence which had been lying under our noses from the first. Behold a miracle dropped into our laps. We are given hanging evidence by word of mouth. We apply it. We arrange the bits in order. We hand them to the prosecuting counsel. And"—he made a gesture—"we draw the bolt of the gallows-trap."

"You got your evidence at the inquest?" repeated Murray, staring at him. "Evidence from whom?"

"From Knowles," said Dr. Fell.

A whimpering kind of cry came from the butler. He took a step forward, and put his hand up to his face. But he did not speak.

Dr. Fell contemplated him.

"Oh, I know," the doctor growled. "It's sour medicine. But there you are. It's an ironical turn of the screw. But there you are. Knowles, my lad, you love that woman. She's your petted child. And by your testimony at the inquest, in all innocence, in all desire to tell the truth, you have hanged her as surely as though you drew the bolt yourself."

Still he kept his eyes fixed on the butler.

"Now, I daresay," he continued comfortably, "that some people thought you lied. I knew you didn't lie. You said that Sir John Farnleigh had committed suicide. You clinched your story by saying—something you had remembered in your subconscious mind—that you saw him fling away the knife. You said you saw the knife in the air.

"I knew you weren't lying, because you had had exactly the same trouble with that point when you talked to Elliot and me the day before. You had hesitated. You had groped after an uncertain memory. When Elliot pressed you about it, you puzzled and shook. 'It would depend on the size of the knife,' you said. 'And there are bats in that garden. And sometimes you can't see a tennis-ball until it's—' The choice of words is significant. In other words: *at about the time of the crime you had seen something flying in the air*. What puzzled your subconscious mind was that you saw it just before the murder rather than just afterwards."

He spread out his hands.

"A very remarkable bat," said Burrows, with shrill sarcasm. "A still more remarkable tennis-ball."

"Something very like a tennis-ball," agreed Dr. Fell seriously, "though much smaller, of course. Very much smaller.

"We will return to that. Let's go on and consider the nature of the wounds. Already we have heard much astonished and feeling comment about those wounds. Mr. Murray here maintained that they were like the marks of fangs or claws; he maintained that the blood-stained clasp-knife found in the hedge could not have produced them. Even Patrick Gore, if you have correctly quoted him to me, made a very similar comment. And what did he say? 'I never saw anything like this since Barney Poole, the best animal-trainer west of the Mississippi, was killed by a leopard.'

"The claw-mark motif runs all through the case. We find it coming out with curious guardedness and in a strikingly suggestive way in Dr. King's medical evidence at the inquest. I have some notes here of his testimony. Harrumph! Hah! Let me see:

" 'There were three fairly shallow wounds,' says the physician." Here

Dr. Fell looked very hard at his audience. " 'Three fairly shallow wounds, beginning at the left side of the throat and ending under the angle of the right jaw in a slightly upward direction. Two of the wounds crossed each other.' And presently this still more damning statement: 'There was much laceration of tissue.'

"Laceration of tissue, eh? Surely that is odd, gents, if the weapon were that exceedingly sharp (if notched) knife which Inspector Elliot is showing you now. Laceration of the throat suggests—

"Well, let's see. Let's return to the claw-mark motif and examine it. What are the characteristics of wounds made by claws, and how are they fulfilled in the death of Sir John Farnleigh? The characteristics of marks left by claws are these:

"1. They are shallow.
"2. They are made by sharp points which tear and scratch and lacerate rather than cut.
"3. They are not separate cuts, but are all made at the same time.

"Every one of these qualifications, we find, is fulfilled by the description of the wounds in Farnleigh's throat. I call your attention to the somewhat odd testimony given by Dr. King at the inquest. He does not tell a direct lie; but he is obviously working like blazes and talking wildly in order to make Farnleigh's death a suicide! Why? Observe—he, too, like Knowles, has a petted child in Molly Farnleigh, the daughter of his oldest friend, who calls him 'Uncle Ned' and whose traits of character are probably known to him. But, unlike Knowles, he screens her; he does not send her out to have her neck cracked in two at the end of a rope."

Knowles put out his hands as though in supplication. His forehead was smeary with perspiration; but he still did not speak.

Dr. Fell went on.

"Mr. Murray suggested the basis of our case to us some time ago, when he spoke of something flying in the air and pertinently asked why the knife had not been dropped in the pool if it were really the weapon. But what have we got now? We've got something that flew at Farnleigh in the dusk, something smaller than a tennis ball. We've got something equipped with claws or points which would make marks like claws—"

Nathaniel Burrows uttered a ghost of a chuckle.

"The episode of the flying claws," he jeered. "Really, doctor! And can you tell us what the flying claws were?"

"I'll do better than that," said Dr. Fell. "I'll show them to you. You saw them yesterday."

From his capacious side-pocket he took out something wrapped in a large red bandana handkerchief. Unfolding it so that the needle-sharp points should not catch in the handkerchief, he disclosed an object which Page recognized with a shock, even though it was a puzzled shock. It was one of the objects which Dr. Fell had unearthed from the wooden box put away in the book-closet. It was (to be precise) a small but heavy leaden ball into which at intervals had been set four very large hooks of the sort used to catch fighting deep-sea fish.

"Did you wonder at the purpose of this singular instrument?" asked the doctor amiably. "Did you wonder what earthly use it could be to anybody? But among the Middle-European gipsies—among the gipsies, I repeat—it has a very effective and dangerous use. Let me have Gross: will you, inspector?"

Elliot opened his brief-case and took out a large flat book in a grey jacket.

"Here," pursued Dr. Fell, juggling the book, "we have the most complete text-book on crime ever compiled.* I sent to town for it last night to verify a reference. You'll find a full description of this leaden ball on pages 249–50.

"It is used by the gipsies as a throwing weapon, and accounts for some of their mysterious and almost supernatural thefts. Into the other end of this ball is fastened a long length of very light but very strong fishing-line. The ball is thrown; and, at whatever it is thrown, the hooks lightly catch no matter in what direction they fall—like a ship's anchor. The leaden ball lends the necessary weight for throwing, and the fishing-line draws it back with the booty. Hear Gross on the use of it:

" 'As regards the throwing, gipsies, especially the children, are remarkably skilful. Among all races children amuse themselves by throwing stones, but their particular object in doing so is to throw them as far as possible. Not so the young gipsy; he gathers together a heap of stones about the size of a nut and then chooses a target, such as a fairly large stone, a small plank, or an old cloth, at a distance of about ten to twenty paces; he then launches his stock of projectiles. . . . He keeps going for hours and soon acquires such skill at this exercise that he never misses anything larger than one's hand. When he reaches this stage he is given a throwing hook. . . .

" 'The young gipsy comes out of his apprenticeship when he is able to strike and carry off a piece of rag thrown upon the branches of a tree among which he has to cast his hook.'

*Criminal Investigation: A Practical Textbook for Magistrates, Police Officers, and Lawyers, Adapted from the System der Kriminalistik of Dr. Hans Gross, Professor of Criminology in the University of Prague, by John Adam, M.A., Barrister-at-Law, and J. Collyer Adam, Barrister-at-Law; edited by Normal Kendal, Assistant Commissioner, Criminal Investigation Dept., Metropolitan Police. (London, Sweet & Maxwell, 1934.)

"Into a tree, mind you! This is how, with amazing skill, he is able to carry off linen, clothes, and so on, through barred windows or in enclosed yards. But as a throwing weapon you can imagine its horrible effectiveness. It will tear the throat from a man, and back it goes—"

Murray uttered a kind of groan. Burrows did not speak.

"H'mf, yes. Now, we've heard of Molly Farnleigh's uncanny and amazing ability at throwing, a trick she learned among the gipsies. Miss Dane told us of it. We know of her deadly snap-judgments, and the suddenness with which she could strike.

"Where, then, was Molly Farnleigh at the time of the murder? I hardly need to tell you: she was on the balcony of her bedroom overlooking the pool. My eye, *directly* above the pool; and her bedroom, as we know, is built over the dining-room. Like Welkyn in the room below, she was much less than twenty feet away from the pool, and raised above it. Very high up? Not at all. As Knowles here—invaluable at giving us hints on how to hang her—as Knowles told us, that new wing of the house is 'a little low doll's house of a place,' the balcony hardly eight or nine feet above the garden.

"So there she is in the dusk, facing her husband below, and raised up high enough to give purchase to her arm. The room behind her is dark—as she admitted. Her maid was in the next room. What brought her to that deadly snap-decision? Did she whisper something to make her husband look up? Or was it because he was already looking at a star, with his long throat upturned?"

With an expression of growing horror in her eyes, Madeline repeated: "Looking at a star?"

"Your star, Miss Dane," said Dr. Fell sombrely. "I've talked a good deal with the various persons in this case; and I think it was your star."

Again memory returned to Page. He himself had thought of "Madeline's star" when he walked through the garden beside the pool on the night of the murder: the single eastern star to which she had given a poetic name, and which from the pool you could just see by craning your neck to look over the farther chimney-tops of the new wing . . .

"Yes, she hated you. Her husband's attentions to you had done that. It may have been the sight of him looking up, staring at your star and facing her blindly, that brought out murder in a flood. With the line in one hand and the leaden ball in the other, she lifted her arm and struck.

"Gents, I call your attention to the curious, the weird behaviour of that poor devil when something caught him. It has vaguely troubled everybody who has tried to describe it. The shufflings, the chokings, the jerkings of the body before he was yanked forward into the pool—what has it reminded you of? Ah! Got it, have you? Shows clearly, does it? Of a hooked fish on a line; and that is what it was. The hooks did not penetrate deeply: she saw to that. There was a good deal of mauling, on which everybody commented. The direction of the wounds, obviously, was from left to right, running upwards, as he was pulled off balance; and he went into the pool (you recall?) with his head slightly towards the new wing. When he was in the pool she jerked back the weapon."

With a heavy grimness of expression Dr. Fell held up the leaden ball. "And this little beauty?"

"Obviously, of course, it left no blood-trail or any traces when it was pulled back. It had landed in the pool and had been washed clean. You recall that the water in the pool had been so agitated (naturally, by his strugglings) that it was slopped over the sand for some feet round. But the ball did leave one trace—it rustled in the shrubbery.

"Reflect. Who was the only person who heard that curious rustling? Welkyn, in the dining-room below: the only person who was near enough to hear it. That rustling was an intriguing point. Clearly it had not been made by any *person*. If you will try the experiment of attempting to slip through yew hedges as thick as a wide screen (as Sergeant Burton noticed when he later found the knife 'planted' there, with the dead man's fingerprints conveniently on it), you will realize what I mean.

"I spare you details. But that, in essence, is how she planned and carried out one of the wickedest murders in my experience. It was all flash and hate; and it succeeded. She fished for men as she has always done; and she caught her victim. She won't get away, naturally. She will be nabbed by the first policeman she passes. Then she will hang. And all, happily for the cause of justice, because of Knowles's happy inspiration in telling us about the flight of a tennis-ball at dusk."

Knowles made a slight waggling gesture of his hand as though he were trying to stop a bus. His face was like oiled paper, and Page was afraid he was going to faint. But still he could not speak.

Burrows, with his eyes gleaming, seemed inspired.

"It's ingenious," Burrows said. "It's clever. But it's a lie, and I'll beat you in court with it. It's all false and you know it. For other people have sworn things too. There's Welkyn! You can't explain away what *he* said! Welkyn saw somebody in the garden! He said he did! And what have you got to say to that?"

Page noted with alarm that Dr. Fell himself was looking somewhat pale. Very slowly Dr. Fell pushed himself to his feet. He stood towering over them, and he made a gesture towards the door.

"There's Mr. Welkyn now," he replied. "Standing just behind you. Ask him. Ask him if he's now so sure of what he saw in the garden."

They all looked round. How long Welkyn had been standing in the doorway they could not tell. Immaculate, brushed as ever, the overgrown cherubic countenance was uneasy, and Welkyn pulled at his lower lip.

"Er—" he said, clearing at his throat.

"Well, speak up!" thundered Dr. Fell. "You've heard my say. Now tell us: ARE you sure you saw something looking at you? ARE you sure there was anything there to see?"

"I have been reflecting," said Welkyn.

"Yes?"

"I—er—gentlemen." He paused. "I wish you would cast your minds back to yesterday. You all went up to the attic, and I am given to understand that you investigated certain curious articles you found there. Unhappily I did not go along with you. I did not see any of those articles until today, when Dr. Fell called them to my attention. I—er—refer to the black Janus-faced mask which you seem to have found in a wooden box there." Again he cleared his throat.

"This is a plot," said Burrows, looking rapidly right and left like a man hesitating before wild traffic in a road. "You can't get away with this. It's all a deliberate conspiracy, and you're all in it—"

"Kindly allow me to finish, sir," retorted Welkyn with asperity. "I said I saw a face looking at me through the lower panel of the glass door. I know what it was now. It was that Janus mask. I recognized it as soon as I saw it. It occurs to me, as Dr. Fell suggests, that the unhappy Lady Farnleigh—in order to prove to me the presence of someone actually in the garden—merely let down that mask on another length of fishing-line; and unfortunately sent it too low against the window, so that . . ."

Then Knowles spoke at last.

He came up to the table and put his hands on it. He was crying; and for a moment the tears would not let him speak coherently. When the words did come out, they shocked his listeners as though a piece of furniture had spoken.

"It's a bloody *lie,*" said Knowles.

Old and muddled and pitiful, he began to beat with his hand on the table.

"It's like Mr. Burrows said. It's all lies and lies and lies and lies. You're all in it." His voice grew frantic, rising to a quaver, and his hand beat frantically on the table. "You're all against her, that's what you are. You none of you will give her a chance. What if she did carry on a bit? What if she did read them books and maybe carry on with a lad or two? What difference is it, much, from the games they used to play when they were kids? They're all kids. She didn't mean any harm. She never meant any harm. And you sha'nt hang her. By Christ, you sha'nt. I'll see nobody harms my little lady, that's what I'll do."

His voice grew to a scream through the tears, and he waggled his finger at them.

"I'll fool you, with all your grand ideas and your grand guesses. She didn't kill that crazy silly beggar that came here pretending to be Master Johnny. Master Johnny my foot! That beggar a Farnleigh? *That* beggar? He got just exactly what he deserved, and I'm sorry he can't be killed all over again. Came out of a pig-sty, that's where he came from. But I don't care about him. I tell you you're not going to hurt my little lady. She never killed him; she never did; and I can prove it."

In the vast silence they heard the tap of Dr. Fell's stick on the floor, and the wheezing of his breath, as he walked over to Knowles and put his hand on Knowles's shoulder.

"I know she didn't," he said gently.

Knowles stared at him with blurred frenzy.

"Do you mean," shouted Burrows, "that you've been sitting here telling us a pack of fairy-tales just because—"

"And do you think I like what I'm doing?" asked Dr. Fell. "Do you think I like one word I've said or one move I've had to make? Everything I told you about the woman and her private witch-cult and her relations with Farnleigh was true. Everything. She inspired the murderer and directed the murder. The only difference is that she did not kill her husband. She did not make the automaton work and she was not the person in the garden. But"—his hand tightened on Knowles's shoulder—"you know the law. You know how it moves and how it crushes. I've set it in motion. And Lady Farnleigh will hang higher than Haman unless you tell us the truth. Do you know who committed the murder?"

"Of course I know it," snarled Knowles. "Yah!"

"And who was the murderer?"

"That's an easy one," said Knowles. "And that silly beggar got everything that was coming to him. The murderer was—"

IV

THE FALL OF A HINGE

There was one thing which Flambeau, with all his dexterity of disguise, could not cover, and that was his singular height. If Valentin's quick eye had caught a tall apple-woman, a tall grenadier, or even a tolerably tall duchess, he might have arrested them on the spot. But all along his train there was nobody who could be a disguised Flambeau, any more than a cat could be a disguised giraffe.
—*G. K. CHESTERTON, The Blue Cross*

Chapter XXI

Being a letter from Patrick Gore (born John Farn-
leigh) to Dr. Gideon Fell.

Outward bound,
At a certain date.

M y dear doctor:
     Yes, I am the culprit. I alone killed that impostor, and pro-
duced all the manifestations which seem to have alarmed you.
   I write you this letter for a number of reasons. First: I retain (however
foolishly) a genuine liking and respect for you. Second: You have never
done anything better. The way in which you forced me step by step
through every room, through every door, and out of the house into flight,
rouses my admiration to such an extent that I should like to see whether I
have correctly followed your deductions. I pay you the compliment of
saying that you are the only person who has ever outwitted me; but then I
have never been at my best against schoolmasters. Third: I believe I have
found the one really perfect disguise, and, now that it is no longer of use
to me, I should rather like to brag about it.
   I shall expect an answer to this letter. By the time you receive it, I and
my adored Molly will be in a country which has no extradition-treaty with
Great Britain. It is rather a hot country, but then both Molly and I are fond
of hot countries. I will drop you a line as to the address when we are
settled in our new home.
   One request I should like to make. In the *débâcle* of horrified talk
which will follow our flight, I shall doubtless be presented by newspapers, judges, and other distorters of the public eyesight as a Fiend, a
Monster, a Werewolf, and so on. Now, you are quite well aware that I am
nothing of the sort. I have no liking for murder; and if I cannot feel any
repentance over the death of that swine it is, I hope, because I am not a
hypocrite. Certain people are constituted in certain ways, like Molly and
myself. If we prefer to make the world a more exciting place with our

studies and our day-dreams, I should think it would be an inspiration to Suburbia and a hint towards better things. When, therefore, you hear someone indulging in maudlin speech about the Fiend and his Witch-bride, kindly inform the person that you have had tea with both of us, and perceived no sign of horns or stigmata.

But now I must tell you my secret, which is also the secret of the case you have been so earnestly investigating. It is a very simple secret, and can be expressed in four words:

I have no legs.

I have no legs. Both of them were amputated in April, 1912, after being crushed by that swine in a little affair aboard the *Titanic,* which I shall describe in a moment. The admirable set of artificial legs I have since worn have not altogether, I fear, disguised this disability. I saw that you noticed my walk—which is not exactly a limp, but is always clumsy and sometimes awkward enough to betray me if I attempt to move rapidly. I cannot, in fact, move rapidly; and with this also I shall deal in a moment.

Have you ever thought of the remarkable opportunity presented by artificial legs for the purposes of disguise? We have had mummeries of wig and beard and grease-paint; we have had faces altered with clay and figures with padding; we have had the subtlest turns to the subtlest illusion. But, astonishing to state, we have never had the eyes deceived in the simplest way, and there has always been the statement, "This and that a man can do, but there is one thing he cannot disguise: his height." I beg leave to state that I can make my height anything I please, and that I have been doing so for quite a number of years.

I am not a tall man. That is, to be strictly accurate, I believe that I should not be a tall man had I any means of estimating what my height would have been. Let us say that, without the interference of my small friend on the *Titanic,* I should have been about five feet five inches tall. The removal of under-pinning (observe my delicacy) leaves my actual body less than three feet high. Should you doubt this, measure your own height against a wall and observe the proportion taken up by these mysterious appendages we call legs.

With several sets of limbs made to order—this was first done in the circus—and a good deal of painful practice in the harness, I can make my height what I choose. It is interesting to discover how easily the eye is deceived. Imagine, for example, a small and slender friend of yours appearing before you as a six-footer; your brain would refuse to take it in, and the smallest dexterity in other branches of disguise would render him completely unrecognizable.

I have been several heights. I have been six-feet-one. And again, in my famous role as "Ahriman," the fortune-teller, I was almost a dwarf: with such success as completely to deceive the good Mr. Harold Welkyn, when I later appeared before him as Patrick Gore.

Perhaps it would be best to start with the business aboard the *Titanic*. Now, when I returned to claim my inheritance the other day, the story I told to the assembled gapers in the library was true—with one slight distortion and one notable omission.

We changed identities, as I said. The gentle-hearted lad did in reality try to kill me, as I said. But he attempted to do it by strangling, since he was at that time the stronger. This little tragic-comedy was played among the pillars of high tragedy; and you have guessed its background. Its background was one of the great white-painted steel doors, bulkhead doors, which shut a liner into compartments and can swing several hundred-weight of ponderous metal against the creeping water. The crumpling and dissolving of its hinges as the ship lurched was, I think, as terrifying a spectacle as I have ever seen; it was like the breaking of all ordered things or the fall of the gates of Gath.

My friend's purpose was of no great complexity. After squeezing my windpipe until I was unconscious, he meant to shut me into the flooding compartment and make his escape. I fought back with anything within reach—in this case, a wooden mallet hanging beside the door. How many times I hit him I cannot remember, but the snake-dancer's son did not even seem to mind it. I was able to dodge, unfortunately for myself, to the outer side of the door; the snake-dancer's son threw himself against it, and, with the settling of the ship, the hinges gave. All of me, I need scarcely say, got out of the way of it except my legs.

It was a time of heroisms, doctor: heroisms never set to music or told afterwards except stammeringly. Who rescued me—whether it was a passenger or one of the crew—I do not know. I recall being picked up like a puppy and carried out to a boat. The snake-dancer's son, with his blood-stained head and wandering eye, I thought had been left behind to die. That I did not die myself I suppose I must attribute to the salt-water, but it was not a pleasant time for me and I remember nothing of what happened until a week later.

In my story to the group at Farnleigh Close some nights ago, I told of my reception as "Patrick Gore" by old Boris Yeldritch, since dead, the proprietor of the circus. I explained something of my state of mind. If I did not explain my entire state of mind, you know the reason. Boris easily found a use for me with the circus, since I was (not to put too fine a point on it) a freak with a knack for telling fortunes gained from my studies back home. It was a painful and humiliating time, especially in learning to "walk" by using my hands. I do not dwell on this part of it, for I would not have you think I am asking for pity or sympathy: the notion angers me furiously. I feel like the man in the play. Your liking I will have if I can.

Your respect I will have or kill you. But your pity? Damn your impudence!

It occurs to me, too, that I have been posturing like a tragedian over something which, after all, I had almost forgotten. Let us take matters more amiably and be amused at what we cannot correct. You know my profession: I have been a fortune-teller, a bogus spiritualist and occultist, and an illusionist. I somewhat imprudently hinted at this when I came to Farnleigh Close the other night. Yet I have been so many different persons, and served under so many different aliases as He Who Knows All, that I did not greatly fear detection.

I cheerfully assure you that the absence of legs has been, in fact, a boon to me in my business. I would not have it otherwise. But the artificial ones always hampered me; and I fear I have never learned to manage them properly. I early learned to move myself about by the use of my hands: with, I venture to think, incredible speed and agility. I need hardly tell you in how many ways this was useful to me in my business as a fraudulent spiritist medium, and what remarkable effects I was able to produce for my sitters. Reflect on it a while; you will understand.

Whenever I am up to such tricks, I am in the habit of wearing under my artificial limbs and ordinary trousers close-fitting breeches equipped with leather pads, which serve as my limbs and leave no traces on any sort of ground. Since speed in change has often been of the utmost necessity, I have learned to remove or put back my artificial harness in exactly thirty-five seconds.

And this, of course, is the painfully simple secret of how I worked the automaton.

A word concerning it, since history has repeated itself. It not only could have happened before; it did happen before. Are you aware, doctor, that this was how the automaton chessplayer of Kempelen and Maelzel was run?* With the simple assistance of a man like myself inside the box on which the figure sat, they baffled Europe and America for fifty years. When the hoax deceived men of such different temperaments as Napoleon Bonaparte and Phineas Barnum, you need not feel cast down if it deceived you. But it did not, in fact, deceive you; and this you gave me clearly to understand by your hints in the attic.

---

*Mr. Gore is telling the truth. I first came across this explanation in an old edition of the *Encyclopaedia Britannica* (ninth edition, published in 1883). The writer, J. A. Clarke, says: "The first player was a Polish patriot, Worousky, who had lost both legs in a campaign; as he was furnished with artificial limbs when in public, his appearance, together with the fact that no dwarf or child travelled in Kempelen's company, dispelled the suspicion that any person could be employed inside the machine. This automaton, which made more than one tour to the capitals and courts of Europe, was owned for a short time by Napoleon I, was exhibited by Maelzel after the death of Kempelen in 1819, and ultimately perished in a fire at Philadelphia in 1854."—Vol. XV, p. 210.

I have no doubt that this was the original secret of the Golden Hag in the seventeenth century. Do you see now why the automaton fell into such disrepute when my respected ancestor Thomas Farnleigh, after buying it for a whacking price, learned the truth? He had been told the inner mystery; and, like many others who have learned inner mysteries, he was furious. He thought to get a miracle. Instead he paid for an ingenious trick with which he could not hoax his friends unless he kept a special kind of operator on the premises.

This is how the whole effect was originally managed: The space inside is big enough, as you have observed, for a person like myself. Once you are inside the box or "couch," and the door closed, the shutting of the door opens a small panel in the top of the box communicating with the works of the figure. Here—worked by simple mechanical weights— are a dozen rods communicating with the hands and body. Concealed holes by the knees of the automaton, which can be opened from inside, allow the operator to see. That was how Maelzel's dummy played chess; and how the Golden Hag played the cittern over a hundred years before.

But, in the case of the hag, one of the best features of the illusion was the device by which the operator was conveyed inside the box unseen. There, I think, is where the inventor of the hag outdid Kempelen. At the beginning of the performance the magician in charge opened the box and let everybody inspect the inside to show that it was empty. How, then, was the operator spirited in?

I don't need to tell *you*. By your remarks in the attic the day after the murder—carefully aimed at me—about the costume worn by the exhibitor, you demonstrated that you knew; and *I* knew that my goose was done to a cinder.

The traditional wizard's costume, as everybody knows, consists of a huge flowing robe covered with hieroglyphics. And the original inventor merely applied a principle later used by the somewhat clumsy Indian fakirs. That is, the robe was used to cover something: in the case of the fakir, a child who climbs into a basket unseen; in the case of the exhibitor of the hag, the operator who slid into the machine while the magician in his great robe fussed with it at the dimming of the lights. I have made use of the trick successfully in many of my own entertainments.

To which history of my life I must return.

My most successful rôle was in London as "Ahriman," if you can forgive the name of a Zoroastrian devil as applied to an Egyptian. Poor Welkyn, whom you must not suspect of any part in my dirty work, does not know to this day that I was the bearded dwarf of whom he took such good care. He defended me nobly in that libel suit; he believed in my psychic powers; and, when I reappeared as the missing heir, I thought it only fair to make him my legal representative.

(Magister, that libel suit still tickles my fancy. I hoped fervently that I should be able to give some demonstration of my psychic powers in court. You see, my father had been at school with the judge; and I was prepared to go into a trance in the witness-box and tell his Lordship some realistic things about himself. My father, indeed, had been well-known socially in London during the nineties: which fact is less a tribute to Ahriman's awesome insight into his sitters' hearts than to the power of information on which he had to draw. But a weakness for spectacular effect has always been one of my characteristics.)

It is as Ahriman, then, that my story properly begins.

I had no notion that "John Farnleigh" was supposed to be alive, much less that he was now Sir John Farnleigh, baronet—until he walked one day into my consulting-room in Half-Moon Street, and told me his troubles. That I did not laugh in the man's face I simply state as a fact. Monte Cristo himself never dreamed of such a situation. But I think, I say I *think,* that in applying balm to his fevered mind I contrived to give him some unpleasant days and nights.

However, the matter of importance is less that I met him than that I met Molly.

On this subject my views are too fervent to be fashioned into smooth prose. Don't you see that we are two of a kind? Don't you see that, once having found each other, Molly and I would have come together from the ends of the earth? It was a love-affair sudden, complete, and blinding; there was burning pitch in it; it was, in the terms of an American pastime called Red Dog, "high, low, jack, and the goddam game." I must laugh at this, or I shall find myself fashioning incoherence into poetry and curses into endearments. She did not think (when she learned) my crippled body either funny or repulsive. I had not, before her, to sing the refrain of Quasimodo or He Who Gets Slapped. Do not, I urge you, make light of love-affairs whose inspiration is infernal rather than of celestial gentleness. Pluto was as true a lover as the lord of Olympus, and helped to fertilize the earth; whereas Jove, poor wretch, could go about only as a swan or a shower of gold; and I thank you for your kind attention on this subject.

Molly and I planned the whole thing, of course. (Didn't it strike you that in our thrust-and-parry at the Close we were just a little too much at each other's throats? That she was a little too quick with flat insults and I with elaborate barbs?)

The ironical part was that I was the real heir, yet there was nothing we could do about it except what we did. The swine back there had found out about what you call her private witch-cult; he was using it against her as pure, sharp-clawed blackmail to cling to his place; and if he were dislodged he would dislodge her. If I were to regain the estate—as I was resolved to do—and if I were to regain her for my lawful wife so that we could live without furtiveness in our mutual interests—as I was also resolved to do—I had to kill him and make it look like suicide.

There you have it. Molly could not bring herself to murder: whereas I, with the proper concentration, can bring myself to anything. I say no word of the fact that I owed him something, and when I saw what he had grown into after his pious beginnings I knew what makes Puritans and why they have been wiped from the earth.

The crime was timed to take place at some time on the night it did: I could not lay my plans any more closely than that. It could not take place before then, because I must not *appear* at the Close or risk showing myself prematurely; and the fellow could hardly be expected to commit suicide until he knew the weight of evidence against him. You know the admirable opportunity afforded me when he walked into that garden during the comparison of the fingerprints.

Now, my friend, a word of congratulation to you. You took an impossible crime; and, in order to make Knowles confess, you spun out of sticks and stones and rags and bones a perfectly logical and reasonable explanation of the impossible. Artistically I am glad you did so; your hearers would have felt cheated and outraged without it.

Yet the fact is—as you very well know—that there never was an impossible crime.

I simply went up to the fellow; I pulled him down; I killed him by the pool with the clasp-knife you later found in the hedge; and that is all.

Knowles, by either bad or good luck, saw the whole affair from the window of the Green Room. Even then, had I not bungled the whole affair with my one great error, the scheme would have been doubly secure. Knowles not only swore to the world that it was suicide: he went out of his way to give me a gratuitous alibi which astonished me not a little. For he, as you have observed, always disliked and distrusted the late incumbent; he never really believed the man was a Farnleigh; and he would have gone to the gallows rather than admit that the real John Farnleigh had killed the fraudulent one who had stolen his patrimony.

I killed the fellow, of course, minus my artificial legs. That was only common sense, since I can move with rapidity and ease only on my leather pads; and in the artificial legs I could not have bent down so as not to be seen by anybody behind those waist-high hedges. The hedges afforded an admirable screen, as well as innumerable alleys of escape in case of danger. In the event that anybody should see me, I took along under my coat the sinister-looking Janus-mask from the attic.

I came on him, actually, from the north side of the house: that is, from the direction of the new wing. I must, I think, have been a sufficiently unnerving sight. It so paralyzed our impostor that I pulled him down before he could move or speak. The strength developed in my arms and shoulders through these years, doctor, is not negligible.

Afterwards, regarding this part of it—the attack on him—the testimony of Nathaniel Burrows gave me a few uneasy moments. Burrows was standing at the garden door some thirty-odd feet away; and, as he himself admits, his eyesight is not good in semi-darkness. He saw unusual occurrences which he could not explain even in his own mind. He could not see me, since waist-high hedges intervened; yet the victim's behaviour worried him. Read over his testimony again and you will see what I mean. He concludes: "I cannot give an exact description of the movements he made. It was as though something had got hold of his feet."

And something had.

Nevertheless, this danger was negligible compared to what Welkyn almost saw from the dining-room a few seconds after the killing. Doubtless it has been apparent to you that what Welkyn saw, through one of the lower glass panels of the French window, was your obedient servant. It was foolhardy of me to let anyone get so much as a fleeting glimpse of me, but at that time (as you shall see) I was upset over the ruin of my plan; and, fortunately, I had my mask on.

His actual glimpse of me was not so dangerous as the interpretation of a shade of words—an impression—put on this incident when it came to be discussed next day. Here my old tutor Murray, that eternal trafficker in words, was the offender. In Welkyn's description of the incident Murray caught an echo of what Welkyn was (gropingly and uncertainly) trying to convey. And Murray said to me: "On your homecoming you are greeted by a crawling *legless* something in the garden—"

That was disaster fine and full. It was the one thing which nobody must suspect, the one suggestion which must not be implanted. I felt my face contract, and I know that I lost colour like a spilled jug, and I saw you looking at me. I was foolish enough to flare out at poor old Murray and call him names for a reason which must have been inexplicable to everybody but you.

All the same, I feared that by this time I was finished in any case. I have referred to the colossal blunder I made at the outset, which ruined the case I was attempting to build up. It was this:

I used the wrong knife.

What I had intended to use was a common clasp-knife I had bought for the purpose. (I took this one out of my pocket and showed it to you next day, pretending it was my own knife.) I then intended to press his hand on it and leave it by the pool, completing the picture of suicide.

What I actually found in my hand, when it was too late to draw back, was my own clasp-knife—the knife I have owned since I was a boy—the

knife a thousand people have seen in my hand in America, with Madeline
Dane's name cut into the blade. You remember that your most diligent
efforts could not trace that knife to the impostor. But you would have
traced it to me fast enough.

It was all the worse because, on the very night of the murder, I had
gone so far as to mention this same knife to the group in the library. In
telling my story of the affair aboard the *Titanic,* I told how I had met the
real Patrick Gore, how we had fought at sight, and how I had been with
difficulty prevented from going for him with my clasp-knife. A surer
indication of character and weapon it would be difficult to beat. It came
of trying to make too artistic a lie, and of telling all the truth except the
part you mean to suppress. I warn you against the practice.

So here was I, with the infernal thing in my gloved hand by the pool,
after pressing his fingerprints on it; and people running towards me. I was
compelled to make a snap-decision. I dared not leave the knife. So I
wrapped it in my handkerchief and put it into my pocket.

Welkyn saw me when I went to regain my harness at the north side of
the house. I therefore thought it best to say I had been at the south side. I
didn't dare carry the knife about with me, so I had to hide it until I could
find an opportunity to get it away undetected. And I maintain that,
theoretically, I chose an undetectable hiding-place. Your Sergeant Burton
acknowledges that except for one chance in a million he would never
have found the knife in the hedge without systematically rooting up every
foot of hedge in the whole garden.

Were the Parcae, do you say, giving me some particularly nasty
breaks? Oh, I don't know. It is true that I was obliged to alter my whole
plan at the outset and express a belief in murder. Yet Knowles, with noble
instincts of sacrifice, straightway provided me with an alibi; he conveyed
a hint before I had left the house that night; and I was ready for you next
day.

The rest of it is simply indicated. Molly insisted on trying to make our
case better by stealing the Thumbograph, once I had privately made it
clear that this must be murder: for, you observe, *I* could not be accused of
stealing a Thumbograph with evidence of my own identity. We were
going to return it anyway, and with double quickness when it was
discovered to be a dummy.

Molly acted well all the way through, don't you think? That little scene
in the garden just after the discovery of the body ("Damn him for being
right!") had been carefully rehearsed beforehand. Interpreted, it was
meant to convey that I had been right when I said before all the company
she had never been really in love with her husband (another rehearsed
scene), and that she had always been in love with an image of me. We
could not have the widow *too* inconsolable, you know. We could not

have her so prostrated with grief that she might be expected to retain an enmity towards me forever. It was a far-sighted plan, directed towards bringing us together when animosities had been smoothed down in the future—and yet how we wrecked it!

For there was that final unfortunate business next day, when Betty Harbottle caught me tinkering with the automaton in the attic. I must mutter *mea culpa* again. As a matter of strict fact, I had gone up to the attic to get the Thumbograph. But it suddenly occurred to me, when I saw the hag, that I could bring her to life at last. As a boy I knew her secret; but at that time I had not been small enough to get inside the box. So nothing would do but that I must tinker about with it, like a respectable husband with a respectable clock in a respectable attic.

Molly, finding me gone an unconscionable time, came upstairs. She was just in time to find Betty Harbottle investigating the book-closet. And at this time I was actually inside the automaton.

Molly, I honestly believe, thought that I would deal with the little girl as I had dealt with another person. Molly saw that Betty was inside and locked the door. But I had no wish to hurt her. The girl could not, of course, see me: yet I was most badly afraid she would see my harness, propped into the corner behind the machine. I think you know what happened. Fortunately it was not necessary to hurt her; a few movements sufficed; though I could have sworn she saw my eyes through the peep-holes in the automaton. Afterwards Molly and I were in no vast danger. Had you pressed us too hard as to our whereabouts at the time, we should simply have provided each other with a reluctant and grudging alibi. Still, it was a mistake to forget that girl's apron—the hag's claws tore it off as part of the pantomime—and leave it behind when we cleared out.

Well, I had been foolish; and there you are. I saw as soon as the day after the murder that I was, in the simple phrase, for it. You found the knife. Though I made light of it as one the impostor had taken from me years ago, and though Murray assisted me with some unconsciously helpful suggestions designed to make you suspicious of the knife as a real weapon, I was following you and I knew that you had seen through the absence of legs.

You brought up the subject of Ahriman the Egyptian. Inspector Elliot followed with his questioning of Welkyn about the hopping thing in the garden. You returned with some pressing questions on the subject of witchcraft, and neatly brought Molly into it. I questioned in reply; and you conveyed some suggestive hints. Next you stressed the connection between all these points, beginning with Victoria Daly, passing to the late Patrick Gore's behaviour on the night of his murder, and going on to trace Betty Harbottle to the book-closet in the attic.

Your remarks when you saw the automaton were the penultimate give-away. You intimated that the murderer had been doing something here with the automaton which would betray him; and yet at the same time Betty Harbottle had not seen him at all—in the sense that it was not necessary for the murderer to silence her. I then challenged you to show how the automaton worked. You paid little attention, merely remarking that you supposed the original exhibitor wore the traditional magician's costume. And you concluded with a few words designed to show Molly's private witch-cult was about to be discovered. That was when I pushed the automaton downstairs. Believe me, my friend, I had no thought of damage to your person. But I did definitely want to damage the automaton beyond repair, so that one guess as to how it worked would be as good as another.

The inquest showed two more points next day. Knowles was obviously lying, and you knew it. Madeline Dane knew much more about Molly's doings than we could afford.

I am afraid Molly does not like Madeline. Her scheme was to ensure silence on the latter's part by terrorization, followed by real trouble if it became necessary. Hence Molly's not altogether inspired device of a faked telephone-call purporting to come from Madeline, and asking for the automaton at Monplaisir: she knew Madeline's rooted horror of the machine, and made me promise to bring it to life again for Madeline's edification. I did not do that; I had better fish to fry.

Fortunately for Molly and myself, I was in the garden at Monplaisir when you and the inspector had dinner there with Madeline and Page. I overheard your conversation; and I knew that it was all over as regards your knowing everything—the question was what you could prove. When you and the inspector left the house, I thought it much more profitable to follow you through the wood and listen.

After contenting myself merely with pushing out the harmless old hag by the windows, I went after you. Your conversation, properly interpreted, showed my that what I had feared about your manner of proceeding was correct. I now know fully what you did, though I had more than a glimmer then. I knew your objective: Knowles. I knew my weak link: Knowles. I knew where there was a witness who could hang me: Knowles. I knew that he would be tortured rather than admit under mere ordinary pressure who had committed the crime. But there was one person he could not see touched or even breathed upon: Molly. There was only one way to make him speak. That was to make a garrotte for her neck and tighten the screw by degrees until he could not stand the sight of it any longer. That was what you were going to do; I was intelligent enough to read evidence as well as you; and it occurred to me with some realism that we were done for.

Only one thing was left to us, which was to get away. Had I been the bowelless and altogether unbelievable person you will probably hear described, I should without doubt have decided to kill Knowles as casually as paring an onion. But who could kill Knowles? Who could kill Madeline Dane? Who could kill Betty Harbottle? These are real persons I have known, not dummies to pad out a chapter; and they are not to be treated like stuffed cats at a fair. I was tired and a little ill, to tell you the truth, as though I had got into a maze and could not get out again.

Following you and the inspector, I came to the Close and saw Molly. I told her our only course was to get away. Remember, we believed we had ample time; you and the inspector had intended to go to London that night, and we did not fear disclosure for some hours. Molly agreed it was the only thing to do—I am given to understand that you saw her leaving the Close, with a suitcase in her hand, when you looked down from the windows of the Green Room. I think it was unwise, though, deliberately to let us get away so that we should damn ourselves by quick flight. Such a course is wise, doctor, only if you are certain of nailing the quarry when you want him.

In one respect, to conclude this account, I had difficulty with Molly. She did not find it easy to go without a final word to Madeline. When we were driving away in the car she was filled with fantastic notions (I can say this because the lady knows I love her) for getting back at the "cat" at Monplaisir.

I could not prevent her. We arrived there within a very few minutes, leaving the car in the back lane by Colonel Mardale's old house. We arrived, in short—and stopped to listen. For we were being treated to a very lucid account, heard through the half-open window of the dining-room, of the death of Victoria Daly and the probable character of the witch-mistress responsible for it: it was being delivered by Mr. Page. The automaton was still there; and I pushed it back into the coal-house only because Molly wanted to smash it through the windows at Madeline. Such behaviour is childish, no doubt; yet my lady's quarrel with Madeline is of a personal nature—as mine was with the late Patrick Gore; and I tell you that nothing which had occurred so far in the case infuriated her as much as that talk in the dining-room.

I did not know, at the time, that she had brought a pistol with her from Farnleigh Close. I realized this only when she took it out of her handbag and rapped it against the window. Whereupon I realized, doctor, that immediate action was necessary for two reasons: first, that we wanted no women's flaming row at this moment; and, second, that a car (Burrows's) had just stopped at the front of the house. I put Molly under one of my arms and I urged her away with some haste. Fortunately a wireless was going inside and we escaped detection. It was, I am convinced, only a subsequent love-scene of outstanding incoherence—a scene taking place in the window—which caused her to escape my vigilance and fire into the dining-room as we were about to leave. My lady is a good shot and she had no intention whatever of hitting anyone; she wishes me to say that she meant it merely as a comment on poor Madeline's morals, and that she would jolly well do it again.

I stress these unimportant and even ludicrous goings-on, in conclusion, for one very good reason: the reason with which I began. I do not want you to think that we went away in an atmosphere of high tragedy under the dark mutterings of the gods. I do not want you to think that nature held its breath at the evil of our passing. For I think, doctor—I rather think—that in order to make Knowles confess you must have deliberately painted Molly's character as much more stiff with wicked impulse than it really is.

She is not crafty; she is the reverse of crafty. Her private witch-cult was not the coldly intellectual effort of a woman interested in watching minds writhe; she is the reverse of coldly intellectual, and well you know it. She did what she did because she liked it. She will, I trust, continue to like it. To speak of her as though she killed Victoria Daly is nonsense; and anything concerning the woman near Tunbridge Wells is so cloudy as to be beyond proof or even accusation. That she has much of the Lower Plane in her nature I concede, as I have in mine; but what else? Our departure from Kent and from England was not, as I have tried to indicate, a curtain to a Morality Play. It was very much like the jumbled rush of the ordinary family to the seaside, where father cannot remember what he did with the tickets and mother is certain she left the light burning in the bathroom. A similar haste and overset, I suspect, attended the departure of Mr. and Mrs. Adam from a more spacious garden; and this, the king may say without denial from Alice, is the oldest rule in the book.

Yours sincerely,
John Farnleigh (whilom Patrick Gore).

THE CASE OF THE
CONSTANT SUICIDES

I

The 9:15 train for Glasgow pulled out of Euston half an hour late that night, and forty minutes after the sirens had sounded.

When the sirens went, even the dim blue lights along the platform were extinguished.

A milling, jostling, swearing crowd, mainly in khaki, groped about the platform, its shins and knuckles barked by kit and luggage, its hearing deadened by the iron coughing of engines. Lost in it was a youngish professor of history, who was trying to find his sleeping compartment on the Glasgow train.

Not that anyone had cause for apprehension. It was only the first of September, and the heavy raiding of London had not yet begun. We were very young in those days. An air-raid alert meant merely inconvenience, with perhaps one lone raider droning somewhere, and no barrage.

But the professor of history, Alan Campbell (M.A., Oxon.; Ph.D., Harvard) bumped along with unacademic profanity. The first-class sleepers appeared to be at the head of a long train. He could see a porter, with much luggage, striking matches at the open door of a carriage, where names were posted on a board opposite the numbers of the compartments assigned to them.

Striking a match in his turn, Alan Campbell discovered that the train appeared to be full and that his own compartment was number four.

He climbed in. Dim little lighted numerals over each door in the corridor showed him the way. When he opened the door of his compartment, he felt distinctly better.

This, he thought, was really first-rate in the way of comfort. The compartment was a tiny metal room, green-painted, with a single berth, nickel washbasin, and a long mirror on the door communicating with the next compartment. Its blackout consisted of a sliding shutter which sealed the window. Though it was intensely hot and close, he saw over the berth a metal ventilator which you could twist to let in air.

Pushing his suitcase under the berth, Alan sat down to get his breath. His reading matter, a Penguin novel and a copy of the *Sunday Watchman*, lay beside him. He eyed the newspaper, and his soul grew dark with bile.

"May he perish in the everlasting bonfire!" Alan said aloud, referring to his only enemy in this world. "May he—"

Then he checked himself, remembering that he ought to remain in a good temper. After all, he had a week's leave; and, though no doubt his mission was sad enough in a formal way, still it was in the nature of a holiday.

Alan Campbell was a Scot who had never in his life set foot in Scotland. For that matter, except for his years at the American Cambridge and a few visits to the Continent, he had never been out of England. He was thirty-five: bookish, serious-minded though not without humor, well-enough looking but perhaps already inclined toward stodginess.

His notions of Scotland were drawn from the novels of Sir Walter Scott or, if he felt in a frivolous mood, John Buchan. Added to this was a vague idea of granite and heather and Scottish jokes—which last he rather resented, showing himself no true Scot in spirit. Now he was at last going to see for himself. And if only—

The sleeping-car attendant knocked at the door, and put his head in.

"Mr. Campbell?" he inquired, consulting the little imitation ivory card on the door, on which names could be written with a pencil and rubbed out.

"Dr. Campbell," said Alan, not without stateliness. He was still young enough to get a thrill at the newness and unexpectedness of the title.

"What time would you like to be called in the morning, sir?"

"What time do we get to Glasgow?"

"Well, sir, we're *due* in at six-thirty."

"Better call me at six, then."

The attendant coughed. Alan correctly interpreted this.

"Call me half an hour before we do get in, then."

"Yes, sir. Would you like tea and biscuits in the morning?"

"Can I get a proper breakfast on the train?"

"No, sir. Only tea and biscuits."

Alan's heart sank along with his stomach. He had been in such a hurry to pack that he had eaten no dinner, and his inside now felt squeezed up like a concertina. The attendant understood his look.

"If I was you, sir, I should nip out and get something at the buffet now."

"But the train's due to start in less than five minutes!"

"I shouldn't let that worry you, sir. We'll not be starting as soon as that, to my way of thinking."

Yes: he'd better do it.

Ruffled, he left the train. Ruffled, he groped along a noisy and crowded platform in the dark, back through the barrier. When he stood at the buffet, with a slopped cup of tea and some dry sandwiches containing ham cut so thin as to have achieved a degree of transparency, his eye fell again on the *Sunday Watchman*. And bile rose again in his soul.

It has been stated that Alan Campbell had only one enemy in the world. Indeed, except for a fight in his school days in which he had exchanged black eyes and a bloody nose with the boy who later became his best friend, he could not even remember disliking anyone very much.

The man in question was also named Campbell: though he was not, Alan hoped and believed, any relation. The other Campbell lived in a sinister lair at Harpenden, Herts. Alan had never set eyes on him, and did not even know who he was. Yet he disliked him very cordially indeed.

Mr. Belloc has pointed out that no controversy can grow more heated, more bitter (or, to a detached observer, more funny) than a controversy between two learned dons over some obscure point that nobody cares twopence about.

We have all, with glee, seen the thing happen. Somebody writes in a dignified newspaper or literary weekly that Hannibal, when crossing the Alps, passed close to the village of Viginum. Some other erudite reader then writes in to say that the name of the village was not Viginum, but Biginium. On the following week, the first writer mildly but acidly deplores your correspondent's ignorance, and begs leave to present the following evidence that it was Viginum. The second writer then says he regrets that an acrimonious note seems to have crept into the discussion, which is no doubt what makes Mr. So-and-So forget his manners; but is under the necessity of pointing out—

And that tears it. The row is sometimes good for two or three months.

Something of a similar nature had dropped with a splosh into Alan Campbell's placid life.

Alan, a kindly soul, had meant no offense. He sometimes reviewed historical works for the *Sunday Watchman*, a newspaper very similar to the *Sunday Times* or the *Observer*.

In the middle of June this paper had sent him a book called, *The Last Days of Charles the Second*, a weighty study of political events between 1680 and 1685, by K. I. Campbell (M.A., Oxon.). Alan's review of this appeared on the following Sunday, and his sin lay in the following words, toward the end of the notice.

> "It cannot be said that Mr. Campbell's book throws any fresh light on the subject; and it is not, indeed, free from minor blemishes. Mr. Campbell surely cannot believe that Lord William Russell was ignorant of the Rye House Plot. Barbara Villiers, Lady Castlemaine, was created Duchess of Cleveland in 1670: not, as the printer has it, 1680. And what is the reason for Mr. Campbell's extraordinary notion that this lady was 'small and auburn-haired'?"

Alan sent in his copy on Friday, and forgot the matter. But in the issue nine days later appeared a letter from the author dated at Harpenden, Herts. It concluded:

> "May I say that my authority for what your reviewer considers this 'extraordinary' notion is Steinmann, the lady's only biographer. If your reviewer is unfamiliar with this work, I suggest that a visit to the British Museum might repay his trouble."

This riled Alan considerably.

> "While I must apologize for drawing attention to so trivial a matter (he wrote), and thank Mr. Campbell for his courtesy in drawing my attention to a book with which I am already familiar, nevertheless, I think a visit to the British Museum would be less profitable than a visit to the National Portrait Gallery. There Mr. Campbell will find a portrait, by Lely, of this handsome termagent. The hair is shown as jet-black, the proportions as ample. It might be thought that a painter would flatter his subject. But it cannot be thought that he would turn a blonde into a brunette, or depict any court lady as fatter than she actually was."

That, Alan thought, was rather neat. And not far from devastating either.

But the snake from Harpenden now began to hit below the belt. After a discussion of known portraits, he concluded:

> "Your reviewer, incidentally, is good enough to refer to this lady as a 'termagent.' What are his reasons for this? They appear to be that she had a temper and that she liked to spend money. When any man exhibits astounded horror over these two qualities in a woman, it is permissible to inquire whether he has ever been married."

This sent Alan clear up in the air. It was not the slur on his historical knowledge that he minded: it was the implication that he knew nothing about women—which, as a matter of fact, was true.

K. I. Campbell, he thought, was in the wrong; and knew it; and was now, as usual, trying to cloud the matter with side issues. His reply blistered the paper, the more so as the controversy caught on with other readers.

Letters poured in. A major wrote from Cheltenham that his family had for generations been in possession of a painting, said to be that of the Duchess of Cleveland, which showed the hair as medium brown. A savant from the Athenaeum wanted them to define their terms, saying what proportions they meant by "ample," and in what parts of the body, according to the standards of the present day.

"Bejasus," said the editor of the *Sunday Watchman*, "it's the best thing we've had since Nelson's glass eye. Leave 'em to it."

Throughout July and August the row continued. The unfortunate mistress of Charles the Second came in for almost as much notoriety as she had known in the days of Samuel Pepys. Her anatomy was discussed in some detail. The controversy was entered, though not clarified, by another savant named Dr. Gideon Fell, who seemed to take a malicious delight in confusing the two Campbells, and mixing everybody up.

The editor himself finally called a halt to it. First, because the anatomical detail now verged on the indelicate; and, second, because the parties to the dispute had grown so confused that nobody knew who was calling whom what.

But it left Alan feeling that he would like to boil K. I. Campbell in oil.

For K. I. Campbell appeared every week, dodging like a sharpshooter and always stinging Alan. Alan began to acquire a vague but definite reputation for ungallant conduct, as one who has traduced a dead woman and might traduce any lady of his acquaintance. K. I. Campbell's last letter more than hinted at this.

His fellow members of the faculty joked about it. The undergraduates, he suspected, joked about it. "Rip" was one term; "rounder" another.

He had breathed a prayer of relief when the debate ended. But even now, drinking slopped tea and eating dry sandwiches in a steamy station buffet, Alan stiffened as he turned over the pages of the *Sunday Watchman*. He feared that his eye might light on some reference to the Duchess of Cleveland, and that K. I. Campbell might have sneaked into the columns again.

No. Nothing. Well, at least that was a good omen to start the journey.

The hands of the clock over the buffet stood at twenty minutes to ten.

In sudden agitation Alan remembered his train. Gulping down his tea (when you are in a hurry there always seems to be about a quart of it, boiling hot), he hurried out into the blackout again. For the second time he took some minutes to find his ticket at the barrier, searching through every pocket before he found it in the first one. He wormed through crowds and luggage trucks, spotted the right platform after some difficulty, and arrived back at the door of his carriage just as doors were slamming all along the train, and the whistle blew.

Smoothly gliding, the train moved out.

Off on the great adventure, then. Alan, pleased with life again, stood in the dim corridor and got his breath. Through his mind moved some words out of the letter he had received from Scotland: "The Castle of Shira, at Inveraray, on Loch Fyne." It had a musical, magical sound. He savored

it. Then he walked down to his compartment, threw open the door, and
stopped short.

An open suitcase, not his own, lay on the berth. It contained female
wearing apparel. Bending over it and rummaging in it stood a brown-haired
girl of twenty-seven or twenty-eight. She had been almost knocked sprawling by the opening of the door, and she straightened up to stare at him.

"Wow!" said Alan inaudibly.

His first thought was that he must have got the wrong compartment, or
the wrong carriage. But a quick glance at the door reassured him. There
was his name, Campbell, written in pencil on the imitation ivory strip.

"I beg your pardon," he said. "But haven't you—er—made a mistake?"

"No, I don't think so," replied the girl, rubbing her arm and staring
back at him with increasing coolness.

Even then he noticed how attractive she was, though she wore very
little powder or lipstick, and there was a look of determined severity
about her rounded face. She was five feet two inches tall, and pleasantly
shaped. She had blue eyes, spaced rather wide apart, a good forehead,
and full lips which she tried to keep firmly compressed. She wore tweeds,
a blue jumper, and tan stockings with flat-heeled shoes.

"But this," he pointed out, "is compartment number four."

"Yes. I know that."

"Madam, what I am trying to indicate is that it's my compartment. My
name is Campbell. Here it is on the door."

"And my name," retorted the girl, "happens to be Campbell too. And I
must insist that it's *my* compartment. Will you be good enough to leave,
please?"

She was pointing to the suitcase.

Alan looked, and looked again. The train rattled and clicked over
points, swaying and gathering speed. But what he could not assimilate
easily was the meaning of the words painted in tiny white letters on the
side of the suitcase.

K. I. Campbell. Harpenden.

II

In Alan's mind and emotions, incredulity was gradually giving way to
something very different.

He cleared his throat.

"May I ask," he said sternly, "what the initials 'K.I.' stand for?"

"Kathryn Irene, of course. My first names. But will you *please*—?"

"So!" said Alan. He held up the newspaper. "May I further ask whether you have recently taken part in a disgraceful correspondence in the *Sunday Watchman?*"

Miss K. I. Campbell put up a hand to her forehead as though to shade her eyes. She put the other hand behind her to steady herself on the rim of the washbasin. The train rattled and jerked. A sudden suspicion, and then comprehension, began to grow in the blue eyes.

"Yes," said Alan. "I am A. D. Campbell, of University College, Highgate."

By his proud and darkly sinister bearing, he might have been saying, "And, Saxon, I am Roderick Dhu." It occurred to him that there was something vaguely ridiculous in his position as he inclined his head sternly, threw the paper on the berth, and folded his arms. But the girl did not take it like this.

"You beast! You weasel! You worm!" she cried passionately.

"Considering, madam, that I have not had the honor of being formally introduced to you, such terms indicate a degree of intimacy which—"

"Nonsense," said K. I. Campbell. "We're second cousins twice removed. But you haven't got a beard!"

Alan instinctively put a hand to his chin.

"Certainly I have not got a beard. Why should you suppose that I had a beard?"

"We all thought you had. We all thought you had a beard this long," cried the girl, putting her hand at about the level of her waist. "And big double-lensed spectacles. And a nasty, dry, sneering way of talking. You've got that, though. On top of which, you come bursting in here and knock me about—"

Belatedly, she began to rub her arm again.

"Of all the nasty, sneering, patronizing book reviews that were ever written," she went on, "that one of yours—"

"There, madam, you show a want of understanding. It was my duty, as a professional historian, to point out certain errors, glaring errors—"

"Errors!" said the girl. "Glaring errors, eh?"

"Exactly. I do not refer to the trivial and meaningless point about the Duchess of Cleveland's hair. I refer to matters of real moment. Your treatment of the elections of 1680, if you will excuse my plain speaking, would make a cat laugh. Your treatment of Lord William Russell was downright dishonest. I do not say that he was as big a crook as your hero Shaftesbury. . Russell was merely a muttonhead: 'of,' as it was put at the trial, 'imperfect understanding'; to be pitied, if you like, but not to be pictured as anything except the traitor he was."

"You're nothing," said K. I. Campbell furiously, "but a beastly *Tory!*"

"In reply, I quote no less an authority than Dr. Johnson. 'Madam, I perceive that you are a vile Whig.' "

Then they stood and looked at each other.

Alan didn't ordinarily talk like this, you understand. But he was so mad and so much on his dignity that he could have given points and a beating to Edmund Burke.

"Who are you, anyway?" he asked in a more normal tone, after a pause.

This had the effect of putting Kathryn Campbell again on her dignity. She compressed her lips. She drew herself up to the full majesty of five feet two.

"Though I consider myself under no obligation to answer that question," she replied, putting on a pair of shell-rimmed glasses which only increased her prettiness, "I don't mind telling you that I am a member of the department of history at the Harpenden College for Women—"

"Oh."

"Yes. And as perfectly capable as any man, more so, of dealing with the period in question. Now will you *please* have the elementary decency to get out of my compartment?"

"No, I'm damned if I do. It's not your compartment!"

"I say it is my compartment."

"And I say it's not your compartment."

"If you don't get out of here, *Dr.* Campbell, I'll ring the bell for the attendant."

"Please do. If you don't, I'll ring it myself."

The attendant, brought running by two peals on the bell each made by a different hand, found two stately but almost gibbering professors attempting to tell their stories.

"I'm sorry, ma'am," said the attendant, worriedly consulting his list, "I'm sorry, sir: but there seems to have been a mistake somewhere. There's only one Campbell down here, without even a 'Miss' or a 'Mr.' I don't know what to say."

Alan drew himself up.

"Never mind. Not for the world," he declared loftily, "would I disturb this lady in possession of her ill-gotten bed. Take me to another compartment."

Kathryn gritted her teeth.

"No, you don't, *Dr.* Campbell. I am not accepting any favors on the grounds of my sex, thank you. Take *me* to another compartment."

The attendant spread out his hands.

"I'm sorry, miss. I'm sorry, sir. But I can't do that. There's not a sleeper to be had on the whole train. Nor a seat either, if it comes to that. They're even standing in third class."

"Never mind," snapped Alan, after a slight pause. "Just let me get my bag from under there, and I'll stand up in the corridor all night."

"Oh, don't be silly," said the girl in a different voice. "You can't do that."

"I repeat, madam—"

"All the way to Glasgow? You can't do that. Don't be silly."

She sat down on the edge of the berth.

"There's only one thing we can possibly do," she added. "We'll share this compartment, and sit up all night."

A powerful shade of relief went over the attendant.

"Now, miss, that's very kind of you! And I know this gentleman appreciates it. Don't you, sir? If you wouldn't mind, I'm sure the company'll make it right with you at the other end. It's very kind of the lady, isn't it, sir?"

"No, it is not. I refuse—"

"What's the matter, Dr. Campbell?" asked Kathryn, with icy sweetness. "Are you afraid of me? Or is it that you just daren't face historical fact when it is presented to you?"

Alan turned to the attendant. Had there been room, he would have pointed to the door with a gesture as dramatic as that of a father turning out his child into the storm in an old-fashioned melodrama. As it was, he merely banged his hand on the ventilator. But the attendant understood.

"Then that's all right, sir. Good night." He smiled. "It shouldn't be so unpleasant, should it?"

"What do you mean by that?" Kathryn demanded sharply.

"Nothing, miss. Good night. Sleep—I mean, good night."

Again they stood and looked at each other. They sat down, with mutual suddenness, at opposite ends of the berth. Though they had been fluent enough before, now that the door was closed they were both covered with pouring self-consciousness.

The train was moving slowly: steadily, yet with a suggestion of a jerk, which probably meant a raider somewhere overhead. It was less hot now that air gushed down the ventilator.

It was Kathryn who broke the tension of selfconsciousness. Her expression began as a superior smile, turned into a giggle, and presently dissolved in helpless laughter. Presently Alan joined in.

"Sh-h!" she urged in a whisper. "We'll disturb the person in the next compartment. But we have been rather ridiculous, haven't we?"

"I deny that. At the same time—"

Kathryn removed her spectacles and wrinkled up her smooth forehead.

"Why are you going north, Dr. Campbell? Or should I say Cousin Alan?"

"For the same reason, I suppose, that you are. I got a letter from a man named Duncan, who bears the impressive title of Writer to the Signet."

"In Scotland," said Kathryn, with cutting condescension, "a Writer to the Signet is a lawyer. Really, Dr. Campbell! Such ignorance! Haven't you ever been in Scotland?"

"No. Have you?"

"Well—not since I was a little girl. But I do take the trouble to keep myself informed, especially about my own flesh and blood. Did the letter say anything else?"

"Only that old Angus Campbell had died a week ago; that such few members of the family as could be found were being informed; and could I find it convenient to come up to the Castle of Shira, at Inveraray, for a family conference? He made it clear that there was no question of inheritance, but not quite so clear what he meant by 'family conference.' *I* used it as a good excuse to get leave for a much-needed holiday."

Kathryn sniffed. "Really, Dr. Campbell! Your own flesh and blood!"

And Alan found his exasperation rising again.

"Oh, look here! I'd never even heard of Angus Campbell. I looked him up, through a very complicated genealogy, and found that he's a cousin of my father. But I never knew him, or anybody near him. Did you?"

"Well . . ."

"In fact, I'd never even heard of the Castle of Shira. How do we get there, by the way?"

"At Glasgow, you take a train to Gourock. At Gourock you get a boat across to Dunoon. At Dunoon you hire a car and drive out round Loch Fyne to Inveraray. You used to be able to go from Dunoon to Inveraray by water, but they've stopped that part of the steamer service since the war."

"And what is that in? The Highlands or the Lowlands?"

This time Kathryn's glance was withering.

Alan would not pursue the matter further. He had a hazy idea that in estimating the Lowlands or the Highlands, you just drew a line across the map of Scotland about the middle; that the upper part would be the Highlands, the lower part the Lowlands: and there you were. But now he felt somehow that it could not be quite as simple as this.

"Really, Dr. Campbell! It's in the Western Highlands, of course."

"This Castle of Shira," he pursued, allowing (though with reluctance) his imagination some play. "It's a moated-grange sort of place, I suppose?"

"In Scotland," said Kathryn, "a castle can be almost anything. No: it's not a big place like the Duke of Argyll's castle. Or at least I shouldn't think so from photographs. It stands at the entrance to Glen Shira, a little way off from Inveraray by the edge of the loch. It's rather a slatternly-looking stone building with a high tower.

"But it's got a history. You, as a historian, of course wouldn't know anything about that. That's what makes it all so interesting: the way Angus Campbell died."

"So? How did he die?"

"He committed suicide," returned Kathryn calmly. "Or he was murdered."

The Penguin novel which Alan had brought along was bound in green for a crime thriller. He did not read such things often, but he considered it his duty, sometimes, in the way of relaxation. He stared from this back to Kathryn's face.

"He was—*what?*" Alan almost yelped.

"Murdered. Of course you hadn't heard about that either? Dear me! Angus Campbell jumped or was thrown from a window at the top of the tower."

Alan searched his wits.

"But wasn't there an inquest?"

"They don't have inquests in Scotland. In the event of a suspicious death, they have what is called a 'public inquiry,' under the direction of a man named the Procurator Fiscal. But if they think it's murder, they don't hold the public inquiry at all. That's why I've been watching the Glasgow *Herald* all week, and there's been no report of an inquiry. It doesn't necessarily mean anything, of course."

The compartment was almost cool. Alan reached out and twisted the mouth of the ventilator, which was hissing beside his ear. He fished in his pocket.

"Cigarette?" he offered, producing a packet.

"Thanks. I didn't know you smoked. I thought you used snuff."

"And why," said Alan with austerity, "should you imagine that I used snuff?"

"It got into your beard," explained Kathryn, making motions of intense disgust. "And dropped all over everywhere. It was horrid.—Big-breasted hussy, anyway!"

"Big-breasted hussy? Who?"

"The Duchess of Cleveland."

He blinked at her. "But I understood, Miss Campbell, that you were the lady's particular champion. For nearly two and a half months you've been vilifying my character because you said I vilified hers."

"Oh, well. You seemed to have a down on her. So I had to take the other side, hadn't I?"

He stared at her.

"And this," he said, whacking his knee, "*this* is intellectual honesty!"

"Do you call it intellectual honesty when you deliberately sneered at and patronized a book because you knew it had been written by a woman?"

"But I didn't know it had been written by a woman. I specifically referred to you as 'Mr. Campbell,' and—"

"That was only to throw people off the track."

"See here," pursued Alan, lighting her cigarette with a somewhat shaky hand, and lighting his own. "Let us get this straight. I have no down on women scholars. Some of the finest scholars I've ever known have been women."

"Listen to the patronizing way he says *that!*"

"The point is, Miss Campbell, that it would have made no difference to my notice whether the writer of the book had been a man or a woman. Errors are errors, whoever writes them."

"Indeed?"

"Yes. And for the sake of truth will you now admit to me, strictly in private and between ourselves, that you were all wrong about the Duchess of Cleveland being small and auburn-haired?"

"I most certainly will not!" cried Kathryn, putting on her spectacles again and setting her face into its severest lines.

"Listen!" he said desperately. "Consider the evidence! Let me quote to you for example, an instance I could hardly have used in the newspaper. I refer to Pepys's story—"

Kathryn looked shocked.

"Oh, come, Dr. Campbell! You, who pretend to be a serious historian, actually give any credit to a story which Pepys received at third hand from his hairdresser?"

"No, no, no, madam. You persist in missing the point. The point is not whether the story is true or apocryphal. The point is that Pepys, who saw the lady so often, could have believed it. Very well! He writes that Charles the Second and the Duchess of Cleveland (who was then Lady Castlemaine) weighed each other; 'and she, being with child, was the heavier.' When we remember that Charles, though lean, was six feet tall and on the muscular side, this makes out the lady to be rather a fine figure of a woman.

"Then there is the account of her mock marriage with Frances Stewart, in which she acted the part of the bridegroom. Frances Stewart was herself no flyweight. But is it reasonable to suppose that the part of the bridegoom was enacted by the smaller and lighter woman?"

"Pure inference."

"An inference, I submit, warranted by the facts. Next we have Reresby's statement—"

"Steinmann says—"

"Reresby makes quite clear—"

"*Hey!*" interrupted an exasperated voice from the next compartment, followed by a rapping on the metal door. "*Oi!*"

Both disputants instantly piped down. For a long time there was a guilty silence, broken only by the flying click and rattle of the wheels.

"Let's turn out the light," whispered Kathryn, "and draw the blackout, and see what's going on outside."

"Right."

The click of the light switch appeared to satisfy the disturbed occupant of the next compartment.

Pushing aside Kathryn's suitcase in the dark, Alan pulled back the sliding metal shutter over the window.

They were rushing through a dead world, pitch-black except where, along a purple horizon, moved a maze of searchlights. Jack's beanstalk went no higher than these white beams. The white lines shuttled back and forth, in unison, like dancers. They heard no noise except the click of the wheels: not even the waspish, coughing drone of *war-war, war-war,* which marks the cruising bomber.

"Do you think he's following the train?"

"I don't know."

A sense of intimacy, uneasy and yet exhilarating, went through Alan Campbell. They were both crowded close to the window. The two cigarette ends made glowing red cores, reflected in the glass, pulsing and dimming. He could dimly see Kathryn's face.

The same powerful self-consciousness suddenly overcame them again. They both spoke at the same time, in a whisper.

"The Duchess of Cleveland—"

"Lord William Russell—"

The train sped on.

III

At three o'clock on the following afternoon, a mellow day of Scotland's most golden weather, Kathryn and Alan Campbell were walking up the hill comprising the one main street in Dunoon, Argyllshire.

The train, due to reach Glasgow at half past six in the morning, actually got there toward one o'clock in the afternoon. By this time they were ravenously, ragingly hungry, but they still got no lunch.

An amiable porter, whose conversation was all but unintelligible to both Campbells, informed them that the train for Gourock left in five minutes. So they piled into this, and were borne lunchless along Clydeside to the coast.

To Alan Campbell it had been a considerable shock when he woke in the morning, tousled and unshaven, to find himself hunched back against the cushions of a railway carriage, and a good-looking girl asleep with her head on his shoulder.

But, once he had collected his scattered wits, he decided that he loved it. A sense of adventure was winging straight into his stodgy soul, and making him drunk. There is nothing like spending the night with a girl, even platonically, to remove a sense of constraint. Alan was surprised and somewhat disappointed, on looking out of the window, to see that the scenery was still the same as it was in England: no granite cliffs or heather yet. For he wanted an excuse to quote Burns.

They washed and dressed, these two roaring innocents, to the accompaniment of a stern debate—carried on through a closed door and above the splash of running water—about the Earl of Danby's financial reconstruction policy of 1679. They concealed their hunger well, even in the train to Gourock. But when they discovered, aboard the squat tan-funneled steamer which carried them across the bay to Dunoon, that there was food to be had below, they pitched into Scotch broth and roast lamb with silence and voracity.

Dunoon, white and gray and dun-roofed, lay along the steel-gray water in the shelter of low-lying, purple hills. It looked like a good version of all the bad paintings of Scottish scenery which hang in so many houses: except that these usually include a stag, and this did not.

"I now understand," Alan declared, "why there are so many of these daubs. The bad painter cannot resist Scotland. It gives him the opportunity to smear in his purples and yellows, and contrast 'em with water."

Kathryn said that this was nonsense. She also said, as the steamer churned in and butted the pier sideways, that if he did not stop whistling "Loch Lomond" she would go crazy.

Leaving their suitcases at the pier, they crossed the road to a deserted tourist agency and arranged for a car to take them to Shira.

"Shira, eh?" observed the dispirited-looking clerk, who talked like an Englishman. "Getting to be quite a popular place." He gave them a queer look which Alan was afterwards to remember. "There's another party going to Shira this afternoon. If you wouldn't mind sharing the car, it 'ud come less expensive."

"Hang the expense," said Alan, his first words in Dunoon; and it is merely to be recorded that the advertising posters did not drop off the wall. "Still, we don't want to seem uppish. It's another Campbell, I imagine?"

"No," said the clerk, consulting a pad, "this gentleman's name is Swan. Charles E. Swan. He was in here not five minutes ago."

"Never heard of him." Alan looked at Kathryn. "That's not the heir to the estate, by any chance?"

"Nonsense!" Kathryn said. "The heir is Dr. Colin Campbell, Angus's first brother."

The clerk looked still more odd. "Yes. We drove him out there yesterday. Very positive sort of gentleman. Well, sir, will you share Mr. Swan's car, or have one of your own?"

Kathryn intervened.

"We'll share Mr. Swan's car, of course, if he doesn't mind. The idea! Flinging good money about like that! When will it be ready?"

"Half past three. Come back here in about half an hour, and you'll find it waiting. Good day, ma'am. Good day, sir. Thank you."

They wandered out into the mellow sunshine, happily, and up the main street looking into shop windows. These appeared to be mainly souvenir shops, and everywhere the eye was dazzled by the display of tartans. There were tartan ties, tartan mufflers, tartan-bound books, tartan-painted tea sets, tartans on the dolls and tartans on the ash trays—usually the Royal Stewart, as being the brightest.

Alan began to be afflicted with that passion for buying things which overcomes the stoutest traveler. In this he was discouraged by Kathryn, until they reached a haberdasher's some distance up on the right, which displayed in its windows tartan shields (Campbell of Argyll, Macleod, Gordon, MacInstosh, MacQueen) which you hung on the wall. These conquered even Kathryn.

"They're lovely," she admitted. "Let's go in."

The shop bell pinged, but went unheard in the argument which was going on at the counter. Behind the counter stood a stern-looking little woman with her hands folded. In front of the counter stood a tallish, leathery-faced young man in his late thirties, with a soft hat pushed back on his forehead. He was surrounded by a huge assortment of tartan neckties.

"They're very nice," he was saying courteously, "but they're not what I want. I want to see a necktie with the tartan of the Clan MacHolster. Don't you understand? MacHolster. M-a-c, H-o-l-s-t-e-r, MacHolster. Can't you show me the tartan of the Clan MacHolster?"

"There isna any Clan MacHolster," said the proprietress.

"Now look," said the young man, leaning one elbow on the counter and holding up a lean forefinger in her face. "I'm a Canadian; but I've got Scottish blood in my veins and I'm proud of it. Ever since I was a kid, my father's said to me, 'Charley, if you ever go to Scotland, if you ever get to Argyllshire, you look up the Clan MacHolster. We're descended from the Clan MacHolster, as I've heard your granddad say many a time.' "

"I keep telling ye: there isna any Clan MacHolster."

"But there's *got* to be a Clan MacHolster!" pleaded the young man, stretching out his hands. "There could be a Clan MacHolster, couldn't there? With all the clans and people in Scotland? There *could* be a Clan MacHolster?"

"There could be a Clan MacHitler. But there isna."

His bewildered dejection was so evident that the proprietress took pity on him.

"What wad your name be, now?"

"Swan. Charles E. Swan."

The proprietress cast up her eyes and reflected.

"Swan. That'd be the MacQueens."

Mr. Swan seized eagerly at this. "You mean I'm related to the clan of the MacQueens?"

"I dinna ken. Ye may be. Ye may not be. Some Swans are."

"Have you got their tartan here?"

The proprietress showed it to him in a necktie. It was undoubtedly striking, its predominating color being a rich scarlet, and took Mr. Swan's fancy at once.

"Now that's what I call something like it!" he announced fervently, and turned round and appealed to Alan. "Don't you think so, sir?"

"Admirable. Bit on the loud side for a necktie, though, isn't it?"

"Yes, I like it myself," agreed Mr. Swan musingly, holding the tie at arm's length like a painter studying perspective. "Yes. This is the tie for me. I'll take a dozen of 'em."

The proprietress reeled.

"*A dozen?*"

"Sure. Why not?"

The proprietress felt compelled to sound a note of warning.

"They're three-and-saxpence each?"

"That's all right. Wrap 'em up. I'll take 'em."

As the proprietress bustled off through a door at the back of the shop, Swan turned round with a confidential air. He removed his hat out of deference to Kathryn, revealing a mop of wiry mahogany-colored hair.

"You know," he confided in a low voice, "I've traveled a lot in my time; but this is the queerest damn country *I* ever got into."

"Yes?"

"Yes. All they seem to do is run around telling each other Scotch jokes. I dropped into the bar of the hotel down there, and the local comedian was bringing the house down with nothing but Scotch jokes. And there's another thing. I've only been in this country a few hours—got in by the London train this morning—but on four different occasions I've been buttonholed with the same joke."

"We haven't had that experience so far."

"But *I* have. They hear me talk, see? Then they say, 'You're an American, eh?' I say, 'No, Canadian.' But that doesn't stop 'em. They say, 'Have you heard about my brother Angus, who wouldn't even give the bloodhounds a cent?' "

He paused expectantly.

The faces of his listeners remained impassive.

"Don't you get it?" demanded Swan. "Wouldn't even give the bloodhounds a cent. C-e-n-t, s-c-e-n-t."

"The point of the story," replied Kathryn, "is fairly obvious; but—"

"Oh, I didn't say it was *funny*," Swan hastened to assure them. "I'm just telling you how queer it sounds. You don't find mothers-in-law running around telling each other the latest mother-in-law joke. You don't find the English telling each other stories about the Englishman getting the point of the joke wrong."

"Are the English," inquired Alan with interest, "popularly supposed to do that?"

Swan flushed a little.

"Well, they are in the stories told in Canada and the States. No offense. You know the kind of thing. 'You cannot drive a nail with a sponge no matter how hard you soak it,' rendered as, 'You cannot drive a nail with a sponge no matter how wet it is.' Now, wait! I didn't say *that* was funny either. I only—"

"Never mind," said Alan. "What I really wanted to ask: are you the Mr. Swan who's hired a car to go out to Shira this afternoon?"

A curiously evasive look went over Swan's leathery face, with the fine wrinkles round eyes and mouth. He seemed on the defensive.

"Yes. That's right. Why?"

"We're going out there ourselves, and we were wondering whether you'd mind if we shared the car. My name is Campbell, Dr. Campbell. This is my cousin, Miss Kathryn Campbell."

Swan acknowledged the introductions with a bow. His expression changed, and lit up with good nature.

"Not the least little bit in the world! Only too pleased to have you!" he declared heartily. His light gray eyes quickened and shifted. "Members of the family, eh?"

"Distant ones. And you?"

The evasive look returned.

"Well, since you know what my name is, and that I'm related to the MacHolsters or the MacQueens, I couldn't very well pretend to be a member of the family, could I? Tell me, though." He grew more confidential. "What can you tell me about a Miss or Mrs. Elspat Campbell?"

Alan shook his head, but Kathryn came to the rescue.

"Aunt Elspat, you mean?"

"I'm afraid I don't know anything about her, Miss Campbell."

"Aunt Elspat," replied Kathryn, "isn't really an aunt, and her name isn't Campbell, though they all call her that. Nobody quite knows who she is or where she came from. She just walked in one day, forty years or so ago, and she's been there ever since. Sort of female head of Shira. She must be nearly ninety, and she's supposed to be rather a terror. I've never met her, though."

"Oh," said Swan, but volunteered no more. The proprietress brought him his parcel of neckties, and he paid for it.

"Which reminds me," he went on, "that we'd better get going, if we want to be in time for that car."

After bidding an elaborate farewell to the proprietress, Swan held open the shop door for them.

"It must be a good way out there, and I want to get back before dark; I'm not staying. I suppose they have the blackout up here too? I want a decent night's rest tonight for once. I sure didn't get one on the train last night."

"Can't you sleep on trains?"

"It wasn't that. There was a married couple in the next compartment, having a hell of a row about some dame from Cleveland, and I hardly closed my eyes all night."

Alan and Kathryn cast a quick, uneasy glance at each other, but Swan was preoccupied with his grievance.

"I've lived in Ohio myself; know it well; that's why I listened. But I couldn't get this thing straight. There was some guy named Russell, and another one called Charles. But whether the dame from Cleveland was running around with Russell, or with Charles, or with this woman's husband, I never did make out. You just heard enough so that you couldn't understand anything. I knocked on the wall, but even after they'd turned out the light—"

"Dr. Campbell!" cried Kathryn warningly.

But the murder was out.

"I'm afraid," said Alan, "that that must have been us."

"You?" said Swan. He stopped short in the hot, bright, drowsy street. His eyes traveled to Kathryn's ringless left hand. They seemed to be registering something, as though writing it down.

Then he continued, with such a jerking and obvious change of subject that even his smooth voice added to the obviousness of it.

"They certainly don't seem to be feeling any shortage of food up here, anyway. Look in these grocery store windows! That stuff over there is haggis. It—"

Kathryn's face was scarlet.

"Mr. Swan," she said curtly, "may I assure you that you are making a mistake? I am a member of the department of history at the Harpenden College for Women—"

"It's the first time I ever saw haggis, but I can't say I like the look of it. It can manage to look nakeder than any meat I ever did see. That stuff that looks like slices of boloney is called Ulster fry. It—"

"Mr. Swan, will you *please* give me your attention? This gentleman is Dr. Campbell, of University College, Highgate. We can both assure you—"

Again Swan stopped short. He peered round as though to make sure they were not overheard, and then spoke in a low, rapid, earnest voice.

"Look, Miss Campbell," he said, "I'm broad-minded. I know how these things are. And I'm sorry I ever brought the subject up."

"But—!"

"All that business about my losing sleep was a lot of bunk. I went to sleep just as soon as you turned the light out, and didn't hear a thing afterwards. So let's just forget I ever spoke about it, shall we?"

"Perhaps that would be best," agreed Alan.

"Alan Campbell, do you *dare* . . ."

Swan, his manner soothing, pointed ahead. A comfortable blue five-seater car was drawn up before the tourist office, with a chauffeur in cap, uniform, and leggings leaning against it.

"There's the golden chariot," Swan added. "And I've got a guidebook. Come on. Let's enjoy ourselves."

IV

Past the tiny shipyard, past the Holy Loch, under heavy timber-furred hills, up the rise past Heath Jock, and into the long, straight stretch beside deep Loch Eck, the car sped on.

They took to the driver at once.

He was a burly, red-faced, garrulous man with a singularly bright blue eye and a vast fund of secret inner amusement. Swan sat in front with him, while Alan and Kathryn sat in the rear. Swan began by being fascinated with the driver's accent, and ended by trying to imitate it.

Pointing to a trickle of water down the hillside, the driver said that this was a "wee burn." Swan seized on the words as a good thing. Henceforward water in any form, even a mountain torrent which would have carried away a house, became a wee burn: Swan calling attention to it and experimentally giving the letter "r" a sound like a death rattle or a singularly sustained gargle.

He did this to Alan's intense discomfort, but Alan need not have minded. The driver did not mind. It was as though (say) Sir Cedric Hardwicke were to hear the purity of his English commented on with amusement by Mr. Schnozzle Durante.

Those who regarded Scotsmen as dour or uncommunicative, Alan thought, should have listened to this one. It was impossible to stop him talking. He gave details of every place they passed; and, surprisingly, as it turned out from Swan's guidebook later, with accuracy.

His usual work, he said, was driving a hearse. He entertained them with a description of the many fine funerals, to which he referred with modest pride, where he had had the honor of conducting the corpse. And this gave Swan an opportunity.

"You didn't happen to drive the hearse at a funeral about a week ago, did you?"

To their left, Loch Eck lay like an old tarnished mirror among the hills. No splash or ripple stirred it. Nothing moved on the slopes of fir and pine, stretching up to a pate of outcropping rock, which closed it in. What deadened the mind was the quality of utter silence here, of barriers against the world, and yet of awareness behind it: as though these hills still hid the shaggy shields.

The driver was silent for so long a time, his big red hands gripped round the wheel, that they thought he could not have heard or understood. Then he spoke.

"That'd be auld Campbell of Shira," he stated.

"Aye," said Swan, with perfect seriousness. The thing was infectious: Alan had several times been on the point of saying this himself.

"And ye'll be Campbells tu, I'm thinkin'?"

"Those two are," said Swan, jerking his head toward the two in the rear. "I'm a MacHolster, sometimes called MacQueen."

The driver turned round and looked very hard at him. But Swan was perfectly sincere.

"I drove one of 'em yesterday," said the driver grudgingly. "Colin Campbell it was; and as guid a Scot as masel', for a' he talked like an Englishman."

His face darkened.

"Such bletherin' and blusterin' ye niver heard! An atheist forbye, and thocht nae shame tae admit it! Cau'd me ivery name he caud lay his tongue tu," glowered the driver, "for sayin' Shira is no' a canny place. And it isna either."

Again there was a heavy silence, while the tires sang.

"Canny, I suppose," observed Alan, "being the opposite of uncanny?"

"Aye."

"But if Shira isn't a canny place, what's wrong with it? Ghosts?"

The driver whacked the steering wheel with a slow and dogged hand, as though he were setting a stamp on it.

"I'm no' sayin' it's ghaists, I'm no sayin' *wha'* it is. I'm sayin' it isna a canny place, and it isna."

Swan, after whistling between his teeth, opened the guidebook. While the car jolted, and the long afternoon light grew less golden, he turned to the section devoted to Inveraray. He read aloud:

"Before entering the town by the main road, the traveler should look (left) at the *Castle of Shira*.

"This building contains no features of architectural interest. It was built toward the end of the sixteenth century, but has since been added to. It will be recognized by its round tower, with a conical slate roof, at the south-eastern corner. This tower, sixty-two feet high, is thought to have been the first effort in an ambitious scheme of building which was later abandoned.

"Tradition has it that in 1692, following the massacre of Glencoe in February of that year—"

Swan interrupted himself.

"Hold on!" he said, rubbing his jaw. "I've heard about the massacre of Glencoe. I remember, when I was at school in Detroit . . . What the devil's the matter with *him?* Hoy!"

The driver, his good humor now restored, was bending back and forth over the wheel in paroxysms of silent inner amusement, so that tears stood in his eyes.

"What is it, governor?" demanded Swan. "What's wrong?"

The driver choked. His inner mirth seemed like torture.

"I *thocht* ye were an American," he declared. "Tell me, noo. Hae ye heard aboot ma brither Angus, who wadna e'en gie the bluid-hoonds a cent?"

Swan smote his forehead.

"Man, dinna ye see it? Hae ye no sense o' humor? C-e-n-t, cent; s-c-e-n-t, scent."

"Curiously enough," said Swan, "I do see it. And I'm not an American; I'm a Canadian, even if I did go to school in Detroit. If anybody Brother-Anguses me again today, I'll slaughter him. Which reminds me. (Stop chortling, can't you? Preserve a proper Scottish gravity!)

"But about this massacre of Glencoe. We acted it out in a play at achool long ago. Somebody massacred somebody. What I can't remember is whether the MacDonalds killed the Campbells, or the Campbells killed the MacDonalds."

It was Kathryn who answered him.

"The Campbells killed the MacDonalds, of course," she returned. "I say: they're not still touchy about it in these parts, are they?"

The driver, wiping the tears out of his eyes and becoming stern again, assured her that they weren't.

Swan opened the book again.

"Tradition has it that in 1692, following the massacre of Glencoe in February of that year, Ian Campbell, a soldier in the troop of Campbell of Glenlyon, was so embittered by remorse that he committed suicide by leaping from the topmost window of the tower, dashing out his brains on the pavingstones below."

Swan looked up.
"That isn't what happened to the old man the other day?"
"Aye."

"Another tradition is that this suicide was not caused by remorse, but by the 'presence' of one of his victims, whose mangled body pursued him from room to room, until he had no alternative to keep it from touching him except to—"

Swan shut up the book with a snap. "I think that's enough," he added. His eyes narrowed, and his voice grew soft. "What happened, by the way? The old man didn't sleep up at the top of the tower, did he?"

But the driver was not to be drawn. Ask no questions, his bearing intimated, and you will be told no lies.

"Ye'll be seein' Loch Fyne i' a moment, and then Shira," he said. "Ah! Luke, now!"

Reaching a crossroads, they turned to the right at Strachar. A glimmer of water spread out before them. And not a person there but uttered an exclamation of sheer appreciation.

The loch seemed long, wide, and southwards, to their left, endless. Southwards it curved in sun-silvered widening, between heavy banks, for miles to join the Firth of Clyde.

But northwards it lay landlocked—narrower, timelessly placid, its glimmering water slate-colored—and ran in the shape of a wedge to its end some three miles away. The smooth-molded hills, black or dark purple except where stray sunlight caught a splashing of pale purple heather or the dark green of pine and fir, closed round it as though patted into shape with a tone of underlying brown.

Far across the loch, along the water's edge, they could dimly see the low-lying white houses of a town, partly screened behind a belt of trees. They saw a church steeple; and, on the dominating hill above, a dot that looked like a watch tower. So clear was the air that even at this distance Alan could have sworn he saw the white houses mirrored in the motionless water

The driver pointed.
"Inveraray," he said.
Their car swept on. Swan was evidently so fascinated that he even forgot to point out wee burns.

The road—a very good one, like all the roads they had seen so far—ran straight along the bank of the loch parallel with its length toward the north. Thus to reach Inveraray, which was on the opposite bank, they would have to drive to the head of the loch, circle round it, and come back on a parallel course to a point opposite where they were now.

This, at least, was what Alan thought. Inverary looked very close now, just across the gleaming water at its narrowest. Alan was leaning back expansively, taking comfort from the vast, strong hills, when the car stopped with a jerk and the driver climbed out.

"Ge' out," he beamed. "Donald MacLeish'll have a boat here, I'm thinkin'."

They stared at him.

"Did you say boat?" exploded Swan.

"Aye."

"But what in Satan's name do you want a boat for?"

"Tae row ye across."

"But the road goes there, doesn't it? Can't you just drive 'way up there, and come round into Inveraray on the other side?"

"Waste petrol when I've got ma arms?" demanded the driver, not without horror. "No si' a fule! Ge' out. It's five, sax miles by the road."

"Well," smiled Kathryn, who seemed to be preserving her gravity only with considerable effort, "I'm sure *I* don't mind a turn on the water."

"Nor me," conceded Swan, "provided somebody else does the rowing. But, my God, man!" He searched the air with gestures. "What's the big idea? It's not your petrol, is it? It belongs to the company, doesn't it?"

"Aye. But the preenciple's the same. Ge' in."

An almost extravagantly solemn trio, with the driver very cheerful at the oars, was ferried across the loch in the hush of early evening.

Kathryn and Alan, their suitcases at their feet, sat in the stern of the boat facing toward Inveraray. It was that hour when the water seems lighter and more luminous than the sky, and there are shadows.

"Brr!" said Kathryn presently.

"Cold?"

"A little. But it's not that." She looked at the driver, now the ferryman. "That's the place, isn't it? Over there, where there's a little landing stage?"

"That's it," agreed the other, craning round to peer over his shoulder. The rowlocks creaked painfully. "It isna much tae luke at; but they do say, mind, that auld Angus Campbell left mair siller than ye caud shake a stick at."

Silently they watched the Castle of Shira grow up and out at them. It was some distance away from the town, and faced the loch. Built of ancient stone and brick painted gray, with a steep-pitched slate roof, it straggled along the water side; Kathryn's word "slatternly" occurred to Alan in connection with it.

Most of all you noticed the tower. Round, and of moss-patched gray stone, it reared up to a conical slate roof at the southeastern angle of the house. On the side facing the loch it appeared to have only one window. This was a latticed window, with two lights, set close up near the roof; and from there to the uneven flagstones which paved the ground in front of the house must have been close to sixty feet.

Alan thought of the sickening plunge from that window, and moved uneasily.

"I suppose," Kathryn hesitated, "it's rather—well, primitive?"

"Hoots!" said the driver, with rich scorn. "They hae the electric light."

"Electric light?"

"Aye. And a bathroom tu, though I'm no' sae sure of that." Again he craned over his shoulder, and his face darkened. "D'ye see the man standin' by the wee pier and lukin' at us? That'll be the Dr. Colin Campbell I was tellin' ye aboot. Practices medicine in Manchester, or some sic heathen place."

The figure by the pier partly blended with the gray and brown of the landscape. It was that of a man short in stature, but very broad and burly, with a dogged, truculent lift to the shoulders. He wore an old shooting coat, with corduroy breeches and leggings, and had his hands thrust into his pockets.

It was the first time in many years that Alan had seen a doctor with a beard and mustache. These, though close-cropped, were untidy and gave an impression of shagginess together with the shaggy hair. Its color was an indeterminate brown, touched with what might have been yellow or more probably gray. Colin Campbell, the first of Angus's two younger brothers, was in his middle or late sixties, but looked younger.

He watched them critically as Alan assisted Kathryn out of the boat, and Swan scrambled after them. Though his manner was not unamiable, there was always a suggestion of a bristle about it.

"And who," he said in a heavy bass voice, "might you be?"

Alan performed introductions. Colin took his hands out of his pockets, but did not offer to shake hands.

"Well," he said, "you might as well come in. Why not? They're all here: the Fiscal, and the law agent, and the man from the insurance company, and Uncle Tom Cobleigh and all. This is Alistair Duncan's doing, I suppose?"

"That's the solicitor?"

"Law agent," corrected Colin, with a ferocious grin which Alan rather liked. "Law agent, when you're in Scotland. Yes. That's what I meant."

He turned to Swan, and his shaggy eyebrows drew together over a pair of leonine eyes.

"What did you say *your* name was? Swan? Swan? I don't know any Swans."

"I'm here," said Swan, as though bracing himself, "at the request of Miss Elspat Campbell."

Colin stared at him.

"Elspat sent for you?" he roared. "*Elspat?* God's wounds! I don't believe it!"

"Why not?"

"Because, barring a doctor or a minister, Aunt Elspat never sent for anything or anybody in her life. The only person or thing she ever wanted to see was my brother Angus and the London *Daily Floodlight*. God's wounds! The old girl's more cracked than ever. Reads the *Daily Floodlight* from cover to cover; knows the names of all the contributors; talks about jitterbugs and God knows what."

"The *Daily Floodlight?*" said Kathryn, with virtuous contempt. "That filthy scandal sheet?"

"Here! Oi! Go easy!" protested Swan. "You're talking about my paper."

It was the turn of all of them to stare at him.

"You're not a reporter?" breathed Kathryn.

Swan was soothing. "Now look," he said with great earnestness. "It's all right. I'm not going to use that bit about you and Doc Campbell sleeping in the same compartment on the train: that is, unless I have to. I only—"

Colin interrupted him with a sudden and unexpected deep-throated bellow of laughter. Colin smote his knee, squared himself, and seemed to be addressing the whole universe.

"A reporter? Why not? Come in and welcome! Why not spread the story all over Manchester and London too? Do us good! And what's this about the two scholars of the family being up to hanky-panky on the train?"

"I tell you—"

"Not another word. I like you for it. God's wounds! I like to see a bit of spirit in the younger generation, the kind *we* used to have. God's wounds!"

He clapped Alan on the back, and put a heavy arm round Alan's shoulders, shaking him. His amiability was as overpowering as his truculence. Then, after roaring all this into the evening air, he lowered his voice conspiratorially.

"We can't put you in the same room here, I'm afraid. Got to keep up some of the proprieties. Let you have adjoining rooms, though. But mind you don't mention this to Aunt Elspat."

"Listen! For the love of—"

"She's a great stickler for the conventions, in spite of being Angus's mistress for forty years; and anyway, in Scotland, she's now got the status of a common-law wife. Come in! Don't stand there making funny faces! Come in! (Throw up those suitcases, Jock, and look sharp about it!)"

"Ma name's not Jock," said the oarsman, jumping up precariously in the boat.

Colin stuck out his bearded chin.

"It's Jock," he retorted, "if I say it's Jock. Just get that through your head, my lad. Do you want any money?"

"Not from you. Ma name—"

"Then that's just as well," said Colin, taking a suitcase under each arm as though they were parcels; "because damn me if I know whether I've got any to give you."

He turned to the others.

"That's the situation. If Angus was murdered, by Alec Forbes or anybody else, or if he fell out of that window by accident, then Elspat and I are rich. Elspat and a hard-working, stonybroke G.P. are both rich. But if Angus committed suicide, I tell you straight we haven't got a penny to bless our names."

V

"**B**ut I understood—" Alan began.

"You understood the old skinflint was rich? Yes! So did everybody else. But it's the same old story." Colin's next remarks were darkly mysterious. "Ice cream!" he said. "Tractors! Drake's gold! Trust a skinflint to be a simpleton when he thinks he can get richer.

"Not that Angus was exactly a skinflint, mind. He was a swine, but a decent sort of swine, if you know what I mean. He helped me when I needed it, and he'd have helped our other brother too, if anybody'd known where to find the bounder after he got into trouble.

"Well, what are we all standing here for? Get on into the house! You—where's *your* suitcase?"

Swan, who had been vainly attempting to get in a word edgeways throughout this, gave it up for the moment as a bad job.

"I'm not staying, thanks very much," Swan replied. He turned to the driver. "You'll wait for me?"

"Aye. I'll wait."

"Then that's settled," roared Colin. "Here—you—Jock. Get round to the kitchen and tell 'em to give you a half. Angus's best whisky, mind. The rest of you, follow me."

Leaving behind them a man passionately announcing to the air that his name was not Jock, they followed Colin to the arched doorway. Swan, who appeared to have something on his mind, touched Colin's arm.

"Look," he said. "It's none of my business, but are you sure you know what you're doing?"

"Know what I'm doing? How?"

"Well," said Swan, pushing his soft gray hat to the back of his head, "I've heard the Scotch were booze-histers, of course; but this beats anything I ever expected. Is half a pint of whisky at one shot your usual tipple in these parts? He won't be able to see the road on the way back, will he?"

"A half, you ruddy Sassenach, is a small whisky. And you!" Colin now got behind Kathryn and Alan, and shooed them ahead of him. "You must have something to eat. Got to keep your strength up."

The hall into which he led them was spacious, but rather musty; and it smelt of old stone. They could make out little in the semi-gloom. Colin opened the door of a room on the left.

"Wait in there, you two," he ordered. "Swan, my lad, you come with me. I'll dig out Elspat. Elspat! *Elspat!* Where the devil are you, Elspat? Oh: and if you hear anybody arguing in the back room, that's only Duncan the law agent, and Walter Chapman from the Hercules Insurance Company."

Alone, Alan and Kathryn found themselves in a long but rather low-ceilinged room with a faintly pervading odor of damp oilcloth. A wood fire had been lighted in the grate against the evening chill. By the light of the fire, and the fainter one which struggled in through the two windows facing the loch, they saw that the furniture was horsehair, the pictures large, numerous, and running to broad gilt frames, and the carpet red but faded.

On a side table lay an immense family Bible. A photograph, draped in black crepe, stood on the red tasseled cloth of the overmantel. The resemblance of the man in the photograph to Colin, despite the fact that he was smooth-shaven and had clear white hair, left no doubt who this was.

No clock ticked. They spoke, instinctively, in whispers.

"Alan Campbell," whispered Kathryn, whose face was as pink as confectionery, "you beast!"

"Why?"

"In heaven's name, don't you realize what they're *thinking* about us?

And that dreadful *Daily Floodlight* will print anything. Don't you mind at all?"

Alan considered this.

"Candidly," he startled even himself by replying, "I don't. My only regret is that it isn't true."

Kathryn fell back a little, putting her hand on the table which held the family Bible as though to support herself. He observed, however, that her color was deeper than ever.

"*Dr*. Campbell! What on earth has come over you?"

"I don't know," he was honest enough to admit. "I don't know whether Scotland usually affects people like this—"

"I should hope not!"

"But I feel like taking down a claymore and stalking about with it. Also, I feel no end of an old rip and I am enjoying it. Has anyone ever told you, by the way, that you are an exceedingly attractive wench?"

"Wench! You called me a wench?"

"It is classical seventeenth-century terminology."

"But nothing like your precious Duchess of Cleveland, of course," said Kathryn.

"I acknowledge," said Alan, measuring her with an appraising eye, "a lack of proportions which would have aroused enthusiasm in Rubens. At the same time—"

"Sh-h!"

At the end of the room opposite the windows there was a partly open door. From the room beyond two voices suddenly spoke together, as though after a long silence. One voice was dry and elderly, the other voice was younger, brisker, and more suave. The voices apologized to each other. It was the younger voice which continued.

"My dear Mr. Duncan," it said, "you don't seem to appreciate my position in this matter. I am merely the representative of the Hercules Insurance Company. It is my duty to investigate this claim—"

"And investigate it fairly."

"Of course. To investigate, and advise my firm whether to pay or contest the claim. There's nothing personal in it! I would do anything I could to help. I knew the late Mr. Angus Campbell, and liked him."

"You knew him personally?"

"I did."

The elderly voice, which was always preceded by a strong inhalation through the nose, now spoke as with the effect of a pounce.

"Then let me put a question to you, Mr. Chapman."

"Yes?"

"You would have called Mr. Campbell a sane man?"

"Yes, certainly."

"A man sensible, shall we say," the voice sniffed, and became even more dry before it pounced, "to the value of money?"

"Very much so."

"Yes. Good. Very well. Now, Mr. Chapman, besides his life-insurance policies with your company, my client had two policies with other companies."

"I would know nothing of that."

"But I tell you so, sir!" snapped the elderly voice, and there was a little rap as of knuckles on wood. "He held large policies with the Gibraltar Insurance Company and the Planet Insurance Company."

"Well?"

"Well! Life insurance now constitutes the whole of his assets, Mr. Chapman. The *whole* of them, sir. It was the sole one of his possessions which he was sensible enough not to throw into these mad financial ventures of his. Each one of those policies contains a suicide clause . . ."

"Naturally."

"I quite agree. Naturally! But attend to me. Three days before he died, Mr. Campbell took out still another policy, with your company again, for three thousand pounds. I should—ah—imagine that the premiums, at his age, would be enormous?"

"They are naturally high. But our doctor considered Mr. Campbell a first-class risk, good for fifteen years more."

"Very well. Now that," pursued Mr. Alistair Duncan, law agent and Writer to the Signet, "made a grand total of some thirty-five thousand pounds in insurance."

"Indeed?"

"And each policy contained a suicide clause. Now, my good sir! My very good sir! Can you, as a man of the world, for one moment imagine that three days after he has taken out this additional policy, Angus Campbell would deliberately commit suicide and invalidate everything?"

There was a silence.

Alan and Kathryn, listening without scruple, heard someone begin slowly to walk about the floor. They could imagine the lawyer's bleak smile.

"Come, sir! Come! You are English. But I am a Scotsman, and so is the Procurator Fiscal."

"I acknowledge—"

"You *must* acknowledge it, Mr. Chapman."

"But what do you suggest?"

"Murder," replied the law agent promptly. "And probably by Alec Forbes. You have heard about their quarrel. You have heard about Forbes's calling here on the night of Mr. Campbell's death. You have heard about the mysterious suitcase (or dog carrier, whatever the term is), and the missing diary."

There was another silence. The slow footsteps paced up and down, carrying an atmosphere of worry. Mr. Walter Chapman, of the Hercules Insurance Company, spoke in a different voice.

"But, hang it all, Mr. Duncan! We just can't go on things like that!"

"No?"

"No. It's all very well to say, 'Would he have done this or that?' But, by the evidence, he *did* do it. Would you mind letting me talk for a minute?"

"Not at all."

"Right! Now, Mr. Campbell usually slept in that room at the top of the tower. Correct?"

"Yes."

"On the night of his death, he was seen to retire as usual at ten o'clock, locking and bolting the door on the inside. Admitted?"

"Admitted."

"His body was found early the following morning, at the foot of the tower. He had died of a broken back and multiple injuries caused by the fall."

"Yes."

"He was not," pursued Chapman, "drugged, or overcome in any way, as the post-mortem examination showed. So an accidental fall from the window can be ruled out."

"I rule out nothing, my dear sir. But continue."

"Now as to murder. In the morning, the door was still locked and bolted on the inside. The window (you can't deny this, Mr. Duncan) is absolutely inaccessible. We had a professional steeple jack over from Glasgow to look at it.

"That window is fifty-eight and a quarter feet up from the ground. There are no other windows on that side of the tower. Below is a fall of smooth stone to the pavement. Above is a conical roof of slippery slate.

"The steeple jack is willing to swear that nobody, with whatever ropes or tackle, could get up to that window or down from it again. I'll go into details, if you like—"

"That won't be necessary, my dear sir."

"But the question of somebody climbing up to that window, pushing Mr. Campbell out, and climbing down again; or even hiding in the room (which nobody was) and climbing down afterwards: both these are out of the question."

He paused.

But Mr. Alistair Duncan was neither impressed nor abashed.

"In that case," the law agent said, "how did that dog carrier get into the room?"

"I beg your pardon?"

The bleak voice rolled on.

"Mr. Chapman, allow *me* to refresh *your* memory. At half past nine that night, there had been a violent quarrel with Alec Forbes, who forced himself into the house and even into Mr. Campbell's bedroom. He was—ah—ejected with difficulty."

"All right!"

"Later, both Miss Elspat Campbell and the maid-servant, Kirstie Mac-Tavish, were alarmed for fear Forbes had come back, and might have hidden himself with the intention of doing Mr. Campbell some injury.

"Miss Campbell and Kirstie searched Mr. Campbell's bedroom. They looked in the press, and so on. They even (as I am, ah, told is a woman's habit) looked under the bed. As you say, nobody was hiding there. But mark the fact, sir. Mark it.

"When the door of Mr. Campbell's room was broken open the following morning, there was found under the bed a leather and metal object like a large suitcase, with a wire grating at one end. The sort of case which is used to contain dogs when they are taken on journeys. *Both women swear that this case was not under the bed when they looked there the night before, just before Mr. Campbell locked and bolted the door on the inside.*"

The voice made an elaborate pause.

"I merely ask, Mr. Chapman: how did that case get there?"

The man from the insurance company groaned.

"I repeat, sir: I merely put the question. If you will come with me, and have a word with Mr. MacIntyre, the Fiscal—"

There were steps on the floor beyond. A figure came into the dim front room, ducking to avoid the rather low door top, and touched a light switch beside the door.

Kathryn and Alan were caught, guiltily, as the light went on. A large, brassy-stemmed chandelier, which could have contained six electric bulbs and did contain one, glowed out over their heads.

Alan's mental picture of Alistair Duncan and Walter Chapman was more or less correct, except that the law agent was rather taller and leaner, and the insurance man rather shorter and broader, than he had expected.

The lawyer was stoop-shouldered and somewhat nearsighted, with a large Adam's apple and grizzled hair round a pale bald spot. His collar was too large for him, but his black coat and striped trousers remained impressive.

Chapman, a fresh-faced young-looking man in a fashionably cut double-breasted suit, had a suave but very worried manner. His fair hair, smoothly brushed, shone in the light. He was the sort who, in Angus Campbell's youth, would have grown a beard at twenty-one and lived up to it ever afterwards.

"Oh, ah," said Duncan, blinking vaguely at Alan and Kathryn. "Have you—er—seen Mr. MacIntyre about?"

"No, I don't think so," replied Alan, and began introductions. "Mr. Duncan, we are . . ."

The law agent's eyes wandered over to another door, one facing the door to the hall.

"I should imagine, my dear sir," he continued, addressing Chapman, "that he's gone up into the tower. Will you be good enough to follow me, please?" For the last time Duncan looked back to the two newcomers. "How do you do?" he added courteously. "Good day."

And with no more words he held open the other door for Chapman to precede him. They passed through, and the door closed.

Kathryn stood staring after them.

"Well!" she began explosively. "Well!"

"Yes," admitted Alan, "he does look as though he might be a bit vague, *except* when he's talking business. But that, I submit, is the sort of lawyer you want. I'd back that gentleman any time."

"But, Dr. Campbell—"

"Will you kindly stop calling me 'Dr. Campbell'?"

"All right, if you insist: Alan." Kathryn's eyes were shining with a light of interest and fascination. "This situation is dreadful, and yet . . . Did you hear what they said?"

"Naturally."

"He wouldn't have committed suicide, and yet he couldn't have been murdered. It—"

She got no further, for they were interested by the entrance of Charles Swan from the hall. But this was a Swan with his journalistic blood up. Though usually punctilious about his manners, he had still neglected to remove his hat, which clung in some mysterious fashion to the back of his head. He walked as though on eggshells.

"Is this a story?" he demanded: a purely rhetorical question. "Is this a *story?* Holy, jumping . . . look. I didn't think there was anything in it. But my city editor—sorry; you call 'em news editors over here—thought there might be good stuff in it; and was he right?"

"Where have you been?"

"Talking to the maid. Always go for maids first, if you can corner 'em. Now look."

Opening and shutting his hands, Swan peered round the room to make sure they were alone, and lowered his voice.

"Dr. Campbell, Colin I mean, has just dug out the old lady. They're bringing her in here to put me on view."

"You haven't seen her yet?"

"No! But I've got to make a good impression if it's the last thing I ever do in my life. It ought to be a snip, because the old lady has a proper opinion of the *Daily Floodlight,* which other people," here he looked very hard at them—"don't seem to share. But this may be good for a daily story. Cripes, the old dame might even invite me to stay at the house! What do you think?"

"I think she might. But—"

"So get set, Charley Swan, and do your stuff!" breathed Swan in the nature of a minor prayer. "We've got to keep in with her anyway, because it seems she's the autocrat of the place. So get set, you people. Dr. Campbell's bringing her along here now."

VI

It was unnecessary for Swan to point this out, since the voice of Aunt Elspat could already be heard outside the partly open door. Colin Campbell spoke in a low-voiced bass rumble, of which no words were audible, evidently urging something under his breath. But Aunt Elspat, who had a particularly penetrating voice, took no trouble to lower it.

She said:

"Adjoinin' rooms! Indeed and I'll no' gie 'em adjoinin' rooms!"

The bass rumble grew more blurred, as though in protest or warning. But Aunt Elspat would have none of it.

"This is a decent, God-fearin' hoose, Colin Campbell; and a' yere sinfu' Manchester ways canna mak' it any different! Adjoinin' rooms! *Who's burnin' ma guid electric light at this time o' the day?*"

This last was delivered, in a tone of extraordinary ferocity, the moment Aunt Elspat appeared at the door.

She was a middle-sized, angular woman in a dark dress, who somehow contrived to appear larger than her actual size. Kathryn had suggested her age as "nearly ninety"; but this, Alan knew, was an error. Aunt Elspat was seventy, and a well-preserved seventy at that. She had very sharp, very restless and penetrating black eyes. She carried a copy of the *Daily Floodlight* under her arm, and her dress rustled as she walked.

Swan hastened over to extinguish the light, almost upsetting her as he did so. Aunt Elspat eyed him without favor.

"Swi' on that light again," she said curtly. "It's sae dark a body canna see. Where's Alan Campbell and Kathryn Campbell?"

Colin, now as amiable as a sportive Newfoundland, pointed them out. Aunt Elspat subjected them to a long, silent, and uncomfortable scrutiny, her eyelids hardly moving. Then she nodded.

"Aye," she said. "Ye're Campbells. *Our* Campbells." She went across to the horsehair sofa beside the table which held the family Bible, and sat down. She was wearing, evidently, boots; and not small ones.

"Him that's gone," she continued, her eyes moving to the black-draped photograph, "caud tell a Campbell, our Campbells, i' ten thousand. Aye, if he blacked his face and spoke wi' a strange tongue, Angus wad speir him."

Again she was silent for an interminable time, her eyes never leaving her visitors.

"Alan Campbell," she said abruptly, "what's yere releegion?"

"Well—Church of England, I suppose."

"Ye suppause? Dinna ye ken?"

"All right, then. It *is* Church of England."

"And that'd be your releegion tu?" Aunt Elspat demanded of Kathryn. "Yes, it is!"

Aunt Elspat nodded as though her darkest suspicions were confirmed.

"Ye dinna gang tae the kirk. I kenned it." She said this in a shivering kind of voice, and suddenly got steam up. "Rags o' Popery!" she said. "Think shame tae yereself, Alan Campbell, think shame and sorrow tae yere ain kith and kin, that wad dally wi' sin and lechery i' the hoose of the Scairlet Woman!"

Swan was shocked at such language.

"Now, ma'am, I'm sure he never goes to places like that," Swan protested, defending Alan. "And, besides, you could hardly call this young lady a—"

Aunt Elspat turned round.

"Who's yon," she asked, pointing her finger at Swan, "wha' burns ma guid electric light at this time o' the day?"

"Ma'am, I didn't—"

"Who's yon?"

Taking a deep breath, Swan assumed his most winning smile and stepped in front of her.

"Miss Campbell, I represent the London *Floodlight,* that paper you've got there. My editor was very pleased to get your letter; pleased that we've got appreciative readers all over this broad country. Now, Miss Campbell, you said in your letter that you had some sensational disclosures to make about a crime that was committed here—"

"Eh?" roared Colin Campbell, turning to stare at her.

"And my editor sent me all the way from London to interview you. I'd be very pleased to hear anything you'd like to tell me, either on or off the record."

Cupping one hand behind her ear, Aunt Elspat listened with the same unwinking, beady stare. At length she spoke.

"So ye're an American, eh?" she said, and her eye began to gleam. "Hae ye heard—"

This was much to bear, but Swan braced himself and smiled.

"Yes, Miss Campbell," he said patiently. "You don't need to tell me. I know. I've heard all about your brother Angus, who wouldn't even give the bloodhounds a penny."

Swan stopped abruptly.

He seemed to realize, in a vague kind of way, that he had made a slip somewhere and that his version of the anecdote was not quite correct.

"I mean—" he began.

Both Alan and Kathryn were looking at him not without interested curiosity. But the most pronounced effect was on Aunt Elspat. She merely sat and stared at Swan. He must have realized that she was staring fixedly at the hat still on his head, for he snatched it off.

Presently Elspat spoke. Her words, slow and weighty as a judge's summing up, fell with measured consideration.

"And why should Angus Campbell gie the bluidhoonds a penny?"

"I mean—"

"It wadna be muckle use tae them, wad it?"

"I mean, *cent!*"

"Sent wha'?"

"C-e-n-t, cent."

"In ma opeenion, young man," said Aunt Elspat, after a long pause, "ye're a bug-hoose. Gie'in' siller tae bluidhoonds!"

"I'm sorry, Miss Campbell! Skip it! It was a joke."

Of all the unfortunate words he could have used in front of Aunt Elspat, this was the worst. Even Colin was now glaring at him.

"Joke, is it?" said Elspat, gradually getting steam up again. "Angus Campbell scarce cauld in his coffin, and ye'd come insultin' a hoose o' mournin' wi' yere godless *jokes?* I'll no' stand it! In ma opeenion, ye skellum, ye didna come fra the *Daily Floodlight* at all. Who's Pip Emma?" she flung at him.

"Pardon?"

"Who's Pip Emma? Ah! Ye dinna ken that either, du ye?" cried Aunt Elspat, flourishing the paper. "Ye dinna ken the lass wha' writes the column i' ye're ain paper! Dinna fash yeresel' tae mak' excuses!— What's yere name?"

"MacHolster."

"Wha'?"

"MacHolster," said the scion of that improbable clan, now so rattled by Aunt Elspat that his usually nimble wits had deserted him. "I mean, MacQueen. What I mean is: it's really Swan, Charles Evans Swan, but I'm descended from the MacHolsters or the MacQueens, and—"

Aunt Elspat did not even comment on this. She merely pointed to the door.

"But I tell you, Miss Campbell—"

"Gang your ways," said Aunt Elspat. "I'll no' tell ye twice."

"You heard what she said, young fellow," interposed Colin, putting his thumbs in the armholes of his waistcoat and turning a fierce gaze on the visitor. "God's wounds! I wanted to be hospitable, but there are some things we don't joke about in this house."

"But I swear to you—"

"Now will you go by the door," inquired Colin, lowering his hands, "or will you go by the window?"

For a second Alan thought Colin was really going to take the visitor by the collar and the slack of the trousers, and run him through the house like a chucker-out at a pub.

Swan, breathing maledictions, reached the door two seconds before Colin. They heard him make a speedy exit. The whole thing was over so quickly that Alan could hardly realize what had happened. But the effect on Kathryn was to reduce her almost to the verge of tears.

"What a family!" she cried, clenching her fists and stamping her foot on the floor. "Oh, good heavens, what a family!"

"And wha' ails *you*, Kathryn Campbell?"

Kathryn was a fighter.

"Do you want to know what I really think, Aunt Elspat?"

"Weel?"

"I think you're a very silly old woman, that's what I think. Now throw me out too."

To Alan's surprise, Aunt Elspat smiled.

"Maybe no sae daft, ma dear," she said complacently, and smoothed her skirt. "Maybe no' sae daft!"

"What do you think, Alan?"

"I certainly don't think you should have chucked him out like that. At least, without asking to see his press card. The fellow's perfectly genuine. But he's like the man in Shaw's *The Doctor's Dilemma:* congenitally incapable of reporting accurately anything he see or hears. He may be able to make a lot of trouble."

"Trouble?" demanded Colin. "How?"

"I don't know, but I have my suspicions."

Colin's bark was, obviously, very much worse than his bite. He ran a hand through his shaggy mane of hair, glared, and ended by scratching his nose.

"Look here," he growled. "Do you think I ought to go out and fetch the fellow back? Got some eighty-year-old whisky here, that'd make a donkey sing. We'll tap it tonight, Alan my lad. If we fed him that—"

Aunt Elspat put her foot down with a calm, inplacable arrogance that was like granite.

"I'll no' hae the skellum in ma hoose."

"I know, old girl; but—"

"I'm tellin' ye: I'll no' hae the skellum in ma hoose. That's all. I'll write tae the editor again—"

Colin glared at her. "Yes, but that's what I wanted to ask you. What's all this tommyrot about mysterious secrets you will tell the newspapers but won't tell us?"

Elspat shut her lips mulishly.

"Come on!" said Colin. "Come clean!"

"Colin Campbell," said Elspat, with slow and measured vindictiveness, "du as I tell ye. Tak' Alan Campbell up tae the tower, and let him see how Angus Campbell met a bad end. Let him think o' Holy Writ. You, Kathryn Campbell, sit by me." She patted the sofa. "Du ye gang tae the godless dance halls o' London, noo?"

"Certainly not!" said Kathryn.

"Then ye hae never seen a jitterbug?"

What might have come of this improving conversation Alan never learned. Colin impelled him toward the door across the room, where Duncan and Chapman had disappeared a while ago.

It opened, Alan saw, directly into the ground floor of the tower. It was a big, round, gloomy room, with stone walls whitewashed on the inside, and an earth floor. You might have suspected that at one time it had been used for stabling. Wooden double doors, with a chain and padlock, opened out into the court on the south side.

These now stood open, letting in what light there was. In the wall was a low-arched door, giving on a spiral stone stair which climbed up inside the tower.

"Somebody's always leaving these doors open," growled Colin. "Padlock on the outside, too, if you can believe that! Anybody who got a duplicate key could . . .

"Look here, my lad. The old girl knows something. God's wounds! She's not daft; you saw that. But she knows something. And yet she keeps her lip buttoned, in spite of the fact that thirty-five thousand pounds in insurance may hang on it."

"Can't she even tell the police?"

Colin snorted.

"Police? Man, she can't even be civil to the Procurator Fiscal, let alone the regular police! She had some row with 'em a long time ago—about a cow, or I don't know what—and she's convinced they're all thieves and villains. That's the reason for this newspaper business, I imagine."

From his pocket Colin fished out a briar pipe and an oilskin pouch. He filled the pipe and lit it. The glow of the match illumined his shaggy beard and mustache, and the fierce eyes which acquired a cross-eyed expression as he stared at the burning tobacco.

"As for me . . . well, that doesn't matter so much. I'm an old war horse. I've got my debts; and Angus knew it; but I can pull through somehow. Or at least I hope I can. But Elspat! Not a farthing! God's wounds!"

"How is the money divided?"

"Provided we get it, you mean?"

"Yes."

"That's simple. Half to me, and half to Elspat."

"Under her status as his common-law wife?"

"Sh-h!" thundered the quiet Colin, and looked round quickly, and waved the shriveled match end at his companion. "Slip of the tongue. She'll never put in a claim to be his common-law wife: you can bet your boots on that. The old girl's passion for respectability verges on the morbid. I told you that."

"I should have gathered it, somehow."

"She'll never admit she was more than his 'relative,' not in thirty years. Even Angus, who was a free-spoken devil, never alluded to it in public. No, no, no. The money is a straight bequest. Which we're never likely to get."

He flung away the spent match. He squared his shoulders, and nodded toward the staircase.

"Well! Come on. That is, if you feel up to it. There's five floors above this, and a hundred and four steps to the top. But come on. Mind your head."

Alan was too fascinated to bother about the number of steps.

But they seemed interminable, as a winding stair always does. The staircase was lighted at intervals along the west side—that is, the side away from the loch—by windows which had been hacked out to larger size. It had a musty, stably smell, not improved by the savor of Colin's pipe tobacco.

In daylight that was almost gone, making walking difficult on the uneven stone humps, they groped up along the outer face of the wall.

"But your brother didn't always sleep clear up at the top, did he?" Alan inquired.

"Yes, indeed. Every night for years. Liked the view out over the loch. Said the air was purer too, though that's all my eye. God's wounds! I'm out of condition!"

"Does anybody occupy any of these other rooms?"

"No. Just full of junk. Relics of Angus's get-rich-quick-and-be-happy schemes."

Colin paused, puffing, at a window on the last landing but one.

And Alan looked out. Remnants of red sunset lay still ghostly among the trees. Though they could not have been so very high up, yet the height seemed immense.

Below them, westwards, lay the main road to Inveraray. Up the Glen of Shira, and, farther on, the fork where Glen Aray ascended in deep hills toward Dalmally, were tangled stretches where the fallen timber now rotted and turned gray. It marked the track, Colin said, of the great storm which had swept Argyllshire a few years back. It was a wood of the dead, even of dead trees.

Southwards, above spiky pines, you could see far away the great castle of Argyll, with the four great towers whose roofs change color when it rains. Beyond would be the estate office, once the courthouse, where James Stewart, guardian of Alan Breck Stewart, had been tried and condemned for the Appin murder. All the earth was rich and breathing with names, with songs, with traditions, with superstitions—

"Dr. Campbell," said Alan, very quietly, "how did the old man die?"

Sparks flew from Colin's pipe.

"You ask me? *I* don't know. Except that he never committed suicide. Angus kill himself? Hoots!"

More sparks flew from the pipe.

"I don't want to see Alec Forbes hang," he added querulously; "but he's ruddy well got to hang. Alec 'ud have cut Angus's heart out and never thought twice about it."

"Who is this Alec Forbes?"

"Oh, some bloke who came and settled here, and drinks too much, and thinks he's an inventor too, in a small way. He and Angus collaborated on one idea. With the result usual to collaboration: bust-up. He said Angus cheated him. Probably Angus did."

"So Forbes came in here and cut up a row on the night of the— murder?"

"Yes. Came clear up to Angus's bedroom here, and wanted to have it out. Drunk, as like as not."

"But they cleared him out, didn't they?"

"They did. Or rather Angus did. Angus was no soft 'un, for all his years and weight. Then the womenfolk joined in, and *they* had to search the bedroom and even the other rooms to make sure Alec hadn't sneaked back."

"Which, evidently, he hadn't."

"Right. Then Angus locks his door—*and* bolts it. In the night, something happens."

If his fingernails had been longer, Colin would have gnawed at them.

"The police surgeon put the time of death as not earlier than ten o'clock and not later than one. What the hell good is that? Eh? We know he didn't die before ten o'clock anyway, because that's the last time he was seen alive. But the police surgeon wouldn't be more definite. He said Angus's injuries wouldn't have killed him instantly, so he might have been unconscious but alive for some time before death.

"Anyway, we do know that Angus had gone to bed when all this happened."

"How do we know that?"

Colin made a gesture of exasperation.

"Because he was in his nightshirt when they found him. And the bed was rumpled. And he'd put out the light and taken down the blackout from the window."

Alan was brought up with something of a start.

"Do you know," Alan muttered, "I'd almost forgotten there was a war going on, and even the question of the blackout? But look here!" He swept his hand toward the window. "*These* windows aren't blacked out?"

"No. Angus could go up and down here in the dark. He said blackouts for 'em were a waste of money. But a light showing up in that room could have been seen for miles, as even Angus had to admit. God's wounds, don't ask me so many questions! Come and see the room for yourself."

He knocked out his pipe and ran like an ungainly baboon up the remaining stairs.

VII

Alistair Duncan and Walter Chapman were still arguing.

"My dear sir," said the tall, stoop-shouldered lawyer, waving a pince-nez in the air as though he were conducting an orchestra, "surely it is now obvious that this is a case of murder?"

"No."

"But the suitcase, sir! The suitcase, or dog carrier, which was found under the bed after the murder?"

"After the death."

"For the sake of clearness, shall we say murder?"

"All right: without prejudice. But what I want to know, Mr. Duncan, is: what *about* that dog carrier? It was empty. It didn't contain a dog. Microscopic examination by the police showed that it hadn't contained *anything*. What is it supposed to prove anyway?"

Both of them broke off at the entrance of Alan and Colin.

The room at the top of the tower was round and spacious, though somewhat low of ceiling in comparison to its diameter. Its one door, which opened in from a little landing, had its lock torn out from the frame; and the staple of the bolt, still rustily embedded round the bolt, was also wrenched loose.

The one window, opposite the door, exerted over Alan an ugly fascination.

It was larger than it had seemed from the ground. It consisted of two leaves, opening out like little doors after the fashion of windows in France, and of leaded-glass panes in diamond shapes. It was clearly a modern addition, the original window having been enlarged; and was, Alan thought, dangerously low.

Seen thus in the gloaming, a luminous shape in a cluttered room, it took the eye with a kind of hypnosis. But it was the only modern thing here, except for the electric bulb over the desk and the electric heater beside the desk.

A huge uncompromising oak bedstead, with a double feather bed and a crazy-quilt cover, stood against one rounded wall. There was an oak press nearly as high as the room. Some effort had been made toward cheerfulness by plastering the walls and papering them with blue cabbages in yellow joinings.

There were pictures, mainly family photographs going back as far as the fifties or sixties. The stone floor was covered with straw matting. A marble-topped dressing table, with a gaunt mirror, had been crowded in beside a big roll-top desk bristling with papers. More correspondence, bales of it, lined the walls and set the rocking chairs at odd angles. Though there were many trade magazines, you saw no books except a Bible and a postcard album.

It was an old man's room. A pair of Angus's button boots, out of shape from bunions, still stood under the bed.

And Colin seemed to feel the reminder.

"Evening," he said, half bristling again. "This is Alan Campbell, from London. Where's the Fiscal?"

Alistair Duncan put on his pince-nez.

"Gone, I fear, home," he replied. "I suspect him of avoiding Aunt Elspat. Our young friend here,"—smiling bleakly, he reached out and tapped Chapman on the shoulder—"avoids her like the plague and won't go near her."

"Well, you never know where you are with her. I deeply sympathize with her, and all that; but hang it all!"

The law agent drew together his stooped shoulders, and gloomed down on Alan.

"Haven't we met before, sir?"

"Yes. A little while ago."

"Ah! Yes. Did we—exchange words?"

"Yes. You said, 'How do you do?' and, 'Good-by.' "

"Would," said the law agent, shaking his head, "would that all our social relations were so uncomplicated! How do you do?" He shook hands, with a bony palm and a limp grasp.

"Of course," he went on. "I remember now. I wrote to you. It was very good of you to come."

"May I ask, Mr. Duncan, why you wrote to me?"

"Pardon?"

"I'm very glad to be here. I know I should have made my acquaintance with our branch of the family long before this. But neither Kathryn Campbell nor I can seem to serve any very useful purpose. What did you mean, precisely, by a 'family conference'?"

"I will tell you," Duncan spoke promptly, and (for him) almost cheefully. "Let me first present Mr. Chapman, of the Hercules Life Insurance Company. A stubborn fellow."

"Mr. Duncan's a bit stubborn himself," smiled Chapman.

"We have here a clear case of accident or murder," pursued the lawyer. "Have you heard the details of your unfortunate relative's death?"

"Some of them," Alan answered. "But—"

He walked forward to the window.

The two leaves were partly open. There was no upright bar or support between them: making, when the leaves were pushed open, an open space some three feet wide by four feet high. A magnificent view stretched out over the darkling water and the purple-brown hills, but Alan did not look at it.

"May I ask a question?" he said.

Chapman cast up his eyes with the expression of one who says, "Another one!" But Chapman made a courteous gesture.

"By all means."

Beside the window on the floor stood its blackout: a sheet of oilcloth nailed to a light wooden frame, which fitted flat against the window.

"Well," continued Alan, indicating this, "could he have fallen out accidentally while he was taking down the blackout?"

"You know what we all do. Before climbing into bed, we turn out the light, and then grope across to take down the blackout and open the window.

"If you accidentally leaned too hard on this window while you were opening the catch, you might pitch straight forward out of it. There's no bar between."

To his surprise Duncan looked annoyed and Chapman smiled.

"Look at the thickness of the wall," suggested the man from the insurance company. "It's three feet thick: good old feudal wall. No. He couldn't possibly have done that unless he were staggering drunk or drugged or overcome in some way; and the post-mortem examination proved, as even Mr. Duncan will admit—"

He glanced inquiringly at the lawyer, who grunted.

"—proved that he was none of these things. He was a sharp-eyed, sure-footed old man in full possession of his senses."

Chapman paused.

"Now, gentlemen, while we're all here, I may as well make clear to all of you why I don't see how this can be anything but suicide. I should like to ask Mr. Campbell's brother a question."

"Well?" said Colin sharply.

"It's true, isn't it, that Mr. Angus Campbell was what we'll call a gentleman of the old school? That is, he always slept with the windows closed?"

"Yes, that's true," admitted Colin, and shoved his hands into the pockets of his shooting coat.

"I can't understand it myself," said the man from the insurance company, puffing out his lips. "I should have a head like a balloon if I ever did that. But my grandfather always did; wouldn't let in a breath of night air.

"And Mr. Campbell did too. The only reason he ever took the blackout down at night was so that he should know when it was morning.

"Gentlemen, I ask you now! When Mr. Campbell went to bed that night, this window was closed and its catch locked as usual. Miss Campbell and Kirstie MacTavish admit that. Later the police found Mr. Campbell's fingerprints, *and only Mr. Campbell's fingerprints, on the catch of the window*.

"What he did is pretty clear. At some time after ten he undressed, put on his nightshirt, took down the blackout, and went to bed as usual." Chapman pointed to the bed. "The bed is made now, but it was rumpled then."

Alistair Duncan sniffed.

"That," he said, "is Aunt Elspat's doing. She said she thought it was only decent to redd up the room."

Chapman's gesture called for silence.

"At some time between then and one o'clock in the morning he got up, walked to the window, opened it, and deliberately threw himself out.

"Hang it all, I appeal to Mr. Campbell's brother! My firm want to do the right thing. *I* want to do the right thing. As I was telling Mr. Duncan, I knew the late Mr. Campbell personally. He came in to see me at our Glasgow office, and took out his last policy. After all, you know, it's not *my* money. I'm not paying it out. If I could see my way clear to advise my firm to honor this claim, I'd do it like a shot. But can you honestly say the evidence warrants that?"

There was a silence.

Chapman finished almost on a note of eloquence. Then he picked up his brief case and bowler hat from the desk.

"The dog carrier—" began Duncan.

Chapman's color went up.

"Oh, damn the dog carrier!" he said, with unprofessional impatience. "Can you, sir—can any of you—suggest any reason for the dog carrier to figure in this business at all?"

Colin Campbell, bristling, went across to the bed. He reached underneath and fished out the object in question, which he regarded as though he were about to give it a swift kick.

It was about the size of a large suitcase, though somewhat wider in box shape. Made of dark-brown leather, it had a handle like a suitcase, but two metal clasps on the upper side. An oblong grating of wire at one end had been inset for the purpose of giving air to whatever pet might be carried.

To whatever pet might be carried. . . .

In the mind of Alan Campbell there stirred a fancy so grotesque and ugly, even if unformed, as to come with a flavor of definite evil in the old tower room.

"You don't suppose," Alan heard himself saying, "he might have been frightened into doing what he did?"

His three companions whirled round.

"Frightened?" repeated the lawyer.

Alan stared at the leather box.

"I don't know anything about this man Alec Forbes," he went on, "but he seems to be a pretty ugly customer."

"Well, my dear sir?"

"Suppose Alec Forbes brought that box along with him when he came here. It'd look like an ordinary suitcase. Suppose he came here deliberately, pretending to want to 'have it out' with Angus, but really to leave the box behind. He distracts Angus's attention, and shoves the box under the bed. In the row Angus doesn't remember the suitcase afterwards. But in the middle of the night something gets out of the box . . . ."

Even Alistair Duncan had begun to look a trifle uncomfortable.

And Chapman was eying Alan with an interest which all his skeptical and smiling incredulity could not conceal.

"Oh, see here!" he protested. "What are you suggesting, exactly?"

Alan stuck it out.

"I don't want you to laugh. But what I was actually thinking about was—well, a big spider, or a poisonous snake of some kind. It would have been bright moonlight that night, remember."

Again the silence stretched out interminably. It was now so dark that they could barely see.

"It is an extraordinary thing," murmured the lawyer in his thin, dry voice. "Just one moment."

He felt in the inside breast pocket of his coat. From this he took a worn leather notebook. Carrying it to the window, and adjusting his pince-nez, he cocked his head at an angle to examine one page of the notebook.

" 'Extracts from the statement of Kirstie MacTavish, maidservant,' " he read, and cleared his throat. "Translated from the Doric and rendered into English, listen to this:

> " 'Mr. Campbell said to me and Miss Campbell, "Go to bed and let's have no more nonsense. I have got rid of the blellum. Did you see that suitcase he had with him, though?" We said we had not, as we did not arrive until Mr. Campbell had put Mr. Forbes out of the house. Mr. Campbell said: "I will bet you he is leaving the country to get away from his creditors. But I wonder what he did with the suitcase? He was using two hands to try to hit me when he left." ' "

Duncan peered up over his pince-nez.

"Any comments on that, my dear sir?" he inquired.

The insurance agent was not amused.

"Aren't you forgetting what you pointed out to me yourself? When Miss Campbell and the maid searched this room just before Mr. Campbell retired, they saw no suitcase under the bed."

Duncan rubbed his jaw. In that light he had a corpselike, cadaverous pallor, and his grizzled hair looked like wire.

"True, he admitted. "True. At the same time—"

He shook his head.

"Snakes!" snorted the insurance agent. "Spiders! Dr. Fu Manchu! Look here! Do you know of any snake or spider that would climb out of its box, and then carefully close the clasps of the box afterwards? Both clasps on that thing were found fastened on the following morning."

"That would certainly appear to be a stumbling block," conceded Duncan. "At the same time—"

"And what happened to the thing afterwards?"

"It wouldn't be very pleasant," grinned Colin Campbell, "if the thing were still here in the room somewhere."

Mr. Walter Chapman hurriedly put on his bowler hat.

"I must go," he said. "Sorry, gentlemen, but I'm very late as it is and I've got to get back to Dunoon. Can I give you a lift, Mr. Duncan?"

"Nonsense!" roared Colin. "You're staying to tea. Both of you."

Chapman blinked at him.

"Tea? Great Scott, what time do you have your dinner?"

"You'll get no dinner, my lad. But the tea will be bigger than most dinners you ever ate. And I've got some very potent whisky I've been aching to try out on somebody, beginning with a ruddy Englishman. What do you say?"

"Sorry. Decent of you, but I must go." Chapman slapped at the sleeves of his coat. Exasperation radiated from him. "What with snakes and spiders—*and* the supernatural on top of it—"

If the scion of the MacHolsters could have chosen no more unfortunate word than "joke" in addressing Elspat Campbell, Chapman himself in addressing Colin could have chosen no more unfortunate word than "supernatural."

Colin's big head hunched down into his big shoulders.

"And who says this was supernatural?" he inquired in a soft voice.

Chapman laughed.

"*I* don't, naturally. That's a bit outside my firm's line. But the people hereabouts seem to have an idea that this place is haunted; or at least that there's something not quite right about it."

"Oh?"

"And, if I may say so without offense,"—the insurance agent's eye twinkled—"they seem not to have a very high opinion of you people here. They mutter, 'a bad lot,' or something of the sort."

"We are a bad lot. God's wounds!" cried the atheistical doctor, not without pride. "Who's ever denied it? Not me. But haunted! Of all the . . . look here. You don't think Alec Forbes went about carrying a bogle in a dog box?"

"I don't think, frankly," retorted Chapman, "that anybody carried anything in any box." His worried look returned. "All the same, I should feel better if we could have a word with this Mr. Forbes."

"Where is he, by the way?" asked Alan.

The law agent, who had shut up his notebook and was listening with a dry, quiet smile, struck in again.

"That, too, is an extraordinary thing. Even Mr. Chapman would admit something suspicious—something just a trifle suspicious—about Alec Forbes's conduct. For, you see, Alec Forbes can't be found."

VIII

"**Y**ou mean," asked Alan, "he did go away to escape his creditors?"

Duncan waved the pince-nez.

"Slander. No: I merely state the fact. Or he may be on a spree, which is possible. All the same, it is curious. Eh, my dear Chapman? It is *curious*."

The insurance agent drew a deep breath.

"Gentlemen," he said, "I'm afraid I can't argue the matter any further now. I'm going to get out of here before I break my neck on those stairs in the dark.

"Here is all I am able to tell you now. I'll have a word with the Fiscal tomorrow. He must have decided by now whether he thinks this is suicide, accident, or murder. On what he does must necessarily depend what *we* do. Can I say any fairer than that?"

"Thank you. No, that will suit us. All we ask is a little time."

"But if you're sure this is murder," interposed Alan, "why doesn't your Fiscal take some real steps about it? For instance, why doesn't he call in Scotland Yard?"

Duncan regarded him with real horror.

"Summon Scotland Yard to Scotland?" he expostulated. "My dear sir!"

"I should have thought this would have been the very place for 'em," said Alan. "Why not?"

"My dear sir, it is never done! Scots law has a procedure all its own."

"By George, it has!" declared Chapman, slapping his brief case against his leg. "I've only been up here a couple of months, but I've found that out already."

"Then what are you going to do?"

"While all the rest of you," observed Colin, throwing out his barrel chest, "have been doing nothing but fiddle-faddling about and talking, other people haven't been idle. I won't tell you what I'm going to do. I'll tell you what I *have* done." His eye dared them to say it wasn't a good idea. "I've sent for Gideon Fell."

Duncan clucked his tongue thoughtfully.

"That's the man who—?"

"It is. And a good friend of mine."

"Have you thought of the—ah—expense?"

"God's wounds, can't you stop thinking about money for five seconds? Just five seconds? Anyway, it won't cost you a penny. He's coming up here as my guest, that's all. You offer him money and there'll be trouble."

The lawyer spoke stiffly.

"We all know, my dear Colin, that your own contempt for the monetary side has not failed to prove embarrassing to you at times." His glance was charged with meaning. "You must allow *me,* however, to think of the pounds, shillings and pence. A while ago this gentleman,"—he nodded toward Alan—"asked why this 'family conference' had been summoned. I'll tell you. If the insurance companies refuse to pay up, proceedings must be instituted. Those proceedings may be expensive."

"Do you mean to say," said Colin, his eyes starting out of their sockets, "that you brought those two kids clear up from London just in the hope they'd contribute to the basket? God's wounds, do you want your ruddy neck wrung?"

Duncan was very white.

"I am not in the habit of being talked to like that, Colin Campbell."

"Well, you're *being* talked to like that, Alistair Duncan. What do you think of it?"

For the first time a personal note crept into the law agent's voice.

"Colin Campbell, for forty-two years I've been at the beck and call of your family—"

"Ha ha ha!"

"Colin Campbell—"

"Here! I say!" protested Chapman, so uncomfortable that he shifted from one foot to the other.

Alan also intervened by putting his hand on Colin's shivering shoulder. In another moment, he was afraid, Colin might be running a second person out of the house by the collar and the slack of the trousers.

"Excuse me," Alan said, "but my father left me pretty well off, and if there *is* anything I can do . . ."

"So? Your father left you pretty well off," said Colin. "And well you knew it, didn't you, Alistair Duncan?"

The lawyer sputtered. What he attempted to say, so far as Alan could gather, was 'Do you wish me to wash my hands of this matter?' What he actually said was something like, 'Do you wash me to wish my hands of this matter?' But both he and Colin were so angry that neither noticed it.

"Yes, I do," said Colin. "That's just what I smacking well do. Now shall we go downstairs?"

In silence, with aching dignity, the quartet stumbled and blundered and groped down some very treacherous stairs. Chapman attempted to lighten matters by asking Duncan if he would care for a lift in the former's car, an offer which was accepted, and a few observations about the weather.

These fell flat.

Still in silence, they went through into the sitting room on the ground floor, now deserted, and to the front door. As Colin and the law agent said good night, they could not have been more on their dignity had they been going to fight a duel in the morning. The door closed.

"Elspat and little Kate," said Colin, moodily smoldering, "will be having their tea. Come on."

Alan liked the dining room, and would have liked it still more if he had not felt so ruffled.

Under a low-hanging lamp which threw bright light on the white tablecloth, with a roaring fire in the chimney, Aunt Elspat and Kathryn sat at a meal composed of sausages, Ulster fry, eggs, potatoes, tea, and enormous quantities of buttered toast.

"Elspat," said Colin, moodily drawing out a chair, "Alistair Duncan's given notice again."

Aunt Elspat helped herself to butter.

"A'weel," she said philosophically, "it's no' the fairst time, and it'll no' be the last. He gie'd me notice tu, a week syne."

Alan's intense discomfort began to lighten.

"Do you mean to say," Alan demanded, "that that business wasn't—wasn't serious?"

"Oh, no. He'll be all right in the morning," said Colin. Stirring uncomfortably, he glowered at the well-filled table. "You know, Elspat, I've got a bloody temper. I wish I could control it."

Aunt Elspat then flew out at him.

She said she would not have such profane language used in her house, and especially in front of the child: by which she presumably meant Kathryn. She further rated them for being late for tea, in terms which would have been violent had they missed two meals in a row and emptied the soup over her at the fourth.

Alan only half listened. He was beginning to understand Aunt Elspat a little better now, and to realize that her outbursts were almost perfunctory. Long ago Aunt Elspat had been compelled to fight and fight to get her own way in all things; and continued it, as a matter of habit, long after it had ceased to be necessary. It was not even bad temper: it was automatic.

The walls of the dining room were ornamented with withered stags' heads, and there were two crossed claymores over the chimneypiece.

They attracted Alan. A sense of well-being stole into him as he devoured his food, washing it down with strong black tea.

"Ah!" said Colin, with an expiring sigh. He pushed back his chair, stretched, and patted his stomach. His face glowed out of the beard and shaggy hair. "Now that's better. That's very much better. Rot me if I don't feel like ringing up the old weasel and apologizing to him!"

"Did you," said Kathryn hesitantly, "did you find out anything? Up there in the tower? Or decide on anything?"

Colin inserted a toothpick into his beard.

"No, Kitty-kat, we didn't."

"And please don't call me Kitty-kat! You all treat me as though I weren't grown up!"

"Hoots!" said Aunt Elspat, giving her a withering look. "Ye're *not* grown up."

"We didn't decide on anything," pursued Colin, continuing to pat his stomach. "But then we didn't need to. Gideon Fell'll be here tomorrow. In fact, I thought it was Fell coming when I saw your boat tonight. And when *he* gets here—"

"Did you say Fell?" cried Kathryn. "Not Dr. Fell?"

"That's the chap."

"Not that horrible man who writes letters to the newspapers? *You* know, Alan."

"He's a very distinguished scholar, Kitty-kat," said Colin; "and as such you ought to take off your wee bonnet to him. But his main claims to notoriety lie along the line of detecting crime."

Aunt Elspat wanted to know what his religion was.

Colin said he didn't know, but that it didn't matter a damn *what* his religion was.

Aunt Elspat intimated, on the contrary, that it mattered very much indeed, adding remarks which left her listeners in no doubt about her views touching Colin's destination in the afterlife. This, to Alan, was the hardest part of Elspat's discourse to put up with. Her notions of theology were childish. Her knowledge of Church history would have been considered inaccurate even by the late Bishop Burnet. But good manners kept him silent, until he could get in a relevant question.

"The only part I haven't got quite clear," he said, "is about the diary."

Aunt Elspat stopped hurling damnation right and left, and applied herself to her tea.

"Diary?" repeated Colin.

"Yes. I'm not even sure if I heard properly; it might refer to something else. But, when Mr. Duncan and the insurance fellow were talking in the next room, we heard Mr. Duncan say something about a 'missing diary.' At least, that's how I understood it."

"And so did I," agreed Kathryn.

Colin scowled.

"As far as I can gather,"—he put a finger on his napkin ring, sending it spinning out on the table to roll back to him—"somebody pinched it, that's all."

"What diary?"

"*Angus's* diary, dammit! He carefully kept one every year, and at the end of the year burned it so that nobody should ever find it and know what he was really thinking."

"Prudent habit."

"Yes. Well, he wrote it up every night just before he went to bed. Never knew him to miss. It should have been on the desk next morning. But—at least, so they tell me—it wasn't. Eh, Elspat?"

"Drink your tea and dinna be sae daft."

Colin sat up.

"What the devil's daft about that? The diary wasn't there, was it?"

Carefully, with a ladylike daintiness which showed she knew her manners, Elspat poured tea into the saucer, blew on it, and drank.

"The trouble is," Colin continued, "that nobody even noticed the absence of the diary until a good many hours afterwards. So anybody who saw it lying there could have pinched it in the meantime. I mean, there's no proof that the phantom murderer got it. I might have been anybody. Eh, Elspat?"

Aunt Elspat regarded the empty saucer for a moment, and then sighed.

"I suppause," she said resignedly, "you'll be wantin' the whisky, noo?"

Colin's face lit up.

"Now there," he boomed, with fervency, "there, in the midst of this mess, is the idea that the world's been waiting for!" He turned to Alan. "Lad, would you like to taste some mountain dew that'll take the top of your head off? Would you?"

The dining room was snug and warm, though the wind rose outside. As always in the presence of Kathryn, Alan felt expansive and on his mettle.

"It would be very interesting," he replied, settling back, "to find any whisky that could take the top of my head off."

"Oho? You think so, do you?"

"You must remember," said Alan, not without reason on his side, "that I spent three years in the United States during prohibition days. Anybody who can survive *that* experience has nothing to fear from any liquor that ever came out of a still—or didn't."

"You think so, eh?" mused Colin. "Do you, now? Well, well, well! Elspat, this calls for heroic measures. Bring out the Doom of the Campbells."

Elspat rose without protest.

"A'weel," she said, "I've seen it happen befair. It'll happen again when I'm gone. I caud du wi' a wee nip masel', the nicht bein' cauld."

She creaked out of the room, and returned bearing a decanter nearly full of a darkish brown liquid filled with gold where the light struck it. Colin placed it tenderly on the table. For Elspat and Kathryn he poured out an infinitesimal amount. For himself and Alan he poured out about a quarter of a tumblerful.

"How will you have it, lad?"

"American style. Neat, with water on the side."

"Good! Damn good!" roared Colin. "You don't want to spoil it. Now drink up. Go on. Drink it."

They—or at least Colin and Elspat—were regarding him with intense interest. Kathryn sniffed suspiciously at the liquid in her glass, but evidently decided that she liked it. Colin's face was red and of a violent eagerness, his eyes wide open and mirth lurking in his soul.

"To happier days," said Alan.

He lifted the glass, drained it, and almost literally reeled.

It did not take the top of his head off; but for a second he thought it was going to. The stuff was strong enough to make a battleship alter its course. The veins of his temples felt bursting; his eyesight dimmed; and he decided that he must be strangling to death. Then, after innumerable seconds, he opened swimming eyes to find Colin regarding him with proud glee.

Next, something else happened.

Once that spiritous bomb had exploded, and he could recover breath and eyesight, a fey sense of exhilaration and well-being crawled along his veins. The original buzzing in the head was succeeded by a sense of crystal clearness, the feeling which Newton or Einstein must have felt at the approaching solution of a complex mathematical problem.

He had kept himself from coughing, and the moment passed.

"Well?" demanded Colin.

"Aaah!" said his guest.

"Here's to happier days too!" thundered Colin, and drained his own glass. The effects here were marked as well, though Colin recovered himself a shade more quickly. Then Colin beamed on him. "Like it?"

"I do!"

"Not too strong for you?"

"No."

"Care for another?"

"Thanks. I don't mind if I do."

"A'weel!" said Elspat resignedly. "A'weel!"

IX

Alan Campbell opened one eye.

From somewhere in remote distances, muffled beyond sight or sound, his soul crawled back painfully, through subterranean corridors, up into his body again. Toward the last it moved to a cacophony of hammers and lights.

Then he was awake.

The first eye was bad enough. But, when he opened the second eye, such a rush of anguish flowed through his brain that he hastily closed them again.

He observed—at first without curiosity—that he was lying in bed in a room he had never seen before; that he wore pajamas; and that there was sunlight in the room.

But his original concerns were purely physical. His head felt as though it were rising toward the ceiling with long, spiraling motions; his stomach was an inferno, his voice a croak out of a dry throat, his whole being composed of fine wriggling wires. Thus Alan Campbell, waking at twelve midday with the king of all hangovers, for the moment merely lay and suffered.

Presently he tried to climb out of bed. But dizziness overcame him, and he lay down again. It was here that his wits began to work, however. Feverishly he tried to remember what had happened last night.

And he could not remember a single thing.

Alan was galvanized.

Possible enormities stretched out behind him, whole vistas of enormities which he might have said or done, but which he could not remember now. There is perhaps not in the world any anguish to compare to this. He knew, or presumed, that he was still at the Castle of Shira; and that he had been lured into quaffing the Doom of the Campbells with Colin; but this was all he knew.

The door of the room opened, and Kathryn came in.

On a tray she carried a cup of black coffee and a revolting-looking mixture in a glass eggcup. She was fully dressed. But the wan expression of her face and eyes strangely comforted him.

Kathryn came over and put down the tray on the bedside table.

"Well, Dr. Campbell," were her first unencouraging words, "don't you feel ashamed of yourself?"

All Alan's emotion found vent in one lingering, passionate groan.

"Heaven knows *I've* no right to blame you," said Kathryn, putting her hands to her head. "I was almost as bad as you were. Oh, God, I feel *awful!*" she breathed, and tottered on her feet. "But at least I didn't—"

"Didn't what?" croaked Alan.

"Don't you remember?"

He waited for enormity to sweep him like the sea.

"At the moment—no. Nothing."

She pointed to the tray. "Drink that prairie oyster. I know it looks foul; but it'll do you good."

"No: tell me. What did I do? Was I very bad?"

Kathryn eyed him wanly.

"Not as bad as Colin, of course. But when *I* tried to leave the party, you and Colin were fencing with claymores."

"Were what?"

"Fencing with real swords. All over the dining room and out in the hall and up the stairs. You had kitchen tablecloths slung on for plaids. Colin was talking in Gaelic, and you were quoting *Marmion,* and *The Lady of the Lake.* Only you couldn't seem to decide whether you were Roderick Dhu or Douglas Fairbanks."

Alan shut his eyes tightly.

He breathed a prayer himself. Faint glimmers, like chinks of light in a blind, touched old-world scenes which swam at him and then receded in hopeless confusion. All lights splintered; all voices dimmed.

"Stop a bit!" he said, pressing his hands to his forehead. "There's nothing about Elspat in this, is there? I didn't insult Elspat, did I? I seem to remember . . ."

Again he shut his eyes.

"My dear Alan, that's the one good feature of the whole night. You're Aunt Elspat's white-haired boy. She thinks that you, next to the late Angus, are the finest member of the whole family."

"*What?*"

"Don't you remember giving her a lecture, at least half an hour long, about the Solemn League and Covenant and the history of the Church of Scotland?"

"Wait! I do seem vaguely to—"

"She didn't understand it; but you had her spellbound. She said that anybody who knew the names of so many ministers couldn't be as godless as she'd thought. Then you insisted on her having half a tumbler of that wretched stuff, and she walked off to bed like Lady Macbeth. This was before the fencing episode, of course. And then—don't you remember what Colin did to that poor man Swan?"

"Swan? Not the MacHolster Swan?"

"Yes."

"But what was *he* doing here?"

"Well, it was something like this: though it's rather dim in my own mind. After you'd fenced all over the place, Colin wanted to go out. He said, 'Alan Oig, there is dirty work to be done this night. Let us hence and look for Stewarts.' You thought that would be a perfectly splendid idea.

"We went out the back, on the road. The first thing we saw, in the bright moonlight, was Mr. Swan standing and looking at the house. Don't ask me what he was doing there! Colin whooped out, 'There's a bluidy Stewart!' and went for him with the claymore.

"Mr. Swan took one look at him, and shot off down the road harder than I've ever seen any man run before. Colin went tearing after him, and you after Colin. I didn't interfere: I'd reached the stage where all I could do was stand and giggle. Colin couldn't quite manage to overtake Mr. Swan, but he did manage to stick him several times in the— in the—"

"Yes."

"—before Colin fell flat and Mr. Swan got away. Then you two came back singing."

There was obviously something on Kathryn's mind. She kept her eyes on the floor.

"I suppose you don't remember," she added, "that I spent the night in here?"

"*You spent the night in here?*"

"Yes. Colin wouldn't hear of anything else. He locked us in."

"But we didn't . . . I mean . . . ?"

"Didn't what?"

"You know what I mean."

Kathryn evidently did, to judge by her color.

"Well—no. We were both too far gone anyway. I was so dizzy and weak that I didn't even protest. You recited something about,

>" 'Here dies in my bosom
>The secret of heather ale.'

"Then you courteously said, 'Excuse me,' and lay down on the floor and went to sleep."

He became conscious of his pajamas. "But how did I get into these?"

"I don't know. You must have waked up in the night and put them on. I woke up about six o'clock, feeling like death, and managed to push the key in the door out, so it fell on the outside and I dragged it under the sill on a piece of paper. I got off to my own room, and I don't think Elspat knows anything about it. But when I woke up and found you there . . ."

Her voice rose almost to a wail.

"Alan Campbell, what on earth has come over us? Both of us? Don't you think we'd better get out of Scotland before it corrupts us altogether?"

Alan reached out for the prairie oyster. How he managed to swallow it he does not now remember; but he did, and felt better. The hot black coffee helped.

"So help me," he declared, "I will never touch another drop as long as I live! And Colin. I hope he's suffering the tortures of the inferno. I hope he's got such a hangover as will—"

"Well, he hasn't."

"No?"

"He's as bright as a cricket. He says good whisky never gave any man a headache. That dreadful Dr. Fell has arrived, too. Can you come downstairs and get some breakfast?"

Alan gritted his teeth.

"I'll have a try," he said, "if you can overcome your lack of decency and get out of here while I dress."

Half an hour later, after shaving and bathing in the somewhat primitive bathroom, he was on his way downstairs feeling much better. From the partly open door of the sitting room came the sound of two powerful voices, those of Colin and Dr. Fell, which sent sharp pains through his skull. Toast was all he could manage in the way of breakfast. Afterwards he and Kathryn crept guiltily into the sitting room.

Dr. Fell, his hands folded over his crutch-handled stick, sat on the sofa. The broad black ribbon of his eyeglasses blew out as he chuckled. His big mop of gray-streaked hair lay over one eye, and many more chins appeared as his amusement increased. He seemed to fill the room: at first Alan could hardly believe him.

"Good morning!" he thundered.

"Good morning!" thundered Colin.

"Good morning," murmured Alan. "Must you shout like that?"

"Nonsense. We weren't shouting," said Colin. "How are you feeling this morning?"

"Terrible."

Colin stared at him. "You haven't got a head?"

"No?"

"Nonsense!" snorted Colin, fiercely and dogmatically. "Good whisky never gave any man a head."

This fallacy, by the way, is held almost as a gospel in the North. Alan did not attempt to dispute it. Dr. Fell hoisted himself ponderously to his feet and made something in the nature of a bow.

"Your servant, sir," said Dr. Fell. He bowed to Kathryn. "And yours, madam." A twinkle appeared in his eye. "I trust that you have now managed to settle between you the vexed question of the Duchess of Cleveland's hair? Or may I infer that at the moment you are more interested in the hair of the dog?"

"That's not a bad idea, you know," said Colin.

"No!" roared Alan, and made his own head ache. "I will never touch that damned stuff again under any circumstances. That is final."

"That's what you think now," Colin grinned comfortably. "I'm going to give Fell here a nip of it tonight. I say, my boy: would you like to taste some mountain dew that'll take the top of your head off?"

Dr. Fell chuckled.

"It would be very interesting," he replied, "to find any whisky that could take the top of my head off."

"Don't say that," warned Alan. "Let me urge you in advance: don't say it. *I* said it. It's fatal."

"And must we talk about this, anyway?" inquired Kathryn, who had been eying Dr. Fell with a deep suspicion which he returned by beaming like the Ghost of Christmas Present.

Rather to their surprise, Dr. Fell grew grave.

"Oddly enough, I think it would be advisable to talk of it. Archons of Athens! It's quite possible the matter may have some bearing on—"

He hesitated.

"On what?"

"On Angus Campbell's murder," said Dr. Fell.

Colin whistled, and then there was a silence. Muttering to himself, Dr. Fell appeared to be trying to chew at the end of his bandit's mustache.

"Perhaps," he went on, "I had better explain. I was very happy to get my friend Colin Campbell's invitation. I was much intrigued by the full details of the case as he wrote them. Putting in my pocket my Boswell and my toothbrush, I took a train for the North. I beguiled my time rereading the great Doctor Johnson's views on this country. You are no doubt familiar with his stern reply when told that he should not be so hard on Scotland since, after all, God had made Scotland? 'Sir, comparisons are invidious; but God made hell.' "

Colin gestured impatiently. "Never mind that. What were you saying?"

"I arrived in Dunoon," said Dr. Fell, "early yesterday evening. I tried to get a car at the tourist agency—"

"We know it," said Kathryn.

"But was informed that the only car then available had already taken a batch of people to Shira. I asked when the car would be back. The clerk said it would not be back. He said he had just that moment received a telephone call from Inveraray from the driver, a man named Fleming—"

"Jock," Colin explained to the others.

"The driver said that one of his passengers, a gentleman called Swan, had decided to stay the night in Inveraray, and wanted to keep car and driver to take him back to Dunoon in the morning. This, with suitable costs, was arranged."

"Infernal snooper," roared Colin.

"One moment. The clerk said, however, that if I would come to the agency at half past nine in the morning—this morning—the car would be back and would take me to Shira.

"I spent the night at the hotel, and was there on time. I then observed the somewhat unusual spectacle of a motorcar coming along the main street with its one passenger, a man in a gray hat and a very violent tartan necktie, standing up in the back seat."

Colin Campbell glowered at the floor.

A vast, dreamy expression of pleasure went over Dr. Fell's face. His eye was on a corner of the ceiling. He cleared his throat.

"Intrigued as to why this man should be standing up, I made inquiries. He replied (somewhat curtly) that he found the sitting position painful. It required little subtlety to get the story out of him. Indeed, he was boiling with it. Harrumph."

Alan groaned.

Dr. Fell peered over his eyeglasses, first at Alan and then at Kathryn. He wheezed. His expression was one of gargantuan delicacy.

"May I inquire," he said, "whether you two are engaged to be married?"

"Certainly not!" cried Kathryn.

"Then," Dr. Fell urged warmly, "in heaven's name *get* married. Do it in a hurry. You both hold responsible positions. But what you are likely to read about yourselves in today's *Daily Floodlight,* at risk of libel or no, is not likely to find favor with either Highgate University or the Harpenden College for Women. That thrilling story of the moonlight chase with claymores, with the lady shouting encouragement while the two cut-throats pursued him, really did put the tin hat on it."

"I never shouted encouragement!" said Kathryn.

Dr. Fell blinked at her.

"Are you sure you didn't, ma'am?"

"Well . . ."

"I'm afraid you did, Kitty-kat," observed Colin, glaring at the floor. "But it was my fault. I—"

Dr. Fell made a gesture.

"No matter," he said. "That was not what I wanted to tell you. Intrigued and inspired by this revival of old Highland customs, I spoke with the driver, Mr. Fleming."

"Yes?"

"Now here is what I most seriously want to ask. Did any of you, last night, at any time go up into the tower? *Any of you, at any time?*"

There was a silence. The windows facing the loch were open to a clear, cool, pleasant day. They all looked at each other.

"No," returned Kathryn.

"No," stated Colin.

"You're quite sure of that, now?"

"Definitely."

"Mr. Swan," Dr. Fell went on, with a curious insistence which Alan found disturbing, "says that the two men were 'dressed up' in some way."

"Oh, it's silly and horrible!" said Kathryn. "And it's all Alan's fault. They weren't exactly 'dressed up.' They had checkered tablecloths draped over their shoulders for plaids, that's all."

"Nothing else?"

"No."

Dr. Fell drew in his breath. His expression remained so grave, his color so high, that nobody spoke.

"I repeat," Dr. Fell continued, "that I questioned the driver. Getting information out of him was rather more difficult than drawing teeth. But on one point he did give some information. He says that this place is not 'canny'—"

Colin interrupted with a fierce grunt of impatience, but Dr. Fell silenced him.

"And now he says he's in a position to swear to it."

"How?"

"Last night, after they had put up at Inveraray, Swan asked him to drive back here. Swan was going to have another try at getting in to see Miss Elspat Campbell. Now let's see if I've got the geography straight. The road to Inveraray runs along the back of the house, doesn't it?"

"Yes."

"And the front door faces the loch, as we see. Swan asked the driver to walk round and knock at the front door, as a sort of messenger, while Swan remained at the back. The driver did so. It was bright moonlight, remember."

"Well?"

"He was just about to knock at the door, when he happened to look up at the window of the tower room. And he saw somebody or something at that window."

"But that's impossible!" cried Kathryn. "We were—"

Dr. Fell examined his hands, which were folded on the handle of his stick. Then Dr. Fell looked up.

"Fleming," he went on, "swears he saw something in Highland costume, with half its face shot away, looking down at him."

X

I t is all very well to be hardheaded. Most of us are, even with headaches and shaky nerves. But to find a breath of superstitious terror is far from difficult here.

"Were you thinking," asked Kathryn, "of that story of what happened after the massacre of Glencoe? That the ghost of one of the victims pursued a man called Ian Campbell, who—"

Despairing of words, she made a gesture as of one who jumps.

Colin's face was fiery.

"Ghosts!" he said. "Ghosts! Look here. In the first place, there never was any such tradition as that. It was put into a lying guidebook because it sounded pretty. Professional soldiers in those days weren't so thin-skinned about executing orders.

"In the second place, that room's not haunted. Angus slept there every night for years, and *he* never saw a bogle. You don't believe such rubbish, do you, Fell?"

Dr. Fell remained unruffled.

"I am merely," he answered mildly, "stating what the driver told me."

"Rubbish. Jock was pulling your leg."

"And yet, d'ye know,"—Dr. Fell screwed up his face—"he hardly struck me as a man addicted to that form of gammon. I have usually found that Gaels will joke about anything except ghosts. Besides, I think you miss the real point of the story."

He was silent for a moment.

"But when did this happen?" asked Alan.

"Ah, yes. It was just before the two cutthroats with their lady came out of the back door and set on Swan. Fleming didn't knock at the front door after all. Hearing the shouts, he went to the back. He started up his car and eventually picked up Swan on the road. But he says he wasn't feeling too well. He says he stood in the moonlight for several minutes after he'd seen the thing at the window, and didn't feel too well at all. I can't say I blame him."

Kathryn hesitated. "What did it look like?"

"Bonnet and plaid and face caved in. That's all he could tell with any distinctness."

"Not a kilt too?"

"He wouldn't have been able to see a kilt. He only saw the upper half of the figure. He says it looked decayed, as though the moths had got at it, and it had only one eye." Again the doctor cleared his throat, rumblingly. "The point, however, is this. Who, beside you three, was in the house last night?"

"Nobody," replied Kathryn, "except Aunt Elspat and Kirstie, the maid. And they'd gone to bed."

"I tell you it's rubbish!" snarled Colin.

"Well, you can speak to Jock himself, if you like. He's out in the kitchen now."

Colin rose to find Jock and end this nonsense; but he did not do so. Alistair Duncan, followed by a patient but weary-looking Walter Chapman, was ushered in by the maid Kirstie—a scared-eyed, soft-voiced girl whose self-effacing habits rendered her almost invisible.

The lawyer made no reference to last night's rumpus with Colin. He stood very stiffly.

"Colin Campbell—" he began.

"Look here," grumbled Colin, shoving his hands into his pockets, lowering his neck into his collar, and looking like a Newfoundland dog which has been at the larder. "I owe you an apology, dammit. I apologize. I was wrong. There."

Duncan expelled his breath.

"I am glad, sir, that you have the decency to acknowledge it. Only my long friendship with your family enables me to overlook a piece of ill manners so uncalled-for and so flagrant."

"Hoy! Now wait a bit! Wait a bit! I didn't say—"

"So let us think no more about it," concluded the lawyer, as Colin's eye began to gleam again. Duncan coughed, indicating that he had left personal matters and now dealt with business.

"I thought I had better inform you," he went on, "that they think they may have found Alec Forbes."

"Wow! Where?"

"He's been reported to have been seen at a crofter's cottage near Glencoe."

Chapman intervened.

"Can't we settle it?" the insurance man suggested. "Glencoe's no great distance from here, as I understand it. You could drive there and back easily in an afternoon. Why not hop in my car and run up and see him?"

The lawyer's manner had a sort of corpselike benevolence.

"Patience, my dear fellow. Patience, patience, patience! First let the police find out if it *is* Alec. He has been reported before, you remember. Once in Edinburgh and once in Ayr."

"Alec Forbes," struck in Dr. Fell, "being the sinister figure who called on Mr. Campbell the night the latter died?"

They all swung round. Colin hastily performed an introduction.

"I have heard of you, Doctor," said Duncan, scrutinizing Dr. Fell through his pince-nez. "In fact, I—ah—confess I came here partly in the hope of seeing you. We have here, of course," he smiled, "a clear case of murder. But we are still rather confused about it. Can you unriddle it for us?"

For a moment Dr. Fell did not reply.

He frowned at the floor, drawing a design on the carpet with the end of his stick.

"H'mf," he said, and gave the ferrule of the stick a rap on the floor. "I sincerely trust it is murder. If it is not, I have no interest in it. But—Alec Forbes! Alec Forbes! Alec Forbes!"

"What about him?"

"Well, who is Alec Forbes? What is he? I could bear to know much more of him. For instance: what was the cause of his quarrel with Mr. Campbell?"

"Ice cream," replied Colin.

"What?"

"Ice cream. They were going to make it by a new process, in great quantity. And it was to be colored in different tartan patterns. No, I'm perfectly serious! That's the sort of idea Angus was always getting. They built a laboratory, and used artificial ice—that chemical stuff that's so expensive—and ran up bills and raised merry blazes. Another of Angus's ideas was a new kind of tractor that would both sow and reap. And he also financed those people who were going to find Drake's gold and make all the subscribers millionaires."

"What sort of person is Forbes? Laboring man? Something of that sort?"

"Oh, no. Bloke of some education. But scatty in the money line, like Angus. Lean, dark-faced chap. Moody. Fond of the bottle. Great cyclist."

"H'mf. I see." Dr. Fell pointed with his stick. "That's Angus Campbell's photograph on the mantelpiece there, I take it?"

"Yes."

Dr. Fell got up from the sofa and lumbered across. He carried the crepe-draped picture to the light, adjusted his eyeglasses, and puffed gently as he studied it.

"Not the face, you know," he said, "of a man who commits suicide."

"Definitely not," smiled the lawyer.

"But we can't—" Chapman began.

"Which Campbell are you, sir?" Dr. Fell asked politely.

Chapman threw up his arms in despair.

"I'm not a Campbell at all. I represent the Hercules Insurance Company and I've got to get back to my office in Glasgow or business will go to blazes. See here, Dr. Fell. I've heard of you too. They say you're fair-minded. And I put it to you: how can we go by what a person 'would' or 'wouldn't' have done, when the evidence shows he *did* do it."

"All evidence," said Dr. Fell, "points two ways. Like the ends of a stick. That is the trouble with it."

Absent-mindedly he stumped back to the mantelpiece, and put the photograph down. He seemed very much disturbed. While his eyeglasses came askew on his nose, he made what was (for him) the great exertion of feeling through all his pockets. He produced a sheet of paper scrawled with notes.

"From the admirably clear letter written by Colin Campbell," he went on, "and from facts he has given me this morning, I have been trying to construct a précis of what we know, or think we know."

"Well?" prompted the lawyer.

"With your permission,"—Dr. Fell scowled hideously—"I should like to read out these points. One or two things may appear a little clearer, or at least more suggestive, if they are heard in skeleton form. Correct me if I am wrong in any of them.

"1. Angus Campbell always went to bed at ten o'clock.
"2. It was his habit to lock and bolt the door on the inside.
"3. It was his habit to sleep with the window shut.
"4. It was his habit to write up his diary each night before going to bed."

Dr. Fell blinked up.

"No misstatement there, I trust?"

"No," admitted Colin.

"Then we pass on to the simple circumstances surrounding the crime.

"5. Alec Forbes called on A. Campbell at nine-thirty on the night of the crime.
"6. He forced his way into the house, and went up to Augus's bedroom.
"7. Neither of the two women saw him at this time."

Dr. Fell rubbed his nose.

"Query," he added, "how did Forbes get in, then? Presumably he didn't just break down the front door?"

"If you'd like to step out of that door there," responded Colin, pointing, "you can see. It leads to the ground-floor of the tower. In the ground-floor room there are wooden double-doors leading out to the court. They're supposed to be padlocked, but half the time they're not. That's how Forbes came—without disturbing anybody else."

Dr. Fell made a note.

"That seems to be clear enough. Very well. We now take arms against a sea of troubles.

"8. At this time Forbes was carrying an object like a 'suitcase.'

"9. He had a row with Angus, who evicted him.

"10. Forbes was empty-handed when he left.

"11. Elspat Campbell and Kirstie MacTavish arrived in time to see the eviction.

"12. They were afraid Forbes might have come back. This becomes more understandable when we learn of the isolated tower with its outside entrance and its five empty floors.

"13. They searched the empty rooms, and also Angus's room.

"14. There was nothing under the bed in Angus's bedroom at this time.

"Still correct?" inquired Dr. Fell, raising his head.

"No, it isna," announced a high, sharp, positive voice which made them all jump.

Nobody had seen Aunt Elspat come in. She stood sternly on her dignity, her hands folded.

Dr. Fell blinked at her. "What isn't true, ma'am?"

"It isna true tae say the box tae carry the dog wasna under the bed when Kirstie and I luked. It was."

Her six auditors regarded her with consternation. Most of them began to speak at once, a frantic babble which was only stilled by Duncan's stern assertion of legal authority.

"Elspat Campbell, listen to me. You said there was nothing there."

"I said there was nae *suitcase* there. I didna say aboot the ither thing."

"Are you telling us that the dog carrier was under the bed before Angus locked and bolted his door?"

"Aye."

"Elspat," said Colin, with a sudden gleam of certainty in his eye, "you're lying. God's wounds, you're lying! You said there was *nothing* under that bed. I heard you myself."

"I'm tellin' ye the gospel truth, and Kirstie will tu." She favored them all with an equally malignant look. "Dinner's on its way, and I'm no' settin' places for the parcel o' ye."

Inflexible, making this very clear, she walked out of the room and closed the door.

The question is, thought Alan, does this alter matters or doesn't it? He shared Colin Campbell's evident conviction that Elspat was lying. But she had one of those faces so used to household deceit, so experienced in lying for what she believed a good purpose, that it was difficult to distinguish between truth and falsehood in anything.

This time it was Dr. Fell who stilled the babble of argument.

"We will query the point," he said, "and continue. The next points define our problem squarely and simply.

"15. Angus locked and bolted his door on the inside.
"16. His dead body was found by the milkman at six o'clock on the following morning, at the foot of the tower.
"17. He had died of multiple injuries caused by the fall.
"18. Death took place between ten p.m. and one a.m.
"19. He had not been drugged or overcome in any way.
"20. The door was still locked and bolted on the inside. Since the bolt was rusty, difficult to draw and firmly shot in its socket, this rules out any possibility of tampering with it."

In Alan's mind rose the image of the shattered door as he had seen it last night.

He remembered the rustiness of the bolt, and the stubborn lock torn from its frame. Jiggery-pokery with string or any similar device must clearly be put aside. The image faded as Dr. Fell continued.

"21. The window was inaccessible. We have this from a steeple jack.
"22. There was no person hiding in the room.
"23. The bed had been occupied."

Dr. Fell puffed out his cheeks, frowned, and tapped a pencil on the notes.

"Which," he said, "brings us to a point where I must interpose another query. Your letter didn't say. When his body was found in the morning, was he wearing slippers or a dressing gown?"

"No," said Colin. "Just his wool nightshirt."

Dr. Fell made another note.

"24. His diary was missing. This, however, might have been taken at some subsequent time.
"25. Angus's fingerprints, and only his, were found on the catch of the window.
"26. Under the bed was a case of the sort used to carry dogs. It did not

belong in the house; had presumably been brought by Forbes; but was in any case not there the night before.

"27. This box was empty.

"We are therefore forced to the conclusion—"

Dr. Fell paused.

"Go on!" Alistair Duncan prompted in a sharp voice. "To what conclusion?"

Dr. Fell sniffed.

"Gentlemen, we can't escape it. It's inevitable. We are forced to the conclusion that either (a) Angus Campbell deliberately committed suicide, or (b) there was in that box something which made him run for his life to escape it, and crash through the window to his death in doing so."

Kathryn shivered a little. But Chapman was not impressed.

"I know," he said. "Snakes. Spiders. Fu Manchu. We were all over that last night. And it gets us nowhere."

"Can you dispute my facts?" inquired Dr. Fell, tapping the notes.

"No. But can you dispute *mine?* Snakes! Spiders—"

"And now," grinned Colin, "ghosts."

"Eh?"

"A rattlebrain by the name of Jock Fleming," explained Colin, "claims to have seen somebody in Highland dress, with no face, gibbering at the window last night."

Chapman's face lost some of its color.

"I don't know anything about that," he said. "But I could almost as soon believe in a ghost as in a dexterous spider or snake that could close up the clasps of a suitcase afterwards. I'm English. I'm practical. But this is a funny country and a funny house; and I tell you *I* shouldn't care to spend a night up in that room."

Colin got up from his chair and did a little dance round the room.

"That's done it," he roared, when he could get his breath. *"That's torn it!"*

Dr. Fell blinked at him with mild expostulation. Colin's face was suffused and the veins stood out on his thick neck.

"Listen," he went on, swallowing with powerful restraint. "Ever since I got here, everybody has been ghosting me. And I'm sick of it. This tomfoolery has got to be blown sky-high and I'm the jasper to do it. I'll tell you what I'm going to do. I'm going to move my things into that tower this very afternoon, and I'm going to sleep there henceforward. If so much as a ghost of a ghost shows its ugly head there, if anybody tries to make *me* jump out of a window . . ."

His eye fell on the family Bible. The atheistical Colin ran across to it and put his hand on it.

"Then I hereby swear that I'll go to the kirk every Sunday for the next twelve months. Yes, and prayer meeting too!"

He darted across to the door to the hall, which he set open.

"Do you hear that, Elspat?" he roared, coming back and putting his hand on the Bible again. "Every Sunday, and prayer meeting on Wednesdays. Ghosts! Bogles! Warlocks! Isn't there a sane person left in this world?"

His voice reverberated through the house. You might have imagined that it drew back echoes. But Kathryn's attempt to shush him was unnecessary. Colin already felt better. It was Kirstie MacTavish who supplied the distraction, by thrusting her head in at the doorway and speaking in a tone not far removed from real awe.

"That reporter's back again," she said.

XI

Colin opened his eyes. "Not the chap from the *Daily Floodlight?*"

"It's him."

"Tell him I'll see him," said Colin, straightening his collar and drawing a deep breath.

"No!" said Alan. "In your present state of mind you'd probably cut his heart out and eat it. Let *me* see him."

"Yes, please!" cried Kathryn. She turned a fervent face. "If he's dared to come back here, he can't have said anything very awful about us in the paper. Don't you see: this is our chance to apologize and put everything right again? Please let Alan see him!"

"All right," Colin agreed. "After all, you didn't stick him in the seat of his pants with a claymore. You may be able to smooth him down."

Alan hurried out into the hall. Just outside the front door, clearly of two minds on how to approach this interview, stood Swan. Alan went outside, and carefully closed the front door.

"Look here," he began, "I honestly am terribly sorry about last night. I can't think what came over us. We'd had one over the eight . . ."

"You're telling *me?*" inquired Swan. He looked at Alan, and anger seemed less predominant than real curiosity. "What were you drinking, for God's sake? T.N.T. and monkey glands? I used to be a track man myself, but I never saw anybody cover ground like that thick-set old buster since Nurmi retired to Finland."

"Something like that."

Swan's expression, as he saw that he was dealing with a chastened man, grew increasingly more stern.

"Now look," he said impressively. "You know, don't you, that I could sue you all for heavy damages?"

"Yes; but—"

"And that I've got enough on you to make your name mud in the press, if I was the sort of a fellow who bears malice?"

"Yes, but—"

"You can just thank your lucky stars, Dr. Campbell, that I'm *not* the sort of a fellow who bears malice: that's all *I* say." Swan gave a significant nod. He was wearing a new light-gray suit and tartan tie. Again his gloomy sternness was moved by curiosity. "What kind of a professor are you, anyway? Running around with women professors from other colleges—always going to houses of ill fame—"

"Here! For the love of—"

"Now don't deny it," said Swan, pointing a lean finger in his face. "I heard Miss Campbell herself say, in front of witnesses, that that's exactly what you were always doing."

"She was talking about the Roman Catholic Church! That's what the old-timers called it."

"It's not what the old-timers called it where *I* come from. On top of that, you get all ginned up and chase respectable people along a public road with broadswords. Do you carry on like that at Highgate, Doc? Or just in vacations? I really want to know."

"I swear to you, it's all a mistake! And here's the point. I don't care what you say about me. But will you promise not to say anything about Miss Campbell?"

Swan considered this.

"Well, I don't know," he said, with another darkly significant shake of his head, and a suggestion that, if he did this, it would be only from the kindness of his heart. "I've got a duty to the public, you know."

"Rubbish."

"But I tell you what I'll do," Swan suggested, as though suddenly coming to a decision. "Just to show you I'm a sport, I'll make a deal with you."

"Deal?"

The other lowered his voice.

"That fellow in there, the great big fat fellow, is Dr. Gideon Fell: isn't it?"

"Yes."

"I only discovered it when he'd slipped away from me. And, when I phoned my paper, they were pretty wild. They say that wherever *he* goes, a story breaks with a wallop. They say to stick to him. Look, Doc. I've *got* to get a story! I've incurred a lot of expense over this thing; I've got another car that's eating its head off. If I fall down on this story I won't get the expenses O.K.'d, and I may even get the air."

"So?"

"So here's what I want you to do. Just keep me posted, that's all. Let me know everything that goes on. In return for that—"

He paused, shying back a little, as Colin Campbell came out of the front door. But Colin was trying to be affable: too affable, massively affable, with a guilty grin.

"In return for that, just keeping me posted," resumed Swan, "I'll agree to forget all I know about you and Miss Campbell, and,"—he looked at Colin—"what you did as well, which might have caused me a serious injury. I'll do that just to be a sport and show there are no hard feelings. What do you say?"

Colin's face had lightened with relief.

"I say it's fair enough," Colin returned, with a bellow of pleasure. "Now that's damned decent of you, young fellow! Damned decent! I was tight and I apologize. What do you say, Alan Oig?"

Alan's voice was fervent.

"I say it's fair enough too. You keep to that bargain, Mr. Swan, and you'll have nothing to complain about. If there are any stories going, you shall have them."

He could almost forget that he had a hangover. A beautiful sense of well-being, a sense of the world set right again, crept into Alan Campbell and glowed in his veins.

Swan raised his eyebrows.

"Then it's a deal?"

"It is," said Colin.

"It is," agreed the other miscreant.

"All right, then!" said Swan, drawing a deep breath but still speaking darkly. "Only just remember that I'm straining my duty to my public to oblige you. So remember where we all stand and don't try any—"

Above their heads, a window creaked open. The contents of a large bucket of water, aimed with deadly and scientific accuracy, descended in a solid, glistening sheet over Swan's head. In fact, Swan might be said momentarily to have disappeared.

At the window appeared the malignant face of Aunt Elspat.

"Can ye no' tak' a hint?" she inquired. "I tauld ye to gang your ways, and I'll no' tell ye again. Here's for guid measure."

With the same accuracy, but almost with leisureliness, she lifted a second bucket and emptied it over Swan's head. Then the window closed with a bang.

Swan did not say anything. He stood motionless, and merely looked. His new suit was slowly turning black. His hat resembled a piece of sodden blotting paper from beneath whose down-turned brim there looked out the eyes of a man gradually being bereft of his reason.

"My dear chap!" bellowed Colin in real consternation. "The old witch!

I'll wring her neck; so help me, I will! My dear chap, you're not hurt, are you?"

Colin bounded down the steps. Swan began slowly, but with increasing haste, to back away from him.

"My dear chap, wait! Stop! You must have some dry clothes!"

Swan continued to back away.

"Come into the house, my dear fellow. Come—"

Then Swan found his voice.

"Come into the house," he shrilled, backing away still farther, "so you can steal my clothes and turn me out again? No, you don't! Keep away from me!"

"Look out!" screamed Colin. "One more step and you'll be in the loch! Look—"

Alan glanced round wildly. At the windows of the sitting room observed an interested group of watchers composed of Duncan, Chapman, and Dr. Fell. But most of all he was conscious of Kathryn's horror-stricken countenance.

Swan saved himself by some miracle on the edge of the pier.

"Think I'll go into that booby hatch, do you?" Swan was raving. "You're a bunch of criminal lunatics, that's what you are, and I'm going to expose you. I'm going to—"

"Man, you can't walk about like that! You'll catch your death of cold! Come on in. Besides," argued Colin, "you'll be on the scene of it, won't you? Smack in the middle of things alongside Dr. Fell?"

This appeared to make Swan pause. He hesitated. Still streaming like an enthusiastic fountain, he wiped the water from his eyes with a shaky hand, and looked back at Colin with real entreaty.

"Can I depend on that?"

"I swear you can! The old hag has got it in for you, but I'll take care of her. Come on."

Swan seemed to be debating courses. At length he allowed himself to be taken by the arm and urged toward the door. He ducked quickly when he passed the window, as though wondering whether to expect boiling lead.

A scene of some embarrassment ensued inside. The lawyer and the insurance man took a hasty leave. Colin, clucking to his charge, escorted him upstairs to change his clothes. In the sitting room a dejected Alan found Kathryn and Dr. Fell.

"I trust, sir," observed Dr. Fell, with stately courtesy, "you know your own business best. But, candidly, do you really think it's wise to antagonize the press quite so much as that? What did you do to the fellow this time? Duck him in the water butt?"

"We didn't do anything. It was Elspat. She poured two buckets of water on him from the window."

"But is he going to—" cried Kathryn.

"He promises that if we keep him posted about what's going on here, he won't say a word. At least, that's what he *did* promise. I can't say how he's feeling now."

"Keep him posted?" asked Dr. Fell sharply.

"Presumably about what's going on here, and whether this is suicide or murder, and what you think of it." Alan paused. "What do you think, by the way?"

Dr. Fell's gaze moved to the door to the hall, making sure it was firmly closed. He puffed out his cheeks, shook his head, and finally sat down on the sofa again.

"If only the facts," he growled, "weren't so infernally simple! I distrust their simplicity. I have a feeling that there's a trap in them. I should also like to know why Miss Elspat Campbell now wants to change her testimony, and swears that the dog carrier *was* under the bed before the room was locked up."

"Do you think the second version is true?"

"No, by thunder, I don't!" said Dr. Fell, rapping his stick on the floor. "I think the first is true. But that only makes our locked-room problem the worse. Unless—"

"Unless what?"

Dr. Fell disregarded this.

"It apparently does no good merely to repeat those twenty-seven points over and over. I repeat: it's too simple. A man double locks his door. He goes to bed. He gets up in the middle of the night without his slippers (mark that), and jumps from the window to instant death. He—"

"That's not quite accurate, by the way."

Dr. Fell lifted his head, his underlip outthrust.

"Hey? What isn't?"

"Well, if you insist on a shade of accuracy, Angus didn't meet an instant death. At least, so Colin told me. The police surgeon wouldn't be definite about the time of death. He said Angus hadn't died instantly, but had probably been alive though unconscious for a little while before he died."

Dr. Fell's little eyes narrowed. The wheezing breaths, which ran down over the ridges of his waistcoat, were almost stilled. He seemed about to say something, but checked himself.

"I further," he said, "don't like Colin's insistence on spending the night in that tower room."

"You don't think there's any more danger?" Kathryn asked.

"My dear child! Of course there's danger!" said Dr. Fell. "There's always danger when some agency we don't understand killed a man. Pry the secret out of it, and you're all right. But so long as you don't understand it . . ."

He brooded.

"You have probably observed that the very things we try hardest to avoid happening are always the things that do happen. *Vide* the saga of Swan. But here, in an uglier way, we have the same wheel revolving and the same danger returning. Archons of Athens! What **COULD** have been in that dog carrier? Something that left *no* trace, nothing whatever? And why the open end? Obviously so that something could breathe through the wire and get air. But what?"

Distorted pictures, all without form, floated in Alan's mind.

"You don't think the box may be a red herring?"

"It may be. But, unless it does mean something, the whole case collapses and we may as well go home to bed. It has got to mean something."

"Some kind of animal?" suggested Kathryn.

"Which closed the clasps of the box after it got out?" inquired Dr. Fell.

"That may not be so difficult," Alan pointed out, "if it were thin enough to get out through the wire. No, hang it, that won't do!" He remembered the box itself, and the mesh. "That wire is so close-meshed that the smallest snake in existence could hardly wriggle out through it."

"Then," pursued Dr. Fell, "there is the episode of the Highlander with the caved-in face."

"You don't believe that story?"

"I believe that Jock Fleming saw what he says he saw. I do not necessarily believe in a ghost. After all, such a piece of trickery, in the moonlight and from a distance of sixty feet up in a tower, wouldn't be very difficult. An old bonnet and plaid, a little make-up—"

"But why?"

Dr. Fell's eyes opened wide. His breath labored with ghoulish eagerness as he seemed to seize on the point.

"Exactly. That's it. Why? We musn't miss the importance of the tale: which is not whether it was supernatural, but why it was done at all. That is, if it had any reason at all in the way we mean." He became very thoughtful. "Find the contents of that box, and we're on the view halloo. That's our problem. Some parts of the business, of course, are easy. You will already have guessed who stole the missing diary?"

"Of course," replied Kathryn instantly. "*Elspat* stole it, of course."

Alan stared at her.

Dr. Fell, with a vast and gratified beam, regarded her as though she were a more refreshing person than even he had expected, and nodded.

"Admirable!" he chuckled. "The talent for deduction developed by judicious historical research can just as well be applied to detective work. Never forget that, my dear. *I* learned it at an early age. Bull's-eye. It was Elspat for a fiver."

"But why?" demanded Alan.

Kathryn set her face into its severest lines, as though they had again returned to the debate of two nights ago. Her tone was withering.

"My *dear* Dr. Campbell!" she said. "Consider what we know. For many, many years she was rather more than a housekeeper to Angus Campbell?"

"Well?"

"But she's horribly, morbidly respectable, and doesn't even believe anybody's guessed her real thoughts?"

(Alan was tempted to say, "Something like you," but he restrained himself.)

"Yes."

"Angus Campbell was a free-spoken person who kept a diary where he could record his intimate—well, you know!"

"Yes?"

"All right. Three days before his death, Angus takes out still another insurance policy, to take care of his old-time love in the event of his death. It's almost certain, isn't it, that in writing down that he did take out an insurance policy he'll make some reference to *why* he did it?"

She paused, raising her eyebrows.

"So, of course, Elspat stole the diary out of some horrid fear of having people learn what she did years and years ago.

"Don't you remember what happened last night, Alan? How she acted when you and Colin began talking about the diary? When you did begin to discuss it, she first said everybody was daft and finally headed you off by suggesting that wretched whisky? And, of course, it did head you off. That's all."

Alan whistled.

"By gad, I believe you're right!"

"Thank you so much, dear. If you were to apply a little of that brain of yours," remarked Kathryn, wrinkling up her pretty nose, "to observing and drawing the inferences you're always telling everyone else to draw—"

Alan treated this with cold scorn. He had half a mind to make some reference to the Duchess of Cleveland, and the paucity of inference K. I. Campbell had been able to draw there, but he decided to give that unfortunate court lady a rest.

"Then the diary hasn't really anything to do with the case?"

"I wonder," said Dr. Fell.

"Obviously," Kathryn pointed out, "Aunt Elspat knows *something*. And probably from the diary. Otherwise why all this business of writing to the *Daily Floodlight?*"

"Yes."

"And since she did write to them, it seems fairly clear that there wasn't anything in the diary to compromise her reputation. Then why on earth doesn't she speak out? What's the matter with her? If the diary gives some indication that Angus was murdered, why doesn't she say so?"

"Unless, of course," said Alan, "the diary says that he meant to commit suicide."

"Alan, Alan, Alan! To say nothing of all the other policies, Angus takes out a last policy, pays the premium, and then writes down that he's going to kill himself? It's just—against nature, that's all!"

Alan gloomily admitted this.

"Thirty-five thousand pounds in the balance," breathed Kathryn, "and she won't claim it. Why doesn't somebody tackle her about it? Why don't you tackle her, Dr. Fell? Everybody else seems to be afraid of her."

"I shall be most happy," beamed Dr. Fell.

Ponderously, like a man-o'-war easing into a dock, he turned round on the sofa. He adjusted his eyeglasses, and blinked at Elspat Campbell, who was standing in the doorway with an expression between wrath, pain, uncertainty, and the fear of damnation. They caught only the tail of this expression, which was gone in a flash, to be replaced by a tightening of the jaws and a determination of granite inflexibility.

Dr. Fell was not impressed.

"Well, ma'am?" he inquired offhandedly. "You really did pinch that diary, didn't you?"

XII

Twilight was deepening over Loch Fyne as they descended through the gray ghostly wood of fallen trees, and turned northwards along the main road to Shira.

Alan felt healthily and pleasantly tired after an afternoon in the open. Kathryn, in tweeds and flatheeled shoes, had color in her cheeks and her blue eyes glowed. She had not once put on her spectacles for argument, even when she had been clucked at for being unfamiliar with the murder of the Red Fox, Colin Campbell of 1752, who had been shot by nobody knows whose hand, but for which James Stewart was tried at Inveraray courthouse.

"The trouble is," Alan was declaring, as they tramped down the hill, "Stevenson has so cast the glamour over us that we tend to forget what this 'hero,' this famous Alan Breck—one '1,' please—was actually like. I've often wished somebody would take the side of the Campbells, for a change."

"Intellectual honesty again?"

"No. Just for fun. But the weirdest version of the incident was in the film version of *Kidnapped*. Alan Breck, and David Balfour, and a totally unnecessary female, are fleeing from the redcoats. Disguised up to the ears, they are driving in a cart along a troop-infested road, singing 'Loch Lomond'; and Alan Breck hisses, 'They'll never suspect us now.'

"I felt like arising and addressing the screen, saying: 'They damn well will if you insist on singing a Jacobite song.' That's about as sensible as though a group of British secret service agents, disguised as Gestapo, were to swagger down Unter den Linden singing, *There'll Always Be an England*."

Kathryn seized on the essential part of this.

"So the female was totally unneccessary, eh?"

"What's that?"

"The female, says he in all his majesty, was totally unnecessary. Of course!"

"I only mean that she wasn't in the original version, and she spoiled what little story was left. Can't you forget this sex war for five minutes?"

"It's you who are always dragging it in."

"Me?"

"Yes, you. I don't know what to make of you. You—you *can* be rather nice, you know, when you try." She kicked the fallen leaves out of her path, and suddenly began to giggle. "I was thinking about last night."

"Don't remind me!"

"But that's when you were nicest, really. Don't you remember what you said to me?"

He had thought the incident buried in merciful oblivion. It was not.

"What did I say?"

"Never mind. We're terribly late for tea again, and Aunt Elspat will carry on again, just as she did last night."

"Aunt Elspat," he said sternly, "Aunt Elspat, as you very well know, won't be down to tea. She's confined to her room with a violent and hysterical fit of the sulks."

Kathryn stopped and made a hopeless gesture.

"You know, I can't decide whether I like that old woman or whether I'd like to murder her. Dr. Fell tackles her about the diary, and all she does is go clear up in the air, and scream that it's her house, and she won't be bullied, and the dog carrier *was* under the bed—"

"Yes; but—"

"I think she just wants her own way. I think she won't tell anybody anything just because they want her to, and she's determined to be the boss. Just as she finished off in real sulks because Colin insisted on having that poor inoffensive Swan man in the house."

"Young lady, don't evade the question. What was it I said to you last night?"

The little vixen, he thought, was deliberately doing this. He wanted not to give her the satisfaction of showing curiosity. But he could not help it. They had come out into the main road only half a dozen yards from the Castle of Shira. Kathryn turned a demure but wicked-looking countenance in the twilight.

"If you can't remember," she told him innocently, "I can't repeat it to you. But I can tell you what my answer would have been, if I had made any answer."

"Well?"

"Oh, I should probably have said something like, 'In that case, why don't you?' "

Then she ran from him.

He caught up with her only in the hall, and there was no time to say anything more. The thunder of voices from the dining room would have warned them of what was in progress, even had they not caught sight of Colin through the partly open door.

The bright light shone over a snug table. Colin, Dr. Fell, and Charles Swan had finished a very large meal. Their plates were pushed to one side, and in the center of the table stood a decanter bearing a rich brown liquid. On the faces of Dr. Fell and Swan, before whom stood empty glasses, was the expression of men who have just passed through a great spiritual experience. Colin twinkled at them.

"Come in!" he cried to Kathryn and Alan. "Sit down. Eat before it gets cold. I've just been giving our friends their first taste of the Doom of the Campbells."

Swan's expression, preternaturally solemn, was now marred by a slight hiccup. But he remained solemn, and seemed to be meditating a profound experience.

His costume, too, was curious. He had been fitted out with one of Colin's shirts, which was too big in the shoulders and body, but much too short in the sleeves. Below this, since no pair of trousers in the house would fit him, he wore a kilt. It was the very dark green and blue of the Campbells, with thin transversing stripes of yellow and crossed white.

"Cripes!" Swan muttered, contemplating the empty glass. "Cripes!"

"The observation," said Dr. Fell, passing his hand across a pink forehead, "is not unwarranted."

"Like it?"

"Well—" said Swan.

"Have another? What about you, Alan? And you, Kitty-kat?"

"No." Alan was very firm about this. "I want some food. Maybe a little of that alcoholic tabasco sauce later, but a very little and not now."

Colin rubbed his hands.

"Oh, you will! They all do. What do you think of our friend Swan's getup? Neat, eh? I fished it out of a chest in the best bedroom. The original tartan of the Clan MacHolster."

Swan's face darkened.

"Are you kidding me?"

"As I believe in heaven," swore Colin, lifting his hand, "that's the MacHolster tartan as sure as I believe in heaven."

Swan was mollified. In fact, he seemed to be enjoying himself.

"It's a funny feeling," he said, eying the kilt. "Like walking around in public without your pants. Cripes, though! To think that I, Charley Swan of Toronto, should be wearing a real kilt in a real Scotch castle, and drinking old dew of the mountain like a clansman! I must write to my father about this. It's decent of you to let me stay all night."

"Nonsense! Your clothes won't be ready until morning, anyway. Have another?"

"Thanks. I don't mind if I do."

"You, Fell?"

"Harrumph," said Dr. Fell. "That is an offer (or, in this case, challenge) I very seldom refuse. Thank'ee. But——"

"But what?"

"I was just wondering," said Dr. Fell, crossing his knees with considerable effort, "whether the *nunc bibendum est* is to be followed by a reasonable *sat prata hiberunt*. In more elegant language, you're not thinking of another binge? Or have you given up the idea of sleeping in the tower tonight?"

Colin stiffened.

A vague qualm of uneasiness brushed the old room.

"And why should I give up the idea of sleeping in the tower?"

"It's just because I don't know why you shouldn't," returned Dr. Fell frankly, "that I wish you wouldn't."

"Rubbish! I've spent half the afternoon repairing the lock and bolt of that door. I've carried my duds up there. You don't think *I'm* going to commit suicide?"

"Well," said Dr. Fell, "suppose you did?"

The sense of uneasiness had grown greater. Even Swan seemed to feel it. Colin was about to break out into hollow incredulity, but Dr. Fell stopped him.

"One moment. Merely suppose that. Or, to be more exact, suppose that tomorrow morning we find you dead at the foot of the tower under just such circumstances as Angus. Er—do you mind if I smoke while you're eating, Miss Campbell?"

"No, of course not," said Kathryn.

Dr. Fell took out a large meerschaum pipe with a curved stem, which he filled from an obese pouch, and lighted. He sat back in his chair, argumentatively. With a somewhat cross-eyed expression behind his eyeglasses, he watched the smoke curl up into the bright bowl of the lamp.

"You believe," he went on, "you believe that your brother's death was murder: don't you?"

"I do! And I thundering well hope it was! If it was, and we can prove it, I inherit seventeen thousand five hundred pounds."

"Yes. But if Angus's death *was* murder, then the same force which killed Angus can kill you. Had you thought of that?"

"I'd like to see the force that could do it: God's wounds, I would!" snapped Colin.

But the calmness of Dr. Fell's voice had its effect. Colin's tone was considerably more subdued.

"Now, if anything should by any chance happen to you," pursued Dr. Fell, while Colin stirred, "what becomes of your share of the thirty-five thousand pounds? Does it revert to Elspat Campbell, for instance?"

"No, certainly not. It's kept in the family. It goes to Robert. Or to Robert's heirs if he's not alive."

"Robert?"

"Our third brother. He got into trouble and skipped the country years ago. We don't even know where he is, though Angus was always trying to find him. We do know he married and had children, the only one of us three who did marry. Robert would be—about sixty-four now. A year younger than I am."

Dr. Fell continued to smoke meditatively, his eye on the lamp.

"You see," he wheezed, "assuming this to be murder, we have got to look for a motive. And a motive, on the financial side at least, is very difficult to find. Suppose Angus was murdered for his life-insurance money. By you. (Tut, now, don't jump down my throat!) Or by Elspat. Or by Robert or his heirs. Yet no murderer in his senses, under those circumstances, is going to plan a crime which will be taken for suicide. Thereby depriving himself of the money which was the whole motive for the crime.

"So we come back to the personal. This man Alec Forbes now. I suppose he was capable of killing Angus?"

"Oh, Lord, yes!"

"H'm. Tell me. Has he got any grudge against you?"

Colin swelled with a kind of obscure satisfaction.

"Alec Forbes," Colin replied, "hates my guts almost as much as he hated Angus's. I ridiculed his schemes. And if there's one thing one of these moody chaps can't stand, it's ridicule. I never disliked the fellow myself, though."

"Yet you admit that the thing which killed Angus could kill you?"

Colin's neck hunched down into his shoulders. He stretched out his hand for the decanter of whisky. He poured out very large portions of it for Dr. Fell, for Swan, for Alan, and for himself.

"If you're trying to persuade me not to sleep in the tower—"

"I am."

"Then be hanged to you. Because I'm going to." Colin scanned the faces round him with fiery eyes. "What's the matter with all of you?" he roared. "Are you all dead tonight? We had things better last night. Drink up! I'm not going to commit suicide; I promise you that. So drink up, and let's have no more of this tomfoolery now."

When they separated to go to bed at shortly past ten o'clock, not a man in that room was cold sober.

In gradations of sobriety they ranged from Swan, who had taken the stuff indiscreetly and could barely stand, to Dr. Fell, whom nothing seemed to shake. Colin Campbell was definitely drunk, though his footstep was firm and only his reddish eyes betrayed him. But he was not drunk with the grinning, whooping abandon of the night before.

Nobody was. It had become one of those evenings when even the tobacco smoke turns stale and sour; and men, perversely, keep taking the final one which they don't need. When Kathryn slipped away before ten, no one attempted to stop her.

On Alan the liquor has having a wrong effect. Counteracting the weariness of his relaxed muscles, it stung him to tired but intense wakefulness. Thoughts scratched in his mind like pencils on slate; they would not go away or be still.

His bedroom was up on the first floor, overlooking the loch. His legs felt light as he ascended the stairs, saying good night to Dr. Fell, who went to his own room (surprisingly) with magazines under his arm.

A lightness in the legs, a buzzing head, an intense discomfort, are no tonics for sleep. Alan groped into his room. Either out of economy or because of the sketchiness of the blackout, the chandelier contained no electric bulbs and only a candle could be used for illumination.

Alan lit the candle on the bureau. The meager little flame intensified the surrounding darkness, and made his face in the mirror look white. It seemed to him that he was tottering; that he was a fool to have touched that stuff again, since this time it brought neither exhilaration nor surcease.

Round and round whirled his thoughts, jumping from one point to another like clumsy mountain goats. People used to study by candlelight. It was a wonder they hadn't all gone blind. Maybe most of them had. He thought of Mr. Pickwick in the Great White Horse at Ipswich. He thought of Scott ruining his eyesight by working under "a broad star of gas." He thought of . . .

It was no good. He *couldn't* sleep.

He undressed, stumbling, in the dark. He put on slippers and a dressing gown.

His watch ticked on. Ten-thirty. A quarter to eleven. The hour itself. Eleven-fifteen . . .

Alan sat down in a chair, put his head in his hands, and wished passionately for something to read. He had noticed very few books at Shira. Dr. Fell, the doctor had informed him that day, had brought a Boswell along.

What a solace, what a soothing and comfort, Boswell would be now! To turn over those pages, to talk with Doctor Johnson until you drifted into a doze, must be the acme of all pleasure on this night. The more he thought of it, the more he wished he had it. Would Dr. Fell lend it to him, for instance?

He got up, opened the door, and padded down a chilly hall to the doctor's room. He could have shouted for joy when he saw a thin line of light under the sill of the door. He knocked, and was told to come in in a voice which he hardly recoginzed as that of Dr. Fell.

Alan, strung to a fey state of awareness, felt his scalp stir with terror as he saw the expression on Dr. Fell's face.

Dr. Fell sat by the chest of drawers, on top of which a candle was burning in its holder. He wore an old purple dressing gown as big as a tent. The meerschaum pipe hung from one corner of his mouth. Round him was scattered a heap of magazines, letters, and what looked like bills. Through a mist of tobacco smoke in the airless room, Alan saw the startled, faraway expression of Dr. Fell's eyes, the open mouth which barely supported the pipe.

"Thank God you're here!" rumbled Dr. Fell, suddenly coming to life. "I was just going to fetch you."

"Why?"

"I know what was in that box," said Dr. Fell. "I know how the trick was worked. I know what set on Angus Campbell."

The candle flame wavered slightly among shadows. Dr. Fell reached out for his crutch-handled stick, and groped wildly before he found it.

"We've got to get Colin out of that room," he added. "There may not be any danger; there probably isn't; but, by thunder, we can't afford to take any chances! I can show him now what did it, and he's got to listen to reason. See here."

Puffing and wheezing, he impelled himself to his feet.

"I underwent the martyrdom of climbing up those tower stairs once before today, but I can't do it again. Will you go up there and rout Colin out?"

"Of course."

"We needn't rouse anybody else. Just bang on the door until he lets you in; don't take no for an answer. Here. I've got a small torch. Keep it shielded when you go up the stairs, or you'll have the wardens after us. Hurry!"

"But what—"

"I haven't time to explain now. Hurry!"

Alan took the torch. Its thin, pale beam explored ahead of him. He went out in the hall, which smelt of old umbrellas, and down the stairs. A chilly draught touched his ankles. He crossed the lower hall, and went into the living room.

Across the room, on the mantelpiece, the face of Angus Campbell looked back at him as the beam of his torch rested on the photograph. Angus's white, fleshy-jowled countenance seemed to stare back with the knowledge of a secret.

The door leading to the ground floor of the tower was locked on the inside. When Alan turned the squeaky key and opened the door, his fingers were shaking.

Now the earthen floor under him felt icy. A very faint mist had crept in from the loch. The arch leading to the tower stairs, a gloomy hole, repelled and somewhat unnerved him. Though he started to take the stairs at a run, both the dangerous footing and the exertion of the climb forced him to slow down.

First floor. Second floor, more of a pull. Third floor, and he was breathing hard. Fourth floor, and the distance up seemed endless. The little pencil of light intensified the coldness and close claustrophobia brought on by that enclosed space. It would not be pleasant to meet suddenly, on the stairs, a man in Highland costume with half his face shot away.

Or have the thing come out of one of the tower rooms, for instance, and touch him on the shoulder from behind.

You could not get away from anything that chose to pursue you here.

Alan reached the airless, windowless landing on which was the door to the topmost room. The oak door, its wood rather rotted by damp, was closed. Alan tried the knob, and found that it was locked and bolted on the inside.

He lifted his fist and pounded heavily on the door.

"Colin!" he shouted. "Colin!"

There was no reply.

The thunder of the knocking, the noise of his own voice, rebounded with infernal and intolerable racket in that confined space. He felt it must wake everybody in the house; everybody in Inveraray, for that matter. But he continued to knock and shout, still with no reply.

He set his shoulder to the door, and pushed. He got down on his knees, and tried to peer under the sill of the door, but he could see nothing except an edge of moonlight.

As he got to his feet again, feeling lightheaded after that exertion, the suspicion which had already struck him grew and grew with ugly effect. Colin *might* be only heavily asleep, of course, after all that whisky. On the other hand—

Alan turned round, and plunged down the treacherous stairs. The breath in his lungs felt like a rasping saw, and several times he had to pull up. He had even forgotten the Highlander. It seemed half an hour, and was actually two or three minutes, before he again reached the bottom of the stairs.

The double doors leading out into the court were closed, but the padlock was not caught. Alan threw them open—creaking, quivering frames of wood which bent like bow shafts as they scraped the flagstones.

He ran out into the court, and circled round the tower to the side facing the loch. There he stopped short. He knew what he would find, and he found it.

The sickening plunge had been taken again.

Colin Campbell—or a bundle of red-and-white striped pajamas which might once have been Colin—lay face downwards on the flagstones. Sixty feet above his head the leaves of the window stood open, and glinted by the light of the waning moon. A thin white mist, which seemed to hang above the water rather than rise from it, had made beads of dew settle on Colin's shaggy hair.

XIII

D awn—warm gold and white kindling from smoky purple, yet of a soap-bubble luminousness which tinged the whole sky—dawn was clothing the valley when Alan again climbed the tower stairs. You could almost taste the early autumn air.

But Alan was in no mood to enjoy it.

He carried a chisel, an auger, and a saw. Behind him strode a nervous, wiry-looking Swan in a now-dry gray suit which had once been fashionable but which at present resembled sackcloth.

"But are you sure you want to go in there?" insisted Swan. "I'm not keen on it myself."

"Why not?" said Alan. "It's daylight. The Occupant of the box can't hurt us now."

"What occupant?"

Alan did not reply. He thought of saying that Dr. Fell now knew the truth, though he had not divulged it yet; and that Dr. Fell said there was no danger. But he decided such matter were best kept from the papers as yet.

"Hold the torch," he requested. "I can't see why they didn't put a window on this landing. Colin repaired this door yesterday afternoon, you remember. We're now going to arrange matters so that it can't be repaired again in a hurry."

While Swan held the light, he set to work. It was slow work, boring a line of holes touching each other in a square round the lock, and Alan's hands were clumsy on the auger.

When he had finished them, and splintered the result with a chisel, he got purchase for the saw and slowly sawed along the line of the holes.

"Colin Campbell," observed Swan, suddenly and tensely, "was a good guy. A real good guy."

"What do you mean, 'was'?"

"Now that he's dead—"

"But he's not dead."

There was an appreciable silence.

"*Not dead?*"

The saw rasped and bumped. All the violence of Alan's relief, all the sick reaction after what he had seen, went into his attack on the door. He hoped Swan would shut up. He had liked Colin Campbell immensely, to much to want to hear any sickly sentimentalities.

"Colin," he went on, without looking round to see Swan's expression, "has got two broken legs and a broken hipbone. And, for a man of his age, that's no joke. Also, there's something else Dr. Grant is very much excited about. But he's not dead and he's unlikely to die."

"A fall like that—"

"It happens sometimes. You've probably heard of people falling from heights greater than that and sometimes not even being hurt at all. And if they're tight, as Colin was, that helps too."

"Yet he deliberately jumped from the window?"

"Yes."

In a fine powdering of sawdust, the last tendon of wood fell free. Alan pushed the square panel inwards, and it fell on the floor. He reached through, finding the key still securely turned and the rusty bolt shot home immovably in its socket. He turned the key, pulled back the bolt; and, not without a qualm of apprehension, opened the door.

In the clear, fresh light of dawn, the room appeared tousled and faintly sinister. Colin's clothes, as he had untidily undressed, lay flung over the chairs and over the floor. His watch ticked on the chest of drawers. The bed had been slept in; its clothes were now flung back, and the pillows punched into a heap which still held the impression of a head.

The wide-open leaves of the window creaked gently as an air touched them.

"What are you going to do?" asked Swan, putting his head round the edge of the door and at last deciding to come in.

"What Dr. Fell asked me to do."

Though he spoke easily enough, he had to get a grip on himself before he knelt down and felt under the bed. He drew out the leather dog carrier which had contained the Occupant.

"You're not going to fool around with the thing?" asked Swan.

"Dr. Fell said to open it. He said there wouldn't be any fingerprints, so not to bother about them."

"You're taking a lot for granted on that old boy's word. But if you know what you're doing—open it."

This part was the hardest. Alan flicked back the catches with his thumbs, and lifted the lid.

As he had expected, the box was empty. Yet his imagination could have pictured, and was picturing, all sorts of unpleasant things he might have seen.

"What did the old boy tell you to do?" inquired Swan.

"Just open it, and make sure it was empty."

"But what *could* have been in it?" roared Swan. "I tell you, I'm going nuts trying to figure this thing out! I—" Swan paused. His eyes widened, and then narrowed. He extended a finger to point to the rolltop desk.

On the edge of the desk, half hidden by papers but in a place where it certainly had not been the day before, lay a small leather book of pocket size, on whose cover was stamped, in gilt letters, *Diary,* 1940.

"That wouldn't be what you've been looking for, would it?"

Both of them made a dart for the diary, but Alan got there first.

The name Angus Campbell was written on the flyleaf in a small but stiff and schoolboyish kind of hand which made Alan suspect arthritis in the fingers. Angus had carefully filled out the chart for all the miscellaneous information, such as the size of his collar and the size of his shoes (why the makers of these diaries think we are likely to forget the size of our collars remains a mystery); and after "motorcar license number" he had written "none."

But Alan did not bother with this. The diary was full of entries all crammed together and crammed downhill. The last entry was made on the night of Angus's death, Saturday the twenty-fourth of August. Alan Campbell became conscious of tightened throat muscles, and a heavy thumping in his chest, as his eye encountered the item.

"Saturday. Check cleared by bank. O.K. Elspat poorly again. Memo: syrup of figs. Wrote to Colin. A. Forbes here tonight. Claims I cheated him. Ha ha ha. Said not to come back. He said he wouldn't, wasn't necessary. Funny musty smell in room tonight. Memo: write to War Office about tractor. Use for army. Do this tomorrow."

Then there was the blank which indicated the end of the writer's span of life.

Alan flicked back over the pages. He did not read any more, though he noticed that at one point a whole leaf had been torn out. He was thinking of the short, heavy, bulbous-nosed old man with the white hair, writing these words while something waited for him.

"H'm," said Swan. "That isn't much help, is it?"

"I don't know."

"Well," said Swan, "if you've seen what you came to see, or rather what you didn't see, let's get downstairs again, shall we? There may be nothing wrong with this place, but it gives me the willies."

Slipping the diary into his pocket, Alan gathered up the tools and followed. In the sitting room downstairs they found Dr. Fell, fully dressed in an old black alpaca suit and string tie. Alan noticed with surprise that his box-pleated cape and shovel hat lay across the sofa, whereas last night they had hung in the hall.

But Dr. Fell appeared to be violently interested in a very bad landscape hung above the piano. He turned round a guileless face at their entrance, and addressed Swan.

"I say. Would you mind nipping up to—harrumph—what we'll call the sickroom, and finding out how the patient is? Don't let Dr. Grant bully you. I want to find out whether Colin's conscious yet, and whether he's said anything."

"So do I," agreed Swan with some vehemence, and was off with such celerity as to make the pictures rattle.

Dr. Fell hastily picked up his box-pleated cape, swung it round his shoulders with evident effort, and fastened the little chain at the neck.

"Get your hat, my lad," he said. "We're off on a little expedition. The presence of the press is no doubt stimulating; but there are times when it is definitely an encumbrance. We may be able to sneak out without our friend Swan seeing us."

"Where are we going?"

"Glencoe."

Alan stared at him.

"Glencoe! At seven o'clock in the morning?"

"I regret," sighed Dr. Fell, sniffing the odor of frying bacon and eggs which had begun to seep through the house, "that we shall not be able to wait for breakfast. But better miss breakfast than spoil the whole broth."

"Yes, but how in blazes are we going to get to Glencoe at this hour?"

"I've phoned through to Inveraray for a car. They haven't your slothful habits in this part of the country, my lad. Do you remember Duncan telling us yesterday that Alec Forbes had been found, or they thought he had been found, at a cottage near Glencoe?"

"Yes?"

Dr. Fell made a face and flourished his crutch-handled stick.

"It may not be true. And we may not even be able to find the cottage: though I got a description of its location from Duncan, and habitations out there are few and far between. But, by thunder, we've got to take the chance! If I'm to be any good to Colin Campbell at all, I've GOT to reach Alec Forbes before anybody else—even the police—can get to him. Get your hat."

Kathryn Campbell, pulling on her tweed jacket, moved swiftly into the room.

"Oh, no, you don't!" she said.

"Don't what?"

"You don't go without me," Kathryn informed them. "I heard you ringing up for that car. Aunt Elspat is bossy enough anywhere, but Aunt Elspat in a sickroom is simply bossy past all endurance. Eee!" She clenched her hands. "There's nothing more I can do anyhow. *Please* let me come!"

Dr. Fell waved a gallant assent. Tiptoeing like conspirators, they moved out to the back of the house. A brightly polished four-seater car was waiting beyond the hedge which screened Shira from the main road.

Alan did not want a loquacious chauffeur that morning, and he did not get one. The driver was a gnarled little man, dressed like a garage mechanic, who grudgingly held open the door for them. They were past Dalmally before they discovered that he was, in fact, an English cockney.

But Alan was too full of his latest discovery to mind the presence of a witness. He produced Angus's diary, and handed it to Dr. Fell.

Even on an empty stomach, Dr. Fell had filled and lighted his meerschaum. It was an open car, and, as it climbed the mighty hill under a somewhat damp-looking sky, the breeze gave Dr. Fell considerable trouble in its attentions to his hat and the tobacco smoke. But he read carefully through the diary, giving at least a glance at every page of it.

"H'mf, yes," he said, and scowled. "It fits. Everything fits! Your deductions, Miss Campbell, were to the point. It *was* Elspat who stole this."

"But—"

"Look here." He pointed to the place where a page had been torn out.

"The entry before that, at the foot of the preceding page, reads, 'Elspat says Janet G.'—whoever she may be—'godless and lecherous. In Elspat's younger days—' There it breaks off.

"It probably went on to recount gleefully an anecdote of Elspat's younger and less moral days. So the evidence was removed from the record. Elspat found nothing more in the diary to reflect on her. After giving it a careful reading, probably several readings to make sure, she returned the diary to a place where it could easily be found."

Alan was not impressed.

"Still, what about these sensational revelations? Why get in touch with the press, as Elspat did? The last entry in the diary may be suggestive, but it certainly doesn't tell us very much."

"No?"

"Well, does it?"

Dr. Fell eyed him curiously.

"I should say, on the contrary, that it tells us a good deal. But you hardly expected the sensational revelation (if any) to be in the last entry, did you? After all, Angus had gone happily and thoughtlessly to bed. Whatever attacked him, it attacked him after he had finished writing and put out his light. Why, therefore, should we expect anything of great interest in the last entry?"

Alan was brought up with something of a bump.

"That," he admitted, "is true enough. All the same—"

"No, my boy. The real meat of the thing is *here*." Dr. Fell made the pages riffle like a pack of cards. "In the body of the diary. In the account of his activities for the past year."

He frowned at the book, and slipped it into his pocket. His expression of gargantuan distress had grown along with his fever of certainty.

"Hang it all!" he said, and smote his hand on his knee. "The thing is inescapable! Elspat steals the diary. She reads it. Being no fool, she guesses—"

"Guesses what?"

"How Angus Campbell really died. She hates and distrusts the police to the very depths of her soul. So she writes to her favorite newspaper and plans to explode a bomb. And suddenly, when it is too late, she realizes with horror—"

Again Dr. Fell paused. The expression on his face smoothed itself out. He sat back with a gusty sigh against the upholstery of the tonneau, and shook his head.

"You know, that tears it," he added blankly. "That really does tear it."

"I personally," Kathryn said through her teeth, "will be in a condition to tear something if this mystification goes on."

Dr. Fell appeared still more distressed.

"Allow me," he suggested, "to counter your very natural curiosity with just one more question." He looked at Alan. "A moment ago you said that you thought the last entry in Angus's diary was 'suggestive.' What did you mean by that?"

"I meant that it certainly wasn't a passage which could have been written by anyone who meant to kill himself."

Dr. Fell nodded.

"Yes," he agreed. "Then what would you say if I were to tell you that Angus Campbell really committed suicide after all?"

XIV

"I should reply," said Kathryn, "that I felt absolutely cheated! Oh, I know I shouldn't say that; but it's true. You've got us looking so hard for a murderer that we can't concentrate on anything else."

Dr. Fell nodded as though he saw the aesthetic validity of the point.

"And yet," he went on, "for the sake of argument, I ask you to consider this explanation. I ask you to observe how it is borne out by every one of our facts."

He was silent for a moment, puffing at the meerschaum.

"Let us first consider Angus Campbell. Here is a shrewd, embittered, worn-out old man with a tinkering brain and an intense love of family. He is now broke, stony broke. His great dreams will never come true. He knows it. His brother Colin, of whom he is very fond, is overwhelmed with debts. His ex-mistress Elspat, of whom he is fonder still, is penniless and will remain penniless.

"Angus might well consider himself, in the hardheaded Northern fashion, a useless encumbrance. Good to nobody—except dead. But he is a hale old body to whom the insurance company's doctor gives fifteen more years of life. And in the meantime how (in God's name, how) are they to live?

"Of course, if he were to die now . . ."

Dr. Fell made a slight gesture.

"But, if he dies now, it must be established as certain, absolutely *certain*, that his death is not a suicide. And that will take a bit of doing. The sum involved is huge: thirty-five thousand pounds, distributed among intelligent insurance companies with nasty suspicious minds.

"Mere accident won't do. He can't go out and stumble off a cliff, hoping it will be read as accident. They might think that; but it is too chancy, and nothing must be left to chance. His death must be murder, cold-blooded murder, proved beyond any shadow of a doubt."

Again Dr. Fell paused. Alan improved the occasion to utter a derisive laugh which was not very convincing.

"In that case, sir," Alan said, "I turn your own guns on you."

"So? How?"

"You asked last night why any person intending to commit a murder for the insurance money should commit a murder which looked exactly like suicide. Well, for the same reason, why should Angus (of all people) plan a suicide which looked exactly like suicide?"

"He didn't," answered Dr. Fell.

"Pardon?"

Dr. Fell leaned forward to tap Alan, who occupied the front seat, very decisively on the shoulder. The doctor's manner was compounded of eagerness and absent-mindedness.

"That's the whole point. He didn't. You see, you haven't yet realized what was in that dog carrier. You haven't yet realized what Angus deliberately put there.

"And I say to you,"—Dr. Fell lifted his hand solemnly—"I say to you that but for one little unforeseeable accident, a misfortune so unlikely that the mathematical chances were a million to one against it, there would never have been the least doubt that Angus was murdered! I say to you that Alec Forbes would be in jail at this moment, and that the insurance companies would have been compelled to pay up."

They were approaching Loch Awe, a gem of beauty in a deep, mountainous valley. But none of them looked at it.

"Are you saying," breathed Kathryn, "that Angus was going to kill himself, and deliberately frame Alec Forbes for the job?"

"I am. Do you consider it unlikely?"

After a silence Dr. Fell went on:

"In the light of this theory, consider our evidence.

"Here is Forbes, a man with a genuine, bitter grudge. Ideal for the purposes of a scapegoat.

"Forbes calls—for which we may read, 'is summoned'—to see Angus that night. He goes upstairs to the tower room. There is a row, which Angus can arrange to make audible all over the place. Now, was Forbes at this time carrying a 'suitcase'?

"The women, we observe, don't know. They didn't see him until he was ejected. Who is the only witness to the suitcase? Angus himself. He carefully calls their attention to the fact that Forbes was supposed to have one, *and* says pointedly that Forbes must have left it behind.

"You follow that? The picture Angus intended to present was that Forbes had distracted his attention and shoved the suitcase under the bed, where Angus never noticed it, but where the thing inside it could later do its deadly work."

Alan reflected.

"It's a curious thing," Alan said, "that the day before yesterday I myself suggested just that explanation, with Forbes as the murderer. But nobody would listen to it."

"Yet I repeat," asserted Dr. Fell, "that except for a totally unpredictable accident, Forbes would have been nailed as the murderer straight-away."

Kathryn put her hands to her temples.

"You mean," she cried, "that Elspat looked under the bed before the door was locked, and saw there was no box there?"

But to their surprise Dr. Fell shook his head.

"No, no, no, no! That was another point, of course. But it wasn't serious. Angus probably never even thought her glance under the bed noticed anything one way or the other. No, no, no! I refer to the contents of the box."

Alan closed his eyes.

"I suppose," he said in a restrained voice, "it would be asking too much if we were to ask you just to *tell* us what was in the box?"

Dr. Fell grew still more solemn, even dogged.

"In a very short time we are (I hope) going to see Alec Forbes. I am going to put the question to him. In the meantime, I ask you to think about it; think about the facts we know; think about the trade magazines in Angus's room; think about his activities of the past year; and see if you can't reach the solution for yourselves.

"For the moment let us return to the great scheme. Alec Forbes, of course, had carried no suitcase or anything else. The box (already prepared by Angus himself) was downstairs in one of the lower rooms. Angus got rid of the women at ten o'clock, slipped downstairs, procured the box, and put it under the bed, after which he re-locked and re-bolted his door. This, I submit, is the only possible explanation of how that box got into a hermetically sealed room.

"Finally, Angus wrote up his diary. He put in those significant words that he had told Forbes not to come back, and Forbes said it wouldn't be necessary. Other significant words too: so many more nails in Forbes's coffin. Then Angus undressed, turned out the light, climbed into bed, and with real grim fortitude prepared for what had to come.

"Now follow what happens next day. Angus has left his diary in plain sight, for the police to find. Elspat finds it herself, and appropriates it.

"She thinks Alec Forbes killed Angus. On reading through the bulk of the diary, she realizes—as Angus meant everybody to realize—exactly what killed Angus. She has got Alec Forbes, the murderer. She will hang the sinful higher than Haman. She sits down and writes to the *Daily Floodlight.*

"Only after the letter is posted does she suddenly see the flaw. If

Forbes did that, he must have pushed the box under the bed before he was kicked out. But Forbes can't have done that! For she herself looked under the bed, and saw no box; and, most horrifying of all, she has already told the police so."

Dr. Fell made a gesture.

"This woman has lived with Angus Campbell for forty years. She knows him inside out. She sees through him with that almost morbid clarity our womenfolk exhibit in dealing with our vagaries and our stupidities. It doesn't take her long to understand where the hanky-panky lies. It wasn't Alec Forbes; it was Angus himself who did this. And so—

"Do I have to explain further? Think over her behavior. Think of her sudden change of mind about the box. Think of her searching for excuses to fly into a tantrum and throw out of the house the newspaperman she has summoned herself. Think, above all, of her position. If she speaks out with the truth, she loses every penny. If she denounces Alec Forbes, on the other hand, she condemns her soul to hell-fire and eternal burning. Think of that, my children; and don't be too hard on Elspat Campbell when her temper seems to wear thin."

The figure of one whom Kathryn had called a silly old woman was undergoing, in their minds, a curious transformation.

Thinking back to eyes and words and gestures, thinking of the core under that black taffeta, Alan experienced a revulsion of feeling as well as a revulsion of ideas.

"And so—?" he prompted.

"Well! She won't make the decision," replied Dr. Fell. "She returns the diary to the tower room, and lets us decide what we like."

The car had climbed to higher, bleaker regions. Uplands of waste, spiked with ugly posts against possible invasion by air, showed brown against the granite ribs of the mountains. The day was clouding over, and a damp breeze blew in their faces.

"May I submit," Dr. Fell added after a pause, "that this is the only explanation which fits all the facts?"

"Then if we're not looking for a murderer—"

"Oh, my dear sir!" expostulated Dr. Fell. "We *are* looking for a murderer!"

They whirled round on him.

"Ask yourselves other questions," said Dr. Fell. "Who impersonated the ghostly Highlander, and why? Who sought the death of Colin Campbell, and why? For remember: except for lucky chance, Colin would be dead at this minute."

He brooded, chewing the stem of a pipe that had gone out, and making a gesture as though he were pursuing something which just eluded him.

"Pictures," he added, "sometimes give extraordinary ideas."

Then he seemed to realize for the first time that he was talking in front of an outsider. He caught, in the driving mirror, the eye of the gnarled little chauffeur who for miles had not spoken or moved. Dr. Fell rumbled and snorted, brushing fallen ash off his cape. He woke up out of a mazy dream, and blinked round.

"H'mf. Hah. Yes. So. I say, when do we get to Glencoe?"

The driver spoke out of the side of his mouth.

"This *is* Glen Coe," he answered.

All of them woke up.

And here, Alan thought, were the wild mountains as he had always imagined them. The only adjective which occurred in connection with the place was Godforsaken: not as an idle word, but as a literal fact.

The glen of Coe was immensely long and immensely wide, whereas Alan had always pictured it as a cramped, narrow place. Through it the black road ran arrow-straight. On either side rose the lines of mountain ridges, granite-gray and dull purple, looking as smooth as stone. No edge of kindliness touched them: it was as though nature had dried up, and even sullenness had long petrified to hostility.

Burns twisting down the mountainside were so far off that you could not even be sure if the water moved, and only were sure when you saw it gleam. Utter silence emphasized the bleakness and desolation of the glen. Sometimes you saw a tiny white-washed cottage, which appeared empty.

Dr. Fell pointed to one of them.

"We are looking," he said, "for a cottage on the left-hand side of the road, down a slope among some fir trees, just past the Falls of Coe. You don't happen to know it?"

The driver was silent for a time, and then said he thought he knew it.

"Not far off now," he added. "Be at the Falls in a minute or two."

The road rose, and, after its interminable straightness, curved round the slaty shoulder of a hill. The hollow, tumbling roar of a waterfall shook the damp air as they turned into a narrow road, shut in on the right by a cliff.

Driving them some distance down this road, the chauffeur stopped the car, sat back, and pointed without a word.

They climbed out on the breezy road, under a darkening sky. The tumult of the waterfall still splashed in their ears. Dr. Fell was assisted down a slope on which they all slithered. He was assisted, with more effort, across a stream; and in the bed of the stream the stones were polished black, as though they had met the very heart of the soil.

The cottage, of dirty whitewashed stone with a thatched roof, stood beyond. It was tiny, appearing to consist of only one room. The door stood closed. No smoke went up from the chimney. Far beyond it the mountains rose up light purple and curiously pink.

Nothing moved—except a mongrel dog.

The dog saw them, and began to run round in circles. It darted to the cottage, and scratched with its paws on the closed door. The scratching sound rose thinly, above the distant mutter of the falls. It set a seal on the heart, of loneliness and depression in the evil loneliness of Glencoe.

The dog sat back on its haunches, and began to howl.

"All right, old boy!" said Dr. Fell.

That reassuring voice seemed to have some effect on the animal. It scratched frantically at the door again, after which it ran to Dr. Fell and capered round him, leaping up to scrape at his cloak. What frightened Alan was the fright in the eyes of the dog.

Dr. Fell knocked at the door, without response. He tried the latch, but something held the door on the inside. There was no window in the front of the cottage.

"Mr. Forbes!" he called thunderously. "Mr. Forbes!"

Their footsteps scraped amidst little flinty stones. The shape of the cottage was roughly square. Muttering to himself, Dr. Fell lumbered round to the side of the house, and Alan followed him.

Here they found a smallish window. A rusty metal grating, like a mesh of heavy wire, had been nailed up over the window on the inside. Beyond this its grimy windowpane, set on hinges to swing open and shut like a door, stood partly open.

Cupping their hands round their eyes, they pressed against the grating and tried to peer inside. A frowsty smell, compounded of stale air, stale whisky, paraffin oil, and sardines out of a tin, crept out of the room. Gradually, as their eyes grew accustomed to the gloom, outlines emerged.

The table, with its greasy mess of dishes, had been pushed to one side. In the center of the ceiling was set a stout iron hook, presumably for a lamp. Alan saw what was hanging from that hook now, and swaying gently each time the dog pawed at the door.

He dropped his hands. He turned away from the window, putting one hand against the wall to steady himself. He walked round the side of the cottage to the front, where Kathryn was standing.

"What is it?" He heard her voice distantly, though it was almost a scream. "What's wrong?"

"You'd better come away from here," he said.

"What is it?"

Dr. Fell, much less ruddy of face, followed Alan round to the front door.

The doctor breathed heavily and wheezily for a moment before he spoke.

"That's rather a flimsy door," he said, pointing with his stick. "You could kick it in. And I think you better had."

On the inside was a small, new, tight bolt. Alan tore the staple loose from the wood with three vicious kicks into which he put his whole muscle and the whole state of his mind.

Though he was not anxious to go inside, the face of the dead man was now turned away from them, and it was not so bad as that first look through the window. The smell of food and whisky and paraffin grew overpowering.

The dead man wore a long, grimy dressing gown. The rope, which had formed the plaited cord of his dressing gown, had been shaped at one end into a running noose, and the other tied tightly round the hook in the ceiling. His heels swung some two feet off the floor as he hung there. An empty keg, evidently of whisky, had rolled away from under him.

Whining frenziedly, the mongrel dog shot past them, whirled round the dead man, and set him swinging again in frantic attempts to spring up.

Dr. Fell inspected the broken bolt. He glanced across at the grated window. His voice sounded heavy in the evil-smelling room.

"Oh, yes," he said. "Another suicide."

XV

"I suppose," Alan muttered, "it *is* Alec Forbes?"

Dr. Fell pointed with his stick to the camp bed pushed against one wall. On it an open suitcase full of soiled linen bore the painted initials, "A.G.F." Then he walked round to the front of the hanging figure where he could examine the face. Alan did not follow him.

"And the description fits, too. A week's growth of beard on his face. And, in all probability, ten years' growth of depression in his heart."

Dr. Fell went to the door, barring it against Kathryn, who stood white-faced under the overcast sky a few feet away.

"There must be a telephone somewhere. If I remember my map, there's a village with a hotel a mile or two beyond here. Get through to Inspector Donaldson at Dunoon police station, and tell him Mr. Forbes has hanged himself. Can you do that?"

Kathryn gave a quick, unsteady nod.

"He did kill himself, did he?" she asked in a voice barely above a whisper. "It isn't—anything else?"

Dr. Fell did not reply to this. Kathryn, after another quick nod, turned and made her way back.

The hut was some dozen feet square, thick-walled, with a primitive fireplace and a stone floor. It was no crofter's cottage, but had evidently been used by Forbes as a sort of retreat. Its furniture consisted of the camp bed, the table, two kitchen chairs, a washstand with bowl and pitcher, and a stand of mildewed books.

The mongrel had now ceased its frantic whimpering, for which Alan felt grateful. The dog lay down close to the silent figure, where he could raise adoring eyes to that altered face; and, from time to time, he shivered.

"I ask what Kathryn asked," said Alan. "Is this suicide, or not?"

Dr. Fell walked forward and touched Forbes's arm. The dog stiffened. A menacing growl began in its throat and quivered through its whole body.

"Easy, boy!" said Dr. Fell. "Easy!"

He stood back. He took out his watch and studied it. Grunting and muttering, he lumbered over to the table, on whose edge stood a hurricane lantern with a hook and chain by which it could be slung from the roof. With the tips of his fingers Dr. Fell picked up the lantern and shook it. A tin of oil stood beside it.

"Empty," he said. "Burnt out, but obviously used." He pointed to the body. "Rigor is not complete. This undoubtedly happened during the early hours of the morning: two or three o'clock, perhaps. The hour of suicides. And look there."

He was now pointing to the plaited dressing-gown cord round the dead man's neck.

"It's a curious thing," he went on, scowling. "The genuine suicide invariably takes the most elaborate pains to guard himself against the least discomfort. If he hangs himself, for instance, he will never use a wire or chain: something that is likely to cut or chafe his neck. If he uses a rope, he will often pad it against chafing. Look there! Alec Forbes has used a soft rope, and padded that with handkerchiefs. The authentic touch of suicide, or—"

"Or what?"

"Real genius in murder," said Dr. Fell.

He bent down to inspect the empty whisky keg. He went across to the one window. Thrusting one finger through the mesh of the grating, he shook it and found it solidly nailed up on the inside. Back he went, with fussed and fussy gestures, to the bolt of the door, which he examined carefully without touching it.

Then he peered round the room, stamping his foot on the floor. His voice had taken on a hollow sound like wind along an underground tunnel.

"Hang it all!" he said. "This *is* suicide. It's got to be suicide. The keg is just the right height for him to have stepped off, and just the right distance away. Nobody could have got in or out through that nailed window or that solidly bolted door."

He regarded Alan with some anxiety.

"You see, for my sins I know something about hocusing doors or windows. I have been—ahem—haunted and pursued by such matters."

"So I've heard."

"But I can't," pursued Dr. Fell, pushing back his shovel hat, "I can't tell you any way of hocusing a bolt when there's no keyhole and when the door is so close-fitting that its sill scrapes the floor. Like that one."

He pointed.

"And I can't tell you any way of hocusing a window when it is covered with a steel meshwork nailed up on the inside. Again, like that one there. If Alec Forbes—hullo!"

The bookstand was placed cater-cornered in the angle beside the fireplace. Dr. Fell discovered it as he went to inspect the fireplace, finding to his disgust that the flue was too narrow and soot-choked to admit any person. Dusting his fingers, he turned to the bookstand.

On the top row of books stood a portable typewriter, its cover missing and a sheet of paper projecting from the carriage. On it a few words were typed in pale blue ink.

To any jackal who finds this:

I killed Angus and Colin Campbell with the same thing they used to swindle me. What are you going to do about it now?

"Even, you see," Dr. Fell said fiercely, "the suicide note. The final touch. The brush stroke of the master. I repeat, sir: this must be suicide. And yet—well, if it is, I mean to retire to Bedlam."

The smell of the room, the black-faced occupant, the yearning dog, all these things were commencing to turn Alan Campbell's stomach. He felt he could not stand the air of the place much longer. Yet he fought back.

"I don't see why you say that," he declared. "After all, Doctor, can't you admit you may be wrong?"

"Wrong?"

"About Angus's death being suicide." Certainty, dead certainty, took root in Alan Campbell's brain. "Forbes *did* kill Angus and tried to kill Colin. Everything goes to show it. Nobody could have got in or out of this room, as you yourself admit; and there's Forbes's confession to clinch matters.

"He brooded out here until his brain cracked, as I know mine would in these parts unless I took to religion. He disposed of both brothers, or thought he had. When his work was finished, he killed himself. Here's the evidence. What more do you want?"

"The truth," insisted Dr. Fell stubbornly. "I am old fashioned. I want the truth."

Alan hesitated.

"I'm old fashioned too. And I seem to remember," Alan told him, "that you came North with the express purpose of helping Colin. Is it going to help Colin, or Aunt Elspat either, if the detective they brought in to show Angus was murdered goes about shouting that it was suicide—even after we've got Alec Forbes's confession?"

Dr. Fell blinked at him.

"My dear sir," he said in pained astonishment, and adjusted his eyeglasses and blinked at Alan through them, "you surely don't imagine that I mean to confide any of my beliefs to the police?"

"Isn't that the idea?"

Dr. Fell peered about to make sure they were not overheard.

"My record," he confided, "is an extremely black one. Harrumph. I have on several occasions flummoxed the evidence so that a murderer should go free. Not many years ago I outdid myself by setting a house on fire. My present purpose (between ourselves) is to swindle the insurance companies so that Colin Campbell can bask in good cigars and fire water for the rest of his life . . ."

"*What?*"

Dr. Fell regarded him anxiously.

"That shocks you? Tut, tut! All this (I say) I mean to do. But, dammit, man!" He spread out his hands. "For my own private information, I like to know the truth."

He turned back to the bookstand. Still without touching it, he examined the typewriter. On top of the row of books below it stood an angler's creel and some salmon flies. On top of the third row of books lay a bicycle spanner, a bicycle lamp, and a screwdriver.

Dr. Fell next ran a professional eye over the books. There were works on physics and chemistry, on Diesel engines, on practical building, and on astronomy. There were catalogues and trade journals. There was a dictionary, a six-volume encyclopedia, and (surprisingly) two or three boys' books by G. A. Henty. Dr. Fell eyed these last with some interest.

"Wow!" he said. "Does anybody read Henty nowadays, I wonder? If they knew what they were missing, they would run back to him. I am proud to say that I still read him with delight. Who would suspect Alec Forbes of having a romantic soul?" He scratched his nose. "Still—"

"Look here," Alan persisted. "What makes you so sure this isn't suicide?"

"My theory. My mule-headedness, if you prefer it."

"And your theory still holds that Angus committed suicide?"

"Yes."

"But that Forbes here was murdered?"

"Exactly."

Dr. Fell wandered back to the center of the room. He eyed the untidy camp bed with the suitcase on it. He eyed a pair of gum boots under the bed.

"My lad, I don't trust that suicide note. I don't trust it one little bit. And there are solid reasons why I don't trust it. Come out of here. Let's get some clean air."

Alan was glad enough to go. The dog raised its head from its paws, and gave them a wild, dazed sort of look; then it lowered its head again, growling, and settled down with ineffable patience under the dead.

Distantly, they could hear the rushing of the waterfall. Alan breathed the cool, damp air, and felt a shudder go over him. Dr. Fell, a huge bandit shape in his cloak, leaned his hands on his stick.

"Whoever wrote that note," he went on, "whether Alec Forbes or another, knew the trick that had been employed in Angus Campbell's death. That's the first fact to freeze to. Well! Have you guessed yet what the trick was?"

"No, I have not."

"Not even after seeing the alleged suicide note? Oh, man! Think!"

"You can ask me to think all you like. I may be dense; but if you can credit it, I still don't know what makes people jump up out of bed in the middle of the night and fall out of windows to their death."

"Let us begin," pursued Dr. Fell, "with the fact that Angus's diary records his activities for the past year, as diaries sometimes do. Well, what in Satan's name *have* been Angus's principal activities for the past year?"

"Mixing himself up in various wildcat schemes to try to make money."

"True. But only one scheme in which Alec Forbes was concerned, I think?"

"Yes."

"Good. What was that scheme?"

"An idea to manufacture some kind of ice cream with tartan patterns on it. At least, so Colin said."

"And in making their ice cream," said Dr. Fell, "what kind of freezing agent did they employ in large quantities? Colin told us that too."

"He said they used artificial ice, which he described as 'that chemical stuff that's so expen—' "

Alan paused abruptly.

Half-forgotten memories flowed back into his mind. With a shock he recalled a laboratory of his school days, and words being spoken from a platform. The faint echo of them came back now.

"And do you know," inquired Dr. Fell, "what this artificial ice, or 'dry' ice, really is?"

"It's whitish stuff to look at; something like real ice, only opaque. It—"

"To be exact," said Dr. Fell, "it is nothing more or less than liquefied gas. And do you know the name of the gas which is turned into a solid 'snow' block, and can be cut and handled and moved about? What is the name of that gas?"

"Carbon dioxide," said Alan.

Though the spell remained on his wits, it was suddenly as though a blind had flown up with a snap, and he saw.

"Now suppose," argued Dr. Fell, "you removed a block of that stuff from its own airtight cylinders. A big block, say one big enough to fit into a large suitcase—or, better still, some box with an open end, so that the air can reach it better. What would happen?"

"It would slowly melt."

"And in melting, of course, it would release into the room . . . what would it release?"

Alan found himself almost shouting.

"Carbonic acid gas. One of the deadliest and quickest-acting gases there is."

"Suppose you placed your artificial ice, in its container, under the bed in a room where the window is always kept closed at night. What would happen?

"With your permission, I will now drop the Socratic method and tell you. You have planted one of the surest murder traps ever devised. One of two things will happen. Either the victim, asleep or drowsy, will breathe in that concentrated gas as it is released into the room; and he will die in his bed.

"Or else the victim will notice the faint, acrid odor as it gets into his lungs. He will not breathe it long, mind you. Once the stuff takes hold, it will make the strongest man totter and fall like a fly. He will want air—air at any cost. As he is overcome, he will get out of bed and try to make for the window.

"He may not make it at all. If he does make it, he will be so weak on the legs that he can't hold up. And if this window is a low window, catching him just above the knees; if it consists of two leaves, opening outwards, so that he falls against it—"

Dr. Fell pushed his hands outwards, a rapid gesture.

Alan could almost see the limp, unwieldy body in the nightshirt plunge outwards and downwards.

"Of course, the artificial ice will melt away and leave no trace in the box. With the window now open, the gas will presently clear away.

"You now perceive, I hope, why Angus's suicide scheme was so foolproof. Who but Alec Forbes would have used artificial ice to kill his partner in the venture?

"Angus, as I read it, never once intended to jump or fall from the window. No, no, no! He intended to be found dead in bed, of poisoning by carbonic acid gas. There would be a post-mortem. The 'band' of this gas would be found in his blood as plain as print. The diary would be read and interpreted. All the circumstances against Alec Forbes would be recalled, as I outlined them to you a while ago. And the insurance money would be collected as certainly as the sun will rise tomorrow."

Alan, staring at the stream, nodded.

"But at the last moment, I suppose—?"

"At the last moment," agreed Dr. Fell, "like many suicides, Angus couldn't face it. He had to have *air*. He felt himself going under. And in a panic he leaped for the window.

"Therein, my boy, lies the million-to-one chance I spoke of. It was a million to one that either (a) the gas would kill him, or (b) the fall would kill him instantly as he plunged out face forwards. But neither of these things happened. He was mortally injured; yet he did not immediately die. Remember?"

Again Alan nodded.

"Yes. We've come across that point several times."

"Before he died, his lungs and blood were freed of the gas. Hence no trace remained for the post-mortem. Had he died instantly or even quickly, those traces would have been there. But they were not. So we had only the meaningless spectacle of an old gentleman who leaps from his bed in order to throw himself out of the window."

Dr. Fell's big voice grew fiery. He struck the ferrule of his stick on the ground.

"I say to you—" he began.

"Stop a bit!" said Alan, with sudden recollection.

"Yes?"

"Last night, when I went up to the tower room to rout out Colin, I bent down and tried to look under the sill of the door. When I straightened up, I remember feeling lightheaded. In fact, I staggered when I went down the stairs. Did *I* get a whiff of the stuff?"

"Of course. The room was full of it. Only a very faint whiff, fortunately for yourself.

"Which brings us to the final point. Angus carefully wrote in his diary that there was a 'faint musty smell in the room.' Now, that's rubbish on the face of it. If he had already begun to notice the presence of the gas, he could never have completed his diary and gone to bed. No: that was only another artistic touch designed to hang Alec Forbes."

"And misinterpreted by me," growled Alan. "I was thinking about some kind of animal."

"But you see where all this leads us?"

"No, I don't. Into the soup, of course; but aside from that—"

"The only possible explanation of the foregoing facts," insisted Dr.

Fell, "is that Angus killed himself. If Angus killed himself, then Alec Forbes didn't kill him. And if Alec Forbes didn't kill him, Alec had no reason to say he did. Therefore the suicide note is a fake.

"Up to this time, d'ye see, we have had a suicide which everybody thought was murder. Now we have a murder which everybody is going to take for suicide. We are going places and seeing things. All roads lead to the lunatic asylum. Can you by any chance oblige me with an idea?"

XVI

Alan shook his head.

"No ideas. I presume that the 'extra' thing which ailed Colin, and exercised Dr. Grant so much, was carbon-dioxide poisoning?"

Dr. Fell grunted assent. Fishing out the meerschaum pipe again, he filled and lighted it.

"Which," he assented, speaking between puffs like the Spirit of the Volcano, "leads us at full tide into our troubles. We can't blame Angus for that. The death box didn't load itself again with artificial ice.

"Somebody—who knew Colin was going to sleep there—set the trap again in a box already conveniently left under the bed. Somebody, who knew Colin's every movement, could nip up there ahead of him. He was drunk and wouldn't bother to investigate the box. All that saved his life was the fact that he slept with the window open, and roused himself in time. Query: who did that, and why?

"Final query: who killed Alec Forbes, and how, and why?"

Alan continued to shake his head doubtfully.

"You're still not convinced that Forbes's death was murder, my lad?"

"Frankly, I'm not. I still don't see why Forbes couldn't have killed both the others, or thought he had, and then killed himself."

"Logic? Or wishful thinking?"

Alan was honest. "A little of both, maybe. Aside from the money question, I should hate to think that Angus was such as old swine as to try to get an innocent man hanged."

"Angus," returned Dr. Fell, "was neither an old swine nor an honest Christian gentleman. He was a realist who saw only one way to provide for those he was fond of. I do not defend it. But can you dare say you don't understand it?"

"It isn't that. I can't understand, either, why he took the blackout down from the window if he wanted to be sure of smothering himself with the . . ."

Alan paused, for the sudden expression which had come over Dr. Fell's face was remarkable for its sheer idiocy. Dr. Fell stared, and his eyes rolled. The pipe almost dropped from his mouth.

"O Lord! O Bacchus! O my ancient hat!" he breathed. "Blackout!"

"What is it?"

"The murderer's first mistake," said Dr. Fell. "Come with me."

Hurriedly he swung round and blundered back into the hut again. Alan followed him, not without an effort. Dr. Fell began a hurried search of the room. With an exclamation of triumph he found on the floor near the bed a piece of tar paper nailed to a light wooden frame. He held this up to the window, and it fitted.

"We ourselves can testify," he went on, with extraordinary intensity, "that when we arrived here there was no blackout on this window. Hey?"

"That's right."

"Yet the lamp,"—he pointed—"had obviously been burning for a long time, far into the night. We can smell the odor of burned paraffin oil strongly even yet?"

"Yes."

Dr. Fell stared into vacancy.

"Every inch of this neighborhood is patrolled all night by the Home Guard. A hurricane lantern gives a strong light. There wasn't even so much as a curtain, let alone a blackout, on this window when we arrived. How is it that nobody noticed that light?"

There was a pause.

"Maybe they just didn't see it."

"My dear chap! So much as a chink of light in these hills would draw down the Home Guard for miles round. No, no, no! That won't do."

"Well, maybe Forbes—before he hanged himself—blew out the lantern and took down the blackout. The window's open, we notice. Though I don't see why he should have done that."

Again Dr. Fell shook his head with vehemence.

"I quote you again the habits of suicides. A suicide will never take his own life in darkness if there is any means of providing light. I do not analyze the psychology: I merely state the fact. Besides, Forbes wouldn't have been able to see to make all his preparations in the dark. No, no, no! It's fantastic!"

"What do you suggest, then?"

Dr. Fell put his hands to his forehead. For a time he remained motionless, wheezing gently.

"I suggest," he replied, lowering his hands after an interval, "that, after Forbes had been murdered and strung up, the murderer himself extinguished the lantern. He poured out the oil remaining in it so that it should later seem to have burned itself out. Then he took down the blackout."

"But why in blazes bother to do that? Why not leave the blackout where it was, and go away, and leave the lantern to burn itself out?"

"Obviously because he had to make use of the window in making his escape."

This was the last straw.

"Look here," Alan said, with a sort of wild patience. He strode across. "Look at the damned window! It's covered by a steel grating nailed up solidly on the inside! Can you suggest any way, any way at all, by which a murderer could slide out through that?"

"Well—no. Not at the moment. And yet it was done."

They looked at each other.

From some distance away they heard the sound of a man's voice earnestly hallooing, and scraps of distant talk. They hurried to the door.

Charles Swan and Alistair Duncan were striding toward them. The lawyer, in a raincoat and bowler hat, appeared more cadaverous than ever; but his whole personality was suffused with a kind of dry triumph.

"I think you're a good deal of a cheapskate," Swan accused Alan, "to run away like that after you'd promised me all the news there was. If I hadn't had my car I'd have been stranded."

Duncan silenced him. Duncan's mouth had a grim, pleased curve. He bowed slightly to Dr. Fell.

"Gentlemen," he said, taking up a position like a schoolmaster, "we have just learned from Dr. Grant that Colin Campbell is suffering from the effects of carbonic acid gas."

"True," agreed Dr. Fell.

"Administered probably from artificial ice taken from Angus Campbell's laboratory."

Again Dr. Fell nodded.

"Can we therefore," pursued Duncan, putting his hands together and rubbing them softly, "have any doubt of how Angus died? Or of who administered the gas to him?"

"We cannot. If you'd care to glance in that cottage there," said Dr. Fell, nodding toward it, "you will see the final proof which completes your case."

Duncan stepped quickly to the door, and just as quickly stepped back again. Swan, more determined or more callous, uttered an exclamation and went in.

There was a long silence while the lawyer seemed to be screwing up his courage. His Adam's apple worked in his long throat above the too-large collar. He removed his bowler hat and wiped his forehead with a handkerchief. Then, replacing the hat and straightening his shoulders, he forced himself to follow Swan into the cottage.

Both of them reappeared, hastily and without dignity, pursued by a series of savage growls which rose to a yelping snarl. The dog, red-eyed, watched them from the doorway.

"Nice doggie!" crooned Duncan, with a leer of such patent hypocrisy that the dog snarled again.

"You shouldn't have touched him," said Swan.

"The pooch naturally get sore. I want a telephone. Cripes, what a scoop!"

Duncan readjusted his ruffled dignity.

"So it *was* Alec Forbes," he said.

Dr. Fell inclined his head.

"My dear sir," continued the lawyer, coming over to wring Dr. Fell's hand with some animation, "I—we—can't thank you too much! I daresay you guessed, from the trade magazines and bills you borrowed from Angus's room, what had been used to kill him?"

"Yes."

"I cannot imagine," said Duncan, "why it was not apparent to all of us from the first. Though, of course, the effects of the gas had cleared away when Angus was found. No wonder the clasps of the dog carrier were closed! When I think how we imagined snakes and spiders and heaven knows what, I am almost amused. The whole thing is so extraordinarily simple, once you have grasped the design behind it."

"I agree," said Dr. Fell. "By thunder, but I agree!"

"You—ah—observed the suicide note?"

"I did."

Duncan nodded with satisfaction.

"The insurance companies will have to eat their words now. There can be no question as to their paying in full."

Yet Duncan hesitated. Honesty evidently compelled him to worry at another point.

"There is just one thing, however, that I cannot quite understand. If Forbes placed the dog carrier under the bed before being ejected, as this gentleman,"—he looked at Alan—"so intelligently suggested on Monday, how is it that Elspat and Kirstie did not observe it when they looked there?"

"Haven't you forgotten?" asked Dr. Fell. "She *did* see it, as she has since told us. Miss Elspat Campbell's mind is as literal as a German's. You asked her whether there was a suitcase there, and she said no. That is all."

It would not be true to say that the worry cleared away altogether from Duncan's face. But he cheered up, although he gave Dr. Fell a very curious look.

"You think the insurance companies will accept that correction?"

"I know the police will accept it. So the insurance companies will have to, whether they like it or not."

"A plain case?"

"A plain case."

"So it seems to me." Duncan cheered up still more. "Well, we must finish up this sad business as soon as we can. Have you informed the police about—this?"

"Miss Kathryn Campbell has gone to do so. She should be back at any minute. We had to break the door in, as you see, but we haven't touched anything else. After all, we don't want to be held as accessories after the fact."

Duncan laughed.

"You could hardly be held for that in any case. In Scots law, there is no such thing as an accessory after the fact."

"Is that so, now?" mused Dr. Fell. He took the pipe out of his mouth and added abruptly: "Mr. Duncan, were you ever acquainted with Robert Campbell?"

There was something in his words so arresting, even if so inexplicable, that everyone turned to look at him. The faint thunder of the Falls of Coe appeared loud in the hush that followed.

"Robert?" repeated Duncan. "The third of the brothers?"

"Yes."

An expression of fastidious distaste crossed the lawyer's face.

"Really, sir, to rake up old scandals——"

"Did you know him?" insisted Dr. Fell.

"I did."

"What can you tell me about him? All I've learned so far is that he got into trouble and had to leave the country. What did he do? Where did he go? Above all, what was he like?"

Duncan grudgingly considered this.

"I knew him as a young man." He shot Dr. Fell a quick glance. "Robert, if I may say so, was by far the cleverest and brainiest of his family. But he had a streak of bad blood: which, fortunately, missed both Angus and Colin. He had trouble at the bank where he worked. Then there was a shooting affray over a barmaid.

"As to where he is now, I can't say. He went abroad—the colonies, America—I don't know where, because he slipped aboard a ship at Glasgow. You surely cannot consider that the matter is of any importance now?"

"No. I daresay not."

His attention was diverted. Kathryn Campbell scrambled down the bank, crossed the stream, and came toward them.

"I've got in touch with the police," she reported breathlessly, after a sharp glance at Duncan and Swan. "There's a hotel, the Glencoe Hotel, at the village of Glencoe about two miles farther on. The telephone number is Ballachulish—pronounced Ballahoolish—four-five."

"Did you talk to Inspector Donaldson?"

"Yes. He says he's always known Alec Forbes would do something like this. He says we needn't wait here, if we don't want to."

Her eyes strayed toward the cottage, and moved away uneasily.

"Please. *Must* you stay here? Couldn't we go on to the hotel and have something to eat? I ask because the proprietress knew Mr. Forbes very well."

Dr. Fell stirred with interest.

"So?"

"Yes. She says he was a famous cyclist. She says he could cover incredible distances at incredible speeds, in spite of the amount he drank."

Duncan uttered a soft exclamation. With a significant gesture to the others, he went round the side of the cottage, and they instinctively followed him. Behind the cottage was an outhouse, against which leaned a racing bicycle fitted out with a luggage grid at the back. Duncan pointed to it.

"The last link, gentlemen. It explains how Forbes could have got from here to Inveraray and back whenever he liked. Did your informant add anything else, Miss Campbell?"

"Not much. She said he came up here to drink and fish and work out schemes for perpetual motion, and things of that sort. She said the last time she saw him was yesterday, in the bar of the hotel. They practically had to throw him out at closing time in the afternoon. She says he was a bad man, who hated everything and everybody but animals."

Dr. Fell slowly walked forward and put his hand on the handle bar of the bicycle. Alan saw, with uneasiness, there was again on his face the startled expression, the wandering blankness of idiocy, which he had seen there once before. This time it was deeper and more explosive.

"O Lord!" thundered Dr. Fell, whirling round as though galvanized. "What a turnip I've been! What a remarkable donkey! What a thundering dunce!"

"Without," observed Duncan, "without sharing the views you express, may I ask why you express them?"

Dr. Fell turned to Kathryn.

"You're quite right," he said seriously, after reflecting for a time. "We must get on to that hotel. Not only to refresh the inner man; though I, to be candid, am ravenous. But I want to use a telephone. I want to use a telephone like billy-o. There's a million-to-one chance against it, of course; but the million-to-one chance came off before and it may happen again."

"What million-to-one chance?" asked Duncan, not without exasperation. "To whom do you want to telephone?"

"To the local commandant of the Home Guard," answered Dr. Fell, and lumbered round the side of the cottage with his cloak flying out behind him.

XVII

"Alan," Kathryn asked, "Alec Forbes didn't really kill himself, did he?"

It was late at night, and raining. They had drawn up their chairs before a brightly burning wood fire in the sitting room at Shira.

Alan was turning over the pages of a family album, with thick padded covers and gilt-topped leaves. For some time Kathryn had been silent, her elbows on the arm of the chair and her chin in her hand, staring into the fire. She dropped the question out of nowhere: flatly, as her habit was.

He did not raise his eyes.

"Why is it," he said, "that photographs taken some years ago are always so hilariously funny? You can take down anybody's family album and split your sides. If it happens to contain pictures of somebody you know, the effect is even more pronounced. Why? Is it the clothes, or the expression, or what? We weren't really as funny as that, were we?"

Disregarding her, he turned over a page or two.

"The women, as a rule, come out better than the men. Here is one of Colin as a young man, which looks as though he'd drunk about a quart of the Doom of the Campbells before leering at the photographer. Aunt Elspat, on the other hand, was a really fine-looking woman. Bold-eyed brunette; Mrs. Siddons touch. Here she is in a man's Highland costume: bonnet, feather, plaid, and all."

"Alan Campbell!"

"Angus, on the other hand, always tried to look so dignified and pensive that——"

"Alan darling."

He sat up with a snap. The rain pattered against the windows.

"What did you say?" he demanded.

"It was only a manner of speaking." She elevated her chin. "Or at least—well, anyway, I *had* to get your attention somehow. Alec Forbes didn't really kill himself, did he?"

"What makes you think that?"

"I can see it in the way you look," returned Kathryn; and he had an uncomfortable feeling that she would always be able to do this, which would provide some critical moments in the future.

"Besides," she went on peering round to make sure they were not overheard, and lowering her voice, "why should he? He certainly couldn't have been the one who tried to kill poor Colin."

Reluctantly Alan closed the album.

The memory of the day stretched out behind him: the meal at the Glencoe Hotel, the endless repetitions by Alistair Duncan of how Alec Forbes had committed his crimes and then hanged himself, all the while that Dr. Fell said nothing, and Kathryn brooded, and Swan sent off to the *Daily Floodlight* a story which he described as a honey.

"And why," he asked, "couldn't Forbes have tried to kill Colin?"

"Because he couldn't have known Colin was sleeping in the tower room."

(Damn! So she's spotted that!)

"Didn't you hear what the proprietress of the hotel said?" Kathryn insisted. "Forbes was in the bar of the hotel until closing time yesterday afternoon. Well, it was early in the afternoon here that Colin swore his great oath to sleep in the tower. How on earth could Forbes have known that? It was a snap decision which Colin made on the spur of the moment, and couldn't have been known outside the house."

Alan hesitated.

Kathryn lowered her voice still further.

"Oh, I'm not going to broadcast it! Alan, I know what Dr. Fell thinks. As he told us going out to the car, he thinks Angus committed suicide. Which is horrible, and yet I believe it. I believe it still more now that we've heard about the artificial ice."

She shivered.

"At least, we do know it isn't—supernatural. When we were thinking about snakes and spiders and ghosts and whatnots, I tell you I was frightened out of my wits. And all the while it was nothing but a lump of dry ice!"

"Most terrors are like that."

"Are they? Who played ghost, then? And who killed Forbes?"

Alan brooded. "*If* Forbes was murdered," he said, half-conceding this for the first time, "the motive for it is clear. It was to prove Angus's death was murder after all, like the attempt on Colin; to saddle Forbes with both crimes; and to clean up the whole business."

"To get the insurance money?"

"That's what it looks like."

The rain pattered steadily. Kathryn gave a quick glance at the door to the hall.

"But, Alan! In that case . . . ?"

"Yes. I know what you're thinking."

"And, in any case, how *could* Forbes have been murdered?"

"Your guess is as good as mine. Dr. Fell thinks the murderer got out by way of the window. Yes, I know the window was covered with an untouched grating! But so was the end of the dog carrier, if you remember. Twenty-four hours ago I would have sworn nothing could have got out of the dog carrier grating, either. And yet something did."

He broke off, with an air of elaborate casualness and a warning glance to Kathryn, as they heard footsteps in the hall. He was again turning over the pages of the album when Swan came into the sitting room.

Swan was almost as wet as he had been after Elspat's two pails of water. He stamped up to the fire, and let his hands drip into it.

"If I don't catch pneumonia one way or the other, before this thing is over," he announced, shifting from one foot to the other, "the reason won't be for want of bad luck. I've been obeying orders and trying to stick to Dr. Fell. You'd think that would be easy, wouldn't you?"

"Yes."

Swan's face was bitter.

"Well, it isn't. He's ditched me twice today. He's doing something with the Home Guard. Or at least he was before this rain started in. But what it is I can't find out and Sherlock Holmes himself couldn't guess. Anything up?"

"No. We were just looking at family portraits." Alan turned over pages. He passed one photograph, started to turn the page, and then, with sudden interest, went back to it. "Hullo," he said. "I've seen *that* face somewhere!"

It was a full-face view of a light-haired man with a heavy down-curved mustache, *circa* 1906, a handsome face with washed-out eyes. This impression, however, may have come from the faded brown color of the photograph. Across the lower right-hand corner was written in faded ink, with curlicues, "Best of luck!"

"Of course you've seen it," said Kathryn. "It's a Campbell. There's a resemblance, more or less, in every one of our particular crowd."

"No, no. I mean——"

He detached the photograph from the four slits in the cardboard, and turned it over. Across the back was written, in the same handwriting, "Robert Campbell, July, '05."

"So that's the brainy Robert!"

Swan, who had been peering over his shoulder, was clearly interested in something else.

"Wait a minute!" Swan urged, fitting back the photograph again and turning back a page quickly.

"Cripes, what a beauty! Who's the good-looking woman?"

"That's Aunt Elspat."

"*Who?*"

"Elspat Campbell."

Swan winked his eyes. "Not the old hag who—who—" Wordlessly, his hands went to his new suit, and his face became distorted.

"Yes. The same one who baptized you. Look at this other one of her in Highland costume, where she shows her legs. If I may mention the subject, they are very fine legs; though maybe on the heavy and muscular side for popular taste nowadays."

Kathryn could not restrain herself.

"But nothing, of course," she sneered, "to compare to the legs of your precious Duchess of Cleveland."

Swan begged their attention.

"Look," he said impressively, "I don't want to seem inquisitive. But—" his voice acquired a note of passion—"who *is* this dame from Cleveland, anyhow? Who is Charles? Who is Russell? And how did you get tangled up with her? I know I oughtn't to ask; but I can't sleep nights for thinking about it."

"The Duchess of Cleveland," said Alan, "was Charles's mistress."

"Yes, I gathered that. But is she your mistress too?"

"No. And she didn't come from Cleveland, Ohio, because she's been dead for more than two hundred years."

Swan stared at him.

"You're kidding me."

"I am not. We were having a historical argument, and——"

"I tell you, you're kidding me!" repeated Swan, with something like incredulous horror in his voice. "There's *got* to be a real Cleveland woman in it! As I said about you in my first story to the *Floodlight*——"

He paused. He opened his mouth, and shut it again. He seemed to feel that he had made a slip; as, in fact, he had. Two pairs of eyes fastened on him during an ominous silence.

"What," Kathryn asked very clearly, "what did you say about us in your first story to the *Floodlight*?"

"Nothing at all. Word of honor, I didn't! Just a little joke, nothing libelous in it at all——"

"Alan," murmured Kathryn, with her eye on a corner of the ceiling, "don't you think you'd better get down the claymores again?"

Swan had instinctively moved away until his back was shielded against the wall. He spoke in deep earnest.

"After all, you're going to get married! I overheard Dr. Fell himself say you had to get married. So what's wrong? I didn't mean any harm." (And clearly, thought Alan, he hadn't.) "I only said——"

"What a pity," continued Kathryn, still with her eye on the ceiling, "what a pity Colin hasn't got the use of his legs. But I hear he's a rare hand with a shotgun. And, since his bedroom windows face the main road——"

She paused, significantly musing, as Kirstie MacTavish flung open the door.

"Colin Campbell wants tae see you," she announced in her soft, sweet voice.

Swan changed color.

"He wants to see who?"

"He wants tae see all o' you."

"But he isn't allowed visitors, is he?" cried Kathryn.

"I dinna ken. He's drinkin' whusky in bed, annahoo."

"Well, Mr. Swan," said Kathryn, folding her arms, "after giving us a solemn promise, which you promptly broke and intended to break; after accepting hospitality here under false pretenses; after being handed on a plate probably the only good story you ever got in your life; and hoping to get some more—have you the courage to go up and face Colin now?"

"But you've got to look at my side of it, Miss Campbell!"

"Oh?"

"Colin Campbell'll understand! He's a good egg! He . . ." As an idea evidently occurred to him, Swan turned to the maid. "Look. He's not pickled, is he?"

"Wha'?"

"Pickled. Soused," said Swan apprehensively, "cockeyed. Plastered. Full."

Kirstie was enlightened. She assured him that Colin was not full. Though the effectiveness of this assurance was somewhat modified by Kirstie's experienced belief that no man is full until he can fall down two successive flights of stairs without injury, Swan did not know this and it served its purpose.

"I'll put it up to him," Swan argued with great earnestness. "And in the meantime I'll put it up to both of you. I come up here; and what happens to me?"

"Not a patch," said Kathryn, "on what's going to happen. But go on."

Swan did not hear her.

"I get chased along a road," he continued, "and get a serious injury that might have given me blood poisoning. All right. I come round the next day, in a brand-new suit that cost ten guineas at Austin Reed's, and that mad woman empties two buckets of water over me. Not *one* bucket, mind you. *Two*."

"Alan Campbell," said Kathryn fiercely, "do you find anything so very funny in this?"

Alan could not help himself. He was leaning back and roaring.

"Alan Campbell!"

"I can't help it," protested Alan, wiping the tears out of his eyes. "It just occurs to me that you'll have to marry me after all."

"Can I announce that?" asked Swan instantly.

"Alan Campbell, what on earth do you mean? I'll do no such thing! The idea!"

"You can't help yourself, my wench. It's the only solution to our difficulties. I have not yet read the *Daily Floodlight,* but I have my suspicions as to the nature of the hints that will have appeared there."

Swan seized on this.

"I knew you wouldn't be sore," he said, his face lighting up. "There's nothing anybody could object to, I swear! I never said a word about your always going to bawdy houses. That's really libelous anyway——"

"What's this," inquired Kathryn, breaking off with some quickness, "about you going to bawdy houses?"

"I'm sorry I said that," interposed Swan, with equal quickness. "I wouldn't have said it for the world in front of you, Miss Campbell, only it slipped out. It probably isn't true anyway, so just forget it. All I wanted to say was that I've got to play the game straight both with you and the public."

"Are ye comin'?" asked Kirstie, still waiting patiently in the doorway.

Swan straightened his tie.

"Yes, we are. And I know Colin Campbell, who's as good an egg as ever walked, will understand my position."

"I hope he does," breathed Kathryn. "Oh, good heavens, I hope he does! You did say he'd got some whisky up there, didn't you Kirstie?"

It was, in a sense, unnecessary to answer this question. As the three of them followed Kirstie up the stairs, and along the hall to the back of the house, it was answered by Colin himself. The doors at Shira were good thick doors, and very little in the nature of noise could penetrate far through them. The voice they heard, therefore, was not very loud. But it carried distinctly to the head of the stairs.

> *"I love a lassie, a boh-ny, boh-ny lassie;*
> *She's as puir as the li-ly in the dell!*
> *She's as sweet as the heather, the boh-ny pur-ple*
> *heath-er—"*

The singing stopped abruptly as Kirstie opened the door. In a spacious back bedroom with oak furniture, Colin Campbell lay on what should have been, and undoubtedly was, a bed of pain. But you would never have guessed this from the demeanor of the tough old sinner.

His body was bandaged from the waist down, one leg supported a little above the level of the bed by a portable iron framework and supports. But his back was hunched into pillows in such a way that he could just raise his head.

Though his hair, beard, and mustache had been trimmed, he managed to look shaggier than ever. Out of this, fiercely affable eyes peered from a flushed face. The airless room smelt like a distillery.

Colin had insisted, as an invalid, on having plenty of light, and the chandelier glowed with bulbs. They illuminated his truculent grin, his gaudy pajama tops, and the untidy litter of articles on the bedside table. His bed was drawn up by one blacked-out window.

"Come in!" he shouted. "Come in, and keep the old crock company. Filthy position to be in. Kirstie, go and fetch three more glasses and another decanter. You! The rest of you! Pull up your chairs. Here, where I can see you. I've got nothing to do but this."

He was dividing his attention between the decanter, somewhat depleted, and a very light 20-bore shotgun, which he was attempting to clean and oil.

XVIII

"Kitty-Kat my dear, it's a pleasure to see your face," he continued, holding up the gun so that he could look at her through one of the barrels. "What have you been up to now? I say. Would you like to point out something to me, so that I could have a shot at it?"

Swan took one look at him, turned round, and made a beeline for the door.

Kathryn instantly turned the key in the lock, and held tightly to it as she backed away.

"Indeed I would, Uncle Colin," said Kathryn sweetly.

"That's my Kitty-kat. And how are you, Alan? And you, Horace Greeley: how are you? I'm filthy, I don't mind telling you. Swaddled up like a blooming Chinese woman, though they've got more of me than just my feet. God's wounds! If they'd only give me a *chair,* I could at least move about."

He reflected.

Snapping shut the breech of the shotgun, he lowered it to stand against the side of the bed.

"I'm happy," he added abruptly. "Maybe I shouldn't be, but I am. You've heard, haven't you, about what happened to me? Artificial ice. Same as Angus. It was murder, after all. It's a pity about poor old Alec

Forbes, though. I never did dislike the fellow. Stop a bit. Where's Fell? Why isn't Fell here? What have you done with Fell?"

Kathryn was grimly determined.

"He's out with the Home Guard, Uncle Colin. Listen. There's something we've got to tell you. This wretch of a reporter, after promising——"

"What the devil does he want to go joining the Home Guard for, at *his* age and weight? They may not pot him for a parachutist; but if they see him against the sky line they'll ruddy well pot him for a parachute. It's crazy. It's worse than that: it's downright dangerous."

"Uncle Colin, *will* you listen to me, please?"

"Yes, my dear, of course. Joining the Home Guard! Never heard such nonsense in my life!"

"This reporter——"

"He didn't say anything about it when he was in here a while ago. All he wanted to do was ask a lot of questions about poor old Rabbie; and what we'd all been saying up in the tower room on Monday. Besides, how could he get into the Home Guard in Scotland? Are you pulling my leg?"

Kathryn's expression was by this time so desperate that even Colin noticed it. He broke off, peering shaggily at her.

"Nothing wrong, is there, Kitty-kat?"

"Yes, there is. That is, if you'd just listen to me for a moment! Do you remember that Mr. Swan promised not to say a word about anything that happened here, if we let him get what stories he wanted?"

Colin's eyebrows drew together.

"God's wounds! You didn't print in that rag of yours that we stuck you in the seat of the pants with a claymore?"

"No, so help me I didn't!" returned Swan, instantly and with patent truth. "I didn't say a word about it. I've got the paper, and I can prove it."

"Then what's biting you, Kitty-kat?"

"He's said, or intimated, dreadful things about Alan and me. I don't know exactly what; and Alan doesn't even seem to care; but it's something about Alan and me being immoral together——"

Colin stared at her. Then he leaned back and bellowed with laughter. The mirth brought tears into his eyes.

"Well, aren't you?"

"No! Just because of a dreadful accident, just because we *had* to spend the night in the same compartment on the train from London——"

"You didn't have to spend the night in the same room here on Monday," Colin pointed out. "But you ruddy well did. Eh?"

"They spent the night in the same room here?" Swan demanded quickly.

"Of course they did," roared Colin. "Come on, Kitty-kat! Be a man! I mean, be a woman! Admit it! Have the courage of your convictions. What were you doing, then, if you weren't improving your time? Nonsense!"

"You see, Miss Campbell," pleaded Swan, "I had to get the sex angle into the story somehow, and that was the only way to do it. *He* understands. Your boy friend understands. There's nothing at all to worry about, not the least little thing."

Kathryn looked from one to the other of them. An expression of hopeless despair went over her pink face. Tears came into her eyes, and she sat down in a chair and put her face in her hands.

"Here! Easy!" said Alan. "I've just been pointing out to her, Colin, that her reputation is hopelessly compromised unless she marries me now. I asked her to marry me——"

"You never did."

"Well, I do so now, in front of witnesses. Miss Campbell: will you do me the honor of becoming my wife."

Kathryn raised a tear-stained face of exasperation.

"Of course I will, you idiot!" she stormed at him. "But why couldn't you do it decently, as I've given you a hundred opportunities to, instead of blackmailing me into it? Or saying I blackmailed you into it?"

Colin's eyes opened wide.

"Do you mean," he bellowed delightedly, "there's going to be a wedding?"

"Can I print that?"

"Yes to both questions," replied Alan.

"My dear Kitty-kat! My dear fellow! By George!" said Colin, rubbing his hands. "This calls for such a celebration as these walls haven't seen since the night Elspat's virtue fell in 1900. Where's Kirstie with that decanter? God's wounds! I wonder if there are any bagpipes in the house? I haven't tried 'em for years, but what I could do once would warm the cockles of your heart."

"You're not mad at *me?*" asked Swan anxiously.

"At you? Great Scott, no! Why should I be? Come over here, old chap, and sit down!"

"Then what," persisted Swan, "did you want that toy shotgun for?"

" 'Toy' shotgun, is it? 'Toy' shotgun?" Colin snatched up the 20-bore. "Do you know it takes a devil of a lot more skill and accuracy to use this than it does a 12-bore? Don't believe that, eh? Like me to show you?"

"No, no, no. I'll take your word for it!"

"That's better. Come and have a drink. No, we haven't got any glasses. Where's Kirstie? And Elspat! We've got to have Elspat here. Elspat!"

Kathryn was compelled to unlock the door. Swan, with an expiring sigh of relief, sat down and stretched his legs like one completely at home. He sprang up again with deep suspicion when Elspat appeared.

Elspat, however, ignored him with such icy pointedness that he backed away. Elspat gave them each in turn, except Swan, an unfathomable glance. Her eyelids were puffed and reddish, and her mouth was a straight line. Alan tried to see in her some resemblance to the handsome woman of the old photograph; but it was gone, all gone.

"Look here, old girl," said Colin. He stretched out his hand to her. "I've got great news. Glorious news. These two,"—he pointed—"are going to get married."

Elspat did not say anything. Her eyes rested on Alan, studying him. Then they moved to Kathryn, studying her for a long time. She went over to Kathryn, and quickly kissed her on the cheek. Two tears, amazing tears, overflowed Elspat's eyes.

"Here, I say!" Colin stirred uncomfortably. Then he glared. "It's the same old family custom," he complained in a querulous voice. "Always turn on the waterworks when there's going to be a wedding. This is a *happy* occasion, hang it! Stop that!"

Elspat still remained motionless. Her face worked.

"If you don't stop that, I'm going to throw something," yelled Colin. "Can't you say, 'Congratulations,' or anything like that? Have we got any pipes in the house, by the way?"

"Ye'll hae no godless merriment here, Colin Campbell," snapped Elspat, choking out the words despite her working face. She fought back by instinct, while Alan's discomfort increased.

"Aye, I'll gie ye ma blessing," she said, looking first at Kathryn and then at Alan. "If the blessin' of an auld snaggletooth body's worth a groat tae ye."

"Well, then," said Colin sulkily, "we can at least have the whisky. You'll drink their health, I hope?"

"Aye. I caud du wi' that tonight. The de'il's walkin' on ma grave." She shivered.

"I never saw such a lot of killjoys in all my born days," grumbled Colin. But he brightened as Kirstie brought in the glasses and a decanter. "One more glass, my wench. Stop a bit. Maybe we'd better have a third decanter, eh?"

"Just a moment!" said Alan. He looked round at them and, in some uneasiness, at the shotgun. "You're not proposing another binge tonight, are you?"

"Binge! Nonsense!" said Colin, pouring himself a short one evidently to give him strength to pour for the others, and gulping it down. "Who said anything about a binge? We're drinking health and happiness to the bride, that's all. You can't object to that, can you?"

"*I* can't," smiled Kathryn.

"Nor me," observed Swan. "I feel grand!" Swan added. "I forgive everybody. I even forgive madam,"—he hesitated, for he was clearly frightened of Elspat—"for ruining a suit that cost me ten guineas."

Colin spoke persuasively.

"See here, Elspat. I'm sorry about Angus. But there it is. And it's turned out for the best. If he had to die, I don't mind admitting it's got me out of a bad financial hole.

"Do you know what I'm going to do? No more doctoring in Manchester, for the moment. I'm going to get a ketch and go for a cruise in the South Seas. And you, Elspat. You can get a dozen big pictures painted of Angus, and look at 'em all day. Or you can go to London and see the jitterbugs. You're safe, old girl."

Elspat's face was white.

"Aye," she blazed at him. *"And d'ye ken why we're safe?"*

"Steady!" cried Alan.

Even in his mist of good will and exhilaration, he knew what was coming. Kathryn knew too. They both made a move toward Elspat, but she paid no attention.

"I'll hae ma conscience nae mair damned wi' lees. D'ye ken why we're safe?"

She whirled round to Swan. Addressing him for the first time, she announced calmly that Angus had killed himself; she poured out the entire story, with her reasons for believing it. And every word of it was true.

"Now that's very interesting, ma'am," said Swan, who had taken one glass of whisky and was holding out his tumbler for a second. He appeared flattered by her attention. "Then you're not mad at me any longer either?"

Elspat stared at him.

"Mad at ye? Hoots! D'ye hear what I'm saying?"

"Yes, of course, ma'am," Swan replied soothingly. "And of course I understand how this thing has upset you——"

"Mon, dinna ye believe me?"

Swan threw back his head and laughed.

"I hate to contradict a lady, ma'am. But if you'll just have a word with the police, or with Dr. Fell, or with these people here, you'll see that either somebody has been kidding you or you've been kidding yourself. I ought to know, oughtn't I? Hasn't anybody told you that Alec Forbes killed himself, and left a note admitting he killed Mr. Campbell?"

Eslpat drew in her breath. Her face wrinkled up. She turned and looked at Colin, who nodded.

"It's true, Elspat. Come abreast of the times! Where have you been all day?"

It stabbed Alan to the heart to see her. She groped over to a chair and sat down. A human being, a sentient, living, hurt human being, emerged from behind the angry clay in which Elspat set her face to the world.

"Ye're no' deceivin' me?" she insisted. "Ye swear to the Guid Man——!"

Then she began to swing back and forth in the rocking chair. She began to laugh, showing that she had fine teeth; and it kindled and illumined her face. Her whole being seemed to breathe a prayer.

Angus had not died in the sin of suicide. He had not gone to the bad place. And Elspat, this Elspat whose real surname nobody knew, rocked back and forth and laughed and was happy.

Colin Campbell, serenely missing all this, was still acting as barman.

"You understand," he beamed, "neither Fell nor I ever for a minute thought it *was* suicide. Still, it's just as well to get the whole thing tidied up. I never for a second thought you didn't know, or I'd have crawled off this bed to tell you. Now be a good sport. I know this is still officially a house of mourning. But, under the circumstances, what about getting me those pipes?"

Elspat got to her feet and went out of the room.

"By Jupiter," breathed Colin, "she's gone to get 'em! . . . What ails you, Kitty-kat?"

Kathryn regarded the door with uncertain, curiously shining eyes. She bit her lip. Her eyes moved over toward Alan.

"I don't know," she answered. "I'm happy,"—here she glared at Alan—"and yet I feel all sort of funny and mixed up."

"Your English grammar," said Alan, "is abominable. But your sentiments are correct. That's what she believes now; and that's what Elspat has got to go on believing. Because, of course, it's true."

"Of course," agreed Kathryn quickly. "I wonder, Uncle Colin, whether you would do me a big favor?"

"Anything in the world, my dear."

"Well," said Kathryn, hesitantly extending the tumbler, "it isn't very much, perhaps; but would you mind making my drink just a *little* stronger?"

"Now that's my Kitty-kat!" roared Colin. "Here you are . . . Enough?"

"A little more, please."

"A little *more?*"

"Yes, please."

"Cripes," muttered Swan, on whom the first smashing, shuddering effect of the Doom of the Campbells had now passed to a quickened speech and excitement, "you two professors are teamed up right. I don't understand how you do it. Does anybody (maybe, now?) feel like a song?"

Beatific with his head among the pillows, as though enthroned in state,

Colin lifted the shotgun and waved it in the air as though conducting an orchestra. His bass voice beat against the windows.

"I love a lassie, a boh-ny, boh-ny las-sie—"

Swan, drawing his chin far into his collar, assumed an air of solemn portentousness. Finding the right pitch after a preliminary cough, he moved his glass gently in time and joined in.

"She's as pure as the li-ly in the dell— "

To Alan, lifting his glass in a toast to Kathryn, there came a feeling that all things happened for the best; and that tomorrow could take care of itself. The exhilaration of being in love, the exhilaration of merely watching Kathryn, joined with the exhilaration of the potent brew in his hand. He smiled at Kathryn; she smiled back; and they both joined in.

"She's as sweet as the heath-er, the boh-ny pur-ple heather—"

He had a good loud baritone, and Kathryn a fairly audible soprano. Their quartet made the room ring. To Aunt Elspat, returning with a set of bagpipes—which she grimly handed to Colin, and which he eagerly seized without breaking off the song—it must have seemed that old days had returned.

"A'weel," said Aunt Elspat resignedly. "A'weel!"

XIX

Alan Campbell opened one eye.

From somewhere in remote distances, muffled beyond sight or sound, his soul crawled back painfully, through subterranean corridors, up into his body again. Toward the last it moved to the conviction that he was looking at a family photograph album, from which there stared back at him a face he had seen, somewhere, only today . . .

Then he was awake.

The first eye was bad enough. But, when he opened the second eye, such a rush of anguish flowed through his brain that he knew what was wrong with him, and realized fairly that he had done it again.

He lay back and stared at the cracks on the ceiling. There was sunlight in the room.

He had a violent headache, and his throat was dry. But it occurred to him in a startled sort of way that he did not feel nearly as bad as he had felt the first time. This prompted an uneasy flash of doubt. Did the infernal stuff take hold of you? Was it (as the temperance tracts said) an insidious poison whose effects seemed to grow less day by day?

Then another feeling, heartening or disheartening according to how you viewed the stuff, took possession of him.

When he searched his memory he could recall nothing except blurred scenes which seemed to be dominated by the noise of bagpipes, and a vision of Elspat swinging back and forth beatifically in a rocking chair amidst it.

Yet no sense of sin oppressed him, no sense of guilt or enormity. He *knew* that his conduct had been such as becomes a gentleman, even *en pantoufles*. It was a strange conviction, but a real one. He did not even quail when Kathryn opened the door.

On the contrary, this morning it was Kathryn who appeared guilty and hunted. On the tray she carried not one cup of black coffee, but two. She put the tray on the bedside table, and looked at him.

"It ought to be you," she said, after clearing her throat, "who brought this to me this morning. But I knew you'd be disgusting and sleep past noon. I suppose you don't remember anything about last night either?"

He tried to sit up, easing the throb in his head.

"Well, no. Er—I wasn't——?"

"No, you were not. Alan Campbell, there never was such a stuffed shirt as you who ever lived. You just sat and beamed as though you owned the earth. But you *will* quote poetry. When you began on Tenny-son, I feared the worst. You recited the whole of 'The Princess,' and nearly all of 'Maud.' When you actually had the face to quote that bit about 'Put thy sweet hand in mine and trust in me,' and patted my hand as you did it—well, really!"

Averting his eyes, he reached after the coffee.

"I wasn't aware I knew so much Tennyson."

"You didn't, really. But when you couldn't remember, you just thought for a moment, and then said, 'Umble-bumble, umble-bumble,' and went on."

"Never mind. At least, we were all right?"

Kathryn lowered the cup she had raised to her lips. The cup rattled and clicked on its saucer.

"All right?" she repeated with widening eyes. "When that wretch Swan is probably in hospital now?"

Alan's head gave a violent throb.

"We didn't—?"

"No, not you. Uncle Colin."

"My God, he didn't assault Swan again? But they're great pals! He couldn't have assaulted Swan again! What happened?"

"Well, it was all right until Colin had about his fifteenth Doom; and Swan, who was also what he called 'canned' and a little too cocksure, brought out the newspaper article he wrote yesterday. He'd smuggled the paper in in case we didn't like it."

"Yes?"

"It wasn't so bad, really. I admit that. Everything was all right until Swan described how Colin had decided to sleep in the tower room."

"Yes?"

"Swan's version of the incident ran something like this. You remember, he was hanging about outside the sitting-room windows? His story said: 'Dr. Colin Campbell, a deeply religious man, placed his hand on the Bible and swore an oath that he would not enter the church again until the family ghost had ceased to walk in the melancholy Castle of Shira.' For about ten seconds Colin just looked at him. Then he pointed to the door and said, 'Out.' Swan didn't understand until Colin turned completely purple and said, 'Out of this house and stay out.' Colin grabbed his shotgun, and——"

"He didn't——?"

"Not just then. But when Swan leaped downstairs, Colin said, 'Turn out the light and take down the blackout. I want to get him from the window as he goes up the road.' His bed is by the window, you remember."

"You don't mean to say Colin shot Swan in the seat of the pants as he ran for Inveraray?"

"No," answered Kathryn. "Colin didn't. I did."

Her voice became a wail.

"Alan darling, we've got to get out of this insidious country. First you, and now me. I don't know what's come over me; I honestly don't!"

Alan's head was aching still harder.

"But wait a minute! Where was I? Didn't I interfere?"

"You didn't even notice. You were reciting 'Sir Galahad' to Elspat. The rain had cleared off—it was four o'clock in the morning—and the moon was up. I was boiling angry with Swan, you see. And there he was in the road.

"He must have heard the window go up, and seen the moonlight on the shotgun. Because he gave one look, and never ran so fast even on the Monday night. I said, 'Uncle Colin, let me have a go.' He said, 'All right; but let him get a sporting distance away; we don't want to hurt him.' Ordinarily I'm frightened of guns, and I couldn't have hit the side of a barn door. But that wretched stuff made everything different. I loosed off blindly, and got a bull's-eye with the second barrel.

"Alan, do you think he'll have me arrested? And don't you *dare* laugh, either!"

" 'Pompilia, will you let them murder me?' " murmured Alan. He finished his coffee, propped himself upright, and steadied a swimming world. "Never mind," he said. "I'll go and smooth him down."

"But suppose I—?"

Alan studied the forlorn figure.

"You couldn't have hurt him much. Not at a distance, with a twenty-bore and a light load. He didn't fall down, did he?"

"No; he only ran harder."

"Then it's all right."

"But what am I to *do?*"

" 'Put thy sweet hand in mine and trust in me.' "

"Alan Campbell!"

"Well, isn't it the proper course?"

Kathryn sighed. She walked to the window, and looked down over the loch. Its waters were peaceful, a-gleam in sunshine.

"And that," she told him, after a pause, "isn't all."

"Not more——!"

"No, no, no! Not more trouble of that kind, anyway. I got the letter this morning. Alan, I've been recalled."

"Recalled?"

"From my holiday. By the college. A.R.P. I also saw in this morning's Scottish *Daily Express*. It looks as though the real bombing is going to begin."

The sunlight was as fair, the hills as golden and purple, as ever. Alan took a packet of cigarettes from the bedside table. He lit one and inhaled smoke. Though it made his head swim, he sat contemplating the loch and smoking steadily.

"So our holiday," he said, "is a kind of entr'acte."

"Yes," said Kathryn, without turning round. "Alan, *do* you love me?"

"You know I do."

"Then do we care?"

"No."

There was a silence.

"When have you got to go?" he asked presently.

"Tonight, I'm afraid. That's what the letter says."

"Then," he declared briskly, "we can't waste any more time. The sooner I get my own things packed, the better. I hope we can get adjoining sleepers on the train. We've done all we can do here anyway, which wasn't much to start with. The case, officially, is closed. All the same—I should have liked to see the real end of it, if there is an end."

"You may see the end of it yet," Kathryn told him, and turned round from the window.

"Meaning what?"

She wrinkled up her forehead, and her nervous manner was not entirely due to her apprehensions about the night before.

"You see," she went on, "Dr. Fell is here. When I told him I had to go back tonight, he said he had every reason to believe he would be going as well. I said, 'But what about you-know?' He said, 'You-know will, I think, take care of itself.' But he said it in a queer way that made me think there's something going on. Something—rather terrible. He didn't come back here until nearly dawn this morning. He wants to see you, by the way."

"I'll be dressed in half a tick. Where is everybody else this morning?"

"Colin's still asleep. Elspat, even Kirstie, are out. There's nobody here but you and me and Dr. Fell. Alan, it isn't hangover and it isn't Swan and it isn't nerves. But—I'm frightened. Please come downstairs as quick as you can."

He told himself, when he nicked his face in shaving, that this was due to the brew of the night before. He told himself that his own apprehensions were caused by an upset stomach and the misadventures of Swan.

Shira was intensely quiet. Only the sun entered. When you turned on a tap, or turned it off, ghostly clankings went down through the house and shivered away. And, as Alan went down to get his breakfast, he saw Dr. Fell in the sitting room.

Dr. Fell, in his old black alpaca suit and string tie, occupied the sofa. He was sitting in the warm, golden sunlight, the meerschaum pipe between his teeth, and his expression far away. He had the air of a man who meditates a dangerous business and is not quite sure of his course. The ridges of his waistcoat rose and fell with slow, gentle wheezings. His big mop of gray-streaked hair had fallen over one eye.

Alan and Kathryn shared buttered toast and more coffee. They did not speak much. Neither knew quite what to do. It was like the feeling of not knowing whether you had been summoned to the headmaster's study, or hadn't.

But the question was solved for them.

"Good morning!" called a voice.

They hurried out into the hall.

Alistair Duncan, in an almost summery and skittish-looking brown suit, was standing at the open front door. He wore a soft hat and carried a brief case. He raised his hand to the knocker of the open door, as though by way of illustration.

"There did not seem to be anybody about," he said. His voice, though meant to be pleasant, had a faint irritated undertone.

Alan glanced to the right. Through the open door of the sitting room he could see Dr. Fell stir, grunt, and lift his head as though roused out of sleep. Alan looked back to the tall, stoop-shouldered figure of the lawyer, framed against the shimmering loch outside.

"*May* I come in?" inquired Duncan politely.

"P-please do," stammered Kathryn.

"Thank you." Duncan stepped in gingerly, removing his hat. He went to the door of the sitting room, glanced in, and uttered an exclamation which might have been satisfaction or annoyance.

"Please come in here," rumbled Dr. Fell. "All of you, if you will. And close the door."

The usual odor as of damp oilcloth, of old wood and stone, was brought out by the sun in that stuffy room. Angus's photograph, still draped in crepe, faced them from the overmantel. Sun made tawdry the dark, bad daubs of the pictures in their gilt frames, and picked out worn places in the carpet.

"My dear sir," said the lawyer, putting down his hat and brief case on the table which held the Bible. He spoke the words as though he were beginning a letter.

"Sit down, please," said Dr. Fell.

A slight frown creased Duncan's high, semi-bald skull.

"In response to your telephone call," he replied, "here I am." He made a humorous gesture. "But may I point out, sir, that I am a busy man? I have been at this house, for one cause or another, nearly every day for the past week. And, grave as the issue has been, since it is now settled——"

"It is not settled," said Dr. Fell.

"But——!"

"Sit down, all of you," said Dr. Fell.

Blowing a film of ash off his pipe, he settled back, returned the pipe to his mouth, and drew at it. The ash settled down across his waistcoat, but he did not brush it off. He eyed them for a long time, and Alan's uneasiness had grown to something like a breath of fear.

"Gentlemen, and Miss Campbell," continued Dr. Fell, drawing a long sniff through his nose. "Yesterday afternoon, if you remember, I spoke of a million-to-one chance. I did not dare to hope for much from it. Still, it had come off in Angus's case and I hoped it might come off in Forbes's. It did."

He paused, and added in the same ordinary tone:

"I now have the instrument with which, in a sense, Alec Forbes was murdered."

The deathlike stillness of the room, while tobacco smoke curled up past starched lace curtains in the sunlight, lasted only a few seconds.

"Murdered?" the lawyer exploded.

"Exactly."

"You will pardon me if I suggest that——"

"Sir," interrupted Dr. Fell, taking the pipe out of his mouth, "in your heart of hearts you know that Alec Forbes was murdered, just as you know that Angus Campbell committed suicide. Now don't you?"

Duncan took a quick look round him.

"It's quite all right," the doctor assured him. "We four are all alone here—as yet. I have seen to that. You are at liberty to speak freely."

"I have no intention of speaking, either freely or otherwise." Duncan's voice was curt. "Did you bring me all the way out here just to tell me that? Your suggestion is preposterous!"

Dr. Fell sighed.

"I wonder whether you will think it is so preposterous," he said, "if I tell you the proposal I mean to make."

"Proposal?"

"Bargain. Deal, if you like."

"There is no question of a bargain, my dear sir. You told me yourself that this is an open-and-shut case, a plain case. The police believe as much. I saw Mr. MacIntyre, the Procurator Fiscal, this morning."

"Yes. That is part of my bargain."

Duncan was almost on the edge of losing his temper.

"Will you kindly tell me, Doctor, what it is you wish of me: if anything? And particularly where you got this wicked and indeed danger-ous notion that Alec Forbes was murdered?"

Dr. Fell's expression was vacant.

"I got it first," he responded, puffing out his cheeks, "from a piece of blackout material—tar paper on a wooden frame—which should have been up at the window in Forbes's cottage, and yet wasn't.

"The blackout *had been* up at the window during the night, else the lantern light would have been seen by the Home Guard. And the lantern (if you remember the evidence) *had been* burning. Yet for some reason it was necessary to extinguish the lantern and take down the blackout from the window.

"Why? That was the problem. As was suggested to me at the time, why didn't the murderer simply leave the lantern burning, and leave the blackout in its place, when he made his exit? At first sight it seemed rather a formidable problem.

"The obvious line of attack was to say that the murderer had to take down the blackout in order to make his escape; and, once having made it, he couldn't put the blackout back up again. That is a very suggestive line, if you follow it up. Could he, for instance, somehow have got through a steel-mesh grating, and somehow replace it afterwards?"

Duncan snorted.

"The grating being nailed up on the inside?"

Dr. Fell nodded very gravely.

"Yes. Nailed up. So the murderer couldn't very well have done *that*, could he?"

Duncan got to his feet.

"I am sorry, sir, that I cannot remain to listen to these preposterous notions any longer. Doctor, you shock me. The very idea that Forbes——"

"Don't you want to hear what my proposal is?" suggested Dr. Fell. He paused. "It will be much to your advantage." He paused again. "Very much to your advantage."

In the act of taking his hat and brief case from the little table, Duncan dropped his hands and straightened up. He looked back at Dr. Fell. His face was white.

"God in heaven!" he whispered. "You do not suggest—ah—that *I* am the murderer, do you?"

"Oh, no," replied Dr. Fell. "Tut, tut! Certainly not."

Alan breathed easier.

It was the same idea which had occurred to him, all the more sinister for the overtones in Dr. Fell's voice. Duncan ran a finger round inside his loose collar.

"I am glad," he said, with an attempt at humorous dryness, "I am glad, at least to hear that. Now, come, sir! Let's have the cards on the table. What sort of proposition have you which could possibly interest me?"

"One which concerns the welfare of your clients. In short, the Campbell family." Again Dr. Fell leisurely blew a film of ash off his pipe. "You see, I am in a position to *prove* that Alec Forbes was murdered."

Duncan dropped hat and brief case on the table as though they had burnt him.

"Prove it? How?"

"Because I have the instrument which was, in a sense, used to murder him."

"But Forbes was hanged with a dressing-gown cord!"

"Mr. Duncan, if you will study the best criminological authorities, you will find them agreed on one thing. Nothing is more difficult to determine than the question of whether a man has been hanged, or whether he has first been strangled and then hung up afterwards to simulate hanging. That is what happened to Forbes.

"Forbes was taken from behind and strangled. With what, I don't know. A necktie. Perhaps a scarf. Then those artistic trappings were all arranged by a murderer who knew his business well. If such things are done with care, the result cannot be told from a genuine suicide. This murderer made only one mistake, which was unavoidable. But it was fatal.

"Ask yourself again, with regard to that grated window——"

Duncan stretched out his hands as though in supplication.

"But what is this mysterious 'evidence'? And who is this mysterious 'murderer'?" His eye grew sharp. "You know who it is?"

"Oh, yes," said Dr. Fell.

"You are not in a position," said the lawyer, rapping his knuckles on the table, "to prove Angus Campbell committed suicide."

"No. Yet if Forbes's death is proved to be murder, that surely invalidates the false confession left behind? A confession conveniently written on a typewriter, which could have been written by anybody and was actually written by the murderer. What will the police think then?"

"What are you suggesting to me, exactly?"

"Then you will hear my proposition?"

"I will hear anything," returned the lawyer, going across to a chair and sitting down with his big-knuckled hands clasped together, "if you give me some line of direction. *Who* is this murderer?"

Dr. Fell eyed him.

"You have no idea?"

"None, I swear! And I—ah—still retain the right to disbelieve every word you say. *Who* is this murderer?"

"As a matter of fact," replied Dr. Fell, "I think the murderer is in the house now, and should be with us at any minute."

Kathryn glanced rather wildly at Alan.

It was very warm in the room. A late fly buzzed against one bright windowpane behind the starched curtains. In the stillness they could distinctly hear the noise of footsteps as someone walked along the hall toward the front.

"That should be our friend," continued Dr. Fell in the same unemotional tone. Then he raised his voice and shouted. *"We're in the sitting room! Come and join us!"*

The footsteps hesitated, turned and came toward the door of the room.

Duncan got to his feet, spasmodically. His hands were clasped together, and Alan could hear the knuckle joints crack as he pressed them.

Between the time they first heard the footsteps, and the time that the knob turned and the door opened, was perhaps five or six seconds. Alan has since computed it as the longest interval of his life. Every board in the room seemed to have a separate creak and crack; everything seemed alive and aware and insistent like the droning fly against the windowpane.

The door opened, and a certain person came in.

"That's the murderer," said Dr. Fell.

He was pointing to Mr. Walter Chapman, of the Hercules Insurance Company.

XX

Every detail of Chapman's appearance was picked out by the sunlight. The short, broad figure clad in a dark blue suit. The fair hair, the fresh complexion, the curiously pale eyes. One hand held his bowler hat, the other was at his necktie, fingering it. He had moved his head to one side as though dodging.

"I beg your pardon?" he said in a somewhat shrill voice.

"I said, come in, Mr. Chapman," answered Dr. Fell. "Or should I say Mr. Campbell? Your real name is Campbell, isn't it?"

"What the devil are you talking about? I don't understand you."

"Two days ago," said Dr. Fell, "when I first set eyes on you, you were standing in much the same place as now. I was standing over by that window there (remember?), making an intense study of a full-face photograph of Angus Campbell.

"We had not been introduced. I lifted my eyes from studying the photograph; and I was confronted by such a startling, momentary family likeness that I said to you, 'Which Campbell are you?' "

Alan remembered it.

In his imagination, the short, broad figure before him became the short, broad figure of Colin or Angus Campbell. The fair hair and washed-out eyes became (got it!) the fair hair and washed-out eyes of that photograph of Robert Campbell in the family album. All these things wavered and changed and were distorted like images in water, yet folded together to form a composite whole in the solid person before them.

"Does he remind you of anyone *now*, Mr. Duncan?" inquired Dr. Fell.

The lawyer weakly subsided into his chair. Or, rather, his long lean limbs seemed to collapse like a clothes horse as he groped for and found the arms of the chair.

"Rabbie Campbell," he said. It was not an exclamation, or a question, or any form of words associated with emotion; it was the statement of a fact. "You're Rabbie Campbell's son," he said.

"I must insist—" the alleged Chapman began, but Dr. Fell cut him short.

"The sudden juxtaposition of Angus's photograph and this man's face," pursued the doctor, "brought a suggestion which may have been overlooked by some of you. Let me refresh your memory on another point."

He looked at Alan and Kathryn.

"Elspat told you, I think, that Angus Campbell had an uncanny flair for spotting family resemblances; so that he could tell one of his own branch even if the person 'blacked his face and spoke with a strange tongue.' This same flair is shared, though in less degree, by Elspat herself."

This time Dr. Fell looked at Duncan.

"Therefore it seemed to me very curious and interesting that, as you yourself are reported to have said, Mr. 'Chapman' always kept out of Elspat's way and would never under any circumstances go near her. It seemed to me worth investigating.

"The Scottish police can't use the resources of Scotland Yard. But I, through my friend Superintendent Hadley, can. It took only a few hours to discover the truth about Mr. Walter Chapman, though the transatlantic telephone call (official) Hadley put through afterwards did not get me a reply until the early hours of this morning."

Taking a scribbled envelope from his pocket, Dr. Fell blinked at it, and then adjusted his eyeglasses to stare at Chapman.

"Your real name is Walter Chapman Campbell. You hold, or held, passport number 609348 on the Union of South Africa. Eight years ago you came to England from Port Elizabeth, where your father, Robert Campbell, is still alive: though very ill and infirm. You dropped the Campbell part of your name because your father's name had unpleasant associations with the Hercules Insurance Company, for which you worked.

"Two months ago (as you yourself are reported to have said) you were moved from England to be head of one of the several branches of your firm in Glasgow.

"There, of course, Angus Campbell spotted you."

Walter Chapman moistened his lips.

On his face was printed a fixed, skeptical smile. Yet his eyes moved swiftly to Duncan, as though wondering how the lawyer took this, and back again.

"Don't be absurd," Chapman said.

"You deny these facts, sir?"

"Granting," said the other, whose collar seemed inordinately tight, "granting that for reasons of my own I used only a part of my name, what for God's sake am I supposed to have done?"

He pounced a little, a gesture which reminded the watchers of Colin.

"I could also bear to know, Dr. Fell, why you and two Army officers woke me up at my hotel in Dunoon in the middle of last night, merely to ask some tomfool questions about insurance. But let that go. I repeat: what for God's sake am I supposed to have done?"

"You assisted Angus Campbell in planning his suicide," replied Dr. Fell; "you attempted the murder of Colin Campbell, and you murdered Alec Forbes."

The color drained out of Chapman's face.

"Absurd."

"You were not acquainted with Alec Forbes?"

"Certainly not."

"You have never been near his cottage by the Falls of Coe?"

"Never."

Dr. Fell's eyes closed. "In that case, you won't mind if I tell you what I think you did.

"As you said yourself, Angus came to see you at your office in Glasgow when he took out his final insurance policy. My belief is that he had seen you before. That he taxed you with being his brother's son; that you denied it, but were ultimately compelled to admit it.

"And this, of course, gave Angus the final triple security for his scheme. Angus left *nothing* to chance. He knew your father for a thorough bad hat; and he was a good enough judge of men to diagnose you as a thorough bad hat too. So, when he took out that final, rather unnecessary policy as an excuse to hang about with you, he explained to you exactly what he meant to do. You would come to investigate a curious death. If there were *any* slip-up, any at all, you could always cover this up and point out that the death was murder because you knew what had really happened.

"There was every inducement for you to help Angus. He could point out to you that you were only helping your own family. That, with himself dead, only a sixty-five-year-old Colin stood between an inheritance of nearly eighteen thousand pounds to your own father; and ultimately, of course, to you. He could appeal to your family loyalty, which was Angus's only blind fetish.

"But it was not a fetish with you, Mr. Chapman Campbell. For you suddenly saw how you could play your own game.

"With Angus dead, and Colin dead as well . . ."

Dr. Fell paused.

"You see," he added, turning to the others, "the attempted murder of Colin made it fairly certain that our friend here must be the guilty person. Don't you recall that *it was Mr. Chapman, and nobody else, who drove Colin to sleep in the tower?*"

Alistair Duncan got to his feet, but sat down again.

The room was hot, and a small bead of sweat appeared on Chapman's forehead.

"Think back, if you will, to two conversations. One took place in the tower room on Monday evening, and has been reported to me. The other took place in this room on Tuesday afternoon, and I was here myself.

"Who was the first person to introduce the word 'supernatural' into this affair? That word which always acts on Colin as a matador's cape acts on a bull? It was Mr. Chapman, if you recall. In the tower on Monday evening he deliberately—even irrelevantly—dragged it into the conversation, when nobody had suggested any such thing before.

"Colin swore there was no ghost. So, of course, our ingenious friend had to give him a ghost. I asked before: what was the reason for the mummery of the phantom Highlander with the caved-in face, appearing in the tower room on Monday night? The answer is easy. It was to act as the final, goading spur on Colin Campbell.

"The Masquerade wasn't difficult to carry out. This tower here is an isolated part of the house. It has a ground-floor entrance to the outside court, so that an outsider can come and go at will. That entrance is usually open; and, even if it isn't, an ordinary padlock key will do the trick. With the assistance of a plaid, a bonnet, a little wax and paint, the ghost 'appeared' to Jock Fleming. If Jock hadn't been there, anybody else would have done as well.

"And then?"

"Bright and early on Wednesday, Mr. Chapman was ready. The ghost story was flying. He came here and (don't you remember?) pushed poor Colin clear over the edge by his remarks on the subject of ghosts.

"What was the remark which made Colin go off the deep end? What was the remark which made Colin say, 'That's torn it,' and swear his oath to sleep in the tower? It was Mr. Chapman's shy, sly little series of observations ending, 'This is a funny country and a funny house; and I tell you *I* shouldn't care to spend a night up in that room.' "

In Alan's memory the scene took form again.

Chapman's expression now, too, was much the same as it had been. But now there appeared behind it an edge of desperation.

"It was absolutely necessary," pursued Dr. Fell, "to get Colin to sleep in the tower. True, the artificial-ice trick could have been worked anywhere. But it couldn't have been worked anywhere by *Chapman*.

"He couldn't go prowling through this house. The thing had to be done in that isolated tower, with an outside entrance for him to come and go. Just before Colin roared good night and staggered up all those stairs, Chapman could plant the box containing the ice and slip away.

"Let me recapitulate. Up to this time, of course, Chapman couldn't for a second pretend he had any glimmering of knowledge as to how Angus might have died. He had to pretend to be as puzzled as anybody else. He had to keep saying he thought it must be suicide; and rather a neat piece of acting it was.

"Naturally, no mention of artificial ice must creep in *yet*. Not yet. Otherwise the gaff would be blown and he couldn't lure Colin by bogey threats into sleeping in the tower. So he kept on saying that Angus must deliberately have committed suicide, thrown himself out of the window for no cause at all—as our friend did insist in some detail, over and over—or, if there were any cause, it was something damnable in the line of horrors.

"This was his game *up to the time Colin was disposed of*. Then everything would change.

"Then the apparent truth would come out with a roar. Colin would be found dead of carbon-dioxide poisoning. The artificial ice would be remembered. If it wasn't, our ingenious friend was prepared to remember it himself. Smiting his forehead, he would say that of course this was murder; and of course the insurance must be paid; and where was that fiend Alec Forbes, who had undoubtedly done it all?

"Therefore it was necessary *instantly*, on the same night when Colin had been disposed of, to dispose of Alec Forbes."

Dr. Fell's pipe had gone out. He put it in his pocket, hooked his thumbs in the pockets of his waistcoat, and surveyed Chapman with dispassionate appraisal.

Alistair Duncan swallowed once or twice, the Adam's apple moving in his long throat.

"Can you—can you prove all this?" the lawyer asked in a thin voice.

"I don't have to prove it," said Dr. Fell, "since I can prove the murder of Forbes. To be hanged by the neck until you are dead, and may God have mercy upon your soul, is just as effective for one murder as for two. Isn't it, Mr. Chapman?"

Chapman had backed away.

"I—I may have spoken to Forbes once or twice—" he began, hoarsely and incautiously.

"Spoken to him!" said Dr. Fell. "You struck up quite an acquaintance with him, didn't you? You even warned him to keep out of the way. Afterwards it was too late.

"Up to this time your whole scheme had been triple foolproof. For, d'ye see, Angus Campbell really *had* committed suicide. When murder came to be suspected, the one person they couldn't possibly suspect was you; because you weren't guilty. I am willing to bet that for the night of Angus's death you have an alibi which stands and shines before all men.

"But you committed a bad howler when you didn't stay to make sure Colin was really dead after falling from the tower window on Tuesday night. And you made a still worse howler when you climbed into your car afterwards and drove out to the Falls of Coe for your last interview with Alec Forbes. What is the license number of your car, Mr. Chapman?"

Chapman winked both eyes at him, those curious light eyes which were the most disturbing feature of his face.

"Eh?"

"What is the license number of your car? It is,"—he consulted the back of the envelope—"MGM 1911, isn't it?"

"I—I don't know. Yes, I suppose it is."

"A car bearing the number MGM 1911 was seen parked by the side of the road opposite Forbes's cottage between the hours of two and three o'clock in the morning. It was seen by a member of the Home Guard who is willing to testify to this. You should have remembered, sir, that these lonely roads are no longer lonely. You should have remembered how they are patrolled late at night."

Alistair Duncan's face was whiter yet.

"And that's the sum of your evidence?" the lawyer demanded.

"Oh, no," said Dr. Fell. "That's the least of it."

Wrinkling up his nose, he contemplated a corner of the ceiling.

"We now come to the problem of Forbes's murder," he went on, "and how the murderer managed to leave behind him a room locked up on the inside. Mr. Duncan, do you know anything about geometry?"

"Geometry?"

"I hasten to say," explained Dr. Fell, "that I know little of what I was once compelled to learn, and wish to know less. It belongs to the limbo of school days, along with algebra and economics and other dismal things. Beyond being unable to forget that the square of the hypotenuse is equal to the sum of the squares of the other two sides, I have happily been able to rid my mind of this gibberish.

"At the same time it might be of value (for once in its life) if you were to think of Forbes's cottage in its geometrical shape." He took a pencil from his pocket and drew a design in the air with it. "The cottage is a square, twelve feet by twelve feet. Imagine, in the middle of the wall facing you, the door. Imagine, in the middle of the wall to your right, the window.

"I stood in the cottage yesterday; and I racked my brains over that infernal, tantalizing window.

"Why had it been necessary to take down the blackout? It could not have been, as I indicated to you some minutes ago, because the murderer had in some way managed to get his corporeal body through the grated window. This, as the geometricians are so fond of saying (rather ill-manneredly, it always seemed to me) was absurd.

"The only other explanation was that the window had to be used in some way. I had examined the steel-wire grating closely, if you remember?" Dr. Fell turned to Alan.

"I remember."

"In order to test its solidity, I put my finger through one of the openings in the mesh and shook it. Still no glimmer of intelligence penetrated the thick fog of wool and mist which beclouded me. I remained bogged and sunk until you,"—here he turned to Kathryn—"passed on a piece of information which even to a dullard like myself gave a prod and a hint."

"I did?" cried Kathryn.

"Yes. You said the proprietress of the Glencoe Hotel told you Forbes often came out there to fish."

Dr. Fell spread out his hands. His thunderous voice was apologetic.

"Of course, all the evidences were there. The hut, so to speak, reeked of fishiness. Forbes's angler's creel was there. His flies were there. His gum boots were there. Yet it was only then, only then, when the fact occurred to me that in all that cottage I had seen no sign of a fishing *rod*.

"No rod, for instance, such as this."

Impelling himself to his feet with the aid of his stick, Dr. Fell reached round to the back of the sofa. He produced a large suitcase, and opened it.

Inside lay, piecemeal, the disjointed sections of a fishing rod, black metal with a nickel-and-cork grip into which were cut the initials, 'A.M.F.' But no line was wound round the reel. Instead, to the metal eyelet on what would have been the end or tip of the joined rod, had been fastened tightly with wire a small fishing hook.

"A neat instrument," explained Dr. Fell.

"The murderer strangled Forbes, catching him from behind. He then strung Forbes up with those artistic indications of suicide. He turned out the lamp and poured away the remaining oil so that it should seem to have burned itself out. He took down the blackout.

"Then the murderer, carrying this fishing rod, walked out of the hut by the door. He closed the door, leaving the knob of the bolt turned uppermost.

"He went round to the window. Pushing the rod through the mesh of the grating—there was plenty of room for it, since I myself could easily get my forefinger through those meshes—he stretched out the rod in a *diagonal* line, from the window to the door.

"With this hook fastened to the tip of the rod, he caught the knob of the bolt, and pulled toward him. It was a bright, *new* bolt (remember?) so that it would shine by (remember?) the moonlight, and he could easily see it. Thus, with the greatest ease and simplicity, he pulled the bolt toward him and fastened the door."

Dr. Fell put the suitcase carefully down on the sofa.

"Of course he had to take the blackout down from the window, and, you see, could not now replace it. Also, it was vitally necessary to take the rod away with him. The handle and reel wouldn't go through the window in any case; and, if he were to pitch the other parts in, his game would be given away to the first spectator who arrived and saw them.

"He then left the premises. He was seen and identified, on getting into his car——"

Chapman let out a strangled cry.

"—by the same Home Guard who had first been curious about that car. On the way back, he took the rod apart and threw away its pieces at intervals into the bracken. It seemed too much to hope for a recovery of the rod; but, at the request of Inspector Donaldson of the Argyllshire County Constabulary, a search was made by the local unit of the Home Guard."

Dr. Fell looked at Chapman.

"They're covered with your fingerprints, those pieces," he said, "as you probably remember. When I visited you at your hotel in the middle of the night, with the purpose of getting your prints on a cigarette case, you were at the same time identified as the man seen driving away from Forbes's cottage just after the time of the murder. Do you know what'll happen to you, my friend? You'll hang."

Walter Chapman Campbell stood with his fingers still twisting his necktie. His expression was like that of a small boy caught in the jam cupboard.

His fingers moved up, and touched his neck, and he flinched. In that hot room the perspiration was moving down his cheeks after the fashion of side whiskers.

"You're bluffing," he said, first clearing his throat for a voice that would not be steady. "It's not true, any of it, and you're bluffing!"

"You know I'm not bluffing. Your crime, I admit, was worthy of the son of the cleverest member of this family. With Angus and Colin dead, and Forbes blamed for it, you could go back quietly to Port Elizabeth. Your father is very ill and infirm. He would not last long as heir to nearly eighteen thousand pounds. You could then claim it without ever coming to England or Scotland at all, or being seen by anyone.

"But you won't claim it now, my lad. Do you think you've got a dog's chance of escaping the rope?"

Walter Chapman Campbell's hands went to his face.

"I didn't mean any harm," he said. "My God, I didn't mean any harm!" His voice broke. "You're not going to give me up to the police, are you?"

"No," said Dr. Fell calmly. "Not if you sign the document I propose to dictate to you."

The other's hands flew away from his face, and he stared with foggy hope. Alistair Duncan intervened.

"What, sir, is the meaning of this?" he asked harshly.

Dr. Fell rapped his open hand on the arm of the sofa.

"The meaning and purpose of this," he returned, "is to let Elspat

Campbell live out her years and die happily without the conviction that
Angus's soul is burning in hell. The purpose is to provide for Elspat and
Colin to the ends of their lives as Angus wanted them provided for. That
is all.

"You will copy out this document"—Dr. Fell took several sheets
of paper from his pocket—"or else write at my dictation, the following confession. You will say that you deliberately murdered Angus
Campbell . . ."

"*What?*"

"That you tried to murder Colin, and that you murdered Alec Forbes.
That, with the evidence I shall present, will satisfy the insurance companies and the money will be paid. No, I know you didn't kill Angus! But
you're going to say you did; and you have every motive for having done
so.

"I can't cover you up, even if I wanted to. And I don't want, or mean
to. But this much I can do. I can withhold that confession from the police
for forty-eight hours, in time for you to make a get-away. Ordinarily you
would have to get an exit permit to leave the country. But you're close to
Clydeside; and I think you could find an obliging skipper to take you
aboard an outgoing ship. If you do that, rest assured that in these evil days
they won't bring you back.

"Do that, and I'll give you the leeway. Refuse to do it, and my
evidence goes to the police within the next half-hour. What do you say?"

The other stared back.

Terror, befuddlement, and uncertainty merged into suspicious skepti-
cism.

"I don't believe you!" shrilled Chapman. "How do I know you
wouldn't take the confession and hand me over to the police straight
away?"

"Because, if I were foolish enough to do that, you could upset the
whole apple cart by telling the truth about Angus's death. You could
deprive those two of the money and tell Elspat exactly what her cherished
Angus actually did. You could prevent me from achieving the very thing
I'm trying to achieve. If you depend on me, remember that I depend on
you."

Again Chapman fingered his necktie. Dr. Fell took out a large gold
watch and consulted it.

"This," Alistair Duncan said out of a dry throat, "is the most completely illegal, fraudulent——"

"That's it," stormed Chapman. "You wouldn't dare let me get away
anyway! It's a trick! If you have that evidence and held up the confession,
they'd have you as accessory after the fact!"

"I think not," said Dr. Fell, politely. "If you consult Mr. Duncan there, he will inform you that in Scots law there is no such thing as an accessory after the fact."

Duncan opened his mouth, and shut it again.

"Rest assured," pursued Dr. Fell, "that every aspect of my fraudulent villainy has been considered. I further propose that the real truth shall be known to us in this room, and to nobody else. That here and now we swear an oath of secrecy which shall last to the end of our days. Is that acceptable to everyone?"

"It is to me!" cried Kathryn.

"And to me," agreed Alan.

Duncan was standing in the middle of the room, waving his hands. If, thought Alan, you could imagine any such thing as a sputtering which was not funny, not even ludicrous, but only anguished and almost deathlike, that was his expression.

"I ask you," he said, "I ask you, sir, before it is too late, to stop and consider what you propose! It goes beyond all bounds! Can I, as a reputable professional man, sanction or even listen to this?"

Dr. Fell remained unimpressed.

"I hope so," he answered calmly. "Because it is precisely what I mean to carry out. I hope you of all people, Mr. Duncan, won't upset the apple cart you have pushed for so long and kept steady with such evident pain. Can't you, as a Scotsman, be persuaded to be sensible? Must you learn practicality from an Englishman?"

Duncan moaned in his throat.

"Then," said Dr. Fell, "I take it that you have given up these romantic ideas of legal justice, and will row in the same boat with us. The question of life or death now lies entirely with Mr. Walter Chapman Campbell. I am not going on with this offer all day, my friend. Well, what do you say? Will you confess to two murders, and get away? Or will you deny both, and hang for one?"

The other shut his eyes, and opened them again.

He looked round the room as though he were seeing it for the first time. He looked out of the windows at the shimmering waters of the loch; at all the domain which was slipping away from him; but at a house cleansed and at peace.

"I'll do it," he said.

The 9:15 train from Glasgow to Euston slid into Euston only four hours late, on a golden sunshiny morning which dimmed even the cavernous grime of the station.

The train settled in and stopped amid a sigh of steam. Doors banged. A porter, thrusting his head into a first-class sleeping compartment, was depressed by the sight of two of the most prim, respectable (and probably low-tipping) stuffed shirts he had ever beheld.

One was a young lady, stern of mouth and lofty of expression, who wore shell-rimmed spectacles severely. The other was a professorial-looking man with an even more lofty expression.

"Porter, ma'am? Porter, sir?"

The young lady broke off to eye him.

"*If* you please," she said. "It will surely be evident to you, *Dr.* Campbell, that the Earl of Danby's memorandum, addressed to the French king and endorsed, 'I approve of this; C. R.,' by the king himself, can have been inspired by no such patriotic considerations as your unfortunate Tory interpretation suggests."

"This 'ere shotgun don't belong to you, ma'am, does it? Or to you, sir?"

The gentleman eyed him vaguely.

"Er—yes," he said. "We are removing the evidence out of range of the ballistics authorities."

"Sir?"

But the gentleman was not listening.

"If you will cast your mind back, madam, to the speech made by Danby in the Commons in December, 1680, I feel that certain considerations of reason contained therein must penetrate even the cloud of prejudice with which you appear to have surrounded yourself. For example . . ."

Laden with the luggage, the porter trudged dispiritedly along the platform after them. *Floreat scientia!* The wheel had swung round again.